CODY QUAN

RiceDaddy7 Books

*To Mom and Dad
for their unconditional love.*

PREFACE

Cody Quan started out as what psychologists refer to as narrative therapy. I was a lost, unhappy person who one day wanted to write a part of my life down. I wrote with pure emotion resulting in a general disregard for truth. What resulted was a fun house mirror; a deep introspective journey toward all my fears and why I allowed them to control who I am. Warts and all, this was the book I've always wanted to write. It's the proudest thing I've done up to this point. At the very least it answered a question I've always had about how one becomes a writer. The answer, I learned, is that as anything else in life, you choose to become it. When that choice is made, you embrace that journey of enduring the challenges of learning and growing. The same could be said about being Asian-American today. Eastern culture, far more than its Western counterpart, continues to surrender itself to the centuries-old acceptance of parental debt and blind obedience. We aren't the "-American" part of it unless we realize freedom means telling our families to fuck off and owe it to ourselves to choose. At the heart of what this book is about is that simple truth which I found in a complicated way. One day I hope to achieve what Cody achieves, but until then, I will continue putting the pieces together until I am the person that I want to be.

All this being said, not every character in the world of Cody Quan is accurate to their real life counterparts. This is particularly true of the father. On a grander but related scale, not everything in Cody Quan is necessarily reflective of what Asian-America is either. It's impossible to capture such a complicated weave of people into one book. Still, I am a part of that fabric and therefore, my experience lends a small degree of relevancy. Perhaps all I have is one book in me. If that turns out to be the case, I'm still happy to have said some of the most important opinions I have to speak out in the form of fiction. The primary purpose of writing this book was to cleanse me of things that bothered me. Having others read it is a blessed bonus.

- Louis Leung

ACT I:
BROKEN FAITH

CHAPTER 1: BAPTISM

Splash!

The immediate adaptation to cold water from room temperature was intense. After accepting Christ as his savior, Cody Quan had been flung backwards into the baptism pool by the pastor. What followed was shocking to Cody. He had not expected to transcend through time and space. Every prior life event was relived. He felt the soothing comfort of his mother's womb. He felt the pain of falling down from his first bicycle ride. Then came that right hook connecting to Derrick James' face—the day he finally had enough of Derrick's bullying. He saw his first date. Then his first kiss. He recalled all the times in high school when he had snuck out with friends. High school graduation. Art school graduation. College graduation. Thousands of memories flashed through Cody's mind as he experienced a feeling unlike any other.

Finally, Pastor Lu lifted him back up.

The baptism was over. The sounds of the world emerged. It took Cody a while to get used to his senses again. Once he found them, however, the most unexpected thing of all happened. There, standing close to him was Jesus Christ. Jesus was a white guy with the bluest eyes and the sandiest blond hair. He breathed air and had a shadow. Jesus gave Cody the warmest smile he had ever seen.

"You see him now, don't you?" smiled the tubby and jolly Pastor Lu.

"I...I thought it'd just be figurative. You know, God as an invisible force. God as a concept. But...wow," admired Cody.

"Yes, Cody. We see him. Do you still think I'm joking now?" asked his childhood friend Ennis.

Ennis Wong had known Cody since middle school. He immigrated from one of the finest schools in Hong Kong as a teenager, carrying with him a near flawless fluency of the English language. However, Ennis' strong international accent remained. What resulted from his speech patterns was a strange misuse of emphasis on the wrong words. Yet, what stood out about Ennis wasn't where he came from or the unique way in which he spoke—it was the active openness of his Christian faith that defined him. Through persistence and countless personal testimonies, he eventually succeeded in converting Cody as a brother in Christ.

Cody was glad it happened.

Jesus produced an inviting gesture to embrace. As Cody held on to Jesus with tears of joy, he wondered if God's only son spoke English. That's silly, he thought; of course, Jesus spoke English! He's the Creator of all things, right? Now that Cody was a Christian, he stammered for the first thing to say to Christ.

"What's happening, Jesus?!" blurted Cody.

"Okay, okay," chuckled Pastor Lu, ushering Cody away from the podium. "There are a couple more people who can't wait to meet Jesus today too. If you can kindly please get off the stage so that the next person could be baptized..."

Cody apologized and sat back down with his mother. Because she had not been aware of his decision, it was a risk to bring her here. Cody made her promise not to tell his father, a staunch Buddhist. It would break his heart knowing that Cody had accepted Christianity.

Soon after sitting down, Cody felt a tap on his shoulder. It was Luke Lu, the pastor's son and one of Cody's church friends. Cody got up and walked over to him, accepting Luke's handshake as he congratulated Cody on his baptism. Luke had a chiseled, sculptured body. He was tall, handsome, well-built and friendly. Although he was fully Asian, Luke had Caucasian features. Most notable of those Caucasian traits was his Roman-like nose. Many young Asian women in Second Chinese Baptist Church swooned over Luke. He looked like a white guy.

"I love you, Cody," Luke said as he embraced him. "I love you. I love you. I love you."

Luke slowly let go and looked into Cody's eyes. Cody disengaged eye contact, looking at his other church friends who had walked over to congratulate him.

"Cody, you rock, man!" exclaimed Henry Gao.

Henry was one of the few guys who were much shorter than he was. Unlike Cody, though, Henry didn't look very youthful. Although they were of the same age, Henry looked like an old man. He had a whole lot of facial hair and the hairiest arms Cody had ever seen on an Asian man. Henry looked like a smiling troll.

"Congrats!" smiled Marion Yang.

Marion stood in contrast to Henry. She was six-foot-seven, with equal proportions of a normal-looking woman except for her obvious stature. Marion wasn't someone with a lot to say.

"Thanks, Marion," Cody said, stretching his head all the way up. It was like talking to a giraffe.

"Here," Marion beamed, "I brought you a Bible helper book. It has illustrations and quizzes for each part of the New Testament!"

"C.Q.!" shouted a familiar voice next to Cody.

"Felix!" grinned Cody.

"NooooOoOOoo, I wanna hug him first!!!!" intervened a sweet, youthful voice.

The diminutive, spirited body of a beautiful young woman shoved Felix Lin aside, throwing herself onto Cody. Zoey Vu was the prettiest girl in church. She had a reputation of being overly flirty from the way she talked, the provocative way she dressed and her active use of physical touching. Zoey and Felix were the best of friends, almost always being seen together in public.

"I'm so proud of you, baby!" she smiled.

Felix laughed and congratulated him with a handshake.

Another person made his way over for congratulations.

"Hey, Cody, congrats. You're still gonna play ball later, right?" asked Jay Zheng.

"Sure, Jay. Definitely," replied Cody.

Cody liked Jay, but he knew so little about him. Physically, Jay was short but wide, standing out at times because of his weight. His friendly personality, however, was also distant. Jay gave the impression that he simply wanted to fit in, avoiding the spotlight whenever he could. In their age group, he was the only other person besides Cody who was a born- again Christian.

"I'll see you then," answered Jay.

As he was shaking Jay's hand, Cody saw a grumpy individual from the corner of his eye. It was Marco Ling, an often unhappy church member who usually seemed angry at one thing or another. Marco had his arms crossed while leaning against a wall. He gave Cody a piercing stare. His thin, round glasses made his beady eyes appear even smaller. Marco had a lot of pimples on his face, validating hushed giggles among the girls that he was the ugliest man in their church.

"Good to see you, Marco," waved Cody.

Marco expectedly didn't respond back, but even his foul temper could not erase what would be one of Cody's happiest days. Cody had taken a chance believing in Jesus, and now he was rewarded in knowing that it was all true. He looked forward to a secure future, one with happiness and assurance.

———

In the past few years, the popularity of basketball had exploded in the Chinese community. Whether it was in China or anywhere else, almost everyone with a Chinese background, young or old, male or female, was influenced by the shadow of professional basketball player Yao Ming.

That shadow was especially strong in the city of Houston where he played for the hometown Rockets. It was only Yao's third season, but to a lot of Chinese-Americans, it seemed like he had played forever. Like a lot of Asian churches during this time, Second Chinese Baptist Church was eager to have its own indoor basketball court. Congregational demand for its construction caused the weekly donation totals to temporarily spike to ten times the usual amount. In under a year, the indoor basketball court was built. It drew the interest of many local men, including the ones not attending the church. The court was beautiful. It had high-quality equipment and was kept clean. It even had its own set of restrooms and locker rooms. For many of the male church members, an afternoon game of hoops was secretly their favorite part of Sunday.

Cody was amongst the young men bouncing one of the many

basketballs. It was common for everyone to be joking around, doing warm-ups or practicing shots before the first game. What was uncommon, at least to Cody, was Jesus practicing and conversing with them. Had the Son of God been seen like this every Sunday to the ones who were baptized?

Cody realized he had really missed out.

"Alright, everyone!" announced Felix, "Let's gather around and form teams!"

Forming teams meant everyone standing in line and shooting a free throw. The first person who successfully made a free throw would be on Team A. The second who made it would be on Team B. The third successful person would then go to Team A, and so forth. The alternating pattern would continue until both teams had a total of five players each. If anyone missed, he would simply have to go back in line, awaiting his next turn. Sometimes that second chance never came because the line had so many people. There was a high probability that ten people would have already made a successful free throw by then, establishing the rosters of both teams.

Felix was the first one in line. He took his time, focused on the basket, and succeeded in making the shot. He would be on Team A. Several other players were in line ahead of Cody.

"Hey, man, once again, congrats on the baptism," said Jay, who was in front of him.

"Yeah, it's awesome, man," replied Cody.

While Cody was waiting, he saw his crush, Daphne Lee, making her way through the gym as a shortcut from the rain. Daphne was one of the longtime members of Second Chinese Baptist Church. She was baptized early in life, at the age of five. Cody knew very little about her because he was fairly new.

"Hey, Daphne!" laughed Felix, "Came to enjoy the lovely smell of the court?"

"Shut up!" replied Daphne jokingly.

Even when she was shouting, Daphne's voice was soft and even-keeled, never rising a decibel. Daphne's attire was the same as usual: a conservative long-sleeved sweater and modest pants—complemented with a slight use of makeup. When she was close to passing Cody, she did her best to avoid eye contact. Cody greeted her anyway.

"Hello, Daphne," smiled Cody.

Daphne pretended to look distracted.

"Hey, Daphne," Cody repeated a little louder.

"Oh, uh, hey Cody," she halfheartedly offered, "I heard you got baptized today. Congratulations."

She quickened her pace, nodded toward Jesus, and waited outside in the cold, rainy February weather. However, before the gym doors closed all the way back, Cody saw a car pull over to her. The driver was a handsome, young Caucasian man. He looked a little annoyed with Daphne when she got into his car. The gym door came to a full close, obscuring Cody's view.

"CODY!" shouted Felix.

Cody was snapped back to attention. It was his turn.

"You're going to shoot your free throw or what?" Felix teased.

Cody walked up to the free throw line and dribbled a few times. He then held the ball, squatted up and down, and shot the basketball. The ball went through perfectly without touching the rim. Cody was a good shooter; it was his only strength in the sport. He couldn't play very good defense and he lacked a solid command of his dribbling. He couldn't jump very high and wasn't very fast, and he certainly wasn't tall. But the one thing Cody did better than most was making baskets from long range.

"The Asian Steve Kerr makes it again!" declared Felix.

The free throw shooting continued with the line repeatedly rotating. Everyone besides Felix and Cody missed their shots. Fifteen minutes had passed when Felix lost his patience.

Finally, Felix announced, "Okay, okay, okay. Dang. You guys suck! This isn't working. Seeing how just me and Cody—"

"Cody and I," corrected Henry.

"—pshh. Whatever. Seeing how...Cody and I...are the only two who've made shots, we'll just be the team captains and pick four players each," Felix instructed.

As he said that, two young black men walked in. They were not a part of Second Chinese Baptist Church but, like many others, wanted to play a game of basketball.

"Alright! Some black guys to choose from! I'll take you!" pointed Felix.

The chosen young black man laughed and stood next to Felix.

"Luke!" whispered Marco in protest, "They're black! Do something!"

"They're our brothers in Christ, we should welcome them," Luke replied.

"What?!" whispered Marco.

Marco started shaking with anger.

"Okay, Cody. Your turn. Pick someone," Felix said.

"I pick Jesus!" announced Cody.

"WHAT?!" shouted Marco.

A sudden turn of silence fell upon the basketball court.

"Uh...eh..." The words couldn't come out of Felix's mouth.

"That's the Lord and Savior, you can't just..." Henry couldn't finish his sentence.

"No. It's alright. It's alright. If it is Jesus' will," acknowledged Luke.

Jesus nodded.

"Wait, who are you guys talking to?" asked one of the unbaptized players.

"Jesus. Come to our church sometime and we'll tell you all about Him," smiled Luke.

"Okay, this is a special game where Jesus is playing. Those who aren't baptized, sorry, you're going to have to take a seat because you can't see Jesus," said Felix.

"This is absurd," commented another unbaptized player.

Felix and Cody picked out the rest of their team. Jesus magically adjusted his height to six-foot-seven and altered his clothes from white robes to a set of jersey and shorts. The jersey featured the word "Christ" on the back. His jersey number was "1." Cody was super excited about the game. Playing basketball with the Creator of the universe was far more incredible than even playing with Michael Jordan.

"Okay, just to be clear, here are the rules like always," said Felix. "Whichever team that gets to twenty-one points first is the winner. Each made basket counts as one point. Each basket made from behind the three-point line will be counted as two points."

"Duece?" asked one of the players.

"No deuce. Straight up twenty-one points," answered Felix.

When the game began, the mismatch between both teams became evident. Jesus Christ was unstoppable. He did windmill dunks from the free throw line. He blocked every shot by the opposing team. His passes were always perfect. Those on the sidelines who weren't playing saw different versions. For the baptized, they saw Jesus performing miracles on the basketball court. The others, however, saw Cody performing dunks and other illogical actions. All were flabbergasted.

Cody's team eventually won by a final score of twenty-one to zero. As the players lined up at the water fountain, Ennis took Cody aside.

"Hey, don't do that anymore. Serious. Don't," he warned.

"Why not?" asked Cody.

"Because he's God," explained Ennis. "You can't just request and pray for anything. What will you do next, huh? Ask him to get you a nice car? A pretty girl? Don't be so selfish! He is our Lord!"

"He didn't seem to have a problem with it," laughed Cody.

"Tsk. You just don't get it, do you? I'll pray for you," promised Ennis.

Cody shrugged and sipped from the water fountain. When he was finished, he went around looking for Jesus.

"Hey, have you seen Jesus?" Cody asked Henry. "Where'd he go?"

Henry shrugged.

"Have you seen Jesus?" he asked another player. "What about you? Anyone?"

Cody finally came to the conclusion that Jesus had left. Perhaps he had a starving kid to save? Maybe there was a bus about to crash? But couldn't Jesus be everywhere at once? asked Cody to himself. Were there multiple Jesuses?

There were so many questions.

———

Pastor Lu quietly looked out the window as he sat in his chair. The heavy storm that started an hour after service stubbornly remained into the late afternoon. It made it seem like nighttime. The pastor's office was small but well-furnished. The extreme tidiness served as evidence of his attention toward detail and responsibility. Although he was in his late fifties, memories from where he had come from were still fresh in his mind. He remembered growing up in Shanghai while it was being rebuilt. The city had recovered fairly quickly during China's Cultural Revolution, but not fast enough for a man like Wai Li Lu. Lu was interested in the steady quality of education that the United States had to offer. So, like many of his generation during the seventies, he tried to immigrate westward to the other side of the world. Due to an uncle using bribery, Lu's citizenship was approved and he moved to New York City. He was a skinny man back then. However, not long after he arrived, he experienced a tremendous weight gain. Lu interpreted it as a symbol of happier times and opportunities.

From that point on, his story became a boring one. Wai Li Lu studied hard, obeyed his parents, courted the recommended girl from his congregation, married her and then got an accounting job with a Houston gas company. Houston was the city where his son Luke was born. Once he was away from the comfortable surroundings of New York's Chinatown, Wai Li Lu assimilated as Willy Lu. "Please," he would good-naturedly insist to his American coworkers, "Just call me Willy." He saw the Texas oil boom during the eighties as a sign from God. He prospered and moved his family into a good neighborhood. His house was in a recent development in the then obscure city of Sugar Land, Texas. Although Sugar Land was technically its own city, it was considered by everyone to be a part of the greater Houston area. Willy Lu would have remained at his job for the rest of his life, but the industry fell apart from the domino effect of the Enron scandal.

Once again, Willy Lu saw it as another sign from God. He felt a calling to train in a seminary and became part of a big church in the Houston Chinese community. His ascension as a pastor controversially came after the original church had split. There, he took as many ex-members of its congregation as he could, starting a new church.

That was how he became Pastor Lu.

"<This man. This...preacher. I'm not so sure>," opined a member of his staff, Reverend Han, in their native Mandarin Chinese language.

"<This church won't grow fast enough like this. Our members aren't the most evangelistic type, just look at our annual baptism today. That was only five people, two of them were teenagers.>" Pastor Lu paused to take off his glasses. "<I have prayed many nights ...>"

"<I'm sure you have>," interrupted Reverend Han, "<but we are a Chinese church. We are suddenly letting all these...these black people in. Lu, this preacher is not one of us. Our methods may differ.>"

Reverend Han handed back the prospective preacher's resume. Pastor Lu looked at it again. Paper-clipped to the resume was a photo of the recently ordained preacher, a round and youthful black man in his early forties with a smile even jollier than Lu's.

The resume was written by hand.

"<He has beautiful handwriting. And he insists he can bring in fifty regular members from his former congregation. We have around seventy-seven or seventy-eight people. This would almost double our Sundays. Imagine, a morning service with an audience of over a hundred. Doubling the...>" Pastor Lu stopped himself because he was about to mention the obvious increase in donations.

In his heart, he didn't want to think he did his job as a pastor for money, because it wasn't about money for him. The church is new, he thought, justifying all the extra finances the church could spend. Besides, he thought, his anniversary with his wife was coming up in just under two months...it would be nice to get her something special for once.

The other reverend began to speak.

"<All fifty of this new preacher's members are African-American. I've been invited to a couple of their services. They worship very differently. Our conservative Chinese members would be scared off. What would we do if they started leaving and just the black ones are left? I am not going to dance and shake myself. I...I would leave, Lu>," said Reverend Ping.

Pastor Lu silently looked at his desk. In public, he was jolly and charismatic. In the confines of his close friends and congregation, however, he revealed himself to be a man of fierce determination.

"<If we must join with another non-Chinese pastor, couldn't we at least get a white one or what about a Vietnamese one? There are plenty of Vietnamese churches in Houston>," suggested Reverend Han.

"<Yes>," smiled Reverend Ping, "<a white congregation would be good!>"

"<I tried. There was little interest. And Vietnamese people are usually Catholic. I even asked the new Korean preachers. Nothing. The Bible says we are all brothers and sisters. This new preacher is our Christian brother. Now, I...I haven't seen, nor heard, from our Lord in years. But I still feel Him. I believe we get to a certain point where the Lord communicates us with suggestive signs. He reads our hearts as well as our minds. Seeing, I suppose, is for the weaker faith. The stronger ones, like us, we transcend this. That's what I've come to understand, anyway. Brother Han, Brother Ping...I'm certain this is what Jesus wants>," said Pastor Lu. "<I'm certain of it.>"

"<Well, have you at least talked with some other members of the church?>" asked Reverend Han.

Pastor Lu had no answer.

"<They may not be pleased>," Han continued. "<We assured them that this would be a Chinese-only church.>"

Pastor Lu wiped sweat from the corner of his forehead, "<I'm their pastor, am I not? Since when haven't I made decisions that were for the good of our church? I pray for those decisions. I have made my decision, my brothers. First thing I'm going to do tomorrow is have lunch with this preacher. If everything goes well, I will make him co-pastor. Second Chinese Baptist Church will be renamed to Fellowship Communion Baptist Church. Final decision.>"

The lack of democracy created an air of pause in the room.

"<Reverend Han. Lead us to prayer.>"

"<Of course>," Reverend Han replied.

The two reverends and the pastor held hands as Reverend Han recited a long prayer. The old reverend prayed for guidance, understanding and a brighter future for both the church and its individual members. Pastor Lu's eyes slightly opened during the prayer. He closed them again, envisioning the brand new Mercedes that he had always wanted.

———

February weather in Houston is unpredictable. Even within hours on the same day, the temperature sinks to freezing cold from burning hot. Other days, like this particular Sunday, a cloudless morning can transform into an afternoon of ceaseless rain. Before his baptism, Cody would have explained it as precipitation. Now, he defined it as the work of Jesus Christ.

It was now six o'clock and the basketball court had closed for the day. Cody stood outside of it, waiting for the storm to pass. Everyone else had lost patience, fleeing to their cars amid the punishing rain. Poor Henry discovered his car's remote was broken when he reached his little Hyundai Sonata. Marco slipped into a deceptively deep puddle of muddy water. He was so angry he grabbed the person running next to him and forced him into the puddle too. Ennis got soaked running all over the lot, realizing that he had forgotten where he parked. By the time he found his car, Ennis was a total mess. He looked like he had come out of a swimming pool. Luke and Felix, sharing an umbrella, walked across the parking lot and got into Luke's car and waited for the rain to stop. Now there are some people with common sense, thought Cody.

Meanwhile, many questions about Jesus swirled inside of Cody's head. Why did Jesus disappear after the first basketball game? How come some of the baptized couldn't see Jesus? Did Jesus want to be called Jesus? Maybe Mr. Christ, or more likely, Lord and Heavenly Father? It was like logic had flipped upside down for Cody. Nothing made sense. Does he go through life now pretending that things are still the same? Or should he quit his job and tell everyone what he had seen, like Paul from the Bible?

"So many questions," uttered Cody out loud.

Then, something caught his eye.

Someone was moving behind one of the pillars. Because the lighting was poor and the weather conditions were less than ideal, Cody's sight was limited. Determined to find an answer, he squinted his eyes, hoping to improve his vision.

"Jesus?" called out Cody. "Is that you?"

The silhouette came closer to a slightly more lit area. It was enough light for Cody to realize that it really was Jesus. He was now dressed in ragged clothes, far different from the shiny basketball outfit he had worn earlier. More importantly was Jesus' change in expression. Gone was the friendly, inviting smile. In its place was an angry, hateful look. Cody remained still, like a deer in headlights.

"Jesus...Lord...Heavenly Father...why are you looking at me like that?!" Cody asked.

The eerie figure of Jesus silently and slowly walked closer to Cody. He felt spooked now. Jesus finally approached to within a few feet away from Cody and then stopped. Cody blurted out the first question he had wanted to ask.

"Why? Why is there so much pain and suffering in this world when you could just stop it?" he inquired.

Jesus looked at him silently.

"Why are people born only to die?" Cody asked, feeling bolder.

No answer came out of Christ's lips.

"What's the point of heaven and hell if people don't even know you exist?"

Finally, Cody found the courage to ask his most daring question.

"DO YOU EVEN CARE?" he shouted.

And like a tiger, Jesus pounced on Cody and violently punched him until Cody lay shocked and stunned on the ground. What happened? he wondered. He felt Jesus breathe close to his ear.

"Fuck. You," the Messiah replied.

And then Jesus was gone, leaving Cody alone in a bloody pulp.

CHAPTER 2: TIME WAITS FOR NO ONE

If there were one particular word to describe the root of Cody's problems, it would be this: punctuality. It was a concept that he struggled to understand. Perhaps it was a reflection of self-centeredness or the result of being a perfectionist. Neither of these or other reasons, however, interested his supervisor, Rachel Hutchens. To her, Cody was consistently late.

What wasn't so much of a mystery was how Cody kept getting away with it. He was part of a new breed of designers, ones who were as adept in art as they were at programming. Cody's skill set made him the prince of his castle; that castle's name was the University of Houston. There, he was working with soon-to-be senior citizens, pushing past their fifties. To many of them, Cody's talent was a gem. It was Rachel who initially saw Cody's outstanding resume and capabilities. Although he had originally applied for the wrong position, she begged her boss to create a new one for Cody.

It proved to be a big mistake for Rachel.

Her boss and others in their department fell in love with Cody's abilities. They spoiled him by letting him bend rules. He became a nightmare employee for a supervisor like Rachel. Cody's favorite bad habit was intentional tardiness. He deliberately came to work two hours later than he was scheduled. This was done in front of Rachel's face. It made her look powerless and disrespected. It was the same song and dance every time. Cody would come in late, Rachel would ask him why and then Cody would shrug it off.

This particular Monday morning, however, drew Rachel's ire more than usual. As soon as Cody came in, she shot from her desk and walked toward his. Rachel's anger was apparent when she pulled a chair next to him and sat on it with resounding authority.

"You're two hours late. Again. Like you are everyday," she seethed.

"I'm, uh, heh, sorry?" Cody smirked.

"You're sorry? You're sor—. Ugh! You're going down, Cody. Someday, somehow, I'll find a way to bring you down. You are so lucky to be doing what you're doing. Did you know what I did when I was your age? I was a fucking gym teacher. I came to work on time every day. I made something close to minimum wage. And you're trying to convince me that you're 'sorry?' If it was up to me, you'd have already been fired! You're lucky people higher up than me like you, Cody Quan. But you aren't shit to me. You're not!" Rachel's head was about to explode.

"I'm sorry, Rachel. But I always leave two hours after everyone else. It's still eight hours of work that I put in," justified Cody.

"I don't give a rat's ass!" Rachel replied. "You can't just make new rules here! What does that make me? I look like a chump!"

Cody knew what he had done was wrong, but somehow he found it difficult to be punctual. He was never punctual for anything. Not school, not work, not even for his own birth; he was born weeks after his expected due date. Most people who knew him often joked that he'd probably be late for his own funeral. Sometimes his extreme tardiness was humorous. Most times, however, it wasn't. It shocked Rachel that Cody had often gotten away with being late without consequence. He was either incredibly lucky or exceptionally special.

"You missed training the new intern this morning," hissed Rachel.

"Damn," commented Cody, "I'm sorry for that too."

"Stop saying you're sorry, Cody! Because you're not." She paused to calm down. "She's still here. Now be more professional and show her around."

Rachel stood up and went back to her desk.

Moments later, the intern made her way to Cody's cubicle. She was deliberately distant. She sat around quietly, making little eye contact while tightly clutching her belongings. For the first thirty minutes, Cody saw more of her back than her face. He eventually learned that her name was Mindy Cheung.

"So...Mindy, is it?...You're transferred from the optometry department, eh?" asked Cody.

"Yes," Mindy hastily replied. She was fidgeting with the Internet cables of her laptop.

Cody waited for her to follow up on her reply, but soon realized that it was the full extent of their conversation. Slowly, he turned back around to his workstation. Cody skimmed through the clutter of work-related emails. He was hoping for a reply back to a flirtatious lunch invitation he had written to Daphne, his crush from Second Chinese Baptist Church. She often didn't reply back. When she did, however, they were direct and formal answers without a hint of romantic interest.

He decided to write another email:

"Hey babe, how's your body stopping traffic today? Don't break too many hearts. Would like to know if you'd like to have lunch with me

this week. It's not often I get to have lunch with a goddess. Let's make it a habit. Looked hot at church yesterday. - X's, O's and Cheerios, Cody Q."

Cody clicked on the Send icon, casting another line of bait into the cyberspace waters.

"Need any help?" he asked the new intern.

"No," Mindy replied.

She placed her purse between them, creating a barricade. Cody excused himself to go to the restroom. It was a ploy he often used to get out of the building. During the peak hours, the University of Houston was like its own city. Thousands upon thousands of students walked onto its numerous labyrinths of pathways. Previously, Cody had dated one of the students here, but realized someone in his late twenties did not have much in common with girls in their late teens. The school was diverse, but he felt lonely. It was made up of mostly people in their late teens or aged forty and above. Perhaps I've been here too long, thought Cody.

Whenever he wanted to be alone, Cody would walk to one of his favorite places on campus—the old Roy Cullen building. It was musty and relatively ancient, dating back to the late 1930s. The top floor, which was rumored to be haunted, was damp and dark. Because of this, Cody found it to be a great place for solitude. It was the first place he had in mind to collect his thoughts about what had happened at his baptism yesterday.

He was very confused as to why Jesus was friendly enough to play basketball with him, but then would later violently beat him. It was as though Christ was bipolar. More strangely, Cody immediately healed, showing no signs of injury.

"Dear Heavenly Father," he closed his eyes and prayed. "Hallowed is your name. I was wondering if you could, you know, show yourself."

Moments of silence followed. Cody tried again.

"Dear God...Jesus...I need to talk. If you don't mind," he prayed.

He looked around expecting Jesus to be there, but there was nothing. Were the events from yesterday a hallucination? They couldn't be, thought Cody, others saw Jesus too.

Disappointed, Cody headed back.

In his cubicle, he found Mindy doing tutorials for the Adobe Photoshop software. She was noticeably struggling, but her pride prevented her from soliciting help from Cody. In Mindy's mind, he was Asian-American, which meant he probably looked down on her. As a native from Taiwan, she wished there was another Taiwanese worker around to converse with. Instead, Cody was the only Asian in their department, but he was like a banana—yellow on the outside, white on the inside. Mindy took notice that the department was purposely diversified with people of different races, gender and handicap. Clearly affirmative action in place, she thought to herself. She eyed the Americans suspiciously.

"Hey, you're doing it wrong," a voice interrupted her train of thought.

It was Cody. He had been looking at her laptop screen from where he was sitting.

"Um. O-Okay," Mindy muttered, "What am I doing wrong?"

Mindy pretended to fidget with the software, hoping Cody would divert his attention elsewhere. After a minute of acting, she looked back up. Cody was still looking at her, but now he was also eating a box of Pocky.

"You're trying to make a reflection, right? Use the gradient tool for your mask," munched Cody.

"B-but the book says..."

"Here, let me show you..." he insisted.

Cody reached over and did the whole tutorial in a few seconds. While he was doing it, his fingers worked in a blurred motion.

"Wow!" she smiled in admiration.

Cody went back to his computer and started checking his emails. Still no reply from Daphne, he said to himself. Frustrated, he fidgeted around his desk. He yearned for a window. Every other cubicle was located near a window that featured a view of the giant fountain in the middle of campus. Perhaps Rachel did this deliberately? I guess she has subtle ways of getting back at me, thought Cody.

"Hey, hey!" Mindy shook Cody's shoulder.

She was suddenly very close to him.

"Yeah?" he answered.

"You speak Chinese?"

"No."

"Why not? Don't your parents teach you?"

"I speak decent Cantonese. Does that work?"

"You should learn. It's the most important language," she explained.

A sudden burst of energy gave Mindy an animated behavior.

"Hey! Teach me how to double her!" she demanded.

"What? 'Double her?'"

"The picture! Audrey Hepburn! She's my favorite. I'm just trying to learn this other tutorial. Ms. Rachel made me," said Mindy. "Double her picture for me. I need to show Ms. Rachel. Then I get to go home."

Cody began cloning the digitally cutout photo of Audrey Hepburn. Like an art director, Mindy gave directions on how she wanted the canvas to be decorated.

"Okay...move the tree there. Make the background pink...add a sun...no, a moon is better...can you use a different font?...make it glow..."

she instructed.

The final result was amateurish, which made it that more believable that Mindy had done it. She sent it as an attachment to Rachel and started packing up to leave.

"Thanks so much!" Mindy smiled with glee. "Tomorrow, you will do my other tutorials for me! Goodbye!"

"Wait, what...?" asked Cody.

———

Duke wasn't the chosen one.

That distinction belonged to his cousin Cody, who was the last male heir of their family. Cody was an only child, whose father was the only son among his grandfather's six children. In Chinese culture, males who carry the family name are more beloved. Duke would've given anything to be a Quan. Instead, because this was his mother's side of the family, Duke was a Feng.

"<Grandma, it's me, Duke>," he announced in a solemn voice.

The one the family called Skinny Grandma opened her eyes. It was the first time she had smiled since her stay at the hospital. She was lucky. The city of Houston is well-known for its medical center, comprising the best collection of hospitals and medical staff the world has to offer. Because many billionaires and their family members had been saved there, generous donations were often given to the medical center. This made the hospitals seem more like five-star hotels. It was well understood that if someone couldn't be saved at the medical center, funeral services should be in order. Skinny Grandma had been diagnosed with a heart condition. The doctors attributed it to thinning heart vessels, which increased her risk of a stroke.

Duke had brought her congee and egg tarts from Houston's Chinatown. Because he lived in Dallas, he was a bit drained from the long four-hour drive. Yet, nothing was more important to him than being there for the grandmother who raised him and Cody. Duke was a very serious person. His de facto expression was comprised of a frown and an arrogant stare. His posture was as austere as it was stringent.

"Hi there," greeted the heart surgeon, "I was told you were already informed of the specifics of the procedure. The risk is high. She has a lot of blockage. We've tried to do it without surgery, but now it looks like it might come down to that."

The doctor went on to explain the procedure in detail to Duke. Once he finished, he took his leave. Moments later, footsteps could be heard running toward the room. It was Cody.

"Granndddmmaaa!" he smiled.

She laughed while being hugged by Cody. Duke's expression remained unchanged, with only a mere movement of his eyebrow hinting of his disapproval. To him, Cody appeared like a child.

"<My favorite grandson! Turn around and let me spank you!>" requested Skinny Grandma.

Cody turned around while his grandmother playfully spanked him.

"<Spank!>" she laughed.

"Hey, Duke, thanks for making it," said Cody.

Duke shrugged.

"At least one of us cared enough to show up on time. Now she can begin her operation as scheduled. I filled out all the paperwork," Duke said. "Things you should have done but you never do. Because you're a child and you're spoiled. You don't deserve this woman's love."

"Go to hell," remarked Cody.

Duke shrugged.

"<Why do you boys speak so much English in front of your dear old grandmother? I thought I raised you both better than that. Don't forget all of your Chinese, Cody>," requested Skinny Grandma.

"<Yes, Cody. Don't forget all your Chinese, white boy>," Duke sneered.

"<Laugh don't me dare beat for to>," Cody attempted in broken Cantonese.

"<Ai-ya, Cody! It seems that you've forgotten all of your Chinese! You need to get yourself a nice girlfriend from China, so that she can speak Chinese to you all day long. This way, you wouldn't forget>," she advised.

"Heh. A girlfriend. That'll be a long time coming," laughed Duke.

"<And what about you, Gay Wind? What happened to your girlfriend?>" Skinny Grandma asked Duke, using his Chinese name.

Cody chuckled, "Gay Wind."

Duke did not find the verbal jab at his name humorous. He chose to ignore Cody instead.

"<My previous girlfriend. She was...not very virtuous>," Duke explained.

"<I have told you to watch out for those Taiwanese girls, haven't I? Get yourself a nice Chinese girl too, Gay Wind>," she said.

Skinny Grandma paused to collect her thoughts. Cody and Duke knew she was about to delve into a more serious matter.

"<Min-Guang, Gay Wind>," she called both of them

in their Chinese names. "<If your dear grandmother doesn't make it after this operation, just know that I'm okay with it. It could be my time. Everybody has to go someday. If this is my last moment, seeing you both have made me a very happy woman. I would only regret not seeing either of you marry and have grandchildren.>"

"<Time it is not your>," said Cody.

Even though his Chinese was awful, Skinny Grandma knew what he was trying to say.

"<You're such a shoe shine boy, Min-Guang>," his grandmother smiled.

In China, a shoe shine boy was someone who knew how to sweet-talk. The heart surgeon entered the room again, this time with three assistants.

"Okay, guys," he began, "We've got to prep her for her operation tonight. We'd appreciate it if y'all wait outside."

Both cousins walked out of the hospital room. Their body language and distant personal space reflected a long-held animosity towards one another. Neither wanted to leave Skinny Grandma right away.

"You're still gonna stay here?" Cody asked.

"Someone has to," muttered Duke.

"No, no one has to. Methodist is a good hospital. This is a professional facility. One of the best in the world. They can take care of her without your meddling," Cody said.

"Then you can go on with your life and be selfish like you always have," dismissed his cousin.

Cody and Duke stared each other down. Duke had mastered the lion's stare, never backing off from a challenge, real or perceived. He was much bigger in stature than Cody, which helped him intimidate his cousin. Eventually, Cody stared away and directed his attention elsewhere.

"So," Cody broke the silence,"still doing auditing?"

"Yes," Duke replied, giving him a minimal answer.

"What about your dating coach seminars? Still doing those?" asked Cody.

Duke had been holding a series of seminars that focused on the empowerment of Asian men in dating opportunities. His philosophy was to create the identity of the alpha male. It was a state of mind set on establishing a superior position on the totem pole of race dating in America.

"I'm not a 'dating coach.' I hold seminars for empowerment. I save lives. You need to come. You need my help," Duke assured.

Cody paused for a moment.

"Okay. How about this? I'll go to one of your silly seminars if you come to one of our church retreats," offered Cody.

"I'll gain nothing," calculated Duke, "while you'll gain everything."

"What do you mean by that? No one but loser guys attend your seminars. There are actually cute girls in our church retreats. I'm the one with nothing to gain. You get girls and the word of Jesus whom, by the way, I met yesterday," exclaimed Cody.

"You...'met'...Jesus?" laughed Duke.

"Yeah!" smiled Cody.

"Why do you always lie, Cody?" responded Duke. "Lying is a trait of the beta male. You are using a detoured passive-aggressive stance to achieve your goal. This is the kind of habit I wish to remove from you and other weak men. As Asian men, we need to take back what's —"

"Hey, look, it's Pete Mok!" interrupted Cody.

He had spotted their childhood friend Pete from across the hospital floor. Pete, Duke and Cody were once very close. The years had not been kind for the high school dropout. Pete had fallen into the drug-dealing life, resulting in imprisonment for most of his early twenties. Neither cousin had seen him for awhile, but they heard the rumors about what had happened to him. The current incarnation of Pete resembled very little the goofy kid with the heart of gold they once had known. Yet, Cody knew that underneath Pete's tattoos and baggy pants, he was that same person.

"Pete!" shouted Cody from across the hall.

Pete looked around, trying to make sense of his reality. He had a look of disorientation and confusion, which was a result of the daily drugs that he was taking.

"Pete!" Cody continued waving. "Dude, it's me, Cody!"

"Oh whadda C, wha up nigga, been awhile ain't none done," Pete cryptically replied.

Pete gave Cody a unique high five that he had developed from the streets. He attempted to do the same with Duke, but Duke simply greeted Pete with a smileless nod.

"What are you doing here, man? It's been years," asked Cody.

"Ah, you know how it be, nigga. Some nigga clipped my girl's ma tryin' a mug it up in C. Town and we handlin' bizness. What up wit' you, my childhood nigz?" Pete sniffed in between his sentences, an obvious sign of active cocaine use.

"I found Jesus, man," Cody answered with conviction.

"Ah, for real? Dang, nigga. I need sum of dat myself." Pete tapped Duke on the forearm. "My man, ain't seen you since ninety-eight back in the S.W.A.T. Look at choo, bitch azz got married yet? Say, I need a cig break. Y'all wanna cut loose?"

"No, man, we're good. So what have you been up to, Pete?" asked Cody.

Pete raised his voice, "Maaaaannn I—"

"Big P.! Tuan is on the phone!" interrupted one of his friends from across the hall. "He madder dan a motherfuck, nigga."

Forgetting to say his goodbyes, Pete rushed back toward the other end of the hospital floor hallway.

Duke shook his head with judgment and a hint of disgust.

"He's going to be dead before he hits thirty," he estimated.

Cody walked toward the elevators. He didn't wanted to be there with Duke longer than he had to. His cousin was uncomfortable to be around. In fact, thought Cody, if he weren't related to me, I wouldn't even be talking to him. He had always felt a bit of danger around Duke, who had a hyper-competitive streak. It was a result of Duke's superiority complex. While waiting for the elevator, Cody took one final look at the surroundings. On one end of the floor was Duke, standing next to their grandmother's room. He was deep in thought, perhaps bearing the weight of responsibility. On the other end was Big Pete and his entourage, tending to a fallen ally. They were joking and happy. There was a touch of carpe diem about them with a clear disregard for consequence. Both Duke and Pete possessed opposing schools of thought. Was his cousin right to stay responsible at the expense of contentment? Or was it better to be someone like Pete, who was happy and cared so little about the future? These were the thoughts racing through Cody's mind as he waited for the elevator to come.

———————

Houston would not be confused as an extraordinarily beautiful American city. It lacks the majestic mountains and palm trees of Los Angeles. It is devoid of an endless adornment of monolithic skyscrapers like Manhattan. There is a perceived lack of popular history, unlike that of other major American cities such as Chicago, Boston, San Francisco, Seattle or Philadelphia. Above all, it lacks the perception for fun like Miami or Las Vegas. All these viewpoints, however, failed to illustrate what so many Houstonians felt about their city: It would one day be the future of America.

As he made his way across different parts of town, Cody saw glimpses of what would someday be. He drove past the rudimentary monorail that was in its beginning stages of citywide public transportation. He passed by the beautiful lofts that drew the migration of carpetbaggers. The city was constantly bright with electricity, illuminating new ventures and construction projects.

Houston, locals predicted, would be a force to be reckoned with.

Cody loved driving on the city's freeways during the evenings. Catch a perfect winter night and the temperature is ideal, he thought. The drive from the medical center area to his house was approximately twenty minutes. He deliberately took thirty. Relatively speaking, Cody had done well for himself. At the age of twenty-five, he had bought his own place, a beautiful three-story townhouse in a popular part of town. He lived on the strip of Westheimer Road near the Piney Point area. Like most Asian-American men of his generation, Cody had a well-paying job, excellent financial security and medical benefits. Yet, also like most Asian-American men his age, he was prone to spend as much as he made. There was a feeling of financial invincibility, giving him the illusion that he could live above his means.

Cody made his way towards the closed gate of his complex. He stopped right before it to type in his four-digit password. When he couldn't reach the panel, he cursed his shortness and got out of his car to manually enter the numbers in. When the gate finally opened, Cody got back into his car and drove on through. He cranked up the volume of his stereo, navigating his way through the twists and turns of his neighborhood. He was seconds away from home, sweet home.

Then, he noticed a familiar scene which triggered his temper.

"Oh, no. No...NO!" he shouted.

The lights inside Cody's three-story townhouse had been turned on. Through the blinds of the second floor he could make out a silhouette moving around. That person was digging through his belongings. He recognized the figure right away. It was his father. Cody angrily stormed inside, rushing upstairs to the second floor.

"<There you are!>" smiled his father. "<We were wondering when you'd return. Why didn't you answer your phone?>"

Kelvin Min-Lo Quan was a happy, easygoing man. He was well-liked. Cody resembled him in looks, but unlike his father, he was prone to hotheadedness.

"WHY ARE YOU GUYS DOING THIS?! GET THE FUCK OUT OF THIS HOUSE! NOW!!!" Cody screamed in English.

He scanned the second floor where his kitchen and living room were. Food was scattered everywhere. His Playstation 2 was being used as a DVD player on full blast for a Cantonese movie. The stairs leading to the floor above were littered with tied-up grocery bags recycled as trash bags. Cody pushed his father aside and stormed upstairs to the third floor. He wanted to speak with the mastermind behind this latest home invasion.

Finally, Cody located the culprit based on the loud sounds of the washer and dryer along with the running water from the bathtub. There, he confronted his mother. She was rearranging his clothes, sorting out the ones she approved or disapproved of.

"LEAVE THIS HOUSE N—" Cody began in English.

"<HOW MUCH DID THIS NEW SHIRT COST?!!!>" his mother screamed back. "<AND THIS ONE! THIS IS BANANA REPUBLIC! BANANA REPUBLIC IS EXPENSIVE! IT'S AT LEAST FIFTY DOLLARS! WHY DO YOU WASTE SO MUCH MONEY?>"

"I JUST WASHED THAT BANANA REPUBLIC SHIRT! WHY ARE YOU WASHING IT AGAIN?"

Marie Wong was very tiny in stature but possessed a booming presence. She had stayed at four-foot-nine since she was twelve. However, growing up as the second eldest sister of eight siblings had molded her into a naturally domineering person. She was used to looking up at people and wagging her finger at them. Very little intimidated her. Cody, however, was the exception.

"<GIVE ME YOUR WALLET!>" she ordered in Cantonese.

When Cody hesitated, she reached into his left pocket, pulling the wallet out herself. She knew Cody never had much cash in it. She also knew that if there were cash, he would spend it instead of using his credit and debit cards. Cody's mother got her purse and started putting money into his wallet.

"<I gave you thirty-five dollars last weekend and now there's only two dollars left. What did you use the money for?>" she inquired.

Cody was growing very annoyed that she was trying to control every aspect of his life.

"<I ate with it>," answered Cody.

"<That was just two days ago! You spent that much money? I cooked for you! I left you enough food for both lunch and dinner. Why are you eating out, huh?!!!>"

"<'CAUSE I'M SICK AND TIRED OF YOUR COOKING! I WANNA

EAT WHAT I WANNA EAT!>"

"<I'M JUST TRYING TO SAVE YOU MONEY! MY COOKING IS HEALTHIER THAN AMERICAN RESTAURANT FOOD!>"

"YEAH, RIGHT!" Cody screamed. "THIS IS ALL ABOUT CONTROL LIKE IT ALWAYS IS! JUST LIKE THE OTHER DAY WHEN I BOUGHT GROCERIES TO COOK AND YOU JUST CAME IN AND TOOK EVERYTHING BACK TO YOUR HOUSE! YOU DON'T LIKE IT WHEN I COOK, YOU DON'T LIKE IT WHEN I IRON AND WASH MY OWN CLOTHES, YOU DON'T LIKE IT WHEN—>"

"<Hey, hey, hey! Both of you calm down!!!>" shouted Cody's father after he had come up from the second floor. "<Please stop fighting! We've got to have peace!>"

"<QUAN MIN-LO!>" she ordered her husband, "<GET YOUR ASS BACK DOWNSTAIRS AND WATCH TELEVISION!"

"<I just...I just want you both to stop fighting!>" pleaded Mr. Quan.

"<ARE YOU SIDING AGAINST ME? ARE YOU?>" she looked at him, daring him to challenge her.

"<No...I...I'm going back downstairs>," he complied.

The loss of control was too much for Cody to bear. Externally, he resembled his father. Cody had dark olive skin, a similar speech pattern, expressive creativity and a laugh like his dad. But there was much of Cody that resembled his mother, particularly her temper. Cody and his mother were like oil and water. Once Cody reached a maximum boiling point, he did not react verbally—he reacted violently.

"AHHHHHHHHHHHHHHH!!!!!!!" Cody let out a primal scream.

He then punched a hole into his bathroom wall. *WHAM!*

The cheap flimsy plaster made it seem like Cody had super strength. The hole was large, ugly and a sign of more destruction to come.

"<Stop, son, stop! No, no, no!>" his father begged.

Cody repeatedly punched his closet door, smashing it past recognition. He grabbed toothbrushes and deodorant bottles, tossing them randomly throughout the bathroom. He kicked the toilet until his foot started hurting. Cody's mother burst into tears and grabbed her son. Cody flung her to the floor, using what self-control he had left to stop from kicking her. Instead, he started stomping on the tile floor.

"YOU WANT A PIECE OF ME?! YOU WANT TO CONTROL MY LIFE?!!" screamed Cody.

The voice coming out of him was from something else. He sounded like a monster.

"<Please...please...stop!>" His mother grabbed Cody's clothes and wallet.

He grabbed the wallet back and threw it across the room. He followed up with his clothes and did the same.

"NO! I DON'T WANT YOU TO WASH MY CLOTHES! I DON'T WANT YOU TO GIVE ME MONEY!" yelled Cody.

Mr. Quan held his sobbing wife, hoping the sudden silence would cool things down. Fights between Cody and his mother were commonplace. Cody breathed heavily, allowing his heart rate to return back to normal. He had come close to hitting his mother in every fight, but the closest he had come to it was when he pushed her down tonight. It was only a matter of time, he concluded, that he would snap and brutally attack her.

It was the consequence of culture.

When she was growing up in Hong Kong, boys weren't considered men until they were married. Their mothers were expected to coddle them. Then this practice was transferred over to their wives, who spoiled them. Women of her generation were a symbol of power and pride. While American culture's belief that a woman's place in the kitchen was considered sexist, Chinese women of his mother's generation saw it as a forum for control and empowerment. Cody, meanwhile, saw the whole process as emasculating. How could he expect to compete against other men for women? He had parents who were trying to make him as ignorant of basic life skills as possible. They didn't want him to know how to iron, cook, sew or fix things. They expected him to get a degree, work at a high-paying job and provide them with money.

"<Come on, Lai Un>," pleaded Mr. Quan, calling out to his wife by her Chinese name. "<We should go. You know how these young men are now. They want their independence. They don't want you taking care of them. Son, control your temper. I will come back this weekend and fix that door and wall for you.>"

He ushered his silent wife down the stairs. Within a few moments, they were outside. Cody could hear the engine of their Honda CRV starting. Then they pulled out of the driveway. The food and clothes that his mother was supposed to take back remained.

Cody had won the battle.

He looked around and saw the complete and utter destruction of his bathroom. It looked like a war zone. From a distance he heard his cat, Toby, meowing. The feeling of guilt started seeping in. Cody wondered if there would ever be a moment when he and his mother would get along. He
was also angry at his father for letting her get away with such controlling behavior. Twenty-seven years old, he thought, twenty-seven years old and he still had to put up with this. Sometimes he wished he weren't Asian. Do other people go through this? No, he concluded, Chinese people are a unique breed of fucked up.

Cody observed the large hole in his bathroom wall and the broken bathroom door. He couldn't recognize the monster that destroyed his bathroom. After minutes of staring, he went toward his safe haven—his laptop. Computers were his drug. Ever since they had become popular during his teenage years, Cody enjoyed being in front of a monitor's warm glow. Cody opened up his email account and saw, to his surprise, a reply from Daphne.

It read:

January 23, 2005:
"Hey Cody. Thanks for the sweet email. Do you talk to all girls like this? Yes, let's meet up for sushi tomorrow at noon. I prefer Miyako's. See you then!
- Daphne."

Cody's heart skipped a beat. All traces of the angry monster had disappeared. In its place was a bright, Cheshire cat grin.

CHAPTER 3: DAPHNE LEE

Daphne Lee was both beautiful and plain looking. She was born in Beijing but grew up in the States. Her facial structure resembled a look of typical Northern Chinese origin, but her figure hinted of a consistent American diet. She had a set of large, triangular-shaped eyes, shoulder-length hair, dry lips and a round face. At five-foot-four, she was of average height. For someone who rarely worked out, her body was in terrific shape. However, as a result of her conservative attire, nothing much was revealed and what resided underneath her clothes was left for the imagination. Nothing either good or bad stood out about Daphne. Her face was symmetrical enough to resemble beauty, but any traces of charisma seemed purposely restrained. She rarely bothered with much makeup or lipstick.

"You're ten minutes late," she observed.

Cody's timing, as usual, was off. The estimated driving time from the university to Miyako Japanese Restaurant was roughly twenty minutes. Cody left his workplace ten minutes before their noon lunch appointment.

"Well, you know, there was an accident at Highway 59 and they funneled all the ongoing traffic into two lanes. That's not even counting all the construction that's been going on," Cody fumbled.

"Oh," Daphne replied.

She made no eye contact as she spoke. Her bento box was nearly empty, with just a few pieces of salad and half a tomato left. Not surprisingly, all traces of the tempura had disappeared. Daphne loved tempura, particularly the shrimp variety. She also placed things with immense precision. Her napkin was perfectly folded. Her cup of green tea was placed exactly back into the same spot. Her chopsticks, after usage, were gently returned, together in unison, near the side of her bowl. Even the wasabi, ginger and soy sauce stayed separated, unlike most sushi restaurant patrons who ignorantly mix the three together like hot pot sauce.

"Are you finished with your food already? How long have you been here?" asked Cody.

"I came twenty minutes early," she replied in her usual passive voice.

"I love this place," Cody said, giving out a slight pause. "You know they give out Miyako bucks? For every ten dollars you spend, you get one Miyako dollar. I have about a hundred of those collected. This lunch is on me."

"I already paid for it. I'm about to leave."

"Oh. That's...that's okay. Next time then. Dinner is always better for me. None of this 'rush from work' stuff."

"Um...," she replied.

Daphne looked around for the check. There was a lengthy pause.

"Yeah, so hey, I'm baptized now!" informed Cody.

"Good. That's good. I'm glad you've developed a relationship with God. That's important, you know, because we need His love to get salvation. Who shepherded you into accepting?"

"It was Ennis. He and I are childhood friends."

"Oh. Okay."

"Yeah, I was so surprised when I literally saw Jesus. It was awesome!"

"Uh-huh."

"I really haven't seen God since then though. Do you see him? Like, literally?"

Daphne hesitated to answer, "Let's just change the subject."

"Here you are," interrupted their waitress, a young Hispanic woman in her early twenties.

Daphne signed the credit card slip. She calculated the number of reward points today's lunch would give her. Though Cody continued blabbering about various subjects, Daphne paid no attention to him. He was unattractive to her—too intense, too scrubby and too nerdy. He was also too short in stature and too lightweight for Daphne's taste. Most Asian men are ugly, she thought, and Cody was no different. It didn't matter to her that he was second-generation, born and raised in Houston. He would always be Asian. Secondary. Weak. Inferior.

"And what would you like, sir?" the waitress smiled.

"I'll, uh. Just...um," stammered Cody.

He found it difficult to decide between looking at the menu and Daphne picking up her belongings. He had waited a long time for this date. He was hesitant to accept that it would merely last several minutes.

"Just give me some miso soup, some edamame and a bento box," Cody answered.

Daphne stood up to leave.

"Hey wait, Daphne—"

"Sir, would that be Bento Box A, Bento Box B or Bento Box C?" inquired the waitress.

"I...I dunno. C. Let's do C, ok?...Hey, Daphne, wait—"

"Would that be chicken, beef or shrimp, sir?"

"Daphne.......Ugh!"

"Chicken, beef or shrimp, sir?"

Daphne walked out without looking back or saying good-bye. Cody felt a strong urge to chase after her, but he held back. The hostess in front told Daphne good-bye, to which Daphne smiled and replied back to the hostess.

"Sir?" the waitress repeated to him a third time.

"Chicken," he finally answered the waitress. His mind was miles away from his order. "I'm...I'm a chicken."

———

Mindy flashed a smile when Cody returned from lunch. She had brought her own food, which consisted of a home-cooked variety of chicken feet, bok choy and rice. The quantity she brought was enough to feed several people. Mindy ended up finishing it all. Once again, she proved to have a monstrous appetite for an extremely thin girl.

"Hey, Bubblehead!" she laughed.

"Wha—what'd you just call me?" Cody asked.

"Yeah, you got a big head, man!"

"You mean bobblehead," he corrected her.

He started browsing through his emails, hoping that Daphne would return a thank-you. There wasn't one.

"What's a bobblehead?" she inquired.

"That's like those doll things with the giant...just google it," Cody said.

"How do you spell it?"

"I don't fucking know."

An immediate feeling of guilt crept into Cody's conscience. He obviously knew how to spell "bobblehead," but he just wanted Mindy to leave him alone.

Cody decided to remedy the situation by creating conversation with her, "So what's Rachel got you doing today?"

"I just got to do some more tutorials. Hey, do you know how to make an online shopping cart?" she asked.

"Your tutorial is an e-commerce site?!" Cody asked in disbelief.

"No. I know people. They are in Taiwan. They have a shipment. There is a lot of stuff to sell. Maybe you can build a shopping cart. I will split with you. We will BE RICH!!!" she exclaimed.

"Not interested," Cody declined.

"Why not? You don't want to be rich? You would rather want to be...a...a hippie?"

"No, I just want to be content. I don't need money for that."

Cody was still facing his computer screen. Suddenly Mindy whacked him in the back of his head.

"OW! What are you doing?!!" screamed Cody." Why'd you just hit me?"

"Because you are stupid! How can you say you don't want to be rich? You think you don't need money, huh?" Mindy said.

She was a hundred-and-eighty-degree turn from the shy, introverted person she was from the previous day.

"Don't hit me like that again, OK? That hurt."

"Yeah, right! I'm so skinny and your head is so bubble!"

"Look, I've had a bad day. Bad...lunch. Just leave me alone. If you need help, let me know," Cody said.

He started working on his day's assignment. Mindy sat at her seat observing him.

"Do you have a girlfriend?" she asked.

"Oh, my God, you're in love with me," guessed Cody.

"No, STUPID! I am married, OK? I am talking about you. You went to lunch with your girlfriend, huh?"

"Jesus, please remove this woman," he prayed under his breath.

"Huh? What did you say? Something woman? Yes, I am."

"Yeah, I went to lunch with a girl. She was rude to me. I don't think she likes me. She left right away."

"Why'd she leave you? She could get a free lunch!"

"It's not like that. I don't even know why she showed up."

"Man, she sounds weird. What is her name? How do you know her?"

"Daphne. And I met her at church."

"What? You go to a church? I am Buddhist. Have you heard of Soka Gakkai?" asked Mindy as she closed her hands, placed her palms together and imitated a gesture of meditation.

"My family is Buddhist. Especially my dad," Cody revealed.

"How nice," Mindy said. "So you are in love with a girl named Daphne. How come?"

"I dunno. She's pretty. She's trustworthy and nice. Smart. Not too wild. Asian. I like Asian girls." Cody's voice trailed off as he lost track of where he was.

"It's OK, Bubble. If it was meant to be, it was meant to be. When my husband and I met, we got married after six months."

"Six months?!"

"Yes! That is the destiny. Like a red string. You know about red string?"

The red string Mindy was referring to was the Chinese version for soul mate. It was a figurative thread in which two souls were bound together. Regardless of how far apart they were, this red string would inevitably pull the two souls back together, like a rubber band.

"I believe in Jesus," Cody said with conviction. "Daphne is a God-fearing woman and I know she'll make a great girlfriend because God will lead her decisions. If two people in Christ are together, God will make it work."

Mindy reacted with a burst of laughter, covering her mouth with a ladylike politeness. However, she couldn't help but maintain eye contact.

"Ahahahahahaha!" she laughed. "Why do you think like that? She is just a woman like any other woman. Oh, Bobbie! You are such a Bobbie-Bubblehead!"

"I'm serious," countered Cody. "You should see her lead Sunday school. Her heart's in the right place."

"That's so silly, man! She is just a regular person. She is pretty, eh?"

"I think she is. But she doesn't smile enough. And she always glares at people. Like this." Cody imitated Daphne's judgmental glare.

"What? She doesn't seem like such a nice person," reasoned Mindy.

"She's a nice person. Girls from church are always nice people."

"Yeah, right. Is she born here?"

"No. She moved here early on. You know, come to think of it, I don't know much about her."

"So she is American like you. Does she speak Chinese?"

"Yeah. She's very fluent in Mandarin. She was born in China," explained Cody.

"She is from Mainland China? Be careful, Bobbie. Mainland Chinese people cannot be trusted."

Cody knew what Mindy meant by the Mainland Chinese mentality. As a frequent visitor to Hong Kong, a city soaked with Western values from decades of British rule, he had seen firsthand the decline of moral values whenever he crossed over the Mainland Chinese border. Crime was high. Once, he was even mugged there by children no older than ten years. And, Cody had observed, the people there drove with little regard for traffic rules and safety. His Hong Kong relatives had constantly told him that Mainland Chinese people were savages. Mindy, a native of the sovereign nation Taiwan, had similar experiences with the Mainland Chinese as Cody. Much like the people of Hong Kong, the Taiwanese also held a negative image of the Mainland Chinese people.

"Stop calling me Bobbie," Cody paused. "No, she grew up here. She doesn't have Mainland Chinese traits."

"Maybe her parents they teach her the bad things," Mindy stereotyped.

"It doesn't matter. She is Christian. She knows right from wrong."

"I don't think so. I don't think she is different from any other person."

With that spoken, Cody and Mindy dropped the subject. Their conversation evolved into Mindy's daily tutorials. She was in awe of the Adobe Photoshop software's basic features like the lens flare and drop shadow effects. Particularly interesting to her was the feather effect, where the edges of an image were softened from a defined border. Cody was impressive to Mindy. He was smart, creative and energetic. Everything he did felt magical to her. By their second day together, she had already felt comfortable with Cody. Mindy was comfortable enough to lean her head on his shoulder while he explained certain aspects of the tutorial. Whoever this Daphne girl was, she thought, must be lucky to have someone like Cody chasing after her.

Pastor Quentin Washington arrived with grand flair to Second Chinese Baptist Church on Wednesday afternoon. He got out of a limousine along with an entourage of other well-dressed black men in suits and sunglasses. They were mostly clergymen from his former church.

"Dang!" shouted Felix, who was painting one of the outer walls.

"Hey, how're ya doing?" greeted the smiling Pastor Washington.

The new pastor was in his late forties. He looked more like a hip-hop mogul than a man of God.

"What th—?" asked Felix.

"Pastor Washington!" greeted Pastor Lu's voice from behind, "so glad you could make it! Welcome to Second Chinese Baptist Church! Come on in. Let me give you guys a tour."

Pastor Lu was dressed in an unflattering combination of a cowboy hat, a tacky white T-shirt and jeans. The contour of his large belly was visible. Felix observed the strange contrast between the well-dressed black men and the suppressed nervousness of the Chinese congregation. However, not a bit of uncomfortable feeling was visible with Pastor Lu. He began showing his new friends around the church.

"And this stage," Pastor Lu proudly expressed, "also doubles as a baptism pool."

Several of the church members removed key floor boards from the stage, revealing a small pool for baptism. Pastor Washington and his entourage were impressed.

"Now, what about the stage lighting?" asked the new pastor. "Is there a way to dim the overall brightness and focus on the center of a stage? You know, like for dramatic effect and what not?"

"That can be arranged. Our technicians are very talented. A lot of them are electrical engineer graduates, you know," gloated Pastor Lu.

"Excellent. That's excellent," smiled Pastor Washington, scanning the large worship hall. "This is a beautiful church, Willy."

"Thank you. Thank you."

"I mean, you told me you guys don't even have a choir yet. Well, we got a whole choir we can bring...imagine a choir on that stage. Wouldn't that be something!"

A middle-aged Chinese woman, accompanied by Luke, approached the visitors with a plate of snacks.

"Would you like some cookies?" she asked the visitors.

"Oh, yes. Thank you," replied one of Washington's clergymen.

"This is my lovely wife and my son Luke. You mentioned in your letter that you have a child of your own, Quentin?" Pastor Lu asked.

"Why, yes," said Pastor Washington, gobbling on a cookie, "just my teenage daughter, Maple. They grow up so fast. My wife and I don't know what to do with her. You gotta have eyes on children at all times!"

"Oh, I know. We were lucky that Luke wasn't trouble at that age," smiled Pastor Lu.

"How old are you, my man?" asked Pastor Washington.

"Twenty-six, sir," answered Luke.

"Well, well, well. Time to get you a wife! We've got a lot of new God-obedient women that are gonna join soon. Got plenty of girls to introduce to you, son," joked the new pastor.

Polite laughter filled the room.

The rest of the tour included the Bible study halls, the library, the kitchen, the dining area, the day care centers, the indoor basketball court and, finally, the new office for Pastor Washington. The hip new pastor flashed a big, bright smile. He looked at various members of his clergy entourage and they telepathically expressed their heartfelt approval.

"It's yours," offered Pastor Lu. "Welcome to your new home, Pastor Quentin Washington."

———

Toby looked at Cody with an understanding only a cat owner would appreciate. The overweight gray tabby forced her way into his lap and made an intensive vibration with her purring, wagging her tail in a slow and devious pattern. Toby was very selective about when she wanted physical contact. However, she could also be a very affectionate pet when she wanted to cheer someone up. She knew by Cody's unusual silence that he was feeling distraught. As owner and pet, they had developed a psychic bond. It was this perfect balance of independence and well-timed affection that made Cody a fan of cats. What many others perceived as attitude from them, Cody saw it as an understanding of personal space.

Three nights had gone by since Daphne's lunch with Cody. He had sent a short thank-you email to her, hoping to lure a response in return. When she didn't reply back, he sat next to his house phone, contemplating calling her. Phone calls were Cody's weakness. There was something about putting a cold piece of machinery next to his ear that discouraged him from conversation. He preferred face-to-face. Cody started jotting down bullet points on some topics to bring up. He wanted to ask what she thought about God, what her favorite spots in Houston were, cooking, current events and whether or not she enjoyed fine art.

Taking a deep breath, Cody picked up the phone and dialed Daphne's cell number. There was a brief pause as the telephone lines connected. Fear started to grip Cody. What if she were on the phone with somebody else right now? he wondered. What if she's sleeping? What if another man answered the phone? What if—.

"Hello?" answered Daphne.

"Hey, Daphne. It's me, Cody. I just wanted to see if you're okay."

"Um...what do you want?"

"Nothing. I haven't heard from you since we last had lunch. We hardly talked and my emails went unanswered."

"Oh, yeah. I was busy. Sorry," she said, without a hint of remorse.

Cody decided to play the church angle.

"So, you did pretty well last time at Bible study. I really liked your points regarding Corinthians. The definition of love is so deep and really makes us think about society's shallow definition of love. You made a good point about connecting with one another as brothers and sisters of Christ," Cody flattered.

"Yeah. Thanks."

There was a long pause.

"You know, I see Jesus sometimes. Am I crazy or do you see him too?" asked Cody.

"I used to. I used to see him all the time."

"What does that mean? He stopped showing up?"

Daphne ignored his question. "That's good that you see him, Cody. I'll pray that you see him some more."

"What about you? Anything I should pray for on your behalf?"

Daphne let out a long condescending laugh. There was another long pause of silence.

"Let's just drop the subject, Cody."

"Okay. So, you live alone, right?" he inquired.

"Yeah," she answered.

"Any pets?"

"No."

"I live alone too. I've got a cat."

"Ew. Why do you own a cat? Most people own dogs."

"That shouldn't mean I should own a dog just because of it."

"Yeah, it should. There's a reason so many people own dogs. They're friendly, they're outgoing, they're cute and they're smart."

"I don't know," disagreed Cody. "I think they're a bit overrated. I had a Dalmatian for ten years. Well, he was more like the family dog since I didn't take care of him that much. But he was always overly eager, knocked things around, stunk, made the house dirty...just felt more annoyed about him than any other emotion. My dad loved him though. I felt sad the day the dog had to be put to sleep. It was like a family member died."

"Aw."

"Okay. Well, anyway, I'm just calling to let you know that I think you're very attractive and that's why I want to ask you out to dinner with me."

"I know. You already told me all this on the emails, remember?"

"Sure, but you haven't responded much and I thought since we had lunch at least—"

"That's flattering, but I don't feel that way about you. I only like white guys, Cody. I'm sorry. That's just my preference."

"You and every other Asian woman," muttered Cody.

"Excuse me?"

"Nothing," Cody paused," I just want to get to know you a bit. It's, like, every time I pass by you in church, my heart starts fluttering."

"Oh."

"But I have to hide that feeling in front of others because it's weird. They'll start thinking I'm not into you for Christlike reasons. But I don't know how to approach you and tell you in any other way," Cody confessed.

"I see," Daphne replied.

"Maybe all I want to do is know you. I don't know anything about you besides the basic stuff like you sometimes lead Sunday school or that you do investing. You're a year younger than I am, and you graduated with honors from UT. But I don't know what movies you like, your favorite color or why you choose to drive that dorky Volkswagen Passat."

"That's flattering, Cody. It really is. It's sweet that you want to get to know me," she paused. "Tell you what, I'll let you be my friend. Friendship is forever. You can hear about my problems, things like my favorite color and stuff. That could work for me."

"Oh. Okay, well, of course. We've got to be friends first, right? Yeah, we could get to know one another. Be there for each other," Cody convinced himself.

"Exactly. It'll be like that TV show *Will and Grace*," assured Daphne.

"Yeah."

There was a slight pause in conversation.

"Well. It's ten o'clock. I guess I should be getting ready for bed," she said.

"I enjoyed talking with you as well. Let's hope that this is a start of a beautiful, new friendship. And hopefully it'll blossom into something more," he hoped.

"Let's just be friends, Cody. Good night!"

CHAPTER 4: FAMILY

"Don't end up in the friend zone," lectured a stern Duke.

The seminar was held at the smallest conference room in the Doubletree Hotel near the Galleria area. It was attended by an assortment of socially awkward men, most of them Asian-American in their mid-twenties to late thirties. It was his fifth annual Alpha Asian Boot Camp—the most highly attended thus far. The objective of the seminars was to empower these men by converting them into his definition of an alpha male. Cody was also in attendance because of the deal he had made a few weeks earlier.

"Repeat what I just said," Duke barked.

"WE DO NOT END UP IN THE FRIEND ZONE," the attendees shouted in unison.

"Women are our prey. We are, by nature, hunters. Civilized society has made us forget that! This is particularly true if you're an Asian male! Look at the media! Look at what people are saying! White guys laugh at us and take our women! We fight back with stronger game! What did I just say?"

"WE FIGHT BACK WITH STRONGER GAME!"

"Good. First, I'll start by saying what I've said in all these boot camps. Forget romantic fluff. Women measure a man by three things: looks, money and social status. Be honest with yourselves. How many of you have all three? None? I bet for most of you money isn't a problem. You're Asian. You've graduated from top schools, earning good pay, and I know that's true because you're attending this class and paying thousands of dollars for it. You're making me, an alpha male, rich! But you were never taught the fundamentals of what women want. So, continuing what we've been learning, I'm introducing a method called screening," Duke said.

Duke paused so that his students could jot down the word "screening" onto their notes or laptops.

"AMANDA! Come out here," he ordered.

A beautiful blonde woman approached the stage. She had gorgeous hair that fell down to her waist, complemented by her sparkling blue eyes and magnificent smile.

"As you've all noticed, this woman is a perfect ten," explained Duke. "What are most of you? Twos, threes, a four at best. Even I'm a nine-point-five. Amanda? She's a ten. Some of you right now can't even stay conscious looking at her. So what do you do when you see a gorgeous woman like this in a bar?"

A few hands slowly went up. Duke pointed at one of them.

"Kino," suggested the student.

"Kino" was the method of touching a woman during conversation. This was to make her react and imply sexual tension.

"No," replied Duke.

"Negs," blurted another one.

"Negs" was the method of insulting a woman, breaking down her self-confidence. It was the preferred method for jerks.

"Did I point at you?" Duke scowled.

"Sorry," the second student replied.

"No. We don't use negs in this instance."

Duke glanced at the front row until he found whom he considered a weak-looking person.

"You," he said, pointing at the student, "what do you think?"

"We use screening," the student replied. "That's what you just said we're gonna learn, wasn't it?"

The students collectively laughed. Duke did not like to be made fun of. He approached the meek student and gave him a primal stare.

"Yeah. The answer is screening. Good. What's your name?" asked Duke.

"M...Minh," he answered nervously.

"Stand up," Duke commanded.

Minh did as he was told. Duke proceeded to grab him in the crotch, sending Minh screaming in pain. There was a collective wincing among the other students.

"Do you know what I'm doing to you right now?" Duke asserted.

The student fumbled for an answer, but only inaudible words came out of his mouth.

"Right now, I'm squeeeeeezing your dick," informed Duke. "You like that? You like having your dick squeezed?"

Minh shook his head.

"Listen to me and listen to me well. Until the day you're alpha enough to teach this class and not give smartass remarks, I'll stop squeezing your dick. Do you understand?"

Minh nodded in pain. Duke let go of his groin and dismissed him back to his seat.

"Screening," Duke continued, "is making a woman earn you by giving her a trial of tests. Apply this when you're dealing with a ten. Watch."

The blond woman pretended to be someone in a bar. Duke paced back and forth, looking at her, determining if she were worthy of his liking.

"Hello," he said to Amanda, "I'm interested in you. Can I have your number?"

"Ugh," pretended Amanda, "why should I give it to you?"

Duke frowned.

"It's okay. Fine. That's your choice. But just know that if I give you mine, I won't answer you if you call me five times a day. It's beyond my standard."

"What?"

"Yes, even with a beautiful woman like yourself," said Duke, "I have policies. And I only like women who dress in yellow, teal green or mahogany."

"Wow!" she exclaimed, "I've never met anyone like you before. I can meet those standards!"

"Can you? I don't think you can."

"Please, give me a chance," pleaded Amanda. "I'm begging you. You must be an alpha male."

"I am," Duke replied.

He held her close, applying kino, then stronger kino, and finally, maximum kino. When he had her close to him, he unleashed a primal stare. Amanda felt an overflow of wetness inside her panties. A collective "wow" came from the audience.

"Psychopath," coughed Cody.

"Okay, everyone," Duke said, "take a ten-minute break. Use it wisely. Underneath your chairs is a package of Pick Up Artist guidelines and accessories. Like karate, you will seek to ascend into various levels of PUA until you become a master, or what we call an alpha PUA. Memorize the acronyms. Alpha males use acronyms to save time. There's also a chart with a formula for measuring yourself on the ladder. Looks, money and social status. Where does she fit? How does she accurately rank in a scale of one to ten? How do you rank? Can you get the ones who are ranked eight or above? Learn the secrets. Develop your day game. Then night game. Use words as an opening and then unleash various techniques to establish your dominance. Remember, women are our prey. They are to be chased, conquered and enjoyed."

During the break, Cody walked toward Duke.

"That was all bullshit!" Cody exclaimed. "I can't believe people pay you for this!"

Duke shrugged.

He turned his back towards Cody. There was no end of admirers who surrounded Duke with Pick Up Artist questions. They were fascinated by his knowledge in the art of seduction. Duke's methods involved the biological nature of animals, explained and tested through the methods of calculus and statistics. He felt it was his way of giving back to Asian men. Duke believed he gave them empowerment.

––––––––

"Aiya!!!!!"

It was the eve of the Lunar New Year. Cody's mother stared at his father with daggers in her eyes. Marie Un-Mui Wong had been married to Kelvin Min-Lo Quan for twenty-seven years. She had hoped that certain flaws about him would have changed since then.

"<Why did you rearrange every furniture around the house?>" she questioned. "<What's this plant doing in the middle of our kitchen? Why'd you put these cheap battery-operated glowing lotuses everywhere? Our
wedding photo upstairs...it's moved!>"

"<This is proper feng shui>," Mr. Quan explained. "<I am directing as much positivity as I can.>"

"<What? No! Put it all back! You're being a ninny>," replied Cody's mother.

Their house was already compact. Bookshelves and display cases caused the narrow living spaces to be even tighter. It was located in a decent neighborhood with children constantly playing outside, where the home association did a fine job of keeping it in pristine condition.

"<What's going on?>" asked Ace Wong, scurrying downstairs.

Ace was Marie's nephew, a visa-carrying student from Hong Kong. He had been staying with them for the past two years.

"<Your uncle is being overly superstitious again>," explained Cody's mother.

"<Luck is not a superstition>," Mr. Quan defended. "<We are controlling our destiny by mastering the flow of our chi.>"

"<Do you need help?>" inquired Ace.

"<Please don't encourage him>," Cody's mother replied.

As a staunch follower of commercialized Chinese Buddhism, Kelvin Quan revolved his life around it. This meant a minimal focus on traditional Buddhist practices like meditation and mantras. Instead, he had a deep fascination for fortune-telling, charms, numbers, chi and, of course, feng shui. He felt that the fabric of their world was like a safe that could be cracked by a metaphysical master. The answer, he believed, involved proper usage of the elements, timing it with the Chinese lunar calendar, understanding its relations to the four directions, controlling it with karma and then applying any other kooky personal theory he could throw in there. This was what Cody's father loved about mainstream Buddhism; it was like a Lego set that could be assembled any way he saw fit.

"<How much did you spend on these?>" she inquired, referring to the dozens of metallic pinwheels her husband had purchased from the art store.

"<Six dollars>," he lied.

"<You liar! Why do you always buy crap like this? Is that a rocking horse?>"

"<It's a red rocking horse. It'll speed up the flow of our earth energy, which is what we lack in this household.>"

"<Earth energy...>" Cody's mother repeated.

"<Yes. It'll ease up our surplus of fire element energy. See? The pinwheels are fanning out the bad luck. Can you get a Sharpie and help me paint them black?>"

"<This is crazy>," she criticized. "<We do this every year and our luck is still shit.>"

"<But we're close to getting it right. I can feel it. Haven't you noticed a reduction in bad incidents year after year?>"

"<I was hoping it was because you were learning your lesson from all that silly scheming. So, are we going to the temple or what? It's almost seven o'clock. It's going to be packed the closer we get toward lunar midnight.>"

Her husband agreed. Not long afterwards, both of them headed toward their local temple, which consisted of a large series of shrines devoted for mass worshipping. Because it was Lunar New Year's Eve, massive numbers of visitors came to maximize their luck. In Houston, the majority of the Asian population was an entangled mixture of Chinese and Vietnamese. The temple's crowd reflected this, with both languages intertwined among the cacophony of conversations. More noticeable was the massive amount of smoke created by the incense. Visitors grabbed handfuls of the incense to give offering to the various gods.

"<Hey!>" screamed Cody's mother.

She was about to take some incense of her own when a middle-aged woman pushed past her, grabbing handfuls of incense herself.

"<Don't be greedy!>" Cody's mother continued. "<You don't need that much luck!>"

"<Get the hell out of my way!>" the woman retorted.

"<She took all the incense and now there's none left for the rest of us! >" She glared at her husband. "<Do something!>"

"<Er...uh...excuse me, miss. Uh...>" Mr. Quan's voice trailed off.

Cody's mother chased down the woman and began pulling some of the incense away from her. She successfully wrestled a handful.

"<Gimme that!>" she yelled in conquest.

"<Let's not...please...let's not cause a scene. It's the new year>," pleaded Cody's father.

"<We needed incense!>" Cody's mother claimed.

She handed some of it to her husband. "<Here. Start clockwise from the left and I'll move counterclockwise from the right. We'll cover more gods that way.>"

The couple weaved through the large crowd efficiently, placing incense in each of the large pots per Buddhist deity. There was Shui Wei Sheng Niang, the waterfront goddess. Mazu, the protector of the sea. Zao Shen, the lord of the kitchen. Budai, the laughing Buddha. Various deified Chinese lords. The eight immortals. And finally, Guan Yin, the goddess of compassion. Of all these, she was Mr. Quan's most revered bodhisattva.

"<A wife>," he prayed to Guan Yin, "<please give my son a wife. And health. And also, I could use a winning scratch-off lottery ticket every now and then.>"

"<Are we done?>" complained Cody's mother. "<Our clothes smell like barbecue.>"

"<We still have to do some kau chim>," he insisted.

Kau chim is a fortune-telling technique that features hundreds of marked sticks in a long cup. The user prays and repeatedly shakes the cup at a forty-five degree angle until a stick falls to the ground. The user then picks up two wooden blocks and drops them to the ground. If both blocks land facing up or down, it means that the gods approve of the destiny foretold by the stick. However, if the blocks land facing differently from each other, the user has to repeat the process.

"<This is important>," muttered Mr. Quan. "<I wish our son was here for this.>"

"<Just do it for him>," Cody's mother advised.

He kneeled in front of the god statue and shook the cup. Because he was clumsy, multiple sticks fell out at once.

"<Oh, man.>" Mr. Quan hastily picked them up and tried kau chim again.

"<Hurry up and do it right, asshole!>" someone in line shouted.

Mr. Quan tried it again, this time shaking the cup more gently. This time, a lone stick fell down. He picked it up and, using his reading glasses, viewed the number written on it.

"<Number forty-one>," Cody's father read.

They went to the shelf that contained various stacks of pink paper. Each of the stacks was marked with a specific number. Mr. Quan picked up a slip from stack number forty-one.

"<What does it say?>" asked Cody's mother.

"<It's a medium luck one. 'The path you are embracing shall soon meet a fork in the road'>," he read. "<I wonder what that means? That boy better not be getting into any trouble. I think it'll be safer to buy a couple extra pinwheels tomorrow. Just in case.>"

Minutes later, the middle-aged couple walked out of the crowded, smoky temple. They were reminiscing about their early days of dating. She first met him when he was a bank clerk in the North Point district of Hong Kong. Kelvin Min-Lo Quan called her the cutie cat. She looked so young and so beautiful. Even to this day, Cody's mother continued to look ten years younger than she was. Min-Lo was quite the charmer as a teenager. He was adored by plenty of young women who claimed that he resembled Cantopop singer Sam Hui. More importantly, the young Mr. Quan was charming, nice and talkative. However, after years of marriage, his confidence deteriorated when he learned that his pretty cutie cat wife was also a feisty, domineering woman. That was fine for him, though, since his submissive personality led him to fear confrontations.

"<I wonder if he has a girlfriend already>," he wondered. "<I've never seen him with a girl. Do you think our son could be gay?>"

"<Well, he did drive to Montrose several weeks ago>," quipped Cody's mother.

Montrose is a famous gay and lesbian part of Houston.

"<Wasn't that for work though?>"

"<Why would he need to drive anywhere for his work?>" she reasoned. "<He sits in front of a computer all day for his job.>"

"<Our son's not gay>," Mr. Quan confidently believed. "<He can't be. Besides, I'd rather he'd be a homosexual than someone who married a black person. I would disown him if he did that.>

"<He wouldn't marry a black girl>," assured Cody's mother.

"<I know. But if he did. I'd disown him. I would.>"

"<How about a white girl?>"

"<Oh! Now that...that'd make me happy!>" he glowed.

"<Our grandchild would be so beautiful. We'd be so rich.>"

"<I'd honestly rather he'd married a white girl over an Asian one>," she admitted.

"<It doesn't matter to me. You know how I am. I love everyone. But no blacks.>"

Cody's father heard his cell phone ringing. The number was from the hospital. Why would they suddenly be calling me at eight o'clock? he wondered.

"Hello?............yes, this is Kelvin .... yes......... okay....... please repeat, my English suck......okay.......okay.....what happened?.........I thought you said everything is okay? Now it is not okay?.........okay, okay, I'm coming."

"<What's wrong?>" asked Cody's mother.

"<Call Cody. Tell him to meet us at the hospital. My mother's health unexpectedly took a fatal turn.>"

———————

It was midnight at the hospital when the Quan family and other family members gathered around Skinny Grandma. She was in a comatose state, "alive" by only the technical definition of the word. The unified humming and beeping from the medical equipment was heard through the family's silence. In attendance was Cody, both of his parents, a various assortment of aunts and uncles, Duke, their cousin Minston, Minston's much-too-young-for-him girlfriend Wanda, Minston's thirty-year-old ex-girlfriend, Cody's two maternal cousins Ace and Megan, and, finally, his grandfather.

The last one on that list was the most notable in attendance.

It was rare for Cody's paternal grandparents to be in the same place together. For reasons never entirely explained to them, he and his paternal cousins were unclear about why his grandmother held a lifelong grudge against his grandfather. He knew that they had never married, but even in the most contemporary of Chinese culture, couples joined together anyway for the sake of unison. This was especially true for his grandfather's generation. Therefore, an appearance by the elderly man was an indication that Skinny Grandma was lying on her deathbed.

"<Passing away at Chinese New Year, mother>," cried Mr. Quan.

"<How perfect is fate?>"

"<Don't be ridiculous, Min-Lo! >" shouted his older sister Mei. "<How do you know this is it?>"

Cody's Aunt Mei was always bossing around his father. Both Cody and his mother resented her. She was bullheaded, loudmouthed and domineering. There was no doubt she had passed on those values to her son Duke.

"<Because the doctor said so!>" Cody's mother retorted.

"<Yeah? Well, I don't trust that Mexican man>," exclaimed Aunt Mei. "<Oh, why couldn't they have given mother a white doctor? They must want her to die!>"

Mr. Quan nodded in agreement. "<And notice how most of the nurses are black too. This is most definitely a conspiracy.>"

Cody stood there dumbfounded. Just a week ago, the hospital staff had assured him that his grandmother was going to be okay. They had claimed that the heart surgery would only be a minor risk. He had done his best to understand all the medical jargon, but that was the summary of what the doctor had explained. Cody looked at Duke to ensure that he, too, had concluded something similar from the previous doctor's meeting. Though Duke hesitated to make eye contact, the signs of confusion on his face indicated that he had thought the same.

Both of them held a deep love for their grandmother. Without her, their childhood memories would be empty. The original house that Cody grew up in was a very modest one, taken care of by Skinny Grandma. Because Aunt Mei was going through marital issues, Duke, as a child, would spend time living in the home. The old backyard had been practically turned into a farm. Row after row, the soil was used to grow melons and other assorted vegetables. Chickens and pigeons ran around. The two boys were usually sent to the nearby stables, asking local farmers for horse manure that would be used for fertilizer. The Alief area that they grew up in was a different place in the early eighties; it was slightly suburban but still had traces of ruralness. This, however, did not stop either Cody or Duke from proudly revealing that they were from there. Alief was their home, their childhood, their best memories. It reminded them of a time when both were as close as brothers instead of distant cousins.

"We gotta go," whined Minston's ex-girlfriend.

"No, this my grandmother!" responded Minston in broken English. "Late one hour clubbing. Okay today."

"Like we make a difference here!" she pouted. "It's my friend's birthdayyyyy!"

"Ooooh, is it held at the Roxy?" asked Minston's current girlfriend, Wanda.

"Who asked you, bitch?"

"Slut!"

Duke angrily glared at the two scantily dressed women. The one in her late thirties had a horrible boob job. The other one, Wanda, was an underaged girl who had too much makeup on but too little clothing. When she caught Duke's intimidating expression, she leaned closer toward Minston for safety.

"I think your group should leave," Duke firmly commanded.

"Come on, baby. Your cousin is scary," glared Wanda.

"Sigh," muttered an annoyed Minston. "<Okay, okay. She better not be dead when I come back tomorrow!>"

The middle-aged playboy left the room with his two lady friends.

Several hours passed. Each family member procrastinated about leaving, wondering if this would be their last chance with Skinny Grandma. Once one o'clock in the morning came, however, Cody's parents left because of Ace and Megan. His aunts and uncles slowly followed suit. Duke, Cody and their grandfather were the ones left remaining. Finally, their grandfather walked towards her and offered his condolences.

"<I'm sorry>," whispered Cody's grandfather. "<I'm so sorry for what I did to you.>"

Though both cousins were curious about what had happened between their grandparents, they were raised not to ask questions.

"<Min-Guang>," Cody's grandfather commanded to him in his Chinese name, "<Take me home>."

Duke was offended. He was the responsible one. His grandfather would be safer with him instead of his immature cousin. But then again, he wasn't a Quan. This hierarchy by birthright silently angered Duke. Out of obligation, Duke kept silent, exiting the room with them. They left Skinny Grandma, clinging on to life in her hospital bed.

As the elevator took them down, Cody observed how elegant the hospital was. His grandfather silently stood next to him, occasionally muttering a deep, regretful sigh. Whatever was going on in his head, Cody thought, was decades of history about a complicated love affair. It was one that only his grandparents knew about. Sure his parents, aunts and uncles had an idea, but it was probably a summarized version. People kept secrets, Cody surmised. People kept them to their graves.

Once they were in the parking garage, both cousins walked their separate ways.

"You remembered where you parked?" asked Cody.

Duke ignored him and continued walking.

"Okay then," continued Cody, "drive safely. Remember......family dinner tomorrow for Chinese New Year."

Duke felt insulted that his cousin would remind him of things like Chinese New Year. In his mind, he believed that he was more Chinese than Cody would ever be. Duke had values. He had tradition and cultural pride. Cody once joked that they weren't really Chinese because neither of them could name three streets in China. Duke countered that blood decided their nationality. The terms Chinese-American or Asian-American were acceptable, but never just American. The latter symbolized integration, an idea Duke couldn't accept.

Once Duke found his car, he sat in it for a few seconds. He had never been a spiritual or religious person, but for a mere moment he realized it was no good being an atheist either. He cried and mumbled words that resembled prayers. They were wishes to whatever cosmic forces were out there listening. When it came to Skinny Grandma, Duke would do anything, believe in anything, to save her.

———————

It didn't take long for Cody to drop his grandfather off at his retirement complex. Before his grandfather left the car, however, he had a few words for Cody.

"<Please take time to have dinner with me more often>," he insisted. "<Out of all my grandchildren, I love you the most. You are the last remaining Quan. Whatever is mine is yours. Please know that, Min-Guang.>"

"<Yes>," Cody replied.

His grandfather continued, "<You're a good boy. I hope you are obedient. You should find a wife and make some grandchildren to honor me. I would be most happy if you married your cousin in Hong Kong.>"

There was an awkward pause.

"<But improper cousin not love>," protested Cody in broken Cantonese.

"<Improper? What's so improper about it?>" wondered his grandfather. "<Back in my village, everyone married their cousins. Is she not pretty enough for you? Why must you be so picky? It's not like she's your sister.>"

"<Girlfriend already have I.>"

"<Oh, really, you have a girlfriend? Who? Is she Chinese? She must be Chinese, Min-Guang.>"

"<Yes. Beijing born she original.>"

"<Ah! A Beijing girl! That's good! Very good. She can cook dumplings for you!>"

"<No but raise must her in America small since.>"

"<Huh? I didn't understand what you just said.>"

"<She no cook.>"

"<What do you mean she doesn't cook? That's a woman's job.>"

"<Invest. She does.>"

"<I see. Well, maybe when you're both married she can stay home and cook for you.>"

There was a moment of silence.

"<I am tired, Min-Guang>," Cody's grandfather continued. "<I love your grandmother, but things didn't go well between us. I did much to make up for the mistakes of my youth. So, I'm still disappointed and confused why she never forgave me. We could have been a more unified family.>"

"<What happened?>"

Cody's grandfather paused for an answer.

"<Sometimes, small things can seem like bigger things, Min-Guang>," explained his grandfather. "<In the end, they don't matter. Behave and always be obedient. Consider marrying your cousin. That is the best advice I can give you. Good night, Min-Guang.>"

Cody observed his grandfather as he walked into the retirement home's entrance. He had always watched because he never knew if it would be the last time he'd see him. His grandfather was nearly eighty-five years old. Cody was very blessed to see him in such peak health. This brought his mind back to his grandmother in the hospital. The doctors had estimated that she might not make it past the current month. More so, it seemed to Cody that she might not even make through the night. What if, he wondered, she would pass away in a few hours? What if this was his last chance?

Fearing this, Cody drove back to the hospital. Once he was there, he observed his grandmother in her hospital room. There she was, full of tubes and IVs, clinging on to the very end of her life. She looked frail and mortal. He reached out to hold her hand. There was no reaction. He crudely estimated that Skinny Grandma had probably only a five-percent chance of living at this point. Cody realized what he had to do. He kneeled beside his grandmother and sought a higher power.

"Jesus," he prayed, "dear Jesus, save her. Please. I love her."

Cody said it with tears streaming down his closed eyes.

He cried until it became audible. "Okay," he heard a voice say.

Cody opened his eyes and saw Jesus standing across the other side of the bed. He was wearing green hospital scrubs. The medical equipment began beeping louder in unison. Jesus winked at Cody.

"<Min-Guang?>" asked Skinny Grandma suddenly.

She had awakened in full health.

"Thank you," smiled a cheerful Cody. "Thank you!"

"<Min-Guang, who are you talking to?>" asked his grandma.

"<Jesus did I talk to>" he stammered in broken Cantonese.

"<Jesus? That's silly, Min-Guang. We're Buddhist.>"

CHAPTER 5: IN LOVE, IN FAIRNESS

A new scene was awaiting the usual congregation of Second Chinese Baptist Church. For the first time, its large parking lot exceeded full capacity. People were slowly being funneled into its welcoming doors like streams of water flowing into a drain. Most apparent was the unusual mix of Asian and black attendants scattered about, keeping a combination of distance and politeness. Both groups were in stark contrast with one another. The Asian crowd were clad in a near-uniform attire—mostly black suits, white shirts and an assortment of ties for the men; long-sleeved white dresses for the women. The African-American crowd, on the other hand, wore an assorted array of colorful outfits, like a bag of Skittles scattered around the church. Most notable were the fancy hats of the elderly black women. The Asian and black children were sent to the nursery where their color blindness allowed them to mingle without hesitation. The adults, on the other hand, were distracted by their differences, enough to divert their attention from the day's message delivered by the new pastor, Quentin Washington.

"From one man," boomed the affluent black preacher, "He made all the nations, that they should inhabit the whole earth. And he marked out their appointed times in history and the boundaries of their lands. Acts 17:26."

The church was packed to its maximum capacity.

For several weeks, Pastor Lu had been announcing the addition of a new pastor to the current Chinese membership. What he had understated to them, however, were how many new people would immediately join, and more shockingly, that all of them were black.

"<From one man>," followed the translator in Mandarin Chinese, "<He made all the nations, that they should inhabit the whole earth. And he marked out their appointed times in history and the boundaries of their lands. Acts 17:26.>"

To the Chinese crowd, having sermons interrupted for a translation was commonplace in an Asian church. However, the black crowd was far from used to it, and it silently irritated many of them that they were getting pauses in between the pastor's delivery. Some in the black audience also wondered if there had always been a security guard sitting near the front door.

"Since the days of Babel," continued Pastor Washington, "God has made us different. We look different, we speak different languages, we have different tastes. Similarities make us cocky. Makes us self-righteous. But DIVERSITY. Diversity humbles. God may have made us into the image of Him, but we are scattered pieces of Him, like a puzzle. Only by working together and being together can we see a fuller image of Jesus."

"Amen!" "Amen!" "Hallelujah!" shouted various members from the black crowd.

Several of the Chinese congregation looked around and then at one another. Daphne glared at one particular black woman who started shaking up and down like she was being possessed.

"Just look around," insisted the pastor. "Look around and let yourselves know that this...this was meant to be. God doesn't want a bag of flavorless tortilla chips. No. He wants an assorted party mix of Doritos."

"Doritos?" Marco Ling angrily mumbled to himself.

"AMENAMENAMEN!!!" came a squeaky high-pitched male voice.

It was from Herman Shu, a skinny, overly active young member of the Chinese youth congregation. Herman came to church services in spurts. A self-proclaimed prodigy, he liked to view himself as an intellectual, making a habit out of debating and interrupting as many conversations, lectures or events as possible. He was known to love attention. No one quite remembered when Herman had joined the congregation, though he had been there for a very long time. His personal history was a blurry one, and the numerous explanations of his origins contradicted themselves.

"Uh, thank you," replied Pastor Washington. "As I said...today, as we see ourselves as brothers and sisters in Christ, the Almighty, the Lord, the Man Upstairs, just by being together, Chinese and black, we are already doing His work."

"PREACH ON, BROTHER! OHHHHH WEEEEEE!" Herman stood up and started doing a spin dance.

"Herman! Please sit down!" hissed Ennis.

"You sure are pumped up today," chuckled the elderly black woman next to Herman.

The sermon extended past the hour because of the translations. It ended with Luke leading a small band, which was comprised of acoustic guitars and the soft, soprano voice of Henry. After awhile, it transitioned to a makeshift choir group from Washington's previous church. Many of the new black members clapped and shouted at the top of their lungs. Cody stood and watched several of the Chinese members join them, even when their mimicking revealed a lack of familiarity toward such an openly emotional style of worship.

Finally, Pastor Lu concluded the service in prayer.

"Dear Heavenly Father. We do not know why you have put us

together...this, unique...combination of Christians. But we have faith that this is your plan. We thank you for Pastor Washington. Thank you for the challenge of having a larger church. May we grow together and learn about you through these times. May we set an example of what this can accomplish when we put our differences aside and bask in your love. In Jesus' name we pray, amen."

The congregation followed with a collective amen.

———————

"Are you sure you're married?" asked Cody.

"Yes. I am," replied Mindy.

"Then explain to me why the two of us are sharing a table at a five-star steakhouse on Valentine's Day?"

It was the night afterwards: Valentine's Day. Del Frisco's was one of the most expensive steakhouses in Houston, next to Taste of Texas and Perry's, both of which Cody had always believed to be overrated. Located at the side of the famous Galleria mall, it was constantly filled, but never more so than this special holiday for lovers.

"Because you wanted dinner, Bubblehead," Mindy said, browsing through the menu. The menu was short, following the restaurant rule that the higher the class of the restaurant, the fewer choices available.

"Stop calling me Bubblehead. And when I said dinner, I meant Jack in the Box. Maybe Chick-fil-A," said Cody.

"That is unhealthy! Besides, you said you like turtle soup. And this is one of the few places that will have it. I want to try it!"

"So where's your husband? Why isn't HE taking you out tonight?"

"Because he's working, man!"

Cody gave her a skeptical eye.

"Why aren't you wearing a wedding ring?"

"Huh? Are you crazy? What the silly question is that? It can get stolen. I never wear it outside! Man, it's so dark in here. I cannot read the menu. They need to open the lights!"

"Okay, you're paying half. You're not my girlfriend," said Cody.

"Tsk. You make more than me! I am a student. That is not gentlemanly of you, Bubblehead!" explained Mindy.

She leaned closer to him.

Cody was lost in thought. He replayed the events earlier this Valentine's Day when he made a custom CD of carefully selected songs for Daphne. He had gone to her workplace with the CD and fruit flowers. Her initial surprise of seeing him there was quickly replaced with annoyance. She felt embarrassed. Daphne quickly shooed him out of her workplace, giving the fruit flowers to her boss instead. She then tossed the CD into the trash.

"HEY!" Mindy interrupted Cody's thought process, "I want the sixteen-ounce ribeye! That looks good!"

"Can you eat all that?! Where does it all go? You must poop a lot!"

"Ahahahahaha!" giggled Mindy.

The two new friends eventually placed their orders and enjoyed the night away. After her second glass of wine, the lightweight Mindy started feeling buzzed. She carefully glanced at Cody's face amidst the dim, flickering candlelight.

"You know what?" Mindy muttered. "You are my best friend,"

"Oh...that steak was so good. Damn. That steak was fucking good," observed Cody.

"Why do you say so many bad words? I thought you go to church."

"It's okay. I can curse."

"No, it's not, Bobbie. You must set a good example," assured Mindy.

"Oh yeah? You should come to our church some time."

"Haha. No. Church people are mean. Besides, it's so stupid. It doesn't make sense. They just want your money. Have you ever given them money?"

"No. Not yet," replied Cody.

"Good! Because that is how they trick you!"

Cody paused.

"What's your husband's name?" Cody asked her.

"I don't know. Hahaha!"

"What do you mean you don't know? You made him up, didn't you?"

"Hahaha! I'm just kidding, Bubble! His name is Wing Wei. We met singing karaoke. Hey! Wanna hear me sing? I'm good."

"You're drunk, Mindy," Cody flatly replied.

"Am I? The wine taste like grape juice, man. Sorry. HEY! Guess what?"

"What?"

"Tonight we celebrate!" Mindy held her glass toward Cody's glass.

Cody cheered her glass.

"What are we celebrating, buddy?" asked Cody.

"To our new partnership! I am making you the cofounder chief executive vice president of Mosaic Decor!" smiled Mindy.

"I told you I don't want in on any of your kooky business ideas."

"Come on! We are going to be rich! I have it all in my head! You just make the website. We sell it! Okay?"

"And how are we going to find suppliers? What is being sold anyway?"

"Home decor! But modern! That is why I have decided to call it Mosaic Decor!"

"Mosaic doesn't mean modern, dear," corrected Cody.

"It sounds cool, man. It's easy! Come on! I know some wholesalers."

"Okay, okay. Fine. I can use some side income."

Mindy grabbed Cody's hand and placed her head on his shoulder. The waiter came over and handed them their check.

"How was it? Good?" asked the waiter. "You two seem happy. How long have y'all been together?"

"We're not a couple," corrected Cody.

"Oh," paused the waiter, "should I split the check then?"

"No, no. It's alright. I got it," Cody plopped down his credit card.

"I'm already married!" exclaimed Mindy.

The baffled waiter thanked Cody and took his card back to be processed. Mindy stared at the patrons at the table next to them. An older gentlemen in his fifties was feeding chocolate cake to a giggling young woman in her twenties.

"Man," observed Mindy, "that guy. He is too old for her! And that lady, her boobs are fake!"

"Stop staring at people. It's not polite."

"You think I need some fake boobs? Mine are small. My husband give me a nickname. He calls me Ms. A-Minus!" informed Mindy, regarding her breast size.

The waiter returned with Cody's receipt.

"Thank you for dining with us at Del Frisco's. I hope you both have a VERY pleasant evening," smiled the waiter.

Mindy held on to Cody's arm as they walked out of the Galleria steakhouse. The mall was closing, but since it was Valentine's Day, it wasn't as empty as it would have been on an average Monday night. Mindy waited outside while Cody walked around the parking lot trying to find his car. The car was a six-year-old sea green 2000 Acura Integra. It was only a four-cylinder automatic, but its outward appearance made the small sports car appear faster than it was.

Cody finally found his car and drove up to where Mindy was waiting.

"Man, what took you so long?!" quipped Mindy.

They headed west along Westheimer Road—traffic was beginning to thin out for the night. Mindy played around with the radio until she found an adult contemporary station.

"Ooh! My favorite song! It's by Daniel Powter!" Mindy started singing along. "'You had a bad day! La la la la. Ma ma la la...la la la la!'"

"How can this be your favorite song? You don't even know the words."

"I like it, okay?!"

They stopped at a traffic light. A bum walked up to Cody's car, offering to clean his windows. Cody aggressively shook his head in rejection. The bum continued to clean the front window anyway.

"Hey, hey! Stop! I said no!" Cody shouted.

Cody squirted water from his windshield wipers at the bum while he was still cleaning the car window. Soaking wet, he flicked his middle finger at Cody and then extended his other hand for money.

"Give me my dolla, muthafucka!" demanded the bum.

The traffic light turned green.

"Go go go!" insisted Mindy.

Cody drove off.

"Man, why don't they get a real job? That nigger!" blurted Mindy.

"Hey! Don't say that word! It's wrong!" Cody said.

"Why not? I hear them call each other that all the time."

"You just can't. It's...it's a rule."

"Rule, huh? You always call me a fob. How come you can say fob and I can't say nigger?"

"I shouldn't be calling you a fob either."

"But you do! I don't like it when you call me that, Bobbie."

"Okay, okay. I'll stop calling you a fob."

"And I'll stop calling you a nigger."

"You didn't call me that word," insisted Cody.

"What word?" Mindy asked.

"The word that just said."

"How come you can't say it? Say it out loud!"

"No," said Cody.

"Man, this country is so sensitive, man! In Taiwan, we can laugh at those things!"

"Well, in Taiwan, everyone is...Taiwanese!" Cody reasoned.

"What do you mean by that?"

"You're all Chinese!"

"We are not all Chinese!"

"I don't mean politically," Cody said, "I mean—"

"I am not Chinese, Bubble! I am half Japanese and half Korean!"

Cody was stunned.

"Then how come you speak Taiwanese?" he asked.

"Because I grew up in Taiwan! But people can make fun of me and say Korean or Japan joking! No one is in offense!"

A long pause resulted.

Deep down inside, Cody understood what Mindy was talking about. He recalled, once again, the day he punched out the fifth-grade bully, Derrick James. Derrick James was a large black kid, two years older than the average fifth-grader. He remembered Derrick and other black kids beating him up in front of the teachers. They constantly called him several racist names, but the teachers turned the other way. When Cody finally found the courage and anger to stand up to Derrick, Cody screamed the word "nigger" for his first and only time. The school suspended him for what they dubbed "a racial incident." Cody had to apologize to Derrick's family and admit to them that he had a problem and needed help. Memories like these had long been buried. As a young adult, Cody had found closure, but Mindy's reasoning brought the topic back up.

"HEY, LOOK OUT!" screamed Mindy.

A Mexican man, trying to cross the street, suddenly ran in front of Cody's car. Cody instinctively tried to swerve past him, but it was too late. The man was airborne for a split second, landed across the windshield, and then ricocheted onto the pavement, leaving a splattering of blood on the passenger side of the windshield.

"AHHHHHHH!" screamed Mindy.

From his rearview mirror, Cody saw the motionless body lying on the street. Cody stepped on the brakes and got out of the car.

"What are you doing? Don't get out!" pleaded Mindy.

They were in a dangerous neighborhood.

Cody heard a woman scream. A round, middle-aged Hispanic lady ran to comfort the hit pedestrian. Moments later, local residents started to gather around the unconscious man. Cody stood next to him. The man was alive but in critical condition. Several of the neighbors got on their knees, praying for help. Cody slowly spun around; several Jesuses appeared at once to comfort each praying person.

"Who the fuck did this? Who da motherfucka did this?" demanded a skinny, short-haired, spunky and tomboyish teenage girl. She pointed at Cody, "You did this? You hit Gustavo?"

"Yeah, I did," answered Cody. "I just want to make sure he's fine until the ambulance comes."

"Fine? He look fine to you, dipshit?" She whipped out a knife.

"Hey, it was an accident! He shouldn't have run in front of my car!" Cody pleaded.

"*Te voy a arrancar la cabeza!*" the aggressive teenage girl screamed in Spanish.

"Bobbie! HELP!" screamed Mindy from the car.

Cody looked back with terror in the direction of his car where Mindy was still inside. He saw several gangbangers surrounding it. A girl from the crowd yanked Cody aside.

"I just called 911," she explained. "Don't talk back to any of them no matter what they say. Just let them yell at you."

For ten intense minutes, Cody endured a barrage of verbal insults, most of them in Spanish. Inside the car, Mindy repeatedly dialed her husband's cell phone, but he did not answer. The bastard's sleeping, she thought. Finally, flashing red and blue lights from two police cars came to their rescue. Sirens from a nearby ambulance could also be heard.

"What's going on here?" asked one of the officers in a deep Texan twang.

"I was just driving when all of a sudden this guy tried to cross the street. He did it right in front of my car. You have to believe me, it's the truth," explained Cody.

"Oh, I believe you alright," laughed the officer. "This happens once a week in this part of Westheimer. It's always a beaner that gets hit."

"You shouldn't say that word," corrected Cody.

"Son," the officer responded, "I'm going to protect you and clear your name in this here mess. You let me say what I want. Got it?"

Paramedics soon arrived. They carted the injured pedestrian to the ambulance. Mindy and Cody were both escorted away by several policemen from the hostile neighborhood crowd.

"Y'all need a ride back home?" offered a policeman.

"Yes. Can you guys take my friend back home too?"

"She's not your wife?" asked the surprised policeman.

"No, if you had taken down my ID, you would have seen that I'm single."

"Don't worry about that," chuckled the police officer. "We know it's not your fault. Come on, where does she live and where do you live?"

"She lives in Sugar Land. I'm a few blocks away," replied Cody. "You sure you don't want to check our IDs?"

The officer sighed and took Cody and Mindy's license; both cleared.

"Bobbie, you be careful, huh? I'll see you at work tomorrow," Mindy paused. "Thanks for everything. I had a lot of fun tonight. Hope you did too. Sorry about your car."

She looked at the policeman.

"Can I sit in the front?" she insisted.

Daphne felt no remorse about her treatment of Cody earlier in the day; she had already forgotten about it. Her mind was preoccupied with Valentine's Day dinner with Kyle Sawyer and his family—she had just been invited by Kyle to meet them. She had known him since her high school years when Kyle led the Clements High Rangers to successful seasons as the starting quarterback. Tall and well-built with a masculine jaw, the dreamy blue-eyed, blond-haired titan had fallen on tough times after suffering a career-ending injury near the end of his senior year in a playoff game.

Fortunately for him, Kyle was as much brains as he was brawn. He had graduated from the University of Texas with honors, double majoring in business and accounting. His academic success helped ease the pain of his athletic letdown, though a large part of him would always miss playing football. In Texas, football is king, and Kyle was once a part of that royalty. The thought of being just another face in the crowd disturbed him.

Although they had never officially dated, Daphne had interpreted their consistently matching college class schedules as a sign from God. This made her believe that choosing to be a Texas Longhorn instead of an A&M Aggie was the right decision. She had wanted to be wherever Kyle wanted to be. And while he had several other relationships during their time as friends, Kyle was quick to pick up Daphne's passive-aggressive interest in him as a lover. He had asked her to hang out with him on several occasions, appreciating Daphne as a buddy, yet, at certain times, using her as something more. She loved him enough to give up her virginity, though she hid this fact from her family and friends. Besides, she reasoned, this man is destined to be my future husband. She didn't feel like she had sinned as a devout Christian; it was a loophole she'd found.

Hence, when Kyle asked her to join his family for dinner on Valentine's Day, Daphne was delighted. For the first time in a long time, she gave a heartfelt prayer to God. She knew it was putting the cart ahead of the horse, but during her drive to Kyle's house she pictured what their children would look like. Mixed children are so beautiful, she sighed to herself. How many boys? How many girls? Daphne wanted two of each—a family of six, living in a nice three-story home with a white picket fence.

The American dream.

"So, Daphne," smiled Kyle's mother, "thanks for tutoring Kyle with his trigonometry homework. Your math skills really came in handy."

She wore a necklace with large white pearls, which complemented her pink suit and white hair.

"Actually, Mrs. Sawyer, I helped him with his English," corrected Daphne.

"Ah!" exclaimed Kyle's mother, nudging her husband, "see, dear, these Asian kids are taking over our language now! Y'all are so smart at everything!"

Silence followed. The four of them ate their chicken, mashed potatoes and green beans. The rhythmic clinging of silverware could be heard amidst the silence.

"You know, Kyle's changing his job. He just got a job offer from NASA!" said Mrs. Sawyer.

"Oh wow! Really?" replied Daphne. "Gosh, Kyle, I'm so happy to hear that! Does that mean you're moving to the Clear Lake area?"

"Mmm," Kyle said waiting to finish chewing his food. "Well, mom exaggerates. I'm not sure I'm actually going to take it."

"What? Why not, Kyle?!" asked his mother."Surely you can't be happy doing what you're doing right now. You don't make nearly enough that matches your worth."

"I'm planning on trying out for the Canadian Football League next season," declared Kyle.

"You're doing what?" Kyle's father was surprised. "That's a bad idea."   "Kyle, you'll get hurt. You had a serious injury and you're lucky you can still walk like a normal person," reasoned a concerned Daphne.

"Yes, listen to your Asian girlfriend," said Kyle's mother.

He grew irritated. "You guys just don't understand. A large part of my soul has been missing ever since high school. I need football. I had several physical trainers evaluate and tell me I can bounce back and have a good career."

"Kyle...I—" his mother started before getting interrupted.

"It's the Canadian Football League, not the NFL. Who's ever made it to the NFL from that dismal league?" asked his father.

"Warren Moon did. Doug Flutie," answered Kyle.

"Aberrations. Statistically speaking it's one in a million. But you're your own man. You do what you want," said Mr. Sawyer. He looked at Daphne. "Or date whatever kinds of people you want."

Another long moment of silence followed.

"Soooo, Daphne. How do you like the dinner so far?"

"It's very good, Mrs. Sawyer," smiled Daphne.

"You're so polite. So where are you from? Are you Japanese or Korean?"

"I was born in Beijing. But I grew up here," Daphne replied.

"So you're Japanese. My coworker is Japanese. Her name is Oki Mishima. She has two sons. Do you know them?"

"No, Mrs. Sawyer."

"Beijing's the capital of China," corrected her husband. "She's Chinese."

"Isn't that where your brother deployed to in the seventies?" inquired Mrs. Sawyer.

"No, that was Korea," explained Mr. Sawyer. He was getting full.

"Oh, that's right! He has an Asian wife. They met during his time there. That woman has the most beautiful skin. How do y'all keep that skin so smooth and youthful? Look at my arms, they're full of spots. Do you have some kind of secret Asian cream that you can recommend to me?" asked Kyle's mother.

Kyle got up and headed out.

"Where are you going?" asked Mr. Sawyer.

"Leaving," explained Kyle. "Gonna go to Joe's. Think we're gonna shoot the shit and drink a few."

"Well, what about your little Saigon girlfriend here?" asked his father.

"She can help mom clean the dishes. Hell if I care," Kyle shrugged heading out.

Daphne watched as he drove his car out of the driveway. He didn't even bother looking back, she noticed. Her heart sank. She felt lower than dirt.

"You know, I only buy Toyotas. They're great cars!" exclaimed Mrs. Sawyer.

Daphne glared at her.

CHAPTER 6: THE HUSTLE

The Platinum Star was celebrating its second-year anniversary as a dance club in Houston—a long lifespan for a city whose other clubs averaged six months maximum. Because of their frequent changes in ownership, most clubs were, instead, known for their locations. Though The Platinum Star wasn't a decades-long success like the Roxy, people still knew it by its name. They didn't come for its shabby decorations or its mediocre music; it was, however, a place where the best drug deals could be found.

Among its many clubbers that night was Pete Mok. Pete had been out of jail for two months, thanks to an early Christmas Day parole. It was, in his mind, an easy stay. During his stint in prison, he had the luck of being protected by Big Thunder, a large, thick-mustached Hispanic enforcer whom Pete had known from his earlier criminal career. No one had laid a hand on Pete, giving his prison experience the equivalent of an extended bed and breakfast. He had made the survival decision of shaving his head, hiding his natural curly hair. That, along with a body decorated in tattoos, had transformed Pete from looking like the guy who could get mugged to the guy doing the mugging.

Yet, word on the street suggested that Pete was still soft. He was a sheep among wolves, mostly getting by because he was well-liked. He didn't have a malicious bone in his body;

Pete's good heart, however, made up for his timidity. Also, fortunately, he had the added trait of astounding luck, making him the underworld Forrest Gump. Even his criminal peers recognized it. Since there was little for them to take from Pete, they never bothered to hustle him. They recognized him as one of their own, figuring his vulnerabilities gave him some usefulness. That was how Pete originally got into the drug dealing life. He was asked by a local supplier to store cocaine in his family home. At the time, Pete turned out to be a perfect cover for the supplier. While he lived with his mother, he hid tens of thousands of dollars' worth of drugs underneath his childhood bed and, because his household was Asian, was not suspected by police.

Eventually, though, Pete's naivety and carelessness got the better of him. He became addicted to his own supply. Moreover, he openly talked about his drug dealing career, eventually leading to his own capture. One morning, a large narcotics police force stormed into his house and forced his grandparents, little sister, cousins and mother onto the floor. They tore through his family's furniture before finding the cocaine underneath his bed. That was how Pete got caught and sent to prison. Drug dealing and burger flipping were the only two occupations he had ever known. And Pete loved the former.

The familiarity of the club scene distracted him while his good friend Danny, a Cambodian-American friend of similar age, approached the lead bartender named Li'l Bis. Li'l Bis was easily identifiable from his eye patch—a little souvenir from his Vietnam War days.

"My man Li'l Bis. How ya doin'? Brought my boy Pete for Piranha," informed Danny.

"Yeah, I know who he is, Danny. This the dumb motherfucker who got caught with drugs in his own bed," scoffed the bartender.

The grizzled, one-eyed veteran was an old friend of The Platinum Star owner, Piranha, who saved him from an encounter with the Viet Cong over forty-five years ago.

"Nigga, dun gimme that. Pete was just startin' out. Anyway, I asked Piranha to give him another chance," insisted Pete's friend.

"What you want this life fo'? Y'all school boys. Y'all just fuck up again," replied Li'l Bis.

"We already got word he say yea, so just let us in!" demanded Danny.

"Oh, what? Y'all got an appointment? This the doctor's office now?" Li'l Bis barked back. He finished cleaning off the beer mug he was wiping. "Shiiiit. Follow me. Hope he can talk some sense into you."

The bartender led them through a narrow and dark hallway within the back of The Platinum Star. They passed by small rooms where patrons were snorting cocaine on mirrored tables. Pete recognized some of them as celebrities. Li'l Bis brought them to a large, brightly lit office whose entranceway was covered by bead curtains. In the middle of the room lay a large oak desk, occupied by two men on each end. Piranha was a physically imposing middle-aged black man, large and powerful in stature. His body language suggested deep inner strength, forged by the fires of hardened life experience. The choice of his attire included dark sunglasses, a nice white suit and a dark purple tie. Across from him was an equally well-dressed, hefty-looking Asian man, whose choice colors were black suit and beige tie. Li'l Bis removed himself from the office, closing the door behind him. The office walls absorbed most of the club sounds, giving them a resemblance of privacy for conversation.

"Yo, Piranha, man," said Danny, "thanks for giving my nigga Pete a second chance."

The drug baron collected his thoughts. There were no chairs left in the office for either of them, so they remained standing.

"My family," Piranha began, "lives in a modest two-story, three-bedroom townhouse inside of Meyerland. You've been to Meyerland, I'm sure. Not too good, not too bad. Average. Suburban. Safe, but not too safe. Our cars are a Camry, an Odyssey and an old 1996 Eclipse—that one we have for almost ten years. I've got a wife who bakes weekly cookies for her church and a teenage daughter who gossips daily on her phone. Both of them know what I do."

Piranha paused. The hefty Asian man sitting across from him submitted a smirk.

"I don't like drugs," he continued. "They fuck people up, fuck families up, fuck communities up, but at the end of the day, it's a business that gives my family what it wants. The owner of McDonald's doesn't care about making America fatter. This current retarded president, George W., doesn't give a shit about sending kids to war. But you know what? It's business. We gotta do what we gotta do. I make this all work because I see it as that. And that's what you gotta do. You feel me?"

Pete nodded.

Piranha pointed at the stocky Asian man. "This is Andrew. He's going to be heading the operations in Alief, near Chinatown. You and Danny are going to follow him. I'm giving you a second chance, Pete. This is a business. Remember that. Don't fuck this shit up again."

"Ah, man. You know a nigga do, ain't nuthin' but growing pains. But now I'm a grown nigga, you best heard, my nigga," expressed Pete.

The drug baron winced.

"Why do you kids talk like that nowadays? Damn hip-hop," commented Piranha.

With that said, he dismissed the two of them. Pete headed outside past the bustling weekend crowd. It was an early March night, with the last traces of winter found upon the occasional breeze.

"Where to now, nigga?" asked his Cambodian companion.

"Shit, nigga. We back in the game, nigga," smiled Pete. "We celebratin'!"

————————

Cody made the usual call.

He had been phoning Daphne almost every night at fifteen minutes before ten o'clock. There was little advancement made, but the anticipation still gave his life a little flavor. It helped take away the disturbing memories of hitting someone with his car a couple of weeks back. The phone calls usually went unanswered for seven to eight rings before she'd pick up. Cody wondered if she did this on purpose or if her cell phone was left somewhere far from her during this time of night.

Finally, Daphne picked up.

"Hey," she answered.

"Hi, Daphne, it's me Cody," he replied.

"I know it's you, cell phones have caller ID."

"Yeah, sorry. So...how was your day?"

"Oh, you know. Work. Studying for my GMAT."

"And how's that coming along? Need any help?"

"How could you possibly help me, Cody?"

"I don't know. We could play study Monopoly. I usually do that. You could swap out the Community and Chance cards. Replace them with index cards that contain study questions. Have it where property can't be purchased without correctly answering the questions. Those are the rules."

"You're really weird, you know that?" said Daphne.

"I like to think outside the box."

"Why? It makes you strange. I prefer to study like a healthy normal person, Cody."

"Okay. I was just offering a suggestion."

"Yeah. Thanks."

There was a pause in their conversation.

"Hey," asked Cody, "why don't you come to my house some time? Let me cook for you."

"Nice try. No."

"What do you mean 'nice try?'"

"You're just trying to get into my pants. You'll have candles, I'll be trapped in your home, and you'll get my guard down with some wine."

"No, I won't. I thought we were friends. Friends can't invite each other to dinner?"

"It's not a very Christian thing. A guy and a girl can't be alone together. Especially alone in a house."

"Okay, well, I make a killer shrimp scampi. That's too bad. What about a restaurant? We had lunch in public together. How about a restaurant for dinner?"

"It would have to be one where I would have zero chance of being seen with you," she said matter-of-factly.

Cody thought up of a list of places in his head.

"Cafe 101?" he suggested.

"Are you kidding me? That's the most popular Asian restaurant in Chinatown. I'll most likely bump into someone I know. Try again."

"How about, uh, um...do you like Italian?"

"No. I just had that."

"Oh, what about French then? I know a nice French restaurant near our homes. You live a few blocks from me, right?"

"Yeah, how'd you know?"

"I threw a Christmas party at my house a couple of months back and invited some people from church. You didn't come. Felix mentioned how close it was to your house and that you were a couple of blocks near me," explained Cody.

"I see. Felix has a big mouth," she observed.

"It's fine. I was just mentioning it because the restaurant is so close. We can get back to your house before ten o'clock, just the way you prefer."

"Yeah, okay. I guess," she paused. "Okay. It's almost ten. I'm hanging up now."

"What? There's six more minutes," Cody pleaded.

"Close enough."

"Well, when would you like to have dinner then?"

"I'll let you know."

"Will you be going to the church retreat in two weeks?"

"Yeah," she answered, "I'm one of the counselors."

"Oh. I'm going too. I'm bringing my cousin. Alright, is there anything you'd like for me to pray for?"

Daphne let out a judgmental laugh.

"Cody, how long have you been a Christian? How could you possibly know what to pray for?" she asked.

"It's the thought that counts, isn't it?"

"No, it's not. You don't know anything. If I wanted a prayer, I'd ask Luke or Ennis. And anyway, why do you always ask that? Do you think it would score points with me? Honestly."

"I've got little to say. I know nothing about you. You never tell me anything besides very small details, but even then, I don't know much about those things either. I don't know what your favorite color is, what kind of music you like, what types of movies you like to watch, who your best friends are outside of church, let alone anything about your family. All I know is that you're Daphne from church and that you drive a Volkswagen Passat."

"And why should you know any of those other things, Cody? We're just friends," Daphne replied.

"I'm just saying that we—"

"One more minute 'til ten o'clock," interrupted Daphne.

"Wait, wait. Before you hang up. Since you won't tell me much about you, I'll tell you something about me. I was born and raised in Houston, I'm a graphic designer and web developer, I like R&B, I have no siblings, my parents both live here, I like reading books and comics, I like cooking and dining out and my favorite color is black," described Cody.

"Okay," she said. He could picture her on the phone, glaring at an object that represented him. "That's nice to know. Alright, it's ten now. Bye."

Daphne immediately hung up.

———

Cody slowly started waking up from his dream. It was the reoccurring one with the giant boulder rolling behind him as he ran down an endless, spiraling stairway. That was one of his two usual dreams. The other was an absurd dream where he was saving fish from drowning. He had never awakened screaming in any of them. Perhaps he was so used to it that he realized he was dreaming. Whenever it reached that point, Cody would turn around and stop running, letting the boulder pass through him, or, in the case of the second dream, returning the fish back to sea. This ending calmed him. It led him to wake up in a happier mood, knowing his worries were illusions. If only that were the case in reality, he sighed.

It was late Saturday morning.

As Cody rolled the other way to retrieve his glasses, he made out a human figure standing beside his bed, staring at him.

"Aaaahh!" he screamed, quickly putting on his glasses.

It was Mindy.

"Bubble!" she replied, "you scared me! You okay?! You have the nightmare?!"

"What are you doing standing here next to me in my bedroom?!"

"I wanted to see if you would have lunch with me. You are naked!"

"Where're my shorts?!"

"I see them in the other side of the room. Do you just take off your pants at night and throw them around? Hahaha!" laughed Mindy.

"Just hand them over to me," demanded a sensitive Cody, clinging on to his bed sheets tightly. "Please."

Mindy continued laughing and walked over to the opposite side of Cody's bedroom. She picked up his shorts and tossed them at him.

"Oooh. Calvin Klein!" she observed.

"Very funny. Now turn around!" demanded Cody as he started putting on his shorts.

"Why do you sleep naked? Ants may bite you!" Mindy said with her back turned. "Are you done? Can I see you now?"

"Yeah," he replied, getting out of his bed to look for a T-shirt to wear. "How did you get in here anyway?"

Mindy faced Cody, "You gave me your emergency key, remember?"

"Everyone has my fucking keys," muttered Cody.

"You say it is okay because you could be on vacation and I can come feed your cat," explained Mindy.

"Well, I'm not on vacation. You can't just come in here anytime you want."

"Why not? We're friends. I even talk to you on the phone when I pee."

"Please don't tell me these things, Mindy."

"Ahahaha! You are my best friend! Ever since my twin sister in South Africa left me, Bobbie!"

"You...have a twin sister?"

"Yes," she grinned.

"Really?"

"No! I am joking! Hahahaha! I am an only child just like you!"

Cody continued looking for a T-shirt. He headed for his drawer.

"Do you exercise? You have a nice muscle! Can I touch?"

Cody gave her a weird look.

"Huh?" he asked, choosing his favorite blue T-shirt that read "Secret Asian Man."

"Come on, we're best friends!" She walked over and pinched his biceps.

"Whatever. I'm a skinny lightweight toothpick," muttered Cody, putting on the shirt.

The sound of a closing car door came from below, just outside the front door of his three-story townhouse.

"What was that? Did you bring someone with you?" Cody inquired with a worried expression.

Cody heard the front door open; loud footsteps soon followed. Someone was running up to the top floor.

"Yeah, I brought my husband!" Mindy beamed.

"WHAT?!" replied Cody.

A tall, middle-aged Taiwanese man with a giant potbelly walked into Cody's bedroom. He had a chubby face and a happy grin.

"<Why didn't you wait in the car?>" Mindy asked him in Taiwanese.

"<It was hot>," he replied back in their native tongue.

"Hi," Cody interrupted, "Welcome to my home."

"Hi! I'm I-Tsung's husband, Wing Wei!"

"I-Tsung?" asked Cody, looking at Mindy.

"That's my Taiwanese name, Bobbie! I-Tsung Cheung!" laughed Mindy.

"That...rhymes," observed Cody.

"Your name is Bobbie?" asked her husband.

"No, it's Cody. Your wife strangely calls me Bobbie all the time."

"Yeah!" smiled Mindy to Wing Wei, "because his head is giant. Like a bubble!"

"Oh! Bubble! Bubbie! Bobbie!" he laughed, getting the joke.

"AHAHAHAHAHAHAHAHAHAHAHA," they both laughed.

Cody did not find it amusing.

"Come on, Bobbie! Let's go to lunch! We need to talk about our business!"

The married couple waited in Cody's living room on the second floor while he took a bath, put on colored contacts, fixed his hair and selected an outfit. The entire process took half an hour. When Cody was ready, he saw them fiddling with his Playstation 2.

"Hey, how do you turn this on?" Mindy asked.

"The power button is right there," Cody explained, flicking the switch.

"Can we try a game?" she inquired.

"Yeah! I like game! Especially man game!" said Wing Wei.

"I only have 'man' games. This one is a fighting game," explained Cody.

Cody and Wing Wei played a round from a brand new video game named Tekken 5, which was one of Cody's favorite games. Since Cody was familiar with it, he allowed Wing Wei to beat his virtual character.

"Hahahaha! I want to play too, Bobbie!" demanded Mindy.

She grabbed his controller and chose a female character.

"She looks like me, huh?" she asked.

"Um, she's Brazilian," said Cody. "Nothing like you at all."

The virtual match began. Mindy started mashing the controller's buttons, laughing maniacally while she virtually beat up her husband's fighter. Less than a minute later, she won the match.

"Ahahahahahaha! Man, this game is so fun, man! Maaaaan!!!" she shouted.

"Wanna play again?" offered Cody.

"No, one time is fun. Two times, too much. Let's go eat!" Mindy declared.

"Where do you want to go?" Cody asked.

"Cafe 101! That is where all the Asians go!" she smiled.

"Good Taiwanese food too!" exclaimed her husband.

The three of them rode in Wing Wei's SUV. Mindy sat in the back with Cody while her husband drove. During the ride, they discussed various topics including the idiocy of daylight savings, Chien-Ming Wang being the greatest pitcher of all time ("he will be great for the Yankees!" declared Wing Wei, "you watch!"), and Wing Wei's special hot pot sauce recipe.

Upon arrival in Houston's Chinatown, Cody once again marveled at how far the Asian community had come since his childhood days in the eighties. Back then, the original Chinatown was in downtown. It had failed for various reasons, including being placed near dangerous neighborhoods and the lack of a significant Chinese population. Its demise was not surprising. Several years later, however, a modern Chinese shopping center named Dynasty Mall had opened in a suburban area of the Alief district. It included a large Chinese community-oriented bank and what was then the largest dim sum restaurant as part of the mall. This facilitated a foundation for the second attempt at a Chinatown. Thanks to a spurt of population from Chinese and Vietnamese immigrants in the nineties, it soon became one of America's best looking Chinatowns seemingly overnight.

The most famous intersection in Chinatown was also one of Houston's deadliest—the converging points of Bellaire Road and Beltway 8 had attributed to many fatal accidents year after year. It certainly didn't help stifle the stereotype of Asians and their poor driving abilities. Wing Wei was quickly reminded of this when he dodged oncoming traffic, where most of the motorists were following their own rules.

"Crazy drivers!" he muttered, "Chinese people can't drive, you know. That's no lie."

"Man, Cody got into a car accident not too long ago, man! He ran over a Mexican!" blurted Mindy.

Cars everywhere honked at Wing Wei as he nudged his way toward Cafe 101. A tiny old Asian lady driving a pickup truck almost rammed into them. Wing Wei cursed her out. Because parking space was so scarce on Saturday afternoons, he decided to invent one of his own.

"<Are you sure you're supposed to park there?>" criticized Mindy. "<I don't think you can park there.>"

"<Who cares?> " Wing Wei muttered. "<Tow trucks can't get to it.>"

Cafe 101 was best known as a trendy, sexy restaurant. With its dark interiors and neon lights, the decor was reflective of a night club. The waitresses were mostly college-aged Asian women who dressed in seductive, skimpy outfits. Being a woman herself, Mindy didn't care about that. She loved the restaurant because of its food; it was similar to what was served in the food streets of her hometown, Taipei. When they arrived, the three of them were escorted to a table for four. Mindy held Cody's arm and sat next to him, across from her husband. She leaned her head on Cody's shoulder while flipping through the menu.

After they ordered beef tongues, spicy intestines, stir-fried noodles, squid balls and peppered chicken, Mindy brought out a series of pictures from her Mosiac Decor collection. Cody inspected each one of them carefully.

"My CPA has done all the paperwork," she explained. "You be sure to show up and sign them next week, then you help us make a website shopping cart, okay?"

"Who's your supplier?" asked Cody.

"A man," she replied.

"A man named...?"

"He is called Odie."

"Okay, so what does Odie get out of this?"

"Don't worry, we take care of it. You just put it into your garage."

"Say what? Why isn't it in Odie's warehouse? This is shady."

"Man, you shady, man!"

"Where is he getting this stuff?"

"He is in charge of the shipping entry. He put them in box. In secret. Then he give them to us. For a fee."

"In other words, he steals this crap and then it's in my garage. My house becomes a crime scene," Cody deduced.

"Come on! No one's going to find out! Your garage is empty, man!"

Mindy looked at Cody with a stern expression.

"No. I'm not doing it."

"Come on! Man, come on!"

"It's illegal, Mindy!"

"No, it's not! You won't get caught! I already thought it out, Bobbie! Please, please, please, Bobbie!"

"I don't need the money. I already have a good job."

She caressed his arm lightly. Wing Wei read a Taiwanese newspaper, seemingly in his own world.

"Don't you want to be your own boss?" she smiled. "Come on, I see how Ms. Rachel yell at you during work. I am studying for my PhD, but I really want to do this! Have our own business! My own business with my best friend, Cody Quan."

"No."

"Pleaseeeee?" She made a walking motion with her fingers on Cody's lap.

"No."

"Pleeaasssseeeeeeeee?"

"No, Mindy."

"Pleaaasseeeeeeeeeeeeeeeeeee?"

Cody finally gave in.

"Okay. We'll try it."

"THANKS, BOBBIE!"

———

The silver Audi with tinted windows pulled over near the Whataburger parking lot at slightly past seven o'clock in the evening. A week had passed since Pete Mok had been employed again by the local drug lord, Piranha. During that time, Pete and his friend Danny spent the past six nights doing some blow and hitting the clubs with former acquaintances. Both had no qualms about being small-time drug dealers; they knew it paid well. But because Pete had botched his previous gig, he and his friend were reassigned to working under the tutelage of a man named Andrew Huynh.

Andrew was the well-dressed hefty Asian man from their initial meeting with Piranha. Pete and Danny knew little about him except that he was well-trusted by the kingpin. He had been well-dressed both the times that they had seen him, a sharp contrast to their baggy pants and loose T-shirts. Danny was skinny and scrawny, wearing a baseball cap at a forty-five degree angle that covered up the side of his face a bit. Pete was fairly tall, with a near-shaven head and an average body build. Both usually twitched because of heavy drug usage.

The tinted car window rolled down. Andrew was in the passenger seat. His driver was a stern-looking Asian man in his mid-forties. The radio in the car was set to 104.1 FM KRBE, a popular pop station in Houston.

"Get in the back," ordered Andrew.

Both of the young drug dealers got inside of the Audi. Once they were in, the driver headed toward their evening's destination.

"Man, I hate this station!" complained Danny. "Turn it to 97.9. Want something hard, nigga."

Both Andrew and the driver ignored his request. They were in an old area of Alief. Pete recognized the neighborhood.

It reminded him of his childhood with his friends Cody and Duke. He was their lackey, helping them refill their water guns with boiling water, bringing them canned sodas, running bogus errands. Even then, Pete realized he was a tool. He blinked to return to his current reality. Alief had degenerated. The lack of street lights made the late March evening darker than it should have been.

"Say, dawg," Danny inquired, "I don't see why it has to take four of us niggas to do this motherfuckin' deal, you know what I'm sayin'? We been down with this game for a long time, nigga. I don't see what you got to teach us or if Piranha ain't put enough trust for yo' ass to come babysittin' here. Know what I'm sayin'?"

"This isn't a drug deal," replied Andrew.

"What, nigga?" asked Danny.

The sedan slowly pulled into the front driveway of a shabby one-story house. It was among a row of similarly bedraggled dwellings. The look of the area was typical of an old neighborhood in Alief. Pete could hear dogs aggressively barking from everywhere. The driver automatically unlocked the backseat doors, indicating for both the new dealers to get out.

"Ask for a guy named Johnny," instructed Andrew. "Tell him it's time to pay. He owes us forty thousand dollars in coke money. We want to know what happened with it. You'll recognize Johnny as the guy wearing a cast."

"Why we gotta do this?" asked a worried Danny. "We ain't no enforcers."

"Piranha wants both of you to see that this isn't about fun and games. Now go. I'm not going to tell you again," Andrew replied.

Danny and Pete nervously got out of the car and walked toward the front door. The barking grew louder.

"Shit, I ain't never done it like this before, nigga," commented Pete.

"Yeah. The fuck we doin' here?" asked Danny.

A thin, middle-aged Asian man with a reversed V-shaped mustache opened the screen door.

"Ah, whatdoyouwant?" he asked.

"'Sup, my nigga. That nigga Johnny here?" Danny asked.

"Whothefuckareyou?   YouVietChineseLaos? Whothefuckareyou?"

"What the hell matter what the fuck we are, nigga? Is that bitch Johnny here or not?" demanded Danny.

An Asian man with an arm cast appeared alongside the man who had opened the front door. He was holding a lit cigarette in the hand of his good arm.

"Yeah, I'm Johnny," he said. "What do you guys want?"

"We here for Piranha, nigga," replied Pete. "You owe 'em forty G in coke. We here to collect."

"Oh yeah? Tell him I'll have it by next month," replied Johnny.

"You said that last month," informed a voice behind Pete and Danny. It was Andrew; both he and the driver had gotten out of the car.

"Oh, shit," muttered Johnny. He flicked his cigarette toward the ground and stamped on it.

Andrew calmly made his way into the run-down house. A three-year-old girl was playing with an assortment of cars and dolls. A pregnant woman in her late twenties came out of the master bedroom, seeing Andrew and his men in their living room.

"Tell her to take the kid inside and close the door," Andrew ordered.

"Come on, Andrew," pleaded Johnny. "I got the coke. You don't have to do this."

"Well, where is it then? Three months, coke is gone, you've got no money to show for it. It's not apples and apples, Johnny."

The woman, wearing a frightened expression, quickly ushered the child inside the master bedroom and closed the door.

"I-I-I, my cousin has an addiction, he stole it, man! I'm getting the money back from family! I'm selling my car!" stumbled Johnny.

"That little beat-up piece of shit 1989 Camry? I'm surprised that thing still runs, Johnny. Can't be worth more than five hundred dollars in the market. You know we hate doing this sort of thing, don't you?" Andrew calmly explained.

"Please, please, please, mannnnn..." Johnny begged on bended knees.

"We gave you that broken arm last month, just to let you know how serious we were. We did that so you could still find a way to get us either the coke or money back. You remember what I said if you didn't take us seriously. We don't like doing this next thing, Johnny, you understand that, right? There's no profit in it."

"Heycomeonwegotthemoney," interrupted Johnny's companion.

"Shit, dude. This ain't your business, stick-thin nigga." Danny pushed Johnny's skinny friend aside.

Drops of sweat fell upon Johnny's forehead. He continued begging.

"Last chance," explained Andrew. He produced a gun and pointed it at Johnny's forehead.

"NO! NO!" came a shout. It was the pregnant woman. She had opened the bedroom door.

"Please don't kill me. Please don't kill me. Please don't kill me," begged Johnny. "I'll have it by next week. I swear."

"You know what?" asked Andrew. "I believe you."

He turned and shot the pregnant woman in the stomach, sending her collapsing unconsciously on the floor.

"NO!!!!!!!!!!!!!!!!!!!!!!!!!!!!!!!!!!!" screamed Johnny.

"I'll be back next week. If you don't pay us then, I'm killing your other kid," said Andrew.

Pete stood watching the scenario while his companions walked away. Danny nudged him to walk out.

"Come on, nigga," Danny said. "Don't be soft about this."

Pete slowly turned away, walking out of the house with Danny. The driver calmly started the silver Audi and pulled away from the home. Not long afterwards, an ambulance arrived to save the woman. She would survive, but her unborn child was dead upon arrival.

CHAPTER 7: GOD'S PERFECTION

Duke sized up the girls in the group and calculated who would be his prey. He wanted someone wholesome, Cantonese, submissive, educated and short in stature. The thought of knowing about God was of little interest to him; it wasn't why he had agreed to come to the church retreat. He was looking for a wife and it didn't take him long before a prospect caught his eye.

The target was Zoey Vu, one of the prettiest women of the newly renamed Fellowship Communion Baptist Church. Zoey was youthful looking, in her early twenties, tiny and petite. This late afternoon, she was wearing low-cut jean shorts, a revealing white tank top and an extra large pair of Chanel sunglasses. When Duke first spotted her, she was carrying three large plastic bags of groceries to one of the cabins. That was where the cooking was being done. She wasn't meant to be carrying them alone, however; her childhood friend and soul mate, Felix, had forgotten to help her after hearing about the Xbox 360 tournament in one of the front cabins.

"Let me help you with that," Duke offered.

"Oh! Thanks. I didn't see you coming!" exclaimed Zoey.

Duke didn't respond. He removed the grocery bags from her grasp, looking straightforward as he walked. It was important for him to maintain excellent posture and some semblance of masculine dignity. Zoey didn't respond either, still occupying her mind with Felix. Both Felix and she had grown up together in the heart of New York City's Chinatown. They had gone through plenty of good times and bad. When Felix moved to Houston, so did she. How could she leave him? He had been there for her when it counted, which was why Zoey carried such a deep and heartfelt love for her best friend. Once Duke and Zoey approached her designated cabin, she reached out her hand to reclaim the groceries.

"That one," she pointed at the cabin, "and I'll take those bags. Thanks."

"Why were you carrying these bags alone?" he asked.

"Oh, my friend just went and left me alone with them," she replied."Can you believe that? I bet he's playing Xbox 360 with his buddies."

"That's a shame. A man should never leave a woman to do all the work."

"I know! Although I wouldn't call Felix a man, he's more like a big kid," giggled Zoey.

"Is this Felix your boyfriend?"

"No. It's...complicated. He's my best friend. I love him. SO! Are you new to our church? A guest? I'm Zoey, by the way." She extended her hand to shake his.

Duke transferred the bags of groceries into one hand and gave her an unusually firm handshake with the other. He made sure not to smile.

"I'm Duke," he revealed.

"Ow!" moaned Zoey, "you've got a strong grip! Careful there...I'm fragile. Heh."

There was a moment of silence, then Duke let go of her hand.

"To answer your question, I'm here with my cousin Cody," Duke answered.

"Oh, yeah! Cody's a sweetheart. So you came here to share the Word and receive the love of Jesus Christ?"

"Yeah, sure," he shrugged.

A female voice from inside the cabin called out to Zoey.

"Zoey, is that you? Come in here quickly! I need you to help chop some tomatoes. And bring the sauce in here too." It was from Deena Ling, Marco's younger sister and also the head organizer of the church retreat.

"I gotta go," Zoey said, giving Duke a mischievous smile.

"Let me take these groceries inside for you," insisted Duke.

"No, guys aren't allowed. Not that I agree with it. Rules are rules, though. Give them to me, I got it. I may be tiny, but I'm stronger than I look," she replied, flexing her muscles.

"Are you sure?"

"Yeah, I got it. Maybe I'll see you tonight at the group dinner?" Zoey suggested.

"Of course."

With that said, Duke handed the grocery bags back to her and headed toward his own cabin. Inside, Zoey caught up with Deena and the other girls who volunteered to make the nightly dinner for the retreat. Daphne and Marion were preparing ingredients while Maple Washington, the pastor's teenage daughter, helped with the vegetables. Overall, they were making large amounts of spaghetti, ravioli, fish sticks, dumplings and pecan pie. They talked about various subjects including relationships, movies, shopping, cooking and clothes.

"Who were you talking with?" asked Deena.

"Oh, just some guy," dismissed Zoey.
Deena glimpsed through the kitchen window facing the street.

"You shouldn't be flirting with guys, Zoey," commented Deena. "It's not proper Christian behavior."

"I wasn't flirting with him!"

She started taking groceries out of the bags.

"You flirt with everyone, dear," Deena scoffed.

"Deena, how do I chop these onions?" asked Maple.

"Marion, show her how to do it."

Deena took pride in being bossy. Part of it was because she was a natural born leader, but there was a more practical reason. It also compensated for her lack of talent, beauty or wealth. She thrived on her keen intellect, claiming it was her natural gift from God. Deena liked Zoey, more than the others did anyway, but the poor girl seemed lost to her. It was in her opinion that while Zoey was Christian, she was also too easily tempted by the ways of the world.

"You know," Deena gossiped, "I hear one of the teenage girls is letting her boyfriend sleep over in her cabin. I told Pastor Lu about it and he put an end to that."

"Good job, Deena," Marion praised.

"Yeah," said Daphne.

Zoey gave a disagreeing expression, "And what's wrong with that? Doesn't mean they'll be doing anything."

"Oh, you wouldn't understand, would you, Zoey?" teased Deena.

The rest of the girls giggled.

"What do you mean I wouldn't understand?" Zoey asked.

Deena smirked, "Well, if you did, you wouldn't have had—"

"MOMMY!" interrupted a small three-year-old boy.

He ran over and hugged Zoey's legs.

"My point exactly," said Deena.

The child was Little Ryan, Zoey's pride and joy. It seemed to her that he always carried a bright smile. Although Zoey detested Little Ryan's father, she thought the best parts of him were reflected in the boy. To certain people, Ryan's existence was judged as a mistake, but Zoey believed God made no mistakes. After all, she reasoned, Little Ryan was her primary reason to live. He was angelic and well-behaved. A young single mother couldn't have asked for a better child.

"Why aren't you playing with the other kids, Ryan?" Zoey asked him.

"They pick on me," he replied.

"Oh, you know that's not true. Come on, don't be such a baby."

"I'm not being a baby!"

"Come on, girls," sighed Deena. "Everyone's going to be hungry. Looks like Ms. Mom here is going to be distracted while we pick up her slack."

"No, I'm almost done. I can wrap these dumplings up," Zoey insisted.

"Moooommmmmm. I need to pee. I can't pee alone," Ryan cried.

"Oh, my gosh, Zoey, just take him to potty already! Besides, you wrap these dumplings slower than a turtle," laughed Daphne.

"Yeah, shouldn't he know how to pee on his own by now?" teased Marion.

The rest of the girls laughed at Zoey.

"He's already damned potty-trained! He just can't reach the damned light switch! That's all!" Zoey angrily defended.

"Hey, no need to curse! Wow! Gotta pray on that one," laughed Deena.

"Among other things," added Daphne.

"Mommmm," pleaded Ryan.

Zoey picked him up and headed toward the bathroom. It was cramped for space, but far enough from the kitchen where the other girls were cooking. She didn't like what they implied about her and her son. Why did so many Christians forget to reserve judgment? she wondered. A makeshift stool was created from scattered telephone books for Little Ryan to reach and urinate into the toilet.

"Ryan, what did the other kids say to you?"

"They said I have no daddy," he replied. "Then they pushed me."

"That's not true. You see daddy all the time. Did you tell them that?"

"Yes. But they said you're in love with everybody else's daddy. That's why I have no daddy. That's why I'm a sin," he finished peeing.

A tear slowly streamed down Zoey's left eye, ruining part of her mascara. She wiped away the teardrop and helped Ryan pull up his pants, tightly hugging him with one hand while flushing the toilet with the other.

"Listen to me," she assured him, "you are not a sin."

"Then why are the other kids calling me that?"

"Because, baby, they don't recognize God's perfection."

———

It was past supper when they were separated into various fellowship groups based on age and gender. Both Cody and Duke joined the twenty-to-forty men's group, which was led by Ennis. The session was held near the lake due to the perfectly windless weather. It was also close to the basketball court where the guys hoped to slip in a few rounds of hoops afterwards.

They sat around in a circle, singing a few contemporary

gospel songs while Luke played his guitar. Then Ennis closed his eyes and summoned Jesus, their Lord and Savior. When some of them had opened their eyes again, they saw Jesus among them. Cody felt an awe of amazement. He hadn't seen Jesus since his grandmother's miraculous recovery over a month ago.

"Wow! It's Jesus!" blurted Herman.

"Shhhhh!" hushed Felix.

Herman ignored him and started to sing, "You give and take away, You give and take away, my heart will choose to say, Lord, blessed be Your name!!!"

"Herman, shut up!" threatened an angry Marco.

Ennis took on a more calming tone.

"It's okay, Marco. We are here under the Lord's presence," said Ennis gently.

"Amen," the group said together, looking at Jesus.

"Who are they looking at?" whispered Duke. "I don't see anything."

"It's because you haven't been baptized," explained Cody.

"That's the stupidest thing I've ever heard."

What Cody didn't realize was that not all the baptized could see Jesus. One of them was Marco, who had been struggling to witness Jesus for years; it constantly made him frustrated and furious.

"Tonight," Ennis said in a gentle, accented voice, "we've all gathered here to discuss fellowship based on Acts 2:41 to 2:47. We are commanded to be together because we are infused with God's spirit. We know better than worldly people. We see past the illusions. We were chosen to save lives. That's why we're here; so that we can stay strong and keep holy. That's why we're having this retreat. It's what makes us different. As long as Christians stick together, we are infallible, you know? God Power, guys. God Power."

"God Power," they chanted in unison.

"Also," Ennis continued, "tonight we celebrate this fellowship by sharing with Jesus what we're thankful for. Because as Christians, we are free to love on a higher plane of existence. Anyone want to share some things that they're thankful for?"

There were a few seconds of silence. Finally, Ennis decided to speak up on the subject himself.

"I'll begin. I just...I just want to say that...I...I don't know...I love you, Jesus," Ennis paused, trying to continue. He started crying instead.

Felix patted Ennis on the back. Ennis sobbed louder.

"Whoa!" exclaimed Felix, "anyone else wanna give some thanks? I think Ennis has lost it!"

Ennis continued sobbing uncontrollably.

"I'll go next," stood Cody. "About a month ago, my grandma was on her deathbed. She had a very small chance of living. My cousin Duke and I didn't know what to do. She raised both of us, after all. I prayed for Jesus to heal her, and there Jesus was, right in front of me. He said 'okay' and she came back to full health. Thanks, Jesus."

Jesus gave him a thumbs up as he sat back down.

One by one, various members of the group gave a story of thanks. Herman told them about his amazing run for his audition in American Idol. Felix gave thanks for avoiding an accident at the most dangerous intersection in Chinatown. There were over twenty testimonials overall.

Ennis finally got himself back together again, "Anyone else? Please share your experiences with the Lord."

Jay stood up.

"Two years ago, I was going through some very hard times. I was about to take my own life. I came from an abusive father who hurt my mom. I was really addicted to porn. I felt things like homosexuality were right. But then, thanks to Ennis, you guys took me in and I found Jesus. Right now, I'm looking at Jesus and he's looking at me. And the light is there," testified Jay. "The light is there. My life has meaning."

After Jay's testimonial, Jesus got up and ascended toward the sky. Duke felt awkward watching many of them wave goodbye at nothing. Sheer lunacy, he thought.

"Before we say a final prayer of thanks tonight," said Luke, "I see that Cody has brought a guest."

"Yeah, everyone, this is my cousin Duke," introduced Cody.

"Hey, Duke!" smiled Luke. "Glad you could join us. Would you like to hear us share the Word with you about our Lord Jesus Christ?"

"Bullshit," Duke replied.

"Er, uh..."

"I don't believe in an invisible man in the sky. I think your beliefs are a reflection of your weakness. You use them as a crutch. I would prefer you stop peddling lies and be honest with yourselves."

He looked right into Luke's eyes, unleashing a primal stare. Luke avoided eye contact and decided to move on with the next topic.

"Okay, let's, uh, yeah, let's gather around," he said as everyone closed their eyes. "Ennis, would you like to say a prayer for us?"

There was a moment of silence before Ennis collected his thoughts.

"Dear Heavenly Father...we just...we just want to thank You...for being...I mean, Lord, You're just so great. So great. We just take You for granted all the time...and...I just want You to know...we can't ever repay You for dying for our sins...Lord...and I hope, I just hope, God...that...that we all keep receiving Your blessing...and...and that we stay true to whatYou want us to be and let us continue growing with You. In Jesus' name we pray, Amen," Ennis said.

"Amen," the group collectively responded.

Within seconds, the sound of a basketball bouncing could be heard.

The group of young men headed toward the court. Its condition was pristine, with bright lights and a metal fence that prevented the ball from rolling into the lake. Once again, they lined up to shoot free throws to determine who would play the first game. The first ten who made their shots would be qualified while the rest sat and watched. Cody knew better this time than to pick Jesus for a teammate. Eventually, they had selected their ten—shirts versus skins.

The shirtless team consisted of Ennis, Felix, Marco and two other members of the church. The team that kept their shirts on were five regular members who all happened to be white.

"Dang!" joked Felix. "Everyone else versus white guys! Or singles versus the non-singles!"

"That's not funny! Don't make that joke!" growled Marco.

Everyone else laughed.

It was two hours before their eleven o'clock curfew. The familiar sounds of pickup basketball were heard throughout the retreat area. With their fellowship over too, some of the girls came to cheer their boyfriends on. The first game went smoothly, exhibiting a competitive, yet cordial atmosphere. Halfway into it, however, one of the shirt players stole the ball from Marco, which resulted in Marco chasing and shoving him to the floor.

"Hey! What was that all about? I saw that! You pushed him!" yelled a teammate of the shoved player.

"No, I didn't! You're making things up!" responded Marco.

The shoved player got up and waved it off, "I'm fine, guys. It's okay, let's keep playing."

The basketball game resumed. Marco looked around. It seemed like everyone was laughing at him. On one possession he was wide open, but Felix didn't pass the ball to him. Why didn't he pass it? Marco wondered, was it because he didn't trust me? They never trust me! He felt a wave of anger sweeping inside of him. When the same opposing player he was guarding dribbled past him and scored, Marco felt disrespected. He deliberately ran at full speed and tripped the player, giving him a near ankle injury.

"Owwwww!" the opposing player hollered.

"What happened?" asked Felix.

"I dunno. I guess he fell," lied Marco.

"Yeah right, I saw you push him!" declared his teammate.

"No, I didn't. He tried to push me, and he missed. That's why he fell," Marco exclaimed.

"That doesn't even make sense."

"Stop fighting, please," pleaded Ennis.

Herman got up from the sidelines and started dancing randomly. Several of the others who weren't playing looked at one another in disbelief over Marco's blatant denial. Duke sat motionless, observing him.

"Come on, guys," reminded Ennis. "We're brothers in Christ, remember? We just talked about being God's children. We're infused by the Lord's wisdom. We're better than this. The game's almost over. Please don't fight, okay? God Power!"

"God Power!" they echoed.

The basketball game resumed with the race to twenty-one points coming toward an exciting conclusion.

"Nineteen to twenty, guys!" Felix announced as he dribbled the ball forward.

"DON'T SAY THE SCORE OUT LOUD!" shouted Marco.

"Huh?" Felix was confused.

"WE CAN ALL COUNT. WHY DO YOU INSULT US BY SAYING THE SCORE OUT LOUD???"

"Okay, okay, man! I'm just making sure everyone knows."

Marco was boiling with anger. Everything seemed to be in slow motion to him. He hated the way Felix was dribbling the ball. He was dribbling it with his left hand, then with his right. Marco looked at some of the players on the opposing team. One of them was chewing gum. Another was coughing. This made Marco furious. He looked at the sidelines and saw Henry talking on his cell phone. Duke was looking right at him. Why is he looking at me? Marco wondered. Jay was pacing around. This annoyed Marco. Then he saw Herman on the sideline, where he was dancing and singing to himself.

Marco snapped.

"Let's get it started in here! Let's get it started in here—aaaAAHH!" Herman's singing was interrupted by Marco's tackle. Marco inexplicably pinned him to the ground and started beating him. Fortunately for Herman, several of the men immediately restrained Marco, pulling him away from Herman.

Ennis couldn't take it anymore.

"What's your problem, huh HUH HUH HUH?????!!" Ennis scolded, kicking the ground. "IT'S RUINED! THE RETREAT IS RUINED! OH MY GOD!!!"

He ran out of the fenced court, screaming in rage.

"Hey, what's Ennis doing?" inquired Henry, ending his cell phone call.

"FUCK SHIT DAMN ASSHOLE CUNT MOTHERDICK!!!" Ennis yelled, punching the door of a nearby parked car.

"Hey! That's my car, man! Stop!" pleaded the owner.

Ignoring him, Ennis jumped on top of the car and stomped on its hood repeatedly. He shouted more curse words like a man possessed. By now, most of the church members surrounded the car but were afraid of physically stopping him.

"Stop!" the car owner repeated. "Not my car!"

"DAMN ON SHIT IN ASS!!!!!" Ennis roared.

"Ennis! Come on, Ennis!" said Felix.

Finally, Ennis got tired and jumped off.

Luke reached out to him, "Ennis, are you o—"

"BITCHSONOFAHOLETITFUCKFUCKFUCK!!!" Ennis screamed, pushing his hand away.

He continued screaming away at the darkness, disappearing into the woods and presumably toward the cabins. His cursing could be heard from a distance.

"Let's call it a night," Luke concluded. "Sorry about your car, man."

"He was so nice to me the whole day," recalled the car owner. "Then he just changed."

"Hey, is everything alright?" asked one of the fellowship.

"Where's Marco? Weren't you one of the guys holding him?" asked Luke.

"Yeah, he's deceptively strong. He shook us aside and walked away, muttering to himself from here."

One by one, they eventually headed back toward the cabin area. Cody was the last to return. He took a long look at the large car dent created by Ennis. There were some slight blood stains because Ennis had been punching it too hard. To Cody, the bloody dent resembled a Rorschach blot. Regardless of how many times he looked at it, all he could see from the dent was Jesus' face, mockingly laughing at them.

"You're much happier than I thought you would be," observed Cody.

It was the next day. He and Duke were having an early lunch with the rest of the attendees in the main dining area. There were a total of over fifty people from various ages, ethnic backgrounds and gender.

Duke shrugged and offered a rare smile. "I just find all this chaos amusing. While you people brought me here to take a step closer to your world, you're all going to leave one step closer to mine."

Across from their table he spotted Zoey and the group of young women who had been teasing her. Women are different from men, Duke once lectured in his seminar. Biologically, the female gender is empowered by being a part of a collective group. The ones who are loners are weak and ripe for the picking. Duke envisioned the dining hall as a jungle with him as the lion. Soon, he thought, she will be his prey.

At Zoey's table, she was slowly annoying the church girls, particularly Daphne. She didn't approve of Zoey. She didn't approve of the way she dressed. Or the way she sat. Or the way she walked. She might as well be wearing a big scarlet "A" on her forehead, Daphne thought. Her history was well-known among the other girls. She came from a single mother, who also came from a single mother before her. And now she was a single mother herself. Zoey, concluded Daphne, was the rotten apple who hadn't fallen even an inch away from the tree. The girls sneered at her lack of education. While they had graduated from prestigious Texas universities like UT, A&M,

Rice and Baylor, Zoey couldn't even handle community college. She had no significant talent and no significant achievements; all she seemed to be good at was sleeping with thugs.

"Maple, what happened to your arm?" asked Zoey.

Maple fell silent and looked at her new cast she had received that morning. It featured a decent collection of signatures and well-wishes. Though she was new to their church group and far younger, the girls genuinely accepted Maple with open arms. Being friends with the daughter of the pastor had its perks. They found out things behind-the-scenes and often got their suggestions implemented. Her connections with her dad were an asset to the group. Besides, they figured, she was pure Christian. Just like her father. Maple could be trusted.

"I was just trying to grab something last night," she explained to Zoey. "It was from one of the top shelves. I slipped from the ladder and busted my arm."

"But that doesn't look like the type of cast from a fall," Zoey observed.

"Like you would know. Are you a doctor?" giggled Deena.

"I didn't know they trained orthopedic surgeons at the University of Phoenix, Zoey," added Daphne.

The girls broke into laughter.

"Nooo, all I'm saying is that Felix once fell down and his cast wasn't like that," she clarified.

"Different brands of cast," Deena shrugged.

Zoey took out some Ruffles chips and started eating them.

"Ew, those aren't from Whole Foods," commented Deena.

"No, why? They were on sale for a dollar at Walmart," Zoey replied.

The girls snickered. They knew she had used food stamps to purchase them.

"Oh, nothing," smirked Deena.

"What's wrong with Ruffles? They're delicious," Zoey said.

"I guess. For your kind they are," Deena replied.

Zoey started to feel self-conscious and placed the bag of Ruffles on the side. She switched to the turkey sandwich she had received from the retreat.

Deena paused for a moment and cleared her throat.

"Well, Zoey, this is as good a time as any to tell you. We're not allowing Little Ryan to sleep in our cabin for the rest of the trip."

"What? Why not?!" Zoey asked defensively.

"He's a boy. He's male. He's not supposed to be staying with a cabin full of women. He was watching Marion change clothes last night," explained Deena.

"So? He watches me change all the time. For God's sake, he's only three!"

"Are you going to argue with Scripture? 2 Timothy 2:22."

"Or Matthew 5:29," added Marion.

"Oh, why are we even bringing the Bible up? You don't even study it," expressed Deena. "At any rate, Ryan needs to stay with other men."

"You're talking about my little boy!"

"He can stay with Felix. You trust Felix, don't you? Heh. I'm not even quite sure that he isn't the father, if you know what I mean," Deena blurted.

Everyone within earshot gasped.

"How DARE you!" Zoey shouted.

Silence followed as the others anticipated Zoey's next response.

"Where's my son? Where's Ryan?" she demanded.

Felix rushed up to their table trying to figure out what had happened. Zoey's eyes watered.

"What's happening?" asked Felix. "Why are you crying?"

"Where's Ryan? Somebody please find him for me," Zoey said.

Luke took Ryan to her.

"Mommy, why are you crying?" he asked.

"We have to go now," Zoey said, packing things up. She quickly buttoned her son's coat.

"Why do we have to go?" he pleaded.

"Because we do. They don't want us here, sweetie," she said, fighting off tears.

"But I don't wanna go! I like it here!" cried Ryan.

Zoey picked her son up and headed out of the dining hall. Everyone was watching the scene unfold. She wished Felix would just follow her, but he was too busy arguing with Deena. She loved Felix with all her heart and it wasn't until now that she realized why Deena's statement made her so angry. It wasn't because she implied that Zoey was an easy sexual target; it was because deep down inside, she wished Felix really was the father. It hurt her that she could never have the man she wanted. She knew him too well. Once she was outside, Zoey made her way towards her car that was parked a half mile away.

"Stop," commanded a voice behind her.

Zoey turned around and faced Duke.

"What do you want?" she asked.

"The question is, what do YOU want? I see you leave here, all alone, a single mother with a child. You are in need of my protection," he replied.

Duke walked up to Zoey and grabbed her hand that wasn't holding her son.

"I can provide for you. I'm well-educated, well-financed, well-groomed. I am tall, physically above average and disciplined. Someone like you would be lucky to have someone like me. You are the type I'm looking for. I choose you," he said.

"And what are those things you're looking for?" inquired Zoey.

"Wholesome, Cantonese, submissive, educated.......short in stature. Someone who needs dominance," he listed.

Zoey let out a mocking laugh, "I'm Vietnamese. And I'm not most of those other things either."

"You may not be everything I'm looking for, but I'm willing to let a few things slide as long as there is submission. I see that you're in love with Felix, but let's be honest, what does he have that I don't?" He pulled her close to him. "You need a real man in your life."

"You got that right," Zoey replied.

"Time to ditch coach and fly first class."

Zoey's expression changed from a neutral to an angry one. Duke made a grave mistake by insulting the love of her life.

"Felix will have more class than you ever will," Zoey defended her friend. "You think I'm one of those fragile stuck-up 'Daddy Little Girl' types born with a silver spoon in her mouth, don't you? You're wrong. I'm from the hood of New York Chinatown, man. I've kicked and stabbed a few tough guys in the nuts who grabbed me just like how you're grabbing me now. And don't think I wouldn't recognize cheap pick-up tricks when they're done to me. Take your little alpha male gig elsewhere. I suggest with Deena."

She flung her arm free, staring back at him. She dared him with her eyes to make another forceful move.

Duke was taken aback by her sudden toughness. He was seldom wrong about his prey, but this opposing action of hers left him momentarily defensive. Zoey couldn't be taller than four-foot-eleven, he surmised, but here she was, establishing a position of supremacy.

Duke let go.

"I should've known you were a hood rat," he barked at her.

"I'm not a hood rat. I'm a single mother," Zoey said with pride. "And I've dealt with a lot of shit. Shit that you can't handle."

She turned around and walked away. Duke did not pursue.

"Mom, I didn't get to eat. I'm hungry," Little Ryan complained.

"How about McDonald's?" grinned Zoey.

"We're not going back?"

"No, mommy wasn't treated very nice here. We're going to find a different church. A church where people will treat mommy nicer."

And with that, Zoey strapped her son into the safety seat inside her 2001 Dodge Neon and drove away.

———————

The lake at the retreat was a beautiful place to be on a cloudless, warm spring night. It was the second and last night of the weekend retreat. What had started out so promising ended up in a disaster. Numerous incidents of drama and disagreement had broken out. A few friendships were ruined. Several of the retreat's attendees took an early leave. Rather than go on with the activities, the planning committee decided to impose a strict ten o'clock curfew. All the members were asked to stay inside their cabins during lockout. Yet, two of them wondered, how can anyone waste a gorgeous March evening like this?

Hence, silhouettes of the clandestine duo made their way past the small patch of trees dividing the cabin area and the lake. The retreat was several hours from town, enough to be serenaded by the rhythmic orchestra of assorted chirping and croaking. The flawless reflection of the moon from the lake was even more beautiful than the moon itself.

"What a weekend, huh?" Luke asked.

"We tried our best. Guess there're a lot of things we need to work on. Maybe we should start with a smaller group next time," suggested Felix.

Luke gave a moment's pause.

"Just between us," the preacher's son began, "Marco really bothers me. I don't know what's wrong with him."

"Luke, he's almost thirty-five years old. He's never had a relationship."

"You really think that's it? He just lacks being loved?"

"What else could it be? He has a good job, a supportive family."

"I think he's bipolar," suggested Luke.

"Maybe."

"Even then, sometimes Deena needs to keep her brother in check. It's getting embarrassing. Did you know he yelled at one of the elementary school kids last Sunday? He accused the boy of taking the last carton of milk. But there were cartons everywhere. He almost attacked that child."

"He wasn't like that before, man. That's why I don't think he's bipolar," contemplated Felix.

Luke and Felix sat in brief silence looking at the lake and the moon. Finally, Felix spoke.

"You know, sometimes it's harder than we think to be alone. I hate what I'm putting Zoey through," Felix muttered.

"Don't feel guilty about that. It's not your fault. She understands."

"No, it's not that. She can never get enough credit, you know? I get a lot of praise for taking care of her after the drama with her son's father, but she always protects me too and nobody knows it. She does it for me."

"Felix..."

"So it must be hard for Marco and Zoey. To be all alone. Unlike us..."

Felix leaned close to Luke. He felt safe in Luke's well-toned arms and pressed his ear next to Luke's chest to hear his gentle heart beating. As hard as it was for Felix to hide his secret, it must have been even more difficult for a pastor's ideal son to keep it from the world.

It was the perfect night for romance, one that was irresistible for even the most covert of lovers. Slowly, Felix lifted his lips and met Luke's. They kissed passionately under the midnight glow. The temporary feeling of freedom made them forget the past and future; it was only the moment that mattered.

"Mmmm...ahhh...oooh," moaned Luke.

"Huuuuhhhhh...ooooooh," smiled Felix.

From a distance, another pair of eyes was watching them. Jay Zhang had also snuck out his cabin to hike around the lake area. His cabin mate, Henry, had fallen asleep, but Jay was a night owl who couldn't stand being awake with little to do. He had not expected to see this private display of homosexuality between two prominent church members, both of whom he had grown to trust as brothers through fellowship. Felix and Luke continued to caress and kiss one another for twenty more minutes, but Jay had long left them by then, terrified with what he had seen.

CHAPTER 8: JUST FRIENDS

Cody couldn't remember the last time he had alcohol. Or intimacy. Or anything else that was fun, for that matter. He was beginning to have doubts about Christianity. Not the kind of doubt in regard to faith. It was the kind of doubt that was about dogma. He was still unclear of whether or not the modern concept of church was even mentioned in the Bible, let alone all the rules that were loose interpretations of the Ten Commandments. For example, he began to enjoy cursing again. Did saying the word "fuck" really equate to saying the Lord's name in vain? Did it lead people into thinking it was of less Christlike behavior? He wondered about that. And why must they be absolutely obedient to Pastor Lu and Pastor Washington anyway? Words like "flock" and "sheep" bothered Cody a great deal more than words like "shit" and "ass." Then there was also the genuine unhappiness surrounding most of the church members as well. The whole situation seemed like a clean room with dirt swept under the rug.

It was mid-April now. Although only two months had passed since his baptism, Cody had actually given his life for Christianity the prior year. He had been recruited by Ennis, his longtime friend since middle school, for a game of "church basketball." There, he had learned about religion as often as he played. He had sensed the church basketball group's ulterior motive was to convert him, but Cody wanted to be pursued. He loved the attention he received, and that was how he ultimately gave his heart to Jesus. It had made him feel accepted. He thought he had made friends.

Cody knew better now. He was still alone.

Physically at the moment, he wasn't. He was sitting around waiting for Daphne at a cozy sushi restaurant named Sasaki. It was one of those hidden gems where it looked modest and "invisible" from the outside, but pleasantly wonderful and authentic on the inside. It didn't feel like one of the trendy lounge "Japanese" restaurants that were rapidly spreading like a virus across contemporary America. Sasaki had the homely feel that kept things simple and didn't start naming their rolls based on city or states.

Psychologically, however, Cody did feel alone.

Once he had verbally committed to accepting Christ, the fellowship had moved on. It felt like a sales job. What Cody wanted more than anything was a deep friend. Perhaps, he realized, that was why he endured Daphne's consolation prize for friendship status. It was better than feeling lonely.

"Sorry I'm late. It's usually the other way around, isn't it?" asked Daphne.

She came in a jogging shirt and unflattering sweat pants. Her hair was unkempt and she didn't bother with even a trace of makeup. That was all Cody needed to know about how important he was to her. Conversely, he was dressed for the occasion. He didn't overdo it, but he did choose a decent dress shirt, had on colored contacts and fixed his hair.

"So what's the occasion?" she asked. "Why'd you invite me to dinner? You made it seem like it was an emergency."

"No emergency at all," Cody corrected. "Can't two friends go out for dinner?"

"Not together alone."

"What happened to being friends like Will and Grace?"

"Okay, what do you want? Do you need me to pray for you? Questions about Scripture? You could've gotten Ennis for that," she said, taking a menu being handed to her by the restaurant's staff. "Thank you."

"What would you like to drink, please?" asked the Japanese waitress in a polite Japanese accent.

"Ah, I dunno. Green tea," Daphne decided.

The waitress walked away, leaving them unbothered.

"Hey, I got something for you," Cody said. He took out a small wrapped object that was equivalent to the size of an engagement ring box.

"What's that? What's going on?" Daphne was cynical.

Cody placed the gift down and extended both his hands across the table.

"First, hold my hands," he instructed.

"Why?" she hesitated. "Cody, this is awkward."

She slowly placed her left hand on his, and her right one on his other hand.

Cody looked her in the eye. "Daphne, will you be my girlfriend?"

Daphne felt insulted, but she also felt flattered for the effort.

"Eh...no," she quickly replied.

She immediately let go of his hands as fast as she could. Was that it? she wondered, did this guy take me here just to ask me that?

"Okay, good. I knew you'd answer it like that. Now open this box," Cody said, handing it to her.

"Cody, this is weird. Please don't do anything to embarrass me."

"Just open it," he insisted.

The waitress came by with Daphne's green tea.

"Are you ready to order now?" the waitress smiled.

"No, please give us ten more minutes," Cody requested.

The waitress smiled and walked away.

"Cody, what's in that box? That better not be a ring," she said. "I'm serious. Take that thing back to whatever pawn shop you bought it from."

"It's not a ring," Cody insisted.

"Then what is it?"

"You'll find out once you open it."

"I'm not opening it until you tell me what it is, Cody."

"It's the reason I asked you to come here. It wasn't because I wanted to ask you to be my girlfriend. I knew you'd say no."

Daphne gave Cody a skeptical eye. She slowly reached out for the box and unwrapped it. It was a transparent plastic box with a piece of paper inside.

"What the heck?" Daphne muttered.

She opened the box and picked up the strip of paper.

"FRIENDSHIP," she read.

Cody smiled.

"Huh? I don't get it. We already are friends," Daphne replied.

"I just thought from this moment on, we could be real friends. You know, not 'friends in Christ' but real friends. You just rejected me. You made it official that my romantic aspirations are dead. So let's move on and get to know one another as human beings. What are you afraid of?" asked Cody.

Daphne glared at him in silence.

"I'm just a person, Daphne."

"You need to be taller and weigh at least a hundred and sixty pounds," she answered. "And you look like you're still in high school."

"So we can't be friends? Because I embarrass you when you're with me? This was never about Christian ideals, was it?"

"And your dad and mom are uneducated and your family is poor," she added.

"So?" Cody said, looking at her eyes.

"As a child of Christ, I deserve the best. Even my friends need to be ideal," she answered.

"I don't understand the logic here. I don't understand all this unnecessary hostility. I'm a child of Christ too," Cody said.

"You're an adopted child of Christ. And you should feel lucky."

The waitress interrupted their conversation by taking their orders. Cody ordered several of their finest sashimi. It was an assortment of ika, toro, unagi, hotategai, sabi, hamachi and, his favorite, sake (salmon). Daphne was disappointed about the absence of fried rolls. They did have plenty of tempura though. And she loved roe.

The rest of their conversation was composed of small talk. The distance between them that Cody had hoped to eliminate continued to exist; it may have even grown wider after the dinner. He had done all that he could to break the barrier, but it was up to her to make an effort. As long as she chose to remain unapproachable, tonight was as far as they would get. The question remained: Why wouldn't she give them a chance to know one another? Was it merely attraction? Attraction, according to research Cody had read, was not so much physical beauty, but how looks complement one another. They were both youthful looking and Asian, and had the same tone of olive skin and similar facial features. Daphne, however, did not feel the same way. It was curious to Cody as to why she viewed him as the most hideous thing on Earth. Indeed, he was noticing that he was getting a similar vibe from Asian-American women throughout the city.

———

The phone calls came in the middle of the night. On the third call Cody was finally awakened. This was not surprising. He had taken a long time to fall asleep, but once he had gone into Slumberland, it was difficult to wake him up. When he finally heard the last call, he had to stumble downstairs to the second floor where his home telephone was. His naked body knocked around a few random objects in the darkness, causing his cat, Toby, to flee for safety. Finally, he reached the phone.

"H-Hello?" he answered.

There was crying on the other end.

"Hello?" Cody repeated.

"Sniff...sniff...sniff..."

"Who's this?"

"It's Daphne," she said.

The reply stunned him for a moment.

"Are you there? Say something," Daphne demanded.

"Daphne, what's wrong?"

"I... " Daphne broke down and cried some more.

"Where are you? What's going on? Are you in danger?" asked Cody.

"I'm at home," she sniffled.

"You're scaring me," he said, "Was there a burglar?"

"No."

"Did you hurt yourself?"

"No."

"Then what is it?"

"............It's my ex," she answered. "I went to his house today and...and...he totally ignored me. Then he brought home another girl. Then I just left. I feel like shit."

It was the first time Cody heard her curse. So there was another side to Daphne, he realized.

"You're not shit," he countered. "You're the opposite of that. You're the prettiest girl in church."

"No, I'm not. Zoey is. Every guy ogles her. Before she left anyway," Daphne sniffed. "Maybe I should be a slut like her."

"Hey, don't say that, Zoey's a good person."

"She's a shameless, un-Christian flirt, Cody!"

"But this isn't why you're crying, is it? This is about your ex."

"Right."

"What about me? You know I think the world about you. Every minute of every day, you're on my mind. You know that's no bullshitting. I enjoy being around you. You're special to me."

"No, I'm not, you like Zoey. You should date Zoey too. She's short like you and she's more of your type," she replied. "Every...every guy wants a...wants a flirty girl. They don't...they don't want a good girl...a good girl like me!"

"Hey, it's his loss, OK? If he can't recognize a great catch like you he doesn't deserve you. It's his loss, Daphne. Some people don't know what they've got."

"I know! It's like he wants trash! You should've seen this girl, Cody. She was like Zoey...she was...she was... " Daphne lost herself in tears.

"Okay, okay. It's not the end of the world, sweetheart. Who is this guy? Tell me about him. I never knew you were seeing someone."

"He's someone I knew...since high school. We...saw each other off and on...in college. This was our......fifth time together......we never officially dated."

"Sounds like he considered you his backup plan."

Daphne sniffed.

"You should be no one's backup plan. You should be their number one priority," assured Cody.

Silence followed.

"You know what you just did?" Daphne asked.

"What?"

"You just made me smile."

Cody silently smiled in the darkness.

"Hello?" asked Daphne.

"No, nothing. I was just smiling too."

"Oh," Daphne paused, "I don't know why I'm so attached to him, Cody. I just wish he would just tell me to get out of his life forever."

"What do you see in him?"

"I dunno. I guess...I guess I just want to see him meet his potential to succeed. He's got such a good upbringing. He's so tall and athletic. Smart—"

"—white."

"Yeah. Dreamy eyes. Have you ever heard of this new show that just came out called *Prison Break*?"

"I've seen promos for it," mentioned Cody.

"I just love the main actor, Wentworth Miller. If I ever see him, I would...I would tell him to meet me at a hotel room," cooed Daphne.

"..."

"..."

"..."

"Cody, can you do something for me?"

"Sure, what is it?"

"Let's role-play. I'm going to hang up and call you back," she said. "You pretend to be someone else."

"What do you mean?"

"Just stay near the phone."

"Okay."

Daphne hung up.

Cody hung up the phone too and sat next to it. Ten minutes went by. He felt silly sitting next to his phone in the dark, naked as a jaybird. He was about to head back upstairs when the phone rang.

"Hello?" he answered.

"Hi," Daphne replied, "Is this 911? I've got an emergency."

"What's your emergency?"

"I'm tied up in my bed.

"And what are you wearing while tied up to the bed?" grinned Cody.

"Don't be crass. That's not a very professional answer, Officer..."

"Miller. Wentworth Miller."

"Oh, in that case, I'm wearing a see-through nightie, navy blue to complement my black toe polish."

"That's nice and everything, but I'm afraid I can't help you."

"Why not, Wentworth?"

"Because I don't know where you live," laughed Cody.

"25061 Woodchase Drive."

Cody paused.

"Come over here, and free me," giggled Daphne.

"Are...are you serious?"

"Yes," she replied, "I am."

Daphne hung up the phone. Cody froze for a moment before realizing what he was being invited to. He quickly ran back upstairs and found some decent clothes to wear. Once again, Toby ran for cover, fearing for her life. The cat eyed Cody's actions curiously, wondering why her owner was heading out during this peculiar time of the night. Through constant observation, she knew this was an unusual circumstance.

The squealing of tires could be heard along the empty

lanes of Westheimer Road. Cody breezed his way through rows of green traffic lights, hoping the entire time he wouldn't suddenly hit another Mexican. The political incorrectness of the thought made him laugh. He didn't care. This was the night he had been waiting for. He opened up his Integra's sunroof, enjoying the wonderful air. The mid-April weather felt like summer already.

Once he had arrived in front of her townhouse, Cody quickly made short work of the gate and approached her front door. Before he could even knock, Daphne opened the door, wearing a worn-out, burnt-orange University of Texas T-shirt and sweatpants. It was hardly the transparent navy blue nightie she had described.

"Hey," said Cody.

"Hey," replied Daphne.

"You're not wearing a nightie."

"And you're not Wentworth Miller."

"Fair enough. Can I come in?"

"...........okay. Sure." She took a few steps back from the door.

Neither seemed to care they both had to go to work the next morning; things had gotten a little interesting. Daphne's one-bedroom townhouse was two stories, compact and surprisingly empty. Cody had expected stacks of Bibles everywhere with a giant cross in the middle of her living room. Instead, it turned out she was a minimalist. Even though she lived there for years, it seemed like she had just moved in.

"Don't you ever buy stuff?" laughed Cody.

"Haha! I know! Ironic, huh? I work in the Galleria and I don't ever shop!"

"See? This isn't so bad. A guy and a girl under the same roof. It's not a sin."

"I've had guys in here before," grinned Daphne.

"So it's all an act, eh? The goody-good church girl."

"No, I mean, I love Christ with all my heart, but..."
Daphne paused. "Come over here."

Daphne directed Cody around the corner of her living room where a grand white piano was the centerpiece of attention.

"Wow!" exclaimed Cody.

"Do you play?"

"No, I was in marching band. That was it. First chair clarinet," Cody smiled.

"My mom made me take lessons since I was five years old."

"Oh?"

"She was very hard on me, but it was tough love, you know?"

"Can you play something now?" asked Cody.

"Are you kidding me? The neighbors would complain!"

"Oh. Of course. Duh."

"Cody...I'm sorry I said your family was poor. I don't know why I'm like that sometimes. I pray for it constantly. I'm aware of how stuck-up I am. I've been told by people about how I think I'm better than everyone," Daphne explained.

"It's okay. I see past that. I know you're a good soul."

She looked him in the eye for the first time and smiled.

"Aside from my grandma, I don't have any family here in the U.S. My parents spent every dime they had to support me. They demanded excellence. I've always been the good girl. The model child. It's hard for me to see anyone else who have lower success and acknowledge them as my equal."

"Is that why you're always against Zoey?" asked Cody.

"Sort of. I mean, I think she milks it. She completely changes around Felix. Do you ever notice this?"

"Yeah, what's the deal with those two anyway? Are they dating or not? Is Little Ryan really Felix's..."

"No, he's not Felix's kid. I don't know. They've got a weird friendship. I have no idea why," said Daphne. "I'm pretty sure Felix is still a virgin."

"Are you a virgin?"

Daphne glared at Cody for asking such a question.

"I'm sorry if I've overstepped my boundaries," Cody apologized.

"Of course, I am," she lied. "It's all about chastity, Cody."

"You had a different tone when we were role-playing."

"We were just playing, Cody. What are you saying?"

"Nothing. It's just...refreshing to know that you may have a wild side, I suppose."

They both paused. With the exception of the piano, the living room was close to empty. There was a small glass table used for dining and a couple of generic photos of random still objects. The entire home, thought Cody, lacked personality.

"You should come by this weekend," Daphne suggested.

"I'd love to," replied Cody.

"I have the whole Season 1 DVD collection of *Sex and the City*. Watch it with me. It's my favorite show. I also love *Nip/Tuck*."

Cody laughed.

"What's so funny?" she asked.

"It's just...I just thought you sit around all day reading the Bible."

"Haha. I...do that too."

"And then you watch *Nip/Tuck*?"

"Yes."

They both laughed.

"I hate my dad," Daphne admitted.

"Don't say that. He's your dad."

"He lives with my mom in China. Every time my mom and I would speak on the phone, she would tell me he beat her. He's handicapped, you know. He had an accident a long time ago, which prevents him from finding work. He takes his frustrations out on her by throwing stuff. It's hard for me to trust men. I...I hate men, sometimes. I don't know how Zoey does it," she said.

"Stop bringing her up. You talk about her quite a lot. Do you think she even thinks of you half as much as you think about her?" Cody countered. "Anyway, I'm sorry to hear about your dad doing that to your mom."

"It's okay. He's an asshole," Daphne said with conviction.

"Is that why you don't like Asian men?"

"Because they remind me of my father? Not sure. All I know is that I've never been attracted to one."

"My cousin Duke blames the media."

"Was Duke the guy you brought to the retreat last month?"

"That's the one."

"I don't like him. He scares me. He stares at people like a serial killer."

Sunlight was seeping through the windows; morning had come.

"Okay," Daphne said, "you have to go now. Sunrise."

She led Cody to the front door. When she opened it, the glare of the rising sun was blinding. Early morning joggers were everywhere. They looked at one another for a moment, not as lovers but like two very good friends.

"Thanks for coming. Have a good day at work," she smiled.

"You too."

Cody reached for a hug, but Daphne pushed him away.

"No, we can't do that. It's not godly."

"Okay. Didn't know. *Sex and the City* marathon viewing at your house this weekend?" asked Cody.

"Sure, can't wait," Daphne smiled.

CHAPTER 9: WILL AND GRACE

Cody had never been in an arms deal before. This wasn't an arms deal, of course, but if he were to imagine what one would be like, it would probably resemble the situation he was in this early June afternoon. At a back alleyway in the Harwin wholesale district, his parked car was facing another parked car. He could only guess who was in the other one. All he knew was that these persons were the carriers of some stolen decor merchandise from Taiwan.

"So how does this work?" he asked Mindy. "We all come out at the same time? I hope they don't expect us to have a briefcase of cash."

"You go. I stay," she instructed.

"What? But they're your 'friends.' Wouldn't it be better if you talked to them? We're partners in this remember?"

"No, no, no. You go. I stay here, man."

"Why do you have to stay?"

"Because I am shy."

Cody gave Mindy a confused look. Doors were heard opening and closing from the opposing car. Three middle-aged Asian men began to approach them.

"Come on!" insisted Cody. "Let's go together, I don't speak Taiwanese."

"No! You go! He speak good English, Bobbie," Mindy promised.

Cody got out of his car and walked over to them,

aiming toward the one in the middle who appeared to be their leader.

"Hey, sorry, my partner's kinda shy. So where are you guys storing this stuff?" asked Cody.

"<Who are you? Where is the woman who said she would meet with us?">·asked the ringleader in Taiwanese.

Cody did not understand a word they said.

"Um, any of you speak English?" asked Cody.

"<Do you speak any Chinese?>"

"English anyone?"

"<You have a Chinese face, but you don't speak any of it. Why is that? >"

"I...don't think we're communicating," replied Cody.

Cody motioned for Mindy to get out of the car. She vigorously shook her head in rejection.

"Money, yes. Stuff, yes," explained the leader in broken English. "No money, no stuff."

"Woman in car," gestured Cody, "have money."

The three Taiwanese men talked amongst themselves. Cody stood and watched. Cody's cell phone rang. It was Mindy.

"What's going on, Bobbie? Did they bring the furniture or not?" she asked over the phone.

"First of all, it's not furniture. It's home decor. Secondly, none of them speak decent English. You need to come out here and talk with them," Cody demanded.

"Yes, they can speak English. I heard them," Mindy said.

"Where?" asked Cody.

"On Skype."

"You've only talked with them over the Internet?"

"Yes."

The ringleader gestured for Cody to hand over the phone. Cody complied.

"<Hey, is this a joke?>" he scolded her. "<Are you joking with us? Our time is valuable and we will not be wasting any more of it.>"

"<This is my associate, he knows what to do, just lead him to the merchandise and then I'll give you the check>," she answered.

"<Are you the same woman from Skype and the phone? Why can't you come out? We're only trusting you because you know our connection in Taipei>," the ringleader angrily replied.

"<He's okay. I trust him. I don't like being out in the summer sun. It tans my skin.>"

The ringleader turned around and shared her absurd answer with the other two Taiwanese men. "<Can you believe this princess? She doesn't want to come out because of a tan!>"

All three men laughed. The ringleader handed the mobile phone back to Cody.

"What'd you say to him? Why are they laughing at us?" asked a concerned Cody.

"Don't worry about that. I told them that they can trust you, Bobbie."

"And that's why they're laughing?!"

"No, just...come on. Just get the furniture, okay?"

"It's not fur—"

Mindy hung up.

"Ha ha. Women. Many trouble, eh?" The ringleader put a friendly arm around Cody's neck. "Come. We give stuff."

The four of them weaved their way around the labyrinth of warehouses and wholesale buildings until they came upon an unassuming closed storage garage. Taking out a small key from his pocket, the ringleader unlocked the keypad. He then slid the storage garage door upwards, revealing a stolen cache of sealed home decor merchandise.

"Use hand," motioned the ringleader, encouraging Cody to inspect a vase with his hands.

Not one to look like a fool, Cody attempted his best acting. He gently tapped the vase with his knuckles and squinted his eyes, attempting to give off the look of a counterfeit expert. He counted to fifteen before he turned around and nodded with approval.

"No more?" asked the surprised ringleader.

"Oh. Uh. Yeah, let's inspect a couple more," Cody replied.

This time he opened a box containing a picture frame. He continued the charade by holding it toward the sunlight, once again counting to fifteen inside his head. The three men chuckled at Cody. After probing a few more items, Cody gave his thumbs up approval.

"Okay? Good?" smiled the ringleader.

Cody smiled back, "Yeah, good."

The four men helped carry the boxes of merchandise to Cody's little Integra. It was surprisingly able to hold it all. Strutting towards the open window of the passenger side, the ringleader began making conversation with Mindy.

"<Okay, it's all loaded.>" He grinned. "<Do you have our check?">

"<Here>," Mindy said, handing him a check from her purse. Mindy found nothing appealing about his appearance. The man had oily skin, bad teeth and an overall dirty look.

"<Is that your husband?>" the ringleader asked, nodding toward Cody.

"<No>," replied Mindy with a serious expression. "<He is my bodyguard.>"

As he accepted the check, the ringleader observed Cody's clueless expression.

"<I don't think he's your bodyguard>," he smirked. "<Next time, you might have to write a bigger check. You're lucky we're nice.>"

The three Taiwanese men headed back toward their own car, laughing and slapping each other on their shoulders.

"What was that all about?" asked Cody. "What did you guys say to one another?"

"Just drive," instructed Mindy.

Cody started the engine and backed the car out. They were silent for a few minutes, reflecting on their first deal. Then he decided to break the silence.

"Why do you keep secrets from me?" asked Cody.

"It is not a secret! I did not know, okay?"

"You've never met that guy. You totally have never met that guy!"

"Hey, I don't want to do the big argue, okay? Let's listen to your CD," she said.

She popped in a random CD from Cody's collection. Mindy winced, finding the music unbearable.

"Man, what kind of singer is she?! She sound like she shout loud, man!"

"That's Mary J. Blige. She's expressing emotion. Her man just left her in this song. So she's got to find herself a better man," explained Cody.

"I don't like it! She is screaming!" criticized Mindy.

"Okay, fine, fine. I prepared for this." Cody ejected the CD and took out another. "I made this CD just for you. It's got all the crap you like. A whole collection."

Cody popped in the CD. Her eyes grew wider when she realized it was a song she liked.

"Oh, Norah Jones! Yes, Bobbie!" she smiled, turning up the volume.

"I also have that sissy thousand miles song in there too. Track six, I think," he said.

Mindy fiddled with the playlist, "Do you have—"

"YOU HAD A BAD DAY, YOU'RE TAKING ONE DOWN, YOU SING A SAD SONG JUST TO TURN IT AROUND," the stereo blared.

Mindy squealed with approval.

"I love you, Bobbie! You pay attention!"

"Yeah, yeah."

Though they didn't know it, some of the merchandise was already cracking from the slightest bumps of the ride. They were indeed counterfeit.

———

Within the crowded merchant markets in India, a shirtless young man is seen running away from his pursuers. He dodges moving carts, bystanders and other obstacles, hoping he can successfully escape before completely losing his breath. Amid a background of colorful tapestry of primary and secondary colors, he finally finds a narrow alleyway to make his escape. He uses whatever remaining energy he has left to make a permanent getaway. Unfortunately for him, the corridor leads to a wide dead-end area where the chasing men catch up and surround him.

The pursuers begin shouting for him to die with great fervor. The young man, however, raises a hand to demand silence. A unique beat begins to play. He suddenly breaks out into a hip-and-shoulder gyrating dance motion that perfectly fits within the soundtrack of techno and traditional Indian music. From out of the dead-end shadows, exotically dressed Indian women wearing silk saris and ghagra choli join him. Together, they bob their heads and skip around in unison, singing the main chorus of a modern Indian song.

"That's ludicrous!" blurted Cody.

Daphne had declared June as Bollywood month. Both she and Cody had been spending weeknights together, sharing her quirky obsession for the popular Indian musicals. She would pick the movie while he did the cooking at his home.

"They were about to kill him and then he just starts dancing? This isn't a movie. It's a Smooth Criminal video!" criticized Cody.

Daphne shrugged. "You need to add more salt into your French onion soup."

Though she had gotten comfortable with their friendship, their actions and arrangements reflected a continued enforcement of her strict Christian beliefs. They sat on opposite sides of the sofa, said grace before every meal and avoided any form of physical contact, hugging or otherwise.

Their usual routine consisted of movie watching, television shows, board games, and helping Daphne study for her GMAT test. He knew those activities were mundane, but being with her somehow circumvented that personal perception. Things did get interesting on a conversation scale. They spoke openly on many subjects, especially their experiences growing up Asian-American. They were the same race, but their genders gave them vastly different perspectives.

"Hey, what's that?" asked Daphne in disgust.

It was the first time she had seen Cody's cat, Toby. The overweight gray tabby was usually introverted around visitors, but it appeared she finally deemed Daphne worthy enough to be touched.

"That's just my cat," reminded Cody. "I mentioned her to you before, remember?"

"She's so freaking fat. Shoo! Go away, you ugly thing!"

Toby stopped and glared at her. She was insulted by Daphne's rejection. The cat changed her mind, making her way to the stairs where she gazed at Daphne with unreserved judgment.

"She's just glaring at me. How rude!" said Daphne.

"Now you know how it feels," laughed Cody.

Daphne turned and glared at him, aggravated that he would take sides against her.

"Yeah?" she retorted. "Well, you know what? There's nothing in your house that suggests you have other girls coming here. I don't feel threatened. You need to make a girl feel competition. The only challenge I'm getting is from your cat!"

Cody scratched his head. "Well, isn't it better if you're the only one that mattered?"

"I guess. I dunno. I do, but I don't," Daphne answered cryptically. "Also, I just hate that you even have a cat. Can't you be like a real guy and get a dog?"

"One cat for a guy's alright. No one's ever criticized the Godfather or Dr. No for having a cat. Besides, isn't it more feminine when a guy has little girly dogs running around his house?"

Daphne loathed being disagreed with and chose to respond to him with silence. They didn't speak again until a particularly romantic scene in the movie that left her with a despairing sigh.

"Penny for your thoughts?" he asked.

"What? Sorry I was distracted."

"I said, 'Penny for your thoughts?'"

"My thoughts are only worth a penny? How low."

"Okay, a dollar for your thoughts then."

"Heh," she chuckled, "can you imagine someone being named Dollar? Makes them feel cheap. My mom almost named me Darcy. How retarded is that?"

Cody noticed she was trying to change the subject. He decided to cut to the chase.

"So what's going on in your mind right now? You're obviously sad," he asked.

"It's Deena. She just got a boyfriend."

"Nice."

"Not nice. How come God gives everyone boyfriends but me?"

"What do you mean? I asked you out numerous times..."

"I meant a real man, Cody," Daphne discounted. "Someone who knows how to take care of things. Someone ideal. Someone who's best for me that I deserve...I don't know. It's like God hates me. He wants me to feel miserable."

Cody frowned. They'd had this same conversation several times.

"We've been through this topic before. Maybe you're just too picky," he suggested. "Maybe...maybe what's best for you isn't what you think it is."

"It makes me lose faith in Him."

"Because you didn't get what you want? What do you pray for? Don't you worry about the homeless or orphans? What about sick people?"

"We're also told we get rewarded for our faith, Cody. There's a reason why certain people are chosen to be baptized. It's part of God's plan."

They both paused.

"You think it's all corrupted sometimes? The church, that is," asked Cody.

"It...crosses my mind," she answered.

"Yeah."

"Like, I'm sure you've seen that commercial with the bald guy and those third world country kids. You think that's real?" asked Daphne.

"Not likely."

Another pause. Daphne returned to her original thought.

"Deena's new boyfriend looks like Jesus," she laughed.

"Really?"

"Yeah, haha."

"MAYBE THAT'S WHY DEENA WENT FOR HIM!" they both said at once, breaking into laughter.

"Hey, what do you want to do this weekend?" asked Cody.

"I dunno. I was thinking about studying. The GMAT's important," she replied. "You can watch."

"Again?"

"What's the matter? I thought you liked helping me succeed."

"I...I do, it's just..."

"You're my friend right?"

"Why couldn't we, like, watch a movie in a theater or something? I know you have to study, but take a break, Daphne."

"I don't think that's a good idea.......I don't know. It would feel like a date."

"Then let's bring one of our friends. Like Ennis or Marion," he insisted. "Why do we always have to meet in secrecy?"

"The GMAT is so important. I don't know. I'll...I'll have to think about it."

Once ten o'clock came, Cody went through the usual routine of walking Daphne to her car. He stayed to watch her pull away from his driveway. As expected, she ignored his waves of goodbye and carried herself with an act of entitlement. The terms of their friendship were unfair. As long as he was nice to her, she was reluctant to show warmth to him.

Skinny Grandma had represented mortality to the Quan family.

Although she had always been a frail woman, she received the "Skinny" moniker for a less obvious reason. During the Japanese-occupied China days, Cody's grandmother worked night and day, sheltering her fellow countrymen in underground tunnels. Her tireless dedication and persistency saved hundreds of lives, one of whom was a surviving American journalist who dubbed her the Chinese Harriet Tubman. The "Skinny" nickname, however, turned out to be the more popular choice. It led survivors to symbolically equate her thinness to a vigorous dedication.

The family found out just how true that nickname was after her miraculous recovery. Since her homecoming from the hospital a few months ago, Skinny Grandma exhibited an energy and metabolism unlike anyone else her age. She cooked large family meals by herself, played mahjong on a daily basis, walked for miles around her retirement home, and constantly desired to see her two favorite grandchildren: Cody and Duke.

"<Why isn't Min-Guang here?>" asked Skinny Grandma, referring to Cody by his Chinese name.

It was another weekly dinner with her only son and daughters, but the eighth straight week missed by Cody. Duke occasionally made it but usually didn't because he lived in Dallas.

"<He's with his friend. Again. So he says>," answered Mr. Quan in a disappointed and frustrated voice.

"<Are you sure it isn't because he's dating someone?>" teased Skinny Grandma.

"<Impossible. We would've known. We constantly check up on him. Every good Chinese child knows that he's supposed to report back to his parents for approval>," boasted Cody's father. "<After all, we know better. So we can ensure that he doesn't make mistakes. We approve of his friends too.>"

"<Girlfriend? Ha!>" dismissed Mei. "<How can your short, stupid son have a girlfriend before my perfect boy?>"

"<And what's so perfect about your son?"> challenged Cody's mother.

"<Which one graduated from UT? Who's taller? Who makes more money? Of course, girls are going to pick my son first! It's just a fact. I wish you could just accept it. I'm not trying to argue with you>," Duke's mother said while chewing a bite of pork chop.

"<They're both good kids>," explained Skinny Grandma. "<It's just embarrassing to me that Min-Guang can't come to eat with his grandmother anymore. I also desire to see him get married and bring over a nice Hong Kong girlfriend for once. Have her make me some tea. Ask me how I'm doing. My health may be okay right now, but who knows how many years I have left?>"

Boiling anger rose inside of Mr. Quan. It was disheartening for him to know how much Cody displeased his grandmother. He wondered if it were too much to ask for a little obedience. His son had an easy life and a well-paying job. Certainly women would be flocking to him if he had made an effort to get one. How hard could it be for Cody to find a nice Cantonese girlfriend and bring her over for family dinner? When their visit was over, each attending family member politely bid their farewell to Skinny Grandma for the evening.

"<Don't worry, mother>," assured Aunt Mei. "<By the end of the year, my son will find himself the perfect fiancée. He'll make you proud.>"

Strolling around the parking lot of the retirement home, Cody's father felt the fates assigning a mission to him. It was to find his son a perfect wife. One calculated according to Chinese superstitions. He would match lucky numbers, harmonious elements and, most importantly, compatible Chinese zodiac signs.

"<Someone born from the Year of the Rooster>," he muttered.

"<Why are you suddenly smiling?>" inquired Cody's mother.

"<Because, it's up to us to find our son a wife!>"

"<Can you please stop doing that sort of thing? I know this is all about competition with your sister, but these are modern times. Even people in China don't even take this sort of thing seriously anymore. Let our son be.>"

It was pointless reasoning on her part; she knew her husband was too preoccupied with his scheming to listen to her.

Skinny Grandma watched from her third-story window as her adult children searched for their cars in the parking lot. Though it was almost eight-thirty in the evening, the Texas summer sun stubbornly refused to set. It resulted in an enduring sunset, one that seemingly never ended. But inevitably night would occur, she reasoned, and after that, the morning after. The contrast between the sun's immortality and her lack thereof did not escape her notice. She was not jealous, however, because she accepted that a finite lifespan was preferable to a never-ending one. It was the sun that felt envy. People, Skinny Grandma believed, received the gift of reincarnation. Life after death. Death after life.

Getting ready for bedtime, she lit some incense to give thanks to Guan Yin, the goddess of compassion. Then she called it a night. Once she fell asleep, the figure of Jesus entered her bedroom. He looked at her for a moment before placing a hand over her head. In an instant, a shiver ran through her body. The perfect health she had enjoyed took a turn for the worse.

Cody's grandmother started dying.

———

Daphne came out of the movie theater with a grin on her face. It was near the end of June now, weeks after she and Cody talked about watching a movie together. Summer nights in Houston were hotter than most daytime temperatures in other cities. The heat, however, didn't bother either of the long-time Houstonians.

"That was an awesome movie!" she exclaimed.

"Yeah!" smiled Cody. "You know what made it so great? They took a popular comic book and gave it the indie touch. They resisted going the commercial route and stuck with a long-term goal in setting up a trilogy. This is going to change things for superhero movies."

"I'm glad you talked me into coming to the theater with you."

"Well, it's your birthday. I just didn't expect you to pick Batman."

"Why not? Just because I'm a girl?"

"No. Because you have shitty taste in movies."

They laughed.

"You really seem to like reviewing things, Cody. Maybe you should start a blog."

"A blog, eh? Isn't that something all the church people at Fellowship are getting into nowadays?" asked Cody.

"Yeah, but you know...they write about boring stuff," Daphne giggled.

Her body movements were noticeably different that evening. She twirled her hair while she talked and fiddled often with her jean pockets. Even her preferred degree of personal space extremity was momentarily absent.

"Okay, sure," considered Cody, "I'll start a blog."

"Well...it's almost ten o'clock..."

"Aw, really? Come on, I'm hungry. Let's go to IHOPs."

"It's 'IHOP,' Cody," she corrected. "There's no 's' in it."

"Alright, let's go to IHOP."

"Can't. I really shouldn't. I want to, but I shouldn't. It's ten. I need to get enough sleep for work tomorrow."

"No, hey, wait. At least...come on over with me to my car real quick," he insisted. "I've got your birthday present in the trunk."

Daphne followed him through the outdoor parking lot. Cody opened his car's trunk and produced a large box. It required both of his arms to carry, because of its sheer size and weight.

"Wow, what is it?" wondered Daphne.

"I don't think you should open it here," Cody advised while carrying the box to her car.

"Should I open it at my house?"

"Yeah, I think so."

She unlocked and opened the trunk of her Passat for Cody. The box fell gently in with a slight thud. They both sheepishly smiled at one another in silence. She hesitated for a moment, but then approached Cody and gave him a hug.

It was a long deserved one.

"You're the best friend a girl could ever have, Cody. I mean it," she said with a heartfelt confession.

She let go of him and headed toward the driver's side door. Cody stood and looked at her, feeling like he was lost in time and space. The engine of Daphne's Passat started.

"Well, aren't you going to move? I'm going to run over you, haha!" she shouted.

Cody snapped out of his trance and got out of the Passat's way. He waved goodbye to her, then got into his own car. Not long after he arrived home, the phone rang. It was Daphne.

"Hey," she said.

"Hey."

She giggled. Sounds of her unwrapping the present could be heard.

"This isn't just a big box with a piece of paper that says 'Friendship' in it, is it?" she joked.

"Haha. No," laughed Cody.

It took a minute for Daphne to entirely unwrap the large box. Once she used her car keys to cut through the thicker taping, she opened it and found it contained an assortment of smaller wrapped boxes.

"It's twenty-six presents," explained Cody. "One for every birthday of your life that I've missed."

A long silence followed. Daphne could be heard fighting tears through the phone.

"I'll never forget you, Cody Quan," Daphne whispered. "Not in a million years."

She offered a comment of delight with each opened present. Some were silly, some were expensive, some were handmade. Each carried a symbol of their time together. It took a total of forty-five minutes for her to open them all.

"Thanks for remembering my birthday," said Daphne. "No one ever does. When it's yours, I'm going to give you the best present ever. I'm going to throw you a party!"

"But mine's all the way in December."

"I know. But our friendship should last that long, right?"

"Of course," said Cody, "Why wouldn't it?"

"BOBBIE, WAKE UP!" screamed Mindy.

Cody could hear her pounding on his bedroom door. He had long since learned to lock it even though he lived alone. On this early September morning, he was glad that he did.

"Come on! Come on! Come on!" she insisted.

"Okay, okay. What...what time is it? What's going on?"

Cody took a glance at his digital clock: 7:32 am. Too early, he thought. He quickly put on his glasses and searched for some clothes.

"Come on, Bobbie!"

After finally finding a decent T-shirt and shorts, he opened his door.

"WHAT?!" he demanded. "Why the hell are you in my house at seven-thirty in the morning? You know what? Give me my emergency keys back—"

"THIS IS AN EMERGENCY!" Mindy interrupted.

"What's the emergency?"

"Man, watch the news, man! There's a Category Four hurricane coming! The same size as Katrina!"

This was important news. The announcement of a hurricane coming so soon to Houston after Hurricane Katrina would cause major panic in the city. Everyone had seen what happened to New Orleans and they were not going to accept a similar fate.

"But I thought it was just a tropical storm," he muttered.

"No! It's big! Real big! They say it will destroy the city, man!"

"You're exaggerating."

"No, I am not!"

Cody went downstairs and turned on his television. Every major news channel, both local and national, was discussing the projected impact of the coming hurricane. The graphics of the meteorologist's radar screen showed it floating above the Gulf of Mexico. It was almost half the size of Texas. This was serious, he realized.

Mindy wasted no time in panicking. "Quick, you gotta pack! Call your family! Call your friends! Call—"

"OKAY OKAY! STOP TALKING, I CAN'T THINK!" shouted Cody.

A thought suddenly occurred to Mindy.

"Oh, my God, Bobbie! What do we do about the Mosiac Decor stuff? I paid a lot of money for them!"

"We're talking about a fucking hurricane here," Cody said, packing his Playstation 2. "We can only take what's important."

The media continued feeding them images. They saw Mayor Bill White explaining evacuation routes and ordering mandatory abandonment of the city. The hurricane's name flashed in big bold letters across the screen.

"Rita," read Cody.

Millions of thoughts raced through his head as he stuffed his car with clothes, personal belongings and food supplies. Meanwhile, Mindy was on her cell phone, yelling instructions to her husband in Taiwanese. It triggered Cody to make a call of his own. He wanted to make sure Daphne was safe. Her phone went unanswered.

"Hey.......hey!" Mindy interrupted his thoughts, "my husband says we need to get gas as quickly as possible. There are long lines in the gas stations."

Cody stared at his cell phone with a worried look.

"You're thinking about the Daphne girl?"

"Yeah," he replied, "she's not answering. I want to check up on her."

"No, no! You can't do that! You must think of your family and best friend first!"

"God, where is she?" Cody wondered out loud to himself.

Mindy slapped him on the back of the head.

"HEY! PAY ATTENTION!" she demanded.

"STOP HITTING ME!"

"CHECK WITH YOUR FAMILY FIRST! NOT SOME STUPID GIRL, OKAY?"

Mindy gave him a stern look.

".......okay. You're right," Cody said.

They spent the next half hour looking for the cat. Toby had climbed on top of the kitchen cabinets and was meowing frightfully. Mindy grabbed a nearby broom and poked at the feline, trying unsuccessfully to get her to jump down. Cody did a better job at convincing Toby by squirting her with a spray bottle. With Cody's perfect catch, the cat was now safely in his arms, though she unkindly repaid him by shredding the top portion of his shirt.

"OW! AWHAA!!!" he hollered in pain, "damn cat!"

When blood immediately began to seep through his shirt, he shoved Toby into the portable cage, locking it tight. Mindy looked after her as Cody went upstairs for a fresh shirt. The cat squeezed her face against the bar doors, angrily looking for a way out. Moments later, Mindy heard his returning footsteps.

"Well, are you coming with us?" he asked.

"No, I need to go back to my husband and leave town with him. You take care, eh?"

"You should put tape on the windows of your house. That way, the glass won't shatter."

"There won't be anything left, Bobbie," she paused. "Let me take the decor products home."

"Leave them. I think they're fake anyway."

"How do you know they are fake?"

"Just look how easily they break!"

"I don't care, man! I paid for them!"

"Then be my guest and take them yourself!"

"You have to carry them to my car for me. I have small power. And my nails are still fresh."

Cody looked at her in disbelief.

"How. Do. You. Survive. In. This. World?" he asked.

"Man, come on, man!"

After he had spent twenty long minutes helping Mindy with the decor merchandise, he immediately made his way toward Daphne's neighborhood. Pandemonium was what he found. Most of the residents seemed to have heeded the early warnings and had left, but the remaining few fought, looted or did otherwise destructive behavior. Without disregard to danger, Cody walked past them and knocked repeatedly on Daphne's door. No response. Perhaps she had already left, he hoped.

He gave up after the fifth series of knocking. His motives for saving her were partially subconscious; it was a chance to play hero. More so, it meant rebelling against the Asian structure of "family first." Cody enjoyed the secrecy of their friendship because it was one of the rare things of his choosing. His car and home were picked by his parents. His job was given by a family friend. Daphne's friendship, however, was something he decided and earned. If Hurricane Rita turned out anywhere near as devastating as Hurricane Katrina, he didn't want to spend his last moments with his parents. That would be a typical epitaph for an Asian-American male: found dead hanging out with parents. But now that Daphne was nowhere to be found, his family-oriented inclinations kicked in. Guilt quickly followed.

"Shit," he concluded, "I can't just leave my mom and dad."

He weighed the cell phone in his hand, stalling for an opposing decision. The phone felt clunky and huge—like a metal cucumber in his pocket. Hopefully they'll make them smaller some day, he thought. When his pertinacious accountability for family remained, Cody gave in and dialed his mother's cell phone number. She immediately answered.

"<Where are you?!>" she shouted.

"<I'm right now checking come house to.>"

"<Your Chinese is getting worse and worse! What are you waiting for?! Hurry up and come over here so you can be safe! We'll protect you!>"

It took only those words to remind Cody that he was a child. Whether he was twenty-seven or seventy-two years old, it didn't change. Something was programmed in him to obey and feel like property. Once his parents had him locked on, he struggled to diverge.

"<Okay. Come will I now,>" he said.

His mother responded with broken English, "You here come, ok? Mommy cook soup. Fix you. Good boy."

Cody immediately complied. Whatever opportunity he had about running away with Daphne subsided. Now it became a timeline of hiding out with his family, drinking fish head soup and eating leftover sausage buns. He accepted those would probably be his last memories. The usual twenty-minute trip took over two hours because of the evacuation. When he finally arrived, Cody saw Ace's station wagon parked outside the doorway. He was loading containers of gasoline into his trunk. Look at that, opined Cody, even my cousin has the sense to leave.

"<Hello, eh, fellow cousin! Eh, I'm about to evacuate>," Ace explained.

"Where are you going?" Cody asked him in English.

"<Eh, Dallas, maybe, ehhhh, what about you?>" he replied.

"<My parents where how come no follow?>"

"Sorry? Me no understanding you," answered Ace.

"Okay, you speak Chinese. I speak English, alright?"

"<Alright, ehhh. Your parents aren't leaving and I told them I would feel, eh, safer if I got out of town.>"

"Well, why are they just letting you go? Why are they forcing me to stay?"

"<I don't know. Maybe I'm not their son?">

"Do you have anywhere to go?"

"<Ehhh. Uh...ehh...no. I just thought I could sleep in my, eh, car.>"

The requisite to obey suddenly removed itself from Cody.

"Follow me," he said, "We'll go to my cousin Duke's house in Dallas."

"<Okay, cousin Cody.>"

With a newfound independence, Cody ventured into his parents' home. Upon taking a couple of steps in, he found a bowl of soup shoved in his face.

"You drink now!" his mother ordered in English.

"Mom, this isn't the time for soup!"

"Always time for soup! You drink now!"

Once again, he reverted to compliance.

"<Ah, there you are>," exclaimed his father as came down the stairs. He was holding armfuls of pinwheels and incense. "<You'll be safe here. I've isolated the entire house with maximum Chinese charm protection. The hurricane should bounce right off it like it was a force field.>"

"Dad, we're going to die if we stay here! All the pinwheels, incense and fish head soup isn't going to save us!"

"<Speak Chinese, son.>"

"<YOU TWO LEAVE NEED MUST NOW GO!>"

"<Things will be alright. It's just a hurricane>," shrugged his mother. "<Now, drink more soup.>"

"<Mom. Month to last came hurricane people die kill many. Okay?>"

"< Everything will be alright>," she repeated.

Cody felt frustrated that his parents were living inside their own bubble. Rather than heeding the news reports and meteorology, they were counting on ridiculous feng shui and other nonsense. He wondered why they often overreacted to meaningless things, yet calmly ignored actual danger. It was enough to push him to leave. If they didn't care about dying, he figured, why should he stay? Now there was just one more piece of business to check on: the safety of his grandparents.

"<Where grandma is?>" asked Cody.

"<Your grandparents are both alright>," his mother informed him. "<There's a mahjong tournament going on in Chinatown. People figured they could take advantage of this time off. In fact, Chinatown is busier than ever.>"

The defiant nature of the Asian community appalled Cody. Now he cared about only himself. It made the decision easy for him to turn and leave.

"<Where are you going?! You're staying with us! You're a child! Ace can go, but you can't handle it!>" demanded Cody's mother. "<You come back here right now!>"

"Come on, Ace," Cody said, ignoring his mother. "Start your car and follow mine. We're heading for Dallas."

"<But, ehh, what about your parents?>"

"Didn't you hear them?" he scoffed. "They seemed okay with dying."

Cody was roused from a deep sleep, feeling cold pressurized water hitting his face. He had a second of disorientation before remembering what had happened. By cleverly eluding the stationary traffic the night before, he had successfully made it to Dallas in just under six hours.

"Wake up," ordered Duke, holding a recently used garden hose.

"You...damn it...you couldn't have just tapped me on the shoulder?" responded a wet Cody.

"This is my apartment and we go by my rules."

Duke had honored the obligation of sheltering his cousin and Ace, but he was none too pleased about their unannounced visit. He showed his spite by offering Ace the guest room and forced Cody to sleep in the garage with the animals.

He sprayed Cody again.

"Ah, fuck you, asshole! I'm not an animal! Stop spraying me, you dick!" Cody yelled.

"Why not?" chuckled Duke. "You're sleeping with them, aren't you?"

"I smell like a hobo. Can I please use your damn shower now? I've been stuck in my car and sleeping in your garage for the past twenty-four hours."

"No."

"Yeah? Stop me."

"If you don't like my rules, then feel free to stay at a motel. Oh, wait, those are all booked now because of you refugees, eh?" Duke let out a loud but unnatural laughter, "Hahaha! I like the sound of that. 'Refugees.'"

He continued being amused with himself as he walked outside. Moments later, a stretching Ace came through the door leading to the house.

"<Wow, ehh, what a great night's sleep," the teenager yawned. "<Your cousin has a great bed in his guest room! How was the sofa? Um, why do you smell like, ehh, the toilet?>"

"I slept in here," Cody stated, "with the pets."

"<Because you wanted to look after your cat, right?>"

"No, Duke made me sleep in here."

"<Why would he do that? Eh, he's pretty nice to me.>"

A loud honk interrupted their conversation. Duke forcefully drove his car into his garage, causing Cody to promptly move out of the way. With much amusement, Duke got out of his car laughing. He dangled a bag of food and gestured for them to make their way to the dining table. A collective sigh of relief came from Ace and Cody; neither had eaten for over a day.

"<This one's mine. And this one's yours, Ace>," Duke said, handing out the portions. There were none for Cody.

"Come on, Duke," he said with irritation. "Don't be a dick. Not now."

"<It's okay, cousin Cody. Have one of my egg rolls>," Ace offered.

"Don't give it to him," Duke commanded.

He gave Ace a primal stare. Ace hesitated and stopped.

"<Sorry, eh, Cody. Maybe you can, ehh, eat later on when we are volunteering.>"

"Volunteering?" Cody looked at Duke. "Where are we volunteering?"

"At a center for shelter. I signed us up. It would benefit you to serve society for once."

Cody's stomach began growling as he watched the two of them eat with delightful expressions. Thoughts of robbing Duke for his General Tso's chicken floated in his mind. Or at least robbing the bastard up in his own apartment, contemplated Cody.

Once their meal was over, Duke drove them to the shelter. They passed by flatlands of grass and dirt, leading Cody to conclude that Dallas was a dull city. He made another attempt to call Daphne again, receiving the same unpropitious result: no answer.

"Can we listen to some music, please?" he suggested with an irritated tone. "I'm really tired of your National Public Radio."

Duke's silence served as a no.

"That is some boring shit," Cody added.

"You can learn a lot from National Public Radio. I find its information very useful, especially when it comes to tax deductions and maximizing your 401(k)," replied Duke.

Due to Duke's totalitarian decision, National Public Radio was the station of choice for the remainder of the trip. Thankfully for Cody, the volunteer shelter wasn't much farther. Once they had arrived, he made a brief observation of their surroundings. Most of the Katrina and Rita refugees were black, though enough scattered numbers of Hispanics and whites were there to make up the fabric of a mixed bag. He surmised that all of them shared the common bond of being poor. It also reminded him of something his father once said: In America, Asians were never seen in poverty. This was true in most cases, but Cody didn't subscribe to his father's theory of superiority over other minorities. After all, he had seen some of the worst ghettos in China. Perhaps, he thought, it was much more likely that the more meritorious ones from Asia were allowed to immigrate. Or at least those lucky enough to be connected to someone meritorious. That, and Asians tended to sweep their troubles into the shadows, keeping the rotten apples from public view.

The three of them were assigned the task of distributing donated clothes to the evacuees. In theory, the refugees—as Duke called them—were supposed to fill out forms and wait in line. That system was quickly dissolved once multitudes of them decided not to follow the rules.

"I said I wanted red shoes! These are orange-red!" shouted an ungrateful evacuee. She threw them back at Duke.

"They're shoes," Duke retorted. "Maybe if you weren't so used to receiving free things, you would appreciate what is given to you."

"WHAT?! What'd you say to me, Bruce Lee?! I'll fuck you up!" shouted the woman.

Security came and removed her from the line.

"Next!" ordered Duke.

"Yeah, eh, you got some toothpaste, man?" asked the following person.

"We only have Colgate."

"Okay. Nice! Also, man. I could use some T-shirts."

Duke's withdrew his attention for a moment to notice what Cody was doing. He was skipping the line and taking requests on his own.

"Hey, man, you listenin'?" the evacuee asked Duke. "You're zoned out!"

Duke ignored him and turned to Ace beside him, "<Take over for me.>"

Cody had found the structure too cumbersome and decided to take things into his own hands. It was more efficient to make a list and retrieve their needs at once. While many of the evacuees seemed to genuinely agree, Duke immensely disliked that they were breaking the rules. Not only were they there to prevent chaos, it was also a means to rule the masses and let them know who was in charge.

Without hesitation, he grabbed his cousin's list and crumpled it up.

"Hey! My list!"

"You're breaking rules," replied Duke. "Don't be a part of the problem or I'll find another solution. Get back to the table and take requests like you were told."

"That method's too slow," countered Cody.

"Yeah! It's too slow!" the evacuees echoed.

Duke stared them down.

"You will do as you're commanded, Cody Quan."

"Man, enough of your bullshit!" Cody replied, leaving the area. "I'm gonna go eat some chili cheese nachos."

"We will have words about this later. Remember, you are staying in my apartment. I am your breadwinner," reminded Duke.

Cody dismissed him as he headed for the food court. He surmised his cousin's ego would be more tolerable after eliminating his hunger. Meanwhile, back in the volunteer booth, Duke sought out a head organizer.

"Find us a new volunteer," he demanded. "One of our lazy ones just left. We're down a person."

The head organizer followed his suggestion immediately, pleasing Duke in the process. He was once told that in life one could either be loved or respected. Never both. The choice was clear to Duke; love was highly overrated.

"Why, hello there," chimed a voice with southern belle charm.

He turned around and saw something he didn't expect. The voice belonged to a petite, diminutive pixie of a cowgirl. She had on a western-style hat, with two long pigtails flowing beneath it. The girl was everything one would expect from an old Western movie, except for the glaring fact that she was

Asian.

"Y'all wanted a new volunteer, I heard," she said in a cute southern twang. "Is that right?"

"Yes, of course," Duke replied, immediately getting up to offer her his chair.

"Thanks!" she smiled, "Don't worry about teaching me, I've been here I reckon since seven in th' mornin'."

"I understand, but different booths have different functions. You still might need to be instructed."

"Nope. You'll see. I'm a quick learner."

The girl was headstrong and fiercely independent—Asian on the outside yet Deep South on the inside. He had never seen an Asian woman like her before, certainly not in Houston's Chinatown or from his college days. By all accounts, the spunky southern firecracker wasn't what he'd imagine to be his ideal type. Yet, there he was, feeling the magic of love at first sight.

"By the way, name's Annebelle," she introduced herself. "Annebelle Wu."

Duke gave her a strong, yet assuring handshake.

"Duke Feng," he smiled.

"Is that plural for fang?" she joked.

"No, why would it be? The plural for fang is fangs," he said, confused.

"It was a joke. I'm giving you sass," she smiled.

Duke tried his best to laugh like a normal person.

Concurrently, on the other side of the shelter, Cody was sitting in the food court, enjoying a plate of chili cheese nachos and chicken fried steak. Ace came over to him and snacked on some nachos.

"Hey, aren't you supposed to be helping out?" asked Cody.

"<Eh, a new person came and helped. I can take a break.>"

Cody took interest in the television showing the local news. It suddenly occurred to him that he had forgotten his own family the entire time. A wave of fear brushed over him. Today was supposed to be the day Hurricane Rita made landfall in Houston.

"<Hey, eh, how come the weather, eh, looks so nice in Houston?>" asked Ace.

He was right, observed Cody. The live footage from Houston showed sunshine and blue skies. It also switched to a clear picture of Galveston Island, showing happy pedestrians waving in the background.

"Son of a bitch," muttered Cody, "it didn't hit."

———

Daphne distanced herself from her coworkers at the tacky Las Vegas airport bar. She was tired of their gossip, mostly because she had no drama of her own to contribute. She was counting every hour, every minute and every second for their business trip to mercifully end. It wasn't like she had passion for what she did either. The world of finance was so dreary and dull—its people so focused on money. What she wanted was adventure.

That was what made the entire trip to Las Vegas so disappointing. She cursed Jesus again for not giving her that perfect boyfriend. It was the ideal setting. She imagined a charming rogue playboy in a casino, whisking her off her feet. They would do daring things, perhaps a secret society of witty and handsome thieves involving her in an elaborate but zany plan to rob the Bellagio or Caesar's Palace. Like Ocean's Eleven. Daphne sighed, reminiscing that fantasy. It was far better than her current reality of eating peanuts and watching news clips of Hurricane Rita. She knew she should have worried a bit more about Cody, but he was probably safe.

"Anything for you?" asked the bartender.

"No, I'm fine," she replied.

"Sure? Not even a glass of water? Those peanuts can make you awfully thirsty."

"Alright," sighed Daphne, "I'll have a glass of milk then."

The bartender gave her an odd glance, then complied anyway. He couldn't remember the last time anyone ordered milk.

"Gin and tonic," ordered a new voice, "and a Washington apple for the lady."

She frowned when the incoming stranger wasn't handsome and white. He was a hefty-looking Asian man, one she correctly guessed to be in his early forties. She gave him points for being well-dressed, however. The dark gray blazer that matched his black vest, white-collared shirt, emerald tie and black slacks weren't cheap.

"Where are you heading to?" the man asked.

"Houston."

"I'm from there too. What's a beautiful woman like yourself doing alone in a bar?"

"I'm sorry, you should stop. I only date white guys."

The hefty man chuckled.

"Here you go," the bartender said, placing their respective drinks in front of them. "Gin and tonic, sir. Washington apple for the lady. And her milk too."

"Cheers," the stranger offered as a toast.

Daphne stayed put, glaring at him. He toasted her glass that was sitting on the table instead.

"You should try that, see if you like it," he insisted.

"I won't."

"Why not?"

"Cause I know I won't."

"You're religious or just an uppity bitch?"

Daphne didn't reply. She felt no attraction for him.

"What are you afraid of, Ms. Goody Two-Shoes?" he asked, "It's just a drink."

She felt that there was something dangerous about him. Not the charming type she was used to in movies or television shows, either. He carried himself with indifference and an unusual calmness, as though he could turn emotions on and off like a faucet. But there was something greater than that which bothered her more, Daphne realized. His entire presence mocked everything she believed in. He reminded her of how boring she was. She decided to defy him by doing exactly what he wanted. Picking up the glass of the Washington apple, she made the drink disappear in three large gulps, slamming the empty glass down with a resounding bang.

"Is that goody two-shoes enough for you?" she mocked with a naughty smirk.

"What did you think of it?"

She shrugged, "It was okay."

Her face was red and hot; she could feel her heart rapidly trying to free itself from her chest.

"You don't drink often, do you?" the man teased.

"I do," she lied. "I drink with my friends all the time."

"Oh, yeah?"

"Yeah," she gleamed, "all the time."

"So what are you doing here in Vegas? You know there was a hurricane in Houston, right?"

"Duh. It's just all over the news and everything. Heard it was a false alarm."

"Oh, it hit somewhere. Probably the countryside. Houston got lucky."

"So what are you doing in Vegas?" she wondered.

"Business."

"What.......kind of business?"

The man paused for a moment. "I own a company that makes identification tags."

"Wow, a big shot CEO, eh?"

"You can say that. Another drink?"

"I...um...no. No, I got to go. My flight is almost ready," she insisted. "Are we on the same plane?"

"No, I'm heading to Phoenix."

"I thought you said you live in Houston?"

"I do. But I have business to attend to in Phoenix, first."

"Oh," Daphne replied, somewhat disappointed, "well, I've got to go now. Bye."

The hefty gentleman took out a business card from his wallet. "Call me."

Daphne read the card, "Andrew Huynh, eh?"

"Yeah."

"Don't you want to know my name?"

"No, we'll talk again. I'm sure of it."

"Yeah, right," she mumbled.

Daphne left the bar, returning back to her coworkers.

———————

Sometimes Maple Washington hated what she was: short, stocky and geeky. It was cruel, she supposed, that she was part of a community that celebrated athleticism over academics. At least it seemed that way in southwest Houston, whose African-American community spotlighted the women's dominance in sports. It made someone so extraordinary like her seem ordinary. She hid her writing and art abilities not so much out of shyness, but because she was afraid that no one would care and understand. To a creative talent, apathy was worse than death.

That was why she favored herself a proud Pisces. Her father discouraged her from astrology, but it didn't make her sign any less true. She liked it best when her head was in the clouds, conjuring up ideas and scenarios for her secretly drawn manga series. Her constant daydreaming, of course, was also the culprit for her average grades. Maple supposed she could make more A's if she put her mind to it, but studying was so mundane. Lord knows her existence was lonely enough, she figured.

Things became a little less solitary when her father became co-pastor of Fellowship Communion Baptist Church. What she could hardly find in the black community, she found in abundance in the new Asian one. There were nerds galore, teens her age who were fluent in Yu-Gi-Oh! and Fullmetal Alchemist. She found girls who crushed on Bi Rain and knew the Korean lyrics to BoA's Girls on Top.

It was not surprising, then, that she had developed a best friend from the church in Jay Zheng. Jay might have been ten years older than her, but he was one of the first ones who reached out. Even though everyone was Christian at their church, Maple could tell there was hesitance for the Asian and black members to get along. Jay, however, had no reservations about talking with her when the church merging first started. She figured it was probably her No Face from Spirited Away earrings or her doodles of Itachi Uchiha from the Naruto series. Those were all the icebreakers they needed to develop a trusting friendship. It was because of it that Maple decided she would choose Jay to reveal her secret.

Her email took no longer than a minute to write; the video file required just a few seconds more to attach. She exhaled after clicking the Send button, knowing a big weight had been lifted from her young shoulders. The secret she had sent would cease being one by tomorrow. It was something that everyone in their church needed to know. Nothing would be the same again.

Five hours later, just after midnight, Jay returned home and opened the email and its attachment. What he read shocked him; what he saw from the video horrified him. The time stamp in the video suggested that it was made at the time of their spring retreat. Its background featured Maple's cabin. The clip started out innocently enough, but things soon escalated when Maple walked past the door, beaten and bruised. Pastor Washington followed, hitting her repeatedly with his belt. The abuse stopped only after he had grabbed and broken her arm. The pastor's expression changed after he realized what he had done. He looked around for witnesses, believing there were none. What he didn't see was the laptop camera recording the assault.

The email read:

Oct. 3, 2005 -

dear jay,
i know we haven't talked much in church and know each other 4
long.

but u r a good friend 2 me. i know we r around 10 years apart, but i feel like ur the one i trust the most. i need 2 tell u my secret. 4 the past 3 years, my father has been beating me up and abusing me. remember my cast? i lied 2 y'all. i didn't fall. it was bcz of him. he is a fraud. he continues 2 hit me. mom knows about it, but is on his side. please send the video 2 the rite people. i trust u.

    ur friend,
    maple

CHAPTER 11: JESUS STRIKES

Usually, Skinny Grandma didn't like nursing homes. They were a big contrast to the mirthful nature of retirement homes, which celebrated life instead of foreshadowing death. It had taken some time for her to get used to the hospital beds and the withering "residents." The loud, unified ticking of the clocks certainly didn't help, either. After several months of it, though, it had evolved into a tolerable experience. The one constant happiness she found was television shows. She had never watched so much American TV before, but she was a fan now, particularly enjoying *The Price Is Right* and *Wheel of Fortune.* Their rules were a bit foggy to her, though it was fun screaming "Come on Down!" or "Big Money!" She also found Bob Barker irresistibly charming.

The other constant was her elderly Hispanic roommate, the one she dubbed "the Mexican lady." Through hand gestures and the simplest of English, they were able to concoct an amenable acquaintanceship. It was all Skinny Grandma could do to decipher the basic details about her: eighty-four years old, two adult daughters and a late husband who passed away seven years ago. The woman's name was unpronounceable by her Chinese tongue. She figured it was something like "Ianamoosa" or "Ismasala"; it was easier just to wave or call out "wai," the Cantonese equivalent to "hey." Only one of the Mexican lady's grown daughters visited her often. The other, she had seen only once. Some nights, the woman would cry, though Skinny

Grandma didn't console her. She figured it wouldn't make a difference.

By now, she had accepted the finality of her life; more so, she was sick of its drama. Life or death, she wished fate would make up its mind. Being confined to a nursing home bed wasn't living. If anything, she cherished the serenity of isolation, especially sleeping. She wished her own adult children would understand that; their visitations and overworrying, frankly, annoyed her. It seemed they were more afraid of death than she was, making her wonder why the ones who weren't dying feared death the most.

She couldn't stand their theater of sympathy. Had her son and daughters come for genuine conversation, their stopovers would have been met with more anticipation. Instead, Min-Lo and Mei held suffering contests, masquerading as tragic people who couldn't bear life's final curtain call. What did they know about suffering? she thought. Skinny Grandma had known real torment in her youth. There were hundreds of times during the war when she could have been shot, raped, starved, stabbed, beaten or drowned. Life had been a blessing for her. An extended life should be celebrated, not pitied.

"<She's sleeping>," informed Aunt Mei.

Cody's father had entered the hospital room with a large thermos filled with congee. He knew how much Skinny Grandma hated the nursing home's food.

"<How'd you get here before me? You don't get off work until six. Today's my day off and it's only six-fifteen!"> cried Mr. Quan.

"<Well, maybe it's because I love her more. You can take your congee back home. I already fed her and I made extras",> she boasted. "<Poor me, how I have to do all that AND work. It's so hard. But I got to do it. I have no choice.>"

"<Hey, this congee took a lot of effort on my part too!>"

"<You didn't suffer as much as I did.>"

"<That's what you think. I've built up a lot of karma points!>"

"<Just go back home, little brother. I've got this handled.>"

Their bickering woke Skinny Grandma up. She was weak with low amounts of energy. It was enough to let out a cough.

"<MOTHER!>" they both shouted.

"<I swear>," she muttered, "<the two of you haven't changed. Six or sixty years old. It doesn't matter. Still children.>"

"<Oh, mother! The doctor says you'll be alright, mother! He says you're improving!!!>" beamed Aunt Mei, nudging her brother.

"<Oh, yes. Yes! In fact, he says you seem more like a visitor than a patient!>" Cody's father grinned.

"<I don't like liars. I raised you better than to be liars>," scowled Skinny Grandma. "<My time is short. Whatever made me heal suddenly made me sick. But I've always decided to be thankful. Remember, the only thing you can control in this life is your attitude. I don't need pity—>"

Aunt Mei jumped in, "<Not pity, mother. I thank you—>"

"<—nor your thankfulness. I hate being old. I can't wait for the next life. So be happy for me when I'm gone.>"

The passion from her speech exhausted her. Cody's grandmother did little to resist sleeping again. She spent her last remaining moments dreaming. It was ironic how most people imagined their last hours awake in a hospital bed when they were more likely to pass away in their sleep. Knowing it was the end, she was thankful to be spending it in her subconscious where she was able to fantasize for a final time. She was a young woman again, running in a field among daisies and dandelions. Everything was perfect and peaceful, free from pain and suffering. There was no rush to leave, but she wanted to eventually. Perhaps just a little longer.

Hours after everyone had left, deep in the middle of the night, her heartbeat came to a conclusive, eternal stop.

———

The routine had lost its luster by now. In fact, it had turned frustrating.

Cody punched the dashboard of his car as the White Sox scored another run against his hometown Astros in Houston's first ever World Series game. It made him furious that he couldn't watch his team play. Like so many of these kind of nights, Mindy had sent him alone on a last-minute supply run. Their company was making decent money, but garnering stolen goods at odd times in strange places had worn thin. He couldn't even remember the last time she had gone with him. True, it was dangerous work and Mindy wouldn't be of much help, but it was the principle of it, he thought. Besides, he was tired of her inconsiderate nature. He figured, at the very least, she should schedule the meetings better. Sometimes the locations would be in the Harwin warehouses, other times it was near the Houston Ship Channel. Once, it was even in the Third Ward. Tonight, it was in a nondescript warehouse near downtown. All of the meetings were held in the evenings where trouble was most imminent. After the last out of the baseball game was made, Cody angrily turned the radio off and sat in silence.

"Shit," he muttered.

Suddenly, he heard another car arrive pull up across from his. As per usual practice, it kept its lights off, but flashed them twice to signify its purpose. Its door opening and closing could be heard. Cody could barely make out the approaching silhouette against the night sky. Cody got out of his car and met the figure halfway. Once they were closer, the seller turned on a flashlight, shining its beam at Cody.

"<You speak Chinese?>" he asked.

"Not very well. Do you speak English?" Cody responded, blocking the light with his arm.

"Yes," replied the man in a perfect American accent.

He shined the flashlight toward the ground. Cody could see that he was an Asian man in his thirties.

"Good," the man smiled, "I'll give you the supplies when you show me the money."

The man motioned for Cody to follow him. The northeast part of downtown was a very dangerous area. Its shadows played tricks on the mind, amplifying paranoia. When Cody heard more than two pairs of footsteps, he knew that it wasn't his imagination. The man stopped and shined the flashlight back into Cody's eyes, blinding him from the glare. Instinctively, Cody knew he was surrounded by multiple people, but it was a mystery as to who they were.

"What's going on here?" he asked. "Who are you people?"

"Shut up and put your hands up," the man instructed.

Cody did as he was told. One of the figures, another similarly aged Asian man, patted him down. Feeling Cody's wallet, he took it out and inspected it.

"I don't have much cash on me," Cody announced.

"We're not looking for your money," said the man holding the flashlight.

The man with Cody's wallet nodded his head to the man holding the flashlight. More flashlights turned on. Cody counted at least ten of them total.

They were wearing police uniforms.

The undercover officer read Cody his Miranda rights while another officer slapped a pair of handcuffs on him. Beads of sweat flowed down his forehead. He had never been treated like a criminal before. The police entered his information into their computer systems and ushered him into the back of a police car. He was soon hauled to the local HPD jailhouse. Never in his dreams would Cody imagine he'd have a mug shot. They took his front and side photos along with his fingerprints. It was a lot like the movies, except it wasn't as cute. He was then locked in a large cell alongside thirty or so other people.

"Hey!" called out an intimidating Caucasian man with tattoos covering his face. "Hey! I'm talking to you!"

Scared out of his mind, Cody continued looking down to avoid eye contact.

"What are you in for?!" asked the tattooed-face man.

He repeated the same question for awhile until he lost interest in Cody and pestered another. Cody tried to keep a positive mind, but he cursed himself for watching too many prison documentaries about inmate raping and the legend of jelly and syrup.

"Please, Jesus, please," he muttered in tears. "You said you'd be there if I needed you. You could show up in a basketball game. Why couldn't you show up now?"

"Jellyyyyy..." chimed in a skinny black man sitting across from Cody.

"Please, please, please, please," whispered Cody to his savior.

"Jellllyyyyyyyyyy..."

"Please, Jesus, please." He was noticeably audible now.

"Gonna put some jelly in my ass for ya!"

"Why aren't you showing up?!"

"Make ya eat it!"

"No! Aw, God, nooooo..."

The skinny black man cackled, "Ah, I'm just playin' wit' ya, ya dumb motherfucka!"

Forty-five minutes passed before Cody was allowed to make his only phone call. He didn't want to upset his parents. He didn't want to show this embarrassment to Daphne. He called the only person he could think of: Mindy.

"Bobbie, what's going on? How did the deal go? Did you get the stuff?"

"Mindy, I'm in jail," Cody said.

"Whaaaat?"

"Yeah, I'm in jail. Thanks to you. I told you I never wanted to do this shit."

"But how come you are in the jail?"

"You think I just walked in here on my own? They had an undercover cop."

"Undercover? I thought that was for drugs!"

"Oh, my God...You're so dumb."

"Hey, hey! I'm your best friend, okay? You do not call me a dummy."

"Why did I let you talk me into this?"

"Well, you did not complain when we made a lot of money, eh?"

"Whatever. I need bail."

"Bail? Bobbie, you know I'm not rich. Why don't I call your parents for you and have them bail you out?"

"No! Not only would they panic the hell out of themselves, but the fact is, we're partners and you're partly responsible for this! You've got to come here with five thousand dollars and bail me the fuck out," demanded Cody.

"Stop saying those bad words."

"I'm sorry. Can you please just come over here and bail me? Please, I can't stay overnight with these thugs. There's minimal police protection. They're gonna..." Cody held back tears.

"They're gonna what, Bubble?"

"They're gonna...jelly..."

"Huh? Jelly?"

"Please, Mindy. Bail me. I'll pay you back."

"But I'm wearing my pajamas. My makeup is all washed off."

"Fucking A, Mindy. You're my best friend. You're going to let your best friend and business partner be stuck in a cell full of hardened criminals and thugs? They're going to rape me. They'll stick a dick inside of me, Mindy."

"Huh? Why would they do that? You are not a girl."

"Come on, I can't believe you have to even think about it! I gotta work tomorrow too! How am I going to tell our boss Rachel about this?"

"...five thousand dollars, right?"

"Yes."

"You must pay me back. Immediately. Write me a check."

"Of course."

"With a fifteen percent interest."

"What? You serious?"

"Yes."

"Come here and bail me out. And I'll write you a check for five thousand dollars. None of this interest nonsense. Are you my friend or not?"

"......fine. Give me an hour."

"An hour?!"

"Yes, an hour. I need to fix my hair and put on the makeup, man."

"What...ah..." Cody glanced back at the cell with the skinny black man chanting "jelly." "Okay, one hour. Please hurry."

As promised, Mindy arrived at the downtown jail house a little past midnight. Despite the abundant police presence, she felt a bit vulnerable with so many eyes looking at her from the waiting area. Catcalls and whistles were thrown her way while she posted bail at the counter. Not long afterwards, Cody came out, looking like a mess.

"Maaaaaaannnnnnnnnn," was all Mindy could utter.

Cody didn't respond. She handed him a ziplock bag filled with cookies.

"What's this?" asked Cody.

"Taiwanese coconut cookie," Mindy replied. "I knew you'd be hungry, Bobbie."

"You made it?" he asked, munching on two of them at once.

"Yeah.   I   made   it......with   money. HAHAHAHAHAHA!"

Cody glared at her with an odd look, "Where's your husband?"

"He's sleeping. He has to go to work tomorrow."

"Can't believe you came here alone, it's dangerous," Cody paused. "Um, did you...bring any water by any chance?"

"Oops."

They sat on a bench right outside of the police department. Cody stopped eating the cookies because they made him thirsty.

"Let's not do Mosaic Decor anymore," suggested Cody.

"Why not? We make money!"

"Yeah, but I do all the work."

"That's not true. I call them and I email them!"

"You weren't the one who just got arrested with some guy chanting 'jelly' at you for a few hours. It's not worth it."

"But, Bobbie, don't you like the freedom of owning your own business?"

Cody reflected on the pros and cons. "It does feel good to not answer to someone. We can set our own rates."

"And later hire more people. Then we don't have to do anything! Imagine, we go to vacation every week. People put money in our bank accounts! How lovely, huh?"

"You're already not doing anything, Mindy."

They both laughed.

"Okay. Fine, Bobbie. We will stop the Mosaic Decor. No more," Mindy replied. "But maybe someday, when you are more ready, you will have your own company, with employees, your own office and everything, right?"

Cody paused.

"You know," he smiled, "I never really thought about that before."

The business card was dark silver and slick, simplistic in design, yet strong in presence. It was no different from the hefty Asian man who had given it to her last month in Las Vegas. For at least once a day since then, Daphne had pulled it out of her purse and examined it. No one had challenged her to chase before. She was used to either the stumbling shy types or the overly zealous ones who exhausted their list of pick-up lines.

"Andrew Huynh," she read out loud.

It didn't sound anything like "Kyle Sawyer," the starting quarterback with the dreamy blond hair, broad shoulders and piercing blue eyes. Heck, she thought, it didn't even sound like "Cody Quan," nerdy and fun-to-talk-with web developer. Andrew could hide behind the nice suit and eloquent vocabulary, but Daphne knew a thug when she saw one. A CEO of a company that made identification tags? Yeah right, she thought, more like someone who probably stole car parts and sold jail-broke cell phones.

Her own cell phone suddenly vibrated.

It was Cody again; she had been ignoring him for weeks now. Even though they had seen one another in church, she had barely spoken to him. She didn't know why. It had all changed for her since meeting Andrew. When the vibrating finally stopped, Daphne glanced at the screen of her cell: Missed Call (18). It was part of a collection of unanswered replies. Deena: 22 missed calls. Ennis: 9 missed calls. Marion: 17 missed calls. Overall, there were around a hundred missed calls. Daphne didn't know what she was feeling. She had never felt this way before. Not even for Kyle. It certainly wasn't love.

She sighed and placed her phone down; but, just as soon, she found herself picking it back up again. As if in a trance, she started dialing the number on the card; she knew it by memory. With each ring that went by, Daphne fought herself to end the call.

"Hello?" answered the voice that had been replaying in her head.

".......hi," she finally replied.

"The girl from Vegas."

"Yes. Yes, it's me," Daphne nervously spoke. "I-I don't know why I'm calling."

"Join me for dinner."

"Right now? It's nine o'clock in the evening. I already ate."

"You can watch me eat."

Daphne wanted to reply that she needed to be home in bed by ten o'clock. She wanted to tell him that she wasn't interested and that his response was more rude than humorous.

"Okay," she answered instead, "where are you?"

"IHOP."

"Are you alone?"

"Yes."

"Okay," Daphne paused, "tell me which one and I'll join you."

The IHOP he selected was a long ways from her townhouse, halfway across town. It was also particularly notorious for its loud customers and rude waitresses, seven days a week. For a presentable and sexy outfit, Daphne chose an olive green shirt matched with a tight pair of expensive jeans. She also put on makeup—not exactly knowing why, but did so anyway. Upon arrival, she saw him sitting at a center booth, busy in mid-conversation on his cell phone. It was unbelievable that this was the man who had been on her mind since Vegas.

"Yes...yeah...I see," Andrew continued on the phone. "Pete's been having cold feet. I don't know if he's cut out for this line of work. His friend's even worse...no...no, that's not the reason...his friend is the opposite problem. He's too daring...yeah...I suppose. Okay. Alright."

She ended up waiting for him for over thirty more minutes, listening to him chat about peculiar topics over the phone. When the conversation ended, he signaled for the check. None of the waitstaff had bothered to ask Daphne for an order.

"So," Andrew finally spoke to her, "what are we doing tonight?"

"I should go back home. I have to work tomorrow."

"Interesting. When do you work?"

"I have to get up at seven," she replied. "I arrive to work at around eight-thirty."

"That's ten hours from now."

"Yeah."

"That's no problem. Here... " He pulled out two pills from his pocket and handed them to her. "These will keep you up."

"What are these?"

Andrew gave her a confused look.

"They're ex," he answered.

"These are ecstasy pills?!"

"Yeah. Good ones too. Let me know if you have friends that need any."

Daphne politely handed them back to Andrew.

"No, thanks," she replied.

"The milk drinking girl," he observed, "I see."

He kept silent while the waiter came back with his credit card. This was unfamiliar territory for Daphne. She expected attempts at small conversation, things like how her day went, what she believed in—details to woo her defenses down. When they had first met, he bought her a drink and shamelessly flirted with her. Tonight, however, he didn't even bother to ensure she had a glass of water. Some nerve, she thought.

"Well," he said getting up, "I'm heading out."

"Where are you going?"

"The Platinum Star."

"Isn't that a bad club? I hear bad things go on in there."

Andrew chuckled and shook his head. They both walked outside.

"You 'heard?'" he asked. "So that implies you've never been."

"No."

"Then how do you know it's 'bad?'" he asked, pulling out a cigarette and lighting it.

"I can't go with you. I have to go to work tomorrow."

He made a consistent stream of smoke come out from his lips.

"You work hard, but do you play hard?" he asked.

"I don't even know what that means."

With a cocky swagger, he unlocked his car via remote and left Daphne staring at him near the restaurant's entranceway. He rolled down the passenger side window while warming up his car.

"Choice is yours," he offered.

Daphne hesitated for a moment, clutching her crucifix necklace. She was seriously considering the devil's invite to hell. Satan was a hefty, unattractive, sleepless Vietnamese-American man who smelled like an ashtray and looked like vice. There were many reasons to fear him, but her soul would have none of it. She walked up to his passenger side door, opened it and, like Alice in Wonderland, descended into the rabbit hole.

"Let's roll," Andrew announced.

He set the stick shift to reverse, hightailing the car backwards from the parking lot. In a matter of seconds, the car was traveling over a 110 miles per hour on the beltway, prompting Daphne to hastily buckle her seat belt. The rush of air from the opened windows gave the superfluous speed its presence. Music pounding from amped-up audio systems— from radio station 104.1 KRBE, Daphne's favorite—gave the ride a melodramatic feel.

"Aren't you afraid of cops?" Daphne shouted in competition with the loud thumping sounds.

Andrew puffed on his cigarette and ignored her.

"I said 'Aren't you afraid of cops?'"she repeated.

"Cops?" He looked at her. "Cops are afraid of me."

Upon arriving and entering the notorious club, she discovered many of The Platinum Star's disreputable features were true. The people there were so different from her—

inviting sin with their lascivious clothes and prurient movements. There was little class in them, so much that she couldn't relate and felt out of place.

"Go sit in the bar and ask for a man named Li'l Bis," Andrew instructed. "He should be the main bartender. Old black guy with an eye patch."

Daphne did what she was told and sat on one of the few vacant stools in the bar. She dreaded that her clothes would be reeking of the club's smell the next morning. None of the bartenders resembled anything like the description of Li'l Bis; they were all tough-looking girls who appeared hardened from years of no-nonsense bullshit. She was in mid-thought when suddenly a hand slipped underneath her and firmly squeezed the base of her buttocks. With a sudden reflex, Daphne infuriately confronted the culprit, bringing her face to face with a young weasel-looking Asian man.

"What say you and me pop some sugar, li'l mama?" he suggested.

She impulsively shoved him away, only to find that it encouraged him to try harder. Apparently, this was the culture of The Platinum Star.

"Come on, baby. You fine as hell!" the man insisted.

A firm hand placed itself atop his shoulders and moved him aside. The knight in shining armor was Andrew.

"Fuck!" The skinny man confronted him. "Nigga, ain't you believe you should think twice before layin' a hand on a nigga? This nigga spittin' game here, nigga!"

He invited Andrew to a challenge by flashing a pocket knife. Andrew smirked and revealed his Smith and Wesson Sigma SW40VE.

"Shit," the man replied, "this your lucky day, fat nigga."

He retreated back into the crowd, looking for another woman to harass.

"I couldn't find Li'l Bis," Daphne said.

"Must be his off night," Andrew shrugged, "or he's taking a dump."

He ordered a shot of straight Grey Goose for Daphne. She wavered, but then gulped it down. Andrew held out two fingers to one of the bartenders, signifying two more shots.

"Andrew..." Daphne protested.

The bartender placed two more shots on the counter. Andrew gestured for her to drink another. Without hesitation this time, she drank it down. Four more shots came. Then another two. Then another three. By the time her brain could no longer count, she was led by her hand to an exclusive area behind the horde of dancers.

"Haha...hahaha!!!" The laughter was involuntarily coming out of Daphne.

Fragments of her reality defied any similitude for comprehension. She gathered that she was in a private room with men and women, most of whom were naked or partially naked. It was also odd that clones of her were in the room, eerily emulating her exact movements. Then a loud, unrecognizable roar of laughter came out from her. She realized she had been staring at her own reflections from the circumferential array of wall mirrors. By constantly blinking, she helped herself regain some partial awareness from her state of dizziness. Sex, she realized. The men and women were having sex. It was so difficult to think with fractions of information coming into her head. The white stuff on the glass tables—she shook her head—it was cocaine.

"Andrew, I don't...I don't want to do this..." muttered Daphne.

"I don't care."

He rolled up a hundred dollar bill and took a whiff of the drug. She saw herself doing the same. The shock to her nervous system quickly made her drop the rolled bill, sending her hands across the small heap of white powder. By the time she partially collected herself, she noticed her fingers smothered in cocaine, causing her to unleash a flurry of tears from guilt. Andrew gently slid a hand down her jeans and inserted a finger inside her. Without hesitation, his other hand began removing her shirt, all done without any request for permission.

It made Daphne feel like a whore.

"Please stop," she begged. "I don't know if I want to do this."

He motioned for one of the other girls to join. A blonde, Daphne was able to comprehend. Naked and kissing her too. It was all too fast, too sudden, too illogical. She was beginning to give in to the euphoria of meaningless, intuitive intercourse. Her morals meant nothing— her integrity an illusion. Perhaps, she feared, the main catalyst wasn't even the alcohol or drugs; it was a concealed desire within the depths of her soul.

"Andrew..." she repeated. This time her tone changed. She was no longer rejecting but inviting.

The exit sign visible from the corner of her eye no longer served as an appealing option. All she wanted to do now was swim in the madness that would set her free. She felt tongues encircling the circumference of her nipples until the arousal resulted in an out-of-body experience. Amid the iniquitous exchanges between male-to-female and female-to-female, Daphne felt the shame of hypocrisy bearing down on her conscience. It was hardly a week ago that she had taught a Sunday school class about virtue and chastity. Now she was a peddler of lies.

The sin had made her see that.

"Are...are you okay? Do you want to stop? You don't have to do this," assured the blonde girl.

That statement couldn't have been more wrong, thought Daphne. Nothing could substitute unrestrained freedom. Not the independence that compensated for a lost childhood from Beijing. Not the no-strings-attached conditions that Kyle Sawyer thought would be adequately befitting. And certainly not Jesus, who was more deadbeat than her own father. All she wanted for an imperfect life was the ideal boyfriend to fix it all. Someone who'd one day appear in her life and make it all worthwhile. Instead, Jesus couldn't even get that right. He gave her Cody Fucking Quan.

"YOU GAVE ME CODY FUCKING QUAN!" Daphne screamed.

"What?" asked the other girl, with a confused expression.

Daphne nudged her away and claimed Andrew as her own. Where her mind had seen scattered truths, the cocaine had clarified the truth. She closed her eyes and opened them again, knowing Jesus would be there. He was in the mirrors looking at her, looking at all the sinners engaging in a symphony of beautiful, emotion-filled sex and drugs. This kind of emancipation was what knowing Christ should have been. Too bad he never was. She climbed on Andrew, taking a long look at his body. He was fat, ugly and old; his naked body made him look like a whale. But she wanted so desperately to pleasure him in the dirtiest of ways. She belonged to him—an object without self-respect. A woman beneath a man.

"It's Daphne," she whispered, finally revealing her name to him. "My name is Daphne Lee."

———————

All Jay Zheng ever wanted to know was the truth. He thought he would find it six years ago when he had run away from home. The sheltered Asian-American life wasn't for him; he needed to make mistakes. His parents, of course, had thought otherwise. Being perfect meant never making an error; being errorless meant living in protection. What it did was arouse his curiosity towards forbidden things—one of which was a drug habit. Running away from home had not taken much courage. It was an idea that had popped into his mind when he had first seen his favorite movie, *The Truman Show*. He had related to the concept of living in a bubble, unhappy with hiding in ignorance. It was tiring to hear everyone tease him about how innocent he was, so he did something about it.

And for a while he was right. The adventures of drug addiction and street hustling were a complete reversal from his pedestrian life. He learned more about reality in those two years than he had from the totality of his previous existence. In time, however, it introduced Jay to a different kind of misery. A worse kind. Drugs had enslaved him, forcing him to engage in embarrassing situations for every next high. The next destination was suicide; he couldn't imagine anything else.

Then he reunited with his old college friend Ennis, a devout Christian who brought him the teachings of Jesus. The concept was exemplary. It called for everyone to forgive themselves because Christ had forgiven them. Success was not measured financially but through living selflessly for others. The idea was inspirational; it simply asked for believers to give themselves entirely, unequivocally to Jesus.

The new purpose became his reality.

As a born-again Christian, he traded drug parties for soup drives, breaking comfort zones to explore his altruistic peak. The Word of Jesus was more addicting than the most potent heroin. It was a life that he had given himself into completely—a trust that transformed into dependency.

But then came the realization that some of his fellowship were keeping secrets. Some were homosexuals. Others were active fornicators. And then there were the child abusers. How could all this exist under the auspices of Fellowship Communion Baptist Church? Jay gave them the benefit of the doubt. He had to; his world would unravel.

It had crumbled earlier in the afternoon when he had sought a church official.

"Hello, Jay. Come. Sit down," the elder Reverend Han said. "I know what you're here to talk about."

It had been four weeks since Jay contemplated what he should do with Maple Washington's email. He figured it was better to give it to the senior church officials rather than local law enforcement. To his surprise, nothing happened. He wanted to know why.

"Jay," the stoic reverend began, "sometimes in order to do right, you have to make a bigger right. It forces hard decisions to be made. The kind of hard decisions for the long term, do you follow me?"

He paused and cleared his throat before continuing.

"Pastor Washington may have done a sin, but he is a good pastor. Because of him, church attendance has doubled and donations have tripled! We were very hesitant to bring in a black group, but we realize now that our black membership is much more generous than our Chinese membership. To cut off this pastor is to cut off our budget. Look at how many new members we are able to bring in now because of our wealthy status! Nobody wanted to come to a low-financed church before. But now... now we are growing! Pastor Washington is God's blessing. Sometimes God wants us to turn a blind eye upon the imperfections of His gifts because there's a bigger gift."

Satisfied with his own answer, the reverend proceeded to ask if Jay had sent the video to anyone else.

"Only you, Reverend Ping and Pastor Lu," he replied.

"Good. That's good," murmured Reverend Han. "I want you to do one more favor for me. Log on to your Gmail account here on my computer and delete the email. For good."

After Jay did what he was told, the reverend clasped his hands together and smiled.

"Everything will be alright," smiled the reverend. "You'll see. It was just an overreaction on Maple's part."

Jay left the office unsatisfied. It was now clear to him that the church was a business. A crooked one at that, thought Jay. A haven for liars and crooks who hid behind the name of God and the good intentions of people—a green light for their character flaws.

Now that his reason for clean living had ceased, he set out to do the one thing he had never done: he wanted to get laid. It was funny, he realized. There was never an opportunity or desire to have intercourse before. Until tonight, sex had been such a sacred thing. His parents forbade it, his drug habits took priority over it, and his church taught him to save it for marriage. None of that mattered anymore; he decided he might as well experience it. It was interesting how the trip from his home to the district with the neon-lit homes was just twenty minutes away. There were so many of them, in fact, that he drove past twice trying to make a decision. Each of the signs looked so similar: Jade Spa, Eternal Massage, Happy Paradise...there were fifteen to twenty in one block alone. Jay finally decided on a smaller one, a place called Oriental Endings.

Upon arrival, he took a deep breath and let the remaining nervousness remove itself from his body. He found the front door was a bit of an enigma for a first-timer. It was sealed by an iron gate with a security camera tracking him from the top. The doorbell was concealed rather astutely, disguised as a plastic flower petal on the wall. Seconds after he had rung it, a pretty Thai girl in a bikini opened the door. She was beyond gorgeous, thought Jay, so attractive that he didn't feel worthy of her friendliness. That opinion quickly explicated when a line of other pretty young Asian women marched in front of him inside the massage parlor.

"You can choose as many as you want. Each for a hundred and sixty dollars an hour," informed the smiling Thai girl.

Jay took his time to decide. He eyed each girl carefully. Some of the girls giggled, some looked tired and some looked angry. He eventually decided on who he thought was the friendliest-looking girl.

"I'll take her," he replied.

She led him to a private massage room where he was asked to pay first. After taking his money, the girl left him alone to remove his clothes. Then he wrapped a towel around his private parts and waited. He silently laughed at all the sexually suggestive decorations; there were lava lamps, naked figurines, displayed champagne bottles, Kenny G CDs. All of these served as entertaining distractions until the sound of the door opening interrupted his thoughts. The girl he had chosen signaled for him.

"Please, come with me," she smiled. "What is your name, sir?"

"Jay, what's yours?" he said, walking around the spa's hallways with both hands holding his towel.

"Flower."

"That's a pretty name."

"Thank you."

On their way to the shower rooms, they passed by other men and giggling spa girls, who were venturing both directions of the hallway. It was disturbing that most of the men looked like they were likely married with children; a majority of them were twice the ages of the young women. Flower made sure Jay was comfortable as he lay across the wet plastic shower bed before bathing him with a gentle stream of water and her soft fingers. Her fingernails teased his buttocks as she applied soap and rubbed his genitals clean. Throughout the shower, she retained a plastered smile, which made Jay wonder how she could maintain it in a job like this.

"Where are you from?" asked Jay.

"I am from Thailand," she answered. "What about you?"

"I was born and raised here in Houston."

"But you are Chinese or Korean or what?"

"My parents are from China."

"Oh. Chinese customers usually do not tip so well. Will you tip me well?"

"Of course," smiled Jay, "pretty girl like you deserves it."

"Thank you! Thank you!"

After the table shower, they retraced their steps back from the same hallway and returned to their private room. This time instrumental covers of classic love songs were playing in the background. Jay enjoyed himself while lying face down in the sensual bed, relishing the oil rubdown Flower gave him. He was impressed with the vigorous strength she was able to muster from her tiny body. When she felt that he was at ease, she dipped her body closer, pressing her perky breasts across his back. This triggered a natural erection from Jay, which she encouraged by playing with his genitals in an alternating pattern between her left and right hands. Knowing he was ready, she gently kissed his ear and asked him to turn over.

"I know what you want. I know why you really came here," she whispered.

Using her mouth, she applied a condom on him with a skill that dazzled Jay with its precision as much as it had aroused him. The girl closed her eyes, engaging in her usual motions of impersonal intercourse. There was a rehashing of the same sounds and grunts she had memorized over the years of her occupation. It distracted and unnerved Jay, knowing sex was just another fabricated gratification in his life.

"Oh, baby, come on, come on. Please cum. Oh yeah, you're the best, so good," she chanted emotionlessly. It was in the tone of a parent hurrying a child to eat vegetables.

He made the most of it by focusing on her bouncing breasts. It helped when he dismissed the higher functions of his brain and delved into its primitive urges to dominate and replicate. Soon enough, in one explosive, calming conclusion, Jay enjoyed the biological benefits of emancipating his urge. Flower's acting immediately ended. She quickly slipped into her nightgown and flushed the condom down the bathroom toilet.

"Do you still want some more massage? You have ten minutes left," she informed.

"No, it's okay," Jay replied. "Hey, what's your real name?"

"I...cannot tell you."

"That's alright. Why do you do this job? Do you like it?"

Flower's expression changed to a serious one.

"Of course, I don't like it. No girl here like it. All we do is fuck, fuck, fuck. We have no choice."

She spent the remaining time giving him a solid back massage until a buzzer sounded.

"Okay, put on your clothes. It's time to go," instructed Flower.

Her sudden impersonal demeanor only added to Jay's rediscovered cynicism. The door slammed shut behind him immediately after he had left the property. He knew he would never enter through it again. Still, he thought, there was plenty of time left before his planned objective for the evening. He decided not to rush it, sitting outside the spa's parking lot and enjoying the cloudless night sky. It was a shame that he knew

God existed, only to realize the guy was a jerk. How could an omnipresent being so sagacious leave the world in such an imperfect state? He could create millions of stars, yet was incapable of preventing war and poverty. If Jay hadn't given up so dispiritedly, he might have felt a tinge of confounding disappointment. Not anymore. Instead, he basked in the sign's neon glow, enjoying its uniquely soothing comfort.

He would sit there for a few hours.

Just around midnight, Jay arrived in front of his church, carrying a large tote bag. Despite its fancy new security systems, it was no sweat for him to breach the building. He did feel a tinge of rust from his breaking and entering days, but it was mere child's play, nonetheless. Besides, he wondered, how much faith did the congregation really have if it depended on security systems anyway?

Using a combination of hairpins, a small knife and a screwdriver, he was able to pick the locks, making his way into the church. Things felt different at night. Without its crowds and lighting, Fellowship Communion Baptist Church lost its mystique. Jay couldn't resist walking up to the podium, imagining what it would feel like to preach on a Sunday morning. There was a powerful presence to it, he felt, no doubt about that. Unfortunately, the feeling wasn't spiritual; it was authoritative. With such a rush of power, Jay realized, it was inevitable that even the best-intentioned pastors would eventually turn to corruption.

When he finally had enough of the podium, he decided it was time to accomplish his primary mission. He made his way toward several of the Bible study rooms, observing their ceiling fans and optimal visibility from the entrance. He found just the one in the children's day care center, which offered the closest distance between its own doorway and the front. There, he collected the teacher's stool and calculated weight comparisons. It was perfect, he determined, though he regretted it would be done in the room where he once substituted for Sunday school. He reminisced about it as being one of his more happier memories, teaching Noah's ark to eager children who held on to every word he said. One day they'll know it was a lie; he wished he could be there to apologize.

But he wouldn't.

Jay plopped down his tote bag and removed a laptop and rope from it. While waiting for the computer to load, he wasted no time in contriving a perfect noose from the rope. It was made from good material, admired Jay—very sturdy and capable of doing its job. Turning his attention back to the laptop, Jay entered the wi-fi codes of the church and logged into his email account. Though Reverend Han had asked him to delete the email, he had never asked Jay if he had saved it on his hard drive. Composing a long and detailed email about what happened to Maple and his grievances with the church, he felt proud to contribute one last act of greater good before expiring from the world. He attached Maple's video and retrieved the email contacts from the church's directory. Jay reviewed it one final time, took a deep breath and clicked Send All.

Now for the second part, he thought.

He took out a handwritten letter from his pocket, placing it underneath the stool. Then, without hesitation, he made his way on top of the stool and adjusted the rope and noose accordingly for a good hang. Before his departure, however, he waited for the figure to walk into the room. He knew Jesus would come; he wanted the Messiah to see this. They looked at one another in silence, both knowing it would not be stopped. Without breaking eye contact, Jay kicked the stool out of the way, allowing gravity to do its job. Jesus stood and watched as the body became lifeless, hanging like a puppet on a broken string.

CHAPTER 12: THE END

The first screams were heard at approximately seven-thirty in the morning. They came from a church member who was in charge of xeroxing the service programs. The second person to scream was one of the choir women. She had come over to the day care room only because she had heard the previous woman scream. Neither of the pastors had arrived yet. Jay's lifeless body remained slowly twirling from the rope—a haunting visage that was covered by a partially closed door until emergency workers arrived.

"Did you know how the deceased person came in?" asked the policeman.

"N...no..." stammered the crying Xerox lady.

"When was the last time you had interaction with this individual?"

"I'm not...sure...I...I even recognize..."

"What's going on here?" chimed in Pastor Lu, who had just arrived.

"Sir, who are you?" asked the officer.

"I'm the pastor of this church!" he declared. "Members were calling me, telling me what had happened! I came as fast as possible!"

The officer led the pastor to a quieter outdoors area to question him. The abundance of police cars and crime scene tape quickly drew the curiosity of the locals. Through the windy mid-November weather they looked onward, clutching their coats in a struggle to observe what had happened. Rumor had it that someone was murdered. Another suggested an armed lunatic was on a shooting spree. By the time Cody had arrived, it was a challenge to separate truth from fiction.

"Oh, Lord, I saw...that body too..." cried one of the black women he often had seen there.

"What's going on? I heard the word 'body.' Did someone die?" asked Cody.

"Yeah, they found Jay's body," Felix softly replied. "He committed suicide."

"Inside of the church?!"

Felix nodded, "There...there was a note."

"A note?"

"Cody, did you check your emails this morning?"

"No, but what did the note say?"

"It said for us to check our emails."

Cody caught sight of a person heading in their direction. It was Marco, boiling with anger as he charged through the crowd.

"TELL ME IT'S A LIE!" he ordered Felix.

"What's a lie?" Felix questioned.

"THE EMAIL JAY WROTE!"

"What? Calm down, man!"

He shoved Felix down to the ground, prompting others to hold and restrain him.

"Dude, what are you mad about?!" asked Felix.

"YOU'RE A FAGGOT. A HOMOSEXUAL! JAY SAW YOU INAPPROPRIATELY KISSING LUKE!" Marco shouted.

Felix was at a loss for words.

"SO IT'S TRUE?!" pushed Marco.

"Yes, it's true," spoke another voice. It was Luke.

"Oh, my gosh," gasped one of the church members.

"The pastor's son..." commented another.

Luke helped Felix up.

"Felix and I," Luke declared, "are lovers."

Hearing that detail sent Marco into a bolt of rage. He found the strength to free himself, charging at Luke like a bull.

"Marco, no!" screamed Ennis, tackling Marco in mid-charge.

"THEY'RE GOING TO HELL! BOTH OF THEM! I'M SERIOUS!" he screamed.

Several police officers intervened, preventing further attack. Marco was shaking so hard he turned red. Several church members glared at Luke and Felix, uncertain of their trust in them after their deception.

"Look, everyone!" interrupted Marion.

A collective gasp erupted as the covered body of Jay Zhang was seen being carted off into an ambulance.

"It's...oh, my Lord...it's Jay's body," muttered Henry.

"Hey, has anyone seen Pastor Washington?" interrupted one of the church members.

"Didn't you read the email sent by that boy?" replied another.

"No, what happened?"

"He was beating Maple."

"For real?"

"It was caught on tape. Figured it was recorded by the girl herself."

Back in Quentin Washington's home, the guilty pastor looked into his own red eyes in the mirror and acknowledged his shame. The email from Jay had reached him that morning just as it had reached the others, including the news of Jay's self-demise. Washington's heart knew the consequences of his mistakes weren't premeditated, but nevertheless his ungodly decisions were still influential in what resulted. The pastor knew he was partially to blame for the disillusions that caused the young man to take his own life. He figured there was only one remaining thing left to do now before police arrived. The Bible commanded him to make peace; it was time to give a heartfelt apology to his daughter. Maple had barricaded herself in her room the whole morning, perhaps in fear of his retribution. He wanted to make sure she knew he had no such intention. He struggled with the words he needed to say, but he found them once he approached the front of her locked door.

"Daddy's probably going to get into a lot of trouble for this. But I just want you to know," Washington said in tears, "that I love you, Maple. And I'm sorry for what I did."

"YOU'RE SORRY THAT YOU GOT CAUGHT!" Maple screamed.

"One day, I'll hope you'll forgive me."

It was the last time most of the members from Fellowship Communion Baptist Church would hear from the pastor. It wasn't too long before the rumor mill also got a hold of the other leaders withholding evidence. Both Chinese and black members left the church and joined other congregations. At the height of its short-lived popularity, Fellowship Communion Baptist Church had grown to 253 members. By the end of the week following Jay's death, the membership was down to 35. The mid-sized church soon closed until further notice.

———————

A week after Jay's death, it was Skinny Grandma's funeral. The Buddhist chants stretched into long monotonous sessions—sounds not designed for audio gratification but for clear passageways of the soul. Every now and then, there would be a chime, a slight pause, and the same repeat of jumbled words foreign to Cody's ears. These were his first impressions of his grandmother's funeral, contrasting it between today and Jay's Christian funeral from a day before. As much as one can "enjoy" a funeral, he found the Christian customs more positive. The usually dry Pastor Lu gave a surprisingly ardent sermon about seeing rare blessings in dark times. It was ironic how they celebrated more of Jay's life in death than in person; yet it was an honorable celebration, nonetheless.

Not so with Skinny Grandma's Buddhist funeral.

There was a deliberate gloom to it as if sadness and suffering pleased the deceased. A certain power and allure resulted from its sturdy mystique. After awhile, all of its participants fell into a spell, chanting along with the monks. Cody momentarily resisted the hypnotizing effect by focusing on the others who were there. Duke stood statue-like, impenetrable but visibly saddened. His grandfather was lost in memory, with each tear a remembrance of times past. Most notable was the melodrama coming from his aunts and father who treated the funeral like it was a stage audition.

"<Shout louder and cry louder>," his father encouraged him. "<We want her spirit to know how upset we are. It'll make her take pity on us and bring good luck. More money. A new car. Your grandmother has the power to bless us with such things now, son!>"

The eulogy after the chant session gave the funeral a momentary resemblance of normalcy. One of Cody's more charismatic uncles delivered a heartfelt speech, though Duke's stoic translation rendered it colorless. The uncle mostly stammered, ultimately repeating his only point four times more than necessary.

"<No matter how much we love life and the people in it>," he said for a final time, "<in the end, we all must part ways.>"

Afterwards, the funeral participants gathered in line, paired through individual families. They were each given some incense and a rose—the former for bowing and placing in the thurible, the latter for the open casket. Every now and then the line stalled because a relative had fainted or had trouble moving on. Cody was near the end of the line. When it was his turn, he barely made more than a passing glance at his grandmother's body. He felt it was better to deal with his emotions this way. After all, he thought, the body was nothing more than a lifeless husk whose omnipresent soul anticipated its next destination. He made a halfhearted bow of respect to the body and dropped his rose in, watching it land closely to her crossed arms.

"Goodbye, mah mah," he muttered.

By design, the last person in line was Cody's grandfather. The elderly Quan stood and stared at the casket for what seemed like an eternity. He stared with a concentrated focus, seemingly to bid his final farewell telepathically. It was a gesture far more genuine and powerful than the showy pantomimes that promulgated the funeral. Then, with a calm release from his fingertips, the last rose was gently dropped and landed near her heart. With that done, the funeral director took over and closed the casket.

Cody, the last male heir, was given the task of holding his grandmother's portrait during the walk to the incinerator room. The rest of the family followed with the casket in tow, carried by Duke, Cody's father and two of his uncles. At first, Cody thought the constant chills up and down his body came from the monks' chanting in front of him. He then realized the cold feeling was literal; the sections away from the chapel had piercingly low temperatures.

It was enough to let his guard down, allowing sentiment to ride with him the rest of the way. He owed his grandmother that much. They were all good memories, even the bad ones. Sometimes they were simple like dribbling a basketball in the parking lot. Others were humorous, like the childhood pranks Duke and Cody had pulled on the old woman. These fragments of yesterday collided together in a place that was forever accessible. It was where Cody wanted to be after he died—a better afterlife than the exclusive heaven of Christian lore. Jesus, he thought, could have Marco, Pastor Washington, Daphne and Deena. Let those hypocrites congregate inside of their own corner of eternity. For him, the choice was simple: He wanted to reside in unconditional love.

The incinerator room could only be described as a decoration-less area that made no apologies for its purpose. It was located apart from the main building, residing in a warehouse that also held extra furniture and supplies. At the end of the room was the incinerator itself. It was a rusty metallic furnace attached to a conveyor belt where the casket would be placed and later dropped. While the four casket holders prepared the positioning of the coffin for the final fallout, the monks maximized the volume and speed of their chanting. The service had arrived to its dramatic conclusion where nary a dry eye remained. As they watched the casket slide into the idle incinerator, Cody stood next to his grandfather and grasped his arm as a show of support. The funeral director led Cody's father to the power button, indicating it was time to turn the furnace on. With a deep breath and wobbly knees, Mr. Quan closed his eyes and quickly pressed it.

In a moment of efficiency devoid of hesitation—one in which only a machine could provide—the incinerator wasted no time coming to life.

The raw reality of hearing the strong flames engulf Skinny Grandma's body was enough to send Cody's heart fainting. He repeatedly uttered Jesus' name as a means for comfort, partially praying for illogical wishes like turning back time or realizing it was a dream. Eventually, the family members left the incinerator room one after the other. Cody and his grandfather were the last to go.

Once outside, he saw distant relatives he hadn't visited with since childhood. Most of them had crossed into the married-with-children life, finding him difficult to relate to. Duke, however, was showered with congratulations as he flaunted his new girlfriend, Annebelle, around. He presented himself with a dignified pose, absorbing their praises as though they belonged to him. Seeing his cousin alone, Ace offered conversation.

"<Hey, ehh, cousin Cody, ehh, sorry about your grandmother>," said Ace.

"It's okay, man," waved off Cody. "Life goes on. Thanks for coming. I know this isn't your side of the family, but I appreciate it anyway."

"<Do you, ehh, want some time alone? Eh, can I pray for something?>"

"Trust me, the last thing I want to do is pray."

"<Ehh, okay. I'm just checking. Eeh, cousin Cody, may I ask you a small question?>"

"Yeah?"

"<I heard that someone died in your church and then it closed. Do you want to go to mine?>" offered Ace.

"No, thanks," answered Cody, "I'm done with churches."

———

"Yo, look this way you li'l bitch!" demanded Danny.

The tiger glared at him, hoping its stare would be ample warning. Danny ignored it and continued taunting.

It was his way of staving off boredom on a cool December morning, where he and Pete were early for a drug meeting at the Houston Zoo. A zoo employee on Piranha's payroll had let them in, leading them to the tiger exhibit where they would meet Andrew. The two had an idea about why they were summoned here. Danny had been attracting attention with his lavish drug parties—ones where he often gave away free cocaine. Pete repeatedly warned his young Cambodian friend about his bold attitude, but it only strengthened Danny's resolve.

"Damn, nigga," cautioned Pete, "stop pissin' that tiger off. We in trouble enough as it is."

"Why you all scared of them niggas, bra?" Danny countered. "You knew they just gonna tell us to lay back!"

"Morning, gentlemen," interrupted a voice. Andrew and his associate had just arrived on the scene. As usual, he was dressed in nice business attire. Both held a cup of coffee.

"Heh," snarled Danny, "I see you tryin' to get all Scarface on us with this tiger. Trying to make you look like a bad muthafuck. Ain't gonna work, my nigga."

Andrew smirked, staring at his coffee.

"You gotta excuse Danny," intervened Pete. "He been a bit high these couple of days, heard?"

"Oh, yeah," chuckled Andrew, "I heard."

"For the real tho'," insisted Danny, "y'all ain't our mommy and daddy. We grown ass niggas. We done deal how we done deal, y'all feel me?"

Andrew calmly finished his coffee and responded, "You know what's the problem with getting cookies from the jar?"

"What, this Pillsbury doughboy the Riddler now?" laughed Danny.

"One forgets to leave tips," replied Andrew. "I thought I taught you both better than that. Throwing parties, giving away free shit."

"Oh, so what now, nigga, you gonna shoot us hea in th' zoo?" commented Danny. "You outta ya damn mind!"

The high he was under made Danny dangerously braver than he had reason to be, strutting around the edge of the exhibit.

"Go ahead an' shoot me then, nigga!" he continued. "I'm bulletproof, fool!"

Andrew's associate took out a gun and pointed it at Pete instead.

"Ay ay ay!" protested Pete, "what you pointin' that at me fo'? I ain't start shit! Them parties weren't my idea, nigga!"

The associate continued holding Pete at gunpoint while walking towards him. He then surprised Pete by pulling out a pair of scissors.

"Hahaha! He gonna cut off your li'l dick, man!" Danny laughed.

Pete heard the scissors trimming off pieces of his hair. The associate gathered samples of it until he had the small quantity that he needed.

"Dang, yo, I was gonna cut my hair anyway!" grinned Pete. "I do it once every Tuesday. What's going on here?"

The associate nodded to Andrew, who took out his own gun and pointed it at Danny.

"Nigga, what the hell is going on?!" Danny asked.

Pieces of Pete's hair were sprinkled over Danny's clothes. It was enough to discourage suspicion. A fifth person joined them—a police officer.

"Meet one of HPD's finest on our payroll," introduced Andrew. "He's going to serve witness to Pete murdering you."

"Huh? You clownin' or what, you fat motherfucka?" Danny taunted.

With a sudden motion, the associate grabbed Danny, flinging him into the tiger's den. The fall injured the young Cambodian's leg. He watched helplessly as the tiger approached him.

"Ah shit, nigga! Ah damn, nigga!" screamed the Cambodian youth.

Pete flinched in horror as he heard inhuman screams of agony and pain. The sounds of bones crunching and blood squirting ensured an inerasable memory.

Then there was silence.

"Officer," Andrew ordered, pointing at Pete, "arrest this man."

The setup had begun. Pete would take the rap and the corrupted officer would make the paperwork legit. There wasn't any use for squealing either; Piranha had deep reaches into Pete's family.

"If you stay low and keep silent, we'll get you out in about five to seven years. Even at first-degree," winked Andrew. "We have friends in high places."

He departed with his associate, leaving the officer to report on the crime.

———

Cody lay awake in the middle of the night while his home phone was left ringing. He knew who it was, but he was too angry to answer her. After a long week that spanned through two funerals, he was also too emotionally exhausted to care. When the ringing stopped, the calling pattern alternated to his cell phone. They were guilt calls from Daphne, he knew. Ever since her surprising infatuation with her new "friend" Andrew, she had forgotten anyone else existed. He was tired of her selfish nature; the only thing she was entitled to was his cold shoulder. She had intentionally ignored his calls, and to top it all off, she had forgotten his twenty-eighth birthday. The least she could do, thought Cody, was stick with her self-centeredness and leave him alone. When the calls continued coming an hour afterwards, her persistency finally won out over his stubbornness.

"Hi," he answered.

"Hi, Cody. Happy birthday," said Daphne in her familiar passive voice.

"Hey."

"Why.......haven't you been returning my phone calls?"

"..."

"Cody?"

"I thought you slept before ten o'clock on Mondays."

"It's a winter holiday, Cody."

"Okay. Well, thanks for remembering."

"Why would I forget? We're friends, remember?"

"Yeah? Friends who ignore each other's calls now."

"You're the one who've stopped picking up. I've called you and called you."

"And who was ignoring who between September and November?"

"That's different, Cody. I got so much to share with you."

"About your new boyfriend, I'm sure. I've heard the rumors, Daphne."

"He's not my boyfriend. He's just my friend."

"Hah!...ha....ehhhh.......Jesus Christ," Cody said.

"I don't know what's wrong with me these days, Cody. I miss you so much. I miss our friendship. Do you wanna have some coffee with me sometime? Please?"

"You're begging me now? That's fucking rich."

"I just don't understand why you're so mad. I don't want you to hate me, Cody."

"I don't hate you. I just don't give a damn anymore."

"..."

"It's liberating."

"Cody, I need to tell you about my...friend Andrew. I don't know what he does."

"Well, where's your so-called friend now?"

"That's the thing. He constantly comes and goes. He's so mysterious. I don't know what's wrong with me, Cody. Tell me what's wrong with me, please?"

"You don't know what he does?"

"He says he sells I.D. tags, but...okay, like once he went to the zoo in the early morning. And he told me it was for I.D.'s. But who does that? He's already lied to me about so many things. About his age, his motives, everything. And the friends he has are so suspect. They just play poker all the time and smoke."

"And you go with him to these poker games?"

"Yes, Cody. I would stay with him until sunrise. I couldn't go to work so I quit my job. I don't know what to do with my friend Andrew."

"Daphne, what do you see in this guy?"

"What?"

"You're obviously in love with him. What do you see in him?"

"I'm not in love with him!" giggled Daphne.

"..."

"I mean, he's a leader. He's got the nicest dog in the world. He cooks for me—"

"I cook for you too."

"Yeah, but I mean, he also cooks for his dog!"

"......are you on crack?"

"A little," laughed Daphne, "I'm just kidding! That was a joke, Cody. Oh, I missed talking with you so much. Andrew doesn't talk much."

"You heard what happened to the church, right?"

"I think so. Isn't it time for the Christmas bake sale?"

"Daphne, Pastor Washington was caught abusing Maple. She told Jay, who in return told church officials, who tried to bury it, and then he goes and hangs himself."

"Oh? Is Jay okay?"

"He's dead, Daphne! While you were on your little rendezvous with your 'friend' Andrew, shit went down. Your little friends from church had been worried sick about you. Who the fuck is this Andrew guy? Why is he so important to you that you abandoned your friends, your job and even your own dreams?"

"I...I don't know. I just...it's just the way he makes me feel, I guess. You know just the other day he took me out to the gun range. He was SO good with his gun. He taught me how to fire. I loved the gun range! But he also does gentle things like golf too. Every day is a new experience with him!" Daphne smiled.

"Jay died. Do you...understand that?" Cody repeated. "And our friendship died as well."

"Of course, I'm shocked that Jay died. Cody, I miss you. Can you buy some of my time shares? It would help pay rent. Andrew borrowed money from me, but he'll pay me back soon."

"You don't even sound like you anymore. It's like I'm talking to a different person. A person who's lost it."

"Maybe you can get me into your home decor business."

"So this is who you really are. That whole Christian persona was just bullshit. This is you. The real you. I gotta say I'm not impressed, Daphne."

"Are you going to abandon me now? We're friends, Cody. You're not supposed to abandon me."

"I was a friend who had feelings for you. I was a friend to you because it was the only way to get you to talk with me. And now you just want to be friends because you're dating a suspect guy and you quit your damn job and you want money from me, is that it?"

"No, of course not—"

"I love you, Daphne Lee."

"You're...you're so silly, Cody," giggled Daphne.

A door opening could be heard. A dog barked.

"Why do I hear a dog barking?" asked Cody.

"He's back! I'll call you later, okay?"

"You live with him now?! Is that his dog?"

"Hey, do you want to go on a ski trip with my friend Andrew and I?"

"Why the fuck would I want to go on a ski trip with you and that guy together?"

"Who's that?" Andrew said in the background.

"Just a friend," replied Daphne, "hey, I made you some dinner. It's on the kitchen table."

Daphne returned to her phone conversation with Cody.

"Sorry about that. Where were we?" she asked. "Hello? Cody, are you there?"

Cody had hung up.

"January 9, 2006. Monday.

I don't know how to start this blog. I suppose for my first entry I'll summarize my day back at work. Rachel Higgins, my supervisor, came to me with a smile. Usually when she smiles, that signifies bad news. Sure enough, they've successfully assigned a new supervisor to me. It's that asshole from the I.T. department. Forgot his name at the moment. But that was a move to make my life hell. Also, Mindy stopped interning and she'll focus full-time on her doctorate. We'll still talk, but probably not on a day-to-day basis.

First day alone sucked. Not much to look forward to anymore. I used to be so excited when I thought God was in my life. I can't say I don't believe in the existence of God, but I don't believe I'm cared for. Ennis lied to me. He said if I gave my heart up to Jesus, better things would happen. All I saw was hypocrisy. It isn't so much with Jay dying or Washington beating up his kid. It wasn't just Daphne falling for a bad guy or Zoey leaving the church or basketball games erupting in violence. It wasn't Jesus miraculously healing my grandmother only to kill her just as quickly. It wasn't any one thing among many things.......it was just all of those things.

Today, I went to the bathroom and took off my crucifix. Jesus came in and looked at me. He always seems to show up when it doesn't matter or whenever it is too late. Jesus gives me the impression that he's a deadbeat. He might as well wear a wife-beater. Anyway, I looked at him and then I dropped the crucifix into the toilet. I told him to talk to me and give me something, anything, that would stop me from flushing it down into the sewer. If he had just said something meaningful, anything meaningful, I would have dipped my hands into that piss-soaked dump bucket and picked it back up. But he just said nothing and looked on. So I flushed the crucifix down the toilet. Then I closed my eyes, opened them, and Jesus was gone.

I don't know why I decided to make my first entry about my day. I figured it probably contained some of the most important things that mattered to me. It feels good to finally write about them. Free from having to worry about God's wrath. I quit being a Christian. I don't know who'll care to find this blog and read it. But hopefully some day, someone out there can find my words relatable. For now, I'm just putting my thoughts down as therapy.

Well, here's to a life of monotony. When it's all said and done, I'm back to square one again."

- From the first journal entry of Cody Quan.

ACT II:
MOSAIC DESIGN STUDIOS

CHAPTER 13: FOUR YEARS LATER

The weatherman had a cheerful expression about him. Out of all the summers in his thirty-year career, he had never felt more stress-free. His usual routine had now been memorized and rehearsed. Every morning the old codger would give his wife of forty-six years a kiss. Then he would look into the mirror and repeat what he had been saying for the past five months. Then, it was time for work.

"And that's it for sports," one of the anchormen would say. "Those poor Astros. Since their World Series debut, they really haven't caught a break, have they?"

The anchorwoman followed up with a laugh, contributing with "Well, neither can this weather. Geez, has it been five straight months now?"

"Well, let's find out!" the sports anchorman would respond.

Then, acknowledging his cue, the old weatherman dispersed similar news from the day before. Which was the same as the one before that. And the previous one before that.

"Well, guys," the weatherman began reciting, "it's yet another hot and dry day in Houston. Again. Five-day forecast shows not a sign of upcoming precipitation. Back to you!"

He then smiled for the camera. Easiest job in the world, he thought.

Several University of Houston staff members were watching the live broadcast in one of the campus' lounge rooms.

"Shit, more of this goddamn heat," muttered Kirk Santiago, looking at a fellow employee who shook her head in disbelief.

"My underwear gets so sticky," he continued and burped. "It's like melted cheese on my ass!"

Now in his late fifties, Kirk had seemingly worked at the university forever. Over time, he had become extremely fat, exceptionally lacking in hygiene and developed a habit of speaking in crude statements. In short, Kirk didn't care. He broke rules because he was connected with the university higher-ups who protected him. All that brownnosing, however, had made him a natural enemy to the regular employees. It also didn't help that he was assigned the role of supervisor in conjunction with his regular title as I.T. head of security—those combined positions gave him ample opportunity to violate employee and student privacy.

"Ah, well," he concluded with the last bite of his triple meat and bacon cheeseburger. "Guess I don't have to check the weather in the next five fucking days. Same old shit."

Leftover grease from his burger drizzled down his double chin. Rather than using the napkins available to him, Kirk chose to wipe the drippings off with his tie instead. Looking at his phone's clock, he realized he had to return to his office. He pushed himself past a few students as he huffed and puffed his overweight body across campus.

"Hey, you fat jerk!" a female student yelled, "watch where you're going!"

"Squeeze them tittles, honey!" he barked back.

Sweat oozed out of his pores by the time he had reached his desk. Once his perspiration met the leather surface of his chair, he felt comforted by his sanctuary. Like a prison warden, Kirk viewed his collection of webcam feeds from his monitor. Most of the cameras were on the workers he was supervising; he liked to imagine them as pets in their cages.

There was one in particular, a gift from fellow supervisor and drinking buddy Rachel Hutchens, that he enjoyed psychologically torturing than most.

"Hey, Cody!" shouted the hellish supervisor, "stop writing emails to non-university personnel. I can see what you're typing behind that goddamn big head of yours!"

Kirk chuckled as Cody scrambled to follow orders. The fat man pulled out some Ruffles; they were on sale at the local Walmart.

"That dumbass," Kirk muttered at the screen. "Never did understand why Rachel had so much trouble with you."

Cody resumed the usual charade of working on his assignment. Both he and Kirk knew it wasn't a real project. The rotund taskmaster saw fit that Cody was given as much work as possible. Once Friday came, the submitted project would be received by Kirk via USB drive where he would immediately delete the project without checking. Cody discovered this when he decided to test him one week. Rather than putting any real HTML code down, he made a pink and yellow web page with the words "Kirk Couldn't See His Own Dick" repeating in an endless loop. The lack of any reaction confirmed Cody's suspicions.

What an ironic life...I get paid for being miserable, he realized. They wouldn't fire him nor would they allow him opportunity to work on anything significant. He was buried deep in the farthest cubicle in an underground office. The notion of rebelling did not escape Cody, though he couldn't conjure up a point to doing so. He tried to put a positive spin on his spurious work, but pretending to work was work itself. Worse, Kirk rarely left his desk. There were rumors he had inserted hidden cameras throughout the female restrooms around campus. It would certainly explain why Kirk was constantly preoccupied, but so did numerous other things like

StarCraft. Cody only knew that whatever his supervisor really did, it wasn't actually work.

It wasn't unusual around three o' clock in the afternoon or so that Cody heard snoring coming from the fat man's office. It reminded him how much his job was a joke; it reminded him how everyone's job in his department was a joke. The government wasted millions of tax dollars on people like Kirk. And it wasn't that Kirk was any good at his I.T. position either—whenever computers broke or received a Trojan virus, he would frantically search Google for the answer. A little baby could do that, Cody thought to himself.

Regardless, there was an advantage with Kirk's daily naps: It meant ample time for Cody to blog. He found therapy in writing, having amassed close to several hundred journal entries over the past four years. Here, he was writing another one:

"June 25, 2009. Wednesday.

Another day, another dollar. What's the point? It just disappears into my mortgage anyway. A thirty-year mortgage. What kind of investment is that? I'm thirty now. Can't believe that shit. Thought I'd have two kids and a nagging wife by now. Where the hell is my minivan? If I traveled back in time and met my fifteen-year-old self I'd tell him lies. I'm too ashamed of revealing that I make money I barely keep, working for Jabba the Hutt."

Cody continued typing for a few paragraphs more. The snoring grew louder inside of Kirk's office. This made it safe for him to turn on his computer's Instant Messenger. Like the Eye of Sauron, once he made himself available online, everyone started messaging him.

"Bubbleman!" typed RainYSkIEs589.

"Chubs," Cody typed back. He was known online as Quanster7.

"Check out my new artwork!"

The person behind RainYSkIEs589 was Rain Yoon, a talented punky hipster far younger than Cody. Rarely did a conversation begin without a request to check out her new artwork. Or to comment on her long rants in the blogosphere. Or to listen to her sing a new song that she wrote. There was no doubt about Rain's diverse talent, but she couldn't commit to anything without wanting to get into another. Chalk it up to youth, thought Cody.

"It's...um...very avant-garde," he commented.

It was an accurate statement to describe her latest masterpiece. The painting consisted of a metal-skinned mermaid diving into a collage of diamond-encrusted seaweed—all of which was taking place at the bottom of a snow globe being observed by a giant girl.

"LOL! Thanks, dude! Wait...what's 'avant-garde?'" she asked.

"It means it breaks the mold. It blazes trails. Maybe it'll start a movement for metallic mermaids," typed Quanster7.

"How do you pronounce that? Is that like 'garden' without the 'e'?"

"Yeah. Or 'guard.'"

The snoring abruptly stopped from Kirk's office followed by a loud thud. He must've fallen off his chair again, thought Cody.

"And what do you think of the coloring. Do you think it's too dark?"

"Hey Rain, gotta go. Fat man's waking up."

"Wait wait wait, dude! Before you go, can you read my journal entry? My brother's being a moron again."

"Look, just show it to Yuki or something," frantically typed Cody. "I have to log off!"

Kirk swept off the pile of potato chips that had fallen on him after his fall. While he was trying to pick himself back up, he collapsed back down again, giving surrender to his weight. He was successful on the fifth try, finally feeling around the desk for his glasses. Upon finding and putting them on, he was reminded of how good it was to see the world in 20/20 vision again. This was especially true as he inspected the webcam images from his monitor. All the workers were hard at work, a sign that they were probably cowering from fear of him. Even Cody was buried in concentration, programming away on Notepad, though Kirk had no idea Cody was actually typing gibberish since the hefty supervisor couldn't read HTML.

"Hey, Cody! Take a damn break, man!" he shouted. "Don't you gotta pee?"

Cody pretended like he didn't hear him. He enjoyed making the obese supervisor muster his way towards Cody's desk.

"Hey," Kirk repeated, "break time, buddy. I'll let you go a little early today. Think I'll head on over to the nudie bar."

"Didn't you tell me you were gay?" questioned Cody.

Kirk stared at him in silence. Cody forgot to address him as 'sir.'

"Sorry, I mean, didn't you tell me you were gay...sir?"

"No, heh heh. I told you...I'm tri-sexual," corrected Kirk. "I'll TRY ANYTHING! HAHAHAHAHA!"

Cody didn't particularly find his lowbrow humor funny.

"What? Not even a chuckle? Eh...I thought it was funny. Yeah, seriously, you're off now. I'm heading to Richmond Avenue. Going to pound my wood. And by pounding my wood I mean I'm going to stick my dick in some vagina! You know what I mean?! You know what I mean?!" laughed Kirk.

He slapped Cody hard on the back. Cody stared ahead without laughing.

"Go. Shoo. You're free! Do whatever it is you Asians do. Play mah-jong with the Joy Luck Club. Hai-yahh! Gongggg!"

Kirk laughed out loud on his way out, though he had a difficult time squeezing his giant frame past the door. Finally, thought Cody, the fat man was walking out of the building. He attempted to turn on his Instant Messenger again, but the computer became buggy. This was no surprise because it was assembled by Kirk and anything by him never functioned properly. Cody had no choice but to sit and sigh, repeatedly wishing their department had a real I.T. professional. After five more minutes of restarting and failing, Cody decided to heed his raunchy supervisor's advice and walked out for some fresh air.

Seeking shelter under a tree, he wondered what he could be doing with his free afternoon. It was far too hot to do anything. He eventually decided it was best to avoid breaking out into a sweat. After all, he had a date later on in the evening. That wasn't very exciting news, however; Cody was on a streak of bad dates. Seventeen by his count.

Perhaps, he believed, tonight would be different.

———

Wynn Chou would not stop talking.

The date had already become a disaster. She seemed to be an angry woman by nature, occasionally slamming the palm of her hands onto the restaurant table. Regardless of what topic they were talking about, Wynn would find a way to negatively spin it with her circular logic. It would not have surprised Cody if she suddenly got up and punched him in the face; fortunately, that didn't happen. Not literally, anyway.

The sushi dinner ended with a nod and a handshake along with a familiar helping of the "I only date white guys" speech. Cody estimated he could've saved three thousand dollars by now if these girls would've just told him that before agreeing to dinner. The only thing higher than the temperature during the summer of 2008 was yellow fever. Or perhaps it was white fever. Cody had never quite figured out which way it went.

Bitterness was the default attitude for those who felt neglected by the modern progression of interracial dating. For them, it was a foe rather than a friend—a further dissipation of an already narrowed selection. Or was it really that simple? wondered Cody. Was dating for Asians in America an exclusive club with a sign reading "Asian Women Only"? It appeared that way. For Asian men of his generation, it seemed like a far steeper climb. He was only limited to his perceptions, of course. Then again, if it weren't generally true, why were so many young Asian men attending his cousin Duke's dating seminars?

"Hey, wait," Cody stopped Wynn as she headed for her car.

"Whatdoyou mean heywait youdon'ttellmeheywait becauseifthisisaboutwhyyouthink—"

"I just...want...to wish you a good night," he explained.

"......oh okay. Bye!" Wynn replied.

Though she was merely a few feet from him, the chasm might as well have been miles apart. He stood and watched Wynn turn her back towards him, walking away with an air of entitlement to her step. For a brief moment he saw the specter of Daphne Lee in her place. Shaking off that brief moment of dispirited nostalgia, Cody returned to the sushi restaurant, this time to its bar.

"Struck out again, eh, Romeo?" asked the bartender.

He poured Cody a cold Sapporo and gently slid it toward him.

"This is pathetic. I should have more self-respect than this," Cody muttered.

The Asian bartender nodded in agreement. "She gave you the 'I only date white guys' speech, didn't she?"

"Yep," responded Cody. He downed the bottle of beer, bottoms up. "The thing I don't understand is, why is it never a black guy or a Hispanic guy? If Asian-American women don't like us, okay, but what's the deal with this exclusivity towards white guys? And we're not just talking about good- looking white guys either. If Usher and George from Seinfeld both flirted with an Asian girl, Jason Alexander would win. This shit's way beyond me."

"Want my opinion?" chimed in the bartender.

"Sure," replied Cody.

"You believe in the illusion."

Cody raised an insulted eyebrow. "Come on, man. Look at all these tables behind me."

The surreal pattern of most of the couples in the sushi restaurant was of the white male/Asian female pairing.

"And they believe in that same illusion too," continued the bartender.

"You know, you're just like my cousin Duke. He blames the media."

"No. No no. I'm not blaming the media. The media's too dumb to start trends. I'm suggesting that you should undo the illusion about fitting into whatever society is telling you to fit."

"Pardon?"

"Look—if I told you that beer suddenly cost forty dollars, would you just pay me that absurd amount?"

"I thought it was free—ahh, I see what you're getting at," said Cody. "But what if it said forty dollars on the menu?"

"Does the law say that only white men can choose whoever they can date and no one else can?"

"Well, I'm clearly trying," countered Cody. "It's not like I'm not trying."

"Then try harder," answered the bartender. "Look, real talk...we're both Asian. Our parents were immigrants. They drilled assimilation into our heads. When we take 'no' for an answer, that's our parents talking. That shit may work in China or Vietnam, but no motherfucking way do we survive with that mentality here in Texas. The only person that can stop you from being you is YOU."

The bartender's advice immediately put Cody to the test when a couple occupied the stools beside him. Like a majority of the couples that night at the restaurant, the woman was Asian and the man was Caucasian. He should be happy for them, of course, but he couldn't help but feel a little envious. Were they genuinely in love or were they trophy lovers—she, the prototypical "Asian girlfriend" and he the "white boyfriend?" These thoughts shouldn't have been in Cody's head. But they were.

"Just remember," reminded the bartender as he passed by Cody. "Illusion."

It was then that Cody remembered a saying he once heard: The best magic doesn't trick you; it causes you to believe.

———

One o'clock. An hour after midnight.

Toby, his longtime feline companion, lay purring herself to sleep on his stomach. The cat had not a care in the world. The same couldn't be said for Cody; this was the time of night he felt his weakest. The redundancy of his life only amplified the fears that played upon themselves in his mind. His sanity was fragile. He started believing the supposed clairvoyance of his half-awakened dreams. His good friend Mindy would one day have twins. He saw what they would look like at the ages of three, nine, seventeen and twenty-five. It was like watching a nature show where the fast-forwarding footage of plant life made them appear to grow at super speed. That was one of the two common dreams he had. The other was so depressing that it woke him up every time he dreamt it.

"Daphne..." he muttered in his sleep.

In every incarnation of this dream, he was a guest at Daphne's wedding. The church where it was taking place was gorgeous; the weather outside was perfect, giving just the right amount of sunrays seeping through the windows. He looked at the bride's guests. All his former church friends were there. He tensed up when the organ started playing—Cody knew who would be walking down the aisle.

"Daphne!" he yelled out.

Family members of the wedding couple walked toward the altar; their look alternated between dream to dream since Cody didn't truly know their real life counterparts. Once they were seated appropriately in their sections, the hefty Asian man—the groom—confidently approached the altar. The soon-to-be-husband's side of the wedding was composed of Asian thugs, hooligans and gangsters. In these dreams they were always hollering around, firing their guns at the ceiling. Nothing they said was ever comprehensible. Idiots, dismissed Cody. The best man, bridesmaids, groomsmen, and a generic maid of honor were next to breeze themselves past him. Finally, the blushing bride-to-be walked in—Daphne Lee, at the pinnacle of her beauty, at the apex of her happiness. She was joined together at the altar with the hefty Asian man in upcoming matrimony.

"Don't do it, Daphne!" cried Cody.

He had reached the height of his insecurity. He could barely hear or see Pastor Willy Lu ceremoniously overseeing the marriage vows. Even in dreams, Cody could feel faint. He didn't care that it felt selfish to begrudge Daphne of her happiness. In truth, he already knew that it was a dream, but the dream was based on a reality where she was effervescent. The bad guy won. The nice guy, whom Cody designated himself as, finished last.

"You're wrong," a voice corrected him.

It was a familiar one, confined only within his dreams now. Yet it was still as powerful as ever.

"Nice guys," explained Jesus, "get their ass kicked for my amusement."

The violence of the punching and kicking from Jesus compounded when the rest of the wedding attendees joined in. The towering Marion held him while the diminutive Henry threw a barrage of haymakers. Ennis' kicking kneaded Cody's stomach until it was soft as dough. Felix. *Punch.* Deena. *Punch.* Zoey. *Punch.* Cody was discovering he could black out in his own dreams. When enough of them had gathered in their furious binge, Jesus retreated into the background where the mayhem was given remote encouragement. Finally, after a second wave made up of thugs and brutes had finished, Jesus ordered them to stop and handed the defeated Cody a whip. To his horror, the mob ushered in the innocent personage of Maple Washington.

"Beat this girl," Jesus ordered, pointing at the young girl.

"No, I can't. I won't," replied Cody.

"Do it," Jesus laughed. "It's okay. I'll let it happen. After all, her dad got away with it, didn't he? Hahaha!"

"No!"

"Fine," responded Jesus angrily, presenting a noose. "Then go hang yourself. Go ahead. I'll watch it happen like I watched it happen to your friend Jay."

The wedding day party cheered for the kill. Daphne cackled alongside her new husband.

"Do it," incited Zoey's little boy, Ryan. "Jesus doesn't love you. Nobody loves you."

"Yeah, listen to my son. Die!" screamed Zoey.

"See if Jesus gives a shit!" laughed Luke.

"Hang yourself! Jesus doesn't love you! Hang yourself! Jesus doesn't love you!" The crowd grew in volume as more people flooded through the chapel doors.

There were family members and friends. Ace. Mindy. Aunt Mei. Cody's mother and father were among the loudest to cheer for his suicide.

"Do it," replied his cousin Duke. "You're not an alpha male. Jesus loves alpha males. That's why everything good happens to me and everything bad happens to you!"

"Yeah," smiled the hefty groom, "I'm fucking Daphne."

"He's sticking his dick in me!" Daphne laughed.

"Bubblehead!" interrupted Mindy, "I only became friends to make money off you. HAHAHAHAHA!"

"NOOOOOOOOOOOOOOOOOOOOOO!"

Cody crashed face first into his living room carpet. It was an unpleasant way of being disrupted from his nightmare, but he nevertheless welcomed the awakening. A mere fifteen minutes had passed since he dozed off, yet he was consumed in cold sweat. Toby approached him and gave him a soft head butt, her way of letting him know that she, at least, loved him.

"A dream," muttered a delirious Cody, petting his tabby, "just a dream. A silly dream. Fearful dreams."

Cody slowly made sense of his surroundings. Why am I hearing Spanish? he wondered, then finally remembering why he had intentionally left the TV tuned to the Telemundo channel. The sounds helped him sleep and his unfamiliarity with the language made it non-distracting. With enough consciousness recovered, he sought the notepad he had kept for almost a month. Upon finding and opening it up, he reached out for a pen to mark a twenty-third stroke to a page with twenty-two tally marks. Nothing. The pen had run out of ink.

"Son of a bitch," he cursed.

He lay upon his sofa for a few moments, contemplating whether or not to go upstairs for a new pen. He cursed himself, knowing he should've put some more of them in the living room. Cody had avoided his bedroom for twenty-two long nights; he knew once he was inside it, the temptation of the Internet would become irresistible. It was easy to stick with looking at work-related sites during his job—Kirk's cameras assured see that. But at home, Cody realized, the draw was too tempting, especially now that a new site called Facebook had grown popular. He cursed the day he ever joined it.

"*Come*," came a whisper from the direction of the upstairs bedroom.

He reminded himself that stairways didn't talk.

"*Come*," it repeated.

Cody couldn't turn his head away from it as he continued glancing at its direction. He wanted to know.

"You want to know," affirmed the stairway. "You need to know."

By the time he further contemplated resisting, he realized he was already upstairs; his legs had made the decision for him. Still, considered Cody, it took his finger to push his desktop's power button and at least he had control over that. Didn't he? The monitor turned on; the Windows interface greeted him. His finger apparently pulled a coup too. His body's rebellion continued when he found himself typing Daphne's name on the search button. He frantically tried telling his mind to block her profile. *Block her profile. Block her profile. Block her profile.* But there it was—her profile. *Damn.*

The streak ended at twenty-two nights. He couldn't overcome his addiction to her happiness, her life, her affiliation with her husband—the hefty Asian man.

"Andrew Huynh," identified Cody.

Daphne Lee was dead; Daphne Huynh was happy. So exhilarant was she that her perfect life was transparent through photos. Cody dug deeper and deeper into her Facebook profile. Why couldn't she have set it to private settings? he wondered. Inevitably, he clicked on one particular album that haunted him—her children. "Perfect," she wrote under one of her daughter's photos, "just like her daddy."

Four hours felt like four minutes; it took sunrise to break the spell. Finally, Cody logged off and made his way downstairs to the second-floor patio. The morning was redundant: hot, dry and predictable. Just like every other day.

If only a storm would come.

CHAPTER 14: LIGHTNING...THEN THUNDER

A few weeks later, the first drops of summer rain fell around three o'clock in the afternoon. Although it was merely a drizzle, many on campus welcomed it with open arms. Kirk celebrated the occasion by turning up the volume of his desktop speakers. Bad techno music blared throughout the department. Two more hours, counted Cody, two more hours before the working day ends. As he was tinkering on yet another spurious project, he had forgotten what it felt like to care. Apathy was torture—perhaps the worst kind. It was usually bearable through instant messaging distractions, but the volume of the techno hinted that Kirk would not be falling asleep.

Then, as if to prove Cody wrong, he suddenly turned his music down.

"Yeah?" Kirk answered his phone. "Hey, Ma."

It was always an amusing treat whenever Kirk's mother called him. Usually, it involved her having trouble with a household appliance and he wouldn't have a clue about how to fix it.

"No...no, press the orange button. Wait, which remote are you using? No, I told you it's the other remote. There's no orange button? Maaaaa..."

The phone calls also afforded Cody and the other workers the best opportunity to sneak in an unsanctioned break. Kirk imposed a three-trip maximum restroom rule because he believed an employee needed to go only that many times. This particular instance, believed Cody, the fat man was right. Cody had exceeded his three trips and he didn't really need to go. But he left anyway because Kirk wouldn't stop him with his mother on the phone.

"I'm going to take a break," Cody whispered, using hand gestures.

Kirk nodded and waved him away, resuming his conversation with his mother. "What? You forgot to open the garage door while you backed the car? Maaa!"

Cody appreciated yet another dose of temporary freedom. It was a far cry from his days in Rachel's office when he was able to walk in and out as he pleased. He missed those five-hour lunch breaks. It was possible he could report Kirk's many infractions or apply to another department, but apathy held him back. A sudden interruption from a sprinkle of rain was met with open arms. It was nice to have cool and crisp Houston weather. Since most of the students were in class, Cody easily became lost in thought while walking around the university. It wasn't until he saw his own reflection in the school store window that he snapped out of his musings.

"The University of Houston," he read out loud from one of the many plastered logos across the store.

Perhaps, realized Cody in a brief moment of clarity, he hadn't switched departments because he was tired of the university itself. He had worked there for so long that he accepted it. Would he be standing in this same spot, looking at his reflection again ten years from now? Twenty? Forty? His mother constantly reminded him of how lucky he had it. Working in a government job was easy and the benefits were excellent. This wasn't the pain his immigrant parents would understand. They worked hard so that he could be where he was today. But was this where he wanted to be? he wondered. What satisfaction was there in a life devoid of challenge?

Perseverance, the older Chinese generation liked to say.

An obsolete word, thought Cody, that had no relevance to the second generation. Making lemonade out of lemons was something to be proud of when it wasn't available in life's supermarket. But Cody's life had aisles and aisles of lemonade already made. He wanted more than lemonade. Life wasn't about lemonades. It was about variety, he thought. Cody wanted orange juice. Perseverance was merely surviving until the threat went away. It wasn't advancement. It was anachronistic endurance.

His thoughts were halted when an approaching figure accidentally bumped into him.

"Oh sorry, sorry," apologized the perpetrator.

Turning to face who had bumped him, he was met with a similarly aged Asian male. The guy was of average height, average build—even his face offered little detail for distinction.

"No problem, man," replied Cody. "It happens."

"Heyyyy. Aren't you—?"

"What?"

"Heh. HAH! It's been so long! You...you remember me, right?"

Cody wore a confused expression.

"Our teacher, Mrs. Frankfurter. Intermediate Chinese. Second semester," he said.

"Yeah," Cody slowly recalled. "The Chinese lady with the German name. She was a hard instructor. That was...wow, that was a while back."

"I was in your class! How could you forget?"

"You were?"

"Come on! Come onnnn!"

"Oh, uh...yeah, I remember," lied Cody. "...uh..."

"M..." helped the stranger.

"Mike?"

"No. Ma..."

"Matthew...?"

"Mar..."

"Martin?"

"—eeee."

"Mart...y?"

The stranger winked and pointed at him.

"Oh, haha. Er, nice to meet you again.......Marty," replied a penitent Cody.

"Wuh huhhuhhuh ha ha," laughed Marty.

Cody observed that he had a strange, yet non-threatening laugh.

"So what have you been up to, man?" Marty asked.

"Ah, just still working here. You know I work here, right?"

"Of course, you told me. Remember?"

"Yeah, I...maybe I did. I don't remember. But if you say so. Just doing the website gig. You ever follow up on Mrs. Frankfurter?"

"Dude, she died!" informed Marty.

"No way!"

"Yeah," sighed Marty. "It was tragic. You know how she was a former sniper in the Chinese army?"

"Uh-huh."

Marty made a gesture of a gun being fired.

"No way! The Commies got to her? I knew she wasn't ordinary."

Marty shook his head in despair.

"Damn, dude," continued Cody. "Sorry to hear that. Really liked her as a teacher. She was tough but fair. Who's teaching the Chinese class now?"

"Some Mexican guy," chuckled Marty.

Cody laughed. He couldn't remember the last time he laughed so genuinely.

"Yeah," Marty sighed. "First the beaners take over our restaurants, now they're teaching our language."

"Haha! Dude, harsh. Watch the language."

"It's like the Secret Invasion. I bet they're Skrulls," Marty said, referencing a popular comic book story.

"No way! You're a comic geek too!"

"Sigh. I thought I was the only one, we're a dying breed."

Cody eagerly shook Marty's hand.

"Hey, listen," Marty said, "I might need your help some time soon. I have a lot of jobs lined up, and I'm looking for a web designer. Maybe you could help."

"Sure, man! That'd be great," beamed Cody.

A loud roar of thunder abruptly interfered with their conversation.

"Holy shit! Did you ever think you'd hear that again?!" quipped Marty.

"No, man! I thought the dry spell would last forever."

"A thunder that loud could only signify the coming of a larger storm. It's going to be a big one. Wah-ha! Stay dry, Sean."

"Cody, you mean. My name is Cody Quan."

"Sigh," chuckled Marty. "Heh. Hah! Sean? I said Quan. You gotta check your hearing, man. Welp, I gotta go."

"Yeah, my supervisor must be pretty pissed by now," realized Cody.

"It's good seeing you again," Marty smiled.

They shook hands.

Cody and Marty walked their separate ways. As Cody headed back to his office, more thunder came. The storm intensified. Cody saw several people running in it, getting soaked from head to toe. They were 'persevering,' he laughed to himself, what foolish people. Cody went back to the store and bought an umbrella. He then proceeded to walk across the campus, staying dry from the weather.

———————

"Rain," typed in MyMelodyBunny, "your art is getting gloomier."

The two bloggers could see one another from their respective webcams. Behind them were the interiors of their individual rooms, each reflecting divergent personalities. The forty-year-old Yuki Yee, also known online as MyMelodyBunny, was secretly young at heart, playfully convincing herself that she must have been Japanese in a previous life. Her compact New York City apartment contained evidence of her "weeaboo-ness." The decorations included giant Asuna and Spirited Away wall scrolls, an impressive collection of My Melody and other Sanrio-related dolls, a miniature bonsai tree, meditation gongs and, of course, the unmistakable Japanese red sun adorned on an ornamental giant fan. As an attribute to her outer appearance, though, there was also an orderly cleanliness to the arrangement. Fairly tall at her height of five-foot-six, the slim woman moved in a mature and exacting way, consuming energy only when needed and always in an efficacious manner. Yuki implemented an air of sophistication, which was complemented always by her unmistakable Manhattan accent.

"Well," replied RainYSkIEs589, "I haven't had much to smile about these days."

Rain's youth often lead her into overdramatizations. Living in a rented garage, her decor included a scattered assortment of pop culture posters, action figures, techware and other—often difficult to identify—objects. Chaos was the preferred atmosphere for the twenty-one-year-old Los Angeles student/artist/scriptwriter/blogger. All of that, of course, was appropriate to her nature because Rain was constantly bouncing around like a fly in a room. Multitasking was her way of life. In contrast to Yuki, Rain was short and stocky but full of constant energy. Where Yuki was conservative and orderly, Rain experimented with a colorful variety of clothes, gadgets and even hair dye.

"Well, I'm not saying it's a bad thing," wrote MyMelodyBunny. "It's just that it makes me notice your current mood reflecting on your art."

Her words took too long for Rain's attention deficit disorder to intercept.

"Hey," she replied, ignoring and changing the subject, "what do you think of this?"

She held up a sketch of a caricature with a large head, climbing the Empire State Building like King Kong.

Yuki shrugged on camera and typed, "It's still gloomy."

"How is it gloomy? It's Bubbleman. Cody would love this."

"Why'd you have to draw all these helicopters shooting at him?"

"Haha. Because he's a hazard."

"I think you need to draw his head bigger then."

"Haha! But then I would need a bigger sheet of paper."

Of course, the two took Rain's remark in jest; after all, Cody was the reason they had met in the first place. It was the result of an unexpected readership that grew out of Cody's blogging. Both had been actively following his writing, relating to the situation of being stuck in life's currentless oceans. Yuki had given up hope long ago on any ambition; she had resigned to starting a family of her own wasn't in the cards. Yet, she realized, there was so much left to do in life that she wouldn't pity herself. Traveling, eating well and making new friends—these things were attainable regardless of age. Rain, meanwhile, felt stuck because of her own indecisions. Yuki believed it was merely Rain's youth and, because the young woman possessed so much talent, her marooned situation would surely come to an end.

"Ugh!" Rain shouted, crumpling up the sketch and throwing it away.

"Hey, come on now!" protested MyMelodyBunny. "That was a good sketch! I can't even draw stick figures."

"It's not tha—" Rain starting saying out loud before she realized Yuki couldn't hear her through the webcam. She started typing, "It's not that. I should be working on my album. I came up with this song today in class, while I was working on my graphic novel."

Yuki watched her search frantically for something through the webcam.

"Can't find my damn guitar," typed RainYSkIEs589.

"Hey ladies," joined in Quanster7.

He had logged in through the webcam program. The three computers could see one another in a three-way video chat.

"Hello," typed MyMelodyBunny.

"Is Rain okay?" he asked.

"She's frustrated about deciding what to do again," responded MyMelodyBunny.

"It must be awful being so talented at so many things."

"It's not fair!" playfully whined MyMelodyBunny. "I suck at everything and she's great with everything!"

"Oh, who knows?" typed Quanster7. "Maybe someday they'll make a Scrabble game where you get to play everyone and you get to show how badass you are. It'll be called *Scrabbling with Friends*. Or something like that."

Yuki nodded. She was fantastic with words, seeing them visually as if they were subatomic particles. She had a sixth sense for noticing misspellings, dangling participles, comma splices and other mistakes.

"Hahaha. Yeah, that'll be the day. That would be great."

"It'd be impactful."

"Stop," corrected MyMelodyBunny. "There's no such word as 'impactful.' It's a common buzzword, created by marketing people in their endless quest to piece together mindless metrics."

"Grammar Nazi."

"Just trying to help. So what have you been up to?"

"Well...I had an epiphany today."

They both paused from their typing while they watched Rain seemingly scream obscenities while searching for her guitar.

"She lost her guitar again, eh?" wrote Quanster7.

"I don't have the heart to remind her that she loaned it to her friend last week. She must've forgotten."

"LOL. You're so mean, Yuki."

"Well, seeing how she was so mad at her friend before, it would trigger another bad memory she had forgotten."

"Ah, okay," he replied.

"So what about this epiphany you had?"

"I've decided to stop making lemonade and venture into orange juice."

"Huh? You're doing what now?"

"Remember I once told you how my friend Mindy and I had our own company?"

"Yeah, you went to jail. So this is about orange juice?"

"No, no. It's about not accepting things. I've been going through life playing not to lose instead of playing to win. It's the difference between the '02-'03 Rockets and the '93-'94 Rockets."

"Rockets pockets sockets. Speak in nonsports lexicon, please. Or at least in Harry Potterese."

"I've got to stop cruise-controlling through life, Yuki. I feel like I've died in my twenties, slowly marching toward my grave."

"So..."

"I'm thinking about taking out my retirement funds and starting my own company with them. A big one. With employees and an office."

"Cody, that would be very brave of you if you did something like that. Most people, myself included, wouldn't have the guts to gamble it all away. May I ask what would your new company be about?"

"Websites. Think about it. There're all those mom-and-pop businesses out there with crappy sites. I want to give them five-star quality stuff for affordable prices. There's a market for that, you know."

Yuki's face displayed a serious expression. She knew Cody well enough to know his mind was stubborn when it was locked onto an idea.

"But you've never ran a company before. You're not even a business major. How would you know how to manage things? What about payroll and taxes?"

"Yuki, Yuki, Yuki...I haven't felt so alive about anything before. That's got to mean something, right? Today, I bumped into this guy on campus. He said he was a former classmate, but I don't quite remember him. Anyway, just talking to the guy made me realize how good it feels to be a person again. How good it feels like to have a fun conversation, not living life so monotonously."

"I'm...I'm not quite sure I follow. It seems like you're deciding out of emotions, Cody."

"I'm thirty-one now, Yuki. I don't have a family. I've got all this money saved up. It's now or never."

"But what about the recession going on? It's dangerous out there. Are you sure you think this is a good idea?"

"All the more reason it would work. People would be willing to spend if I can offer more for less."

Cody stopped typing. He was hesitant to say what he wanted to say next. But Yuki knew anyway.

"This is still about that Daphne girl, isn't it?" correctly guessed MyMelodyBunny.

"You don't understand, Yuki," he responded. "You don't know what it's like to be an Asian male in this society. I've been living the life of the model minority. The thing with Daphne, it's more than Daphne."

"Cody, were you looking at her Facebook page again? You promised you wouldn't be doing that!"

"I know, I know. I went twenty-two nights without looking at it. But I...I can't help it."

"So you're saying that she didn't like you because you weren't interesting, you weren't the bad boy, and now you've finally dealt with this fact and decided to act upon it, am I right?"

"Yes. In so many words."

"Well, it looks like your heart seems to be set on it. I don't think I can change your mind, Cody."

"It isn't just about Daphne though. It's about the plight about being associated with a certain stereotype. Look at me, I'm a web developer. I speak HTML. That's one of the most Asian dude things I could possibly do. I want to be something different. I want to be an entrepreneur."

"And you think that'll land you girls?"

"It's not just about girls. It's about respect."

"Cody, you really should think long and hard about this before you make the jump. I know this whole Asian male discriminatory thing is big with you, but you're slowly evolving into an irrational Angry Asian Man, and that shouldn't impact your decisions. I'm being serious here, as your friend. Think long and hard."

"Long and hard. LOL," typed Quanster7, decorating it with smiley emoticons.

Yuki drew a frowning face emoticon in response to Cody's sophomoric humor.

"Okay, okay," he continued, "I'll think about it. Mindy was right back then, you know. Why should I slave myself working to make other people rich when I could hire people to make me money?"

"I don't think it'll be that easy, Cody," replied MyMelodyBunny.

Rain could be seen popping back in front of her webcam.

"Arrggghh!" she punched on her keyboard, "OMG. Guess what guys?! I just remembered I loaned the guitar to that bitch ex-friend of mine last week! Shit! Motherfuck! Sucking ass!"

"Hey, hey. Cool it with the cussing. We've got a senior citizen here," typed Quanster7.

"LOL. Shut up, Cody," responded MyMelodyBunny. "I'll beat you with my cane!"

The three chatted online for the rest of the night. They were lonely drifters in the sea, but slowly they were beginning to feel a strong current.

———

The drizzle had now turned into a Texas-size downpour. It made a slow day at The Happy Lotus even slower. Quan Min-Lo shrugged it off because it gave him some free time to tinker with the restaurant's dry erase board. Since the hole-in-the-wall Chinese restaurant was located in the middle of Houston's Third Ward, the Happy Lotus was prone to a predominantly lower class African-American customer base. He wrote the word "Fried" in front of everything. If there was anything Quan Min-Lo believed as much as his homeland's superstitions, it was the reliability of stereotypes. All he had to know was someone's race, gender or nationality and he would figure them out in a second. Life was easy that way; the world was stupid for bogging into political correctness.

"<What bad luck, the news didn't even predict the rain>," chimed his working waitress and sister-in-law, Hannah Wong.

"<When did you start trusting the news?>" winced Cody's father. "<Ever since they switched the white weatherman to a black one, the weather has been all wrong. I warned you of that.">

"<Huh?>" she asked.

"<Well, it's obvious, isn't it? That black weatherman got the job because everybody felt sorry for him! If they didn't give him that job, the black people will sue. They will riot! They will kill us all! That's why they gave him that position. They thought it would be dry and sunny for the next few weeks, and the current weatherman took a vacation, so that's a chance to give the job to a black man and say 'hey look, we kiss your ass, black man. Please don't rob us.' Understand? That's America, okay? So now the news is wrong and it's raining and no one's coming to my restaurant. Black man equals bad luck. Bad luck to my restaurant! Bad luck to you because you have no tips today!>"

"<Oh>," replied the simple-minded Hannah, "<I think that makes sense.>"

She wasn't the brightest of Cody's maternal aunts, though the Quan family had to provide a job for her when she gave birth to her daughter Megan in America. Mr. Quan had suspected she did so intentionally to grant herself a quick citizenship. Smart move, he thought, for a dumb woman. Unfortunately, Hannah was a slow worker who, as The Happy Lotus' lone waitress, worked far too inefficiently.

"<Why are you standing still?>" Cody's father cursed at her. "<Wipe some tables, refill the soy sauce bottles...you're still working!>"

Suddenly the attached bell from the front door chimed. Both Mr. Quan and Cody's Aunt Hannah looked up, seeing an unexpected person.

"We have Chinese customers?" Hannah muttered in surprise.

"Oh!......Diana!" recognized Mr. Quan in English.

An old childhood friend of Cody's, Diana Li remained exactly like his father remembered her. She was the twinkle-eyed goody-two-shoes girl, with her identifiable bright smile. Had so many years gone by? he wondered. Diana should be in her early thirties by now, like his son. Yet, her highly successful career as a corporate public relations director hadn't changed her uplifting personality at all.

"<Hello, Uncle>," she said, using "uncle" in a loose sense; he wasn't literally her relative. "<How've you been?>"

"<Same as usual. Same as usual>," smiled Mr. Quan. "<We haven't seen you in years!>"

Hannah wasted no time and interrupted, "<This is...?>"

"<A family friend>," Mr. Quan explained, a bit irritated by her disruption. "<Her mother and I used to wait

tables together. She was such a little girl back then. Twenty...twenty-seven years it's been, I think.">

"<My name is 'Diana'>," she introduced herself to Cody's aunt in perfect Cantonese.

"<Wow!>" admired Hannah, "<your Chinese is perfect! Not a hint of an accent! And you were born here?>"

"<Yes, in the States. I'm originally from Hawaii>," she explained. "<It's a bit slow for you guys today, isn't it? Is it the weather?">

"<It is what it is. We just have to persevere. You picked a good time to visit. So how've you been?>" asked Mr. Quan, signaling for Hannah to get her some tea.

Diana described what she had been up to; there was a lot to catch up about. The conversation lasted for thirty minutes—the two talked about her job, past stories and the state of her family.

"<Tell your parents that I want to take them out for dinner in Chinatown>," offered Mr. Quan.

"<Of course, Uncle. How's Cody been by the way?>"

"<Tsk>," the middle-aged Quan snapped in disappointment. "<My son refuses every girl that I find for him. I don't think he wants to be married. He's too shy. He needs to be more like his cousin Duke. Duke is more assertive. More masculine.>"

"<Heehee. How do you know he isn't hiding a significant other?>" laughed Diana, thanking Hannah as she returned with the tea.

"<His mother and I check on everything in his life! He can't hide a relationship from us! I'll know. Trust me.>"

Diana politely laughed. There was a slight pause in their conversation. Cody's father knew her visit was more than just small talk. She must have needed something.

"<Uncle...the reason I came today is because...I need a favor>," she began.

"<Yes? Sure, sure...anything! Your mother and I go way back.>"

"<Oh, don't worry. It's a small favor. I've got a cousin who just immigrated from Hong Kong. She's still in college. I was wondering if she could maybe find a small part-time job here in your restaurant. Just a couple of dollars a day would be enough for her to buy some books>," Diana insisted.

Hearing this, Cody's aunt felt a little nervous. She knew the little restaurant was slow enough already. A second waitress would further diminish her tips.

"<Well>," slowly answered Mr. Quan, "<Cody's aunt here is our only waitress. And she works every day except Thursdays, when we're closed.>"

"<Please, Uncle. She really needs it.>"

"<Sigh. Well. Okay, okay. Well...okay...she can maybe share some tables with Cody's aunt.>"

Hannah Wong started opening her mouth in protest, but she was interrupted by Diana's jubilation.

"<Thank you, Uncle!!! Are you sure?!!>"

"<Of course! Cody's Aunt Hannah wouldn't mind!>" he assured.

"<Can I bring her in? She's actually in the car. She's kind of shy.">

"<She is? Wow. We made her wait. Yes, yes. I'd like to meet her.>"

"<Okay, one second, okay?>"

As Diana headed back to her car with an umbrella, Cody's aunt took her brother-in-law aside.

"<I don't think it's a good idea for this girl and myself to share tips together. I barely make enough as it is, and Megan is about to be in college. As a single mom, how can I support her?>"

"<But this girl needs it. Okay, okay. Fine. I'll...I'll just...I know! I'll take it out of my pockets. You can show me how

much tips you've made and I'll double it since she's taking your half.>"

"<That's not the point. I—>"

The bell from the front door clanged again. This time, Diana returned with a guest. As Diana closed her umbrella, a tiny, meek girl walked in. She had very thick glasses and a bowl cut.

"<Uncle>," introduced Diana, "<this is my cousin Kiki Tang.>"

The nervous girl snorted a laugh.

"<It's good to meet you>," greeted Mr. Quan. "<What part of Hong Kong are you from?>"

"<Kowloon Bay, Mr. Quan. Emmm, yeah, emmmm.>"

"<Please, call me 'Uncle.' So you're here to study? Where do you take your classes here?>"

"<HCC, but I'm only doing it for the credits and it's cheaper. Then, maybe I'll take a few classes at UT and finish my Master's there.>"

"<Wow, Master's? You know, my son works at UH. Maybe he can show you around campus.>"

Kiki let out a snorted cackle.

"<Emmm, but I have no affiliation with UH>," she insisted.   "<All my core classes can be handled at the community college level, Mr...I mean, Uncle Quan.>"

"<Oh, you know. Just to make friends!>" he insisted.

"<It's really okay, Uncle. I don't want to be a burden...>"

"<No burden, no burden! Hey, how about this. You can start working next week immediately. Cody's auntie will show you how to wait tables.>"

"<Thank you so much, Uncle>," Diana said in her sweetest voice.

They made more small talk until a few customers began showing up for early supper. Cody's father could barely hide his delight. The young girl was studious, polite, Cantonese and her animal zodiac sign even complemented Cody's—he figured this out after he learned her age. Wedding bells were chiming inside the middle-aged man's head. It was followed by the imagined sounds of a mahjong tournament, seven-course traditional Chinese meals, red envelopes and Cody's smiling grandfather.

"<I approve!>" blurted Mr. Quan.

"<What'd you say?>" asked Hannah.

He could answer with only a nod and a highly satisfied smile.

———

The wedding reception two weeks later was rushed, spectacular in some parts, but overall, too little food for too many people. The older Asian relatives grumbled about how it wasn't a traditional Chinese-style dinner; the buffet was a bad idea. Those who stood early in line stuffed their plates with more food than they should have gotten. Some even took two or three plates at once. The banquet hall was filled up to the point that it became standing room only. Not only did the bride and groom invite relatives, friends and work colleagues, but they also invited their hairdressers, third-degree friends of friends and random people they had chatted with at the supermarket. Then there were the wedding crashers.

"Cody!" screamed the bride.

She was a beautiful sight to behold in her white dress, perfect hair, makeup and expensive jewelry.

"Get out of the way!" she said, pushing him aside to make room for the wedding cake.

"<Don't worry about her",> said the groom, Minston Chun. "<She's just being irritable on our wedding day. You know how it is.>"

Cody's playboy cousin had finally married. After a seemingly endless series of women of all ages, colors, nationalities and background, he had chosen Wanda Nguyen to be Wanda Nguyen Chun. Wanda was much younger than Cody while Minston was far older. The couple was almost twenty years apart in age. What was even more unique was that Minston didn't speak much English while Wanda didn't speak any Cantonese. Love, they claimed, was their ultimate communication.

Cody could care less about their reason. He hated weddings. A bachelor like him couldn't be invisible for long. There were constant bombardments of "why are you still single" questions and offerings of blind dates that he knew weren't his type—anyone chosen by prodding relatives wasn't his type. He scoffed at the popular belief that weddings were the best place to meet potential dates. Not in Chinese weddings, dismissed Cody. For one thing, he realized, families watched potential pairings with hawklike intensification. When a girl accidentally looked at his direction, Cody's aunts and uncles immediately analyzed their match potential. His father gave him a disapproving glare—that girl is Vietnamese, he communicated with merely his eyes, I don't want my son marrying a Vietnamese girl. They're crazy. And they're probably in gangs.

"<Good evening, everyone!>" welcomed Minston, covering his ears as the microphone emitted a piercing screech.

"Good evening, everyone!" translated one of the groomsmen.

"<Thank you for showing up to our wedding! Get yourself something to eat from the back. There are king crabs, sushi rolls, sashimi, filet mignon, clams, Cantonese noodles, Vietnamese noodles, Shanghai noodles, curry chicken, ham, shark fin soup, stuffed mushrooms, rosemary meatballs, egg rolls, spring rolls, hors d'oeuvres, fettuccine alfredo, crepes, har gows, shu mais, jalapeno corn muffins, baby back ribs, eggplant rollentino, veal marsala, pecan pie, blueberry pie, coconut ice cream, chocolate ice cream, strawberry ice cream and egg tarts>," finished Minston.

The translator cleared his throat. "There's, uh, a lot of food in the back. Just be sure to get some before it's all taken."

A mass exodus of wedding attendees immediately got up and extended the already long buffet line, resulting in a jam. Some of the elder relatives grumbled about ditching the wedding for Chinatown. Among the people standing in line was Cody. He stood observing various members of his family, particularly Duke who was proudly showing his girlfriend, Annebelle, around to everyone like a prized possession. Duke greeted each and every congratulation with a silent and pretentious stare.

"Wah-hah! Hey!" interjected the person in front of Cody.

"Whoa, hey!" Cody smiled, recognizing a recently familiar face. "Marty! What are you doing here at my cousin's wedding?"

Marty slapped his knee and gave out a hearty chuckle.

"I was, heh, I was just about to ask you the same thing, Cody!"

They shook hands like longtime friends.

"Minston's my cousin," explained Cody.

"My wife works with Wanda at her bank."

"You're...you're married?!"

"Well, heh, yeah! Remember? I told you that the last time we met two weeks ago!"

"You did? I don't remember—"

"Yeah, of course I did! Come on! Don't get all old man on me here, Cody!"

"Oh, yeah. Yeah! I guess you did!"

"Wahuhuhuh. What did I tell you? Early Alzheimer's. So you've been considering about us working together? I've got a few projects lined up and I could really use a web developer."

"Sure. I don't see what's the—DUDE, did you just see that guy grab FOUR plates?"

"Sigh, Asian people," Marty shook his head, "you know what I mean?"

"Man, this buffct thing sounded like a good idea when Wanda told me about it, but now it's a complete disaster."

"Yeah, too many people. I heard they even invited their mailman. It's crazy!"

"So what were you doing in UH that day? Are you still a student there?"

"Me? Heck no! I'm a graduate from the Art Institute, remember?"

"Wait, didn't you just say you had a class with me in UH?"

"Well, wa-hah! I'm from both the Art Institute and UH. Haha!"

"No way! That's freaky man, me too! Class of '98?"

Marty slowly nodded with a smile.

"Cool!"

"Hey, you two! Move forward or get a room!" pushed a man from behind them.

He looked like a character from the X-Men comic books.

"Saber—" began Cody.

"—tooth." finished Marty.

They both laughed.

"The Adam Kubert version of Sabertooth," clarified Cody.

"With a little Jim Lee too, I think."

They spent the next fifteen minutes in line pointing at random people from the wedding, giving them look-alike pop culture matches.

"What about him?" asked Cody.

"The Asian Egon Spangler from Ghostbusters."

"Ah, good one. Old man with a hat right there?"

"Mmm, wah-heh, Darkwing Duck."

Cody smiled and pointed at Duke from across the banquet hall.

"And what about that dickhead?" he pointed at his cousin. "The one with a stick up his ass. Who does he look like?"

"Ricky," replied Marty, "Ricky the Steamboat Dragon."

"That...hahaha...that doesn't even make sense! Hahahaha!"

"Sorry, everybody!" informed one of the venue staff. "We're out of food!"

A large grumbling of complaints of Vietnamese, Cantonese, Mandarin Chinese and English erupted from the crowd.

"Let's go to House of Bowls!" declared someone's uncle.

Minston angrily walked up to the manager of the venue.

"You say good food! Enough for everyone! Why not?" he yelled in broken English.

"Hey, hey! Don't blame us!" replied the staff. "You said there'd be a hundred people. There're over two hundred tonight!"

"Fuck, man! You blame me? You hole! Asssss hole!" cursed Minston.

He then hurried over to his DJ.

"<Hurry, get everyone to the dance floor. Play that 'left, left, right, right' song!>" instructed Minston.

"<You mean 'The Cupid Shuffle'?>" inquired the DJ.

"<Whatever. You're the expert. Do something to take their minds off the food problem. Damn, I need a cigarette!>"

Sheer pandemonium erupted. Angry relatives offered Wanda a condescending lesson about planning beyond her means. Meanwhile, the greedy guests who previously hoarded food were now ironically being mugged for it. A divine miracle in the form of "The Cupid Shuffle" saved the day. The catchy beat drew the guests to the middle of the dance floor like lemmings to the sea. Old and young, male and female, angry and not so-angry joined together to crudely follow the instructions of the lyrics. *To the right, to the right, to the right, to the right, to the left, to the left, to the left, to the left, now kick, now kick, now kick, now kick...*

"<I love this song!!!>" declared Cody's father.

...now walk it by yourself, now walk it by yourself...

Minston and Wanda gave a sigh of relief; the wedding had been saved by the modern day hokey pokey.

Outside of the banquet hall, Cody and Marty took solace among the smokers. Neither smoked, but it was a preferable torture than the generic dance music that was publicly imposed on them thousands of times. The light drizzle and breeze were also a nice welcome from the smothering atmosphere inside.

"So, hey man, I know this sounds crazy, 'cause we barely met, but I'm really thinking about starting my own website company. I saved up enough to get our own office, equipment, employees.......everything. It'll be a blast," Cody told his new friend.

"Okay. Heh...okay. Tell me more," listened Marty.

"'Cause I'm thinking, look at us. Smart, charming talented young Asian-American men. Wasting away our lives. We could be captains of our own destinies, man. We could get a fresh recruit of designers from the Art Institute. Get an assembly line system going. Get a hot-ass secretary. It'll be fun!" exclaimed Cody.

"Yeah. Well, wu-hah, yeah. We shouldn't be wasting our lives. We should be captains of our own destiny! Totally agree."

"Marty," Cody said with a stern look, "I want you to be my business partner."

"Wah-huh! I'm flattered, but I don't have that kind of money, I—"

"Don't worry about the money! I got enough for the both of us. I'll pay for everything! Money's not the issue here! You get a fifty-fifty split in power. What do you think?"

"Well, I...hah! Heh...sure, man...you know...sure! Of course, we'll have to get this thing legal and what not."

"Yeah, man! Of course!"

"Wah-ah, why don't we use my attorney?" insisted Marty. "I trust him. He'll write up all the legal documents and we can get things started."

The bromance was off to a good start; straight men who were best friends were rarer than gold, thought Cody. There wouldn't be an ulterior reason tainting it. Things would be equal, things would be understanding and they were on the same side. He felt an instant kinship about Marty—he was the kind of best friend worth succeeding with.

They shook hands.

"Dude...yeah! Let's do it! Welcome...partner," said Cody.

As he said it, a strong lightning bolt struck dangerously close to the venue. It briefly illuminated the surrounding area like a natural light switch. Inversely, the banquet inside suffered a power failure, which resulted in screams of panic. A moment later, an audio eruption arrived in the form of thunder. It shook the ground so violently that various car alarms blared in the parking lot, sounding like the different instruments of an orchestra. Marty and the smokers covered their ears from the noise. Cody, however, paid no attention to it.

CHAPTER 15: PAYING IT FORWARD

Cody's grandfather looked at his grandson and wondered if he understood the concept of "paying it back." It was the old Chinese retirement plan—a Confucian-based tradition where the younger generation spent a lifetime taking care of the old until they, too, became old. Then they were taken care of by the newer generation, a newer generation that obeyed them with unquestionable respect. This was especially necessary with the immigrant experience. The survival of Cody's grandfather and father depended on Cody's advantage of knowing America's language and culture. Unfortunately, Cody's grandfather had discovered Americans tended to discard the elderly like used batteries. His grandson was no different. He acted like a prince—unresponsive to the needs of senior family members, yet always looking to take as much as possible.

Still, thought his grandfather, regardless of role reversals and the dissolving of customs, he loved Cody because blood was thicker than water. This, in turn, had transformed him into a new kind of Chinese grandparent—one who was kind, patient and understanding. He had never beaten or scolded his grandson, even during times when Cody needed an obvious berating. Even if Cody had to be coaxed into having a weekly dinner with him, his grandfather didn't mind and didn't take it personally. Spending time with his grandson was all that mattered to him. He knew which hole-in-the-wall restaurants that Cody loved—the kind where Cody wouldn't know how to order. The kind of restaurants where the best dishes weren't on the menu, where one had to have a certain affiliation with the Chinese community to request them. And Cody, despite outer appearances, wasn't Chinese enough to know that.

"<Eat! Eat!>" insisted Cody's grandfather.

"<Full am stomach can impossible>," explained Cody in broken Cantonese.

"<Then take some home! I know you can't cook Chinese food very well. How is my favorite grandchild supposed to succeed on an empty stomach?>"

There was something natural and genuine about their bonding. Cody's relationship with his grandfather was an amity where actions spoke louder than words.

"<How's work going?>" he asked Cody.

"<Fine is going, grandpa>," Cody answered.

"<Good. Good. It's your seventh year now, right?>"

"<Yes.>"

"<For twenty years, I worked for an umbrella company in Hong Kong and I was proud of it! I never missed a day of work and whatever my boss told me to do, I was obedient in doing it. You should embrace your longevity. Always be obedient and do whatever your boss tells you to do. You take care of your job, and your job will take care of you.>"

Though his grandfather meant well in giving advice, Cody didn't have the heart to tell him how much he disagreed. Being stuck working in the university for twenty or more years was the last thing he wanted; it certainly wasn't a badge of honor for him. There was no desire to end up like his coworkers—routine government employees who stayed until retirement. It wasn't either the American or Chinese dream; it was cowardice.

"<Grandpa...>" Cody began.

"<Yes?>"

"<...start new my company I want.>"

"<What?>"

"<Start...new...my company. I want.>" Cody repeated in broken Cantonese.

"<You want to start a new company? Why would you want to do that? You already have a great life. It's a government job. It's safe.>"

"<Wasted potential my.>"

"<Potential. You have already achieved such a high climb! Leaving your success would not be a good idea>," advised his grandfather.

His grandfather slowly put his chopsticks down and looked at him for a moment.

"<You are my lifetime's hope. When I survived the war, when I worked for twenty years at that umbrella factory, when I immigrated to New York scrubbing toilets in restaurants, and then when I came to Houston as a cook...it was done so that one day you will have the opportunity to get a good job. And you've done that. You have a lifetime government job. Why do you want to throw it all away?>"

Such a deep question, thought Cody, demanded a greater flexibility with words. It wasn't something he could answer with such a limited vocabulary. Fortunately, the sincerity in his eyes did not betray his feelings to his grandfather. Cody had no idea how truly lucky he was. In previous generations, a youth would have been chastised for wanting something from the elderly. It didn't matter anymore, realized his grandfather. They were in America, and Cody was American. It was his nature to take without full appreciation. This didn't make him a bad person; it just meant that Cody was simply always looking forward instead of behind.

"<Grandpa>," Cody slowly asked, "<this company I money need. In case.>"

He did not know that his grandfather had spent six decades to amass his savings. It was money derived from backbreaking labor and basic government aid.

"<Why do you need so much money? You should just do it alone. Start out small. Earn it>," his grandfather said.

"<But partner. I have.>"

"<You have a partner? Who is your partner?>"

"<A friend new. He's Chinese too. Worry you don't.>"

"<Don't worry just because your partner's Chinese? Haha. Of course I worry! Chinese people can have bad intentions as well. What does he do? How will he help you?>"

"<Sales>," Cody replied.

"<Sales...>" his grandfather echoed.

The feeling gave Cody's grandfather an unpleasant trip down memory lane. During his umbrella factory days, a colleague presented him with a partnership scheme. It involved putting money up front for a business that was "bound to make them rich." Cody's grandfather trusted his instincts and said "no"—even though rejecting the colleague's aggressive advances was difficult to do so. Consequently, he was spared. It turned out to be a scam. The colleague stole a lot of money from a lot of people and disappeared for good. This was a lesson he wanted to bestow upon his grandson, but Cody preferred to hear what he wanted to hear. He knew it would be a bad idea, but it didn't overshadow Cody's unhappiness if he replied "no." The old man cursed himself for giving in; it was a selfish mistake he consciously made.

"<Okay>," his grandfather hesitantly answered, "<I don't have much, but I can ask other relatives from Hong Kong to contribute.>"

Cody's face lit up. It was worth the hefty price, thought his grandfather.

When they returned to his retirement complex, Cody's grandfather did not immediately leave the car like he usually did.

Instead, he grabbed Cody's arm and spoke. If he couldn't stop himself from doing something foolish, he thought, at least he would try and give Cody some wisdom.

"<I, your grandfather, am doing this out of love. If you want money, then I will find a way to get you your money. But know the difference between blood from family and blood from a friend. They're not the same. I hope you realize this difference.>"

Cody silently dismissed the advice as unnecessary paranoia.

"<You have made me so proud. So proud>," he continued. "<I don't need to feel any prouder. I wish you would just start a family instead. I don't know why you need to do this. You should be happy with what you have. I worked hard and your parents have worked hard so that you can have what you already have. I will wonder why it wasn't enough. But your happiness means something to me and if this is what makes you happy, I'll find a way to give you this money. I just hope you know what you've chosen.>"

With those words, he made his way out of the car. Cody watched as the old, withering eighty-five-year-old body of his grandfather slowly made its way past the automatic front doors. It was pride that kept Cody from feeling shameful about taking instead of giving.

———

"He got paid too much money!" someone in the room exclaimed.

"Well, he should," scoffed another. "He's Chinese."

"What does him being Chinese have anything to do with it?"

"Don't you see how many Chinese people are watching these games now? Seventeen million dollars a season wasn't enough! They made millions more off of him! It was a bargain!"

The two debating fans were among a boisterous crowd. There, in the Toyota Center, amidst a sea of No. 11 Houston Rockets jerseys, was the public photo op with injured basketball player Yao Ming. Fans were assigned numbers indicating when they would be allowed to have photos taken with him. There were rumors that his career was close to over. Indeed, he looked sad and uncertain up close in person.

"Marty!" shouted Cody, happy to have found his new best friend. "Come on, I want you to meet my parents, dude."

"Hohhh, man, sorry I'm late. There was an incident at Panera Bread."

"What? What happened at Panera Bread?"

"Psssh. Haha! You wouldn't believe, heh. There was a robbery."

"No shit!"

Marty slowly nodded his head.

"Sigh. I know, dude," Marty exclaimed. "I can't believe my bad luck either. Hah! Can you believe that? This guy wearing a ski mask came in asking for money from the cash register. But guess what?"

"What?"

"He tripped while he ran out!"

"Damn, that's crazy, man. Glad no one got hurt. How could someone just trip up like that?"

"Wu-hah! He had help."

"Help?"

Marty pointed at his left foot. Cody was speechless that his new friend had the guts to stop the robber by tripping him.

"Well," replied Marty modestly, "I would've been much more nervous if it wasn't for my martial arts training. Pshew!"

"You know martial arts?"

"Since I was a kid."

"<Hey!>" interrupted Cody's father. "<We're about to go next! I've been looking all over for you!>"

It was comical seeing his father in a Yao Ming basketball jersey two sizes larger than him. Cody had told him not to purchase one until the store carried his father's size, but Mr. Quan had bought a jersey anyway.

"Dad," introduced Cody, "I want you to meet my friend Marty."

"<Oh, Mr. Quan, it is such an honor. Such an honor, sir>," bowed Marty while shaking his hand.

"<You're Cantonese!>" remarked Mr. Quan.

"<Actually, I was born in 'Detroit'>," Marty clarified.

"<But you speak it so flawlessly. It's like you were born and raised in Hong Kong!>"

"<You humble me, Mr. Quan. Hoo-ha! I'm sure there's an accent in there somewhere. Heh. I give all credit to my wife. She's from Shanghai, but she speaks to me in both perfect Mandarin and Cantonese, heh heh ha!>"

"<Ah, a Chinese wife from China!>" remarked Cody's father. "<See, Cody? Your new friend has taste! He gets a smart and pretty wife from China. He doesn't chase these Asian-American women with their back talk. It saves you a lot of trouble.>"

A Toyota Center employee barked out the Quans' waiting list number. Cody's father had an idea.

"<Do you like professional basketball?>" Mr. Quan asked Marty. "<Why don't you take my ticket and meet Yao

Ming?>"

"<Ah, haha. Ah-ha! No, no, no. This is your day, Mr. Quan. I appreciate your generosity, but I'm already lucky enough to be invited here. Heh.>"

"<Come, I insist—>"

Cody's mother came storming towards the three of them.

"<WHAT THE HELL IS TAKING SO LONG? THEY'RE WAITING FOR US!>" she yelled.

"<This is Cody's new friend>," introduced Cody's father. "<His name is Marty. Look, he's Chinese!>"

"<I can see that>," Cody's mother crisply replied. "<Come on, let's go!>"

The giant's height was even more overwhelming in person than it appeared on television. Cody struggled to comprehend how Yao and he could be from the same species. During the brief photo shoot, they found China's living basketball legend cordial and self-effacing. The height differences didn't seem as noticeable after some friendly conversation.

"<Yao's parents raised him right>," declared Mr. Quan.

Cody left his father and mother to meet Marty at a localcoffee shop near the Toyota Center. There were business plans to discuss.

"Okay," began Cody, sipping a crème brûlée. "So I've decided to start us off as five people. You, me, a secretary and two designers fresh from the Art Institute."

"Uh-huh," replied Marty, eating a bagel.

"This, with our predicted estimate in rent and amenities, takes us to roughly $22,500 we need to match per month. Do you think you, as sales, can get us that much income every thirty days?"

Marty took a long look at Cody's numbers. The planning was done in meticulous detail, color-coded and cleanly sorted. His attention, however, was primarily focused on the word 'secretary.'

"No. I can't do this," Marty replied, "unless I have help."

"Help?" asked Cody.

"Wuh, well, yeah. Um, heh! It's not fair that you get a hot-ass secretary and I get no one right? Hah!" winked Marty.

"Well, yeah, I'd definitely get a hot girl for the job, of course. But the main reason I said we need a secretary is because we'll probably be fielding a lot of calls and emails. We have to make sure that the clients approve the design and functionality of the websites."

"Heh, oh yeah, heh. Ah, well...I mean, that's a lot of sales I need to get! I need a...a mediator, man. Someone to join me in sales so that I can be more efficient in what I do. You know, heh-uh?"

"Yeah, you're probably right," agreed Cody. "Okay, let's add a sixth person on the payroll then. A...what'd you call it...a mediator? But that means you'll have to increase your sales quota."

"Psssh," smiled Marty, "come on, haha, I got this, Cody. I'm good at what I do."

"Okay. Okay, I trust you, man."

"Heh. Ha!"

"Oh, one more thing. I get to name the company. I have chosen to call it Mosaic Design Studios. In honor of the former business a friend of mine and I once started."

"Okay," nodded Marty, who didn't quite get the reference.

The coffee shop waitress came to check up on them.

"Okay, you guys want any more coffee? Any more bagels for you, sir?" she asked.

"No. Phewwww. Six of them...heh...that's enough for me! What about you, Cody?" asked Marty.

"No, I'm not much of a coffee or bagel person," Cody replied, looking at his sheet of paper with the estimated number crunching.

"Well, guys, I'll come by and give you your checks! Split?" asked the waitress.

"Oh yeah, heh, split it, please," Marty replied.

Once the waitress headed back for their checks, Marty hunched over to Cody.

"Eh, heh, Cody?" Marty asked. "Got a bit of a dilemma here."

"Yeah. What's up, man?"

"I...I kinda...sighhhh...this is...this is so embarrassing for me to even say, but...heh...ha!...I forgot my wallet. Can you—"

"Dude, no problem. I'll cover you. We're friends, man. But why'd you go ahead and tell the waitress you wanted to split the check?"

"Uh, you know, I gotta save face. Hah! I'm so forgetful sometimes. You know my wife, Xia, she was, heh, telling me to feed the dogs this morning while I was tending to the garden. Then, heh-ha, I remembered I had promised to meet you here. And halfway to downtown I thought, whoa, heh, I forgot my wallet! Heh."

"It's okay. It's just coffee and bagels, man," waved off Cody. "I mean, you did stop a robbery today, after all. You're a hero!"

"Thanks, buddy, sighhh," Marty chuckled at himself, shaking his head.

"Alright, guys," the waitress came back, "here's your check, and here is yours."

"I'll...I'll be paying for his too," informed Cody.

"Oh?" asked the waitress, "I thought you wanted to split the checks."

"We, uh, heh, just had a little discussion," answered Marty. "And my friend felt bad because I paid for his coffee the other day, right Cody? Right? Right? Heh. Ha!"

Marty secretly tapped one of Cody's feet with his own.

"Sure," Cody played along.

He plopped down his debit card.

———————

The most famous chef in Hong Kong was not a chef at all. Chef Bernie "Sky" Mo became an international sensation when his cup noodle franchise, Chef Mo's Big Wok Ramen, transformed itself into a household sensation. Never someone who particularly enjoyed the spotlight, he nevertheless became a good sport with his fame. He wouldn't decline a photo op or refuse replying to the thousands of Facebook fans who messaged him—even when they numbered into the millions. He accepted that particular consequence for his unforeseen fame; what irked him was the stream of loan requests he kept getting. Bernie's reputation as a good-hearted and nice man made him a target for opportunistic friends and family members alike. It was enough to turn the once extroverted business man into a recluse.

Luckily, his fortune enabled him to assemble a personal condo of solitude. Living space in the grand city of Hong Kong was already incredibly expensive. He counted his blessings to have many homes, including entire buildings, when so many people couldn't afford just one. Even married couples continued living with their parents. Putting that appreciation in perspective, Bernie was glad he had a place alone. It was inspired and designed like a Japanese home, decorated with shoji room dividers, tatami mats, oil warmers and various calligraphy. It was the perfect setting to achieve a zen-like state of peace.

Yet, even that didn't make him immune to investment petitions, for in his mailbox was a handwritten letter. Who knows this address? he wondered. The loft was in his wife's name and it was off the books. One look at the sender's name, however, gave him the answer: his brother-in-law Quan Min-Lo. Bernie knew the man somehow had talked his wife into it. How else would Min-Lo know where to personally contact him? It wasn't that he disliked Min-Lo; his brother-in-law had a good heart. Concurrently, though, Min-Lo was also impulsive and foolhardy. Before he opened the letter, the bogus chef had an inkling as to what it was about. He had heard rumors of Min-Lo's son, Cody, starting a business.

The letter read in Chinese:

"<Mo,

Hope this letter finds you in good health and in good luck. When will you be returning to Texas? I have since found several more gun ranges that you may like. Let me know when you're coming back to visit. We'd be glad to have you again as our guest. We can tour the west side of Texas this time, especially San Antonio. You'd love the River Walk and the Alamo. Plus, the Mexican food there is quite nice, even though I don't prefer it. It looks like diarrhea, but it's considered popular. At any rate, I'm sure you've heard the gossip from our wives and their side of the family. It's true. My son is starting a new company. I didn't think he was serious at first, but then I met his partner, a fellow Chinese guy similar to his age. In fact, they're both Year of Snakes. As I've mentioned to you before, the company will be about websites. They're very in-demand now. Even the local funeral homes are wanting them. With a Chinese partner who has a Chinese mind, I'm sure this will succeed.>"

Bernie temporarily put down the letter and collected his thoughts. He knew what was coming up. He continued reading:

"<And that's when I realize—why settle for winning cents when we could be winning in dollars? Thousands upon thousands of them. My son has put in his entire retirement savings for this, and my father has given what he can as well, but I believe with proper financial backing, he will likely succeed exponentially. You know I'm a humble man, and I would never ask for a loan unless I was positive it would succeed. I've consulted several fortune tellers on this, and all have foretold his guaranteed success.>"

The rest of the letter discussed details of the estimated profits and a timeline for returned payments with interest. Then, finally, he saw the bottom line—the substantial total amount they wanted to borrow. Bernie Mo sat cross-legged on the floor and meditated with his thoughts. It was immediately apparent to him that the math did not make sense. This partner of Cody's was either one hell of a salesmen or his nephew was a victim of gross exaggeration. After much contemplation, the chef decided to give Cody a chance; perhaps, the young man's judgment of character was better than his father's. After all, Bernie wondered, what if Cody wildly succeeded? He couldn't pass up being a part of it. Risking things and going for the win was what made him successful; pulling back from a potential business deal countered that philosophy. Even if it did require a hefty financial accommodation.

Bernie got up and found a few clean sheets of stationery. The Chinese he wrote was crisp and beautiful. Hong Kong natives, he liked to say, kept the traditional way of writing the language. He would never succumb to the butchered look of simplified Chinese the Mainland people were learning. The reply to his brother-in-law was short and to the point. He would soon deposit the amount of the requested loan into Cody's business account. It was in good faith that it would be returned. Mostly, Bernie wished his nephew the best of luck.

———

Luck was a big part of Marty Ho's life.

The thirty-one-year old made his decisions based on his superstitions. In accordance with the luckiest Chinese number, he was obsessed with the number eight. His shirts had eight buttons, he counted to eight before opening doors, he told everybody he was born in '78 instead of '77, he took months to choose a phone number with almost all eights. Conversely, he was also captivatingly fearful of the unluckiest Chinese number: four. He refused to accept change for purchases of four dollars or multiple of four. He wouldn't do anything between four o'clock and five. He never said words like "quartet," "quarter," "quart," "quartz"—even if the last one had nothing directly to do with numbers. Those weren't the only Chinese superstitions he subscribed to, of course.

"Whoa, shit!" he shouted.

He was angry at himself for not seeing the red-and-blue car earlier. It was a fatal color combination, not only for him, but also for his loved ones. All red is fine, even welcomed, he believed. Same for blue. But the two of them together were enough to send Marty into a nervous breakdown. He needed the car to pass by him.

"Wahhh-ahhhh, damn it, hurry up, hurry...up... huh-ah, pass me, you old man!" Marty begged.

Not letting chance decide for him, he took action by pulling himself to the side of the road. It took seemingly forever for the red-and-blue car to drive by. After a few seconds, the gasping salesman closed his eyes and took a deep breath. *Feel the chi. Feel the chi.* Once he was assured the universe was aligned again, Marty resumed his driving. Suddenly, a large ringing noise was heard all around him; it was from the hands-free phone system in his car—or as he dubbed it: "the Batmobile."

"Uh, hello?" shouted Marty.

"<Hey, when are you going to collect the check? It's almost the end of the month>," blared a female voice.

It was his wife, Xia Xiang.

"<Just in time!>" he nervously laughed. "<I'm heading to my meeting now!>"

"<Yeah? Is this one of those meetings where you get paid?>"

"<Wah-ha! Of course, sweetie. This guy...why, let me tell you...this guy, he's a doctor. I think we'll be able to pay all of our bills AND get us that Bahamas vacation.>"

"Wow, really, bay-be?!" Xia exclaimed in English.

Marty smiled. He loved it when he had his wife fooled hook, line and sinker.

"<Ahhh, would I settle for anything less? Heh. It took me months to get him to like me>," proclaimed Marty.

"<Is this the doctor guy from the masquerade party last month?>"

"<Masquer—? Oh, hah! No, not that one. No, no. This one was the mayor's invite!>"

"<Mayor's invite? You didn't tell me you went to something like that. Why didn't you take me?>" his wife asked.

"<Haha. You forgot? Don't tell me you forgot we talked about this.>"

"<What'd we talk about? I don't remember this.>"

"<Sigh>," Marty teased, "<it's because you're always so busy. Heh heh. Always stressing. You forget the little details.>"

"<I guess I do...>" Xia agreed.

"<I only had the one invite. I begged them to give me another, but they said no. You know how politicians are. You know I'd bring you in if I could.>"

"<Yeah. Well, there'll be other opportunities, right?>"

"<Hooah, ffft, of course! There's three more coming up! You're always on my mind. Even when I close my eyes I see you...oop! Look! I'm there with the client.>"

"<The rich doctor guy?>"

"<Heh. You guessed it right. Hawha! I gotta go now, sweetie! I love you, okay?>"

"<Okay! Come back home with a check! Our electricity is about to get shut off!>"

With that, his wife hung up. Marty parked his car and whistled his way across the parking lot. The building he walked into was a modest one. It featured three stories with one tenant on each floor. He made his way to the one on the first floor, the one with the sign that read "Homer Flacco, Attorney at Law." There, sitting inside the waiting room, was Cody.

"Sup, dude," greeted Cody, who was reading an old issue of Sports Illustrated.

"Sighhhh," Marty replied, shaking his head.

"What? What's up?"

"I don't know. It's just...I'm so excited, I guess. I'm nervous! Heh. Ha!"

"I know, man! I'm excited too. Can't wait 'til the day I can tell my asshole supervisor Kirk to stick his fist up his own ass," grimaced Cody.

"Heh...yeah. I mean, no, no, Cody. No. Not that kind of excited."

"What...what do you mean?"

"It's just, like, a month...you know, heh, a month before we start Mosaic Design Studios, that's when we need to, you know, haha, start getting clients, you know?"

Cody thought for a moment.

"You know," said Cody, "that does make sense."

"Heh heh, I know, right? Wouldn't want to feel pressured into meeting the quota from day one, haha. Give me thirty days to prepare and it's better, weh? Wahah?"

"But that's...not too long from now, Marty."

"I know, Cody, I know. But I care about the company. I care about it so much."

"Thanks, man," smiled Cody. "I knew I was right into making you my partner."

Marty shook his head with a humble smile.

"Alright," continued Cody, "thirty days before opening day you should get some clients. Okay. Go for it, dude."

"Uh-hah. Yeah. Sigh. It...it sure would help though... if, heh, if I didn't have to worry about my own problems while I was doing it."

"Well, we've all got to make sacrifices. I'm still doing my job. But we got to do what we got to do, right?"

"Sigh," Marty said, looking at Cody with a puppy dog expression. "It's different when you have a family to raise."

"What do you mean? You've got a kid?"

"Ha! Heh. No, buddy, no. Just me and the wife. But that's considered a family, right? Heh. Well, ffft, I don't know if I can handle the job while providing for her too."

"Provide for her? I thought she worked with Wanda at the bank."

"She does, but she makes next to nothing. She's just a loan officer, Cody. Heh. Ha! Breadwinner. That's me. Sigh. It's such a tough title to take," Marty said it while looking at the floor, shaking his head for effect.

"Hey, I got an idea," Cody suddenly said.

"Yeah? Wuh...what is it?"

"Why don't you just take your salary a month in advance."

"Hooohhh, sigh. Well, does that mean I'll get August's salary for July and so on?"

"Yeah."

"Er, mmm, eh. But that would mean I didn't really get compensated. Eventually we'll bump December to November's salary, so what will I get for December? Nothing?"

"True, but..."

"Come on, heh, we got all this dough lined up. Didn't you just tell me your rich uncle approved a lot of money this morning?"

"Yeah."

"Wah-ha! So! For the sake of our company, wouldn't it benefit us best if I were, weh-hah, to give us a head start and I'm able to already cover for my family? That would allow me to put all my focus on us. Heh? Ha? You know? Hah hah heh?"

"You're right, man. It would give us a boost if we had all these clients lined up for the new employees. Whatever you need to clear you from distractions, man, I'm all for it."

Marty winked and offered him a fist bump. Cody returned it.

"Can we do it in cash?" Marty requested.

"What do you mean?"

"My first salary. It's close to one month before our opening already. Come on, Cody. Hah hah! I need it today. Bills are waiting to be paid and all."

"What's wrong with a check?"

"We don't even have a bank account yet for our company, dude! Heh."

"What about a personal check?"

"Come on, heh. Cash, man."

Cody scratched his head, but decided to give his new friend the benefit of the doubt. "Okay, we'll go to an ATM after this."

"Hehaheehhh, thanks, Cody," Marty grinned happily, knowing he would have the money tonight for his wife.

Echoes of resonating footsteps from the polished wood floors could be heard approaching them. They were from a balding middle-aged man wearing a gray Armani suit.

"Cody, this is my attorney, Homer Flacco," Marty introduced. "Homer, this is my best friend, Cody Quan. Heh heh. He's a really good guy."

"Nice to meet you, Cody," greeted the lawyer. "Why don't you guys come to my conference room and I'll have all the paperwork set up for you."

On their way to the conference room, Cody quietly held reservations about Homer. Everything he did was fast—perhaps too fast. He took two quick steps for each normal one that Cody or Marty took. His speech pattern was also unnaturally fast, even faster than Cody's. It was almost like Homer disliked revealing more than what people were meant to see. Then again, Cody thought, what attorney wasn't secretive in one way or another?

"Please, have a seat. You guys want anything to drink?" offered Homer.

"No thanks," replied Cody.

"Coffee for me. Heh heh. Two creams and a sugar," chuckled Marty.

Homer buzzed the front desk secretary.

"Hey, can you please get us one coffee with two creams and a sugar. And also, I'll have a Diet Coke," ordered Homer.

"Wow, 'Diet' Coke? You, uh, you look fine to me, Homer, heh," complimented Marty.

"Nah, I just gained a couple of pounds over the weekend. Wife and I had our anniversary. Ate a lot of food. I'm a sucker for ham," explained the attorney.

The secretary came in with a cup of coffee and a can of Diet Coke.

"Well, eh, heh, you sure look fit to me! Wouldn't even have noticed, hah," flattered Marty.

"Oh, Marty. You salespeople are such charmers. Now, let's get down to the details of your business, shall we?"

Homer went step-by-step explaining the terminology of their limited liability corporation. He explained how it protected the two of them from having clients and banks seize their assets should they decide to break up the company. Then he explained the various payroll taxes and whether these were paid by the employee or employer or both. Finally, the attorney ended it by explaining their legal titles.

"Wait, wait, wait," interrupted Cody while he was looking at his copy. "This says that Marty is the president of the company. Not me."

"Oh, heh. That. Pssh," laughed Marty.

"Why am I the vice president?" asked Cody.

"Well, Marty told me that you both agreed to it while I was preparing these documents for you," explained Homer.

"No. We...never had a discussion about this," Cody replied.

"Come on, man! Don't you remember?" Marty asked.

"When?"

"At the coffee shop, heh-ha?" Marty winked and pointed.

"No."

"Dude, sigh. I really think you're getting senile. Sigh. Well, hefff, hahh, look, you got Treasurer and I also got Secretary. You can't get all the cool titles, ah-hah?"

"It's...really not a big deal, Cody," assured Homer.

"See? It's just titles. Heh. Semantics," insisted Marty. "Come on, Cody, heh, weh-ha, you're really going to make a deal out of something so insignificant? Haha. We can list us both as CEOs on our business cards. That's what people will see."

"Okay, okay," dismissed Cody, "let's move on. What else do you got, Homer?"

"That's really it. Just sign where I marked an 'X' and we're good to go."

Cody and Marty both signed the paperwork. There were stacks of forms and documents. Once they were finished, Homer congratulated them.

"Oh and one more thing, gentlemen," he said. "Should you both have any disagreements in the future and decide to break up the company, I will need to get you guys together and draft how to divide assets and responsibilities."

Cody laughed. "Why would we fight? Look at us. We're practically joined to the hip!"

"Well, how long have you guys known each other?" asked Homer.

"A couple of months," replied Cody.

"You never know what happens a year from now, guys. That's life."

"I doubt anything bad will happen," smirked Cody.

With that said, he broke out his checkbook and paid the attorney.

CHAPTER 16: CROUCHING SERPENT, HIDDEN AIR

It had been several years since Cody's father had successfully played matchmaker. Since then, of course, Mr. Quan hadn't stopped trying; his son simply had eluded his chosen prospects. This time, however, Cody gave in; over the years, he had had bad luck finding a girl on his own. That disconsolateness made it worthwhile for another try with his father, Cody thought, hoping there was a one-in-a-million chance his dad had gotten it right. To his disappointment, upon arriving at the dim sum restaurant that Saturday afternoon, he execrated himself for having the nerve to hope—sitting across from him was the nerdiest and most socially awkward girl he had ever met.

"<Hi, I'm Kiki! *Snort kak!*>" she greeted.

I want to run away.

"<What'd you say?>" Kiki asked.

"<Hey>," muttered Cody. "<Hi.>"

At first, he squinted at her, hoping her appearance would improve through concentrated eyesight. He tried to make sense of her strange bowl cut, which was probably a botched attempt at a halo. It didn't take long for him to be distracted by her heavy glasses that frequently slid down her tiny nose. She had lousy posture, constant fidgeting, poorly attired color combinations, and worst of all, a nauseating laugh that was half a snort and half a cackle.

To add insult to an already bad date, he discovered they weren't alone. Cody's family and Kiki's family were "coincidentally" at the same restaurant, sitting at the table next to them. He should've known his father would try something like this. Their "date" was soon to be a Facebook status.

"SAY CHEESE!" ordered a laughing Mr. Quan. He took a few photo snaps with his phone's camera. Kiki cackled and made a V for victory sign. Two clicks later, their date went viral. "Having fun?"

"Not really," muttered Cody.

"Just having the fun! Just friend, OK?" advised Mr. Quan in broken English.

"Dad, why are you speaking to me in English? You never do that."

"What you mean? Your dad always say English to you!" his father replied.

Cody gave his father an unimpressed look; he was very used to the passive-aggressive back pedaling.

"<I swear>," Mr. Quan protested, "<I didn't know you two would be here! It's just a coincidence that we came here too!>"

"I should've known better than to assume a normal date," Cody muttered to himself.

"<Haha, it's OK, ummmm>," Kiki interjected. "<We're here. We might as well enjoy it!>"

"You know, my cousin Ace would probably like you a lot," quipped Cody. "Too bad his student visa expired and he had to permanently return to Hong Kong."

His father heard the key word.

"<Yes, yes! Hong Kong! She's from Hong Kong! Ask her about Hong Kong!>" advised Mr. Quan, returning to the other table.

Cody rolled his eyes. "So, what do you like to do?"

"Ummm, well, I like to study. *Snort-keekee-snort!*"

"No, I mean, what do you LIKE to do for fun? Not what do you HAVE to do."

"Studying."

Cody took a deep breath and then responded, "Anything else?"

"Oh, I like to listen to music...especially when I study!"

Kiki continued blabbering about school, the courses she was planning to take, how well she did on her TOEFL, techniques to help read chapters faster, questions about credit hours, grades she received from her past, what days she went to school, her favorite subjects, her favorite teachers; the school-related topics seemingly ran without end. It was almost a welcome distraction when Kiki's younger sister ran over and interrupted her.

"<Sister, look what I bought from the ninety-nine cent store!>" the kid exclaimed, showing Kiki a bracelet.

"<Can I sit next to you guys? Is that your new boyfriend?>"

Kiki let out a big snort-filled laugh, "<Hahaha-*snort*-ha! We're just talking!>"

"<OooOoOoooh, 'talking'>," teased the younger sister.

Kiki's face turned red.

Cody's father frantically dialed his cell phone.

"<Hello?>" answered Cody's mother on the other end.

"<Where are you?>" he asked.

"<I'm almost there! Your father wanted to buy rice cakes from Six Ping Bakery! I couldn't talk him out of it!>"

"<Well, hurry! They're all here!>"

"<I wish you would stop doing this to our son>," Cody's mother said over the phone. "<He can find his own girlfriend.>"

"<That's what I'm afraid of. Hurry up and get my father over here!>"

Cody sat in silence, eating his shu mai. He had grown tired of his father suppressing the modern times, treating the year 2009 like it was early 20th-century China. A little common sense would dictate that dowry accommodation discussions were a thing of the past. A very extinct one too.

"<Hey, your dad said you work in a university. Do you have any interest in academia?>" asked Kiki.

"No," dismissed Cody in English, "it just pays the bills."

"<You should be honored to work for a school. All that education. All those books.>"

In Cody's mind, there was no point to continue the conversation. When he saw his father introducing his grandfather to Kiki's parents, he couldn't take it anymore. Without so much as a good-bye to her, Cody left Kiki and made his way outside of the restaurant. Mr. Quan immediately chased after him, catching up with his son outside.

"<Hey, where are you going? The bathroom is that way!>" informed Mr. Quan.

"<I'm not going to the bathroom! I'm getting out of here>," explained Cody.

"<No no no, we're so close!>"

"Close to what? Your dream marriage, dad?"

"This not a dreaming!" protested his father in bad English. "She perfect for you!"

"Perfect? If you like that Kiki girl so much, you marry her then!"

"Just be friend! Come on!"

"This is an arranged marriage proposal, dad. I'm embarrassed! Do other Chinese families still do this?"

"<Don't be so disobedient! You should be thanking me I found you such a good friend!>"

"Friends...yeah right," replied Cody, before walking farther away.

Disappointed, Mr. Quan walked back into the restaurant. He returned to his chair, defeated.

"<Eat your chicken feet>," insisted his wife with a sly smile. "<They're getting cold.>"

———————

"<Ah-huh, my dear Aunt Juicy, let me get those luggage bags for you, huh>," bowed a humble Marty.

His dear Aunt Juicy stood fanning herself with a folded Hong Kong gossip magazine. It wasn't particularly hot, but from the moment she exited the doors of Bush Intercontinental Airport, she hated the late mid-summer heat. Her son, Guy Tsing, stood dumbfounded in the passenger pickup area as he watched his cousin do all the work. Marty took several of their suitcases and placed them in the trunk of his beat-up Oldsmobile. His wife, Xia, sat patiently in the "Batmobile's" passenger seat, watching the events unfold from the side-view mirror. Once the luggage was situated, Guy made his way to the backseat and immersed himself in his iPod music.

"<Huff...hah...phew>," let out an exhausted Marty.

"<I want to sit in the front>," requested Aunt Juicy.

Marty observed his wife's disapproving expression from the passenger- side mirror. He knew she would not agree to move herself away from her seat.

"<Well, heh, Houston isn't like Chicago, Aunt Juicy>," replied Marty nervously.

"<What do you mean by that? I'm your elder, I want to sit in the front>," she repeated.

"<I...ah...sigh...the sun in Houston...it makes this glare. And a lot of people get skin cancer sitting near the front of the car>," explained Marty.

"<Are you sure?>"

"<Well, yeah. Heh. I'm surprised you didn't know. It's all over the news.>"

"<Maybe you're right...I haven't followed the news in a while. I've been reading too many gossip magazines instead.>"

"<Heh-ha, well, it's up to us younger folk to inform you of what we're told.>"

"<Is that so? Well, then, why is your wife sitting in front? Aren't you afraid she'd be exposed to these cancerous sunrays too?>"

"<Well>," Marty whispered in hush tones, "<your health is a greater concern to me. She's young. You know? She can take it.>"

His aunt gave him an understanding stare.

"<Eh? Haha? Heh?>" he ushered, opening one of the back doors for her. "<Your chariot arrives, Auntie.>"

Small talk kept the mood light and peaceful throughout their ride home. It eased Marty's initial nervousness—not an unusual feeling from him due to his heightened sensibilities. He knew Xia was difficult to deal with, stubborn in her own way. On the other hand, his auntie was immensely assertive.

"<Can you turn up the air conditioner?>" whined Aunt Juicy. "<It's hot.>"

The air conditioner was a level below full blast. He knew his wife wouldn't stand for it getting colder than that. A quick glance at Xia's challenging glare confirmed that her stance remained unchanged.

"<Uh, well, uh, sure>," Marty replied.

You dare? Xia turned her head directly toward him in silence, amazed at her husband's audacity.

"<Why thank you, Marty!>" smiled his aunt. "<You know, you're such a good, obedient boy.>"

"<Heh, huh...heh!>" he chuckled.

The voice of Xia's mother ran through her head. *Why'd you marry this loser?* Her husband was like a puppy dog, eager to please and wanting a pat on the head. He was cowardly too, always taking the path of least resistance. It might have been a bit easier to forgive Marty if he hadn't placed so much pride in those traits. He seemingly enjoyed being a tool—a submissive puppet who made them lose face. How many people have laughed behind their backs? The former Shanghai beauty queen felt she deserved better. Why did she marry this loser indeed?

"<Oh, whoa, oh no! Sigh, heh>," Marty expressed.

"<What? What is it?> asked Aunt Juicy.

"<The knob on the air-conditioner...it's...it's broken! I can't turn it up any higher>," he lied, pretending it was stuck.

That was enough to turn Xia 180 degrees on her opinion. Now her husband was clever and fast-thinking, dissolving tension with passive-aggressiveness. Marty had a way of ensuring drama didn't surface. Perhaps he was protecting her, she reminded herself, in his own indirect little method. Then again, he had always done so when they had fought too. He used his sympathy-generating techniques against her. It was a little overwhelming to think he was incapable of forthrightness when the time called for it.

"<Hey, I think someone is calling you>," Aunt Juicy interrupted.

"<Huh? Wha-what?>" asked Marty.

"<Your phone...I see it flashing and vibrating.>"

Marty fumbled around, searching for it with his hands. He had left the phone in the drink holder.

"H-Hello?" he answered.

"'Sup dude? It's me, Cody."

"Heh! Oh, hey! Heh! HA! Ha...ah...haha. Hey, what...what are you doing?"

Xia raised an eyebrow, "<Who's that on the phone with you?>"

Marty shrugged.

"So yeah," Cody continued, "I just wanted to know if you could hang out tonight, man. We could shoot the shit, talk more about our upcoming company. Oh! And guess what? I've got Street Fighter IV! This guy I know called Herman Shu is coming over. If you make it early, like, around five o'clock, we could play it together. I got lots of beer too. Shiner Bock, good ol' Texas beer."

"Wah, well, yeah, sure...I mean, my cousin from Chicago is here. He might be a burden," warned Marty.

"<I said>," repeated Xia, loud enough for everyone to hear, "<who's that on the phone with you?! >"

"Just bring your cousin!" insisted Cody, "the more the merrier. And we could go for Mexican food afterwards. Let's do this, man!"

"Okay, sure. I'll come," Marty responded.

"<Come where? Where are you going?"> asked his wife. "<It's my shopping night with you, remember?>"

"Badass, man," commented Cody. "Well, you know where the CVS Pharmacy is at by Piney Point? Meet me there. My house is close by."

"Yeah, sorry to hear about that, I'll see what I can do. Tell your wife she has my condolences," Marty replied.

"Huh?" asked a confused Cody. "Sorry about what? I don't have a wife. What are you talking about?"

"I'm losing power. Gotta hang up," said Marty.

He quickly ended the phone call.

"<Sigh>," he said, slowly shaking his head.

"<What's going on? Is something wrong?>" asked Xia.

"<You know my friend from Remax?>"

"<The guy with the one arm?>"

"<Yeah. Sigh. He just blew up his other arm.>"

"<What?! Then how did he call you?!>"

Marty stuck out his tongue and pointed at it.

"<He dialed by using his tongue?>" exclaimed his wife. "<That's incredible!>"

Her husband slowly nodded his head.

"<Sigh. You know how it is>," replied Marty. "<Poor guy can't catch a break. Well, hah-heh, I really want to visit him tonight, but I did promise you that I'd—>"

"<No no no. This is important. You should see how he's doing. I can be with your cousin and Aunt Juicy.>"

"<Well, heh, I have to take Guy too. I mean, he's got to see what tragedy looks like.>"

"<I agree!>" interrupted Aunt Juicy. "<Take my son. Let him know how lucky he has it.>"

She looked at Guy disappointedly. Her son was lost in his own world, immersed in the latest top-40 junk songs. Guy felt no hesitation pulling off imaginary butt-grabbing moves while gyrating his shoulders and hips. His mother wished he had more sense of responsibility, a hint of maturity and above all, an obligation for obedience.

Just like, she thought, Marty Ho.

———

The new Street Fighter was much more difficult than

Cody expected. He enjoyed the classic Street Fighter II of his youth; perhaps he was getting too old to deal with the complexity of modern games. It also didn't help that the most obnoxious person on the planet was shouting at him in his living room.

"Use the Metsu Shoryuken!!!" screamed Herman Shu.

"I'm trying! How the hell do you do it again?!" asked Cody.

"Down swing forward down swing forward all three kicks!!!!!!"

"Down swing what?"

"YOU LOSE!" informed the video game.

Cody had lost the match.

"Agh! Ugh! Aghhhh! WHAT IS WRONG WITH YOU?" screamed Herman.

Herman was from Cody's Fellowship Communion Baptist Church days. There was never a sensible reason for Cody to keep in touch with Herman all these years. Perhaps Cody found some strange sympathy in himself to be Herman's only friend; nobody else could tolerate the guy. He was known to be very loud and, worse, very inconsiderate of personal space. Herman was a habitual line stepper. Cody was reminded of that when he heard loose springs bouncing around behind him.

"Stop jumping on my couch, you prick," Cody commanded.

"But you know how to do the Metsu Shoryuken, don't you? You understand that you have to slide your thumbs in a fast motion and—"

"I don't give a shit about the Matshu Dookey! Stop jumping on my couch, asshole!"

Herman ceased and slid down to where his friend was sitting. He sidled up real close to Cody and playfully gave him a massage. Cody immediately swatted Herman's hand aside and scooted away.

"Come on!" protested Herman. "Why can't I touch you?"

"You sure you ain't gay, dude?"

"No!....okay, seriously, about the Metsu Shoryuken, it's done similar to the regular Shoryuken except—"

Herman's explanation was suddenly interrupted by the doorbell. With a sigh of relief, Cody got up and anticipated who would be on the other side of the front door.

"Marty!" greeted Cody, "so glad you could make it!"

"Heh heh heh. Ah-ha...heh!" chuckled Marty.

"Is that your cousin?" asked Cody.

"Oh hey, I'm Guy..."

The buff third-string Division III quarterback casually gave Cody a warm handshake. He enjoyed claiming his similarities to a particular character from his favorite television show, *Jersey Shore*.

"...aka the Asian Situation," he pointed and winked at Cody.

The three of them took off their shoes and went upstairs where Herman was playing Street Fighter IV on the Playstation 3 console. Herman pretended to be so focused on the video game that he ignored Marty and Guy greeting him. They watched as Herman lost to his computer opponent.

"I HAD IT! I HAD IT!" screamed Herman. "Did you guys see that? The Tatsumaki Senpukyaku fails me every time!"

Guy took the controller and fiddled with the game.

"Hi," Marty offered Herman a handshake. "I'm Marty."

Herman ignored him and screamed at Guy, "Oh my GOD! Use the mid-kick combos and tap it with fireballs! Don't you know how to play?!"

He wisped the controller away from Guy and started playing the game himself.

"Soooo...eh, Guy," inquired Cody, "Marty tells me you're quite an athlete."

"Bro, I wouldn't say that, but, yeah, I play a little quarterback."

Guy made a football throwing motion, celebrating successful catches by imaginary receivers.

"Wow. How much can you lift?" Cody asked.

"I'd say three-hundred-fifty pounds or so benching, max."

"Damn," laughed Cody. "How many Hermans does that translate to?"

"Haha, I don't know, bro. A million?"

Herman shot Guy an angry look. He dropped the controller and walked up to Guy, sizing him up. Both Marty and Cody laughed as the bony Herman gave the football player a stare-down. He then surprised everyone by casually dismissing Guy.

"Pssh. You couldn't handle me," claimed Herman.

"Whatever, bro. I don't even think you can beat me in Street Fighter," Guy joked.

"What?!" challenged Herman. "I'll tell you, aside from being a master singer, dancer, philosopher and intellectual prodigy, I'm also trained in the art of Jeet Kune Do. Whoooooo-ahhhhhh!!!!"

Marty and Cody both looked at one another, laughing hysterically.

"Really?" asked Guy with an amused smirk.

Herman started making snake punch motions in the air.

"Well, heh, actually, that's not Jeet Kune Do," corrected Marty. "Those are snake style kung fu techniques."

"WHAT DO YOU KNOW?" challenged Herman.

"Wuh, eh, I happen to know because I, eh, know martial arts, heh," Marty replied.

Herman looked at him up and down and then did more kung fu poses. He spread his legs wide and extended one hand forward with the other upward.

"What's this style called then?" tested Herman.

"Ah, hmmm heh...that...looks made-up," Marty answered.

"It's called Communist Scorpion!"

Cody and his two new friends burst into laughter.

"I'm serious!" claimed Herman. "I could end your life in two seconds with this move! Be glad my secret master made me vow never to use it."

"Sure, bro," laughed Guy.

Accepting the challenge, Herman immediately leaped at Guy, clinging onto him. His bony arms flailed about, landing punches that didn't seem to affect the gentle giant.

"Hey, hey!" Cody shouted. "Don't go breaking my furniture!"

Both Cody and Marty whisked Herman away from the quarterback.

"Oooooh!" moaned Herman. "Lucky I took it easy. I don't believe in hurting other Asians."

"I've seen children bigger than you," responded Guy.

"Ladies, ladies," Cody chimed in, "let's keep this discussion civilized. Herman, don't try and monkey fuck Guy again, alright?"

Herman responded by doing invisible Street Fighter-type uppercuts into the air.

"I'll take that as a 'yes' from Herman," nodded Cody.

There was a brief moment of silence.

"So, what do you guys wanna do tonight?" asked Guy.

"I dunno, I'm kinda hungry," Cody replied. "What about you, Marty?"

"Shhh, ehh, heh. I don't know. You said Mexican food, right? Up to you, heh."

"Alright, let's do that then. There's a great restaurant a couple of blocks down from my house."

"Cool," agreed Guy. "What about afterwards? We've got all night, bro."

Cody thought for awhile and then he smiled.

"Afterwards," chuckled Cody, "Herman can teach us some martial arts."

———

Usually during his evening shift at eleven o'clock, the manager of the CVS Pharmacy near Piney Point took his smoke break. It was a strategic time, one that protected him from the highest traffic of drunks and loiterers. It was the highlight of his shift, the last moment of peace he would receive for the rest of the night. This time, however, he observed a strange sight behind the dumpster area. As he calmly absorbed the effects of the nicotine, he made note of the four shirtless Asian men jumping in the air, high-kicking it in partially acrobatic moves. The bony one, he observed, seemed to be their leader; he was yelling at them at the top of his lungs. The CVS Pharmacy manager dismissed them as harmless and decided to enjoy their actions as entertainment. Once his ten minutes were up, he stomped his discarded cigarette and returned to the store.

"I want you to focus on me," demanded Herman. "See my stomach? Breathe in and breathe out."

His belly shrank and expanded in rapid motion.

"Okay, like, so when are you going to teach us some cool shit? Show me a move, bro," requested Guy.

"You're not ready," Herman replied dismissively. "You haven't grasped the concept of the golden rule yet."

"Okay, and what's that?" asked Cody.

"The golden rule," revealed Herman in a low tone, "is to know that martial arts isn't really an art.......it's a science."

"Martial science," contemplated Cody.

"Exactly! Think about it," Herman said.

"Okay, so now that we know that," Guy concluded impatiently, "show us a move."

Herman adjusted his thick glasses. He then made a space for himself and did a strange combination of jump kicks, spin kicks, wild punches and finger pokes. It was done in such a blur that none of the others comprehended what he did.

"Woooooohhh, aAAaaahhhh," finished Herman.

"Heh, hah! Ahaha! That was so fast I didn't catch on, heh," Marty said.

"Yeah," egged on Cody, "do it again. But slower."

Herman repeated his attack.

"Fist of North..." he explained, "then...to Claw of Shark...then...Force of Tai...Love of Chi..."

He started spinning over and over.

"And now," he concluded, "Crouching Serpent, Hidden Air!"

It took a lot of willpower for the others to resist laughing. Cody couldn't continue his restraint anymore; he fell to the ground howling hysterically. It was amazing how Herman was oblivious to his own humiliation. Cody concluded he was either too naive or didn't care. Cody decided to find out which one it was.

"So show us how to defend ourselves, Herman," he said, picking up a stick on the floor. "Let's say this stick is a knife and I'm robbing you. How would you stop me?"

"<Hah. Look challenge stick me defy?>" replied Herman in broken Cantonese.

"What?" laughed Cody.

"Learn to speak Chinese!" tsk-tsked Herman.

"You don't seem to speak it very well yourself."

"<What? Laugh you me that is touch heart?>"

"Uh, ok. Anyway. I'm a robber and I have a knife. I'm telling you to stick 'em up and give me your wallet. What do you do?"

"What time of the day is it? How many people are there?" asked Herman.

"You're alone in an alley, and Guy, Marty and I are surrounding you."

"But they're not surrounding me, they're in front of me."

Cody rolled his eyes and gestured for Guy and Marty to form a triangle surrounding Herman. They obliged.

"Okay," Cody said, "there. Now you're trapped. I got a knife—"

"That's not a knife. It's a stick."

"—I know. Pretend it's a knife. So, you're trapped and we're telling you to give us your money. What do you do?"

"Depends on the wind resistance."

"Stop stalling, dickwad. You're being mugged. Who the fuck cares about the wind?"

Herman closed his eyes and started singing.

"It's so hard...to say...goodbye...to yesterdayyyy..." he sang.

"What? Why are you singing Boyz II Men? Hey, pay attention," demanded Cody.

Herman then lunged at Cody by grabbing his wrist. Cody ended up poking the stick at Herman's chest.

"Dude," Guy observed, "he just 'stabbed' you."

The three of them laughed at Herman again.

"But I would've decapitated him first!" Herman insisted. "I would have, look, I would have pinpointed the acupuncture nerves of Cody's wrist and sent his heart exploding after a few steps."

"Heh-wah, like, uh, Kill Bill?" quipped Marty.

More laughter.

"No! Not like Kill Bill!" Herman protested.

"Can't you think of something original?" chuckled Guy.

Herman spun around and tried to attack Marty. Marty dodged him like a matador, sending Herman tripping onto the alleyway pavement. The three laughed at him again.

"Okay," threatened Herman as he picked himself back up, "you want me to take the kiddie gloves off? Is that what you want?!!!!!"

"I'm sorry," laughed Guy, "you were holding back on us?"

Herman ruffled his own hair and growled. He closed his eyes and began hopping around.

"OooOOAAAaa,"   he   moaned.

The sight of his boney, shirtless body along with his serious expressions made him look ridiculous. He pointed at Marty.

"Wah-huh. Me?" Marty asked, pointing at himself with an innocent look.

Herman gestured with his finger for Marty to approach closer.

"Ah heh heh," chuckled Marty.

In a speedy, yet clumsy motion, Herman got on the ground and tried to sweep kick Marty. He ended up missing him, even though Marty hadn't moved.

"Hahahaha!" laughed Guy.

"Ooohhh waaaaa!" shouted Herman.

He approached Marty, poking at him with short kicks.

"Ah ha, stop it, heh...eh...stop it...heh..." Marty flinched.

"Ahh yaaa waa yaa!" Herman continued.

Guy thought it was enough. The big guy calmly walked behind Herman and constrained him from the back. Herman, however, continued flailing his arms and legs at the air.

"Alright, okay. Calm down," suggested Guy.

"Lucky, you're so lucky..." Herman said.

Cody went over to Marty and checked on him. Marty was slouching over and breathing hard.

"You okay?" asked Cody.

"Heh...ah...sigh...he got me in a few places," Marty replied.

"Why'd you let him beat you up like that? I thought you knew martial arts."

"I, wah-huh, I took it easy on him," explained Marty. "You know, it's like beating up on a retarded person. I couldn't do that, you know? Heh?"

Cody turned around and walked toward Herman, who was still being held by Guy.

"Well, Herman," taunted Cody, "you couldn't stop a fake mugging. Guess your little martial arts need a little work, eh?"

He playfully jabbed Herman with the stick from earlier.

"Stab! You're dead," laughed Cody.

"SHORYUKEN!" shouted Herman, stepping on Guy's toes.

"Bro, can you please not step on my new shoes?" requested Guy.

Herman gave him a head butt, using the back of his head. The move surprised Guy and stung him on the bridge of his nose. The impact caused him to loosen his grip, making it easy for Herman to squirm loose.

"You have potential," Herman said, pointing at Guy. "I can train you into becoming a master."

"That was a cheap shot!" Guy claimed.

"Like it?" asked Herman smirking. "It's called Reverse Fortune Cookie."

"I'll turn you into a reverse fortune cookie," threatened Guy.

"Ooooh aaaah!" challenged Herman.

He started throwing random punches and kicks in the air, alternating between Guy, Marty and Cody.

"Toisan Fireball!" he shouted, swinging at Marty.

"Uh hah! Ah!" Marty protested.

"Romance of the Three Kingdoms!" he shouted, kicking Cody.

"Damn it! Stop!" pleaded Cody.

"Su Su Gai!!!" he shouted, flapping his arms around at Guy.

The pattern continued. Chaos ensued. Herman appeared to have a thousand arms, swarming at the other men like locusts invading crops.

"Okay, bro, ow, ooh, it's... not... funny anymore. Stop it, ow, before...you get...hurt," Guy warned.

"Water Meets Wood! Hong Kong Feet!" continued Herman.

Among the turmoil, Marty was given the least attention of the barrage. He, too, was secretly feeling aggravated by Herman's behavior. It was rare for him to feel enough hostility where he felt compelled to take direct action—it was tempting, no doubt. Instead, it took an overwhelming need to save face that turned him toward an alternative solution. Marty decided to be suggestive in letting someone else do what he wanted done. As Herman aggressively thrashed himself at Guy and Cody, Marty waited until the right moment when both their eyes were closed. Once the opportunity presented itself, he clenched his fist and gave his cousin a hard right to the jaw.

"OW! DAMN!" shouted Guy. "OKAY, THAT ONE HURT!"

"Monkey Tail Spin! Bamboo Wall!" continued Herman, oblivious to Marty's interference.

"I DON'T GIVE A FUCK THIS TIME."

Without restraint, Guy gave Herman's groin a nice swift kick, sending the frail young man onto the pavement with pain. He added complementary kicks to voice his displeasure.

"WHAT DO YOU THINK OF THAT, HUH? WHERE'S YOUR FLYING DRAGON UPPERCUT NOW?!"

"Heh, wah-huh, whoa, Guy, heh, hey, calm down," Marty advised.

"He hit me! Hard! Right here.......in the jaw!" Guy said, pointing at the side of his mouth.

Cody walked up to Herman and kicked him too.

"That's for hitting my friends!" Cody explained.

"Heh, huh-ha. Come on, Cody. Let's take a breather. Heh?" Marty said. "Violence never solves anything. You guys really have to control your temper. Heh? Ha? Haha?"

Marty helped Herman up.

"Sigh. I guess I'll be the mature one and end the fun, wuh-eh," he said.

"I have to...I have to go to the bathroom," mumbled Herman.

"There's one in the CVS," informed Marty.

He helped Herman up and patted him on his back. They watched as Herman limped his way around the corner and disappeared toward the front of the pharmacy.

"Man," Guy commented, "how'd you meet this douche bag?"

"Church," answered Cody.

"For real? Haha."

"Sigh, you really shouldn't get so carried away, Guy. You're three times his size," said Marty while shaking his head.

"He really hit me. That last punch...it wasn't like his other punches..."

"I'm sure it wasn't that bad," replied Marty.

"Let's leave him," Cody commanded. "What a loser."

The three friends headed back to Cody's apartment with Herman already erased from their minds. They discussed plans for the upcoming weekend and fantasized about the pretty women they were going to hire.

At two hours past midnight, the CVS Pharmacy manager was lucky enough to sneak in a second cigarette break. It was a rarity for him. It seemed like the late-night customers were scarcer than usual. Before he could light his cigarette, however, he heard a soft whimpering behind the dumpster. Curious, he approached it and saw Herman, whimpering alone with a blank stare in his eyes.

CHAPTER 17: LOOSE ENDS

"<Perfect>," Cody's Aunt Hannah commented, "<just like the American catalog pictures from my childhood.>"

For a moment, all she could notice was the two-story, red-bricked town house in front of her. To an objective eye, the home was modest and unassuming; to Hannah, it was Monticello itself. It was a lifetime reward for penny-pinching and countless overtime hours at the Happy Lotus. Never having to live in another person's house again was an idea she could get used to. At the crossroads age of fifty-two, the single mother required only a few things to make her life complete: a house of her own, her teenage daughter Megan and love. At the present, she was around all three.

Megan didn't share her mother's optimism. Growing up in the information age only accelerated her maturity; the independent eighteen-year-old had sought out a wealth of information online. It was enough for her to know that her mother was getting a shabby deal. Worse, the real estate agent who was snake-oiling Hannah had charmed her heart as much as her wallet.

"<But mom>," reasoned Megan, "<this particular home is priced almost twenty percent more than its market value. There's nothing special about it. I'm sure we could find a better deal elsewhere.>"

"<Nonsense>," Aunt Hannah dismissed, smiling at the man responsible for the laudable find. "<What does a kid like

you know about homes anyway? Tell her how foolish she is, Mui.>"

Patrick Mui had sold fewer homes than any other realtor in Sugar Land, Texas. He was, by definition, unsuccessful. Megan had never understood what her mother saw in him. Everything about him looked recycled—from his patched-up hobo-looking jacket to his taped-up glasses. The middle-aged loser with the salt-and-pepper hair had nothing physically, financially or personality-wise going for him. Surely her lonely mother couldn't have sunk so low?

"<Well>," laughed the duplicitous agent, looking at Hannah's eyes, "<your mother has good instincts. The exorbitant markup was based on its popularity. Where you see just a number, your mother sees its magnetism, its concealed desirability, its...magic. Some things, dear girl, are beyond the logic of price alone.>"

Hannah found it impossible to camouflage her blushing.

"<Come>," Patrick said, taking a hold of the flushed woman's hand. "<Let me lead you both around the house one more time.>"

The tour failed to convince Megan the house had hidden charm. In fact, she realized, it looked even more vulnerable than the first time they had inspected it. Vulnerable also reminded the teen of her mother—the loser salesman had her melting like putty. They stopped at the upstairs bathroom where Patrick paid an unusual amount of attention to the individual air conditioner unit.

"<Remember these in Hong Kong?>" he asked, pointing at it.

"<Oh, I do, I do! That was decades ago though. They used to blow the stink right back at me!>" Aunt Hannah laughed.

"<I'm sure glad we don't have to squat anymore.>"

"<Hahaha! What are you talking about? They helped improve our leg muscles!>"

They have chemistry, Megan admitted to herself, I'll give them that. Then again, Patrick coincidentally related everything to her mother. Either the stars astonishingly aligned in their favor or, more likely, he reacted with lie after lie. Her mother was just as guilty of it too; nobody falls for people like Patrick Mui, she realized, unless they willingly let themselves.

"<My dear daughter>," Hannah insisted with a noticeable giggle, "<why don't you venture around on your own? See if you like the guest room. That would be your room. Mr. Mui and I will be checking the living room downstairs.>"

With her natural tendency towards obedience kicking in, Megan did as she was told—even at the expense of possible trouble. The two adults were heard laughing on their way downstairs. The lanky teenager distracted herself by imagining how she could furnish the small guest room.

"<Oh, Patrick!>" Megan heard her mother's voice, "<that's silly!>"

Meanwhile, in the empty living room below her, Hannah lay on some of the plastic boxes. It was her makeshift sofa.

"<I'm so tired>," she sighed. "<All this walking up and down the stairs. I love this house. I just love it. Too bad Megan's stuff is so heavy; we'll need to carry it upstairs. At our age, our muscles easily cramp. Especially the arms and legs.>"

"<Speaking of leg muscles...>" suggested Patrick, leaning to massage one of Hannah's thighs, "<...perhaps yours could use a little tender care.>"

"<Oooh>," Aunt Hannah giggled.

"<Mom, I have choir rehearsal in thirty minutes!>" Megan interrupted from upstairs.

Aunt Hannah leaned over and gently pushed Patrick off her.

"<Yes...yes, I suppose we must get going>," she said.
"<I love this house though.>"

"<So is that a yes on the purchase?>" asked Patrick with eyebrows raised. "<You should claim it soon if you decide. A lot of people were looking at this house. I can't guarantee that you'll get it. You'll have to act fast.">

"<Really?>"

"<Yes, you and this house fit like a hand in a glove. I knew it was meant for you the moment you saw it.>"

"<You know what? I felt the same thing!>" Aunt Hannah said in amazement.

"<Then what's there to hold you back?>"

"<Mom>," reminded Megan, "<let's go.>"

"<Your daughter>," he observed, glancing at the upstairs direction,"<she's seventeen by now, isn't she? Shouldn't she have her own car to drive?>"

"<Ah, you know, giving a teenager a car is just asking for trouble, perhaps—>"

"<She should work for it then>," continued Patrick. "<That way she can find something useful with her time.>"

Megan came downstairs and approached them with a frown.

"<Monkey>," he said.

"<Pardon?>" asked Aunt Hannah.

"<Your daughter is Year of the Monkey, isn't she? She's seventeen. Monkeys have mischievous personalities.>"

"<Haha. You sound like my brother-in-law, Min-Lo. He's very superstitious>," laughed Aunt Hannah. "<But I don't believe in any of that. I say if it feels good and you want it, go after it.>"

"<Of course. Life is short.>"

Patrick Hui gave her calf muscles a tight squeeze. Megan rolled her eyes as her mother exaggerated a swoon.

"<Come on, Mom...>"

"<Yes, yes>," Hannah brushed her daughter aside as she got up, "<I suppose she's right. We do have to go. I had a great time today, Mui.>"

They left the house together. Patrick watched both her and Megan as they walked toward their navy blue Toyota Celica. It was a good day for him, knowing he had sold his first house in ages—but perhaps just as important, he also won his first heart in ages.

Now all he had to do was conceal it from his wife.

———————

"I haven't seen you in days," typed MyMelodyBunny.

Yuki's tiredness was evident on webcam; she had been waiting for Cody to go online for most of the night. There was a noticeable change to him, but it wasn't necessarily for the better. Though he might have embraced his newfound confidence, she liked her Internet friend better when he was his humble, doubting self. Before then, they were kindred spirits, two souls behind the looking glass understanding one another. She knew there would be a day they would drift apart, but she had hoped it wasn't she who would be left behind. Now that Cody was busy planning for his new company and constantly hanging out with his new friend Marty, she wondered where their friendship fit in. She hoped their time together hadn't completely dissipated.

"I've been busy," answered Quanster7.

"How's the company coming along? It's called Mosaic Design Studios, right?"

Cody seemed distracted or disinterested in talking with her; she wasn't sure which one it was.

"Marty's been fantastic," Quanster7 typed, ignoring her question. "Let me tell you. He's already started looking for clients a month before we start. I like having a partner who's as passionate about succeeding as I am."

"I see. So everything's all set up?"

"Oh yeah, we've found the perfect office. It's right in the middle of the Sugar Land Town Square. My office view is fantastic. I can see the mayor's office from my window. LOL."

"So everything's ready? Furniture, legal documents, employees?"

"Eh, well, we're probably going to IKEA next week. They have fantastic furniture for affordable prices. As for legal documents, we've already taken care of that with Marty's lawyer. For employees, we're going around notifying people about our job openings."

"Marty's...lawyer?"

"Yeah. His name is Homer. Seemed like he knew what he's doing."

"I'll bet he does. Why couldn't Marty get a neutral attorney? One that neither of you knew?"

"Because," Cody felt annoyed, "he just trusts this guy, okay? Why should we go to someone we didn't know? That's just ridiculous."

"I'm sure there're a lot of attorneys capable of helping you out, Cody. Any one of them would know how to file proper paperwork for new businesses."

"Yeah, but it's less hassle going with someone that we know."

"You mean someone that HE knows."

"Why are you so paranoid, Yuki? Geez. Guess I shouldn't tell you we're using his I.T. friend too."

"Well, I'm just playing devil's advocate here," she typed. "For all I know he's really this great guy as you say he is, but it's always best to err on the side of caution."

"He IS a great guy, Yuki, and I wish you would trust me on this."

"Well, I mean, hey, it's your business, not mine. I'm just looking out for you. We haven't talked in awhile. I just...I just missed the way we used to talk."

Yuki wished she hadn't typed that. She didn't like revealing emotion. It was important for people to see her as a strong, independent woman. Telling someone they were missed was fluffy and sentimental. At best, it was awkward as platonic friends; at worst, it was an inappropriate statement.

"Yeah, I miss you too, Yuki."

"Who said I missed you? I just said I missed the way we talked."

She smiled, knowing it gave her a loophole for her momentary display of weakness.

"And wouldn't talking to each other require me?" Cody said. "Wouldn't that, by extension, mean you miss me?"

"Yeah, yeah. Don't flatter yourself, Cody Quan."

Cody smiled. Yuki was proof that when one good friend moves along, another one takes her place. Of course, she and Mindy were very different people. Whereas Mindy was openly emotional, aggressive and insensitive, Yuki was reserved, independent and respectful of emotional space. She was the perfect companion for Cody after the fiasco with his former church. Their friendship was good for her as well. Yuki had recently slammed past the forty-year-old wall. Grey hairs, farsightedness, an aching back; how did the years go by so fast? she wondered. Cody, being much younger than her, had an energy that excited her. His bits and pieces of naïveté made him less pessimistic; it kept her feeling young—even when she wasn't.

"I want to tell you something," typed MyMelodyBunny.

"Yeah?"

"The anniversary of my mother's passing just came."

"Oh, shit. I'm so sorry, Yuki. Here I am always telling you about my upcoming company and you've got real pain to deal with."

"No, no. It's nothing like that. I mean, I accepted it. It is what it is. It's just, I don't know. I guess that's how life is sometimes."

"You know, you should hold on to my number. Let me give it to you."

"Please don't give it to me. It's just..look, Cody...why is it with men it's always about fixing things? I'm just telling you all this because I want to share it with you. That's all. I just wanted you to know that I was a little bummed that night and that it's okay. It's only natural because I loved the memory of my mother."

There was a slight pause between their typing.

"Yuki? Can I honestly ask you about something?"

"Sure."

"Why do you still call yourself a Christian?"

"Because we're both baptized, Cody. And that makes us Christian."

"No, it doesn't," typed Quanster7. "In fact, you walked away like I had. That's how we first met in these blogs, remember? 'Dear Alice'?"

Dear Alice. Cody had forgotten the name of that advice columnist for years. He had forgotten the question Yuki submitted; he remembered only commenting on it because he considered Dear Alice's advice poorly given. It was amusing how important people come from the least important moments.

"That isn't related to the Christian thing," explained MyMelodyBunny. "It wasn't Dear Alice. It was your entry about a rant to all your 'fellow Christians.' You told them you had quit because they were hypocrites. You asked them to change their ways, be less judgmental, be more active in philanthropy, that sort of thing. I agreed with you and said I left for the same thing. That's why we became blogging buddies. It was...admirable."

"So, then, why do you still believe?" asked Quanster7.

"Because when we're baptized, we are told that we're Christian for the rest of our lives."

"But we both gave it up. We can't still be something we no longer believe."

"It's not that. It's hard for me to explain."

"Well," he typed, "regardless of whether or not you're just trying to share, you should take my number anyway."

"Cody, it was your idea not to take each other's phone numbers. It made it safe that we didn't cross into each other's worlds, so that we can talk about each other's lives without fear. That our confessed secrets wouldn't come back and haunt us."

"Yes, but what if it was an emergency and suddenly we needed to talk to each other?"

"I can handle it. It's never that bad, Cody."

"Well, what if it was me that needed to talk with you?"

"You can handle it too. Besides, we also have Rain."

Cody typed himself groaning. He then added a frowning emoticon.

"What are you groaning about?" asked MyMelodyBunny. "I can see you making a pouty face on webcam."

"Rain...she's a nice person. But I wouldn't go to her in my greatest time of need."

"So you choose the old woman instead."

"Stop calling yourself that."

"It's true, Cody," she typed. "I'm old enough to be your mom."

"LOL. No, you're not. You're just a decade older. Maybe an older, wiser sister."

"ROFL!"

"Besides, it's not how old you are, but how old you feel. Your real age inside seems to be younger. Much younger."

"That's sweet talk to an older woman like me. Thanks."

"It's true."

"Well...I guess we're the same age then, if you put it that way. Still, I do like the term 'cougar.' It sounds menacing, Cody."

"Well, Ms. Cougar, it's getting late there in the Eastern Time Zone, isn't it?"

"Yeah. I'm feeling droopy. Let me know how the company goes."

With that said, Yuki disconnected herself from the webcam. This was how two close friends say farewell. No words were needed. They simply understood.

———————

"Let's only hire white chicks," suggested Guy.

It was seven o'clock the next evening. He placed an unlit cigar between his lips, the one he bought from the shop next door. Reflections of Hooters waitresses were seen from the surface of his sunglasses.

"Sigh...Guy, stop posing with that cigar. You look like a douche," observed Marty.

The quarterback ignored his cousin, distracted by the sea of blondes and brunettes walking past him. Their presence had made him twist his head from side to side; it was so frequent that he feared it would come off his shoulders.

"Check out this one," Cody insisted, handing a resume over to Marty. "Web and graphic design skills. Three years professional experience. Knows a bunch of useful software and his samples look incredible. Human Resources from the Art Institute highly praised him."

Marty skimmed through the resume with a disapproving look. The name on the resume indicated the person was most likely male. Men, he believed, were hungry for power. If he and Cody were to be president and vice president respectfully, they needed to be free from male employees who could potentially usurp their authority.

"No," he replied, shaking his head.

"Why not? He seems to be very useful. We could—"

Marty shook his head again.

"How about this one then," Cody asked, pointing at a resume with a female name. "Waverly Jong. Oooh, aside from her design background she's also a former chess champion. It hints she's übersmart."

Marty shuddered at the idea of an overly intelligent woman. The last thing he wanted was someone who questioned him.

"Hey, huh, what about this one?" Marty insisted, pointing at a resume of his choice.

"Hmm. A Flash specialist. Patricia Aguilar."

"Yeah. Lots of sites done in Flash these days. Fancy graphics, wah-ha."

"No, Flash is going to be obsolete. You can't update it easily. I don't think we'd need a Flash specialist."

"Um, well, that's not what I heard."

Cody grew defensive. "What? Where'd you hear that? You don't trust me?"

"No...no! Heh. I mean, no, I trust you. It's just, heh, I wanted our company to get the best. Sure, Flash graphics are a hassle, but I'm sure our employees will respect you enough as a leader to make changes."

Cody didn't seem so sure, especially on any mention of leadership.

"I don't know," he said, "fancy or not. Flash is a hassle. We could make similar effects with Ajax. That's why I'd rather hire that guy over this Patricia girl."

"Wuh-eh. But we could charge extra if the clients want Flash changes," Marty insisted.

"I don't know, dude."

"And she could be a hot one, heh. Every Patricia I know is hot. Ever known one that wasn't? Eh? Ah heh heh."

"Actually," interrupted Guy, "I know this ugly chick named Patricia."

Marty quickly lifted his right foot and gave Guy a silent but impactful kick.

"Ow, bro!" howled his cousin, "I mean, this Patricia was an Asian chick. We don't count Asian chicks, right, guys?"

"Wuh-eh, yeah, I meant other girls," said Marty.

"Interesting rule," Cody commented.

"Heh, just think. Heh. An office full of hot women." Marty waved a hand around the Hooters restaurant.

Cody laughed.

"Ah? Huh-ah? Ehhah?" winked Marty.

"Hahaha! Damn, you're right. You're so right," Cody said, lifting a bottle of beer.

The three of them clanged their bottles and finished them, bottoms up. They imagined coming to an office every morning, greeted by an all-star lineup of beautiful women. Each gave the other a nodding approval, knowing they were thinking the same thing.

"One redhead..." said Cody.

"...one brunette..." replied Guy.

"...and, wuh-eh, one blonde," finished Marty.

They looked around the man's paradise and exhaled. Life was going to be good from now on, they predicted. The ease with which the gorgeous women made them feel assured their confidence. Indeed, amid a succession of greasy buffalo wings and pitchers of beer, the men drowned themselves in an euphoria of testosterone. Marty's own confidence boost gave him encouragement in snagging their table's waitress. She was everything he secretly crazed for: tall and leggy with long blonde hair flowing down to her waist.

"Anything else for you guys?" she giggled. "Would y'all like any more beer?"

"Nah, babe," flirted Guy, "don't think I need beer goggles to appreciate looking at you."

The big guy tilted himself on his stool, pretending to puff on his unlit cigar. Marty gave it a slight nudge, sending his cousin toppling toward the floor. Their leggy blonde waitress let out a hearty laugh.

"Ah-heh, whaoh! You've got to forgive my cousin," apologized Marty sarcastically for his cousin. "All that porn he watches makes him socially awkward."

Guy slowly picked himself back up.

"It's okay," she continued giggling. "I wasn't bothered by his comment at all. It's natural for us to be hit on in this job, heehee."

"Wah, er, HAH! I'm sure you must love it all the time then, heh, ha! Haha! Wa-huh, I mean, I would sure love it if I got hit on by everyone in my job. Men or women! Yuh-hah?"

She giggled in agreement. "Tee-hee-ha!"

"By the way," Marty offered a handshake, "eh, don't you hate it when people forget to introduce themselves? I'm Marty. Marty Ho. The goofy big guy that fell down is my cousin Guy, and this, heh, is my best friend, Cody. He's a good guy."

"Nicky. Nicky Zeigler," she answered, shaking his hand.

"Wauh-hmmm. Zeigler," echoed Marty.

"Yes. Guess the origin," Nicky smiled.

Marty nodded.

"You already know?" she laughed. "Get the hell out of here!"

"Heh. Eh..."

"Australia!" blurted Guy.

"No...it's European," she hinted.

"Poland," guessed Cody.

"No..."

"Alaska!" Guy shouted.

"Guy, that's not in Europe," chided Marty.

"France," guessed Cody again.

"Nope."

"Sighhh. I guess I'll just have to say it..." Marty shook his head.

"What is it?" laughed Nicky.

Marty smiled.

"You know it, don't you?"

Marty nodded.

"Oh my God!" laughed Nicky, "how did you know 'Zeigler' was a German name?"

"Ah heh heh heh!" Marty laughed. "Well, don't let me keep you from this happy job. Lots of people need to be hitting on you. Sigh. Hufff...heh!"

Nicky hesitated to move on. Her fluffy demeanor had now turned into a serious one.

"Actually," she confessed, "I hate this job."

"Wah? Whoa?!!!" Marty appeared surprised.

"Yeah. Some days I could use a little more respect."

"That's right!" exclaimed Guy. "You tell 'em--"

"Mm-ah, that's a coincidence, Nicky," interrupted Marty, "because Cody and I here happen to be starting our own company."

"Really?!"

"Yeah! In fact, wah-eh, we're here at Hooters to celebrate it."

"Heehee! Congrats!" she smiled.

"Yeah, but, sigh, well, we are missing a few pieces..."

He smiled, knowing he had his prize. It was only a matter of time before she said yes to accepting a job interview, possibly by the end of this conversation.

"Few missing pieces?!" she gasped. "Do you think you have room for me? I'm good with people!"

"Well, eh, ahhh, I would, but heh, it's a job that's constantly out of the office. You'd have to dress up a lot, meet classy people, I mean...sales...it's, heh, not something I want to burden you with..."

"No, no!" Nicky insisted, "let me know if you guys need help! I can charm the skin off a rattlesnake!"

"Hell!" blurted Guy, "It would be so awesome if you could join us! We—"

"Oh shh! Mmah, shh!" hushed Marty. "Heh-ha! You have to excuse my cousin. He gets too excited with the opposite sex—"

"Yes!" replied Nicky, "I'll definitely do it!"

"Oh. Eh, wow. Haha! Well, um, eh, what do you think, Cody?" nodded Marty.

"I don't know," Cody hesitated. "We'd have to formally do a job interview first."

No big deal, thought Marty. All he had to do later on was set the fix and she would be hired, regardless of whoever else applied. After that, he excitedly realized, he could talk her into doing anything with him as his sales assistant.

"Sigh," Marty responded, looking back at Nicky. "I guess he's right. Look, why don't you give me your phone number and we'll set you up for an interview. Eh? Aheh?"

"Oh, SHIT you guys are the best!" she said, covering her mouth. "Sorry for my cussing. Can't do that in front of my new employers now, can I?"

Marty chuckled. Mosaic Design Studios had now added its first employee. She was blonde, bubbly, gorgeous and, most important to him, probably more attractive than anything Cody could find as his secretary.

—————

A few days later, Kirk Santiago awoke in the middle of his afternoon hangover. He knew drinking on the job was prohibited, but no one dared to squeal on him. The distinct sound of humming computers gave him an indication that something was wrong. Very wrong. Sweeping a pile of empty Oreo boxes from his desk, the overweight supervisor leaned his face closely at his enormous monitor. One by one, he inspected each of the workers' desks. *Cubicle one.* Check. *Cubicle two.* Check. *Cubicles three, four and six.* Check. *Cubicles eight and nine.* Check. Wait a minute, he muttered to himself. *Cubicle seven was empty.* That was Cody's desk.

"Where is he?" bellowed Kirk, storming out of his personal office.

He walked up to the intimidated intern from cubicle six, who looked clueless.

"Did you see where the Asian guy went?"

Before the intern could say no, Cody came back, snacking on a donut.

"Why did you leave your desk?!" demanded Kirk.

Taking his time to answer, Cody finished his donut and licked the leftover frosting from his thumb.

"I was hungry," shrugged Cody, adding, "you fat fuck."

"What?! You know you're supposed to tell me whenever you leave the office!"

"Well...Kirk...I figured you suffered a heart attack and died."

"I was sleeping!"

"Sleeping, eh?...With a bottle of Coors in your hand. Don't you know you could get in trouble with that? It's against university policy. Tsk tsk."

The fat man looked at Cody up and down. He couldn't believe Cody's bold new attitude. Had he paid attention from the past three weeks, he would have noticed Cody's change. Instead, it came to him as a surprise and an enigma.

"Don't test me," he threatened Cody. "I have friends in high places you didn't even know I had!"

"I thought that was crabs, dickface."

Kirk approached himself inches away from Cody, staring at him eye-to-eye.

"Trying to get yourself fired, my friend?" challenged Kirk. "Where are you going to go? You'll never get a good referral from anyone in this university for as long as I'm here! And I'm going to be here for a long, long time. The rest of your life, at least. You can't survive away from this nest. Where will you go? No one will ever hire you in this town again!"

Without breaking eye contact, Cody dug through his pockets and produced a folded letter. He placed the letter into his supervisor's hands. Kirk slowly looked down, then back up at Cody.

"What's this?" Kirk inquired.

"My two week notice."

"You're leaving town?"

"No. I'm leaving UH."

"But you're staying in town?"

"Yeah."

Kirk laughed. "Are you deaf? Didn't you hear me? Who would hire you? How would you get referrals from us?"

"I don't need any. I'm tired of this charade. I'm tired of the bamboo ceiling. I'm tired of it all. I'm starting my own company, tweedleballs."

"Heh...heheheh...hehehehehahaha! Yeah? Then why wait two weeks? Get the fuck out of here, Jackie Chan!"

Cody smirked and walked over to his desk. He had already backed up all of his projects, burning them onto coordinated CDs. He removed the Dilbert calendar from his cubicle wall and packed the rest of his belongings into a large cardboard box. Kirk walked up to Cody's desk and threw a small box next to him.

"Fits your little penis," he laughed.

"Funny comment coming from a fat man that can't find his own dick."

Cody placed his packed belongings onto a dolly, making his way toward the exit.

"You'll be back," predicted Kirk.

Cody let out a long, emancipated laugh.

"No, I won't," he smiled.

———

It was well-known that Kirk made a nightly habit of attending the pack of dive strip clubs along Telephone Road. Even though he was a frequent visitor, the owners continued to dislike him with a passion. For one thing, the butterball was cheap; the dancers hated his stingy tipping. The other reason was that he was loud with poor alcohol control. It was that carelessness, however, which helped a peculiar unlicensed van find him tonight. By the time he had exited his final dive strip club, Kirk was too intoxicated to hear the approaching footsteps.

Stumbling with his balance across the makeshift dirt parking lot, the drunken fat man needed to relieve himself. He bumped into a large steel object, something that turned out to be the side of someone's parked truck. Kirk, however, thought it was a metal bush. As he unzipped his pants and searched himself, he realized that Cody was right about the difficulty of him finding his penis. His soon-to-be-kidnappers waited patiently behind him as a steady stream of urine was heard splashing on the ground. *Tapppppppppppppp. Tap tap tap.* Once the ordeal was over and his pants were back in place, the two ski-masked figures grabbed him and forced him into their van. Through his intoxicated state, Kirk was able to make note of the discrepancy in the size of his captors. One was a big guy, strong in build; the other was short and light—suspiciously about the same size as Cody. Before he could observe more, he was blindfolded with a piece of cloth, had his arms secured together with rope and was tied onto the backseat.

"Drive!" ordered the smaller kidnapper, after slipping into the front passenger seat.

The van burned rubber and headed toward the I-45 South Freeway where they would later head up the Beltway 8 Tollway and eastward toward La Porte.

"Hey, bro, is it 225 West or 225 East?" asked the larger kidnapper.

"East."

"Are you sure? Because I could swear the map said 'west.' Let me check the GPS on my iPhone—"

"Can you please not talk so much? We want to be a little mysterious here."

"Sorry, man."

"Cody?" shouted Kirk. "Look, I know it's you, Cody."

The smaller kidnapper turned his head toward the larger one.

"I thought you duct-taped his mouth!" he inquired.

"Yeah I did!" protested the larger kidnapper. "It must've came off. He was kinda greasy, dude."

"I'd recognize your voice anywhere, Cody," Kirk claimed. "Where are you taking me?"

Cody cleared his throat. He attempted a deeper voice to disguise himself.

"You're going to be quiet and do as we say!" boomed Cody.

"Hahahaha!" laughed Kirk. "What are you...Batman? Was that Batman's voice?"

A long moment of silence followed the question.

"Shit," teased Kirk, knowing he had guessed correctly. "This is pathetic. Is this your revenge plan? I'm gonna so put a lawsuit on you when we get back."

"Oh, yeah?" replied Cody in the same hoarse and deep voice. "What proof do you have?"

"Who the fuck else would do this?"

"You don't have any witnesses, Kirk."

Cody and Guy decided to keep quiet for the remainder of the trip. Kirk, meanwhile, continued asking questions or insulted them with crude comments. Once they had finally arrived at the Houston Ship Channel, the van weaved its way onto a non-disclosed dock. Soon there was a complete stop.

"Where am I? Tell me!" demanded the blindfolded Kirk. "This fucking sounds like the Ship Channel. What the fuck do you think you're doing, Cody?"

Kirk heard various people speaking in Taiwanese. He felt pairs of hands grabbing him; this time it was a lot more hands than just the previous kidnappers. The new kidnappers made the overweight man waddle for a few steps until they led him inside a large shipping container that was sixty yards in length. Cody had known the owner of this port since his days of buying forged home decor. He slipped two thousand dollars in cash to the lead stevedore.

"Damn it! No! What's going on?" asked Kirk. He was now nervously sweating.

"We're sending you to Taiwan," growled Cody in a deep voice.

"What? Are you fucking serious?"

They were, he realized. More conversations in Taiwanese between the stevedores could be heard. The blindfolded fat man swallowed deeply when he heard the shipping container being closed. A few moments later, he felt the container being hoisted by a crane and loaded onto a large cargo ship. The defiant sound of a loud foghorn blew; Kirk began wetting his pants even though he had peed a short while back. It would be quite some time before the ship would arrive in Taipei. Until then, the stevedores planned on keeping him alive, feeding Cody's former supervisor a steady diet of water and ramen noodles.

CHAPTER 18: PURCHASES

Jack Tsing was the black sheep of his family. His worth was based on the people he scammed. His close friends jokingly labeled his flimflamming as his full-time job. He didn't have bank accounts or money in his pockets; instead, he charmed others into covering for him. He reflected on those scamming skills proudly as he looked at his latest masterpiece. She was half-asleep next to him: a beautiful Japanese exchange student whose name he struggled to recall. Miko? Machiko? Mahoko? It didn't matter. For the past five months she had paid their rent, food, entertainment expenses and alcohol habits. Her name might as well have been Yen, because she was money.

"Mr. Jack?" whispered his temporary meal ticket, "can they please be a little more....... quiet?"

She was referring to another one of those parties she and Jack often threw outside of their rooftop swimming pool. Jack never understood why she made such a big deal out of them. If her rich parents in Japan were going to splurge on one of the most expensive Houston penthouse suites, they might as well throw as many parties as they could. Besides, he thought, the parties made them—at least him—very popular. Jack knew he wasn't the handsomest guy, but he had a talent for rubbing people the right way. He often wondered if it was something inherited from his cousin Marty. The difference, he believed, was that he didn't bother deluding himself that his scams were benefitting others.

"Mr. Jack...please," Miko/Machiko/Mahoko repeated, interrupting his chain of thought.

"Sure...hey, uh, Mik—Mach—honey, have you seen my pants? I was sure they were somewhe—...eh, who cares. I'll just go out there naked. I don't give a fuck."

Jack grabbed a cigarette and his lighter, making his way past a living room full of empty vodka bottles and other trash. The sliding glass doors did not do a good job of muffling the sound of the thumping music from the pool party. There must have been at least a hundred guests. When the drunken partygoers caught glimpse of Jack coming out, they greeted him with loud "woohoos" and "fuck yeahs." Walking with a notable swagger, he lit a Marlboro and puffed it with a smile.

"Hey Jack!" shouted someone from the party, "we're hell outta pot!"

"Yeah? Then fucking buy some fucking more, damn it," Jack replied, facing the crowd. "Can we get this guy some cash so he can buy more weed?"

"I've got a twenty..."

"Fifty bucks here..."

"Yeah," Jack encouraged with a cigarette dangling from his lips." Pass a cup around like a collection plate from church."

A styrofoam cup was handed around until it returned to Jack. He counted the bills.

"Thirty...forty...sixty...THERE," Jack declared, handing the money to the designated marijuana courier," five hundred and sixty dollars. Go get us something nice."

"Yeah! Go Jack!" shouted a random person from the crowd.

Jack continued strutting around in the nude, taking a few breaths in before making his announcement like a king. The partygoers were waiting for him to speak.

"Ladies and gentlemen!" he began, "we start out as babies, thinking that the world...THIS world...revolves around us. Then...then we learn that life isn't like that. And that's why we cry. That's why we get mad. Because we're told to think we can't do what we want to do."

Someone handed him a bottle of Crown Royal. He took a long sip.

"But I say," he continued, "fuck all that shit! I'm gonna do what I fucking want! No responsibilities! No consequences! Let others clean up our mess! 'You Only Live Once'! Y.O.L.O., motherfuckers!"

"WOO-HOOOOOOOO!"

He had a crazy thought.

"Someone hand me that garbage bag full of trash right there!" ordered Jack.

With lighter in hand, he set the garbage bag on fire.

"OH SHIT!" someone shouted in admiration.

"I'M GONNA BURN THIS MOTHERFUCKIN' PLACE DOWN!" Jack screamed, "Y.O.L.O. MOTHERFUCKAS!!!"

The trash and traces of remaining alcohol from the near-empty vodka bottles gave immediate life to the fire. This was unexpected, he thought, I was just going for effect. Realizing he had to think of a fast solution, Jack headed back into his apartment and came out through its front door. The burning trash bag illuminated the dim hallways. Panicking, Jack made his way to the building's public laundry chute and tossed the burning bag into it.

"Hey you!" scolded a witnessing tenant. "What are you doing?"

"Y.O.L.O.!!!!" screamed the intoxicated and naked Jack.

Twenty minutes later, fire trucks surrounded the expensive apartment complex. Amid the chaos were screaming residents, including a petrified Miko/Machiko/Mahoko. More were coming out, thanks to the brave firefighters who risked life and limb for their safety. The particularly devastating fire devoured most of the high-rise, resulting in millions of dollars of property damage. Police found many eager witnesses willing to describe Jack Tsing's appearance.

Meanwhile, hiding inside the bathroom of a nearby gas station, Jack frantically dialed his brother's number for help. It had been awhile since Guy heard from him, and it was never a good thing whenever Jack called.

"Come on answer...answer..." Jack pleaded.

"What do you want?" answered his little brother. "What kind of shit are you in now?"

"Deep shit. Don't tell mom. Where's Marty?"

"I'm in a car with him and Xia. Why haven't we heard from you in years?"

"I need you to come to this address I'm about to text you. It's a gas station. I'm hiding in the bathroom stall. Bring a hoodie sweat shirt and some pants. I need to conceal my identity."

"Dude, what the fuck?"

"Just do it!"

When local law enforcement arrived at the gas station, the employee at the cash register decided the facial composite sketch looked enough like the naked young Asian man who had stormed into the men's restroom. The police officers rushed into the stalls, finding only one of them locked and a visible pair of feet near the bottom of the stall door.

"HPD!" screamed one of the officers with authority.

"Huh?" came a voice from the stall.

"Come out with your hands up!"

Without another moment of hesitation, one of the officers gave the stall door a hard kick, shattering the lock. The door swung wide open, revealing a middle-aged Indian man sitting on the toilet, paralyzed with fear.

"That ain't him," observed a policeman.

"No shit, Sherlock," replied the officer who had kicked the door.

Jack had just made his way out, running among the shadows. He was wearing his newly-acquired hoodie sweat shirt from his brother Guy. Together, the two Tsing brothers snuck away through the back streets where Marty's car awaited them. Jack let out a long sigh of relief when he made it into the backseat. His cousin Marty was driving while Marty's wife Xia angrily glared at him from the passenger seat.

"Okay, first question, how the hell did you get into a gas station naked?" asked Guy.

"I don't know. I just did. The employees didn't stop me though."

"I ask the second question!" insisted Xia in her buttery Shanghainese accent. "You responsible for fire?"

"..." Jack was speechless.

"Oh fuck, bro," Guy realized. "You did that shit? That was you?!"

Xia lost her cool. "You stupid milky boy! You set fire to building, eh?!"

"Now, weh-uh, let's all settle down here," Marty said. "Jack, what happened?"

"I fucking...uh, God...okay, I fucking got a little crazy and set a trash bag on fire. It was full of leftover vodka bottles. I then tossed it into the laundry chute."

"You're kidding me!" Guy said, looking at his brother in awe.

"No. No, I'm not. I'm fucking not. Look, the cops are after me. You guys gotta hide me."

"I should let mom decide that!"

"Ah, damn, you guys haven't told her, have you?"

"Heh ha...heh!" laughed Marty. "Just calm down, shhh. How could we've told her if we didn't know what happened?"

"Yeah, that's true," replied Jack. "But what am I going to do now? The girl I was staying with probably wouldn't want anything to do with me anymore."

Marty had a worried look on his face. It dawned on him that he would have to look after his troublemaking cousin. "Well, eh, don't you have any other friends you can stay with, Jack?"

"Come on, Marty! You're family. You guys gotta help me lay low for the next few months."

"You're so in deep shit," predicted Guy. "Mom's gonna tell Dad back in Chicago and it's over for you, bro."

"Fine then, tell them!" responded Jack. "See if I give a shit! Just cover for me."

"Heh heh, Jack, just...please...calm down..." pleaded Marty.

"You're going to have to help us then!" Guy blurted.

Marty looked at the quarterback incredulously, frustrated that he couldn't keep Mosaic Design Studios a secret. "Wah, no, Guy. Eh, Guy? Don't tell him—"

It was too late.

"—Marty and his best friend are starting their own company! Marty is the president. You're going to help us, bro," splurged Guy.

Marty's heart dropped.

"What?!" shouted Xia. "Own company? What own company?"

"Nuh-wah, er, ah, Guy was just saying...um, that is, freelance-wise I am figuratively my own company, um—"

Xia recognized that tone; her husband was being deceitful again.

"Don't shit-talk me! I will slap you!" she threatened in broken English.

"Sighhhhh," Marty huffed.

"Man," said Guy, "I can't believe you hadn't told your own wife this the whole time. You and Cody planned the company for months."

"MONTHS?" exclaimed Xia. "And who is Cody?"

"Well, uh, you know how I said I had a surprise for you?" explained Marty.

"Yes?"

"Um...surprise?" Marty chuckled nervously. "Ah huh ha? Ah heh heh ha ha? P-Please honey, let's speak in *zhong wen*."

She was glad to oblige. English frustrated her anyway.

"<Why didn't you tell me this?>" she said, growing madder. "<You always lie to me! Don't think I'm stupid! I can bring up divorce papers again if I have to. How much money are you putting down for this business? What is it about?>"

As the couple conversed back and forth in Mandarin Chinese, the two brothers began discussing the upcoming company. The more Guy spoke of it, the more Jack grew excited about the freeloading opportunities. This new partner of Marty's, Cody Quan, seemed wealthy from how his brother had described him.

"I want in!" Jack demanded.

The next few weeks passed in a blur. Cody not only dared to dream; he felt entitled to it. As he and Marty's family were doing a massive office shopping spree, his vision of the office kept getting bolder. He wanted custom granite floors, walls with flowing water, giant monitor touch screens. The other guys had similar thoughts, but it was the lone woman, Xia, who kept their purchases realistic.

"You cannot waste the money," she claimed. "You need to save some."

They settled for self-assembled furniture from IKEA, Super Target and Sam's Club. Marty talked his way into the Apple Store, at least. Even with the pressure from Xia to keep the budget low, Cody insisted on splurging whenever she wasn't around.

"Don't worry about it!" he kept saying. "Money's not an issue."

Indeed, he had never seen so much in his bank account before; it was easy to forgive him for thinking there was an infinite supply of funds. Just when he, Marty and Guy had grown exhausted from splurging, they went out and splurged some more. There were new wardrobes and fancy restaurants, cool gadgets and company car leasing. Marty enjoyed taking Nicky Ziegler out for shopping and dates—it was part of her job interview, he claimed.

All that fun eventually gave way to work. Once the construction company had finished their office's setup, the two best friends and business partners began blueprinting which furniture went where. Cody sighed and smiled as he envisioned the area where his lovely future secretary would be. *Hello, Mr. Quan,* she would greet him. *Hey baby, you're a sight for sore eyes,* he would respond to her. *Want a massage? Why don't you tell me all about it, Mr. Quan?* He could hardly contain his excitement; it was all going to happen very soon.

"Self-assembly office furniture coming through!!!" barked Guy.

The big lug's booming presence curtailed Cody's daydreaming. His mind was back in the office where a makeshift crew was putting the IKEA purchases together.

"This is the job your I.T. man did?" pouted Herman as he inspected the computer cables. "You should have asked me to do it. I'm the master at I.T.!"

"The hell you are," critiqued Guy. "The only thing you master is masturbation."

Guy bellowed at his own joke, believing it was more clever than it actually was.

"Real classy," commented Herman.

"I'm all about class," Guy said, chugging a carton of milk.

The office was like their own tree house—a place to call their own. There was no boss, no clock, no meddling elders telling them what to do. Everyone was happy and in good spirits. Even Marty's cousin, Jack, whom Cody had just met that same evening, contributed without complaining. The self-assembled furniture was put together in an efficient time frame, enough to call for an early dinner of shrimp fried rice and sticky buns, courtesy of Cody's father at the Happy Lotus.

"No...yer, ah...no..." Marty was hovering around the desks, looking for various other ways to arrange the furniture.

"What is it? What's going on?" asked Cody. "Come eat with us, man."

"Probably a luck thing," muttered Guy. "Hey, we got any more sriracha sauce?"

Marty muttered random comments about poor feng shui and the number of desks. When he started arranging the desks himself, Cody approached him and placed a hand on his shoulder.

"Hey, it's okay. You're from Detroit, man," Cody said. "We don't believe in that old world superstition here."

Marty wasn't hearing it; he was too lost in his own irrationalities.

"We can't have the desks facing north. It...doesn't it

look like a classroom format to you? We want them to face us. This way. East."

"Okay, well, duly noted," Cody shrugged. "We can do that after dinner."

"No, it's...heh, well, we got to do it now. It's like a running faucet. We're pouring bad luck into our office."

"Jesus, you're like my dad."

Cody walked back to the others and continued eating with them. Every once in awhile, he turned around and observed Marty's obsessive compulsiveness. He seemed possessed, revealing a vulnerable, superstitious side to him.

"You know what this place needs?!" Guy declared, clearing the air of awkward silence. "A little Akon!"

He began playing an Akon song on his new Apple laptop. He set the volume to maximum, turning the office into a club. Guy grabbed a sticky bun and began dancing to the music. He swung his hips and rubbed his nipples, lip-synching to the lyrics.

Girl, I can't notice but to notice you... noticing me...

"Mmmahhhuhhhh-auh! Baby baby baby!" sang Herman off-key. His words were not a part of the song.

"And you know what else this place needs?" added a smiling Jack. He took out a large bottle of whiskey from his backpack. "A little Southern Comfort."

"Hey! Where you get it?" inquired Xia.

"Swiped it with Marty's Mosaic Design Studios credit card. I knew they'd use the Sugar Land Town Center zip code for their verification," he said proudly.

"What?!" she gasped. "You steal it from my husband?"

"Hey, I slipped it back to him," shrugged Jack. "All's good."

He began pouring shots into disposable plastic red cups, handing one to each of them.

"Come on, Marty!" he insisted. "Leave the feng shui shit alone for a moment and join us."

Marty had single-handedly finished moving all of the desks to face eastward, although he still wasn't satisfied that there were four of them. Four. Death. This was a bad omen.

"Dude!" ushered Jack.

"Mm-ha, okay, heh," Marty obliged, joining them.

Jack began with a toast, "To a great and—"

"TO ASIANS KICKING ASS AND NOT TAKING SHIT FROM ANYONE!" interrupted Herman.

Jack glared at him in silence. The toast started over again.

"To a great and prosperous beginning," said Jack, "and a special thank-you to Marty for starting this company."

"Well, uh, heh, it's not just my company..." smiled Marty, looking at Cody.

Cody smiled back, thinking he was given credit.

"...it's also made possible by all of you helping my company," Marty finished instead.

Cody's smile quickly turned into a confused frown.

"*Gan Bei*!" screamed Xia, which meant 'bottoms up' in Mandarin Chinese.

"GUN BOY!" imitated Guy in bad Chinese.

They all drank their cups in one gulp.

"Eh, Jack?" observed Marty. "This, heh, this tastes like apple juice."

"Yeah, apple juice..." Xia agreed.

"Shhhh..." Jack winked.

They watched as Herman walked toward the other side of the room. Jack signaled for the rest to be in on the joke as he poured a bigger portion of whisky into another cup. He walked up to Herman, offering a second shot.

"You...you think I can't handle this?" Herman shouted. "I drink straight vodka, son! I'll outdrink all of you!"

Jack repeated the shots until Herman became drunk, half shouting and half singing barely recognizable Michael Jackson songs. Cody and Jack led their wasted friend outside where he began serenading the people around Town Square.

"Why? Why?" Herman lunged himself toward a woman holding shopping bags. "Tell them it...tell them that it's human nature...I like it this way!!! Hic."

"Get away from me!" the woman cried, hitting him with her shopping bags.

From the second-floor office window, the rest of Cody's friends laughed at Herman.

"This so mean!" Xia protested. "But so funny!"

"You are not alone...oooooh ahhhh," Herman sang, grabbing a black security guard. "Mr. Black Guy Police Officer! They don't...they don't care about us!"

"Oh, shit," muttered Jack, who walked back to the office. "That cop is going to arrest that fucker."

"Nah, he'll be okay, it's just a security guard," observed Cody.

They witnessed the security guard talking with the intoxicated young man. Then Herman did something unexpected—he pointed at the direction of their office window.

"Shut off the lights! Shut off the lights!" ordered Cody.

Marty quickly shut them off. From the window, they witnessed a drunk Herman leading the guard toward their building. Minutes later they heard knocking on the office front door. After two more knocks and no response, they heard footsteps walking away. Minutes later, Jack slowly opened the door. In front of them, they found a nearly passed-out Herman outside. He was rubbing his genital area.

"Well, bros," quipped Guy, "I guess he really is the master of masturbating."

"Hey," suggested Jack, "let's drag him somewhere."

"A horse stable," laughed Cody.

"Gay bar bathroom," brainstormed Guy.

"I know!" laughed Jack. "How about—"

"No no no!" lectured Xia. "This too much joke already! You take Herman to his home now!"

"Aw, come on, Xia..." protested Jack.

"NOW!" she ordered.

The boys collectively wished Marty's ball and chain hadn't tagged along; she was never any fun. Following her demands, they carried the unconscious Herman to Marty's Oldsmobile. Once in, Cody led them to Herman's residence— the one he shared with his mother. With little regard for subtlety, Guy repeatedly nudged and tapped his face.

"Hey! Wake up, bro!" urged the big guy.

"Hunh?" uttered Herman.

"You're home, Herman," explained Cody. "Go home."

The intoxicated debauchee stumbled outside. The others watched from the car as he looked around and then took off his pants. Herman then proceeded to squat in his neighbor's flower bed and answered nature's second calling.

"Dang!" observed Guy. "He's like an animal!"

"Why he not use his house bathroom?" wondered Xia.

"I dunno," Cody shrugged. "Guess he didn't know people were watching."

"Let's get out of here," Jack suggested.

The Oldsmobile drove off, leaving Herman to do his business.

Time froze the next night when Sonia Rodriguez walked into the lobby of the Sugar Land Marriott hotel. The bellboys collided with one another, trying to be the first to offer help. This, of course, was natural for one of the most beautiful young women in Texas. Whoever claimed that beauty was subjective hadn't met Sonia. She had a perfectly symmetrical face, an irresistible voluptuous body, smooth tan skin, alluring eyes and a Cindy Crawford mole. Most of all, Sonia boasted the one important feature that men primarily care about: a perfect pair of colossal-sized breasts. Her low-cut dress shirt accentuated that asset. Complementing it was a skirt that looked like business wear except for its unusually short length. Her attire was slightly unfitting for a job interview, but she didn't think her potential employers would mind.

"Sonia!" Cody fought himself from slobbering. "So glad you could make it!"

Their location for the job interviews was suggested by Cody; the hotel lobby near their office building was so much cozier and spacious. It also allowed the fun of surprise once their new employees saw the office on their first day of work. Sonia was curious to find another though less-attractive girl sitting along for the interview. The idea of interviewing rival candidates together was Cody and Marty's way of having girls grovel over them.

"Hi, I'm Sonia, nice to meet you," she smiled, shaking the other girl's hand.

The other girl contrasted her; she was dressed conservatively professional with portfolio in hand. By all means, she exemplified class, but that probably escaped the notice of her two enraptured interviewers. Sonia knew she was going to destroy this young woman.

Cody started the dialog rolling. "Since we've got a lot of interviewees today, we're conducting our interviews with two of you at a time."

"Mm-huh, let's start," nodded Marty. "What do you feel that you can contribute to this position?"

"Well—" they both began, then stopping to let the other go first.

"No, no. You go ahead," insisted a smiling Sonia.

The other girl gladly accepted.

"Well," she began, "as someone who has had vast experience doing secretarial work, I offer not only proven skills directly related to the job but also additional skills that would benefit the goals of the company. These skills, as stated on my resume, include extensive knowledge of all of the Microsoft Office products, Adobe Acrobat, Quickbooks, Peachtree, general HTML and MySQL database languages."

She sat upright, impressed with herself. The two men frowned.

"And, heh-eh, what about you Sonia?" smiled Marty.

"Well," Sonia grinned. "As for me, I've been known to give a fax or copy machine a nice swift kick whenever it was needed. And maybe I'm not as tech savvy as Ms. Microsoft Excel here, but sometimes what a customer really needs is a calm, warm voice. A voice that makes them feel like they're cared for. Caressed. Touched."

Guy's jaw dropped. Cody and Marty immersed themselves into her charm.

"Any more questions?" laughed Sonia.

"Well, uh, yes, certainly," stumbled Marty. "Heh. Ha...haha. Okay, wuh-heh, what would you say are your greatest strengths and weaknesses?"

Both girls hesitated to answer before the other.

"Why don't you go first, Sonia?" insisted Cody.

"Oh, this one's easy," she laughed. "My greatest strength is that I know what my weaknesses are. And then I turn them into strengths."

The three men nodded to one another in agreement. It became clear to Sonia that what she said made sense to them even when she didn't. Cody gestured for the other girl to respond.

"I guess how I would describe my strengths," the other girl began, "would be my ability to time manage and multitask. When I'm given a deadline, I aim to finish my tasks way before the given time limit. This way, there's plenty of room for fact-checking so that I'm ensured that everything is done right. And, above all, help maintain an overall positive image for the company. As for my weaknesses, my drive to succeed may sometimes override my calmness. I understand that while everyone in the company will want to do his or her job, sometimes I have to remind myself that everyone's passions manifest themselves differently."

"Wow," Guy said, still thinking about Sonia's answer. "Changing weaknesses to strengths so that there are no more weaknesses. That's deep."

The busty vixen tilted her head and winked at him.

While Marty conducted the rest of the interview, Cody found himself mesmerized by Sonia's allure. She was the one in his previous daydreaming—the one who asked how his day went and gave him a massage. The faceless secretary in his fantasies now had a face. It was more than enough for him to make up his mind about hiring her.

"Okay uh, that, well, that concludes our interview for today," Marty nodded. "Cody and I will, heh, uh, evaluate who we think is best for the, uh, job and we'll let you both know."

"Well, it was so nice meeting the three of you," Sonia said in a sweet tone. "It would be a shame if this was the last time that we met."

"Oh, trust me. It won't," chuckled Guy, ogling her with his eyes.

They had almost forgotten they had more interviews for the secretary and mediator positions. A whole lot more. There were forty women in all, most of them pretty and all of them giving the three men their utmost attention. Cody was on top of a pedestal, happy to wield so much power and persuasion. If only Daphne Lee could see me now, he sneered to himself. The river of beautiful women came to its end two hours later when they reached their final interview. The guys discovered it was possible to overdose on the opposite sex.

"So," asked an exhausted Marty of their final two candidates, "how would you breast evaluate success?.......I mean, heh-ha, best evaluate success, heh."

"Success," repeated the latest interviewee, "is something that I strive for no matter what I'm doing. Whether if it's in your office or simply going out and running in triathlons. I want to be the best. It's how I'm wired. And nothing would please me more than to win with your new company."

Perhaps, thought Cody, it was the fatigue in him, but the woman who said that stood out. She was absolutely ravishing, with movie star looks, perfect almond eyes, smooth skin and perfect long black hair. And, of course, lovely breasts—that detail was inescapable to him. However, those details alone, at least for a night filled with beautiful women, didn't make her stand out. This particular young woman also possessed a keen intellect and articulation. He took a look at her resume and reminded himself of her name once more.

April Finley.

When the interview ended, the three men walked over to Starbucks. They had experienced a well-found high, realizing it was possible to consistently enjoy the company of beautiful women. Each was eager to share their experience.

"So," Cody started, stirring his coffee with a swaggering expression, "what do you guys think?"

Guy could barely wait for Cody to finish before responding. "Oh my God!!! I could fuck that Sonia girl in half! I mean, did you see her tits? Did you? Did you?!"

"Guy," Marty pleaded, "heh-ah, keep it civilized, ok?"

"I'm serious, bros!" Guy continued. "I had a boner the whole time!"

"Ugh!" Cody flinched. "Marty? What do you think?"

"I think...sigh...it's too bad I already made a deal with Nicky Ziegler, heh."

"It's not too late," mentioned Cody. "She didn't sign anything."

"True," Marty replied. "But, I'll look like the bad guy. I can't do that. What would she think of me? Sighhhh."

"Who cares what she'll think of you? Choose whoever you want to choose," reasoned Cody.

"I can't...I just...huh-ah...I just can't."

"You liked that April girl, huh?" pried Cody.

"Oh maaaan, April," interrupted Guy, "I'm so gonna whip my dick out tonight and think about her. First thing I'll do tonight!"

Cody and Marty continued to ignore the quarterback's overt self-romancing.

"Well-yuh, yeah. Heh. HA! But. But no...no, no...I can't ask for a second sales assistant. That...that would affect our, heh, quota. No," Marty said.

"Which one do you like more?" inquired Cody.

"Sigh. I'll just...I'll just stick with Nicky."

"You didn't exactly answer the question, Marty."

"Well, they both have different strengths. Heh. Can't say which one I like more. It would be good to have both. It would certainly, muh-uh, triple our sales, heh heh ha."

"No, we can't have both," replied Cody.

"Mmm, you sure? I mean...heh...you sure?" Marty started getting defensive. "Dude, it's...that is to, uh, say...it's not fair that you have three girls and I only get one. Three to two...that's all I'm saying, Cody. Heh...you know? Hah? Wuh-ah?"

"Three girls? I thought I get to choose our secretary. That's it."

"Mm, well, what about the two designers?"

"Marty, we're a design and web company!" explained Cody. "I'm choosing those two based on individual skill. It's one thing to have hot girls as our secretary and sales assistant, but the designers will be sitting behind a computer all day long. No one will care what they look like."

"Except for you."

"What?"

"No, um, heh. Haha, it's okay, Cody. Shhh. Heh, ffft. I get it."

"Get what?"

"I saw that Flash specialist when you were interviewing her the other day. Come on, Cody, she's a looker, heh. HA!"

"What do you mean?!" asked Cody. "You were the one who recommended her at Hooters. You said we should hire a Flash specialist."

"Okay, whatever, huh...it's okay, heh. HA! Wuuuhhh...hah!"

"Guy, isn't that what he said that day?" Cody asked, looking at Marty's cousin for confirmation.

"Well, to be honest," Guy admitted, "I wasn't paying any attention, bro. Too many hot Hooters waitresses when we were there."

"See?! Huh-heh, you've got some selective memory, Cody. I, hah, I never said that. Seriously."

"I swear, I wasn't picking that Patricia girl out for looks," Cody protested. "And, if it makes you feel better, the other designer I chose isn't a looker at all."

"Oh-ah, don't tell me you picked that ugly flat-chested little Asian girl," Marty said.

"Hey, Lydia is very skilled. You should have seen her portfolio! It's important to have someone with experience to help Patricia out."

"Sigh. Well, I guess. You still have two hot girls. It's not fair."

"They're not MY hot girls. They're OUR hot girls, Marty. You can still talk with them."

"Well, I'm just, heh, it's about fairness. We're partners. Okay, I, eh, I guess I'll be the mature and understanding one and let you have two. Sigh. I really wanted that April girl too. But, in the interest in preserving our budget..." Marty shook his head in sadness.

"Geez, Patricia is pretty and all, but I wouldn't call her hot," Cody reasoned.

"Hey!" Guy proclaimed, "I've got an idea! Why don't we remove that ugly designer and replace her with April! We can teach her how to design, right?"

"It doesn't work that way," Cody scoffed. "It's a skill you develop."

"Right. Develop. We can train a hot girl to design, can't we? I mean, how difficult could it be?" asked Guy.

"No. Just no. We're trying to actually succeed here. That means getting people who can do the job."

"Just sayin', bro," Guy shrugged.

It was getting closer to the start of the first day. Cody and Marty excitedly spoke about the good times they anticipated for their company. So far it was smooth sailing. And now, it was time for celebration.

The following Saturday evening, the assembled staff, close friends and family of the new company celebrated at The Oceanaire. They had reserved a large table with the best view of the five-star restaurant. Each business partner was on opposite ends of the table, sitting next to the ones they were most associated with. Cody sat next to Herman and his longtime friend Mindy Cheung, whom he hadn't seen in awhile. Marty sat close to his wife, Xia, along with his cousins Guy and Jack. The middle part of the table was reserved for the new employees: Sonia, Nicky, Patricia and Lydia. Marty, in a classy new Banana Republic suit and tie, lifted a glass of red wine to toast the occasion.

"Wuh-ha, several months ago, Cody and I found out that we were pregnant." Marty let a few seconds for the laughter to die down, then continued. "Mm-huh, no not that kind. We were about to give birth to an idea, and that idea, heh, is born today."

Sonia began clapping. The others followed with polite applause.

"And here we are," Marty grinned, "reality."

Louder applause came, joined with whistles, hoots and hollers.

"<FEEL GOOD SPIRIT WE LIFT>!" screamed Herman in incomprehensible Chinese.

Their jubilation caught the attention of several patrons, who viewed their table with curiosity.

"Er, hah, yes, Herman. Yes," Marty sheepishly replied.

"OHHHHH, LET'S STAY TOGETHERRRR," sung Herman, "...LOVIN' YOU WHETHER, AHH-EHH, WHETHER TIMES ARE GOOD OR BAD OR HAPPY OR SAD AHHH..."

"MAN, SHUT THE FUCK UP AND LET HIM TALK!" Guy hissed from across the table.

Herman slumped back down into his chair.

"Heh heh...ah heh heh...thank you, er, ah Guy," Marty cleared his throat and resumed. "Yes, uh, we're very lucky to have you all here. I spoke with Cody and we both agreed that, haha, that you all are our best choice in who we wanted. And without further ado, Cody, do you, ah, have a few words you'd like to say? Ah-heh? Haha?"

Cody finished off his red snapper and slowly got up, wiping his mouth with his napkin. He thought for a moment about what he would say, looking at each and every one of them. This was the moment he had waited for all his life. King of his castle. Captain of his own destiny. He lifted his glass of cabernet franc and said the first thing that came to his mind.

"I really don't have anything to say," Cody toasted. "Good luck to us all."

The rest of the evening, they ate imported oysters from the East Coast, freshly cooked lobsters and other fine seafood delicacies. Mindy looked at Cody with a twinkle in her eye.

"Bobbie, I am so happy for you!" she kept repeating.

His longtime friend poured herself another glass of wine and uncharacteristically devoured it. Mindy then entertained Sonia and Lydia with stories about how she and Cody met. With each retelling, Mindy clutched Cody's hand and warmly smiled at him.

"So, like, yuuh," Sonia asked, replacing the word "yeah" with "yuuh." "Are you two a couple?"

"Hahahahaha!" laughed Mindy. "What?! Of course not! I am married! With twins!"

It was a deliberate opportunity for her to whip out her little girls' photos and pass them around like business cards. Sonia and Patricia oohed and awed at the adorableness of her children—it was even enough to get a word out of the shy Lydia.

"How precious... how old are they?" she asked.

The pixie-like Thai-American appeared different from the other girls. She wasn't nearly as attractive or assertive. Cody could only best describe her so far as invisible, though she boasted one hell of a design portfolio.

"They are both just two-and-a-half years old," proudly answered Mindy. "Cody's the godfather! He and I are best friends!"

"Wow, Cody!" admired Sonia. "You're popular. You've got so many best friends here at this table. Mindy...Marty..."

"No, no," corrected Mindy. "He only has one best friend: me."

The other side of the table could care less about best friends and babies. The Tsing brothers and Herman took liberty in their obvious pursuit of Nicky. It didn't take them long to discover the blonde bombshell's alcoholic threshold was four glasses; Jack didn't even have to resort to his usual spiking. Once she informed them of her past as a gymnast, the boys encouraged her to show them her flexibility. Nicky easily obliged their whims, flexing both legs over her shoulders in her chair. This resulted in an assemblage of gawks and disapproving stares from the people at nearby tables. At the north end of their table, Marty's wife looked on with a censured frown. This was the sales assistant her husband had chosen? Xia thought.

She dismissed the former Hooters waitress as a feebleminded airhead. Guy's reaction, however, hinted at his disagreement.

"Holy, yes! That's so damn awesome! That's what I'm talking about!" he expressed.

Jack calmly lit a cigarette and offered one to Nicky.

"Uh, no thanks. I don't smoke," she declined. She unfolded her legs and made herself upright again.

"Come on," insisted Jack. "Life is short. Y.O.L.—"

"Um, excuse me, sir," interrupted the restaurant manager, "but you can't smoke here."

"Of course I can!" Jack said, looking up at him with a smirk.

"No, it's state law," corrected The Oceanaire manager. "Besides, this is a classy establishment. Not a drinking hole in Midtown."

"Sigh," puffed Jack, looking at his cousin. "Hey Marty, pay the man."

"Hoah-wuh?" Marty asked.

"I wanna smoke a fuckin' cig. Pay this asshole so that I can!"

"Sir," the manager replied, "I assure you that bribes won't work at The Oceanaire."

Jack rolled his eyes and dumped the cigarette into his glass of water. Satisfied, the manager walked away.

"Teehee! You're so baaaaad," admired Nicky. "I thought Asian guys were supposed to be submissive and good at math."

"I am good at math," Jack agreed. "You plus me equals a family of three."

"Maaaaan," Guy added. "Submissive? Look at us. This is a new world, baby! Asian men rule!"

With the dinner ending, Cody was given the check. Disregarding any existence of a budget, the new boss asked the waiter what the tipping record was. When the waiter halfheartedly revealed the number, Cody wrote twice the amount on the check. Afterwards, the newly forged Mosaic Design Studios crew left the restaurant, waiting outside for their valet cars to arrive. With their expensive and classy attire, they looked ready to conquer the world.

"Remember, everyone," reminded Cody, "ten o'clock sharp Monday morning."

Their first day of work.

CHAPTER 19: GRAND OPENING

The first day didn't go as Cody envisioned; funny how things are always better in the mind, he thought. He had imagined it beginning with a full-body workout before sunrise, followed by a steaming half-hour-long shower to help him meditate over the rousing speech he had prepared. Upon reaching the office, he imagined, he would find his employees standing in a line with a respectful salute. At ease, he'd tell them. Then, with complete certainty and confidence, he would deliver unto them the most gut-wrenching, morale-inducing speech in the history of speeches. It would be right up there, he fancied, in the Mount Rushmore of Public Speaking alongside of Douglas MacArthur's *Farewell Speech*, Martin Luther King's *I Have a Dream* and Abraham Lincoln's *Gettysburg Address*.

Reality, however, had a different plan.

In the early morning hours of the company's opening day, much of the furniture still had to be assembled. There were plenty of desks, but no chairs. Worse, the computers didn't work properly and neither did their network connectivity. The company's first morning lay in the hands of the volunteer crew. Marty's I.T. friend and Herman, who expectedly talked more than he worked, scrambled to get the computers working. Xia, who had sacrificed some much-needed sleep, perspired heavily as she assembled the rolling cabinets. She proved herself to be more effective than Guy, whose blundering repeatedly caused him to reassemble things. Marty and Cody tended to most of their own desk equipment. Jack was totally useless, mostly walking in and out for cigarette breaks.

"Shit!" exclaimed Guy.

"What?" Cody asked, looking in the big guy's direction.

"Sighhhhh. I see—" observed Marty, "—the chair you made is backwards."

Guy grew livid. "Bro, how the hell can I understand these IKEA instructions? They don't have any words in them!!!"

"That's the point, isn't it?" countered Cody. "They're supposed to be so easy that even an illiterate simpleton can understand them."

"Yeah, but I still don't get it," Guy whined.

Xia, wiping sweat off her brow, tossed a bag of White Rabbit candy to him.

"There! More sugar...help you think...maybe it make you smarter!" she laughed.

"White Rabbit candy?" observed Guy. "Isn't this the crap where you eat the wrapping paper too?"

Cody began feeling very frustrated as he noticed the hour hand of the clock reaching five. He appreciated the others helping, but he was annoyed at the ones who lacked urgency. Guy seemed to enjoy the attention he received screwing up. Herman could work faster if he stopped yapping. Jack was completely undependable. And Marty, he realized, seemingly approached the situation without awareness of exigency.

"Argh!" yelled Guy. "Now this lamp is backwards!"

"Eat more White Rabbit candy!" Xia advised again.

"Let me do it," Cody demanded, pushing the big football player aside.

"What do I do now?" the quarterback asked.

"Go find your brother," answered Cody. "We need more manpower. And switch to a different song—we've been hearing that crap over and over again for the past thirty minutes."

"Dude, I love Taylor Swift!" Guy defended.

"Fuck Taylor Swift! Don't you have anything other than top-50 hits?"

"Play my Shanghai hop-pop! Real hip!" Xia recommended.

Without waiting, she fiddled with Guy's Apple Macbook and added her own songs in there. Within moments, the office intercom blared with Chinese rap music. Cody walked around assisting the others on various tasks, pushing them to speed up. Marty, in particular, was working too slowly.

"Please, Cody, heh, don't...heh heh...don't rush me," he pleaded.

"We're opening our doors in under four hours. We need rushing," Cody bossed.

"I'm, haha, I'm going as fast as I can! Heh-ha!"

"Why are you taking so long anyway?" wondered Cody. "I've already put five chairs together, the printer desk, the supply cabinet, our desk chairs and multiple drawers."

"Sighhhh. I guess it happened again then, heh-ha," Marty said, shaking his head. "Just my bad luck, you guys got all the good ones and I happen to have the defective chairs and cabinets."

"Are you sure?" asked Cody suspiciously. "What's so defective about them?"

"Heh-ha! Hey, guess what?" Marty said, ignoring the question. "They should sell special insurance for people like me. Bad luck insurance, I'd call it. Heh heh ha!"

"That's funny, but seriously we have to—"

His sentence was suddenly interrupted by the loss of power in the entire building. Herman could be heard slipping and falling in the darkness. Somebody let out a loud fart; probably Xia, guessed Cody. They heard the door open.

"Dude, what's going on?" they heard Jack asking.

"This was no accident," theorized Marty's I.T. friend. "I think we're pushing the computers too hard. Herman, don't tell me you placed all the plugs into one socket."

Herman got vocally defensive. "DON'T BLAME ME MAN! YOU TOLD ME TO—"

The power immediately resumed; everyone could see one another again.

"Guy, put your shirt back on!" insisted Cody. "Man boobs aren't in season."

"It was hot," the big guy pleaded, covering himself.

"W-What's that noise?" winced Jack.

The power surges began beeping like an army of crickets. Soon, their decibel levels reached an unbearable high, inducing panic among the volunteer staff.

"Oh my God!" screamed Xia. "My ears hurt!"

The temporary I.T. manager fumbled for an explanation. "I...I'm trying, but the power surges are designed to chime during times of emergency, which—"

"I DON'T CARE!" screamed Cody. "JUST FIND A WAY TO TURN THEM OFF!"

Without waiting, he grabbed the closest power surge protector to him and unplugged it. To his horror, Cody discovered that it continued chirping. The rest of the volunteer crew tried a similar tactic, producing the same result.

"Fuck, bro, what do we do?!!" Guy wondered out loud. "Marty? Any ideas?!!"

"Muh-uh, we could...um...uh..."

"Ah, screw this!" Cody threw up his hands. "I'm hungry. Let's grab a bite at Waffle House."

No one disagreed. The power surges were left beeping in the office during their pursuit of food at the popular diner. They entered the nearest Waffle House in a dejected and offensively pungent state.

"How many, sir?" asked the hostess.

"I am a woman," corrected Xia. She looked at a window reflection of herself and flinched.

"Oh, sorry!" the hostess corrected.

"It's okay. Tonight, I am ugly."

The party of seven was taken to the farthest booth from the windows in an effort to prevent scaring potential customers. None of them blamed the diner's precaution; they truly looked awful. Most of them ordered eggs and pancakes. Marty's I.T. friend, however, ordered a full meal of chicken fried steak. His nap immediately afterwards was inevitable and so was the increasing visibility of his armpit stains.

"Dude," flinched Guy as he noticed the I.T. friend's sweat. "I am not carrying him into Marty's car."

"Yes, you are," Cody flatly opposed. "You're the biggest one out of all of us."

"Don't worry about him!" declared Herman. "I can finish networking the comps. Besides, this ass was in my way."

"Your ass is in the way of your face," Guy countered.

"Guy, that...that doesn't even make sense," Jack scoffed. "Anyway, it's not like you guys are going to make it. First day and your company doesn't even have working computers. Real good impression, guys."

"Shut up before we send you to jail!" hissed his brother.

"Ahahahahahaha!" Xia bursted out laughing.

"Fuck you, Guy," Jack sneered, taking out a cigarette."Shit, my lighter's missing. What the hell..."

"Good!" Xia exclaimed. "No chance for you to do another fire!"

"Fuck you too, man-bitch," growled Jack. "No offense, Marty."

"Mm-huh, eh, watch...watch your language, Jack. That's my wife."

Cody slumped his shoulders. "Jack's right. This wasn't how I envisioned our first day. I can barely stay awake."

"Well, uh-ah now, heh heh," Marty patted Cody. "Don't say that. Heh. Eh? Come on...heh...we'll be alright. Ha-uh-hah."

"No, we've got to be ready to roll on our first day. You've already got all these clients lined up for us," reasoned Cody. "We can't fall behind."

"Mmm...huh," understood Marty.

"Speaking of which—," paused Cody. "Can you tell me who some of these clients are? The ones you had a month to get?"

Marty paused and thought.

"Well, uh, heh," he nervously laughed. "Wouldn't want to spoil the surprise, Cody."

"A month head start. I bet a superstar salesman like you must've gotten twenty by now."

"Guh-huh-ha, oh yeah, I've got us a big name too."

"<Really?>" perked Xia. "<I'm your wife and I didn't know?>"

"<I told you!>" insisted Marty. "<You just forgot!>"

"You always say this!" Xia switched to English. "'You forgot, You forgot.' Oh. Maybe...maybe you the one doing forget, huh?"

"Yeah," joined Jack. "I don't remember you mentioning this big name client either. So who's the big name, cuz?"

"Sigh. Pout. Sighhhhh." Marty looked at the ground and shook his head.

"Come on, man! How come we're finding this out after you tell the new employees? Tell us first! Who's this super client?"

Marty closed his eyes and twirled his head. Then huffed a long sigh.

"Why can't you guys just wait?" he pleaded.

"What? Who is it? Come on," pushed Cody.

"Yeah, bro," joined Guy. "Who is it?"

Their voices turned into a cacophony of pleas and random guesses. Marty felt pressured to give an answer.

"Um, ah, huh, ah..." he stumbled.

"Tell me!" Xia ordered.

"H...," Marty blurted the letter again. "H..."

"Holy shit......Home freakin' Depot," guessed Guy.

"It's Hustler, isn't it?!" excitedly screamed Herman. He jumped up and down. "Oh man oh man oh man!"

"Herman, sit down. You're scaring the senior citizens," Cody pointed out.

"Honda, History Channel, Hugo Boss," Jack listed.

"H-E-B Pantry," Cody guessed.

"I know!" beamed Xia. "H-Mart!"

"Er, ahhh." Marty nervously looked around the table. "Yes, er, heh yes! It's H-Mart. Once again, my, eh, beautiful wife is right. But, heh, shhh. Ffft...heh...shhhhhh."

They oohed and aahed at Marty's revelation. H-Mart was the Korean supermarket juggernaut in Houston.

"Fuccccck," Jack marveled. "Hey, you think you can hook me up with those hot Korean chicks that go there? I swear they all look like Hyori Lee."

"H-Mart," reflected Cody. "Marty...you're the fucking man!!!"

The whole crew came alive with excitement. Cody rushed to give his best friend an approving handshake; Marty had delivered. He cursed himself for doubting him. It was the perfect news to tell the new employees. With newfound excitement, the passengers enjoyed a refreshing atmosphere during the car ride back. They were given a friendly greeting by the morning sun, which gave the blasé Texas landscape a beautiful red hue. Cody stopped Guy on one particular song he discovered fiddling with the radio knobs. He didn't know what the name of it was, but the beat had a nice rock-and-roll rhythm—a perfect soundtrack to the scenery. As his left arm was catching the wind from the driver-side window, Cody basked in the excitement of anticipation. A couple more hours and he would be a boss. How would it feel? What would he say? He'd remember this day for the rest of his life.

———————

When the doors of Mosaic Design Studios opened and the girls arrived, things remained far from perfect. However, Cody was determined to make it so. Amid competition from the chirping surge protectors, he gathered his staff in the conference room and let out the earth-shattering speech he had memorized and saved up for just this moment. What came out instead was a collection of bumbling and stammering, partly including a few sensible points within. He was learning the hard way that public speaking without practice was difficult. The girls looked at him, patiently observing his lack of eye contact and constant fidgeting. He also spoke fast, nervously fast.

"—and without further ado," the new CEO concluded, "we have lots of things coming up busy ready for you yeah coming up so be ready big, big things, I mean, clients, which is to say one of them we got was H-Mart and other important customers who we depend on to spread a good rep perhaps I've over-talked and without further ado, wait, I already said that, well, without further ado, Marty will fill you in on how to fill out your W-2 forms and gather your information about W-2 forms of which information will be gathered."

Cody took a well-deserved dose of air. His heartbeat was racing a hundred miles an hour. Marty took over, calmly explaining the instructions for the paperwork. This gave Cody a chance to collect himself within the privacy of his office room. Guy followed him.

"Hey, yo, you okay?" the big guy asked.

"I'm fine," insisted Cody. "I just...didn't imagine I would sound like that. Thought I would be a little more General MacArthur-like."

"Huh? Who?"

"American History. World War II." Cody gave up. "Never mind."

"God, look at Nicky and Sonia," fantasized Guy. "They could both blow me all day long."

"Hey, could you, like, not say that kind of stuff so openly? This is a real company. This a real work environment. Jesus...don't make me fire you, man."

Guy ignored him and added, "You think Sonia's tits are real?"

Cody looked at the jock in disgust and walked back toward the main office. He was in awe of how patient Marty was with them. His partner was a natural at dealing with people, and they seemed to respond better to him. Cody thought it was too bad that they arranged for him to be in the office while Marty was out with clients. But then again, Cody realized, it was a good opportunity for him to learn leadership. Daphne Lee had always criticized him for a lack of it.

"Okay, hah-ah," concluded Marty, "if there're no more questions, you guys have the rest of the day off. Come back tomorrow morning at ten o'clock."

"Wow, the day off already!" exclaimed Nicky. "You're so nice, Marty!"

"Well, ah, I...ah..." he blushed.

"Yeah, this is awesome. Thanks!" appreciated Patricia.

The four employees gathered their purses and other belongings, heading for home. Marty chuckled and waved. Cody watched them go with a wide-eyed stare. He then turned to Marty.

"Why'd you tell them to take the first day off?!" he asked.

"Heh, relax, Cody, heh. Come on, heh. You know? Eh? Ah? Ah heh heh?" Marty pointed to his nose.

"No...what do you mean?"

Marty put his hands together and rested his head on them in a sleeping gesture.

"Eh? Ah?" Marty arched his eyebrows up and down.

"Sleep? We don't need sleep!"

"Come on, Cody, heh heh, sleeping is what you, heh heh, need. You worked hard. You deserve it. Eh! Eh? Eh!"

"I...I guess. We did work for two nights straight," Cody concluded.

Marty patted him on the back and began writing on the dry erase board. He wrote the names of fifty clients, most of them seemingly from the restaurant or oil industry. Some were recognizable; most were not.

"Reliant? Wow. You got us Reliant?!" exclaimed Cody.

"Wah-uh, more like they got us," winked and nudged Marty.

"Wait, where's H-Mart on your board? Why isn't it on there?"

"Eh, they just called me. Remember when you went to the restroom earlier this morning?"

"Yeah?"

Marty made a throat-slashing gesture with his hand.

"They cut us?!" asked Cody.

Marty closed his eyes and nodded his head, sighing for a few seconds.

"It's okay, though," assured Marty. "We don't need them. I got us M.H. Productions!"

"That's great!...Wait, what the hell is M.H. Productions?"

"Ah ha-eh, you've never heard of them? Big production company. Quality work. I'm, heh-huh, frankly surprised. You should go out there more often, hoo-ah."

Guy walked back into the office wearing a tennis outfit. He bounced a tennis ball with one hand while fiddling with a racket on the other. Jack and Xia came in wearing similar attire.

"Wait, what's going on?" Cody asked.

"Relax, Cody...shh....heh-heh...you haven't slept," laughed Marty. "We need to take our minds out of the company. We're playing tennis. Wanna come?"

"Sounds fun," Cody contemplated. "But then again, I don't play tennis."

"Don't worry about it then. You should rest, you really should, hahuh." Once again, Marty patted Cody on the back. "We'll have plenty of days to get serious and celebrate. This is our first day, hmm-ah, heh heh, let's just treat it as a formality and nothing more."

"I guess. Yeah, you're right," agreed Cody. "We were too stressed from this morning to think properly."

"Mmm yeah, haha, see?" Marty gave him a thumbs-up.

———

By the second week, Sonia had gotten familiar with

Lydia and Patricia. She had also convinced Cody to get her a fancier computer, a higher salary and the new title of Executive Secretary. It didn't take the vixen secretary long to realize that both bosses had underestimated her. Men, she grinned, so easy to understand; so easy to control. She evaluated everyone's current strengths and weaknesses and mentally made a list. It was true that she wasn't very knowledgeable about websites and design. It was also true that she had very little working experience. But she knew how to work things to her advantage, to accurately read people and charm others into doing the fighting for her. Ms. Pokerface, she labeled herself with a smile.

She and the two designer girls made a habit of having lunch at Hula Hoop Shakes, a new diner just across the street from the building where they worked. There, the designer girls delightfully ordered from the fun assortment of hot dogs, pancakes, Frito pies and other items typically found in diners. Sonia herself didn't care for fatty fast food, but the restaurant had something else she enjoyed: a handsome, blue-eyed, blond-haired waiter.

"So...the usual?" the waiter recollected. "A cheeseburger with extra onion, no ketchup. Chicago-style hot dogs and tater tots. And for you, Ms. Sonia, a chicken salad with ranch dressing."

"Lite ranch," Sonia winked, "and, of course, my daily dose of cappuccino."

"With cinnamon in the grounds," the waiter winked back, walking away.

She knew she could have him if she wanted to, but she decided to designate him as a reserve. There were already too many men she had taking care of her. Charm, she was taught by her mother at an early age, was beauty plus attitude. However, none of it mattered without the concealing of intelligence. Sonia knew it was best to delude men into thinking she was incapable of bold ideas and keen observations. Ego, after all, was men's kryptonite. Perhaps, she thought, it would be best to share this knowledge with her new coworkers.

"Oh my Gahhd," Sonia pointed at Lydia, "he's so cute like always. I think he likes you, Lydiaaaa!"

Lydia felt herself blushing beyond her control. She rarely heard herself being described as a thing of beauty. The tiny girl had accepted her fate of dating socially awkward geeks and weirdos. It was better this way, she decided—being average looking was a natural filter from superficial men. Whoever ended up loving her, she figured, would care about her for who she was on the inside. Now, however, Sonia had planted a forbidden fantasy into the girl's head—one that she secretly believed could come true.

"He'd...he'd never like me," Lydia said, brushing it off.

"Like yuuuh," Sonia countered, "white guys like Asian girls...it's the new 'thing.'"

"Ha ha ha! Guys are guys! They like pretty girls like you. It would be ridiculous if they passed you for me just because I'm Asian. Ha ha!"

"Totally not!" insisted Sonia. "I just have better game. I think for an Asian girl to get a white guy, all she has to do is stand still and say 'Hi. I'm Asian!'"

The three girls laughed. They were bonding.

"Nooo," Lydia smiled and sighed. "I'm all good. I...probably...wouldn't want a guy like that anyway. All these girls fighting for him if I was his girlfriend. They would always bug him about why he'd be with me. Ha ha. Better leave him to the beautiful ones like yourself, Sonia!"

"Oh, hon, it's all about how you carry yourself," advised Sonia. "Ever notice that whenever I needed something from him, I would slightly bend over and expose a bit of my chest?"

Lydia and Patricia giggled like schoolgirls. They admired Sonia's openness with sexuality and flirting—

something their conservative backgrounds held them back from exploring. Their lunch conversations led them to ask questions they couldn't believe they were asking. Mostly, though, they respected Sonia because she knew how to control men—and that was tradable knowledge for their loyalty.

"The secret to getting men to do what you want," Sonia began, "is to make them feel like kings. This way they won't realize that the queen is always more powerful."

"Like chess," Patricia observed.

"Yuuuh," she nodded, "like getting them to think we work for them when, in fact, they work for us."

The two girls immediately picked up on Sonia's specific meaning.

"I don't think twelve vacation days in a year is enough," Lydia nodded.

"And nine o'clock in the morning for work?" Patricia said. "Ten-thirty is way better."

"Patricia, is getting to work a problem for you?" Sonia asked in a concerned voice.

"Yeah, I have to have my mom drive me. We live in Humble," she replied.

"Don't worry"," Sonia assured her. "Start coming in at ten-thirty then. Eleven if you must."

"Yeah, it's not like Cody comes in before two in the afternoon anyway," laughed Lydia.

"But what if Marty comes in and sees that we're not there?" asked Patricia.

"Seriously, are any of you really afraid of Marty?" smirked Sonia. "I noticed what a pushover he was during the night at The Oceanaire. His wife clearly wears the pants."

Sonia cleared her throat and began imitating Marty. "Um, ahhh, huh, ah huh ha, hahaha, I don't know what I'm doing. I just laugh. Ah ha ha. Ah huh huh. Ha huh ha!"

The girls burst out into a flurry of laughter. It wasn't a bad impression.

"Seriously," she continued, "I don't buy into all this bullshit about him being an experienced salesman. He's been training that Nicky girl for two weeks and they haven't gotten anything."

"Yeah," Lydia agreed. "I think they lied about H-Mart too."

"I bet he's trying to fuck her," said Sonia. "I can tell these things. It's also why they hired me. Like, oh my Gahhd, did you know that weird cousin of his...what's his name, Jack?...the one who's a drunk-ass loser...anyways, did y'all know what he asked me the other day?"

"No, what?" the two of them simultaneously wondered.

"He flat out asked me if I knew why I really got hired, and I said, 'yeah, for my tits'. And he laughed and said 'glad you know.' What a pig."

"I'd never date someone like that guy." Patricia shook her head. "He smells homeless."

"I heard from his brother Guy that he mooches off unsuspecting women and he's also an arsonist," Sonia added.

"Yeah. I can see that," Lydia agreed.

"They're all dumb," declared Sonia. "I can run a company better than any of them could. Nothing's organized. And speaking of dumb..."

Sonia's expression turned serious. She was about to get into the main point of their afternoon conversation.

"...I think Nicky is an absolute moron. There's air in between her ears. Tell you the truth, girls, I'm scared for the immediate future of Mosaic Design Studios if she's our hope for sales. I really am," said Sonia.

"Yeah, I've talked with her," said Lydia. "She's not very bright. She told me she used to be a Hooters girl."

"Not all Hooters girls are dumb," countered Patricia.

"Well, this one most certainly is," Sonia said, "and I got just the right person to replace her. I have a good friend who's smart, brilliant and charming. She would do a helluva better job than this bimbo."

"Here you go, girls!" interrupted their handsome waiter.

As he served their food, the girls were surprised that he was accompanied by a new waitress. Ever since they had started coming regularly, he was their favorite thing about Hula Hoop Shakes. The sign of an apprentice might mean what they had feared: an end to his services.

"So," Sonia observed, "who's this?"

The new waitress was a spunky-looking young woman of Korean descent. She had piercings on the most visible parts of her body, heavy makeup and spiked-up hair. The entire side of her left arm was covered with an interesting tattoo sleeve design.

"This is my replacement, Phoebe," introduced the handsome waiter. "She'll be here from now on. This will be my last week."

The girls' hearts sank; their instincts had been proven correct.

"Where are you going?" Sonia sweetly asked. "You know we'll miss you."

"I just got accepted to work for Halliburton," he explained. "Guess my days of waiting tables are over. I really liked talking with y'all. It was cool to see you girls almost every day."

"It doesn't have to end, you know." Sonia wrote her number on a napkin.

"I guess it doesn't," he laughed, taking the napkin.

Phoebe, the new waitress, refilled their drinks.

"I'll miss you," smiled Lydia.

"So," ignored the waiter, "anything else for you girls?"

"Yes," replied Sonia, "applications to Halliburton, please?"

"Hahaha, I'm sure they could use a hot girl for a secretary in there."

"Executive Secretary," she laughed and corrected him.

———————

It was the scene that Marty loved the most. With only a small hacksaw and a tape recorder to set her free from the dilapidated bathroom, the chained blonde cheerleader realized her only two options. She was either to saw off her own foot or give oral sex to the corpse beside her. Marty salivated when she looked at the camera and gladly chose the latter. The corpse turned out to be alive; swanky guitar music started to play. The video had the three things Marty loved the most: a porno parody of his favorite movie *Saw*, blondes, and the activity the actress was about to perform.

"Uh-ho ho ha! Hooooo!" Marty breathed heavily. "Yeaaaah."

Keep your voice down, he reminded himself, he didn't want people to know he was in the back of his Oldsmobile, relieving himself on his laptop. The pants-less sales director would be embarrassed if anyone discovered this was how he spent his lunch hours. As the video got into its climax, his cell phone unexpectedly rang, causing him to spurt out a surprise both in expression and secretion.

"Huh-ah, h...hello?" he answered, quickly turning down the volume.

"Hey, Marty! It's me, Nicky, I don't see you here at Starbucks in the Town Square. Are you okay?"

"Wh-what? Um, hah. It's...it's only, heh, twelve-thirty," Marty said, glancing at his car's clock.

"Huh? It is? All the clocks in here must be broken then. They all say one o'clock on them," Nicky believed.

Marty silently cursed himself for forgetting about Guy's Jamba Juice accident earlier in the day. The drink had spilled onto the dashboard and damaged the car clock.

"Wuh-ha! Huh huh, mannn, can you believe that?" he laughed. "All the clocks in the Starbucks are wrong at the same time."

"I know!" giggled Nicky. "What are the chances of that happening? Oh, and guess what? Wow! My cell phone's clock is messed up too! So weird!"

"Well, shhh. Um, glad one of us has a working clock then!" Marty laughed.

"I guess I'm early!" she laughed.

"Don't you worry, I happen to be close by! Wait for me for fifteen minutes, okay?"

"Sure! Maybe I can occupy my time by telling everyone that their clocks are wrong," laughed Nicky.

"Er, ah, HA! No no no, don't do that. Shhh. Hush, heh. Heh-ha! They probably won't appreciate you correcting them. I'll be right down there, okay?"

Marty hung up and quickly put his pants back on. He was thankful that Nicky wasn't very bright; in fact, it made it better that she turned out to be a moron. A hot-looking moron, nevertheless. Still, he was a bit disappointed the video session ended prematurely, but then again, at least for once he was able to do something prematurely. The extensive watching of pornography had messed up his sexual appetite. Perhaps he should blame Xia for holding back intimacy during the past year. Didn't she know it tortured a man?

The phone rang again. It was from the office.

"Hey, bro," Guy's voice said, "you better get in here quick. Some crazy motherfucker is starting shit."

"Wuh-uh, what?" Marty couldn't believe it. "Where's Sonia? Why are you on her phone line?"

"You should just come quickly," Guy hinted before hanging up.

Marty contemplated whether he should meet with Nicky or attend to the office emergency. If he ignored either one, he realized, he'd be seen as the bad guy. It was a thought that greatly bothered him. Think, Marty, he pushed himself, think. After a few seconds, he dialed Nicky's number.

"Um, er, Nicky! Do you see me?" he lied. "No? Um, are you sure? I'm at the door...you, um, heh, sure you don't see me?...wait, what Starbucks are you in again?...no, noooo, hah-heh, I told you the one in the Pearland Town Square...see? You're so forgetful.....muh-heh, it's okay...... Well, you just stay there, I'll drive on over to the one in the Sugar Land Town Square..."

This was why he liked her. She wasn't smart enough to question things. Now he needed just an hour to handle whatever was happening at the office.

The scene that awaited him there was a frightening one. An angry, bald and physically imposing Hispanic man was in the middle of their office. He was yelling obscenities and pushing around loose office furniture from rage. Sonia was leaning toward a corner, paralyzed with fear. The two designer girls stayed at their desks, pretending to look at their screens. And for all his muscles and self-boasting bravado, Guy was hesitant to confront the enraged man. Marty recognized him. He was bad news.

"Now, now Jose," he called out, "ehhh, heh, this doesn't have to get violent."

"So you finally show yourself, eh?" Jose scowled. "Good. I was going to hurt your idiot staff and your whore secretary if you had not!"

Guy was offended by those words.

"Bro, I don't think you can hurtOOOF!" The quarterback dropped down after being kicked in his left calf. Jose proved himself a strong and formidable fighter.

Marty continued with the negotiations. "Ah, eh. Come...come on, Jose. Please? Heh. Eh? Ehhh!"

"Where is my website! Why isn't it ready! I paid you guys!" he yelled.

"Well, ah, uh...Lydia...why don't you show him that design you did. Heh-hah," Marty asked nervously.

"Yes, let me bring it up," she said softly.

"Oh no!" Jose stopped her. "I saw that one already! It sucks! Ugly design! Maybe because made from ugly girl!"

Lydia gave an offended expression.

"Ah, I'm...heh-ha-ha, hey, you want anything to drink?" asked Marty. "We have...what do we have, Patricia?"

Patricia cleared her throat. "Grape Capri Sun, Vita, Pepsi..."

"I don't fucking want a drink!" yelled Jose. "I want you to finish my site right now! I paid you two thousand already!"

"Now now, mm-mmm," Marty assured him, "why don't we go to my office and, heh, let me tell you a funny story!"

Behind closed doors, the staff heard Jose screaming at Marty. Even with Guy's assurance of his cousin's martial arts, all of them were certain it was only a matter of time before the giant man lost control and violently injured their boss. However, minutes later, the room fell quiet. He's dead, they thought, perhaps even witnesses to a murder. Then, unexpected laughter suddenly came from the room; it was Jose's voice. Ten minutes later, their boss' door opened; Jose exited in good spirits. He laughed and waved a friendly hello to everyone. Putting his giant arms around Marty's shoulder, they laughed together as he voluntarily left their office.

"I'm sorry, I'm sorry," he laughed and apologized.

"Ah huh-eh! Ha!" Marty said. "No problem, Jose. See? It was all just a little misunderstanding. Heh. Ha! Heh-ha."

With Jose's departure, Marty felt a rush of confidence; he wanted to do something bold, take whatever he wanted. Nicky, he suddenly remembered—she was still at the Starbucks. It was now or never, he realized. He was going to drag her out, take her to his bedroom and make love to her.

The Starbucks was full of people by the time Marty arrived. Occupying the limited tables were mostly college kids and working professionals with their laptops and those new iPads he heard about. He searched for Nicky's blonde hair until finally, near the edge of the coffee shop, he recognized her unmistakable body. This was it, Marty told himself as he made his way closer to her, *Nicky, come sleep with me. Now.*

Unfortunately, at the expense of his heart, he saw a man next to her, holding her hand and kissing her. Marty's confidence was deflated. How did it never occur to him that she had a boyfriend? A black guy too. He shook his head. His drop back to earth was brutal. A slight buzz to his right thigh shook him out of his self-pity. It was his iPhone vibrating. Xia, he read from the caller ID.

"Mm-huh?" Marty answered.

"<Hey, don't forget to help my brother paint his house today while he's away from town. Also, be sure to walk our poodle around the FRONT of the house this time. Then call Wanda and tell her I'll be going to her girls' night out together this weekend. Did you remember to get the Japanese Blossom hand wash from Bath and Body Works? Oh, and hey, get me

those tampons I wanted from the store next to your workplace.>" His wife hung up.

"<Uh-huh, uh-huh>," nodded Marty, talking to an already ended phone call. "<Yes, dear. Anything for you, babe. Mm-huh.>"

He let the phone slip out of his hands and watched it hit the floor. Nicky had a man. Nicky had to go.

———

His feelings didn't get any better later after midnight as he lay awake on his living room sofa. It didn't help that Guy's snoring could be heard from the first-floor guest room or that Jack was equally as loud wheezing in the recliner. A burst of light caught his eye; it was from Xia coming in from a night of clubbing. He could see her silhouette stagger, making its way awkwardly towards the stairs that led to their second-floor bedroom. Marty hated it when Wanda and her girls got his wife drunk.

"<Xia>," Marty called to her.

"<Oh, husband...my nice, nice husband...hicc...did you get my tampons for me?>" She laughed in a buzzed stupor.

"<Wah-oooh. Ooh, no.>" He walked up and consoled her. "<You're drunk.>"

"GET YOUR HAND OFF ME!" Xia yelled in accented English.

"<Mmuh, ah...>"

Xia laughed and copied him, "<Mmuh, ah! Mmuh, ah! Why do you always sound like you're retarded?>"

"<Sighhhh.>"

"<Don't follow me upstairs. You just...help me...if I command you...hicc...>" Xia stumbled her way into her bedroom.

"<Okay.>"

"<Oh...hicc...look>," giggled and pointed Xia. "<Your cousin Guy has fallen asleep with nothing on. But he...hicc...he still has more pants than you do. Hahahahaha!>"

He watched her as she found her way to the bedroom and locked its door. Today I almost cheated on you, Marty thought to himself. She had no idea how much his own family hadn't wanted him to marry her; his mother felt Shanghai girls were a materialistic and fickle bunch. He was told how they'd rather focus on outside appearances and didn't bother with the inside. Marty wouldn't listen at the time because he was in love with her. Or rather, he liked being married to a pretty woman. It gave him face; people patted him on his back. Xia gave him admiration but for a hefty price.

The gloominess of the topic persuaded Marty to distract himself with something else. He flipped his laptop open and went to his browser's favorites. There, in neatly organized links, he snooped at his employee's Facebook pages, blogs, and other personal pages. He had ways of overriding their privacy settings, courtesy of his I.T. friend. Sonia sure took a lot of risqué photos, he smiled, saving them onto his laptop. He also discovered she was a Maxim Hometown Hottie contestant. Nude? He searched deeper into the web. Yes, he excitedly realized. She had nude photos of herself. *Saved.*

As he was about to log off and enjoy the saved nude photos, he noticed Sonia's latest Facebook status from the corner of his eye. There, with Lydia and Patricia also responding, they were making fun of Nicky. *Dumb. Bimbo.*

Brainless. Marty lacks inability to choose good employees. I heard he tried to sleep with her. He hadn't the guts to ask. Shocked that they were making fun of him, he immediately grabbed his iPhone and dialed Cody's number. Luckily for him, the device still worked after it was dropped earlier.

"Hey man, I was just about to call you!" greeted Cody. "We must have ESP!"

"Heh, ah, maybe," Marty agreed, "hey guess what? Jose came today and started shit. Heh. He was mad, but I calmed him down by talking to him."

"Yeah, I heard about that from Lydia," said Cody. "Good job."

"Huh? Heh-ha...Cody, they....they tell you things? They talk with you?" asked Marty.

"Sure. Why not?"

"I mean, ha...uh ha ha...no, no. It's...it's no big deal."

"Okay. Well, anyway, listen, Marty...I've been looking at our bank account and sales charts for the past month and we're not getting anywhere near the quota as we should. And with all the salary the girls eat up we'll—"

Marty needed to change the subject. "Oh, man! Guy and I played this game today. Guess...guess the name. City of Heroes. And then City of Villains. You get to make your own super hero or villain and run around this world. Wild, huh? You should play with us, Cody, you really should, heh. Ha! Heh-ha!"

"Hey, this is serious," Cody said, sticking to the original topic. "Why haven't you and Nicky been getting enough sales? Aren't you guys going around meeting these fifty or so clients? And why hasn't M.H. Productions paid us yet? Lydia and Sonia emailed them the design for approval, but they haven't responded."

"Uh, ah, are you...you sure they, heh, didn't pay...no, no, shh, ffft...they paid. I'm certain of it!"

"No, Marty, I've looked everywhere. It's not there. Can you ask them again just to be sure?"

"Oh, of course. Wah-uh, eh."

"Dude, we're going to be out of money very soon. Haven't you checked the bank account?"

"Well...yer...hoo...ah, I mean, I thought that was your job...I...didn't know..."

"Marty, we used close to a hundred thousand dollars of my family's money in just under a few months. And so far you've only gotten us four thousand dollars in sales. Four thousand! What's happening here?"

"Well, sales take time, eh ah? Yeah?"

"But bills don't take time. We have to pay salary on time. You assured me you could do this."

"Sigh."

"Marty, we won't last past next month. I can't believe you haven't been checking on our bank account."

"Wer, ya...heh...I lost the password!"

"Then click on the button 'Forget Password.'"

"Nicky."

"Pardon me?"

"It's Nicky. She's...heh...she's the problem."

"Yeah, the other girls tell me she's kind of dumb."

"Er...ah...yes. Yes," Marty agreed. "She holds me back. She's not learning anything. Nothing. Sigh."

"I thought you said you liked her. You were telling me that your training was turning her into a killer salesman."

"I, ah, mmmeh, I made a mistake there. She's incapable of learning. Incapable. Heh...ha! So...let's...fire her, man."

"Okay," Cody slowly said.

"April Finley. Let's replace Nicky with her."

"I was going to suggest the same thing. April came across more capable in her interview than Nicky had."

"Woo-ha, okay," Marty nodded. "You, eh, I'll let you do the firing."

"I've never fired anyone before."

"Heh, uh, neither have I."

"Then let's fire Nicky together."

"Wa-ahh...no no. Um, I'll sit next to you while you do it."

"Fine. Okay. Not now though. Let's wait a few weeks later. Close to Thanksgiving."

"Meh...ah...I...okay. Uh, okay," Marty replied.

CHAPTER 20: DAREDEVIL

In the blink of an eye, autumn passed.

As business continued to slide, Cody found himself coping alone most nights at Hula Hoop Shakes. At first, he regularly ate there with Marty after work hours—they had to try it for themselves since the girls wouldn't stop raving about it—but after a couple of trips, its appeal had waned for Marty. Cody, however, made eating there a habit. He had found the Frito pie and chili dogs to die for, but mostly it was because he had fallen for the pretty Korean-American waitress.

He first met Phoebe during Halloween, when he had come along with Marty and Xia to the diner in full costume. Cody wore a giant light bulb over his head. It was held together by the wire of an old coat hanger, which was his idea of an "abstract costume." Xia and Marty came as a pair of Ranma characters: Akane Tendo and her panda Genma. The large doses of cotton and heavy eye shadow caused Marty to scratch himself constantly. Xia's dark purple wig wasn't nearly as troublesome. The heavily tattooed Phoebe, who wore bright hippie clothing and an assortment of body piercings, was at first mistaken to be in costume as well.

"Oh, I'm always like this," she shrugged, snapping around a piece of bubble gum in her mouth. "They let us wear anything tonight because it's Halloween."

Marty had once made fun of Cody for liking women who "seem like they'd knife ya" and perhaps he was right. He liked Phoebe's spunk, her naughty smile and heavy use of mascara. The attraction proved genuine; it passed several weeks' worth of time. He continued seeing her at Hula Hoop Shakes even after windy weather turned into rainy conditions. And then, to everyone's surprise, by December it became a white winter—for the first time in decades, there was an actual snowstorm in Houston, Texas.

As usual, Cody walked into the diner with Phoebe as the first priority on his mind. He shook the snow off his large black overcoat and dusted his gloves. There she was, he saw... his favorite waitress, busy with other tables at the far end of the diner.

"How many people?" asked another waitress.

"Just me," Cody replied.

To his disappointment, the other waitress led him to a booth near the doorway. He initially decided not to request a seat near Phoebe's section; he thought it might make him appear creepy. After fidgeting with the idea for a few minutes, however, he said to hell with it and waved over the nearest waiter.

"Hello, what would like to drink, sir?" he asked.

"You know what?" Cody replied. "I think I changed my mind about this table. Can I just say hello to Phoebe?"

"Oh, sure," replied the waiter.

Making his way toward his crush, Cody found her standing there, pausing for a moment to watch the television's weather forecast. He stopped a few feet from her, waiting for the segment to end. The news report switched to a story of a man found abducted inside of a Taiwanese cargo ship. Cody let out a heartfelt laugh when he saw a desolate Kirk Santiago being interviewed by the Taiwanese media.

Startled by his laughter, Phoebe let out a slight yelp.

"Oh!" she collected herself. "Hey!"

"Hey, hippie-hipster."

"What were you laughing about?" she giggled.

"The guy who got kidnapped to Taiwan." Cody pointed at the television. "That's hilarious. What a prank, eh?"

Phoebe frowned. "No, it's not. He probably had a family that was worried sick the whole time. Whoever did that to him must've been one self-serving bastard."

She was right, realized Cody. In his short-sightedness to get even with his former supervisor, he hadn't considered Kirk's mother worrying herself sick. She had probably cried hysterically for months, dreadfully awaiting word from investigators.

"W...Well," justified Cody, "maybe that Kirk Santiago guy was a jerk and he deserved it. I mean, why else would somebody do that to him?"

"Meh," Phoebe shrugged. "That's still a vengeance-filled thing to do. I hope they catch his kidnapper. Don't you?"

She looked at him with wandering eyes, waiting for his answer. Cody changed the subject before he could get lost in them.

"Anyway, I just...I just came in to say hi," he sheepishly confessed.

"Meh," Phoebe repeated.

"So, hey, you thought about coming to my Christmas party? There's going to be around seventy-five people there. I really want you to come."

"I'll, uh, I'll see. When is that on? Next Saturday, right?"

"Yeah," Cody answered, "I sent you an invite by email. You never wrote back."

Phoebe remembered the email. It was filled with cheesy flirting and numerous references to how beautiful she was. She didn't feel comfortable enough to say yes.

"I probably can't," she replied. "My boss says I've got to work that day."

"Come on, just tell him your grandma's in town."

"Haha! What? Cody, you are something else."

"Please. It's going to be huge. It would mean a lot for me if you came."

"You don't even know me," she smiled, sticking out her tongue in jest. Even her tongue had a piercing in it, he noticed.

"Well, if you change your mind, let me know," Cody laughed.

"Alright."

Cody mentally kicked himself as he turned to leave. He should've just been an assertive jerk and demanded her to come. Maybe his cousin Duke's seminars had a point; passivity doesn't work. As he stood outside lost in thought, the snow started covering the lenses of his glasses. Cody took them off and wiped them clean. It reminded him to keep moving and stay focused.

———

The Christmas party the following Saturday was an extravaganza. It was held at one of the fanciest hotels in town, financed by Cody's personal savings. As an ambitious attempt for a creative twist, both Marty and he bought out the staff and inserted their own. The volunteer waitstaff were dressed in Lone Ranger–type masks as a tribute to the Crazy 88 villains from one of Marty's favorite movies, *Kill Bill*. To accommodate their theme, "Home Cooking," the two also asked some of their guests to bring home-cooked meals. It was a direct violation of the hotel's rules due to safety reasons. Even with that in mind, they succeeded in fooling the hotel management by switching the hotel food with the home-cooked food behind large blue screen curtains. Marty was proud of himself for coming up with that idea.

True to Cody's prediction to Phoebe, there were seventy-five guests that arrived, most of them friends of Cody's and Marty's, although Mosaic Design Studios employees were invited too. Unfortunately, Phoebe wasn't among them; she had declined after all. Guests were treated to a beautiful setup, complete with a sea of wrapped gifts at the back and an open bar. They were also aware that there would be a game of Black Elephant, a twisted version of White Elephant where random guests would later be pitted against one another in various challenges. It was the first time many of Cody's friends were together in the same room.

"Hey!........Hey!" screamed Herman, serving as the usher.

He quickly grabbed the guest who walked past him.

"What's your name?!!!" Herman continued yelling at her. "We have assigned seating here, you know!"

"Assigned seating?"

"Yeah! Bosses' orders. They have a seating chart."

"That's ridiculous. Why can't we just sit where we want?"

"Rules are rules. Tell me your name. Now!"

"Yuki," she said, "Yuki Yee. And I've read all about you, Herman Shu."

Cody's longtime Internet friend from New York had finally made a trip to see him. It was amazing how all the characters he blogged about were now in front of her in the flesh. There was Mindy Cheung and her husband, Wing Wei. His childhood friend Diana Li and her cousin Kiki, the dorky fresh-off-the-boat relative from Hong Kong. She recognized Zoey Vu and her gay best friend, Felix Lin. There were Lydia,

Patricia, Sonia, Marty, Xia, Guy, Wanda...identifying all of them was like a game in and of itself.

"Sit here!" ordered Herman, pointing to her designated chair.

Like hell I'm gonna stay put, she thought. At least she was near the middle of the horseshoe-shaped arrangement of three long tables. It was easy to see everyone from there. As if on cue, her vision went out—someone had suddenly placed a pair of chubby hands over her eyes. Yuki immediately knew whom they belonged to.

"Guess whoooo?" sang a voice.

"I don't need to see you to know that it's you, Rain."

Rain uncovered Yuki's eyes and both women squealed in joy, hugging one another. They couldn't contain their thrill of meeting in person for the first time.

"You look...you look..."

"Chubbier in person?" laughed Rain.

"No," corrected Yuki, "you look even more hip!"

Yuki was telling the truth. Rain had an aura of confidence and a look to her that made it obvious she was bright and talented. Yuki also felt confident too, but it was in a much different way. She was comfortable with herself, even though she was a decade or two older than everyone else in the room. There was something to be said about elegance and class and wearing the proud mantle of a cougar.

"Hello to both of you, la!" interrupted a voice, "my name is Kiki. Are you friends of Cody? Ahehehehehe."

"We're Internet friends with him," Rain explained, shaking Kiki's hand. "We're meeting him for the first time."

"Internet?" Kiki had a confused expression on her face. "Wow! That's so dangerous!"

"Actually," Yuki realized, "you know what? I haven't actually met Cody in person yet. Where is he?"

"Oh, he's walking around somewhere," explained Rain. "I met his best friend, Marty. That's the guy fixing the stereo systems around the stage area. I think they're going to set up the Black Elephant games or something."

Yuki decided to stay and occupy herself with the other guests around her. Rain bounced around the ballroom, making small talk with anyone who was male.

Behind the blue screen "curtains," Cody was a nervous wreck. Nothing was going as planned. Many guests were coming late—on "Asian Time," he'd call it—and the volunteer Crazy 88 staff was slow and incompetent. Worse yet, the deejay had bailed out on them, but that didn't seem to matter anyway since Marty was still struggling to set up the sound system. He found himself orchestrating everything, keeping the party gears in motion, but it seemed to make things worse. He was worried the party would turn into a big disaster.

"Oh, fuck!" shouted Guy, who tripped and spilled someone's large container of soup all over the floor.

"What—what'd you do?!" alerted Cody. "Aw, hell! That was Diana's chicken gumbo soup! She spent the whole day on it."

Making sure no one was looking, he grabbed a stockpile of expensive hotel napkins and soaked up Diana's soup from the carpet. It was enough to make him curse up a storm. Perhaps he needed to push the volunteer staff harder.

"Go go go!" he shouted at them. "Put the food on the plates faster!"

"Hey, Cody, bro," asked Guy, "what do I do with the spilled gumbo soup? Do I just tell them there's no more?"

"No, don't do that! There's some vegetable soup that the hotel made us order," Cody explained, unveiling a hidden cache of it. "Use this. No one's going to know the difference."

Guy scratched his head. "I don't think so, dude. That doesn't look anything like gumbo."

"Then use the rice that Lydia brought and dump it in. There! Gumbo!"

"But that was for Lydia's Thai curry!"

"Well, now it's just curry soup, man! Market it as that!"

"'Curry soup'? What the hell?"

Cody stormed out from behind the blue screens in anger. It was worse than he thought—what was supposed to be a classy and organized evening had turned into a romping free-for-all. No one followed the assigned seating; they weren't even sitting. Worse, there was something about the guests. All the guests appeared more than tipsy—they were as loud as college kids at a frat party. The open bar, he suddenly realized. Jack Tsing had turned it into a constant stream of shots for everyone. Even the Crazy 88 staff were drinking.

"No, stop!" Cody screamed at Jack. "Don't get everyone drunk! You're skyrocketing the tab!"

"Stop?" laughed Jack. "Are you kidding me? This is the best damn Christmas party ever! You're the best!"

Jack ordered a straight shot of vodka and gave it to Cody.

"Drink, motherfucker!" Jack exclaimed.

"No!" refused Cody.

Suddenly a screech from the microphone could be heard from the stage. Marty finally got the stereo system working.

"Mm-hah. Testing, testing," Marty spoke into the microphone.

He stood in the center of the stage, grinning that he had finally gotten something to work. Cody ran up to him.

"Start the games!" Cody ordered off-mike. "Start the games now!"

"Wah-ah, okay we're going to do our Black Elephant event now," Marty announced on the microphone.

Scattered clapping followed. Marty looked at Cody for further instructions. Cody was irritated because he had gone through the Black Elephant details with him several times before. Now it was obvious that Marty's deer-in-the-headlight look meant that he hadn't understood or listened to Cody.

"Er...ah...heh...mah-wuh..." Marty didn't know what to say. From the corner of his eye, he noticed his wife Xia, giggling with one of Cody's male friends.

Cody couldn't wait for Marty to recover. He grabbed the mike and explained the game himself. "Okay, our first Black Elephant game is simple. We're going to draw the names of four guests from this box. If you get picked and you don't want to do it, you can pick a person to go in your place."

He pointed at the big pile of wrapped presents in the left corner of the stage.

"First prize gets to pick first, second picks second, and so forth," he continued.

"Wait, what's the game about?" shouted Zoey.

"Okay, good point," Cody nodded, "the objective of the first game is to do exactly what Herman does. He will perform various kung fu moves and we will have three judges. The highest overall grade wins."

The four who were selected for the game were Sonia, Mindy, Felix and Wanda. Cody handed the microphone back to Marty who announced, "Heh-ha, let the games begin!!!"

Dramatic music played. The lights were dimmed. A spotlight shined on Herman.

"Now I'm gonna start off with something easy!" Herman declared, "OoooooOoooOooOOOOOOOOOOO!!!"

He unleashed a flurry of random spin kicks, roundhouses, punches and cartwheels.

"YOGA BOOM! JADED UPPERCUT! THE TIGER OF SAN PEDRO!" shouted Herman.

Marty added martial art sounds into the mike for effect. "Whaaa! Oooh! Raaaa! Hadouken!"

The room exploded with overwhelming laughter; some of the guests were so amused that they fell off their chairs. One of the Crazy 88 waiters cracked up so hard he spilled his food. Herman repeated what he did slowly for the contestants to understand.

"Okay, Sonia! Heh-ha!" Marty announced. "Ready? You're up!"

Sonia wore a mischievous smile. The beautiful executive secretary slowly walked up to the stage. Marty cued the dramatic music to play again.

"Haiiiii-YA!!!!" she hollered out, unleashing an athletic assortment of well-done martial arts moves. "Hai-ya! YA! YA! KAiiiIII!" It was better than anything Herman did. Sonia apparently had training.

"I just...I think I just got a boner," whispered Guy.

Jack nodded. "I had no idea our secretary was a black belt."

The judges immediately gave her all tens. Sonia ended up winning the first Black Elephant game, taking home a Sony Vaio laptop as her prize. As they went into the other games, Diana tugged Cody's arm and reminded him of the remaining time.

"We've got fifteen more minutes!" she warned. "And half the guests are only served soup!"

"Shit. Shit shit shit," Cody murmured.

The games were getting boring. Marty had spent too much time on each of them. Most of the guests had lost interest. Cody walked toward the stage and grabbed the mike from Marty.

"Sorry, everyone," Cody apologized. "We've only got fifteen minutes left."

A collective groan emerged from the tables.

"We're going to have to skip right to the Secret Santa and the gifts left over from the Black Elephant. So if you...hey...wait...stop...STOP!"

It was too late. The guests—mostly drunk—stampeded toward the gift tables, taking whatever gifts they could. Zoey proved to be the most vicious, throwing her little body into the middle of the melee while nabbing presents away from other people.

"Holy shit!" smiled a lucky guest, "a new Playstation 3!"

"Gimme that!" shoved Zoey. "I have a seven-year-old son!"

Jack leaned back at the bar, enjoying the mayhem while sipping his Crown Royal.

"That right there," he pointed at the pandemonium, "is a thing of beauty."

Finally, the party was over. By the time most of the guests had dissipated, the manager of the hotel entered the room aghast at finding the hotel room torn asunder. It was too late for Cody and Marty to completely remove evidence of their rule breaking.

"What is this?!" scolded the manager. "I heard you paid off our staff and used your own?! You...what did you...ooooahhhh! I charged you extra for this! No excuse!"

"I'm not the person in charge," replied Yuki.

The manager stared at her blankly. "Who then?"

She pointed at her friend Cody whom she still had yet to meet in person.

"Hey!" the manager approached Cody. "I heard what you guys did!"

Cody rolled his eyes, plopping his personal credit card into the manager's hands.

"Give your staff a nice gratuity tip," dismissed Cody.

Money solved everything.

———————

To Cody's relief, he discovered the after-party was much better.

Held at the Happy KTV in Chinatown, the karaoke bar featured private rooms that were spacious and, just as important, soundproof. The remaining few from the Christmas party were mostly from Marty's family, but Cody also had his cousin's wife, Wanda, joining him as well his two Internet friends, Yuki and Rain.

"Why're you feeling bad, man?" Jack asked, plopping a hand on Cody's shoulder.

Cody remained silent, looking at the floor in defeat.

"You want a cig?" offered Jack.

Cody shook his head. He didn't smoke.

"You really need to loosen up," Jack advised.

"The Christmas party was a complete failure," mumbled Cody.

"No, it wasn't, man. Shit, everyone loved the hell out of it."

"Really?"

"Fuck, yeah. I wouldn't lie to you about that. Here, let me get you something to drink. What's your poison?"

Cody finally surrendered. "A Crown and Coke."

"Good shit. Come on, get fucked up like the rest of us and enjoy the night."

Cody walked over and joined the rest of the group. Rain and Herman were having a karaoke showdown.

Herman grabbed the mike and blurted out of tune," jOSiE's On a VaCATion FAr aWaY, cOME iN mY hOuSE and TalK it oVeR. SO mANy tHIngS I LIke tO pLAy, yOU knOw I liKE thOSE gIRls tO bE oLDer..."

"Um, those aren't the exact lyrics," criticized Rain.

Cody approached Yuki and smiled. Finally, they had officially met face-to-face.

"Fancy meeting you here, Ms. Melody Bunny," he smiled.

"You look tired," Yuki observed and smiled. "Are you tired?"

Cody put an arm around her.

"I was tired," he smiled. "Not anymore."

The karaoke waitress entered the room with various drinks. Marty had a Heineken while his wife sipped a margarita. Wanda got herself a gin and tonic. Cody had his Crown and Coke. The rest of them had shots of Grey Goose.

"More! More!" Jack pushed.

It wasn't long before Cody lost count on how many drinks he had. He gave alcohol a rare invitation, allowing it to take over his body and eliminate the night's stress and imperfections. Once again, Jack pushed Herman to exceed his normal threshold. By the time Herman had consumed his twentieth shot, he was drunkenly screaming obscenities at his reflection in the mirrored walls.

"You wanna challenge me?! You wanna challenge me?!" he screamed at himself.

"I love white girls!" cried Guy. "I love them so much!"

The big guy was almost as wasted, unbuttoning his dress shirt and swinging it over his head.

"Woo-hoooooooo!" cheered Rain.

Cody grabbed the nearest female to him: his cousin's wife, Wanda.

"I love you, Wanda," muttered Cody, "you're...hic... my favorite cousin. Cousin-in-law. Hic. Whatever."

He leaned his head on her shoulder and placed his hand on her lap.

"Ew, Cody!" pushed Wanda, "get off me!"

Cody looked at her and continued in his drunken sincerity, "I...mean...I mean if...if it...wasn't...hicc...for your...wedding...Marty and I wouldn't have...met...hicc. And I love him. I love him like my brother. Like he was family."

"Aawwww," nodded Marty who overheard.

Jack wasn't going to let them stop.

"Drink some more! One more time! Come on, assholes!" he continued.

"No more. I drunk I also sleep," Xia replied in her usual broken English.

Herman stopped arguing with his reflection and took additional shots with the others.

"Wimps!" he mocked.

"Fuck you!" cursed Guy. "You were arguing with your own reflection!"

"I'm not...hicc...I'm not...fuck...I...whoa..." Herman muttered.

He crashed to the floor.

"Dude," noticed Yuki, "does he wax his eyebrows?"

In his drunken state, Cody cleared out a large spot on the table. He stood at the top of it and placed a dollar bill over his eyes.

"I'M DAREDEVIL!!!!!!!" he screamed.

"Aha-eh aha-eh, ah, eh, wa-what?" laughed Marty.

Wanda walked up to Cody and pleaded for his car keys.

"You should let me drive," she insisted. "You're smashed."

"Come on, guys! More drinks!" pushed Jack.

"No!" waved off Wanda. "He's drunk. Cody, let me drive you okay?"

Five hours later, Cody woke up with a massive hangover. He was lying on a bench in the area near his office building in the Sugar Land Town Square. The rare winter snow was still there, but thankfully, the bench was in an area where there was shelter provided by some awning. He admired the beauty of the area; it was well-lit by traditional looking street lamps, intended to re-enact the old Texas towns of yesteryear mixed with a modern touch.

"Morning," came a voice next to him.

Still lying on his back and staring straight up into the dark sky, Cody rolled his eyes up and saw the semi-familiar face of the woman looking down at him. The hangover delayed his recognition, but he was used to seeing her from a low-resolution webcam anyway.

"Yuki," he finally recognized, "I'm sorry I only talked with you for a few minutes tonight."

He made himself sit straight up on the bench.

"What are we doing here?" asked Cody, still disorientated. "Sun hasn't come up yet."

"You don't remember at all, do you?"

"No," he replied, rubbing his eyes. "Who took us here?"

"Your cousin's wife, Wanda. She drove your car. Then she called her husband to pick her up."

"My car! Where is it?"

" *T'inquiète pas*," she replied. "Your car is safely in the parking garage."

"I'll be sure to thank her the next time I see her. God, my head hurts like crazy."

"I'll bet it does. That Jack guy made you guys drink shot after shot."

"And I just passed out?!"

"Um...not necessarily, Cody. Not immediately anyway."

"What do you mean by that?"

"We found out you were a happy drunk. Haha. You strutted around telling everyone that you were 'Daredevil: The Man Without Fear.' You held a dollar bill over your eyes and said that it was your 'mask.' Then you flirted with your cousin's wife."

Cody made a disgusted look with his face. "Who? Wanda?! Ewwww!"

"Yeah. But some of the others did worse. I'm not going to get into details with it, but trying to put Guy's clothes back on was like tackling a rhino. He's ridiculously strong. Hard enough to hold him down when it was mostly the women who were left sober."

"What happened to the guys?"

Yuki sighed, "You guys were such lightweights. All of you were knocked out, except—"

"I know, Jack."

"Actually, no. It was Marty."

"Haha. Marty? What? No way."

"Yes," Yuki replied and paused for a moment. "I noticed something weird about him. Each time you guys were picking up your shot glasses, he subtly poured his drink onto the floor with a flick of his wrist. He did it each time. He was deliberately drinking from an empty cup."

"He probably just wanted to stay sober to drive his wife home safely. What a great guy."

"Maybe. But I think it was something more."

Cody felt a little offended that she didn't trust his new best friend. What did she know? he thought. Cody was the one around him seven days a week. Who was she to come up with conspiracy theories? The nerve of this woman.

"Yeah?" Cody challenged defensively. "I'm sure you're reading too much into it."

"Your friend Mindy thought that way about him too."

"Aw, Mindy's just jealous! She used to be my best friend, but then she had her twin girls and stopped talking with me. She's just pissed I didn't make her my business partner."

"Let's just say it wasn't only her and I who shared that opinion, okay?" Yuki shrugged. "I'm just looking out for you, Cody."

"Well, you should. You're like a big sister to me," laughed Cody.

Yuki frowned, but then pretended to laugh.

"It wasn't like that was all we talked about, of course," she continued. "I talked with Zoey the most. We're from the same neighborhood in New York. I knew her when she was a kid, you know."

"Wow, really? Small world."

"Yeah, we went to the same church. She was only a teenager back then. Was Duke there at the party? I didn't see anyone that fit his description."

"Nah," Cody replied, "I asked him to come but he gave a resounding no."

Yuki nudged him to get up.

"Come on," she said, "let's walk. I'm a big city girl. I'm tired of sitting down."

They strolled around the area, making a solid trail of footprints in the snowy ground. The scenery felt like a ghost town. Cody had never seen the Sugar Land Town Square so empty before. They headed towards the City Hall building, a pretty piece of architecture reminiscent of ancient Rome. Near the roof of it sat a giant clock with its hour hand pointing to four o'clock.

"So what do you think of Houston so far?" smiled Cody.

"Dull. Flat. Ugly," she replied. "Reminds me of Maryland."

Maryland was the state Yuki was frequently forced to visit because her cousin lived there.

"Everything reminds you of Maryland," Cody said, rolling his eyes.

"That's right," she shrugged. "If there isn't an adequate public transportation system, it's 'Maryland.'"

"But that limits you to only a few places in the world."

"I prefer to think of it as living in only the most ideal of places."

"What's so ideal about New York City?!!"

Yuki stopped and gave him an incredulous look.

"Convenience, interesting people, skyscraper malls and mass transportation! Hello?!" she threw her hands up in the air. "The fact that I never learned to drive suggests higher civilization."

"The fact that you've never learned to drive only suggests you're living in a big city bubble!" laughed Cody.

Yuki was noticeably irked.

"How can you defend Houston?" she asked. "Every city should be like Tokyo! The Japanese have it right. Futuristic thinking for maximum efficiency! When I went there, it was like...like...I didn't want to leave!"

"That's the place that has square watermelons for the price of a steak," dismissed Cody. "Nope, I love it here."

"Hah!"

"I'm serious."

"Why? Again, it's flat and it's boring."

"I grew up in this city, sweetie," Cody said in seriousness. "My home is where my friends and family are. As long as I'm with them, life's interesting. Besides, New York City has its own flaws. It's stinky and dirty. And a lot of people live paycheck to paycheck just to pay for its extravagant cost of living."

"Yeah, but I'm just saying it's more convenient there," Yuki continued. "Look at where we are now. I couldn't get some soda and fries if I wanted to."

"Well, actually there's an IHOP a block down. Don't let the Town Square scenery fool you. Anyway, I bet you were shocked to learn we have a big Asian population here."

Yuki chuckled. "Yeah. That and I kinda expected people to talk like hicks."

"You're joking."

"You think so?"

"Even the Asians?"

"Yeah."

They laughed and suddenly found themselves holding hands. Cody found something alluring about her. Yuki may have been in her forties, but there was a young woman inside. It was evident in the twinkle of her eye and the sincerity of her smile. She would have been a catch in her youth, he realized, perhaps an unfortunate victim of bad relationships. Now age had finally caught up with her. Whatever the reason, this much was certain: her fate as an unmarried person was not her own fault.

"I see us," she began, "and I see two people that get along. We're able to express ourselves, and laugh about it. Isn't that more than what most people have? We should give it a chance."

Her words took Cody to an unfamiliar place; he wasn't used to being pursued by women. The programming in his head wouldn't allow him to believe what he heard. Media and society had once too often drilled into his head that Asian men were unworthy and unwanted. But now that he was confronted with one who cared for him—an Asian-American woman, no less— he surprisingly felt fear. The bartender at the sushi bar all those months ago was right. What he felt as barriers were lies and he made them real by believing in them. But now that he knew it wasn't completely true, why was he scared? Perhaps men are like dogs that chased after things and when they caught them, they didn't necessarily know what to do next. Nonsense, thought Cody. Perhaps he was just scared of commitment. Perhaps—he couldn't really figure it out at the moment. All he could do was reply with what he felt in his heart, saying it in the way taught to him by Daphne Lee.

"Yuki, you're a great person," he began, "but I'm just not in the time of my life where I'm looking for a relationship. Let's just be friends. Friends are forever. We'll be like that TV show *Will and Grace*. You understand that reasoning, right?"

She looked at him in silence, reading his thoughts, knowing that it was a dishonest statement.

"There's always a reason, Cody," she sternly replied.

"But mine is justified."

"Everything can be justified. So...what do you think?"

"Yuki...I'm not sure. My family. They'd..."

She let go of his hands. It was only a few moments of vulnerability, but that was a lot for Yuki. She knew he would never tell her the real reason for not wanting a relationship. She could only guess. Was it really family? Was it distance? Was it her age? It was probably age, she guessed.

"I mean, we've just met," Cody stammered.

"No," Yuki countered, "we didn't 'just met.' We've been talking almost every night for four years. I know what you look like and you know what I look like. We know each other's life story. And now we're just going to pretend like we're strangers?"

"Yes. I mean...well...yes, because we don't know each other in person. Do you have a problem with unpunctual people? Because I have a lateness problem. Do you like sleeping with a blanket on top of your head? Because I fight for covers. We couldn't know these things unless we met face-to-face."

"And I'm willing to put up with all that. How do you know I wouldn't put up with that?!"

"You couldn't even stand getting out of New York for a few days!"

Cody and Yuki looked at each other angrily for a few moments.

"This isn't about that," Yuki said, "and you know it."

"I...I don't know what it's about. Besides...I thought you liked white guys."

Yuki laughed.

"What?" blurted Cody. "It's true, isn't it? Asian guys are nerdy, short, have small dicks and we beat our women. I've heard it all."

"I don't like white guys, Cody. I've always preferred Asian guys. You Asian guys just don't prefer Asian women unless they're supermodels."

"That's not true—"

"The real reason Asian men are single is because they're picky as hell!"

Yuki stared silently, challenging him for a rebuttal. When it became evident he had none, she smirked.

"I'm forty years old, Cody," Yuki continued. "I notice things. I was hoping you'd be different. But it's your choice. Take a while to decide what feels right for you. Just know that at this moment, I offered and you declined."

They paused, enduring the awkward silence.

"I'm sorry I opened up to you," she apologized, looking down.

"Don't be."

"I mean, I'm old enough to be your auntie."

"Come on, you're exaggerating. No, you're not. Your math sucks."

They both laughed. Yuki smiled and shed a lone tear, letting it flow down her right cheek before wiping it with the tips of her fingers.

"Well," she said, pointing toward the hotel, "I'm staying at the hotel over there."

"I should go get my car," Cody said. "Thanks for coming to Houston to see me."

"No problem. Sorry if I criticized your city."

"Yeah, well, I'm sorry that I said New York smells."

They both stayed a bit longer, staring at one another. Cody reached out and gave her a long hug. Lots of thoughts went inside his head. Could he justify walking away from such a good woman? Wasn't this what Daphne did to him? He wished he knew the right answers. Between the hug, he opened his eyes and looked at the restaurant in front of him. It told him part of the reason: Hula Hoop Shakes.

CHAPTER 21: IN THE RED

The start of the new year picked up where the drama had left off. Although Cody and Marty had given the staff two weeks of paid holiday vacation, Sonia ordered the designer girls not to express their gratitude. It was, she explained, their bosses' way of winning them over so that they could take advantage of them in the long run. The girls had unofficially started a union with Sonia as its leader. Now that it was January and her orchestration of Nicky's firing had been successful, it was time for phase two: getting her own friends into the company. Everything was going according to plan until one morning when a new woman approached the front desk.

"Hello," informed the new employee. "My name is April Finley and I'm here for my first day of work."

Bullshit, Sonia thought. So it appeared Cody and Marty had an ace up their sleeves. The imperious secretary loudly smacked her gum, silently looking up and down at April. April was young, beautiful, fashionable and very sure of herself. She was possibly very independent and intelligent as well. Sonia saw fit to initiate immediate removal of this potential competition; this woman might jeopardize her plans.

"Wait just one moment," Sonia commanded.

She stormed over to the conference room where Marty and Cody were meeting with local bank representatives. It didn't matter that she was given explicit instructions not to interrupt them; she entered with authority anyway.

"Wha-uh?" Marty turned around.

"HEY!" Sonia yelled. "WHO'S THE NEW GIRL, HUH? WHY DIDN'T YOU GIVE AN INTERVIEW TO THE FRIEND THAT I RECOMMENDED TO YOU?!"

"Ah ha ha, hush shhhh," Marty put a finger over his lips.

"Sonia," Cody calmly responded, "we're in the middle of an important meeting. We'll talk after we're done, okay?"

"You just discriminated from interviewing my friend who was a perfect candidate with the right experience and credentials! And I know justtttttt the reason!!!........ It's because she's not a pretty girl!"

The bank representatives slightly gasped.

"We will discuss this after our meeting, Sonia," Cody repeated in a firmer voice.

Marty chuckled and shrugged his shoulders at her in an I-don't-know gesture. Sonia remained infuriated. She continued to show her displeasure by staying in the room a few seconds longer before making her way out. When she arrived back to her desk, an unexpected sight further tested her fury; several more new hires were waiting there.

"Hi," one of them said, "we're here for our first day too."

"They're at a meeting!!!" growled Sonia. "Just sit there and wait!"

"But—"

"Hey!" Sonia snapped. "I'm the executive secretary around here! You'll learn to do as I say, got it?"

She ignored the rest of them, gesturing for Patricia and Lydia to put their headphones down and follow her. They immediately obeyed Sonia's orders, making haste as they walked over to the front desk.

"Girls, we're going to lunch," she commanded. "I've got a lot to say!"

"Who are they?" asked Patricia, pointing at the new employees.

"Overspending," Sonia replied.

———————

"We got the monnnnney!" sang Cody.

Not long after the girls had gone for lunch, he and Marty were at the local tapioca tea house, toasting their transparent plastic cups like wine glasses. It wasn't an actual victory—they had merely suckered a desperate local bank into giving them a significant loan. It was, however, much needed money nonetheless. In a span of four months they had blown through Cody's retirement funds, Cody's grandfather's life savings, the big loan from Cody's uncle and even an additional fifty grand from Guy and Jack's father. They had only proved so far that they were good at borrowing money.

"Wooo...oh, man, sighhh. I thought Sonia almost ruined it when she interrupted the meeting," Marty admitted.

"Yeah," paused Cody, ".......yeah."

"Mu-hah, we gotta do something about her, you know? Eh? Huh-ha?"

"Damn straight. She's smart. She can calculate how much we spend on their salaries versus how many clients are coming through. She can conclude that we're not doing very well."

"Mm-hmm. Uh, hey, speaking of salaries, Cody.

Mmm...eh...sigh, well, the wife's been yelling at me again. I might need to, heh-ha, take an additional paycheck this month."

"Is...everything okay between you and Xia?"

"Sigh, you know...heh....heh heh...no...I mean, I don't want to burden you with it."

"Come on, man, if something's bothering you..."

"Sigh," Marty looked at the floor while slowly shaking his head. "It's just hard on me. I've been sleeping on the couch every night. Last, heh heh, last night she gave me 'the talk'...again!"

"No offense, but your wife's a total bitch!" Cody exclaimed. "You should be firmer with her. Stop letting her run things, man!"

"Sighhhhhhh..." Marty said, looking sad.

"Look, Marty. We were fortunate to get this bank loan. We've recorded loss after loss each month with no signs of improvement. You might have to sacrifice taking paychecks like I've been doing."

Marty's eyes grew wide with fear.

"No...no no no. Wah-uh, no no," he replied. "Can't do that. That's a no. Heh heh. Cody, come on, I have a family to feed. Ah-eh?"

"You have a marriage without children. That's hardly what I would call a 'family.'"

"But we just got this bank loan!"

"Marty," Cody looked at him firmly, "you haven't been getting us a lot of clients. This loan preserves us."

"Huff...sigh..." Marty looked sad. "I'm trying my best."

"Then what's wrong?"

"It's, you know, heh, we take these people's money via contract, then we don't produce finished products. I can't keep giving us new clients when we, heh-ha, you know...you know? Wa-huh? When we don't finish the old projects."

"Well, that's why we've got more employees now. So we can increase production. And April just joined us."

"Yes, I know, I'll have to train her..."

"No. We can't have you spending time training a sales assistant again," Cody explained. "April will have to find her own methods. You go and get us some new clients."

"Come on, can't we take it easy? We just got a bank loan, heh!"

"It's a LOAN, Marty. We have to pay it back someday. Now luckily, I've put together a plan."

Cody opened up a binder and showed him some of the number crunching. They were to use the loan money aggressively, hiring more production people to match sales. Meanwhile, Cody set up new goals for Marty to match.

"Okay," finished Cody, "you said there's a market out there and you're just withholding potential clients from us because we weren't finishing our jobs. Well, now we have the capabilities. Can you meet your new quota?"

"Yes..heh...yeah, heh-ha, of course, yeah. But we...we've really got to get rid of our secretary."

Cody shook his head in disagreement. "Nah. Sonia's got a lot of heart and she does her job. She's just low on morale. We don't need to fire her."

Marty held his breath while looking at Cody. He wanted to tell Cody how much he disliked Sonia's explicit disrespect of him. She intentionally targeted him more than Cody. Perhaps she could change her attitude toward the company, but not toward Marty. He knew when people saw through him, which was what Sonia had done. In time, she would share her opinion on Marty with the new employees. Then they wouldn't respect him anymore. But how could he tell Cody this without losing face?

"Meh-heh," Marty agreed, "yeah, she does her job."

"Yeah, she'll turn around. Especially when she sees you kicking ass in sales!"

"Sure...yeah, wah-uh, I mean, I sure hope so. Mmm-uh, at least she would stop stealing stuff from the office."

"What?!" Cody did a double take. "What do you mean she's stealing stuff?"

"I mean, huh-heh, haven't you noticed we have less rulers and pushpins..."

Cody burst out laughing.

"So she took one or two rulers home," he dismissed. "My mom does the same shit with her factory work. I can't tell you how many staplers I have because of her."

"Wah-er-ahh...well, I mean, heh, that's not all Sonia took, you know? Remember that extra computer we had? Mm-ahhh, eh...no...shhhh...gone."

"Yeah? What about it? Didn't you tell me you took that computer home for your wife?"

"Wha-what?" Marty asked. "I...heh...there goes your memory again, heh."

"No, I'm sure that's what happened. I could ask Xia."

"Oooh! Uh-uh, shhh. Meh-ah, eh? Ahhhhhh...well, ahhhhh...sighhhhh. The truth is complicated, you see, about that computer. Wah-ha, I bought an exact duplicate of it because Xia wanted it, but, heh, I could never give her a company computer. Mmm mmm. No no. But she also doesn't like me using money, so I...heh...you know, heh, ha, I fibbed a little, and said it was the same one from the company."

Cody scratched his head. "So you're saying the extra computer we had since day one has been in our office somewhere the whole time. And the one your wife has is the same model, which you bought with your own money. You hid the original somewhere and somehow Sonia found it and stole it."

Marty smiled and tapped his right pointer finger at the side of his forehead. "Now you're thinking."

"Dude," Cody was skeptical, "are you really sure? Because we'd look like complete asses if we brought that accusation up to her and she's calling us liars."

"Come on, shhh, heh, she'll probably even deny it."

"Look, we're not firing her," Cody repeated. "She cares more about Mosaic Design Studios than our other employees. We just need to channel that intensity and turn it into productivity instead of rebellion. The designer girls listen to her anyway. If we make her happy, then she'll encourage them to be happy."

"Wah-er, arrr, ahh...Cody, heh, uh, come on...she might be too tainted already. Besides, she's a thief. Heh. HA! Enough reason for us to, woo-uh, heh? Ah? You know? Let her go?"

Marty was as nervous as much as he was frustrated. Why was Cody being so stubborn about something so replaceable? It wasn't like lascivious girls were difficult to find to offer a secretarial job to. His insecurities began taking over his thoughts. He wondered if Cody's refusal to let go of her was because she was his pick? Yes, Marty realized, that was the real reason. He wanted to show him up. Maybe she and Cody were secretly working together in an attempt to overthrow him. No...no, he calmed himself down, don't overthink it. He changed his mind; Cody wouldn't do that—Sonia hated him just as much. He quickly searched his thoughts for a way to have his partner agree on letting Sonia go. Something to pull Cody's heartstrings. Yes, Marty suddenly realized, he knew just what to say.

"Phoebe," he winkled. "Ah huh? Heh-eh?"

"What?"

"Er-ah, Phoebe. From Hula Hoop Shakes. The waitress that you're infatuated with."

"How did you know—"

"Mmm shhhh. Shh shh now," Marty smiled proudly. "I have spies all over Hula Hoop Shakes."

"You made the waiters of that restaurant spy on our employees for you?"

"Wah-huh, yeah. I mean, heh, not on any intimate level, of course."

"What else do you do to spy on them?"

"Now now, Cody, we can't have you saying the S-word now...ehhh...eh? EH? We could be in trouble for that..."

"Okay, but they better not find out that you do that, man," Cody insisted.

"Mm-hmm. So, uh-huh, they tell me Hula Hoop Shakes is going to close soon."

Cody's heart sank.

"Really?" Cody asked. "They seem to have good business."

Marty shrugged. "Wah-eh, just letting you know, because Phoebe might not be in your life anymore."

"Man," Cody sighed. "Maybe I can keep in touch with her by text and stuff."

"Ooh-heh, come now, heh-ha! You tried for the last two months. She didn't go to your Christmas party, did she? Heh heh. She never gave you her number and said you guys should hang out, eh? Eh? Ah-ehhhhh?"

"You're right," accepted Cody. "I guess it's over. She was the best part of my week. I'm going to miss her."

"Mm-huh. Too bad she'll be out of a job too."

"No job?" Cody's eyes suddenly widened. Marty had set the trap. "Hey! We could give her a job!"

"Hooooo! Woo-ah! Good thinking!"

"Yeah!" smiled Cody, "I mean, we were talking about that since we first met her, remember?"

"Heh! HA! But that was just you wishing like always."

"Oh, man! Marty, you have to ask her! It'd look too suspicious if I ask her. You do it. Come on!"

"Wah-uh, I don't know, we're already pretty full," Marty sighed. "If only we could, heh, let someone go, you know? Wah-huh-haha!"

"Yeah..." Cody had an epiphany. "We've got way too many new designers just hired. I'm going to let go of one of them and make Phoebe your sales assistant. I'll do the job interview myself! One on one...in a nice restaurant."

"Er, what about Soni—"

"I know just which of the new designers to let go too."

"Ah-heh, I'm sure Phoebe would use her voice well answering phones... "

"Let's do it, Marty! Ask her! Let's give Phoebe a new job as sales!"

———

Guy's final day came two weeks later; he had to return to school in Chicago for the new semester. He didn't want to leave, and the girls didn't want him to leave either. Besides being a useful guy with brute strength, he was also their informant about Cody and Marty. Sonia had secretly gotten to the big guy long ago, as early as their first week at work. With just a well-timed wink and a teasing view of her cleavage, she had made him loyal to her without him realizing it. It was sad that he had to go, but the girls understood and threw a small party for him in the kitchen room.

"We'll miss you, Guy," Sonia smiled sweetly.

She leaned toward him and gave him what he wanted: a tight body-to-body press with her breasts squashed against him. It made him turn into Jell-O.

"Will you come back and visit us?" asked Patricia.

"I want to, but I don't know, girls," Guy replied sheepishly. "Depends on my dad. He's pretty mad at Marty. He loaned Marty a lot of money because this company almost went broke."

"You don't say?" asked Sonia with a lot of intrigue. "And it's only been a few months."

"Yeah," Guy spilled, "and now all of that's gone and my cousin and Cody just borrowed more money from a bank."

"Oh reaaalllyy?" She paused and stopped Lydia from taking the best piece of cake. "Here, why don't you eat this part of the cake and tell us more about it."

She had him now. Sexual innuendos and food—it was all that took for Guy to pour out the details.

"Aw, this cake is so good," commended the quarterback, "...munch...mmm...I love pineapples. Okay, so yeah...Marty and Cody were stressed...munch...so Cody thinks production is the problem because Marty says he's got a lot of...munch...clients lined up if we...munch...finish the projects."

Checkmate. The smoking gun.

"See, y'all?" Sonia looked at the other girls. "We're probably not going to get paid on time this week. It'll take some time for that bank loan to go through. No wonder Cody switched our paychecks from biweekly to monthly. They're broke! They don't know how to run a company."

"Mmm...yeah, oh, and also," Guy continued, "...munch...my cousin has lingerie photos of you."

Sonia's eyes grew wide. The two designer girls snickered.

Guy flashed a smile. "I mean, wow, I didn't know you

were in Maxim, Sonia! It's so awesome having a model in the company."

Sonia's face turned red. Of all the conniving, spying things that Marty was capable of doing, even she didn't expect he would stoop to that level.

"How did he...how did...that asshole...those weren't even published! How did he...?" Sonia was at a loss for words.

"Oh yeah, he also looks at your Facebook page, MySpace, Google Plus...all those things. One time he even typed your name in his Facebook status, mistaking it for the search bar. He had your name as his status for several hours until he noticed it and deleted it."

Guy left her with her thoughts as he felt his phone vibrating in his pocket. When he checked his text and learned that his ride was ready for him, he bid and hugged each of the girls good-bye. They playfully lined up and gave him a salute while he walked past them. He saluted them back. As he was leaving, Sonia had the stereo system play his favorite song: Taylor Swift's "You Belong with Me."

Once he left, Sonia called for a meeting between her and the two designer girls. They needed to discuss what they planned now that they'd received their newly processed information.

"Clearly we have a lawsuit, girls," she explained.

"Oh my God," muttered Patricia, "do you think he looks at our Facebook accounts too?"

"Of course he does. Don't be silly, hon," Sonia replied. "Perverts don't just stop with one woman. We're all in danger. Even the new employees eventually."

"Maybe we should tell Cody," Lydia offered.

"But aren't they friends?" reminded Patricia.

"Not necessarily," Sonia advised. "They're new friends. Did y'all know that Cody and Marty hadn't met until just half a year ago? Maybe we can turn Cody onto our side."

Marty had done Cody a major favor; at least on the surface, it seemed like a selfless act. He had set up a one-on-one dinner interview with Phoebe at a popular hot pot restaurant near his house. Cody relished his first chance at a date with the Hula Hoop Shakes waitress, getting past the job-related topics as quickly as possible before taking in casual conversation. He learned more about her during the first ten minutes than he had in two months from the diner. There were also so many more questions he had yet to ask, starting with why she had so much trouble with chopsticks. He knew she was whitewashed, but no Asian girl was so out-of-touch with her culture that she couldn't even use chopsticks.

"Aaah!" Phoebe screamed, dropping the food on her shirt.

"Here, let me help you with that," Cody said, wiping the food off her like she was a helpless baby. "Maybe we should ask them to give you a bib."

Phoebe laughed. "I had it. It was so close! It was inches away from my mouth!"

"Haha. Seriously, you're going to starve tonight if you keep trying with the chopsticks. Let's...get you a spoon, shall we?"

"No, it's okay," she insisted. "I got this. This is a learning process."

Her answer revealed this much: Behind the multiple piercings, tattoos and wild hair, Phoebe had a scholar's determination to learn. And, more so, there wasn't a hint of malice in her. She was a peacemaker, a neo-hippie with an egalitarian hope for the world. When the subject of her favorite city was brought up, the girl sat up with her heavy mascara eyes wide open.

"Portland," she beamed, "is where I want to eventually be. It's a wild place, man. The bands in the Aladdin Theater, the breweries on Distillery Road, the indie restaurants, pot..."

The subject of marijuana made him flinch. He should've expected it, though—her outer appearance did fit the stereotype. Then again, maybe it was a sign that she had gotten so comfortable, she had forgotten it was still a job interview. With that thought in mind, Cody reminded himself to look at her resume.

"Bowie," he read aloud, "your last name is Bowie?"

"Yeah. I know. Meh. I have a stupid name. Phoebe Bowie. I hardly say it in its entirety."

"No, no", laughed Cody. "I just didn't know that you were married."

"Married—? Oh no! No...ha ha. I'm adopted!" She twirled one of her chopsticks around. "That's why I don't know how to use these."

"Yeah, it all makes sense now actually."

He scooped some food from the boiling pot and offered it to her. Once he got around to looking closely at Phoebe from the table light, he realized she was probably just above legal age—much younger than he presumed. Perhaps just a kid who waited tables and went to school.

"People think it's great to be an orphan," she said with a distant stare in her eyes, "but you can never take away the fact that you were unwanted."

She took one of the chopsticks and twirled it around the hot pot sauce. They stayed silent for a few moments before she realized her comment might have depressed her new employer.

"But you know," Phoebe smiled and continued, "my adoptive parents have been wonderful. I didn't even come to the States until I was three."

"Really? Were you living in Korea?"

"No...haha. I was in Hong Kong. Didn't you say that's where you're from, Cody?"

"That's where my parents are from. I was made in the U.S.A.," he corrected proudly.

"Such a shame," Phoebe muttered, picking up a few raw pieces of beef and stuffing them into the boiling pot.

"W-why's that?"

"I always thought it'd be cooler to be born in an exotic land."

"Hong Kong's not an exotic land, Phoebe."

She shrugged. "Meh. More exotic than St. Louis, Missouri where I'm from. That's why I occasionally just tell people I'm from Hong Kong."

"Oh yeah?" laughed Cody, "how would anyone believe you if you couldn't mutter a word of Cantonese?"

"I can say something in Cantonese."

"Really?"

"Yeah," she smirked.

"Say something."

"<Hi, my name is Phoebe Bowie and if I'm ever lost, my parents live in 29 block C suite 5078 at Tsim Sha Tsui.>"

"Hahahahahahaha!"

"That's...all I can say in Cantonese. My parents taught

me to say that when I was a kid," she grinned. "I've no idea what the individual words mean, but overall it tells them where my address was in Hong Kong."

"You're charming," Cody complimented her. "You'll do well in sales under Marty."

They took a pause in their conversation to order more shiitake mushrooms, raw chicken meat and napa cabbage. Giving the chopsticks one more try, Phoebe attempted to grab a piece of shrimp. Her clumsy attempt was noble, but ultimately futile—she ended up dropping her entire left chopstick into the pot.

"Dang it! I'll never get this right!" Phoebe shook her head.

"Patience. Practice," Cody advised, using one his chopsticks to fish out her dropped one. "That's the secret to mastering everything."

"You seem like a good teacher," she complimented, prematurely grabbing the hot chopstick too quickly. "Ow! Hot!"

"Well, you'll be under Marty anyway. I'm sure you'll pick up sales well."

Phoebe cooled her hand by grabbing her glass of ice water. "And what do you do?"

"Ah, you wouldn't want my job. It's boring. I stare at the computer all night long, sorting through code."

"You know, I've always wanted to program. I was good at it in school."

"I hate it. It's an introverted job."

"Meh, people-person jobs are so overrated. If it was up to me, I'd never want to put on a fake smile and serve people again. I dunno...I...I hate my waitressing job. It sucks. I've always dreamed of a desk job. You'd make my day if I ever got the chance. I'll work so hard for you guys. Really. I'm a fast learner. Can you teach me how to code instead?"

He couldn't imagine a beautiful girl like her sitting behind a desk all day sorting through lines of HTML. What a waste of her natural Korean beauty—she had a gorgeous slim, olive-skinned and toned body, he thought. It was shallow to think so, of course, and he realized maybe he had been seeing her wrong the whole time. Phoebe had an underrated intelligence to her and perhaps it was time someone took notice.

"Okay," Cody finally agreed, "but I gotta warn you, we don't pay much and you'll have to come every day for two weeks to learn from me."

"Anything," she smiled. "Does that mean I get to sit next to you and work?"

"Certainly," he replied, feeling butterflies in his stomach.

After their hot pot dinner, Phoebe let Cody give her a nightly tour around town. They drove through midtown, the medical center, City Centre, the museum district and, finally, the Sugar Land Town Square. She shuttered with anticipation as their elevator transported them up to the second floor where Mosaic Design Studios was. Her first office job, he realized, and he didn't even tell her she was hired. After Cody flipped on the switch, she squealed with delight as she skipped around the office like an excited child. Cody showed her the parts of the office.

"Here we have the kitchen," explained Cody, "and beyond that are the designers' desks. I do have someone coding with me right now, but she's about to go into labor at any time, so her desk will be free for you. Also—"

He looked back and saw Phoebe staring out the window. She was looking at the Hula Hoop Diner from across the street. Cody put a hand on her shoulder and looked at it with her. She leaned a little closer towards him.

"I used to look at you sometimes from out this window," he admitted, "...sorry if that came out creepy."

"Meh," Phoebe replied, "I'm just glad I won't be working there anymore."

———

It didn't take long for Sonia to implement her plan. She decided to unleash it on Valentine's Day, when the girls got flowers and her employers received a letter from her attorney. The courier came at noon, just after the workers had left for lunch. With the exception of April and Phoebe, the rest of them were loyal to Sonia now, joining her for daily lunches at the recently opened hibachi grill.

"Fuck," cursed Cody. "That bitch. Did you read the whole letter?"

Marty nodded while crunching his fried chicken and drinking his venti-sized frappuccino. He had a knack for eating foods that would greatly increase his risk of diabetes.

"Mmm, eh-ah, I told you," Marty agreed. "She's trouble, heh-ha."

Cody pounded his fists together.

"I can't wait until they get back. I'm going to have an immediate meeting and hold everyone accountable! Everyone!"

"Weh-ah, I can't make it. I have an appointment with April to meet our latest client. Guess what her last name is? Heh. Ha!...haha...it's Bigg Decks."

Cody wasn't amused. "Man, this isn't the time for sophomoric humor. We have a lawsuit on our hands. They weren't specific on the complaints though."

Marty looked at the letter again and grew a little worried. It occurred to him as to what Sonia might be referring to.

Cody continued ranting. "I mean, it says that they were working in a 'hostile and sexually inappropriate environment.' Geez, all you did was look at their Facebook accounts and found Sonia's Maxim photos. They're making a mountain out of a molehill."

Marty felt a lump in his throat.

"Wuh-ah, now now shhh heh, you might, eh, you might hear Sonia embellish some more things later on, Cody, but I assure you that when you hear them, she's making them up."

Cody gave his best friend and business partner a quizzical look.

"What...do you mean by that, Marty?"

"Shhh shhh, heh, ha!"

"Stop doing that stupid laugh, Marty. Is there something you aren't telling me?"

Before Marty could answer, April entered the office and urged Marty to head out. They were planning to carpool towards the Pearland area.

"Now now, wah-eh, remember not to believe anything they say, heh!" Marty reminded Cody once more before leaving.

He sat alone in the empty office, wondering what Marty cryptically meant. Forty-five minutes later, to his bewilderment, Sonia returned alone from her lunch break. Perhaps this was better, thought Cody, he could direct all his rage toward her instead of all the employees. He waited until she sat down at her desk before calling her. Knowing it was Cody, the rebellious secretary allowed the phone to ring until he gave up. They stared at one another through his office window. Cody slammed the phone down and made his way over to the front desk.

"Yes?" Sonia sarcastically asked.

"We've received your attorney's letter."

"Oh, good. It was planned that way. We told the courier the exact time."

Cody pulled over a chair and sat across from her. She looked like the boss and he, the lowly employee. How were things allowed to get this way?

"Sonia," he asked, "where's everyone? Why didn't they return from lunch?"

"Oh. I just gave them the day off," she shrugged, turning her attention toward Facebook.

"Haha...you what? You? You gave them the day off? Who the HELL do you think you are?!" shouted Cody, slamming his hand on her desk.

Sonia displayed a momentary expression of shock. She was not expecting him to stand his ground. Taking a moment to collect herself, she resumed her defiant attitude.

"I turned us into a union," she announced. "Not an official one, of course. But real enough that you'll have to follow our demands."

"Demands? What is this? Blackmail?" scoffed Cody.

"No!" she stood and looked angrily at him. "Protection. Protection against HIM."

That last statement confused Cody. "Who?"

"You know who!"

"Marty?"

"Yes!"

Cody was confused. He thought that between him and Marty in the good-cop-bad-cop roles, he was the bad cop. Now he realized the girls weren't mad at him. But what did Marty do?

"Come on, all he did was stalk your Facebook," concluded Cody. "And yeah, he found your Maxim submissions too. You'll have to forgive him. Sure, he was wrong, but he doesn't mean anything from it. I'll get him to apologize, okay? We don't need to get drastic and take this to court."

Sonia stared directly at him and let out a derisive laugh.

"Hah! Hahahahaha, " she laughed. "You think that's what this lawsuit's about?"

"Yeah. That and we didn't give your friend a chance to take over Nicky's vacancy. But I think April is doing a dandy job at sales, don't you?"

"Yeah," agreed Sonia. "You're right. April's good. Real good. She's cool...I admit I felt a bit threatened at first, but she's not exactly Marty's lapdog either. She's independent, but not a rival. I admire that."

She removed a tube of ChapStick between her breasts and moisturized her lips. Then she placed it back in between her breasts.

"What?" she asked, irritated that Cody was staring.

"I've kept you here because I stood up for you, Sonia. But this is crossing the line. You are so fired. Leave this office. Now."

Sonia remained sitting and smirked instead. Her beauty no longer stunned Cody. It hadn't for awhile, but now she was at her utmost peak of unattractiveness. She was evil. No doubt she had planned this coup for a long time.

"Leave!!!" Cody repeated.

"No. I want Marty to come back and tell me to leave. Then I'll leave," she grinned. "But you know what? I bet he won't. He's afraid to hurt people's feelings. He thinks he's some kind of gentleman that cares about people's emotions. He loves to play victim. 'Oh poor Marty. Poor, poor Marty.' Hahahaha."

She stood up and walked over to Cody, pinching him on the left cheek.

"Look, Cody," she said, "the girls and I have nothing against you. In fact, I knew Marty wouldn't be here because I saw his schedule. But you've made a horrible mistake by choosing him as your business partner."

"You're out of line for saying that."

"I'm telling you something that you're too blind to see."

Cody paused and then asked, "What did he do?"

"Well, Cody darling, when you're not around," she continued, "he has made some...let's just say....advances at some of us. He had some disturbing requests for me and the other girls."

"You're lying," denied Cody. "He's in love with his wife. He wouldn't do that."

"Oh?" shrugged Sonia. "I've got a whole group of girls here who are more than willing to swear in court that he has. And you know Lydia wouldn't lie. Or Patricia. Or......Nicky."

"Nicky? Nicky was fired months ago."

"We've kept in touch," Sonia assured him. "He likes blondes a lot."

Sonia picked up her purse and pulled out a box with most of her belongings. It appeared she had been planning to leave Mosaic Design Studios for some time.

"I'll make it real clear," she concluded. "If you lose him as your partner, we'll stay and drop the lawsuit. If you keep him, not only will you lose most of your staff, but we'll be suing you guys too. After all, you guys just secured a large sum of money from the bank, I heard. This isn't about you. It's about him. Make the right choice."

Satisfied, Sonia picked up her stuff and left the office. Cody was alone again.

"Choose my company or choose my best friend," Cody repeated to himself.

Sexual harassment.

His head was telling him something that disagreed with his heart. Mosaic Design Studios making it big was stubbornly still in his hopes. They had every possible opportunity to succeed; why would Marty do something so careless to prevent that? Where was there to go back to? A dingy office job with a meager retirement fund? Sonia had to be lying, she had to. He paced around the empty office trying to convince himself of it. However, her body language and tone suggested she was too sure, too confident that what she claimed transpired actually happened. And what about Lydia and Patricia? They were saints and they claimed it happened too.

Those thoughts were still sticking with him three hours later when Marty came back, laughing and recalling funny incidents from his meeting. His humor charmed Cody enough that he ended up dismissing the incident with Sonia and keeping it a secret from Marty. This was his best friend, he realized, and friends give each other the benefit of the doubt. He decided to take on Sonia's lawsuit, choosing to defend Marty to the bitter end.

CHAPTER 22: THE EMO SAVIOR

After Cody's decision to stick with his best friend, a series of consequences occurred. Sonia followed through on her sexual harassment lawsuit, costing the company both a loss in staff and a chunk of their recent bank loan. The remaining finances for the company were only enough for the rest of the 2010 summer. With each monthly loss worse than the prior one, Marty had exhausted his excuses for the diminishing sales. Even his usual remedy of changing the subject and giving off a hearty chuckle didn't smooth things over with Cody.

Such as they were, there were still thanks to be given; at least, the company had one last chance to survive. The staff wasn't much, but the core components remained. April, now two months pregnant by her new boyfriend, assumed a less physically mobile role as the new secretary. Much to everyone's surprise, Lydia stayed, perhaps to ensure that she was the only one to see her designs to completion. And Phoebe, once the least skilled, had grown leaps and bounds as a web developer. Their loyalty should've been enough to make their final push over the summer worth it. At least, thought Cody, the girls were owed a debt of gratitude from him and Marty for their work ethic and faithfulness.

"Ah heh heh, ah heh ha, bye everyone!" Marty waved from his desk as the girls left the office.

Marty had made this statement on a mid-May afternoon, but it could've been any afternoon, which was what frustrated Cody about his business partner. His demeanor and attitude hadn't changed since day one, when he gave everyone the rest of the day off and left for tennis. A disturbing thought began swimming inside of Cody's head. Perhaps Marty wasn't either malicious or a mad genius—perhaps he was just not a very bright person. Oh sure, Cody realized, Marty may have consistently shown signs of cleverness when it came to manipulating people, but it was usually for shortsighted gains rather than for a bold, grand plan. It was the first time an opinion like that had crept inside of Cody's mind; it was the first time he had seriously doubted his best friend.

"So," Cody leaned forward in his chair after the wave-off. "What do we do now? Any large clients? Does your uncle have any more money to contribute to us? How about another loan from another bank? Maybe we could both put our houses up for sale."

His intention for that last statement was for sarcastic effect; instead, Marty took it seriously and agreed with it.

"Wuh-ah, you know," smiled Marty, "I was just thinking of that. My mom says she can sell her house and move in with Xia and me."

Leaning forward in his chair, Cody gave his best friend an expression of disbelief.

"Gee. I'd really appreciate the sacrifice your mother would make on our behalf, but I would hate it if it came down to that."

"Sigh," Marty expressed, "I know. But, ffft, we would do it. Even if Xia and my mother don't get along very well."

"No one gets along with that high-maintenance wife of yours very well."

"Huh, wah-er, I..."

As if on cue, Marty's phone rang: Xia, read the caller ID. Cody sat and stared at Marty while his wife gave him an earful over the phone.

"<Yes, huh>," he answered, "<oh...oooh, yeah, she, heh, she really shouldn't have called you that word at work...mmm-huh, mmm-huh...ah, wuh, eh, heh...well, I mean, we already have two poodles...uh, yes, sorry, I mean, heh, HA...of course we can have another little dog...sorry, ah-wuh, I...no, I didn't mean to...I didn't...no, we can have a third dog...mmm-ah, paycheck's coming soon...eh...wuh...no, no...please don't hang up...please...huh...heh...ah-meh, please no!>"

She ended the call. In a rare fit of displeasure, Marty displayed a natural reaction of anger.

"That...that BITCH!" Marty screamed.

"Damn, dude, you really shouldn't be calling your own wife a bitch. I mean, it's cool if others do it because she is one, but you shouldn't as her husband."

"Wuh...sighhhh..."

"What? You have to go?"

Marty nodded with a sad puppy face.

"Will she be at home when you get there?" asked Cody.

"No...she...I mean, sigh, there's this guy from her work she now spends time with. She, mm-heh, she wants me to feed our two poodles and have dinner ready for her when she gets, heh, home. Heh-ah."

Cody looked at him with intrigue. How could a man be so whipped? "Damn. That's kinda cold how she treats you."

"Sighhhh," expressed Marty, "I don't know. Gah-eh, huh ha ha, I don't think our marriage can survive if I go home for another month without a paycheck. Heh. Please, Cody, please. Loan me some more of your personal money."

This conversation again, realized Cody.

"Man, look, Marty, you're my friend and you don't have to pay back the money that I've given you, but I'm almost broke now. I've nothing more to give you, dude. I haven't even paid my own mortgage in months, you understand? You're going to have to save us through sales. It's the only way."

"But how?" Marty asked. "How am I going to get sales? Wuh-heh-heh?"

"How are you—?" Cody couldn't believe he heard Marty say that. "Listen, I don't know anything about sales. But you've got to try. This is your strength. It's what you assured me that you did well."

"Sigh..."

"There are no more saviors," Cody continued. "We've used up all of our lifelines. My uncle from Hong Kong...Guy and Jack's dad...the bank loan...all of it is almost gone. Mosaic Design Studios has three more months to get its act together. At some point, we have to save ourselves."

Marty reacted with more pouting noises. "I...I mean, heh, we don't finish our projects...we, mm-ah, we keep taking people's money first. It just stacks up the workload more and more."

"Yes, but we're going to need to keep getting new clients so that our own employees can get paid. Otherwise, we can't catch up."

"Yeah, I mean, heh...sighhhhh." Marty wanted to disagree and express his opinion, but he was afraid of hurting Cody's feelings or starting a fight. "You're right. You're right, man."

Cody gave him a quizzical look.

"Are you sure I'm right?" he countered Marty. "It's okay to speak your mind, you know."

"Wah-eh, well..."

"Okay, so you do have a conflicting opinion. Spill."

"Mah-uh. No no. Shhh. No no, heh. HA!" Marty was nervously shaking. "Don't pressure me, man. Mmm...ffft..."

Cody grew tired of his mind-reading games. "You think getting new clients will only increase our workload, right?

You're worried that it'll be like Tetris and we'll stack and stack until we get in trouble. Is that it?"

"Hey, heh, you said it, not me!" laughed Marty. "You can't quote me on that. No no. Hush hush. Shhhhh."

"Well, I wish we had one more savior, but we don't. So..."

As he mentioned the word 'savior,' Marty had a sudden epiphany.

"Mm-wuhhh!" He raised a finger. "There, heh, there is someone! Heh...HA!"

Cody squinted his eyes and looked at Marty. "You're telling me that you know someone who would give us a shitload of money and save our company? Is...is that what you're telling me?

"You said it, not me!"

"What do you mean?" asked Cody. "You're the one who just said it, I heard you."

"Now now, Cody. Now now. Revisionist history, heh hah hehhh."

"Stop the bullshit! I just heard that you said you know someone who might invest in our company. Who is it?!"

"Really?!" Marty exclaimed. "Well, that's a good question, heh, mmm-ahhh. You're asking me if I may know someone. Good idea."

"The fuck—"

"It was your idea."

"Did I really?" Cody was confused. "Okay, maybe I brought it up first. I don't remember anymore. Anyway, do you know anyone that can help us or not?"

"Hmmmm, wa-uh, there IS someone, in fact."

"Who? God damn it, Marty...don't make me keep asking!"

Marty cleared his throat. "Wang's Restaurant."

The mere mention of the most successful Chinese restaurant in Houston's history made Cody spring up from his leather chair.

"What do you mean?" demanded Cody. "The Chinese restaurant where all the celebrities go to? The one that's internationally known from Houston? Those guys are loaded."

Marty smiled and nodded.

Cody laughed with joy. "You know Mr. Wang?! That guy's super rich!"

"Wah-ehhh, heh, well, ahhh, hmmm, heh. Heh. HA! Haha! Hoo. Fffttt."

"Is he a family friend of yours or something?"

Marty nodded.

"Dude, I...why didn't you mention it before?!" Cody realized. "Let's ask him for financial help! We'll give him partial ownership of the company. Tell him we've got over several hundred clients. Tell him we're doing well and that we need money to...to expand!...yes...that's a good reason. Whatever it is, ask him! He's insanely rich. Everyone in Chinatown knows Mr. Wang. I...I can't believe you know the guy."

Marty loosened his tie a bit; he needed to tell Cody the catch.

"Er, hmmm, heh, ahhh...well, it's...I mean, I'm not that close to Mr. Wang. I, heh, I'm actually just close with his son. We knew each other from a martial arts school when we were kids. Heh hah heh. Mr. Wang, eh, he's very disappointed in his son because, mm, his son doesn't, heh-eh, wanna follow in his footsteps!"

"That's even better!!!" exclaimed Cody. "We'll make his son the partner then!"

"Good idea!"

"What do you mean? It was your idea. How can it be my idea? I didn't even know this son of his existed."

"Huh? What were we talking about? Muh-eh?"

"We were talking about anointing Mr. Wang's son as a third partner if he financially supports us. We'll let this son dip his toes in responsibility and learn how to manage a company! I mean, he's a rich guy's kid, right? I figure he's our age, right? Probably spoiled as hell."

"That's a good idea! Remember, you thought of it!"

"I...what?...stop doing that psychological mindfuck!"

"Huh? Wah-uh? What are we talking about?"

"About making this rich man's son our business partner in exchange for financial help," explained Cody.

"Good idea!"

"Really?"

"Heh, yeah!"

"I know! I must've thought of it...I don't know how it got into my head...I..."

"Let's do it! Wah-huh, you're a genius, Cody!"

"I am!" He was too excited to care about who took credit.

———————

A week later, unfortunately, Mr. Wang agreed to only the unwanted portion of their proposal. The infamous owner hastily accepted bringing his son in as a third partner; however, he refused to offer any financial help. Free labor, Mr. Wang insisted, was value in and of itself. Knowing that it wouldn't be enough incentive, the restaurant tycoon also dangled a grand financial reward—should Marty and Cody manage to do the impossible and prove that his son could responsibly run a company, he would offer to give them one million dollars in support.

Cody found out just how daunting their task was the day Wilbur Wang was brought in. Similar in age to both him and Marty, the overindulging adult child immediately showed his spoiled and high-maintenance side. Sharing wasn't something he knew—not in the partnership and not in the nature of the business. Rather than continue Mosaic Design Studios as a company that made websites, Wilbur demanded that it transform itself into a venture for promotional events.

Ever the neutral party, Marty muttered half-agreements and half-defenses. Cody, on the other hand, couldn't decide what he disliked more about Wilbur—the spoiled brat's obstinacy or his coddled prissiness and constant stuttering. Indeed, he had not met a more conscientious metrosexual. Considering Wilbur's well-maintained and deliberate bed-head hair, subtle use of eye shadow, perfectly moisturized skin, skinny jeans and carefully plucked hairless face, Cody didn't know whether to punch him or kiss him. He was irresistibly pretty, evidenced by the swooning reactions of the female employees. Meanwhile, his Filipina-American girlfriend, Rosie de Rosales—who also came to the meeting—was the epitome of masculinity. She was assertive, crass, vocal, bossy and openly competitive. In addition to the aforementioned traits, she was also physically well-toned, square-jawed and indifferent to fashion, and sported a short-cropped haircut that would fit better on Jack or Herman. Together, the paradoxical couple combined for an overbearing vexation of oppressiveness.

This, along with Cody's lack of an upper hand, resulted in his reluctance to try Wilbur's direction. Without further ado, everyone was mandated to show up for the meeting, including Herman and Jack.

"Alright, everyone," Cody began, handing out copies of the meeting's bullet points, "as you can see to my left, we've got a new member today. This is Wilbur Wang, our new...uh... director of marketing. We're changing the identity of our company to focus on promotions and catering. Marty suggested that we try building retainers as well. These are incomes that we can receive from restaurants and clubs on a monthly basis. Wilbur will be a vital part of our company by helping us establish this direction."

"What about websites?" Lydia asked.

"Yes. We—"

Rosie shoved herself into the forefront and interrupted, "You guys will only be doing design and websites for Wilbur's promotional events."

Cody could hardly contain his displeasure of being cut off in mid-conversation. Who did Wilbur's girlfriend think she was by interrupting? he wondered, she wasn't even a part of the company.

"No," countered Cody, "there are unfinished sites we still have to do. We're still going to be doing websites."

"L-L-Look," stuttered Wilbur, "y-y-you brought m-m-me in here to h-h-help you g-g-guys out. S-s-so we d-d-do this my way!"

"No," Cody repeated, "maybe you misunderstood. Again, we're still a web company but now we'll have a promotional.......side.......to it."

"T-t-this w-w-wasn't the d-d-deal, man!" Wilbur said with an accusing finger.

They both looked at Marty for his opinion on the matter.

"Wah-uh, ahhhhh...mmm...Wilbur has a point, heh," Marty nodded. "And Cody has a point too."

"The hell does that even mean?" Cody wondered out loud.

"God, you people are morons," Jack blurted, leaving the meeting room. "I'm heading out for a smoke."

Marty watched his cousin go without stopping him. "Heh-hmm, ah, heh, you know, heh heh, maybe we can share the staff."

"I wouldn't mind helping Wilbur," answered Lydia sweetly.

"Yeah," added April, "this party promotion thing sounds fun!"

The rest of the staff chimed in their favorable opinions about doing party promotions. Cody found it unbearable that his dream company was suddenly turning into Mosaic Wilbur Wang Party Promotions. He looked at Marty for help, but Marty was busy chuckling instead. Cody felt annoyed. Shouldn't Marty be on his side? Weren't they the best of friends? And why was he no longer surprised if the answer to both of those questions were "no"?

The transfer of power had already been completed by the time the meeting was over. It was manifested in the way the staff overwhelmingly welcomed and unquestionably obeyed any request from Wilbur and Rosie. It was further exhibited when the Mosaic Design Studios sign was taken down and a "Rawr Means I Love You in Dinosaur" sign was temporarily put up in its place.

"What the hell is happening?" commented Cody to Marty. "Didn't you just feel like our company got hijacked?"

"Heh heh, ahhhh, he's such a douche," agreed Marty.

"'Such a—,' dude, if that's how you felt the whole time, why didn't you stand up to him and She-Hulk?"

"Sighhhh. It's, heh, it's...I mean, what was I supposed to do, heh-ah?"

"I don't know! Maybe back me up when I'm defending our company? Show some spine?"

Marty nervously chuckled and shrugged. "I, heh ha ha, I'm doing my best, Cody! Maybe, meh-eh, he took the 'third partner' part a little too literally."

"That's what we said, didn't we? We told him 'third partner,' not 'sole dictator.' Man. I felt like we just exchanged Sonia for this guy! When is it our turn to be the bosses of our company?"

———

Regardless of Cody's fears, the company responded to the new direction with paramount enthusiasm. In less than a week, the now nameless company—temporarily referred to as Rawr Means I Love You in Dinosaur Promotions—had procured its first client: a jazz and sushi lounge called Purple Wasabi. The owner, an impassionate Cantonese entrepreneur named Roy, spared no expense in making the place a grand exhibition. He expected Purple Wasabi to achieve the triple crown of restaurant ownership: nightly packed parties, exemplified culinary delights and, above all, maximum profiteering. Unlike Mr. Wang, however, Roy was not wealthy, but he had so much confidence in his sushi lounge that it was worth gambling away his life savings.

Marty provided the man with every bit of empathy he could muster. It was almost a little too easy. By speaking to Roy in his native tongue and fitting the profile of someone he'd trust, Marty negotiated highly favorable opportunities for Wilbur to appear competent. Of course, the rewards were beneficial to his goals as well and it only made sense to go where his new bread was buttered. If the situation with Purple Wasabi made Wilbur look good, the million dollars his father offered was just three months away. And by then, who needed Cody?

He put all these thoughts aside while the three partners waited for Roy in his restaurant's private meeting room. The room was very well-decorated, luxuriated in the wealthy Hong Kong tradition: giant golden fu dogs, egg-shaped jadeite pieces, figurines of Cai Shen the God of Wealth, elaborately designed fish tanks filled with a thousand gold fish, and a beautiful scroll with four characters that read, in order, "Good Fortune," "Wealth," "Longevity, " and "Happiness." The owner entered with a small entourage—all from his hometown of Hong Kong, of course.

"<I am so glad to meet you guys>," Roy warmly greeted them. "<We Cantonese brothers need to stick together. Look around you. Look at all my employees. All Cantonese. Even the busboys. Hell, even these chairs and tables are made from Hong Kong!>"

Cody and Wilbur looked around their chairs, expecting to find a "Made in Hong Kong" label.

"<Muh-heh, of course, of course>," nodded Marty. "<Heh, if you can't trust your own people, who can you trust? Eh eh?>"

"<Yes>," Roy smiled, "<so happy that you feel what I feel. See what I see.>"

Marty smiled like a puppy dog. "<Wah-eh, you are my brother, Roy.>"

"<Cantonese brothers. For life.>" Roy shook his hand firmly. "<So, let us discuss what you have proposed in agreeable terms.>"

They reviewed giving Wilbur complete control of the event operations, with all external costs provided by Roy himself. The low monthly residual to their company, however, revealed an uncharacteristic stingy side of Roy. He was willing to spend thousands on deejays, photographers and go-go girls, but for the use of their company's services, he offered merely five hundred dollars. Cody immediately saw it as a red flag.

"How are we surviving with this guy?" he asked Marty the next afternoon in their office. "He's barely enough to pay for the printer toner."

"Meh-huh, ehhh." Marty thought about the situation as if contemplating it for the first time. "You're right, I didn't think of that. Heh. You know me. Heh heh heh! I suck at math!"

"What are you—your head in the clouds?" Cody expressed. "Get us some website jobs! We're bleeding all of our leftover money! I haven't paid my mortgage in months!"

"Sighhhhhh." Marty sadly looked at the floor. "I'm trying to, heh, make Wilbur happy. Wasn't that our goal? Meh-eh, wasn't that what you told me to do?"

Cody held back; Marty's point made sense. It was a million dollars or bust.

"Yeah," he nodded, "but what about our immediate survival? How do you know Roy's going to pan out? He gives a good spiel about being Cantonese brothers and all, but I wish he'd back it up with money!"

"Now now now, shh hush hmm-eh," Marty shushed as he checked to make sure their office door was closed. "I...I got us a plan, mm-heh."

"Oh, yeah?!" Cody chewed on the eraser of his pencil. "Tell me this plan, Marty. Does it involve us? Our original vision? Do you know that Wilbur is overriding all of my orders to the staff? They haven't been doing any of our work for days! They've been making his personal portfolio and website. They've been doing strictly Purple Wasabi stuff."

"Wooo, fffft, yeah, heh, that's bad," agreed Marty, "but isn't that what we wanted?"

"They're under the impression that Wilbur is the most important person in this company!!!" Cody said, overreacting. "And what if Mr. Wang sees our numbers and realizes Roy has ripped us off for half a grand a month? You think he's going to be impressed with Wilbur doing that? That's not leadership we're proving, that's foolish cheap labor!"

Marty paused and contemplated whether or not he should tell Cody something he didn't know. Cody knew him long enough to recognize that look.

"You know something more," he accused Marty. "What is it?"

"Er-ah...well...there's a big payoff coming from Roy."

Cody sat on the edge of his chair. It was starting to become a normal thing for him to do when talking with Marty. "What 'big payoff?'"

"Bluefin Tuna Night."

"...what's that?"

Marty took an unnecessary deep breath and then explained the concept of the Bluefin Tuna Night. Roy was planning to import a rare and expensive tuna straight from Japan. It would be gathered fresh from Asia, delivered to Houston in under twenty-four hours. This naturally made it exceptionally expensive, but also unique. Where else in Texas could anyone eat bluefin tuna?

"So you see, heh," Marty continued explaining. "Roy wants to make it a fancy suit and tie event."

"Charging several hundred dollars a person for V.I.P. and seventy-five for regular seats," said Cody, making the calculations on paper. "That's...that's a hell of a lot of money if he sold out."

Marty smiled and nodded.

"So how much did he say he'd give us in sales commission?" asked Cody.

"Well, er, ahhh, hmmm, it's, heh, it's not nice to bring up an exact negotiation amount when we were planning," Marty protested.

"You mean you didn't set a price and agreed to do it anyway?!!"

"Now now, Cody, shh shh, wah-eh, Roy doesn't work like that. He puts his trust in us and if we do well he'll, heh, he'll take care of us after the event is over. Besides, it doesn't matter as long as Wilbur looks good."

"No, this is business," countered Cody. "Enough of this brotherhood crap. We've got two months left or we die as a company. We need an exact amount to pay the employees, pay off rent and other expenses. I know the figure. It's fifteen thousand dollars. That's how much commission we get from Roy or else we take our talents elsewhere. He signs a contract or else."

With that said, Cody started dialing the number to Purple Wasabi. Marty immediately ran up to him and wrestled the phone away from his partner.

"What are you doing?" Cody struggled. "I'm telling Roy he has to sign a contract!"

"No...no...please...Cody... heh... ah-weh...ahh. .. don't... ehhh..."

Cody hung up.

"What else are you hiding from me?" he demanded from Marty. "Why were you so afraid I'd make that phone call?"

"Heh-ahhhh, nothing, no, I mean, he doesn't answer the restaurant line. Eh?" Marty smiled. "Look, I'll, heh, I'll just text his cell and tell him about it!"

Cody eyed his partner suspiciously—he had heard someone mention once that business partnerships were like a marriage. If that were so, they were on the edge of divorce because Cody didn't trust him. Ever since Sonia's warning, he had begun seeing Marty in a different light. As much as he didn't want to believe it, she was right about Marty's motives and nervous laughter seeming suspect. Now he was wondering if there was more going on than he was told. Perhaps adding Wilbur as a partner had been planned all along. To ensure protection in their next meeting at Purple Wasabi, Cody surprised everyone by pulling out a contract in front of Roy.

"<What's this?>" the restaurant owner asked.

"Contract," Cody sternly explained in English. "Marty said he texted you about this."

An offended look fell upon Roy's face. It was obvious that he hadn't been told the contract was coming. Marty gulped.

"<Contract?>" Roy echoed in Cantonese.

"<Ah, heh, Roy, I didn't know...I...>" Marty stumbled to reply.

"Yeah," nodded Cody. "We'll agree to sellout the Bluefin Tuna Night event if you give us a commission of fifteen thousand dollars. That's about a thirty-three percent commission from the total profits. Pretty fair, if you ask me."

Roy looked Cody in the eye; the Asian-American traitor was betraying the gentleman's agreement. This wasn't how the Cantonese brotherhood does things, Roy believed. A contract symbolized a lack of trust, a lack of understanding and, above all, a lack of respect.

"<Okay>," Roy wryly smiled. "<You want to do this the American way. Okay. I thought we were Cantonese brothers. Dragon brothers. But you insult and challenge me with this contract. But okay.>"

He whipped out a pen and scrawled his signature on the contract.

"<Wah-uh>," Marty said, trying to smooth things out. "<You have to excuse my partner Cody here. He's—>"

Roy threw the contract back at Cody. "<Okay. Signed. You'll get your thirty-three percent if you sell out the tickets. All three hundred of them. Show me what you hot shots can do.

Hunh!>"

The sushi restaurant owner got up and attended to his kitchen staff. The three partners were kindly escorted out by Roy's manager. They were left to argue amongst themselves in the parking lot.

"Y-y-you i-i-idiot! N-n-now he's m-m-mad!" stuttered Wilbur.

"Sigh, Cody." Marty shook his head. "You really shouldn't have done that."

"What? This is about principle, isn't it?" Cody defended. "I'm not going to risk using up my staff's time for a petty gentlemen's agreement!"

"Y-y-your s-s-staff?" Wilbur shook a finger at him. "I-i-it's my c-c-company n-n-now!!!"

Cody lost his temper. "WHY YOU SPOILED PIECE OF—"

Marty got between them and played peacemaker.

"Heh, come on guys, we're all on the same side now. Mm-hmm. Mmeh?" Marty looked at Cody. "Mm-hhhehhh...?"

"Yeah," Cody replied breathing hard.

Wilbur gave him a challenging stare.

Marty stammered a noise. "Mm-hhuhhhh."

"Yeah, I'm alright," Cody repeated. "I'm alright. Let's just fucking do this and get it over with."

Marty carpooled with Wilbur on their way to the office; Cody had noticed an obvious bonding between those two. Marty wasn't bright enough to set his Facebook exchanges with Wilbur to privacy, especially photos of their weekend hangouts. It was a clear message that Cody was a third wheel and that, out of everything that had happened, stung the hardest. Marty had merely pretended to sink with the ship, but he was probably abandoning it either way. With a million dollars he could start his own company; with a loss he would run away and scheme with someone else. Regardless of what happened, he had no more need for Cody and the rest of the staff. Now that they were down to nearly their final month, they were set on course for letting the success of the Bluefin Tuna Event determine their fate. All the eggs in one basket, Cody realized, with Marty the least of the victims should it fail.

Three weeks later, the Bluefin Tuna Night event failed.

Blame tumbled from one person to another like a setup of dominos falling. Cody was upset at Marty for not selling the tickets; Marty acted innocent and suggested Wilbur had taken care of it. Wilbur claimed all his time was spent preparing the party buses, dancing girls, band, photographers and a video crew. Meanwhile, Roy felt contempt toward Cody for promising a guaranteed sellout. The event had cost him tens of thousands—they ended up with enough uneaten bluefin tuna to feed the homeless.

In a fit of rage, the infuriated owner demanded that Cody be immediately sent to his office. The manager found him walking Phoebe to her car and delivered the indictment. After making his way through the restaurant, Cody found a hostile atmosphere awaiting him inside the familiar Purple Wasabi meeting room. The silence from everyone signified its seriousness. At the far end of the conference table sat a cigarette-smoking Roy, ready to explode. Beside him were Cody's two partners, seemingly blameless from the fiasco.

"Hey!" Roy barked in a thickly-accented English. "You stupid American boy! You know what you cost me tonight?!!!!!"

Cody stared back at him with equally challenging eyes.

"You say full house!" Roy continued. "I, Roy, I say okay. I believe, you see?! Then I order too much bluefin tuna! You see this? You see this tuna all around the table? All outside?! The bums are eating it!!!!!!!!"

Roy's face was as red as a lychee. One of his staff members urged him to calm down, but Roy pushed him out of the way.

"<That's all homeless food now>," Roy switched back to Cantonese. "<I gave you all so many chances. I even gave you guys an advertising budget! How come I didn't see any ads of my event anywhere, huh?>"

"What advertising budget?" scoffed Cody. "You didn't give us shit!"

"<Don't play dumb with me!>" yelled Roy. "<I'm already pissed!>"

Cody glared at Marty and then looked back at Roy.

"What advertising budget?!" Cody repeated.

Roy pointed at Cody with the cigarette between his fingers. "<Oh, you want to play this game, you bastard? I don't think you do. You've embarrassed me enough tonight. I gave you two thousand dollars—in cash because I trusted you guys—marketing budget...where did you use it?!>"

Cody's jaw dropped and he looked at Marty's eyes across the table. His partner shifted his gaze toward the floor. Marty must've taken the advertising money for himself, realized Cody.

"I see it so clearly now," Cody chastised Marty. "Asian brothers, eh?"

"Ah heh heh, Cody, please...heh...there's been a misunderstanding..."

Cody left the room before Marty could explain himself.

By instinct, he drove to the alleyway behind the CVS pharmacy near his house—the one where he, Marty, and Guy had made fun of Herman a year ago. The friendship back then had felt so real for him; he was naive enough to believe that life was more than people befriending one another just from necessity. He did not want to believe that what his cousin Duke had told him was right—that life was just looks, money and social status. But how else could he interpret this reality? How much smarter would it have been if he started his company without foolishly giving half of it to someone that he had just made friends with? To add insult to injury, his iPhone had been continuously vibrating with Marty's phone calls for the past half hour. It was a feeling of déjà vu; he had gotten used to face-saving apology calls.

"Yeah, man?" finally answered Cody.

"Wooah-ho, pshew, ffft," Marty said in his usual exaggerated tones, "emo boy was crying after we left Roy's place!"

"Who's emo boy?...Oh, you mean Wilbur."

"Yeah, shhh, heh! Yeah! Oh, man! He was stuttering even more than normal! Heh, he was devastated about it! Apparently he asked, like, a hundred friends to come and none of them showed up! Hah ha! That was why we didn't sell out!"

"That's still not the reason, Marty. We failed as a team. What'd you do, huh? What did you do this whole time we were organizing that event? At least Wilbur tried, as prima donna as he was."

"Huh," Marty struggled for words. "Er, ah, come on, heh heh, Cody. I was at the office taking care of production."

"Your title says 'CEO Sales Director'! That means you get sales!!!!" Cody lost his temper.

"But the workers needed me, they—"

"Yeah right. I saw you. You usually just sat there in the office, socializing with everyone! Not a damn time did you do anything, especially in the last month when we needed you the most! This is OUR company, man!!! And then you just sit there and crack jokes while Rome burned! I believed in you. I believed we had the opportunity of a lifetime to write our own path, create our own destiny, to escape this notion that people like us have to accept the role of a model minority!"

At this point, Cody wished Marty would respond with anger. A deep part of him hoped his best friend would care enough to defend a similar concern for their company. Marty didn't, of course. Instead, like always, he laughed it off.

"Well, ah, it's not, come on...it's not like that. Heh," was all Marty could reply with. "Oh man, heh, you should've seen Roy's expression when you left. Wuh-eh-ah!"

Cody expected to crush his iPhone with his bare hands as his grip tightened from displeasure.

"Listen, you asshole," he seethed at Marty. "We've inconvenienced a lot of people as a result of this company. We just lost Roy's bid and, by default, we've also lost Mr. Wang's confidence. I don't understand why you stole the advertising budget or how you could so casually laugh at what happened to us, but you are completely stupid for taking short-term rewards for long-term consequences!"

"Aarr-ah, now now Cody," Marty responded. "I mean, I believe in that too. Freedom, man. It's what it's all about. Breaking the bamboo ceiling! Heh! We can't give up what we built, muhhh, not without a fight we're not! I'm with you all the way, man! Heh, you know what really? Fuck Wilbur! We never should've catered to his party bus shit in the first place, huh?"

"Oh yeah? You really believe that? You seem to have gotten pretty chummy with 'emo boy.'"

"Ffft, come on, heh. Chummy. Me? Him? I was always on your side, man."

"You're on everybody's side, Marty. That means you're on nobody's side."

"Heh-ha! Yer-ah, you don't understand. I really am on your side."

"Really...prove it. I want you to tell Wilbur that he's no longer welcome in our company tomorrow. Tell all the girls that the event was a disaster and that we're broke. You're going to let April, Lydia and Phoebe go. You're going to be the bad cop this time. Then we're going to run the company together, just you and me."

"Er, ahhh, yeah, I got it, man! No problem! Psssh! Fuck emo boy. We're going to save this company, heh, you and me together! Like real Cantonese brothers, man! Not that fake brother stuff that Roy was spouting! Heh! Like Double Dragon, man!"

CHAPTER 23: DISAPPEARING ACT

With his stomach in knots, Marty was dreading to tell the girls it was all over; yes-men like him always did. But with four kamikaze shots already, he really couldn't continue with a fifth one. As for the news Cody asked him to deliver, he had been trying to do so, but the timing was never right for Marty. They usually ended up talking about something else, watching a movie or, like the present moment, celebrating his birthday with drinking games. There was no choice, Marty convinced himself, he just couldn't think of a nice way to tell them they were laid off. So he never told them.

As a result, he had a good birthday, the best one he ever had. Rosie bought him a Batman-themed cake, Wilbur bought him free shots, the girls sang "Happy Birthday" together and that was enough for him to believe it was better to remain the good guy.

"T-t-to my b-b-best friend, M-M-Marty Ho! A b-b-brother to me," Wilbur toasted.

"Maw-uh, ah! Heh!" Marty gushed. "HA!"

"D-d-drink!" Wilbur insisted. "Drink drink d-d-drink!"

Rosie and the girls joined the chant. "DRINK! DRINK! DRINK!"

Succumbing to their persistency, Marty unwisely gulped down the fifth shot. It was all that his lightweight threshold could withstand. His defenses had raised a white flag. In those rare times that he had gotten drunk, Marty found alcohol to be a truth serum—dangerous to someone who was used to filling every sentence with half-truths and tactical cognizance. Worse, it made him into even more of a yes-man. In a state of embarrassment, he began muttering incoherently and stumbled his way upon a rotating world.

"Wha-uhhhh...ahhhhhhh....hehhhh...haaaaaa."

As April waved her hand in front of his face, the trail of motion from the movement seemingly created ten hands.

"Areee youuuuuu oookkkaaaayyy?" Her words came across to him in slow motion.

"Merrrrr-ahhhhh....woooo..." Marty found his own words taking their time to come out as well. As he looked down and focused on her dazzling cleavage, the drunken Marty felt drool descending from his mouth.

"Ohhh myyyy Godddd." Who was it? Marty figured it was Rosie who said that.

His current dizziness notwithstanding, the birthday boy was ignored for a moment when Wilbur loudly declared that he had an announcement. The staff and Wilbur's girlfriend gathered around him as well as some curious nearby bar patrons.

"M-M-Marty a-a-and I are gonna s-s-s-s-s-s-s-sssss...ssssss—"

"'Start', hic," helped Marty.

"—s-s-start our o-o-o-o-o-o-o-o—"

His stuttering only heightened the anticipation of whatever news he was trying to spew. After a few more 'o's, the group lost patience and began guessing his next word out loud. Fortunately, Wilbur blurted out the word he wanted to say.

"—o-o-OWN company! Y-y-yeah t-t-that's r-r-right! A c-c-company! This t-t-time we're gonna d-d-do it r-r-right."

Even in his less than perceptive state, Marty wished Wilbur wouldn't have announced their new business so soon. After all, he hadn't even told Cody he was leaving his current one yet. And how confused would the girls be as they still believed they were on Mosaic Design Studios' payroll? Ah well, dismissed Marty, that was his former best friend's problem, not his.

"Cool," remarked Rosie. "What'll it be called?"

Wilbur gave a proud smile and replied, "'Y-Y-You're t-t-the C-C-Celebrity'!"

"Wait, what about the current company?" questioned April.

Wilbur gave a smug shrugging of his shoulders. Several days ago, he had demanded that Marty leave Mosaic Design Studios and join him. Marty, as always, agreed, but he balked at informing Cody like he promised.

"A-A-And I'm g-g-gonna g-g-give L-L-Lydia the honor t-t-to m-m-make my l-l-logo!" beamed Wilbur.

"Awesome!" The lilliputian designer held her smile, forgetting for a moment to conceal her crush on him.

"Wow, a company designed to make people feel special," April replied.

"Y-y-yeah!" proudly proclaimed Wilbur. "B-b-because we believe that p-p-people should be t-t-treated right! Unlike how C-C-Cody runs his business! F-f-fuck Cody, man!!!"

"Heh, ha!" agreed the drunken Marty, toasting an empty shot glass to Wilbur's empty shot glass. "Yeah, fuck him, heh! Woo-HA! Wah-uh, he doesn't have your vision, Wilbur! He doesn't know how to, wa-eh, treat people right like you do!"

"F-F-FUCK MOSAIC DESIGN STUDIOS! FUCK THAT SHITHEAD C-C-CODY QUAN!" Wilbur toasted with a sixth round of kamikaze shots.

Marty chuckled, "Wah-heh-ha, er ah-hah!"

The interns and employees hesitated for a moment and weakly toasted back.

"I...I have to go," Phoebe excused herself as she left the bar.

The former waitress had been quiet for most of Marty's

little birthday bash. She was as queasy as much as she was confused. Unlike Lydia and April, she had seen a lot of Cody's good side. But then again, she was often inclined to see everyone's positive side, including Wilbur's and Marty's. It was disheartening for her to witness a splitting of the company; worse yet, her immediate future was in question. Reverting to her usual habit, she treated herself to a cigarette and, after it was down to its last inch, discarded it for another one. The events that had transpired frustrated her. Cody had promised her a better future if she gave him her best. She was peeved that her new job had likely ended prematurely because of childish bickering. The thought of it was so distracting that she barely made out the footsteps from behind her.

"Hey!" called out Lydia.

Phoebe fumbled to put her cigarette out, dropping and stepping on it on the sidewalk. Although everyone knew she was a chain smoker, she was still ashamed of being seen with a Marlboro in hand.

"Oh, uh, hi," Phoebe stammered. "I thought...I thought you were still with them, Lydia. Are they done?"

It was rare for them to have a conversation together; Phoebe suspected it was because Lydia figuratively looked down on her. Of course, there wasn't any actual evidence to support that feeling of insecurity. Her coworker seemed nice enough, but she was always distant—much more so than with the others. It was also natural for girls who were polar opposites to misjudge and make assumptions. Phoebe knew that Lydia had come from a good family and had a great education; Lydia had never mentioned taking a blue collar job before and with her talent she might never have to. It was only natural if Lydia considered Phoebe beneath her, even if she failed to see Phoebe's positives. After all, she thought, Lydia wouldn't be the first one or the last.

"No, they're still drinking," Lydia answered with a reserved tone. "I felt a little unnerved. I can't drink, you know. Christian upbringing and all. So...what are you doing out here? Smoke break?"

Phoebe gave off a look of shame. "I was hoping you wouldn't catch that. But yeah. I was...I needed a cig."

The two young women stood silently on the sidewalk, watching a few people pass by as they struggled to come up with conversation.

"You can smoke inside the bar, you know," Lydia finally said, suggesting the obvious.

Phoebe rolled her eyes but remained composed on being nice. She knew her diminutive coworker didn't mean to sound as condescending as she did. "I...um...well, I just didn't want them to see me. None of you guys smoke, so I just didn't want you all to think that I'm a bad person. I know it's silly. But I don't like it when...yeah..."

"It's okay," Lydia eased. "I just wanted a proper chance to say it's been nice working with you. Maybe you didn't recognize me back then, but you were our waitress back in Hula Hoop Shakes. We've never talked much and I'm sorry. You probably thought I was a snob."

"Meh," Phoebe shrugged, trying to change the subject. "You're very talented. I wish I had your talent. Cody always assured me that I could one day be as talented as you, but I think that's just pep talk from him."

Lydia waved off her compliment. "Talent's overrated. I guess I just got lucky."

Phoebe appreciated Lydia's olive branch for friendship, but she also knew the timing of it signified the end of Mosaic Design Studios. If she could figure it out, certainly her brainy coworker could as well. Only the most important question remained.

"So...are you gonna join Wilbur and Marty?" Phoebe

asked.

To her surprise, Lydia shook her head. "I think Wilbur's cute but I don't trust Marty."

Phoebe didn't know if it was appropriate to pry about Sonia's sexual harassment accusations, but she secretly wanted to know. It had always seemed a little out of character for Marty, who appeared to be a friendly and caring person. She wanted to believe he was simply misunderstood, but something about the way Lydia spat out his name indicated he wasn't the pleasant person he appeared to be.

Sensing Phoebe's hesitation, Lydia offered an interpretive answer. "He did some...questionable...things before you joined the company. Maybe they weren't that bad. It depends on perspective. To us who were there, I suppose, it was pretty out of line. Maybe you wouldn't have thought so. Maybe we overreacted."

The former waitress appreciated her coworker's attempt for fairness, but both of them knew Lydia felt otherwise.

———

Older men like Patrick Hui knew better than to be frustrated; opportunities for romance did not come often at his age. For over a year, he had remained behaved with Cody's Aunt Hannah, always placing himself within striking distance yet savoring her like a precious bottle of 1982 Chateau Lafleur Pomerol. He made himself believe it was because he wanted her to feel comfortable, but in his own honesty he knew the situation was a tangled web. The problem with romance was that it hinged so much on anticipation. It was why married couples got bored and why Patrick was convinced cheating saved marriages. Loyalty was such an unnecessary ruse; certainly back in the day of concubines, society understood and accepted this necessity to continue a happy marriage. He wondered if it was so wrong to pursue a woman that was happy with him while he was married. Was it so wrong to desire someone who cared when his own wife didn't? These weren't the obstacles, of course. The real problem was because no one else would approve of his pursuit. Hannah's family was a constant thorn. Between her teenage daughter's animosity and her own sister's meddlesomeness, it was enough to consider the romance unachievable. Yet, he had gained her trust and she loved his company. Why else would she frequently invite him to her house—the same house that he sold to her—to fix things? A middle-aged man like himself, he admitted, just desired to be wanted.

"<This door to my daughter's old room>," Hannah complained during a usual afternoon visit, "<it never did completely close. See? You have to force it to close correctly. The home association warned us that a lot of these houses were built from cheap labor. The construction companies contracted illegal Mexicans. Isn't that horrible? I knew you wouldn't have any idea about this and it wasn't your fault.>"

Patrick kept his lips sealed; he had had the house inspected and had known of its flaws and construction shortcuts. Yet, as long as Hannah wasn't aware of his involvement, it was far more convenient to blame phantom illegal Mexicans.

"<You know, this isn't difficult to fix>," observed Patrick.

"<Really?>"

He smiled, assuring her of his confidence. "<Yes, certainly. You just measure the length of the door to the angle and readjust the hinges. The calculations shouldn't be difficult at all. Let me go get the toolbox.>"

As promised, the gray-haired realtor turned handyman came back and re-screwed the hinges on Megan's bedroom door and reapplied them at their appropriate angles. Throughout this process he could feel Hannah's eyes undressing him—a disposition suitable for their first official rendezvous. With an electric screwdriver in hand, he began unbuttoning his shirt only to turn around and discover a teacup inches away from his nose. Hannah insisted that he drink.

"<Hot?>" she inquired. "<Let me turn on the A/C.>"

He reluctantly took the teacup and sipped it as his consolation prize. Funny how the Chinese culture quenches thirst with warm drinks, he mused. A slight moment of doubt arose within Patrick, but he knew his instinct wasn't entirely incorrect. She just needed to be taken slowly, he realized, that's all.

"<I can't thank you enough for helping me once again>," Hannah smiled with a schoolgirl's twinkle in her eye. "<I'm always ashamed that I couldn't repay the favor. It's just that you're so brilliant and I'm such a dummy.>"

Patrick laughed it off with a modest wave. "<It's...it's just a door, Hannah. You give me too much credit. Just a piece of wood held together by screws and hinges. Not like it's a car or rocket.>"

Hannah opened her mouth to say something, but she hesitated for a moment, trying to fight off her better judgment. As if he could read her intentions, Patrick placed his cup on a nearby table stand and happily leaned over to her with a smile. They both giggled like schoolchildren before he initiated some action.

"<Yes?>" Patrick smiled. "< Don't be shy, what's on your mind?>"

"<Well, I...I do have a second favor to ask you this afternoon.>" She bit her lip and continued. "<Remember around last year, while Megan was still in high school...and...and you were showing us this house? And you gave me that quick massage?>"

Patrick replied in agreement with a slow blink of his eyes and a calm nod.

"<I...ahem...I liked it>," Hannah admitted. "<Can you give me another one? My daughter's not here this time around.>"

"<No interruptions>," added Patrick.

She smiled. "<No interruptions.>"

By instinct, he took her by the hand and whisked her downstairs to the living room. The silver-haired realtor hadn't felt so alive in a long time. He couldn't even remember the last time he had made love to his own wife. A decade at least, he calculated. Then, in the same thought, he dismissed it because he didn't care. This afternoon was the moment. He would be lucky and he would be participating in a moment to remember. He vacillated between starting with the main course and soothing her first with his homemade brand of reflexology. Why rush, he ultimately decided.

"<There>," Patrick made her comfortable on her living room sofa. "<Just relax and enjoy the magic.>"

He started rubbing the soles of her feet, soothing pressure points that were specifically designed for sexual arousal. Patrick knew he could make her orgasm with merely a foot massage, a perfect way to start their first encounter of intimacy.

"<OOOOOH>," moaned Cody's aunt.

Mid-fifty-year-olds shouldn't be having THIS much fun, she thought. Meanwhile, Patrick smiled, knowing that an older gentleman uses every tool at his disposal. Within a minute he had worked every sensual nerve in her body by timely-placed pressure points to her left foot. For fifteen minutes they continued this variation of reflexology sex until Hannah could stand it no more—married or not, she demanded Patrick perform intercourse the standard way. With no words needed, the lustful realtor climbed atop Cody's aunt and unbuttoned the rest of his shirt.

"<I am the South China Tiger!!!>" he declared. "<Feel my conquest!>"

In a moment of shock, however, they were unpleasantly interrupted by loud knocking on the front door. At first, they dismissed it as a mere trick of the mind, but the knocking persisted.

"<My sister!>" Hannah gasped. "<She probably brought me some food from Chinatown.>"

"<Oh>," replied Patrick in an icy tone. "<You don't have to answer it, you know.>"

As Hannah wondered whether or not she should heed Patrick's advice, the knocking continued.

"<Damn it, doesn't that woman quit?>" he growled.

Hannah scrambled to the front door and peered through the peephole. She had been correct—Cody's mother was standing outside with plastic grocery bags in hand.

"<Just ignore her>," hissed Patrick.

"<Hey!>" Cody's mother shouted. "<I know you're in there, sister! Your car's outside.>"

Patrick's eyes widened like saucers; he knew he had carelessly parked his car next to hers as well. Hannah looked at him to signify she had a similar realization.

"<Mui's car is here too. Why is he in there with you?>" demanded her sister.

Patrick quickly put on his shirt and signaled for Hannah to open the door.

"<Finally!>" Cody's mother exclaimed, seeing her face-to-face. "<So what's going on?>"

She craned her neck past her nervous sister and caught a glimpse of Patrick in the living room.

"<Well>," Hannah scratched her head. "<Um, Patrick was upstairs fixing my daughter's door. You know how it never closed properly—>"

Cody's mother pushed her aside and wagged a finger at him from the entrance. "<You bastard! What are you doing with my sister? Go back to your wife!>"

"<What?>" the realtor barked back. "< I came to help a friend. I can't help a friend?>"

"<Yes>," Hannah agreed. "<We're just friends. That's all. Just friends.">

Cody's mother let out a mocking laugh."<Hunh! Use your brain, sister! He's a man! Men always want something more!>"

With a lesser restraint on his temper, Patrick walked closer to the two of them in a bid to defend himself. "<Oh, you vile woman! Don't be so jealous! Just because you don't have any friends, let alone male ones, you're thinking the worst intentions! Your sister is every bit more the woman than you are!>"

"<Oh? Is that right?>" scoffed Cody's mother, who never backed down from a challenge. "<Maybe it's better to be friendless than to shame myself in tempting other people to cheat!>"

In a fit of rage, Patrick grabbed and put on his shoes, storming past the two sisters. Hannah served as a human barricade between her secret lover and her enraged sister. Halfway towards his car, however, he turned around and clinched his fist at Cody's mother.

"<Someday you'll know better than to interfere with other people's happiness>," he threatened, "<and I won't promise to be as civil next time.>"

———

It came as no surprise to Cody when he got involved in his first car accident during September; after all, short of death, every other bad thing had happened to him in the year 2010. He didn't believe in curses, though it was probably as good a time as any to explain the worst year of his life. This time he couldn't even blame Jesus; the pursuit of money did this to him. Or rather, as he stood near the wrecked mess that used to be his Integra, he did this to himself. A brief but frightening truth emerged from that realization—maybe anything bad that had ever happened to him he had done to himself; though as much he tried, he wasn't courageous enough to accept that. There was no use contemplating it during this moment, he thought, it was a bigger priority to find a ride home. By instinct, he reached out to Marty, perhaps because he had gotten used to speed-dialing his number or perhaps a part of Cody still considered him his best friend.

"Hey," he barked. "I just got into an accident. Come pick me up."

"Wah-huh, okay," Marty responded.

The ride back to Cody's house started with trivial chatter—no mention of the Bluefin Tuna Event collapse or Wilbur's continual presence at the office. It offended Cody that

Marty tried to skirt the issue, as though they could sit the whole way through without talking about what was important. The growing insult nagged at Cody until he changed his mind and ordered Marty to eat with him somewhere in Chinatown. Always eager to play the role of the harmless nice guy, Marty complied, though he steered their decision to an udon restaurant whose staff were familiar with him—and could protect him should Cody snap and get out of line.

They arrived at the restaurant late afternoon, finding it packed with Mainland Chinese patrons. Cody always felt a bit uncomfortable with these types of hole-in-the-wall eating places because they were openly disdainful toward Asian-Americans. Marty, of course, found it easier to camouflage himself as one of them since he was fluent enough in Mandarin Chinese to blend in. Unbeknownst to Cody, Marty gave a signal to the waiter and hinted for a table near the middle of the packed restaurant. He hoped being surrounded would discourage his partner from displaying open fits of anger, but Cody ended up snapping anyway.

"What have you been doing with your time?!" Cody barked after they ordered food. "I've been seeing you and Wilbur hanging out together. I thought I told you I didn't want him around the company anymore! And don't get me started on the staff still being there."

"Sigh..." Marty protested. "I did, I guess they didn't understand. It's been one big misunderstanding, Cody."

Cody had an expression of disbelief. "What's there not to understand?! Wilbur is worse than ever. He acts like he owns the place!"

"Hah, er...woo-ha! Oh that!" chuckled Marty. "Let me tell you a funny story—"

"I DON'T WANT ANY FUNNY STORIES!" screamed Cody, catching the attention of nearby customers. "You never told him he wasn't welcomed anymore, did you?"

Marty started wiping beads of sweat from his forehead with a napkin. "I...no, I, I did! No, I swear, I did! It's just...woo-hah...he's always asking to see me, that's all. You know? I told him 'Now now, Wilbur, you can't keep hanging around the company anymore.' Heh. Mm-huh. But he keeps persisting. I...I have to hang out with him. I don't want to, but he makes me."

"So what the fuck?! Tell him no! What you're doing is disrespectful and insulting! By the end of this month, we'll be owing our employees thousands of fucking dollars, man! Where are we going to get the money to pay them? Holy shit, I thought having zero was bad, but being in the negative! Fuck, man!"

"Muuuh, then why don't you fire the staff yourself already?"

Cody knew it was the smart thing for him to do, but he had been blinded with pride, rather keeping the girls until Marty fired them. He was sick of always being the one who delivered bad news.

"Because I asked you to do it. Because you owe me this. Because you're just going to wait until I do it and then take them out to drinking with you and Wilbur."

Marty adjusted the collar of his shirt. He couldn't believe Cody already knew about his new company.

Cody smirked. "Oh, don't think I don't know."

"Now now, shhh shhh!" Marty replied. "It's all just a big misunderstanding. You're still my best friend. And Wilbur? Shhh. I don't have anything to do with emo boy."

"I wish you did a better job hiding that. Bringing him in and out of the office everyday doesn't help. Laughing and eating with him and posting Facebook photos of yourselves hanging out doesn't help. DO YOU THINK I'M AN UTTER MORON, MARTY?"

"Shhh...shhh...ah heh heh, ah wah uh! Calm down, Cody. You, heh, you sound like a jilted lover."

Cody stood up in anger. "You 'shhh,' you motherfucking strange talking weirdo! How are we paying the staff now? You claimed you have clients. Who have you gotten in the past few weeks?"

"Sighhhh...you don't...sighhh..."

"WHAT?!"

"My mother has cancer!" shouted Marty in uncharacteristic seriousness. "There, heh, I said it, okay? Huh? Huh? It's put so much stress on me! That's what's been happening. Nah nah er, ah!"

Marty had expected Cody to exhibit sympathy. To his surprise, this news somehow made Cody angrier.

"You mean to tell me that you knew your mom had cancer all this time? That you wouldn't be able to get any sales?! That you decided not to tell me?!"

"Wah-huh, please, shush shh! Heh! It's personal! That's why I didn't have time to do anything! I...heh...eh? You just misunderstood!"

"FUCKING ASS MOTHERFUCKER!!!" Cody screamed standing. He had his pointer finger inches from Marty's nose. "We're business partners! You need to tell me this shit! I could've just let all the employees go!!! Now we owe them money we don't have!!!"

"Please, heh, please Cody, my mother..."

"I don't fucking care about your mother! For her sake I hope you're lying like you always do! You didn't have a sale all this time!!! Why the hell didn't you just say so? Are you a fucking idiot?!"

"Ah-wah...er...mahhhh." Marty was at a loss for words. "The doctors said she has a tumor growing behind her left eye. Heh-ha! We couldn't detect it until it was too late!"

Cody dropped his chopsticks and looked at him in disbelief. Marty was giving the best puppy dog expression that he could muster. Cody wondered if it was possible for even Marty to lie about his own mother.

"Have you ever heard of the boy who cried 'wolf,' Marty?" Cody asked.

"Ffft, fine!" Marty rolled his eyes. "It's true. Heh-haw! But you don't believe me."

"You've always lied with every chance you've gotten."

"Hah-waaaaa?!!!!!!! Me?! I...I don't lie!"

"Yeah, you! You're a damn compulsive liar!!!!"

"Mahhh, er, ah, I've never ever told a lie in my life!"

"Fuck you, man!"

"What? What are we talking about? Fuck me about, heh, what?"

"About your shitfaced lying!!!"

"You're a liar? When? Cody, what did you lie about? Heh-wa?"

"Oh no! You're not doing that psychological game with me! Not this time!"

"Mmm heh, wah? You're a liar? Please, shh, shhh! Hush now! Meh-gah, maybe you shouldn't lie so much, ffff."

"I'm not lying! You're the one who's lying! Oh my God! I let you steal from me and my friends! My family! All of it! MY FAMILY TRUSTED YOU! And all you can do is make up some story about your mother having cancer."

"Now now, Cody. If your mom has cancer, you really need to think things through."

"No! What are you talking about? You said YOUR mom has cancer! You said that! How dare you even lie about it? Now you're...wait...ahhh..."

"Cody." Marty put a hand on his shoulder. "It's okay to let it out. Heh, humm. If your mom is going through treatments, maybe you should take it easy."

"My mom," Cody assured, "is a hundred percent okay!!! Don't jinx her! Don't bring her into this game!"

"What game? Why are we in this restaurant? Who are you? I'm me, you're you, you're you but you're not you. Mah-heh. Your name is Cody Quan, your mother just got cancer and I saved you from a car crash."

Whatever mind trick Marty was pulling was finding its way into Cody's head. "Shut up! Shut up! Shut up!"

"Meh-ah, I've never met you, hi, my name is Marty." Marty gave him the friendliest of chuckles. "Don't you remember? You look familiar. Heh, we have the...ah hah!...I know! You were in my Chinese class. Remember? Wuh-hah! What are we talking about? Why are we in this restaurant? Don't you remember me? You're going through a nervous breakdown, Cody. Let me help you, meh-heh. You're going through a nervous breakdown, Cody. Let me help you. Hey, you look familiar, wait, meh-heh, you're in my Chinese class. Hi, I'm Marty. You're going through a nervous breakdown, Cody. Mah-hah, mah-heh—"

"SHUT UP SHUT UP SHUT UP! I'M SANE!"

Cody couldn't take it anymore. Marty was doing something to him and it was working. Whatever control Cody had left demanded him to do one thing: stop Marty from penetrating his mind at all costs. Deep resentment had already bubbled onto the surface of Cody's temper. He found his decision to unleash a good hard right to Marty's jaw a straightforward and effortless one. *POW!* Despite Marty's many claims of mastering martial arts, he was a surprisingly easy opponent. Cody's best friend immediately fell down on the floor.

"<Hey!>" the manager shouted at Cody in Mandarin Chinese. "<I saw what you just did! Get out of this restaurant!>"

Cody could not understand him, but it was universal that fighting in any restaurant was not encouraged. A waitress quickly rushed up to the fallen Marty.

"<Are you alright?>" she asked. "<Oh, you poor soul. You were just talking to him and he hit you.>"

"<Ah-weh, mahhh. It hurts, sigh. It hurts.>" Marty shook his head, managing to extract a tear or two from his eye.

"Aiya!" The manager shook his head. "<How can this be? A Chinese hitting another Chinese!>"

The confrontation drew a crowd; the two of them were smothered with accusing patrons. Cody found himself shaking from the adrenaline of hitting his best friend—perhaps it was now more appropriate to label Marty as his former best friend. From the floor, Marty continued to wail. Come on, thought Cody, it wasn't that good of a punch. Regardless of what he thought of Marty's acting, the mob of customers were quite sold on it, pointing incriminating fingers in Cody's direction.

"STOP IT!" Cody angrily demanded. "STOP SHOUTING AT ME! I HAVEN'T DONE ANYTHING WRONG!!!!!"

"<He doesn't understand Mandarin Chinese!>" observed a patron.

"<Figures>," tsk-tsked another, "<with that temper that guy's obviously corrupted with American influences.>"

"<Ohhh, my jaw, hhhuhhhh.>" Marty continued moaning as he rolled over in pain. "<I need help.>"

"<And this one>," one of the customers pointed at Marty. "<He speaks such fluent Chinese! And well too! He's one of us!>"

One after another the faces of the crowd directed their angry glares in Cody direction.

"<What happened, sir?>" a nearby patron asked Marty.

"<Huh, I...I don't know...>" Marty explained. "<I was just asking how his mother was doing. Then he hit me. She must not be doing well. But still. Heh. Ha...why punch me? You know? Huh-ha? Temper temper.>"

The hostile atmosphere encouraged Cody to back away until he was able to reach the exit. He doubted anyone from the mob of customers would actually attack him, but he ran anyway. He weaved himself between alleyway after alleyway until he was certain he was alone, finally seeking refuge behind a dumpster near the edge of Chinatown. Whatever illusions he had about preserving his friendship with Marty were now completely gone. More importantly, there wasn't time for self-pity or anger; he was facing massive debts and something had to be done quickly. There were salaries to be paid, rent to be covered, not to mention all the massive credit card payments that had piled up. He had no qualms about suing Marty. That was the obvious thing to try and do. But something needed to be done soon and he feared Marty could weasel his way around the loopholes of the legal system. Cody collected himself and accepted that immediate action was needed.

"You want how much again, Bobbie?!" asked Cody's longtime friend Mindy.

Cody stammered for the right words as night-time mosquitoes feasted on his neck outside of her home. She was the first person he could think of when it came to borrowing money. It was frightening how hanging out with Marty had made him accustomed to being a beggar.

"Fifteen thousand dollars," he answered, "I'll...I'll even give you partnership of the company. Half of it. Three-thirds of it. All of it. I don't care."

Mindy silently stared at him with concern as he stood there, occasionally slapping a mosquito or two. She didn't like seeing her friend like this, not when he used to be so confident and financially well-off.

"Bobbie," Mindy replied affectionately, "what is happening to you? You were once so bright. So smart. It hurt me to see you in this way."

"I was a fool, Mindy," Cody humbly responded. "I opened up this company for all the wrong reasons. And now this snake of a partner abandoned me."

"That's right," she tsk-tsked. "He was never your best friend like I was! I told you he was taking advantage of you since that Oceanaire dinner! Now did you regret not choosing me instead?"

"Okay, okay. You were right," Cody paused, "can I, you know, come in or something? These mosquitoes are biting the hell out of me."

Mindy paused for a moment and then finally gave in. "Okay, but please take off your shoes."

Her new house was a decent two-story dwelling, littered with children's toys and old Taiwanese newspapers. Cody figured there must have been several televisions turned on at once because he could hear a dissonance of various TV programs in English and Taiwanese. Somewhere in the back was one of Mindy's twin girls crying, probably because of bath time given the time of night and what appeared to sound like water splashing. Mindy asked him to excuse the mess as they found a resemblance of privacy in the kids' playroom. Cody pulled out two miniature children's chairs while she closed the bifold doors in an attempt to reduce the outer noise. The ridiculousness of two adults squatting on tiny plastic chairs countered the seriousness of Cody's request.

"I cannot give you that much," Mindy began."I save everything and put it into a certificate of deposit account for the girls."

Cody looked at her in disappointment. She was his best hope.

"Well, how much can you loan me?" he asked.

Mindy twitched her eyebrows and gave him a familiar, frustrated look. Like old times, she gave him a loud and hard slap on his shoulder.

"Ow!" yelped out Cody.

"You only talk to me now when you need to borrow money, huh?"

Cody rubbed the spot on his shoulder where Mindy had slapped him. For a thin woman she had an unusual amount of strength. "Could you be a little more understanding? All my time was spent on running a company. You encouraged me to blaze trails."

"Yeah, but I never told you to be stupid and foolish! Okay, okay. I can let you borrow some money. Two hundred dollars."

"That's it?!" Cody tried to remain calm. "Mindy, you know I wouldn't be asking for help if I wasn't in such dire circumstances."

"Bobbie, you should just sue him!"

"These things are harder to prove then you think!"

"Sue him, Bobbie!" Mindy repeated. "Why do you need your friends' money, eh?"

"What about the employees? I can't just delay their paychecks!"

"Yes, you can!"

"Well, I won't do it," Cody dismissed. "That would be something Marty would do."

"Don't be stupid! Protect yourself! Tell them 'Too bad, no paycheck. sorry! This is America. Ha ha!' Just like that."

Cody's glare showed disapproval of her absurd suggestion. "I can't do that. Come on. They'll get pissed! How can you even suggest that, Mindy?"

"Well, you cannot also ask anyone to just loan you fifteen thousand dollars, Bobbie!"

Cody eventually left her house with a check for two hundred dollars. For awhile he cursed Mindy's stinginess but then considered himself lucky she loaned him anything at all. His mind quickly brainstormed on who else could help him—it didn't take long for him to remember Yuki. They hadn't talked since the previous holiday season when he rejected her advances and considered their friendship on hold. Fortunately, he found her to be as goodhearted as usual, despite his sudden awkward return into her life.

"Please," he typed to MyMelodyBunny, "I wouldn't ask this unless I needed it."

"I don't know," she replied. "I haven't heard from you since you rejected me during last Christmas holiday. And now that I finally do, it's for money."

"I didn't reject you!" corrected Cody as Quanster7.

"Call it what you'd like."

RainYSkIEs589 entered their chat room.

"Hey, guys!" she interrupted. "Long time no see! What're you guys talking about? Wanna see my new artwork?"

"Nothing, Rain," they both typed.

"I'll email you about this later," MyMelodyBunny answered.

Yuki ended up contributing a substantially bigger loan than Mindy, though it was still far from the fifteen thousand dollars he needed. After receiving loans from a few sympathetic distant cousins and old high school friends, he had half the amount he needed but time was running out. Frustrated, Cody considered drastic solutions like robbing Marty or kidnapping Wilbur—but he probably wouldn't get much money doing either. It wasn't like Marty had a lot of money or that Wilbur's father would seriously consider saving his kidnapped son. Through his desperation, however, he had sunk low enough to consider a previously forbidden source for money: the reserve account for his grandfather's funeral.

Would he dare?

Granted, his grandfather was in wonderful health, but beyond the principle of taking such sacred money, senior citizens of that age were at risk to pass away at a moment's notice. If his grandfather passed away and his family found out the account was empty, there would be hell for Cody to pay. Ultimately, he decided to risk his luck and empty the money from the funeral reserve anyway.

But first, he decided to pray about it.

CHAPTER 24: LOSS

The familiarity of the scene hit Cody all at once. The beautiful pews, the choir warming up, the exquisite height from floor to ceiling that gave the church just the right amount of echo. As a show of humility, Cody did the one thing that he had rarely done: show up anywhere an hour early. With all the problems that had arisen, he needed Jesus' help and forgiveness. He felt sorry for flushing the crucifix down the toilet and he was sorry for denying Christ—even if the prior relationship had been severely abusive and catastrophic. None of it mattered anymore; he was out of options.

He had selected this particular church, knowing it provided a notably beautiful setting. Indeed, the soothing ambiance briefly erased any reason he had for breaking his spiritual relationship off. It brought back pleasurable memories of his baptism and the sensation of peace. That was when his faith was intact. Cody looked around, observing the scattered early birds who also sought solace amongst God. He had always felt a little envious of these happy Christians. Why didn't Jesus bully them? Then again, Cody realized, who's to say they had never been tested. Perhaps their sense of peace was the aftermath of Jesus' wrath—a challenge that came across to Cody as abuse. Wasn't that the lesson of Job? God purposely allowed the devil to torture this wonderful man beyond the confines of cruelty just to reward him again. It was funny logic without the humor, certainly similar to child abuse.

With those negative questions in mind, Cody decided to pray anyway. It was a good time to speak with Jesus, especially since the church was still barely filled. He found a relatively quiet area near the back where several rows of pews were left unoccupied. There, he slipped into the farthest pew and got on his knees to pray. It was strange what a foreign feeling it was, having never done so for more than half a decade. Slowly, he closed his eyes and spoke from the desires of his heart. Cody prayed for guidance, he prayed for money; mostly, he prayed for an audience with Jesus Christ.

"Dear Jesus," he began, "I..."

Thump. His thoughts were interrupted by an external sound. Yet, what was even more noticeable was the lack of other sounds. The choir had suddenly stopped; the loose chatter had vanished. A chill crept down his spine; something had happened. Cody reluctantly opened his eyes to find a dark, empty church. The walls were a bit distorted as though part of another world; indeed, he realized, it was another world altogether. Cody looked at his watch to confirm what he had suspected—time had frozen. It didn't take long for him to realize it was a mistake to summon Jesus. A very bad one.

"Hello?" Cody inquired out loud. "Anybody here?"

The echoes of the dark, empty church greeted him back. He felt a strong wave of fear seeping into his soul. The floor slowly began rumbling underneath him. Suddenly, there came a crash followed by a succession of crashes. To his horror, Cody caught sight of the empty pews toppling one after another. From the stage, the pulpit fell down. Chandeliers dropped from various parts of the ceiling. The rumbling turned into a violent shaking as though the dark world church was in the middle of a small earthquake. Of all the objects vying for Cody's immediate attention, however, were the locked entrance doors that had him fixated. He saw the attempts of someone—or something— trying to break through; it was only a matter of time before the locked doors gave way. Cody was proved right. No sooner had he convinced himself of this, the doors burst open to a very strong power. Entering through them was an angry Jesus Christ.

"No!" pleaded Cody. "Stay back! Don't hurt me!"

His appeals for mercy seemed denied by Jesus, who wore dark gray garments. The Messiah stared intensely at Cody with a lone eye that shone through his dark and wet long hair. The intimidating Deity calmly walked towards Cody, inching slowly toward him until the distance between them was a mere few feet. For a moment, Jesus stopped, offering nothing but a disapproving frown. Cody was certain punishment would soon come.

"Hahahaha!" Jesus laughed in a gesture that surprised Cody. "AHAHAHAHAHAA!!!!!!"

With uncanny speed, the dark Messiah grabbed Cody and began sprouting a large pair of black wings.

Cody pleaded, though he knew it wouldn't help. "No! Nooooo!!!!"

Without a second's hesitation, Jesus flew upward into the black sky at an astronomical speed. Their flight caused them to crash through the glass rooftop and Cody immediately found himself covered in blood. They soared so high above the clouds that Cody could see Houston as a collection of bright dots. The city, too, seemed frozen in time.

"P...please," begged a semiconscious Cody, "why are you doing this? Why do you...torture...me..."

"Because I can," replied Jesus, tightly holding on to him.

"But all people do for you is love and worship. Why do you hurt them? Why...do...you...hurt...me..." Cody felt himself fainting.

"Because. I. Can. And. I. Don't. Love. You."

"Is that...why you...made us?...to...torture and...and play with..."

"This is going to hurt, Cody. I'm going to drop you and you're going to be in a lot of pain." Jesus let out a malicious laugh. "But please, I insist, keep praying for me. Maybe I'll feel nice someday and follow through. HAHAHAHAHAHAHA!"

"You're...nothing...nothing but a sadist..."

Jesus wouldn't let Cody finish his sentence. Instead, the dark Messiah let go of him, watching him drop quickly down through the Earth's stratosphere. As Cody descended, he made sure to give Jesus a glaring, hateful stare. If God created man simply to make him suffer, then never was there a God so unworthy of praise. He decided he would never give Jesus another chance, even if it meant living in eternal hell. That was all Cody had in mind while his body quickly plunged into the world and promptly into an envelope of darkness.

———

"Cody! Hey Cody!"

It was the next morning, a late October Monday. Cody opened his eyes and found himself staring at Phoebe. He was lying on top of the conference room table.

"Where...where am I?" He sat up, making his way off.

"You're in the office, boss," Phoebe explained.

"Please don't call me that. What happened?"

"I'm not sure. You had me worried," she replied. "I was the first one in.......geez, what happened? You got cuts all over you. Did you crash through a glass window?"

It took Cody a little longer than usual to remember how Phoebe could enter the office. Then he recalled giving her an extra set of keys because the employees had been managing themselves. They were saints for coming to work on time without supervision. It was little wonder that Marty didn't have the heart to let them go; of all the wrong that had happened, they were lucky to have some of the most honest employees a company could ask for. Pity they had to be let go.

"Boss?" Phoebe said, trying to snap him out of his thoughts. "Hey?"

"I don't know what happened," Cody finally replied. "I was in that church..."

"Church? Meh. You were lying here unconscious when I found you."

She sat him down and told him to stay there while fetching him a cup of water. Cody was amazed at how thirsty he was the moment he drank it. A quick look at his reflection on the table glass showed cuts over his visible body, but they were also healing with an astonishing quickness.

"What time is it?" he asked when Phoebe returned with more water.

"Eight-thirty."

"Eight-thirty?!" Cody did a double take at the office clock.

"Yeah, you told us last Friday to come here at nine because you had a special meeting."

The meeting, he realized. After his fight with Marty and his scramble to collect fifteen thousand dollars, he had mandated a meeting for the final Friday of October. Today was the day Cody would deliver the bad news: Mosaic Design Studios was no more. However, because there were still plenty of projects left to be done, he was going to keep one of them for an extra month.

"So you're telling us it's officially over," April summarized once the meeting started and the rest of the girls arrived.

"Yes. In so many words," Cody replied, looking tired and defeated.

Lydia raised her hand. Feeling like a schoolteacher, Cody pointed at her. "Lydia?"

"What happened to Marty?" she asked.

"Marty has...well..." Cody collected his thoughts carefully. He decided to be cautiously candid about it. "We haven't seen him get a sale in the past four months. In the past month, he hadn't even made an effort."

"Did you guys fight?" prodded Lydia.

"That's...not important," he tactically explained. "He's gone. And he won't be with us anymore."

"You know he was working on his own company behind your back," continued Lydia. "I just thought you should know because it was wrong for him to do so."

Cody nodded, confirming that he already knew.

"Yeah," April agreed. "Remember M.H. Productions?"

The three girls paused, letting Cody put the rest together.

"Marty...Ho...Productions," realized Cody. He let out a groan of regret. "Oh, how could I have been so blind and stupid?"

"Hey, it's okay," April offered her condolences. "He's had his own company set up long before Wilbur."

"Well, Sonia should get a lot of credit," replied Lydia modestly. "She discovered his secrets while she was going through the projects. Also, his cousin Guy told her a lot of things as well."

"So he never did get us any clients before opening day," Cody concluded. "That scumbag."

The four of them let out a collective sigh.

"You might want to ask some of the clients what they actually paid too," April insisted. "Some of them have been saying they paid an amount different than what I saw in the contracts. They said they wrote a second check to—"

"Marty Ho Productions," finished Cody.

"Yeah," nodded April, "but there's a line in the contract that says Mosaic would refund the whole amount if either we or Marty didn't fulfill obligations."

"Holy shit," he sighed.

"Is the company broke?" interjected Phoebe.

Cody paused. He didn't think delivering the bad news would be this difficult.

"Yes," he replied after a long silence. "I'm sorry, girls. None of you deserved this. You were all so professional and tried your best. I was lucky to have you all as my employees. After your last paycheck you're free to find work with another company."

Phoebe held back tears.

"However, Lydia, I'd like for you to stay. Just to wrap up loose projects," Cody requested.

"Cody, I..." Lydia paused, "I think you should give the job to Phoebe."

He tried to bring Lydia to her senses, "I'd love to, but—"

"No, I...I figure it's best if I moved on, Cody," she insisted. "I think it's time for me to seek new challenges in my career."

Phoebe smiled, silently thanking Lydia with a slight nod.

"Okay," Cody faced the former Hula Hoop Shakes waitress. "Phoebe, can you stay?"

Excited to know that there was still some resemblance of an office career left, Phoebe joyfully reacted in her own unique way. "Meh. Sure."

When Patrick Mui's cell phone buzzed earlier in the afternoon, he leapt up from his recliner and felt a strong tinge of excitement. It was either a rare call from an interested homebuyer or, better yet, Hannah; secretly, he was hoping it was the latter. To his delight, the caller ID on his phone showed him just that: "Hannah Wong, Calling." He had worried that their last encounter—a passionate rendezvous thwarted by Cody's mother—scared her for good, that it might have been his only chance at making love not only to her but with any woman in general. At his age and modest income, intimate opportunities were miracles.

"<I was hoping I could bother you for a well-needed massage>," Hannah hinted. "<If you don't mind, of course.>"

"<Of course I don't mind>," he grinned.

Neither heaven nor hell would stop him this time around. There was, of course, that accursed sister of hers, he reminded himself. The mere thought of Cody's mother put a frown on his face. *If that woman dare interrupt us again...* He decided to stop thinking about it and resumed his concentration on the upcoming lovemaking instead. Fortunately for Patrick, the distance between his house and Hannah's was a mere fifteen-minute drive. He didn't let the three school zones he breezed through serve as obstacles. Besides, he opined, children in urban cities learned early on to dodge traffic; it was high time suburban kids did as well.

Absorbed in his determination, he paid no attention to a familiar car exiting the post office. Earlier on, Cody's mother had purchased yet another round of groceries for her sister. She knew Hannah gave her the stink eye for being pushy, but Hannah wasn't exactly the most responsible person, in her opinion. Even when they were children, Hannah needed to be taken care of and Cody's mother found it difficult to stop doing so. As she waited patiently at the first red traffic light, she immediately recognized the car in front of hers: Patrick Mui's. She could only take a guess as to what he planned on doing in her sister's neighborhood.

Meanwhile, Patrick glanced at his rear view mirror and noticed Cody's mother. In his frantic state of mind, he could only reason with one explanation why her car was behind his: the intrusive woman was out to stop him. She must've planned it all along.

"<No—"> Patrick damned in revulsion. "<No! NO! How did she realize...>"

Fumes came out of his head. That woman is always cock-blocking me! he cursed to himself. When he arrived in front of Hannah's house, he stormed out of his little gray Kia Optima, ready to confront Cody's mother. With Chinese groceries in hand, she got out of her car too, ready for the confrontation.

"<You BITCH! YOU TOTAL BITCH!>" he yelled.

"<What are you doing here? Stop screaming at me!>"

"<YOU FOLLOWED ME! YOU KNEW ABOUT THIS! WHY DON'T YOU MIND YOUR OWN BUSINESS?!>"

"<What are you talking about? I'm just here to give groceries to my sister! I live in this neighborhood as well!>"

Hannah heard the two familiar voices and shuddered at the worst-case scenario happening in her front yard. She quickly concealed her lingerie with a bathrobe and rushed out of her house to calm the situation.

"<Little Sister!>" scolded Cody's mother when she saw Hannah. "<Why's this married man coming to your house again? And why are you wearing a bathrobe? You never do that!>"

"<It's just a little misunderstanding!>" Hannah insisted. "<He's here to offer some reflexology treatments. He—>"

"<'Reflexology treatments'?! Ha!>" mocked her sister. "<Oh, you always did fall for the wrong men...>"

"<HEY!>" Patrick snapped in her direction. "<What we do is NONE of your business! You better scram! I told you I won't be as civil the next time you stopped us!>"

His threat came across as an empty one as Cody's mother stood her ground.

"<Oh yeah?!>" she exclaimed.

Her defiance inflamed him. Patrick couldn't stand it any longer. "<DON'T THINK FOR ONE MOMENT I WOULDN'T PUSH YOU!>"

He had little reason to be intimidated by her. The woman was tiny, no taller than a prepubescent child and no heavier than a sack of rice. She was foolish to hold her ground; even at his advanced age, Patrick could put her in a world of pain.

"<PUSH ME?!>" challenged Cody's mother. "<I DARE YOU.>"

Her words were an invitation to attack her; with a brutal shove, the silver-haired realtor sent Cody's mother face first into the concrete driveway. She lay still on the ground, absorbing both the physical and psychological damage she immediately suffered. Patrick resumed standing before her, dreaming up of further things he could do. He could kick her in the stomach, he mused to himself, yes, that would show her he meant business. Before he could act on his impulse, however, Hannah came between them and pleaded to him to cool off inside her house. With a tinge of guilt, Patrick obliged but not before he heard Cody's mother surprising them with another bout of determined words.

"<How dare you?>" she shouted at Hannah as she lay there on the driveway. "<Choosing a man, over your own sister!>"

Hannah hung her head in shame as she closed her front door, leaving Cody's mother to recover alone outside. The hurt woman eventually pulled herself up, wiping away the dirt and blood that poured out from the new cuts. It took some effort to get herself into her car. Once she had, she took a long look at herself in the mirror and saw a mess. Mostly scrapes and bruises, she dismissed; maybe back when she was young she cared about her looks, but now she prided herself in her fortitude. She drove herself a block north where her home was and made an immediate phone call to her husband at work. Mr. Quan took awhile to answer.

"<It's me>," Cody's mother replied. "<I was just visiting Little Sister to give her some groceries. Mui was there and he shoved me to the ground.>"

The incident was further explained in detail. Not surprisingly, Cody's father didn't feel the need for action.

"<That doesn't sound good>," he casually answered. "<I hope you're okay.>"

"<Well?>" Cody's mother insisted. "<Aren't you going to do something?">

"<What do you mean?>"

"<That disgusting man just pushed me! Come over here!>"

"<Oh. Okay, I'm coming>," he declared.

Cody's father cancelled his game of Angry Birds and took a detour to the men's room. After reading a funny article about sea monkeys, he headed to Hannah's house while relaying to Cody on the phone the details of the incident.

"What?" Cody asked in disbelief.

"<What do you mean 'what'?>" his father chuckled. "<I'm sure it was nothing. You know how your mother overreacts.>"

Cody didn't feel the same sense of casualness; the news of someone harming his mother was enough to send him into a rage.

"No," he declared, "I'm coming over there."

"<Hey now, hold on—>"

Cody slammed his desk phone down, hurrying to the parking garage where his rental car was. On his way over to his aunt's house—a good half-hour long drive—he continually slammed his fists into the rental car's steering wheel, imagining it was Patrick Mui's face. That slimebag! he cursed to himself, and that floozy aunt of his deserved some yelling too! How could anyone hurt his dear sweet mother? He put the pedal to the metal, ignoring school zones and making the crossing guards earn their pay. It was high time suburban kids learned to cross the street on their own anyway, he thought.

"PATRICK MUI! COME OUT!" Cody screamed once he arrived in front of his Aunt Hannah's house.

He banged continuously on the door until it drove his aunt insane. When she couldn't take it anymore, he heard footsteps rushing downstairs.

"<Please, Cody>," she pleaded from the garden window. "<Be an obedient boy and don't worry about it.>"

This angered him and sent him pounding his fists into the door harder.

"<Go away, boy!>" he heard a man's voice say. Patrick had shown his face next to Hannah's in the garden window. "<Your mother deserved it! She had it coming!>"

"<FUCK HOLE ASS I KICK YOURS!>" screamed Cody in broken Cantonese.

"<Oh yeah?>" mocked Patrick. "<You can't do anything to me!>"

Cody kicked the door until dents started appearing in it. Neighbors were coming out to watch the incident.

"<PLEASE!>" pleaded his Aunt Hannah from the window. "<Cody, this is an adult situation. Be an obedient boy. Please.>"

"<Obedient?!>" scoffed Cody's mother, who was making her way back to Hannah's front yard. "<Why don't you tell your dog of a boyfriend to obey my son's order to come out?!>"

"Mom!" Cody's face lit up. "Are you okay?"

His mother pushed him aside and joined the door banging. "<Come out, you cowards!!! I'm ready for round two!>"

"<Give up!>" advised Patrick. "<This isn't your business! You're not coming through that door!>"

"<Oh yeah?>" defied Cody's mother. "<And how will you get back home to your wife?>"

Her words stung Patrick; the realization hadn't dawned on him that he had trapped himself. The Quans could easily stake outside forever. Besides, there was also Hannah's daughter Megan too. She would eventually be returning home from school.

Hannah attempted to soothe the situation. "<Come on, Big Sister. This is just a minor thing. No need to get worked up about it.>"

"<Oh, I definitely need to get worked up about it>," Cody's mother replied.

As Cody contemplated throwing a brick through the garden window, he heard the screeching tires of his father's car pulling into the driveway. At last, Cody smiled, his father could join him in what surely would be a father and son team-up ass-kicking fest. That dirtball was going to get it now.

"Come on, dad!" Cody encouraged. "I'll throw a brick through the window and we'll rush him out together!"

"<No, no, son>," calmed Mr. Quan. "< Let's just go home and pretend this never happened.>"

Cody paused in surprise, "...what?"

With an apologetic smile he walked toward the garden window where Patrick was and bowed. "<I'm sorry my wife and son has caused this unnecessary disturbance, Mr. Mui.>"

"<You better be!>" Patrick grunted. "<And next time you tell your bitch of a wife that she won't be so lucky! And I'll kick you and your shithead son too!>"

Mr. Quan repeatedly bowed. "<It won't happen again. We don't need to have confrontation. We've embarrassed us all.>"

"What are you doing, dad?!" screamed Cody. "This guy pushed Mom! He pushed your wife!"

Mr. Quan took Cody's arm and pulled him away from the front door.

"<Please, son",> he offered in hush tones. "<This is embarrassing. A bunch of Chinese people yelling at one another. What will the neighbors think? Save face...save face...let's go.>"

Cody refused to leave, picking up a brick instead.

"<No!>" his father stopped him. "<You're going to regret doing that!>"

His father's words carried through; he was right, Cody realized. It would've been an invitation to foolishness to directly attack that treacherous man. They weren't street thugs and who knows what would happen if they actually fought? Patrick Mui wasn't exactly the kind of man who hesitated on suing for preposterous reasons.

Still, something inside nagged him; he couldn't just let Patrick get away with it. Some justice had to be done. Picking up his iPhone, he texted Rain, hoping his long-distance friend was free enough at the moment to respond. She did.

"What's up, Bubbleman?" RainYSkIEs589 responded.

"Hi, Rain," texted Cody, "sorry to bother you but I need an emergency favor..."

Moments later, Cody walked back to face Patrick and Hannah at the garden window.

"Patrick! I just had my friend look up and call the local police number. We filed charges against you! The cops are going to haul your ass to the police station. My friend also looked up your home number and called your wife too! Feel free to explain everything to her when she bails you out of jail!"

As promised, two squad cars arrived ten minutes later. Patrick willingly came out with his hands up. The police interrogated him and eventually hauled him to the station. While it wasn't the action-packed beating that Patrick probably deserved, a part of Cody was nonetheless proud things were resolved in an uncharacteristically refined way.

"You should have been the one doing something," Cody glared at his father.

Mr. Quan replied with a lengthy sigh, staring regretfully at the grassy ground. Cody's father didn't like the way they lost face in front of their neighbors. What transpired was not worthy of the victory his son so proudly cherished. The incident was enough for him to consider looking for another neighborhood, one where no one knew anything embarrassing about the Quans.

———

Cody didn't have too long to dwell on the afternoon incident with Patrick. There was some unfinished business between him and Marty later on in the night in the lobby area of the Sugar Land Town Center Marriott. Neither was prompt as usual—one of the many things they shared in common. However, looking back, Cody realized that their differences, while few and far between, were vast in philosophy and morality. Perhaps those two things were what mattered the most.

As per usual on an uneventful weeknight, the lobby area was quiet and devoid of workers. Even the desk clerk was nowhere to be found. The two former friends sat opposite each other, focusing on the papers scattered across the glass coffee table between them. The document in the center was the most important one, indicating a legal breakup on Marty's behalf of the company. As Cody predicted, his business partner hurriedly agreed to give the entire ownership of the company to Cody now that it was in heavy debt and ruined beyond repair. This was okay, decided Cody, also realizing beforehand that suing Marty would be futile. Like always, Marty put a lot of effort into such an unrewarding hustle, leaving him with intangible triumphs that meant so little to most people. All he had won was an absolved responsibility he could never pay back and the love of Wilbur and Rosie. None of it mattered. Marty was destined to run the same deceit with someone else again and come out happy with only the public acceptance he so pathetically cherished.

"Wah-uh, I'm glad things worked out alright in the end," Marty chuckled.

His laughter sounded so phony to Cody now. Everything about him became so predictable. Once he started out with a lame attempt at humor, Marty would slide in what he really needed to say.

"Er, ah, heh-heh, I made a slight change, ah heh heh," Marty insisted.

Cody gave out a mocking snort, knowing his partner would try something sleazy.

"What change? I told you not to change anything," Cody replied, looking at the first page of the contract.

"Meh-ah," Marty adjusted his collar. "No no. It's nothing bad. See? I just added my middle name. Ah heh."

Cody rolled his eyes and read out loud Marty's full name, "Marty Lai Ying Ho."

"Ha! Yeah. Lai as in 'good intentions.' Ying as in 'brave.'"

"That's ironic. Your full name in English sounds like 'Marty Lying Ho,'" Cody observed.

"Hah! Heh! Good one, Cody!"

"Not funny, because it's true."

Cody thoroughly looked over the rest of the contract papers. Once he was certain nothing seemed awry, he signed his name on the appropriate line. Now it was official: their partnership had ended and, Cody hoped, as was Marty's future presence in his life. Marty seemed more than glad that he was free from responsibility.

"Mm-huh, if it means anything, I'm really sorry that the company fell apart," said Marty. "I mean, heh, if it wasn't for Sonia and emo boy, wah-uh, we'd definitely turn things around together. You know! Eh? Haha, eh?"

Cody silently stared, unmoved by his former friend's spurious comforting.

"Oh, hey!" Marty suddenly announced. "I brought you something."

Cody looked at him suspiciously as he pulled out a wrapped gift from a shopping bag.

"Heh! Thought of you, man!" Marty smiled.

"Why are you giving me this? It's not even Christmas or my birthday."

A reply wasn't need; Cody already knew what it was—a bribe. A bribe for good feelings. A bribe to suggest Marty wasn't the deceitful opportunist that he had proved himself to be. Cody needn't open it; he decided it would be better thrown away unopened.

"Wah-eh, why aren't you opening it?" asked Marty.

"I'll, um, I'll do that... later," Cody replied.

With business taken care of, they both got up from their chairs. Marty offered a handshake, one that Cody ultimately decided to refuse. With his back turned, Cody walked away from his former friend, disgusted at himself for ever trusting someone so noticeably deceitful. He also found a nearby trash can to dump the present in.

"Wuh...uh...hey, wait!" Marty called out to him, his voice echoing across the empty lobby. "I'm not the bad guy, you know! I, heh, I'm not!...Cody?...Cody?...heh heh? Eh?...Cody? Codyyyy!"

Soon he discovered he was talking to only himself.

————————

"Hey, do you need help with that box?" smiled Phoebe the next morning.

It was the second to last day of Mosaic Design Studios. Cody had found Duke, of all people, willing to help out with tomorrow's moving. Until then, only Cody and Phoebe were left to haul the smaller boxes to the front of their building. They both found the temperature outside to be fantastic; the late autumn weather was just cool enough to quell the usual Texas heat.

"Sure," replied Cody, "if you think you can lift it."

Phoebe gave out a teasing laugh. "Hey! I used to lift trays of food heavier than this!"

She helped carry the box and place it with the others sitting on the curb. As she was stacking the rest, Cody couldn't help but notice how spectacularly beautiful she was in her plaid-patterned red shirt and dark blue Wranglers; if only she didn't smell like a ten-gallon ashtray, he thought to himself.

"There," she huffed, "I think that's all of the supplies."

They rested by leaning on the large stack of boxes, facing the second floor window they both once shared. Despite its failure, at least Mosaic Design Studios brought Phoebe into his life, if only temporarily. Cody never stopped appreciating the moment; it was a gift to spend the final moment of his dream company with the waitress he once fawned over. A moving truck pulled up and stopped at the corner of the building. It was from a private charter company that was moving into Cody's office space.

"Prestigious Air Flights," Phoebe read the sign that was being moved upstairs. "What a totally different business than ours."

After Phoebe and Cody watched the movers for the new company make a few trips upstairs with office furniture, their stomachs began to growl.

"You know," Cody suggested, "I've always wanted to try that five-star steak place around here."

"Let's go," Phoebe replied, smiling slyly.

"This late in the morning? It's eleven o'clock!"

"Meh, why not?"

"Because it's still kinda morning...and because... " Cody began feeling his pockets. Something was missing. "Shit."

"What?"

Cody lowered his head in embarrassment. "Phoebe, I think I...I think I lost my wallet."

"Haha. Ah, don't worry, boss," she smiled, holding her paycheck. "My treat."

"You sure? We can just eat at Taco Bell."

"You can't afford Taco Bell," laughed Phoebe. "You're broke. I'm paying, so I get to decide. A steak dinner it is."

"You mean an early steak lunch."

"Meh. Steak's a steak."

Cody sighed. "Alright. But only because I want to end this company on a happy note."

He retrieved his rental car and drove it toward the front of the building. Together with Phoebe's help, they filled it with all the boxes that would later go into public storage. The Mosaic Design Studios office supplies would soon join the Mosaic Decor counterfeit decorations. After parking the car and heading towards the steakhouse, Cody hesitated walking too quickly away from their building. Staring sadly back at their former office, he stopped Phoebe. He knew he would probably never be anyone's boss again. It was back to cubicle jobs and facing that old familiar bamboo ceiling—the life of the model minority.

"I'll miss this place," Cody mumbled. "This will go down as the worst defeat of my life."

"Hey." Phoebe patted his back, trying to cheer him up. "Don't say that. You'll bounce back. Some way. Somehow."

He shook his head. "No, this was a once-in-a-lifetime opportunity and I blew it. I let someone else dictate my fate. I shouldn't have had a partner. I should've been the captain of my own destiny. And now that it's over, I'll never be rich. I'll never amount to anything. And I'm broke. I'm even going to lose my house and live with my parents.

Phoebe leaned in and, to his surprise, planted a soft kiss on his cheek.

"You'll be okay from this," she promised. "You know why?"

"Why?" he asked.

"Because you're Cody Quan."

ACT III:
KARMA

CHAPTER 25: FOUR YEARS LATER

Pity. Logical. Victorious.

These were Duke's feelings as he observed the remaining pile of boxes from his cousin's now defunct company, Mosaic Design Studios. Nothing was a bigger indication of Cody's surrender than his asking for Duke's help. Then again, it also didn't surprise him that Cody would fail; weakest links inevitably snap. Cody's entrepreneurial moonlighting had temporarily given them equal footing. It afforded a silent treatment from Duke as he patiently waited for Cody's silly experiment to crumble asunder. And how spectacular of a failure it was indeed—even Duke couldn't have imagined Cody would come groveling to him. It was better than he had ever imagined. It was a sign of his Manifest Destiny, to take the crown as the most dependable and successful grandchild of the Quan family. The new prince's first order was to establish dominance. He began doing so by teaching Cody the error of his ways.

Cody, of course, had done all that he could to prevent Duke's solo help. It wasn't without effort that he asked as many friends as possible for assistance. However, the leasing management wouldn't permit additional time to catch up on back rent, and there was also the issue of docility—Cody's Asian friends were some of the most obedient people on the planet. He rolled his eyes as grown man after grown man opted out to take their mothers shopping or to mahjong games.

"H-hey, where're you going?!" Cody shouted as the last volunteer suddenly dropped his box down and began running off.

"Sorry, man! My mother called. I gotta go!"

"What?" protested Cody. "You're thirty years old! Learn to tell her no!"

"I...I can't! Sorry!"

Cody sighed as he observed the disoriented box and tilted it upright again.

"Fucking Asians!" he cursed out loud. "Why do they always have to listen to their moms?!"

His embarrassing dependency on Duke's help was all that was left. The necessity of the situation gave Cody more appreciation for his haughty cousin's aid than his pride usually conceded. Whatever Duke's reasons, at least it was better than moving things alone. Fortunately for Cody, his cousin's fiancée, Annebelle, later joined them in the office. She mostly spent her time rearranging the items inside the boxes for better efficiency. More importantly though, her presence somewhat kept Duke from all-out gloating despite his gnawing criticism.

"Just another one of your failed plans," Duke mocked Cody. "The smartest thing you did was seek my help."

It was worth it for Duke to say that. His back had reached close to breaking from the heavy lifting, but helping Cody seal his own fate was the cure. Duke tasted ultimate triumph. He won. Cody lost. Alpha. Beta. Nothing else mattered in the world. Survival of the fittest.

With the moving finally over and the boxes placed in storage, Duke stood in front of Cody and gave his cousin a silent intimidating stare. It would be the last acknowledgement of them as equals. Duke would never again look at him in the eye. It was not surprising when Cody slowly refused to accept Duke's eye-staring contest and offered a handshake instead— Cody was, after all, a beta male. Beta males succumb to last-minute offerings of peace instead of stubbornly fighting to the end. They can't handle competition, thought Duke.

"Thank you," Cody took all his pride to muster. "When nobody helped me, you did."

Duke remained still for a few moments before unleashing a pinpointed projectile of spit onto Cody's right cheek. Cody remained still as he watched Duke slowly turn his back towards him, walking off with Annebelle.

"Duke, that ain't right. You sh'n't have done that," Annabelle insisted in her usual Southern belle voice. "His apology seemed sincere."

He gave her a dominant stare that commanded her to do nothing as they continued walking. Sincerity, Duke knew, was for the defeated.

———————

When he arrived home, Cody saw a forfeiture notice taped to his front door. It was the consequence of exhausting his efforts on trying to save his company instead of his own house. Perhaps, he thought, more of his own irresponsibility than consequence. The forfeiture gave him a week.

"Shit!........shit SHIT SHIT! Fuck!" he screamed as neighborhood dogs barked back in response. "Maaannnnn. I loved this town house. Loved it! SHIT."

His exhaustion from moving company boxes all day made him decide to pack his personal belongings tomorrow. Instead, he spent the next hour sitting on the steps of his second floor with the patio door open. Losing seemed like déjà vu to him. Cody counted the number of years he lived in the house—eight...nine...ten. Ten, he shook his head. Then again, he had been suckered into a thirty-year plan with a whopping 6.7 percent interest before the recession. Maybe it was better off this way, he thought to himself. Before he could counter his optimism with cynical pessimism, his iPhone suddenly lit up with a text message.

":)".

"Phoebe," he realized. He wasn't sure if he should act entirely as her boss anymore or embrace this new part-time friendship they'd developed. As he got to know her, he realized their wide age difference gave them little in common. Calling, for one thing, now seemed generational. She liked to text; he liked to call. He quickly decided to meet both of their preferences by texting her that he would call her. A few seconds went by before he did just that.

"Yeah?" she answered. "Is there an emergency?"

"So people only call each other now if there's an emergency?"

"Meh."

"Don't 'meh' me."

"Sorry, boss."

"This is what us old folks used to do when we were your age. It's called talking on the phone."

"Groovy," she replied laughing. "What's up? Everything okay?"

"I've seen better days. Anyway, I want to go over the leftover projects. Think you can do it all from your laptop? Also, I transferred our old company line into a cell phone. I'll give it to you the next time we see each other. Hopefully we could do that tonight...if you're not too busy."

Cody held back the other reason he wanted to see her. His crush hadn't faded—instead, their previous dinner at the steakhouse planted thoughts into his head that love could work.

"Nah," she replied, choosing her words carefully, "I...kinda promised someone I'd join them for dinner tonight."

He briefly paused to make sense of her words. "'Them'? Sounds plural."

"Meh. You know how it is, boss."

Cody chuckled to himself, realizing a pretty girl like Phoebe was likely a magnet for party invitations. Probably her usual neo-hippie friends, no doubt.

Phoebe interrupted his train of thought, "Boss?"

"...Yeah?"

"I just want you to know...what you did, risking everything to start your own company...even when you lost it all, I admired you for doing that."

"Thank you, Phoebe," Cody responded, feeling genuine gratitude. "I don't think you understand how much that means to me."

"I do. I guess you needed to hear it. Especially from a 'white chick,'" she laughed in reference to her adopted background.

"You're an honorary Asian now, Ms. Phoebe Bowie."

"Thanks. Haha. Well, someone's texting me, I gotta go. Ciao, boss!"

"See ya later," Cody smiled.

Over on the other end, Phoebe ended their call. She was annoyed to find more text messages on her iPhone pushing her to hurry. The messages showed signs of the texter's impatience, the digital equivalent to nervous stuttering.

"Hurry UP! COME ON! ARE U COMING?"

"Hurry UP! COME ON! ARE U COMING?"

"Hurry UP! COME ON! ARE U COMING?"

"Hurry UP! COME ON! ARE U COMING?"

"Okay, OKAY!" Phoebe finally texted back. "I'm coming, Wilbur."

————————

Thanksgiving was observed a few weeks later by everyone in America, including the inmates of Darrington Penitentiary. There, the holiday's prominence differentiated, depending on the inmate. Some had the most profound experiences, staying humble to thwart the vain desires of a better reality. Most, however, felt a high tide of frustration—their usual dissonance unable to protect them from realizing a happier world beyond barbed wires.

All Pete Mok could do was think of Fortress Maximus.

It was the most expensive Transformer one could have as a kid, a giant robot toy that changed into a city. Most mothers wouldn't even consider the near three-hundred-dollar price tag—a huge amount in the mid-eighties—but that didn't stop his mother from surprising him with it on a Thanksgiving afternoon, too eager to wait until Christmas. She had penny-pinched enough tips to afford the toy and it was worth it to see the young Pete smile.

Materialism was the fruit of labor in low-income households. The wealthier families needed to know she sacrificed and bought Pete a toy their children envied. It was her way of telling Pete she loved him. It took twenty-five years, with six of them behind bars, for him to realize it wasn't about

Fortress Maximus. There was something special about being the spoiled poor kid.

His mother hadn't visited him during his time in Darrington Penitentiary—a direct contrast to her weekly visits during his first prison stint in 2004. Back then, she loved him despite his conviction of cocaine trafficking. This time, however, he was framed for a crime he didn't commit; her silence to his innocence was deafening. It was enough for Pete to distract himself with prison work before he drove himself mad. He did laundry and cleaned restrooms, passed out library books and did field work—anything to remove his thoughts from the psychopath who killed his best friend and planted him in jail.

Thus, when he received a surprising notification of a visitor two days later, he dared to hope it was his mother and sister again. Pete quickly dropped his chores and prepared himself for the opportunity. The short walk to the visitor room ill afforded him much time to think of a crisp heartfelt apology, but he tried anyway, starting with owning up to his association with criminals. I've changed, he wanted to them, I've learned the errors of my ways. As he turned the last corner leading up to the visitor room, his stomach butterflies came to a screeching halt when he realized it wasn't his family who had come.

It was Andrew Huynh.

Aside from a few strands of gray hair, the man who had framed Pete for murder looked identical to how he was years before. He was still hefty in build with an air of arrogance around him. Pete greeted Andrew with a hateful glare as he sat himself across from the thick layer of glass. The veteran hit man wasted no time, initiating the conversation by picking up the booth phone from his end. Conversely, Pete went at his own pace, eventually following suit.

"What you want, fat nigga?" Pete frowned with the phone in his ear.

"Now, is that an appropriate way of talking to your employer?" teased Andrew.

"Bitch, fuck you."

"I see you haven't quite expanded your vocabulary in Texas' number one bed-and-breakfast. Anyway, how's life? Got buttfucked yet? Hahaha."

Pete gave him a daggered stare.

"Well," continued Andrew, "I'm happy to report your mother's doing okay, and your sister's looking fine as fuck. In fact, she recently got breast implants, you know."

"Nigga, you got a point, 'cuz I was washing my underwear in my cell," scowled Pete.

"Haha, relax," Andrew snickered. "I've got some good news for you, Petey boy. Piranha thinks it's time for you to go. As promised, we've...arranged...for your early release."

"Yeah? Nigga, what I gotta do once I'm out? Maybe I like it here. At least I ain't gotta worry 'bout no damn tiger eatin' me up, hear?"

"Yes, that was most unfortunate." Andrew gave out a rare frown. "Your friend should've stayed quiet."

"So what I gotta do once I'm out?" repeated Pete.

"Oh, we've got a special assignment for you."

"Yeah? And what might that be, nigga?"

Andrew tapped at the phone. "Can't get into details with it right now, can we? They're listening."

Pete laughed. "So? What you 'fraid of? Y'all motherfuckas already bought out the damn guards."

The hefty assassin gave out a long sigh.

"Look, you've stayed quiet and just the fact that I'm personally here shows how important Piranha thinks of you. We've got big plans. You've proven your loyalty."

"Ain't no loyalty when it's under threat, nigga," hissed Pete.

"You'd be surprised. Snitches snitch no matter what. Anyway, be seeing you in a few weeks, Pete."

With continued eye contact and a snarky smile, Andrew hung up his phone, slightly nodding his head as a "see you later" towards Pete. Pete responded with a scowl, hanging up his end of the phone. He was calmly led out of the visitation booth and returned back to his cell. Piranha was always good with his word; Pete knew he would be out of prison soon, but not necessarily free.

———

"Beautiful. BEAUTIFUL," exclaimed Cody's father.

Mr. Quan was pleased with the realtor; she had really outdone herself this time. Ever since his wife had been pushed by her sister's lover, Cody's father had actively sought out a new neighborhood. Not just any neighborhood, however, one where he could live in his dream home. A home, in his mind, that was surrounded by trees and man-made lakes—the kind of lakes with giant fountains in the middle that suggested luxury and class. And above all, no black people, he smiled to himself, for they were the scourge of society, whose lifeblood was through welfare and crime.

"<I don't know>," rationalized Cody's mother. "<It's undoubtedly expensive. What do you think we are—rich?>"

Her words fell on deaf ears; she knew the lakeside house had entranced him. His mind was transfixed at the possibilities, she observed. It was probably imagining Cody and the girl Cody's father had chosen to be his wife, Kiki, growing old with them.

"<I can imagine it now>," grinned Cody's father. "<Cody and my chosen wife for him, Kiki, living together in this house. All of us growing old together.>"

Cody's mother rolled her eyes. "<Can you stop being so old-fashioned? He'd probably want to move out once he saved his money back. Why would he want to continue living with us?>"

"<Why wouldn't he?! We could take care of his children! Our grandchildren! We would be knowledgeable of all his troubles. Give him advice.>"

"<Even his sex life?!>"

"<Especially his sex life! Of course, we would give them their privacy. We need to encourage them to make grandkids for us, but sometimes kids need a little help.>"

The Caucasian realtor grinned, having no clue as to what they were talking about in Cantonese.

"So...what do you think, Kelvin?" the realtor smiled.

"I like! I like!" he approved with two thumbs up.

The realtor could see that one spouse was more excited than the other, an obvious sign of overreaction. Still, she thought, it was an opening for her to push Mr. Quan's enthusiasm and hoped it would spill over to his wife.

"Well, this one has been VERY popular lately," the realtor smiled. "Everyone wants the lakeside. It's a shame they won't be building anymore neighborhoods by this lake for awhile. And it IS beautiful. Especially if you have a big family. Any grandkids?"

"No!" Cody's mother responded. "No grandson. No granddaughter. Son, no marry. Too picky."

The realtor laughed, "Young people these days tend to marry later on, usually in their thirties. My own son just got married and he waited until thirty-three."

"My son no girlfriend!" she frowned in broken English.

"I'm sure he has one," assured the realtor. "We're always the last to know as parents."

"Last parents?" Cody's mother misunderstood. "No, first parents! Always we first! Take care of us when we old!"

The realtor laughed nervously, deciding it was wiser to change the topic. "You guys really should consider it. The recession has made the prices so affordable now."

Cody's mother saw her husband standing by the lake and glancing into the distance. He was obviously in love with the new home. This gave her the opportunity to negotiate.

"How much?" she whispered over to the realtor.

She almost fainted when she heard the price. It was eight times the value of their current home. Cody's mother was hesitant to commit themselves to another fifteen-year mortgage; she and her husband would be old and feeble by the time it was paid off. This didn't even take into account that her son had also lost his company and house recently. Mr. Quan, however, would hear none of her reservations.

"<We must buy this house! Wow! It's my dream home!>" exclaimed Mr. Quan as he walked back to them. "<Think of our grandchildren playing in the backyard!>"

"<Oh my goddess, do you know how expensive this home is?>" lectured his wife.

"<It doesn't matter! We'll work more hours! We'll persevere!>"

The realtor recognized the universal tone and body language of spouses debating over price. She knew the decision wasn't going to be made at once. It was all about planting a thought in the desiring spouse's ear. Let the enthusiastic one do all the work. If she played her cards right, one would steer the other into buying the house.

"I'll tell you what," the realtor smiled to both of them. "Why don't you both sleep on it, give it a few days and let me know. Just understand that most people consider this home the most beautiful in the neighborhood. It would most certainly sell should you one day decide to let it go. A beautiful investment to live in such a beautiful place."

In one brilliant stroke, she had introduced the possibility of making money to Cody's mother and reinforced the beauty of the home to Cody's father. She knew it was only a matter of time before they would talk themselves into purchasing the new house.

She was right.

———————

Cody knew he was diving headfirst into the deep end. For his own good—and perhaps a little of it from his crush on Phoebe—he took her suggestion and tried networking with her. The early December night saw his introversion given a temporary rest as they wined and dined with the business-to-business elite. It was a bold move, getting new customers while maintaining the remaining projects left undone. Phoebe was convinced it was worth rebranding themselves as a two-person operation, though Cody had experienced that before with his longtime friend Mindy. He was still unsure that she would work past the end of the year, but he was also more open-minded than ever about trying things. The sea of people was confusing and intimidating—a cacophony of voices that competed against his concentration. Cody realized how naive he was believing networking as a series of gentle one-on-one conversations, drinks in hand, laughing at tasteful jokes in an acceptable volume. The reality was maddening.

"Ah hello, my name is Cody and my associate Phoebe and I make websites. And what do you do?" he found himself repeating that same sentence about a hundred times.

They laughed at jokes that were both funny and not. They made themselves more important than they were. Phoebe found herself holding on to his arm like it was a buoy keeping her from drifting off from the crowd. Their alcohol limitations were tested, and it was only a matter of time before Cody became Daredevil: The Man Without Fear. Daredevil would soon have a companion that night in Elektra: the Ninja Assassin. That was what Phoebe called herself after her eighth glass of wine.

"Hey look! Asians!" a drunken Cody pointed at the only other two Asian-Americans in the crowd.

"Hi, I'm Mitch and this is my wife, Doreen," said the Asian man.

Mitch and Doreen were of similar ages to Cody, both of them looking classy and calm. They seemed to have handled their alcohol far better than Daredevil and Elektra.

"Mitch!" laughed Cody. "Babe, this guy's...hic...name is Mitch! I'm Mitch, bitch!!!"

Phoebe exploded in laughter, thinking it was the funniest thing she had ever heard. They laughed and pointed at the newly met couple.

"I'm...hic...Cody...Cody Quan...at your serviceeee," he saluted, "and this...this sexy little...hic...thing here is...Phoebeeeee..."

"So how long have you guys been in Houston? We're from Toronto," smiled Doreen as she shook their hands.

"Ohhhh man...hic...how long?" Cody started counting his fingers, "Thirty...hic...I dunno...thirty-three years..."

"Silly," giggled the drunken Phoebe, "you're thirty-three years old, dude!!!"

"AHAHAHAHAHAHAHA," they both laughed.

"You guys are so happy together," laughed Doreen. "How long have you two been dating?"

Phoebe shook her head and waved her off. "Oh, he's...hic...he's not my—"

To her surprise, Cody grabbed and kissed her. It was their first French kiss, though amnesia would later mercifully remove it from their memories. Mitch and Doreen stood in awkward silence, watching them make out like high school teenagers. Finally, they stopped.

"Ahhhh...hic...anyway, he's...he's just my boss," grinned Phoebe with one eye more opened than the other.

"You...YOU," Cody pointed at Phoebe.

"Me?"

"Yeah you...hic...you taste like ashtrayyyy."

Phoebe playfully pushed him.

"Well, it's...it's good to see another Asian-American couple here," Mitch expressed. "We don't see many of those."

"We are so not a couple...hic...ah ha hahahaha!" Phoebe laughed.

"I'm sorry...I'm sorry I'm sorry I'm sorry," apologized Cody to Mitch and Doreen. "She's...she's drunk!"

"Noooo...hic...you're drunk!" poked Phoebe.

"I-I think you're BOTH a little drunk," corrected Doreen. "Honey, why don't we get them some water..."

Mitch took the cue and sought the bartender. Doreen smiled and continued her part in a civilized conversation with the two drunks.

"Where in town do you two live? You guys should show us around!" she requested.

"Well, I...hic...I live with my parents...in...Katy," nodded Phoebe. "And this...this man...hic...he's about to move back in with his mom and dad. I dunno where they...hic...live..."

"Moving in with...parents...hic...bankrupt...hic..." Cody frowned. "God, I need another drink."

"Oh my God," expressed Doreen.

Mitch came back, handing Cody and Phoebe each a glass of water.

"Honey," said Doreen, "they just went bankrupt."

"Wow," replied Mitch, "my condolences."

"It's...hic...damn it, let's change the subject! Woooo!" Cody was still clearly drunk.

"No," shook Mitch, "in fact, we have to go, our baby Papyrus needs to be picked up from her nanny before the hour ends."

"Papyrus! Their baby's name is Papyrus! Ahahaha!" Phoebe laughed.

"Walk like an Egyptian!!!" Cody sang and gestured in a King Tut pose.

"Well," said Doreen, "like I said we're new in town and we haven't bumped into many Asian couples—"

"We're not a couple...hic...," corrected Phoebe.

"Okay, well, Asian friends then," corrected Doreen, "that look and act like drunken couples. We'd like to get to know you two when...when you're more sober."

Cody stumbled for his business card from his suit pocket.

"Here," he said, finally finding one. "Call...hic...call us..."

"Thanks, man!" smiled Mitch, accepting the card and shaking both of their hands. "Nice meeting you guys!"

The attendees of the networking party eventually dissipated, leaving Cody passed out on Phoebe's shoulder. She noticed his head was bigger and heavier than it initially appeared. Like a bobblehead.

An hour later, the bar was soon empty as closing time neared. Cody was still knocked out while Phoebe had sobered up.

"Hey, want me to call a cab for him?" offered the bartender.

"Meh," shrugged Phoebe, craving a cigarette. "Sure. Thanks. His address is in his wallet."

She slowly moved Cody out of the way and made him lean unconsciously toward the counter. She gave him a kiss on his cheek and patted him on the head.

"Love you, boss. You're the best," she whispered.

CHAPTER 26: LOOKS, MONEY AND SOCIAL STATUS

Marty would never admit it in their newly formed partnership, but he couldn't stand Wilbur. It didn't take long for him to learn that Wilbur lived in a different world. There, it was a shallow, illogical existence, one where vanity and impatience had its place. Wilbur enjoyed sending streams of texts and selfies, and entire conversations written in acronyms and exclamation marks. Indeed, he loved exclamation marks—the more, the better. Nothing could get by him without drama. All of these vexations tested Marty's arsenal of phony laughs and rehearsed assurances to their limit. Wilbur was like a fourteen-year-old girl trapped inside of a twenty-seven-year-old metrosexual.

Fortunately, the shifty salesman's passive-aggressive stance paid off when Wilbur introduced him to the owner of the The Platinum Star. The prestigious dance club had endured the strains of time, immovable like a boulder in the middle of an economic typhoon. It remained the thriving drug laundering capital of the Houston underworld, now needing a cover-up as a legit entertainment business more than ever. Marty had no qualms taking advantage of The Platinum Star's underground wealth. The good clubs, after all, had healthy levels of corruption.

They were summoned on a weeknight, instructed to find their lead at the bar. Marty ignored his discomfort with the sticky carpeting as he and Wilbur wallowed through hundreds of dancing customers. He barely made sense of Wilbur's remarks within the loud noise, unable to piece together the combination. Once they reached the bar, it didn't take long for Wilbur to get the attention of the lead bartender. Li'l Bis was easily recognizable with his eye patch; he was also the lone male within a handful of pretty barmaids.

"H-h-h-hhey, I-I-I-I-I need to s-s-see your b-b-bbbbbbb...bbbbbbbb—"

"Boss," finished Marty.

"—b-b-boss." Wilbur took a deep breath.

Li'l Bis took his time wiping the glass while giving them a disapproving stare with his remaining good eye. His only greeting came in the form of a scowl, particularly directed toward Wilbur. Measuring an exact six-foot-two with skin darker then molasses, the native Alabamian remained as intimidating as ever since his tour in Vietnam half a century ago. The veteran found it unpleasurable that the testosterone in Asian men had evaporated. The Viet Cong soldiers he had fought were tough sons of bitches. Now Asia spawned beautiful boys like Wilbur—self-centered narcissists that knew more about changing eye shadow than changing oil.

"I expected two men," growled Li'l Bis. "Not a fool and his bitch."

Despite his insults, the two patiently waited for him to finish his cleaning. When he was done, he subtly motioned for them to follow. Marty and Wilbur made a path around the counter and accompanied Li'l Bis through a hallway. There, they passed by private rooms with opened doors, witnessing multitudes of nude men and women engaged in activities conjunct with sex and cocaine. Both visitors found it irresistible to stare in awe.

"Haul yo' ass," Li'l Bis commanded.

The two men quickened their pace like children playing catch-up with an irritable adult. A few steps later, they were led into an empty room decorated by mirrors from wall to ceiling. It was similar to the other private rooms they'd seen except this one was better shielded from the dance floor noise—ideal for conversation. Wilbur wasted no time making himself comfortable on the red velvet sofa; Marty did the same by sitting a small distance from him. They noticed the crabby bartender had left and, in his place, a pretty waitress in a revealing outfit walked in.

"Can I get you two anything to drink?" she offered.

"Wah-huh, well, uhh, heh! What do you like to drink?" Marty asked her back.

"Um, I like girly drinks," she laughed, twirling her hair. "You should just order what you like."

"Er, heh, hah!" Marty laughed. "Ooh-hah! HA! Good one! In that case, eh, I'll take, mm-huh, a Heineken then. Huh-eh."

"A-a-and I-I-I'll have a-a-a Hennessy," answered Wilbur.

The waitress nodded and left them in seclusion. Marty placed his hands together and twiddled his thumbs. He silently went through how he planned to sell and rehearsed what he was going to say. The plan should work, he thought to himself, but Wilbur's ego and stuttering outbursts were potential elements for disaster. Quickly approaching footsteps, however, immediately quelled his worrying, forcing him to focus on the situation at hand. The steps belonged to a sophisticated-looking, well-dressed businessman in his early thirties. Both Wilbur and Marty found his attire sharp, particularly the no-nonsense white suit and slacks, complemented by a sleek, dark purple tie.

"Hi, my name is Dimitri," he introduced himself with hand extended. He had a noticeable Russian accent. "You are Wilbur Wang, yes?"

"Well, heh," clarified Marty, "actually I'm Marty and he's, muh-hah, Wilbur."

"My apologies, gentlemen," said Dimitri.

"S-s-s-so l-l-let's get down to b-b-b-business," stuttered Wilbur.

Marty flinched at yet another one of Wilbur's annoying outbursts. Had Emo Boy quickly forgotten their discussed strategy? They had agreed to soften up the prospective client with small talk and then move to the heart of the negotiations—the plan was off to a bad start.

"As you wish," Dimitri replied.

The Russian took out his laptop and turned its power on. The three sat waiting for the operating system to load along with the local Wi-Fi to connect. During this time the skimpy waitress returned with their drinks, smiling as she handed Marty his Heineken and Wilbur his Hennessy. After a few moments, the browser was fully operational and the website of The Platinum Star came up in short time. It looked ancient; Marty estimated it to be circa 1998. The social media pages were also in need of updates and sported a surprisingly low number of followers.

"Foo-huh, hoo-boy...hah. Mmmm," Marty commented.

"I think this speaks for itself, yes?" asked Dimitri. "The Platinum Star needs to catch up with the world."

"I'm surprised, pshew-ffft," expressed Marty. "I, heh, I thought you guys would have a top-notch website design and tons of Twitter and Facebook followers. Hooo, hmmm..."

"Well, that's why my associates and I pushed for better marketing when we merged with the club. We would like to grow from the usual crowd that comes here."

"M-m-m-merged?! I-I-I thought you w-w-were an e-e-employee!!!" overreacted Wilbur.

"Heh, Wilbur," pleaded Marty, "shhh shush."

"No, it's quite alright, Mr. Ho," assured Dimitri. "I am working for a group that is in a beneficial business relationship with the owner of this club. Our main concern at the moment is expanding the base of our customers. In fact, we are redecorating the main dance floor area if you may have noticed. What we are looking for is getting promoters and generating new customers. That is why we are inquiring about your website skills along with your marketing expertise."

"Well, mmm, we certainly can, hmm-ah, help," Marty assured. "Our 'You're the Celebrity' model is scientifically proven, heh, to assure the latest promotional methods and the maximization of crowds."

He was rather proud of his latest statement. It was his fancy way of saying Wilbur's expansive network of friends would be relieved of some of their money. Of course, he realized, in order for it to work he would have to continue nourishing Wilbur's self-importance. So far it didn't seem to be a challenge at all—far easier than with his former partner Cody. Wilbur only cared about prestige and the prudish prince was willing to work hard for it. Once that happened, Marty believed, all he had to do was sit in the background and enjoy the money.

"You said it is scientific," inquired Dimitri. "What kind of scientific data?"

Marty swallowed hard, feeling a lump in his throat. He had not expected the young Russian to question him. For him, usually having a good-natured tone and a wink were good enough to get by.

"Wuh-eh, well, heh, ah-heh," he stalled, "heh...ummmm...these are times of reality television shows, you know?"

Dimitri looked at him with intrigue. "I do not really know, but in general, yes. How does it relate?"

"Well, mmm, it shows people want the center of attention. It's part of the entitlement, heh." Marty's eyes quickly darted in Wilbur's direction.

"I see," Dimitri hesitated, "so it is catering to the attention-craving psychology of the average American person, yes?"

Marty silently smiled and nodded, "People like it when it's all about them."

"This is true," agreed Dimitri. "When we give someone attention, they will crave more."

Marty nodded his head in agreement, encouraging the businessman to turn the gears in his head. The more Dimitri believed it, the more he would find ways to rationalize it. The explanation was vague enough for any loose interpretation.

"I'm sure I don't have to, meh-hah, tell you how the algorithm works," Marty winked at the Russian.

"Well, if you are referring to that same area of the brain which controls emotional rewards with pleasure, then I understand," Dimitri agreed and winked. "People's minds are generally weak. But not all."

He gave back a nod of understanding; Dimitri may not have been as susceptible to mind games as he seemed.

"Wah hah hah hah! There we go!" Marty opened his arms wide open. "You got it!"

"T-t-that's not a-a-all!!!" interrupted Wilbur.

Once again, Marty let loose a visible flinch at his partner's outburst.

Dimitri smiled, suspecting bullshit. "Yes, I am sure there is more to it. Mr. Ho, you seem to be a very knowledgeable person about psychology and how the brain works. Please tell me more."

"Ah, ffft." Marty looked at Wilbur. "Come on, man! Stop joking around! You know how the, heh, you know, how the science of 'You're the Celebrity' works! Ah heh heh! Eh? Why make a conversation out of complicated details?"

He silently prayed Wilbur wouldn't respond; the prayers went unanswered.

"S-s-see this is h-h-how it w-w-works... " Wilbur began.

Marty resisted the urge to tackle and shut his new partner up.

"Mah-hah, now now Wilbur, heh—"

"M-m-my p-p-program is b-b-based on the l-l-limbic s-s-system in our b-b-brain, motivating a-a-any behavior t-t-t-that makes us f-f-feel good. This i-i-in turn s-s-stimulates w-w-what is c-c-commonly known as the f-f-five senses by the c-c-cerebral cortex, a-a-affecting the ability to p-p-plan. So w-w-we attract t-t-the g-g-guests by t-t-treating them well l l like the celebrities they u-u-urge to be from T-T-TV!!!"

Both Dimitri and Marty found themselves unexpectedly impressed. A thorough scientific explanation was the last thing they thought would venture from Wilbur's mouth. He brought more into the 'You're the Celebrity' idea than Marty realized; it was a fantastic sign of luck for Marty. He attributed it to all the perfect feng shui he noticed in the room.

"I must say," Dimitri slowly nodded with genuine approval, "I was skeptical, but it appears both of you seem to know what you are doing."

"Er-hah, good. Heh! Good," Marty rubbed his hands. "We could, heh, show you the ideal business plan I drew up!"

He seized the moment by handing Dimitri the business plan. It was cleanly typed, coil bound and printed from FedEx Office.

"Meh-heh, ah, of course the overall estimate is a little lower than we usually charge," greased up Marty, "but I figured, heh, it's The Platinum Star...why not show them we're more interested in helping them than worrying about the finances, eh eh? Just the honor of having The Platinum Star alone as a client...heh, ya know? Heh. Hah!"

Marty had actually never quoted so much in his life; the "discounted price" he mentioned was five times higher than any he had negotiated in the past.

"This price," Dimitri opined, "is very fair."

The answer sent Marty's heart pounding. It didn't take him long to realize the payment probably had come from drug money, but he quickly disregarded the questionable morality in favor of a soon-to-be fortune. He could finally flaunt for his wife the social status she craved: BMWs, expensive jewelry, lakeside property, name-brand clothes, travels to exotic destinations...Xia would love him forever.

"However," the Russian continued, "I want to see results first."

"Y-y-your club b-b-better m-m-make my f-f-friends happy!!!" demanded Wilbur.

Marty rolled his eyes. Wilbur was taking his ultra-simplistic friends-treating-friends-well philosophy a bit too far. He would have a talk with his new partner later. For now, it was all about sealing the deal.

"Wuh-ha, Wilbur, I'm sure The Platinum Star knows what they're doing," he assured.

"I-I-I want at l-l-least t-t-three p-p-party buses and a p-p-party helicopter!"

"Heh heh," Dimitri calmed him down. "You are very enthusiastic, my friend. That is good. But do not test our limits and we will not test yours, you understand?"

The meeting ended with an immediate small payment up front as a statement of trust. Although it was merely five percent of the high six-figure price tag negotiated, it was more than enough to substantially carry Marty and his wife for a few months. At the very least, it would stop Xia from having "the talk" with him. Perhaps he wouldn't even need her once the big payday came. The Russian was very clear about their criteria. He wanted a better website, a citywide brand recognition and, most importantly, crowd attendances that matched a demanding quota. The Platinum Star was about to turn big. It had to be in order to hide the even bigger plans that were about to happen in the Houston criminal underworld.

"Why are you helping me?"

It was the only question Cody could muster when Duke surprisingly reached out to him after the spitting incident. The two cousins reunited on a wintry afternoon inside of a beautiful indie coffeehouse with an industrial chic and eco-friendly layout—the kind Cody loved. There were just enough patrons to make it feel public, yet it was also quiet enough for a long overdue discussion. Now that Duke had declared victory in an imagined war, it aroused Cody's curiosity as to what was left to discuss.

"Because you need to accept who you are," Duke finally answered. "A loser."

A predictable answer, shrugged Cody. He wondered why he bothered expecting something other than a stern lecture from his serious cousin. Perhaps this was Duke's unique way of caring, through chiding and reminders of his superiority. After all, what he did wasn't too much different than zealots. Cody was no fan of "Duke-ism," although, if he filtered enough of the egotistical bigotry, he might acquire some useful advice. His cousin's tone, however, made things harder to swallow.

"A loser..." contemplated Cody, "really, Duke, you can go kiss my ass."

His cousin quickly gave him a familiar dominating stare.

"You will stay," Duke ordered, "and you will listen."

With those words spoken, Cody's voice was locked inside of him; his body was now obeying his cousin's strident commands.

"Stay there," repeated Duke, "and do nothing but listen. I am your superior. I am authorizing you. You will do as I say because you fear me and it is now in your nature to fear me. Like a rabbit to a lion. Like a man to a god. I have a high paying job. I am taller than you. I have a fiancée. I am dominant."

This act had grown tiresome, but strangely it was the first time Cody succumbed to it. There was something eerily familiar about the enchantment, which was the kind he had felt around Jesus and Marty Ho. With what little willpower he had left, he reached out for his coffee, hoping it would release him from Duke's spell. Duke immediately swatted down Cody's wrist, exponentially magnifying his psychological snare.

"You will drink your coffee when I allow you to drink it," ordered Duke. "Right now, you listen. It shall be all you do."

Cody paused for a moment, wondering how a man can have the audacity to hold another man's wrist and give orders.

"Do you have any idea how insane you sound?" whispered Cody.

"Nothing is more insane than a beta male defying the hierarchy of looks, money and social status."

"So I dared to dream," Cody spoke, slightly louder than his previous hushed tone. "What's wrong with failing?"

"Everything," Duke hissed, letting go.

"No."

"Yes."

"You're just jealous because I'm the last male Quan. And they'll love me no matter what a 'loser' I am."

Duke gave Cody a hard slap across the face. "Supercilious!"

"Look who's talking..."

Duke slapped him again, this time following it with a primal stare that froze Cody in his place. How Duke could do this so often, Cody couldn't understand. But it always worked.

"There is a war, Cody. A war between Asian-Americans and everyone else. We're on the same side, but weak men like you are ill fit to lead. I will not have your failures diminish us. I will not have anyone giving you any more advantages. You will go get a regular job and you will respect your family. You will get married to a Chinese wife and prolong our people. You will take care of your elders when they're old. You will stop embarrassing me and every other Asian. You will listen to me because I know what's good for you and what's good for you is to be the model minority. Do you understand?"

"I don't want to be like you, Duke. Why do people have to be rich and good-looking and famous just to be loved?"

Duke slapped him a third time. Cody clinched his fist and prepared for retaliation.

"Unclench your fist," commanded Duke.

Cody found himself unclenching it.

"It's not about being loved, Cody. It's about being feared. My viewpoint is reality while yours is a child's fantasy. Grow up. Grow up like you've never grown up before. Do something for others for once and stop being so vain. Know your place and accept it because all you've done is hurt and burn our family's money. You were never cut out for dreams; you never were and you never will be. It's high time someone told you this. I do not respect you and my opinion about you is all that matters, because I am alpha and you will obey. I am commanding you to stop and accept my orders. I am better looking than you. I make more money. People know me. You will never be on my level. I am king of our family now and you will accept your place beneath me."

Whatever rebellion had stirred inside of Cody disappeared after those words. In one submissive sigh of acknowledgment, Cody nodded in shame and accepted his fate.

———

Cody's father could never forget Earl Fletcher, the first black man he ever met. It was during a visit to a Houston Oldsmobile dealership in 1977 where he and his new pregnant wife were shopping for a car. He was not prepared for Earl—a whirlwind of gregarious smiles, preposterous size and skin darker than he thought possible for a person—who immediately came at the newlyweds with a friendly fervor that both surprised and intimidated them. Earl gave plenty of reasons to choose the newest Cutlass Supreme, from its improved interior trim to its optional five-speed manual transmission. They were hi-tech features for the time, but Mr. Quan paid no attention to any of it, mesmerized instead by Earl's vainglorious Afro, colorful bell-bottoms and, of course, the rambunctious manner in which he talked. Cody's parents politely stopped Earl in the middle of his sales pitch and spent the next three hours at a friend's house dissecting the encounter. Mr. Quan did not expect to meet blacks in America, and now that he had, they were a fascinating enigma. Were there a lot more of them in Houston? Why were they so translucent with their feelings? He had heard there was a war and the blacks lost—didn't they have a king named Martin Luther and he died? Where was Sammy Davis Jr.? What was Motown? But most importantly, did the Quans have anything to fear? Did the blacks have anything against Chinese people? There were so many questions in 1977 and so little resources.

Within short time, he realized there was a significant black population in Texas, and he found it difficult to distinguish them from one another; they all looked like the Oldsmobile salesman. At Montgomery Ward's, one Earl Fletcher was in line in front of them, openly upset at a cashier's error. The young Quan Min-Lo couldn't follow most of the angry black man's words, but he heard the last few lines clearly: "IT'S BECAUSE I'M BLACK, ISN'T IT?"

The sentence repeated in his head over and over again. What did that mean? White people had always treated Asians well; did they not do the same to blacks? Perhaps the Earl Fletchers were misbehaving members of society, branded in a lower caste like the Indians and Filipinos in his native Hong Kong. They probably didn't have much money and their dark skin was ugly. This, he concluded, was why blacks had to be louder, had to be angry and most likely selfish by nature. He found his answer early in America about them—they were dangerous and they would hurt anyone who wasn't of their race.

As the years passed, he found what he believed to be ample evidence of the evilness of African-Americans—the safe term he learned to call blacks—from the numerous news reports and the stories of Chinese neighbors who were robbed and hurt by them. His son Cody had even come home beaten and bruised, always from black kids and always because they had started trouble with him. Then came the riots of Los Angeles fifteen years later, where he saw Koreans being robbed and beaten on live television. *IT'S BECAUSE I'M BLACK.* Mr. Quan had come to see the sentence spoken so long ago in another meaning now: Being black meant they couldn't be made fun of. Being black meant being everyone else's enemy. Being black meant being entitled to hurt other people—hurting Asians on live television without anyone doing something about it.

After more than three decades, Cody's father had come to a conclusion about his reality. Asians worked hard and stayed quiet; their children would grow up and get into top universities. They would be respected members of society, beloved by white America who would do nothing less than love Asians without prejudice. With every news footage he had seen of black people robbing and killing, Mr. Quan grew delighted that it strengthened his theory. Perhaps if the rest of America grew sick of black people, they would cease their charade of political correctness and exterminate blacks like termites from a home. Then America would be crime-free.

It was wishful thinking on his part anyway as he stood and mopped up a recently spilled drink in the middle of his restaurant, the Happy Lotus. He hated that his restaurant was in the Third Ward, hated that most of the customers were low-income blacks who did nothing but exemplify obnoxious behavior. If he were asked to come up with a good opinion of them, he couldn't think of one. Maybe they could dance and play basketball well, he thought, but nothing useful for society.

"Hey! HEY!" shouted one of the black customers, "there's a cockroach in my fried rice!"

Mr. Quan rolled his eyes and nodded at his waitress Kiki to solve the problem.

"Yes, sir, what is the problem?" she asked.

"I want a free plate to go!" demanded the same customer.

"But, ummm, why did you wait until you finish your plate to say so?"

Foolish girl, thought Cody's father, *don't challenge these people. They will only complain more.*

"What the fuck you sayin', you four-eyed bitch?!" shouted the man.

Kiki scooted back in fear, too raw and stunned to handle a bully. He approached her and raised his voice, "Are you accusing me of lying?!!"

"N-n-no I'm just—"

As she took a step farther back, she tripped on the shoe of another customer, crashing backwards toward the floor along with the plates she was holding. The customer whose foot Kiki tripped on got up and kicked her.

"Maaaan, clumsy four-eyed chinky chong!" He flipped over his table and yelled, "I ain't paying for this shit. Motherfuckin' was probably a dog!"

As the table of black customers left, another black customer walked in. His look frightened the Happy Lotus workers, with the large noticeable scar across his face among his scariest features. Mr. Quan stopped mopping and observed him with suspicion, mentally check-marking every physical trait that disgusted him: cornrows, oily skin, multiple tattoos, scars, bulging muscles, tall height and a frown that stayed on his face at all times.

"<You clean that mess up>," the veteran waitress Hannah offered to Kiki in Cantonese. "<I'll handle that scary-looking one who walked in.>"

"<Thank you>," whispered Kiki.

Hannah looked at Mr. Quan before tending to the new and frightening customer. They both knew they were thinking the same fears. She then approached him and asked the usual question of how many. The intimidating man did not respond; he merely blinked his eyes within a cold stare. Hannah decided to assume it was just he and led him to a corner seat.

"What do you want to drink?" she asked.

The man stared at her and nodded at a glass of water from the next table.

"Water?"

"..."

"Okay...water."

As she made her way near the counter, Mr. Quan mopped near her and gave her some advice without looking at her, "<Careful with that big one. He probably just got out of prison.>"

Everywhere and everything he did, Mr. Quan thought about Earl Fletcher. Earl was in black pens and black piano keys, black sesame soup and dark chocolate candy. More so, he thought of Earl Fletcher in shoot-outs and gang violence, loud athletes who shouted "black is beautiful" on television, and the rap videos that bragged about snorting drugs and killing policemen. If he could put on a mask and get away with hurting as many black people as he could, he would do it. Kelvin Min-Lo Quan didn't want to be racist; he just felt it was honest to be one.

CHAPTER 27: ASIAN PENIS

The Year of the Rabbit was not supposed to be a good year for a Rooster—at least, that's what the magazine claimed that Diana Li was flipping through. Though it occupied her time during takeoff from Miami to Houston, she wished there was something less trite as a distraction. The Chinese New Year predictions called for her having a series of bad health, bad financial decisions, a bland love life and an uphill struggle with her career. She found amusement reading the sidebar remedies of proper feng shui protections and recommended charms. Fortunately, she needed none of it because the nonsense was inapplicable to her. Diana's success had long been hinged on an unwavering, relentless attitude towards higher achievement. Everything had a reason, and that reason came from sensible logic. It was through this belief that she had not only achieved career success but had also won a bout against cancer. By the middle of the article, her disinterest in luck, fate and cosmic fortune had reached its threshold; she quickly dismissed it in hopes of finding an upgraded substitute. She found an adequate one flipping through the end of the magazine in the saving form of sudoku. There, the puzzles were more to her liking, exercising her memory and problem solving.

Some of the passing coach passengers cast envious stares as she stretched her legs around her spacious first-class seating, revitalizing in her mental element. Business first class was heaven for her; sometimes on afternoon flights like this one, there was a chance she would enjoy the entire section to herself. Even if there were fellow passengers, however, they had always been nice people who kept to themselves. Diana found no reason to put her guard up with this comfort in mind—and it was at that moment when her stability was shattered.

She didn't like to profile, but it would've been dishonest to suggest previous experiences didn't alter her prejudices. Besides, she thought, the immediate actions of the man plopping himself down next to her did not exactly give her reasons to remove doubt. Diana was brought back to an unpleasant familiar territory, a Caucasian man in his early thirties—her age group—whose unrelenting stare was joined by a desirous smile and disregard for personal space. A part of her hoped he would be an anomaly, or at least that she would be proven wrong about such fears—that this would be the man to alleviate them. Instead, it took under a second after he had made himself comfortable to justify her continued biasness.

"Man, I love Asian women," he opened.

She knew better than to accept the statement as a face value compliment. Perhaps on the lips of the many white men who had given similar endorsements, they had done so with innocent, albeit naive, intentions. She had heard it all before in restaurants, in shopping malls, in subway stations, on Internet message boards and anywhere else there were people. What always followed was a storm of awkward courting, filled with harsh innuendos, blatant presumptions—and the displeasured stench of entitlement.

"You mean you love women," she politely smiled, burying her attention inside the sudoku puzzle.

It was small hope that he would take the hint or perhaps even turn it around into a pleasant, civilized conversation. Instead, the man grabbed a hold of her wrist and leaned over.

"You remind me of a delicate peony," he whispered in her ear, "soft and gentle upon the cool summer rain, wanting to be plucked and sheltered."

Diana rolled her eyes and forcefully flicked her wrist away. She leaned toward the opposite edge of her seat—away from his breath—and continued pretending to be honed in on her puzzle. It was a meaningless gesture at this point, she knew, but direct confrontation was not her style. Of course, she knew deep in her heart that he wasn't entirely at fault. It was a day and age where so many of her female Asian contemporaries dated white men en masse. Threw themselves at them, she wanted to say. Was it any wonder no other types of men solicited her when they assumed she was spoken for by Caucasian men? Maybe the passenger beside her couldn't be blamed; he was merely acting out of a public trend. But then again, she realized, it was not her job to be politically correct; she had every right to be annoyed.

"*Em la ngot nhu ca phe sua da*," the man said in heavily accented Vietnamese.

"Please stop," Diana pleaded, smiling politely.

"Oh, you're smiling. I knew you'd like that," he incorrectly guessed. "*Bạn thích những người đàn ông mỹ?*"

"I'm not Vietnamese. I don't know what you're saying."

"Oh? Sorry, what are you then?" He decided to switch to Korean. "*Ahn nyeong, nuh gwi yub da!*"

His persistency eventually removed the courtesy of her smile. "Stop. Don't do this."

She gave a sigh of relief as the airplane's loudspeaker came on and the lead flight attendant gave the usual information about flight safety and weather conditions. It lasted long enough for her to lean towards the window and pretend to fall asleep during takeoff. The peace was short-lived once she heard the snack cart roll along the aisleway. The man called her bluff with a sharp pinch to her right buttock, sending her to immediate attention as she sat straight up and gave him a daggered look.

"Stop!!!" she uncharacteristically shouted. "I'm not kidding! I'm going to complain to the flight crew!"

"Relax," he laughed, "I just wanted to make sure you got your drink. Vodka? Brandy? What's your poison, honey?"

"No! I don't want anything!"

"Ah, an Asian woman that doesn't drink," he declared, believing he had her figured out. "You must be Chinese."

The snack cart rolled next to them. It was their turn.

"And what would you two like to drink?" smiled the flight attendant.

With a grin that was all at once arrogant as it was defiant, he waved a twenty-dollar bill and ordered a Jack Daniel's.

"Sure thing," replied the flight attendant, "and what about your wife?"

The assumption shocked Diana; she knew she was risking overreaction, but she could hardly contain her displeasure. The stewardess didn't mean anything by it, she told herself. Bad guessing happens all the time. But then again, has society shifted so far that this was the norm? And if she and other Asian women didn't speak up, would it be accepted that Asian women belonged to white men? The thought of belonging to any men in general was an insult to gender progression.

"I'm not his wife, I don't even know his name," seethed Diana. "And I'll have an orange juice."

"Sorry, it's a common mistake, I assure you," apologized the flight attendant.

"No, it's not!" Diana blurted, shocked at the rise of her own voice.

She immediately felt guilty, seeing the flight attendant's embarrassment.

"Well, I just thought...you know...it's just so common these days..." stammered the flight attendant. "I-I'm sorry."

They were quickly given their respective drinks and left alone. The outburst had made the incident worse, and if she could apologize to the woman, Diana would. By this time, the cart had already breezed through the aisle, leaving her to seek refuge once again behind the sudoku puzzle.

"You're so good at math," the man observed.

As she turned to look at him, he made it obvious to her that he was also eyeing her body; Diana was, after all, blessed with a pair of considerably generous-sized breasts. He had hoped she understood. Were not most men attracted to those features, regardless of race and ethnic background? And considering he had done the same to other women during his Miami trip—including two very receptive off-duty Japanese stewardesses who found it an honor to be his playthings—was it only natural for him to succumb to a feeling of invulnerability? He felt no reason to pardon himself as he once again leaned toward her and advanced his solicitations.

"I'm sure," he nodded, "you find white guys irresistible. All Asian women do. That's a statistical fact."

Diana let out a snort. "'All' means one hundred percent."

"That's correct."

"No, it's not correct, because I don't, so that's at least ninety-nine point nine nine percent right there. Like my math now?"

Diana had no more reservations about being upfront with him; he had already made it clear that cordialness had long passed. Still, she wished there would be some other Asian woman in first class for him to bother. It was selfish to unleash such a vexatious man on someone else, but at least she wouldn't have to endure five hours of ceaseless wooing. Diana looked around and felt disappointment once she realized she was the only woman in her section.

The man unbuckled his seat belt and leaned over, placing a palm on her thigh. He slowly placed his other arm around her shoulders and pressed his nose inches from hers.

"Do you have anywhere to stay in Houston?" he offered. "I have a penthouse room at the Derek Hotel near the Galleria. Maybe we can spend a night together...you'd love my giant cock."

"OH MY GOD!!!" she screamed, shoving him away.

By instinct, she clutched the closest thing resembling a knife—it was a pen from her purse, but she figured it would puncture quite a hole into his shoulder should he attempt to infringe upon her again.

"Shhh, shhh. Don't get too excited."

"I'm not! Oh my God! What the hell?"

"Eight inches," he proclaimed, pointing at his crotch. "I'll prove it to you tonight."

Diana immediately grabbed his arm and threatened him with her pen. To his surprise, she had an unexpectedly strong grip, one derived from adrenaline and anger. This was not the treatment he got from the Asian women he pursued in Miami. Or Atlanta, Los Angeles, Washington D.C., San Francisco, Philadelphia, New York City, Boston, New Orleans or Houston. He gave Diana a confused look, one that caused her pity and guilt. The man truly was naive in his actions, she realized.

"Hey hey! What are you doing?" he asked incredulously. "I'm just...I'm just trying to be friendly here. What's your problem?"

Diana let go of him, while loosening the grip of the pen from her other hand. "Sorry. Perhaps I overreacted."

"I'll say!" the man said, resuming an entitled glare. "I offer a lucky night to an Asian girl and she says no? Who do you think you are?! Do you know how many Asian women I've slept with?"

Diana clutched her teeth, regretting her brief moment of pity.

"I don't care! Besides, I have a fiancée," she proudly proclaimed.

"Oh." He could picture Diana's fiancée now, a big muscular blond-haired, blue-eyed Greek god.

"And he's Asian," Diana added.

The man exploded with laughter. "Hahahahaha! Is that all? And here I thought it'd be some REAL competition! Haha! Let me guess, arranged marriage?"

"No, of course not. Why would you even think that?"

"Seriously, why?"

"What do you mean 'why'? Because we connect and get along."

"I mean, physically. You know...certainly he couldn't satisfy you with his..."

"With his...?"

"Duh. Little Asian penis. Helllooooo..."

He flashed a smile and she grew angry. Very angry. Not at him or for any men like him, but for so many of the women—Asian or otherwise—who gave him the impression that his words and actions were okay. Why else in today's world would such things be said so freely toward a stranger? Diana didn't know what to think; instead, she began planning for an escape.

"Oh honey," he continued, "you have no idea how many women that look like you I've slept with. They always tell me they love white men. In fact, this Asian girl I recently had—"

"Look, I don't care," she interrupted. "I love my fiancée, he's Asian, I'm happy with him in every way and that's all you need to know. It's none of your business."

"But doesn't he beat you? I hear Asian men beat their girlfriends. The Asian women I've dated told me so."

"No, he doesn't beat me," replied Diana, "but I sure wish he was here so he could beat you."

"Hah! I'm six-foot-three, my Asian dear," boasted the man. "I bet your Asian boyfriend is four-foot-nine."

She rolled her eyes, wishing he'd stop putting the word "Asian" into everything he said. She thought of revealing that her fiancée was six-foot-five, but what would be the point? This Neanderthal clearly wanted to turn everything into a pissing contest, she realized.

"So what do you say?" he continued. "Tonight. You. Me. You know you want it."

"I want—" she raised her hand, signaling the nearest flight attendant.

"Yes?" a flight attendant asked.

"I want to change seats," requested Diana. "This man...is a delusional pervert!"

———

Cody's tardiness, as usual, was impeccable.

His six o'clock promise to pick up Diana from Bush Intercontinental Airport had run on Asian time. Like always, Diana forgave him for his tardiness—their lifetime friendship had earned them that understanding. It was through it also that Cody had sensed something was bothering her. Diana's smile was a little too wide and her optimism overly done. While she may have appeared to be happy, Cody correctly interpreted her jovial mood as a defensive mechanism.

"What's wrong?" he asked her on the drive back.

"Nothing," she beamed, "nothing's wrong! It's so GREAT here! I missed my city so much!"

"Yeah yeah. Whatever," dismissed Cody. "You were just in Miami."

"I know! But I miss Houston too! I was thinking all about it when I was watching the Heat play!"

"What?! You mean...from a television set, right?"

"No. I was given front row VIP tickets. I really didn't want to go. I even got to meet the players. They were so nice."

"Ahhhhhh, I hate you. You suck," joked Cody.

"Really, I was bored. There were too many superstars. I couldn't keep track of their names," Diana replied modestly. "Maybe if I had met them one at a time."

She was sincere in her modesty. Although Diana had the greatest job in the world as one of the nation's top biochemical research auditors, she somehow kept levelheaded about it. Cody had never quite understood how she remained so humble; he had long been a proponent of nurture over nature. Yet, Diana was a rare exception to this. It seemed she was born a caring person, with enough intelligence to go far but enough wisdom to remain unpretentious. He knew she would counter otherwise, believing that anyone can choose to be what they are. Perhaps, he realized, it was something he could learn. Something opposite of fate.

"Where should we go for food?" he finally asked.

Diana smiled, turning around to face him before she answered, "Um, Buca di Beppo?"

"An excellent choice."

Buca di Beppo was Cody's favorite restaurant—and Diana's least. Yet, it was another under-the-radar deferment to please the people she cared about. Besides, Diana knew, Cody was in a new phase in his life: thriftiness. Maybe he didn't quite know, but she needed to look out for him. The man who once threw lavish Christmas parties needed to adapt to saving money. He needed to decide on things based on value and good prices. That was Buca di Beppo—a restaurant he loved that was merciful to his wallet.

When they arrived, Cody poured out what he was holding inside of his soul. He described the events of the last ten years, from the incident with Fellowship Communion Baptist Church, Daphne, Mosaic Decor with Mindy, the kidnapping of his supervisor, and Mosaic Design Studios. Throughout it, Diana listened with focused intensity.

"...and that's when I signed that contract and dissolved my partnership with Marty," concluded Cody.

"Oh man, I'm really sorry that happened, Cody," Diana offered her condolences. "I didn't know it was that bad. My fiancée said your ex-partner wasn't very impressive at that Christmas party several years back. He said Marty looked like someone from the bottom end of the totem pole."

Cody wanted to change subjects. He had finally exhausted himself that night recalling his past. "Enough about me. What's bothering you, Diana?"

Diana smiled nervously. "Haha. Nothing. Everything's going great!"

"No, it isn't."

"Of course it is!"

Cody frowned and glared at her. Maybe she fooled the world, but she didn't fool him. Slowly, Diana's bright smile diminished as she slumped her head down. When she raised it back up again, her expression was replaced with one of agony. She knew it was okay with Cody.

"There was...this guy, on the plane ride..." she hesitantly began, "...a white guy."

She paused and began rotating a nearby fork with her fingers.

"Again?" Cody asked. "I mean they're not all like that."

Diana dropped the fork on the tablecloth and looked angrily at Cody. "Spare the political correctness. Why does it keep happening? Why do they think Asian women will gravitate towards them?!"

Cody looked around to see if any nearby tables were listening in. When he was sure that there wasn't, he leaned in and answered her.

"Because," he replied, "they do gravitate towards white guys. Everyone knows that. This is just something that happens. We deal with it. Some of these types of couples are in love. Nothing wrong with that. So this is what's been bothering you?"

"But it's not true!"

"True enough. It gets to the point that whenever an Asian-American woman mentions her boyfriend or husband, people automatically assume he's white."

"I know, isn't that awful?!" Diana blurted. "I mean, isn't there something shady about that particular pairing?"

"It's a complicated issue," replied Cody. "I'm surprised you feel you have to bring it up. Why does it bother you anyway? You're an Asian woman. You get all the attention."

"Because I'm tired of feeling like a sex object!" Diana exclaimed.

"Hah!" Cody let out a heartfelt laugh. "I wish women looked at me like a sex object. That would be hot."

"I'm serious. No, it's not! You imagine it would be beautiful women seeing you as a sex object. But what if most of them weren't? What if most of them were obnoxious and unattractive?"

"I...I think that would be okay, Diana. I'd feel flattered if most people found me attractive. Do you know how it feels to be unattractive? It sucks ass, Diana."

"It's creepy."

"Look, if a bunch of white women somehow mistook me as a sexy ninja," Cody laughed, "I'd roll with it. What's the problem? Asian women have it good these days."

Diana felt annoyed by Cody's dismissal. Why did he have such a difficult time taking seriously what bothered her? Perhaps today's incident on the plane was harmless, but there were times they were dangerous. Being seen as a fetish made her a target and she often traveled alone during work. All it would take would be a crazy taxi driver, a shady hotel manager, a false policeman—it could be anyone. Cody's problem, she thought, was that he saw it in terms of sex. He needed to see it from the viewpoint of safety and privacy, she thought. How wonderful it must be for him to walk into a department store and not be harassed? Cody didn't know how good Asian men had it, and he had the audacity to say she was lucky?

Their conversation continued after dinner as they sat out on the restaurant's open patio, watching traffic go by on Highway 59. The night sky was absent of stars and the moon was too shy to expose itself. Diana couldn't drop the subject; it was the only chance she had to let loose her thoughts.

"I'm serious, Cody!" she explained. "It's dangerous!"

"What were we talking about aga—oh yeah. White guys obsessing over you. Haha. I don't know. Just get pepper spray, I guess" he shrugged. "Besides, not all these guys that hit on you are ugly. I bet some of them are lookers, right?"

Diana let out a polite laugh. "Doesn't matter, I'm married. Best if they were all ugly to stave off temptation. Anyway, I'm tired of it. I want to be known as Diana Li. Not 'the Asian girl.'"

"And I want to be someone's boyfriend. Not 'that guy who probably has a little penis because he's Asian.'"

"Haha! Well...do you have a little penis?"

Cody looked at her and rolled his eyes. "Nothing wrong with having a compact penis. Not saying I do or don't. But it isn't a bad thing, like a Mini Cooper or a 4-gig flash drive. You know what? Next time I see Jesus and I'm not getting beat up, I'll ask why penises weren't created super small and large at the same time—just an absolute design flaw to be stuck as one size or another. Not a great engineer, that guy."

Diana fell down from laughter. She loved talking about sex because she felt inhibited bringing up the subject herself.

"You know, it's funny," Cody recalled while she continued rolling around on the ground. "I met this couple at a networking event who said they didn't see many Asian-American couples around. I thought they meant in the event. I now realize they meant in Houston itself.......and they're right."

"And probably most of America," added Diana, picking herself back up and sitting next to him. "Maybe that'll one day change."

"Why should it change?" asked Cody.

"What do you mean?"

"Maybe it's better if people dated whoever they wanted. That's not the tragedy of it. Asian women can date other guys. Asian men should be able to easily do the same. Including dating Asian women."

The scene at The Platinum Star was a kaleidoscope of eye candy. Marty couldn't turn around without swimming among a sea of beautiful women; they were of all shapes and colors, sandwiching themselves in gyrating motions in front and parallel to his spine. This, he realized, was what it felt like when the universe aligned itself, when his positive karma was perfect, and he was concurrent with his personal chi. That had to be the explanation—all those lucky numbers he requested as his cell phone digits finally paid off.

"Wah-guuhh, ahhh," he sighed, rolling his eyes to the back of his sockets as he felt random women press upon him one after another. His dancing was left a bit to be desired—he clucked his arms as he spun them in circular motions, appearing like a Tyrannosaurus rex dancing—yet no one cared from the dimness of the dance floor.

When the DJ switched to the next song, Marty took it as a cue to stop and give his libido a rest. The newly redecorated Platinum Star was grand; Dimitri and his partner Piranha had not spared any expenses. The club was drawing in higher-class clientele, positive media coverage, and more prestige for Marty than he had ever thought possible. He glimpsed at himself in the club's mirrored walls, admiring his own white suit and pants. Marty thought he looked like the Asian John Travolta, coming into a scene fresh out of *Saturday Night Fever*. Five grand, he smiled to himself recalling the outfit's price tag, all paid for by his new company expenses. It was fun strutting for the first time in his life as he made a beeline toward the most ostentatious VIP booth in the club. There, surrounded by water walls and elaborately reserved brightness, was his beautiful wife, Xia. She was laughing and socializing with important people. *The Pride of Shanghai*, he playfully called her these days. This was what she wanted; this was what they both wanted: mingling with socialites and celebrities, living off the spoils of high society.

"Oh my dear, my dear, my dear!" Xia waved to Marty. "Everyone! This is my husband, Marty! He is the host of this club!"

"Pleasure to meet you," smiled one of the socialites, raising a martini-filled glass to him. "I hear you're the big promoter in town."

"Wah-huh, psssh, heh!" Marty responded. "I'm just, heh, I'm just trying to make sure everyone has a good time!"

"Oh don't sell yourself short," countered another socialite. "You and your partner Wilbur have made this the hottest place in town!"

Marty excused himself as he went back towards the dance floor. Something magnetized him about it, as though he emanated sexuality and required receptors before it faded away from him. But as he resumed delivering his fluttering style of dancing underneath the rotating disco lights, he realized he was not alone. It was something he'd never thought he'd see in America—Asian men in the company of women, any women they wanted. They could touch them anywhere, do anything to them. In the moment of deliriousness, Marty found it natural to reach out to the best-looking blonde in front of him and cupped his arms around her large, soft breasts. As the music thumped and shook everything around him, he closed his eyes and pressed the side of his head within her long, flowing hair. She didn't care, flinch, or slap him aside like he was some Chinaman. The blonde gave his hands full access as he gripped the edges of her V-neck. A long, fluidic string of saliva dripped from of his mouth as he immersed himself in ecstasy. Gravity took its time tugging the drool, allowing it to sway back and forth across his face. Marty imagined himself in his mother's womb again, protected from all the dangers of the world.

To his surprise, a soft pair of arms reached out from behind him and held him close. By the tender way they felt, he knew they were female.

"Uh-heh, now now, Xia," he babbled, "no need to get jealous. I was just—"

He turned and realized the arms belonged to a woman he had not seen before. He admired her perfect ebony skin, her large dark eyes staring into his soul, the lovely curly texture of her hair, the perfect contrast of her bright pink lipstick. She wanted him, and her hands reaching inside of his pants left nothing beyond doubt.

"I don't know who Xia is," whispered the sensuous black woman, "but she has EVERY right to be jealous."

She tugged the part of him between his legs in rhythmic sessions, allowing Marty to enjoy the pleasurable procession as his own fingertips gently twisted the outer circumferences of the blonde's nipples. He turned his head and found himself locking lips with a third woman—an attractive Latina woman who devoured his drooling saliva and tasted his tongue. Marty's consciousness temporarily escaped him as he unleashed an explosion of warm fluid, pouring it all over the hand that was encouraging it to flow out.

"Maaaggaahhhh-uhhhhh..." he moaned.

The conclusion of the lustful session coincided with the ending of the song, and the deejay briefly paused to announce something Marty didn't care to listen to. As the three women departed, Marty slowly opened his eyes again in the middle of the dance floor, grinning like a puppy dog, not minding much the newfound stickiness in the crotch of his pants.

Making use of his time between the announcements, Marty walked over to the other side of the club where Wilbur was entertaining guests in a game of giant Jenga blocks. It was a mystery to Marty why anyone enjoyed it, let alone pay top cover prices to be in a club and play a fifteen-dollar board game. Yet, it didn't matter as long as they were entertained and having a great time. Whatever Wilbur's magic was within his dominoes, giant Jenga blocks and silly beer pong, it was working to bring crowds in. Marty spotted two familiar faces within Wilbur's group: his cousin Jack and Phoebe, Cody's supposed new business partner in crime. Well, that wasn't true, he corrected himself, Phoebe was merely Cody's employee. Whenever she was off the clock, her preferences clearly showed she'd rather be with Wilbur and himself. A smile appeared on his lips as he realized this. It must have wounded Cody to see his *cheri amor* choosing to hang with Marty over him. She probably doesn't even tell him where she goes on weekends; such a revelation would crush his dear former partner's heart.

"W-w-watch out!!!" Wilbur teased a pretty girl as she attempted to take out a fragile Jenga block.

His warning proved prophetic as her effort caused the whole tower of blocks to come tumbling down.

"N-N-Now y-y-you gotta d-d-d-d-d-d-drink!!!" declared Wilbur.

"I'm bored. Let's play some beer pong!" shouted another person.

"B-B-beer p-p-pong it i-i-is!"

Marty walked over to his new puppet and patted him on the back.

"Wah-huh, looks like you guys are, heh, having a good time!" Marty congratulated.

"O-o-oh hey!" greeted Wilbur. He pulled a young man wearing a pair of headsets around his neck to him and introduced him to Marty, "DJ Zack, t-t-this is m-m-my p-p-partner and b-b-best f-f-friend, Marty H-H-Ho."

"Oh hey, how are you?" nodded Marty, offering a handshake.

DJ Zack gave signs of delayed reactions; Marty wasn't quite sure if it was an indication of drug use or mental retardation. Wilbur's deejay friend eventually comprehended the situation and shook Marty hand.

"Oh...yeah....hey," nodded DJ Zack, partly looking at the ground.

"Wah-ah, if you're supposed to be a deejay, why aren't you on stage playing something?" teased Marty.

"Huhhhhhh?"

"I, heh, I, eh, I said if you're supposed to be a deejay, ah, why aren't you on stage playing something. You know, eh?"

DJ Zack stared at him blankly and then looked at Wilbur, "Where am I?"

Marty dismissed Wilbur's deejay friend and observed what Jack was doing instead. He was glad to see his opportunist cousin finding a wealth of impressionable young women to target—in particular, the same waitress who had served Marty drinks during their initial meeting with Dimitri a couple of weeks back. He witnessed Jack's hands making themselves into her skirt while he made out with her in public.

"Smile!" interrupted a photographer as Jack gave the picture a middle finger.

Marty embraced the madness; Wilbur's "You're the Celebrity" idea was skyrocketing towards Dimitri's imposed sales quota. In a couple of months they would fulfill their contract and make a fortune. As the photographer made his way among Wilbur's extensive group of friends, Marty called out to him and plotted one last salt to the wound on his dear former partner Cody.

"Ah-huh, hey! Come take a photo of me and her," he said making his way toward Phoebe.

He brought Phoebe close to him, one hand around her shoulder, the other holding a bottle of Absolut vodka.

"Heh, make it a big smile, Phoebe, wah-uh. You're having a great time, right? Eh?"

With a flash of the camera the moment was forever preserved in time, but not before going to where Marty knew the photographer was posting it: through the viral channels of social media—Facebook, Twitter, Instagram. There was no chance Cody would miss it. There was no chance his soul wouldn't break knowing Phoebe was on Marty and Wilbur's side all along.

"I...I gotta go," Phoebe apologized. "I was only going to stay for awhile."

"H-H-hey Phoebe!" Wilbur called out to her, "dominoes!"

Phoebe hesitated for a moment before considering her feelings. Well, she thought to herself, I am having fun. Indeed, she realized she was meeting interesting people—an Asian crowd for once who accepted her as one of them. She immediately turned around and joined everyone for a game of dominoes. One game led to another. And then another.

"I won!" she laughed after winning five times in a row. "I won again!"

Searching for his wife, Marty scanned the VIP area, wondering where she went. The lounge chair she was in before was now replaced with other socialites that weren't there earlier. After a couple of minutes of fruitless searching, he figured Xia had probably gone to the dance floor for a good time. As he scanned the club once more, he noticed Dimitri talking to someone in his office on the second floor. The conversation was with a hefty Asian man, probably in his early forties, and an Asian woman, seemingly around Marty's age, but whose tired demeanor showed advanced aging through stress and fatigue. Their conversation looked serious, far removed from the joyous celebrations below. While Marty was observing the peculiar meeting above, he was unaware he had made his way onto the edge of the dance floor.

"<Where were you?>" interrupted a familiar voice in Mandarin Chinese.

This time he recognized the arms embracing him from behind. It had been awhile since they caressed him in that way, but memories last for a long time. It was Xia. Her tone was not only one of love, but of deep respect—something Marty had long craved, but seldom found in his life of lies and manipulation. He slowly turned around and pulled her close to him, treating her for once with the direct aggression and assertiveness she had long craved from her husband. They kissed and felt time freeze as Marty reached the top of his world and claimed her as his own.

———————

Six years.

That's how short Pete's prison time ended up being for purportedly murdering his best friend. It was all, of course, part of the corruption. Even his parole office promised to "turn the other way" should Pete feel the necessity of "violating" his newfound freedom. Piranha had so many people on his payroll that Pete wondered if anyone wasn't. A sense of déjà vu returned when he got off the bus to Houston; this time, however, he felt shame and disharmony. He wanted to rise above his circumstances and avoid becoming another victim of his violent environment.

There was little surprise when no one came to pick him up from the bus station. He would have to walk home, regardless of the many hours it would take to get there. At least, he chuckled to himself, he wouldn't fear criminals putting a move on him. He was, after all, still their kind.

"Say...say!" hollered someone from the street. "You one of Piranha's boys. Ey, hit me some, mang."

The voice came from a ragged old man who was standing under the streetlight across from him. Pete tried his best to recognize the elderly drug user, but he had served so many addicts in the past that their faces became a blur. The old man tagged along behind him as he kept walking.

"I'm clear, old man," Pete finally replied without turning back. "Ain't got shit. Just got outta prison."

"So ya sayin' ya fresh out?"

Pete grew irritated, stopped and faced him. "What I just tell you, nigga? Shoo."

"Come on, man! Ain't dat some dumb hell luck! Holla at ya boy. Hook me some sumthin' some."

"Shoot, ma-fucka, it ain't about that, no mo', 'sides, nigga, I'm quittin' the game, nigga."

"Hahaha, talkin' 'bout retirin'? Now y'all knaw y'all can't do dat."

"And why the fuck not?" challenged Pete. "Ain't that nigga Piranha's whipping boy no mo'. A tiger and some prison time changed my perspective, hear?"

The elderly addict gave out a haunting laugh. In the dull illumination from the streetlight Pete could see that the old man was missing most of his front teeth.

"That raw," the addict acknowledged. "Respect. But check it, youse do what they call lifetime work. KnawhaImean?"

Pete gave the old druggie a silent, challenging look.

"Wat?" the man grinned toothlessly, "don't act like it ain't known."

"Not exactly, nigga," Pete replied. "Must be a way."

"Ain't no 'other' way, my boy. 'Sides, way I figured it, y'all ain't got 'nother trade."

"Rules meant ta be broken, my nigga. Way of the world."

"Truth," acknowledged the junkie, "but still..."

"Ol' man, why y'all worry fo' anyway?!" Pete asked defensively. "All you want was dust and I ain't got shit, nigga. You deaf? Flipmode, nigga, don't make me fast and furious."

"Jus' concerning, man. Is all."

"Nigga, I deal with the consequences involved. Catch, nigga? Best reverse."

The old junkie tsk-tsked him and left him alone. Pete resumed heading towards the direction of his neighborhood. The walk itself was one of the finest presents he had experienced in a long time. He was both excited and nervous to see his mother and sister again; they probably were still angry but he was confident he could mend fences with them. Regardless, he would take advantage of the long walk and collect his thoughts. Pete had never been much of a planner—perhaps, he realized, that had always been the problem. It was time he took control of his life, one where he dictated it before someone else did it for him. "Someone" like Andrew Huynh and his boss, Piranha.

Several blocks in, his growling stomach was fortuitous enough to encounter an unexpected and eye-catching sight. There, amid a well-lit area, was a food truck unlike any he had seen before. He observed the state-of-the-art, black and gold vehicular restaurant, staring at it with wide-eyed amazement. What shocked him most were the high prices, more expensive than most establishments in town.

"Kobe beef burgers and red wine?!" he read out loud.

"Can I help you, sir?" asked a voice.

Pete looked up at the truck counter and saw a woman dressed in a waitressing outfit.

"Yo, what the hell is this?" laughed Pete. "Y'all niggas got any common shit for regular niggas like me?"

"No, sir, this is Millionaire Munchies, the food truck for the distinguished class."

Pete broke into laughter. "This for real?"

As if on cue, a limousine pulled up near the food truck. Pete was flabbergasted as the tinted windows slowly rolled down and the smiling head of a middle-aged gentleman popped out.

"Hi there!" he greeted, "you guys serve steak?"

"Yeah! Check us out!" shouted the vendor.

"Ridiculous!!!" commented Pete. "This can't be real!"

He would soon find out that the food trucks were not only very real, but increasingly popular in the city of Houston. Half a decade of incarceration had Pete catching up to what he had missed. A few blocks later, he encountered two more food trucks. Then three more. Then dozens. They were near nightclubs and other restaurants, bars and apartment complexes. Hundreds of nocturnal big spenders were willing to pay top dollar for food that satisfied their hunger. There were gimmicks that tiptoed on the imaginative—Eskimo pizzas, Italian egg rolls—to the ones that were common—hamburgers and fries. It was enough of an epiphany that Pete stayed for hours, long after the trucks had left and daylight had come.

CHAPTER 28: LIKE A CAT

Ace couldn't believe his eyes. The newly purchased house in front of him was a dream—three stories, eight bedrooms, a beautiful garden surrounding the driveway, and most of all, wonderful proximity to the beautiful lake behind it. His uncle may not have been rich, but it was amazing what a good credit score and a crafty loan officer could come up with. He was mostly happy that Cody's family had upgraded their standard of living, but a part of him wished it had happened earlier when he was an international student living with the Quans. He remembered the cramped town house and its thin walls, and his fear that the structure might have been fragile enough to come crashing down upon him at any moment.

"<Just wait until you see the kitchen!>" Mr. Quan proudly proclaimed. "<It's bigger than your father's entire apartment in Hong Kong!>"

Cody's father did not speak out of exaggeration as they walked in for a tour. The kitchen space was vast—1500 square feet by Ace's approximation—with walk-in pantries, tiled backsplashes, and eco-friendly bamboo flooring. Ace was led to other parts of the home that had equally impressive architecture, though he felt a little annoyed that Mr. Quan continually bragged that in America one doesn't need to be rich in order to live rich.

"<All you have to do is borrow, borrow, borrow!>" smiled Cody's father. <"It's so incredibly easy, I didn't know why I didn't think of it before!>"

His uncle had a childlike gleam in his eye, a long-lost happiness that Ace didn't want to interrupt. Besides, he thought, who was he to question his uncle anyway? Cody's father had been through life. Ace looked up to him as an elder, someone who felt a reason to mortgage the Quans' future into something that was far beyond their means of living. Perhaps if he remained submissive and obedient, he might learn the lesson his uncle was trying to teach him. Was it getting everything he wanted before he was too old to enjoy life? Was it making his own family look well-to-do on the surface while hiding the struggles from the public eye? Before Ace could contemplate any further, his focus was taken in by the brilliant backyard. There, the giant lake was mere yards away from them. Cody's father nudged his bewildered nephew and gestured at the surrounding serenity. They heard only the chirping of birds, nothing else. Ace was led to the farthest side of the yard where he saw a canoe and a rifle lying beside it. A short distance out on the lake, Ace saw several rubber ducks floating, most likely placed there by his uncle. They remained stationary on the current-less water, seemingly as if they were on solid ground itself.

"<See those rubber ducks in the distance?>" Mr. Quan inquired, picking up the rifle and clacking it. The gun had been loaded all this time, Ace realized.

"<Ehhhhh, yes, Uncle, but, ehh, what are they doing there?>"

"<I put them there this morning by way of this canoe. Target practice.>"

Ace took a few steps back as Cody's father aimed the rifle at the ducks. Guns had always made the young man nervous, particularly from their use in sport. His uncle closed one eye; a twisted smile crept across his face.

"<Relax, don't be scared>," laughed Mr. Quan, opening his eye again as he looked at his nephew. "<Here, hold it. It'll make you feel powerful.>"

He slowly passed the rifle to Ace, helping the young man adjust to the correct posture. The rifle felt heavy and alive, willing to obey anything that its handler demanded. Mr. Quan was impressed at how Ace picked up the correct stance; he thought his nephew looked stylish in his current pose.

"<Good...you're holding it exactly right>," Mr. Quan instructed. "<Now aim with one eye. Look at the rubber duck.>"

Ace continued holding on to the rifle steadily with his non-firing hand with the butt of it pressed firmly against his firing shoulder. His breathing was growing heavy with nervousness, but otherwise he had one of the ducks locked in his sight.

"<Now squeeze the trigger>," his uncle whispered.

Ace's shooting finger froze and remained still on the cold metal. He was conflicted between listening to Cody's father or succumbing to his desire to stop.

"<Squeeze the trigger>," repeated Mr. Quan.

His nephew closed his eyes and did as he was told. *BLAM!!!* Within the moment of firing, the recoil surprised him and sent his aim several degrees off. The ducks remained still and not a ripple had appeared. Nevertheless, Ace felt immense power as he felt his heart beating faster than he could imagine.

"<That was fun, wasn't it?>" Mr. Quan congratulated, patting him on the shoulder.

"<Ehhh, uncle, ehhhh, wouldn't it be illegal to be shooting this gun right now?>"

Cody's father shrugged. "<It's Texas. No one will care.>"

Ace gave him a rare, quizzical look.

"<I'm sure, okay?>" assured his uncle. "<I've been firing it here all week.>"

"<Really?>"

He nodded. "<Of course, whenever I'm shooting it's not rubber ducks that I see. It's niggers.>"

The sudden statement almost made Ace drop the rifle.

"<Ehhh, uncle. Uhhh, you just said—>"

"<What?>" snorted Mr. Quan. "<It's why I bought the gun. I couldn't have a nice house without fearing black people trying to steal things now, could I?>"

"<Perhaps you are overreacting, uncle.>"

"<Hey, trust me, you don't see them everyday like I do. It's their nature. Why do you think this black president is trying to remove guns? It would enable his people to more easily steal from everyone else. I know these things. Think about it. It makes sense.>"

The logic of the speech left its mark on the impressionable young man. Ace pulled the rifle back up, repeating the same stance that he had just been taught. Again, he pointed the gun at one of the rubber ducks, aiming at it through the scope of the rifle. Something was different this time. His breath was calm, his hands were steady—he felt empowered by the emotion of fear. As Ace blinked his eyes, the rubber duck was replaced by a threatening black man. The imaginary invader was wearing a hooded sweatshirt and baggy pants. As he walked on top of the water, heading towards Ace, the black man removed his hood, revealing a head with cornrows and tattoos across the side of his face. The figure began charging at him, exposing a knife in hand, leaving no doubt that he was after Ace's money and life. The young man felt a seeping adrenaline rush, allowing the right for self-defense to be joined by an inner hatred he never knew he had.

It was kill or be killed.

"<Die!!!!!!>" Ace screamed as he squeezed the trigger and sent the bullet tearing a clean hole through the rubber duck.

The action shook him to the core, as he slowly lowered the rifle, eyes wide open at the devastation he had caused. He felt his shoulders moving up and down, a result of the heavy breathing that ensued after firing the gun. Cody's father slowly walked over to his nephew and took the rifle back.

"<Good, good. We're going to have to work on your aim later. But that was very good. Come>," he motioned back toward the house. "<There's more inside I want to show you. On the second floor there's a gorgeous Buddha room I had custom made.>"

As Mr. Quan led his nephew back into the new house, he patted Ace's back like he was his own son. He liked Ace, feeling a better connection with him than Cody. For one thing, there wasn't a language barrier. But more importantly, Ace was obedient, like a loyal dog that was easily trainable and aimed to please people. Ace was led to a dark room illuminated by dim red light. It was generously spacious, set up almost like a temple within the house. At the far end of the wall, close to the center part of the wall, rested the largest personal statue he had ever seen of the Buddhist goddess of compassion.

"<The new Guan Yin statue is beautiful, isn't it?>" admired Cody's father. "<She'll bring so much luck. So much longevity and babies.>"

"<It is beautiful, uncle>," agreed Ace.

Mr. Quan paused and gave his nephew a stern expression. "<We get good fortune because we are good people. My heart is pure and karma takes care of us in the end. Do you understand?>"

Ace nodded, appreciating what his uncle had taught

him. Surely everything he was told to accept or fear was said for his own good. Elders were always right. A sudden noise sent their attention toward the illuminating statue. There, a large gray figure slowly emerged from the altar, making its way onto the large Guan Yin statue's lap. It was Toby, Cody's cat.

"<HEY!!!>" Mr. Quan screamed, shooing off Toby. "<No! Get off! Go!>"

The old cat refused to budge, blankly staring at the middle-aged man instead.

"<Move!>" he repeated, moving his hand back to slap her. "<Or else!>"

The cat ignored him and went back to sleep. Cody's father dropped the charade of attacking her and, instead, attempted to lift the feline with his hands.

"<Come on...come on!......Damn, I hate this cat. I hate all cats! They act like they can do whatever they want! Like my son!>"

He took Toby and dropped her to the floor. She landed upright and took her time walking away.

"<Anyway>," he continued looking back at Ace, "<we always got to treat our deities well. By doing well, we get better things. By taking luck seriously, we can receive an ultimate life. And we do so with compassion.>"

He lit some incense and placed it in a thurible in front of the statue. Mr. Quan bowed to it several times.

———

Cody finally felt the receiving end of tardiness; though it was long overdue, it hurt just the same. It left him with a concoction of disrespectfulness, abhorrence and negligence. Phoebe's tardiness was a new trait for her, something he feared that could lead to repeating incidents. He impatiently tapped his right foot on the marble floor of the Town Square Starbucks, hoping it was the only nervous sign displayed to their newest client, Maxine Walters. Cody was thankful one of the most prominent African-American businesswomen in Houston had given their two-person operation a chance. Strokes of luck were a rarity for Cody, which made Phoebe's lackadaisicalness even more frustrating. Perhaps he deserved this for all the times he had been late for his old job and the careers of other people he had risked.

"I'm...I'm really sorry, Maxine," Cody repeatedly apologized. "My associate is usually not late. Maybe her car broke down. She drives a crappy Kia..."

"No, no, it's okay. I know how it is," Maxine smiled, though he realized it was more out of politeness than forgiveness. "You guys do good work and I think the quality makes up for the punctuality."

"Thanks, maybe we should start without her. This isn't fair for you. Phoebe has the nice laptop, but maybe I can show you your site on my iPhone."

"No, I'd rather see my site on the laptop," calmly requested Maxine. She looked at Cody and read his mind. "Go easy on her. She's young."

"I know. It's just...it isn't fair to you, Maxine. I appreciate the chance you're giving us. I understand how important you are."

Maxine calmly patted Cody's knee and offered a suggestion. "Maybe you should ease up on the stress a little. You know what I do when I'm stressed? I pick a famous movie star and come up with ten movies that he or she starred in."

Cody smiled at the suggestion. It appealed to his geeky nature.

"That should be easy," he laughed.

"It's actually not," Maxine assured. "I find I usually tap out around seven or eight."

"Really?"

"Sure. For example, Tom Cruise."

"Piece of cake," scoffed Cody, "*Days of Thunder...Jerry Maguire... Rainman... Minority Report*...um... *Top Gun*...uhh...*War of the Worlds*... uhhhh...ummm...*Vanilla Sky*.......*Eyes Wide Shut*...uh...uhhh...hmmmm.."

Cody began to struggle.

"Hahaha. See?!" laughed Maxine.

"*Tropic Thunder*...and...uh...*Austin Powers*."

Maxine continued laughing. "Those last two don't count! They were brief cameos! Amazing you remembered *Vanilla Sky* though. How did you miss *Risky Business*?"

"Oh yeah. Good one. Give me another movie star," Cody insisted. "I'm not a big Tom Cruise fan."

"Okay," Maxine replied, "Leonardo DiCaprio."

"Easy. *Titanic, Shattered Island, The Departed, Gangs of New York, Basketball Diaries, Romeo + Juliet, The Quick and the Dead*...and...damn it...what's up with you and pretty white boys?"

A burst of laughter came out of Maxine. "Well, being black, I didn't want to pick a black actor."

"Oh, come on! I just wanted an easier one like Samuel L. Jackson. That guy's in everything!"

Before Cody could come up with ten Samuel L. Jackson movies, they saw Phoebe walking into the coffee shop. She looked untidy; her hair was a mess and her face was devoid of makeup. Cody had never seen her put forth such minimal effort into her appearance. Both Maxine and he flinched as a strong stench of cigarettes reeked from Phoebe sitting next to them.

"Coming in a little late, are we?" Cody said in a disapproving tone.

"Meh," she shrugged.

The response offended Cody. "Maxine was kind enough to wait for half an hour."

Phoebe ignored him and opened up her laptop, fidgeting for the proper Wi-Fi connection.

"Apologize to her—"

"It's alright, Cody. Really," assured Maxine.

"Sorry, Maxine." Phoebe rolled her eyes. "I was just...eh..."

"It's okay, no need to explain," Maxine smiled. "Must've been a nice party last night."

"Yes," agreed Cody in an icy tone.

The next hour was spent discussing details about Maxine's website. Fortunately for Cody and Phoebe, she was pleased with the progress. After the meeting ended and their client left them, Cody took his former crush aside and let her have it in the nearby parking lot.

"Why were you so late?" Cody scolded, feeling more than a touch of irony in his words.

"Sorry, boss," she shrugged. "I woke up late."

"And why did you wake up late?"

Phoebe hesitated for a moment in telling him the truth, but lying wasn't in her nature. ".......Because I was partying with Marty and Wilbur last night."

She immediately regretted telling him that as he displayed an expression of heartfelt pain.

"YOU WHAT?!" Cody blurted. "W-what have you told them? What details about our clients have you revealed?"

"I didn't tell 'em nothing, man!" Phoebe protested. "Besides, why did you fight with them? I want you guys to be friends again!"

"Friends again?! Marty left us when the ship was sinking!!!"

"Well, that's because he told me you kicked him out!"

"That was before I kicked him out!"

"Whatever," Phoebe rolled her eyes. "I need a cig."

She quickly dug through her purse and found a pack of cigarettes, lighting one up as quickly as she could. Cody knocked it out of her hand.

"Hey!" she screamed, picking it back up off the ground.

"You're not seriously putting that back into your lips, are you?!"

Phoebe shook with anger, but decided not to incite him further with the cigarette. She flicked it back to the ground.

"Marty," Cody explained, "started his own company when he was still with ours. He continued giving us false information about having clients and left me with a large hole in our account that was over fifteen thousand dollars in debt! My friends and family all chipped to cover the expenses!!!"

"I just...I mean, I just don't get it," she quivered. "Why would you be partners with someone you barely knew?"

Cody paused, acknowledging the legitimacy of her question.

"Yeah. I was...I was stupid, okay?" he replied. "I thought I knew the guy."

"But you only befriended him for a few months before making him the partner of your company?!"

"I said I was stupid."

"Yeah? Well, maybe Marty was equally as stupid for trusting you!"

Cody's jaw dropped. "What?! How could you even defend him?!"

"I'm not defending him......BOSS!!!"

"That fucking guy doesn't care about you! He's using you as a tool to get back at me! He knows I like you!!!"

Phoebe looked at him and paused. She secretly felt flattered every time he admitted his feelings for her. "Boss...Cody... how can you be such a paranoid person?"

"I thought we were a team," Cody confessed. "And teams have loyalty. You are either with me or against me."

"Of course, I'm with you," assured Phoebe. "But I also make friends with whoever I want."

"I understand that but did it really have to be those two?!"

Phoebe gave him a look of anger.

"What's your problem?!" she shouted, her voice echoing across the parking lot. "It's my life! I can do whatever I want!"

"So if I wasn't supplying you with paychecks, you wouldn't be talking to me? Is that how it goes? How come you never hang out with me when I ask?"

"MAYBE IT'S BECAUSE THEY'RE FUN AND YOU'RE NOT!!!" Phoebe blurted.

Cody silently looked at her and struggled to find further words. Was that how she truly felt about him? Did she party and drink with Marty and Wilbur, screaming "fuck Cody Quan" to one another? How could he have been such a fool? he wondered. Phoebe was a peacemaker. She'd never understand the point of choosing sides.

"Did you tell them anything about the company?" Cody finally asked.

"What? No! How could you even think of that?" Phoebe asked. "What makes you think that, huh?!"

"Oh my God, I trusted you..."

"I didn't tell them anything!" she assured him.

"Well, maybe you should hang with them more!!! Then it'll come out! Why are you even wasting our time together, huh?!!!! Go!...Go!!!"

"Meh! MEHHHHHHH!" Phoebe turned around and stormed away.

"Go ahead and text your two new friends!" Cody shouted at her. "Tell them we've just had a fight! They'll be delighted to hear that!"

Phoebe felt her entire body shaking with rage as she made her way out of the parking lot. When she was out of Cody's sight, tears began flowing and she was glad she didn't have mascara on. The sudden honk of a car scared her as she leapt away from the middle of the road and onto its grassy sides. She faced the Sugar Land Town Square, cursing she had ever known of its existence—everything from Hula Hoop Shakes to Mosaic Design Studios. If Cody thought paying her was charity, she thought, and if all she was to him was deadweight, unworthy of being trusted, then he could try and run his company by himself. She took out her business cards from her purse and tossed them in the street.

Phoebe Bowie and Cody Quan were no more.

———

Cody flipped his pillow over, hoping the coldness of the other side might comfort him. No such luck, he realized. He wanted to blame his insomnia on the new house; it was unrecognizable and devoid of memories, no different from a hotel room that wasn't his own. The walls of his new room were adorned with familiar personal items, some of which were a bit embarrassing—like the first shoes he wore as a baby, and paraphernalia from eighties' morning cartoons like *Thundercats*, *DuckTales* and *The Real Ghostbusters*. He supposed that was how his mother best wanted to decorate it; she would always see him as the child she remembered, resisting the inevitable pull of change like most parents do. Yet, although those private belongings and more were in his new room, they felt like they should be somewhere else—perhaps even in another time. He didn't belong there and he didn't belong living with his parents again. It was a reality he was struggling to comprehend.

"The universe is against me," he muttered aloud in the darkness. "Jesus hates me. Nothing ever works right in my life."

He paused in fear for a moment, wondering if Jesus might suddenly appear and attack him again. Once moments had passed and nothing happened, he breathed a sigh of relief, though it wasn't before long that a wave of sadness came over him. Cody missed Phoebe; he wasn't quite sure why. She was not a kindred spirit by any means nor had their brief time together developed any fond memories. It also wasn't Cody's style to enjoy playing the savior and besides, he thought, the poor girl wasn't necessarily dependent. So why did he miss her? he wondered. Regardless, he concluded it didn't matter anymore because she was tainted with the stain of Marty and Wilbur's world.

Was that really it then? Cody realized.

Phoebe was the last reminder of a dream that failed, a foolish hope that his time here on Earth could be something more. His current situation—with everything lost and living with his parents in a house paid for by credit—was the reality. The only successes that Cody had felt were the ones he imagined and hoped for that never came true—intangible things that didn't exist. He believed in a lie that told him he was special, that he was better than people deemed him to be.

"But what is the reality?" Cody could see his cousin Duke asking him. "The reality is that you are a loser. A beta male, not fit to dare think you are anything more. Let go and quit...and accept it for the rest of your life."

Cody closed his eyes and finally gave in. In the upcoming week he would terminate his business and run away from all the angry former clients and their growing pile of lawsuits. He would get a job in a cubicle and hide away from reality, putting himself where the world thought he should be. Many years ago, his friend Jay Zheng hanged himself when he had realized the world was cold and indifferent to him. Cody Quan decided to kill himself in a much slower, more painful way—enduring life on cruise control for the rest of his remaining days.

———

It was three in the afternoon when he woke up. Cody felt neither hot nor cold, neither hungry nor full. Worse, something was missing in the mirror while he was brushing his teeth—it showed everything but his reflection. He looked around and observed the additional absence of his shadow, the contortion of gravity, and most of all, his lack of concern for any of the unusualness. This, he realized, was the result of a disappearing soul.

"<Hi, cousin Cody>," greeted Ace.

Cody squinted at him, raising one eyebrow in suspicion.

"You see me?" he asked his cousin, toothpaste foaming out of his mouth.

"<Ehhh, of course.>"

Cody turned around and rinsed his mouth. He wiped his face with a towel, still minus his reflection in the mirror.

"<Do you want to play *Grand Theft Auto?*>" asked Ace, looking at his reflection.

Clearly nothing was different to the boy, observed Cody.

"Yeah...yeah, sure. Let's do that, Ace."

Cody and Ace spent the rest of the afternoon playing games, vegetating on their violence and repetitive action. Cody hardly made conversation with his cousin, who occasionally gestured with an imaginary rifle and made shooting sounds from his mouth. Cody was comfortable leaning his head at the bottom of the dining room sofa, his body lateral with the floor. His cat made her way on top of his stomach, enjoying the wavy motion of his stomach as she slept soundly on it.

Hours later, when his father came back and discovered them in the same position, Mr. Quan held no verbal restraint in telling them what was on his mind. Sensing his uncle's rage, Ace excused himself and headed upstairs, where his room provided adequate shelter from the upcoming ruction he predicted would occur.

Cody, now soulless, felt indifferent to his father's disapproval.

"<Why are you sitting here playing games?!!>" Mr. Quan began scolding his son.

"Hello, dad."

Cody turned off the Playstation 3 and stared at his father with a wide-eyed expression.

"<What are you doing? Why are you acting so strange?>"

"I don't know. I'm shutting down the company."

The unexpected news caused Cody's father to smile. Finally, his son was smart enough to give up his foolish ambitions, he thought. Luck was, indeed, on his side.

"<Good...I see you've come to your senses. Find yourself a nice job again. One with health insurance and a retirement plan. Why, you can even pay off your uncle in Hong Kong after a few years.>"

Cody looked down and nodded in silence. His father was holding a full plastic bag of groceries he had purchased from Chinatown.

"<Look what I've brought you, son. Tangerines. They'll give you good luck and longevity. You be obedient...come on, eat some.>"

He watched as his son picked up a tangerine and peeled it.

"<You'll be good now, you hear? Get a job, listen to your parents, give us things with your paycheck. In return, we'll guide you and reward you if you follow what we say.>"

Cody munched on a slice of tangerine and nodded again.

"<First you'll get a job, then you'll date Kiki. You remember Kiki, don't you, son? Your grandfather likes her...I like her.>"

"<Yes, father.>"

"<Good. You were like a cat before, always doing what you wanted, never putting up with what people did to you. It's best to be submissive. You don't have to think, you don't have to care. It's wonderful, son.>"

With the lecture over, the Quans and Ace had a quiet dinner. Cody ate two bowls of rice and balanced portions from the other dishes—just as he was instructed. The food was tasteless; the moment was joyless. It was one beautiful display of Confucianism at its finest.

CHAPTER 29: TRUTH IS LIKE THE CLOUDS

The late morning sunlight pried opened Daphne Huynh's eyes. It was such a rare experience for her now, one that reminded her of a life that had long since passed. These days, it was either Helen or Winnie that served as the alarm clock. Helen, because the six-year-old was usually up before dawn, making a mess of the kitchen while watching morning cartoons. Winnie, because she had the habit of gently kicking inside of Daphne's stomach right around sunrise. She could tell the latter child was opposite of her first one; the soon-to-be-born was calm and collected, patient in getting what she wanted. It was a good balance from Helen, who was fierce and careless like her father.

Altogether, it was what the thirty-two-year-old mother considered the perfect life. She was the wife of a mobster, a fearless and powerful man who made her the most untouchable possession in a world of danger. It was the primary justification of a life supported by drugs and murder—God's way of sorting out the deserved and undeserved. It blessed Daphne with a life of riches and protection. Their family's lifestyle was one of underground royalty—the king being a cold-hearted, yet sociable man who often ignored her and spent his time trying to satisfy his demeritorious appetites. And on the rare occasion Andrew Huynh was home, he brought with him an ever-changing array of like-minded marauders. They played high-stakes poker games and smoked exorbitantly premium cigars until she could not stay awake a moment longer, heading to bed alone, where he seldom returned to her. Still, she liked to say, their two thoroughbred Rottweilers kept her safe upstairs and watched the master bedroom doorway like personal soldiers trained to kill on sight.

Yes, she admitted, it had made her unpopular to fall for a bad man, a real bad man who did bad things. Andrew would sometimes tell her of the evil he had done—usually moments after they had finished making love—and expressed his joy about his homicidal moments, between maiming and torturing, and listening to the last breaths of the soon-to-be deceased. Through it all, Daphne listened to his stories, happy and honored that she was privileged to be the one this killer told his secrets to. She was the special woman who stood in the eye of his whirlwind of madness, who could observe the carnage and excitement of men and the violent games they played.

It was through that love that she understood why this morning, like most mornings, the other side of the bed was empty. He was God's pick for her as a husband and God could never be wrong, because she was taught that everything happened for a reason. Daphne wouldn't question the honor of serving him and being submissive as his wife—this was love, and she was only sorry that once upon a time at first sight, she had initially denied him.

"Daddy!"

Her daughter's excited announcement downstairs snapped her away from her thoughts.

Daphne's eyes lit up. She slowly got out of bed, a slight challenge for a woman several months pregnant. The stairs were a bigger test, but one easily conquered with well-paced waddling. Andrew slowly appeared to her with each step. When she finally got a good look at her husband's face, it revealed a tired expression, though it offered little information about whether or not his fatigue came from work or pleasure. Daphne knew better than to ask; his outbursts of temper were few but memorable in their marriage. As he sat on the living room sofa bouncing Helen on his knee, she approached him in her bathrobe with a smile and nod.

"Morning," greeted Daphne.

His response was null, ignoring her existence; Helen giggled uncontrollably as she seesawed on the knee of the dangerous hit man. Andrew abruptly stopped and produced a life-sized Woody doll from the *Toy Story* movies his daughter loved. As predicted, the six-year-old flashed a large smile and took the figure into her tiny hands with delight.

Daphne, too, was overjoyed about the new gift, forgetting for a moment that her husband did not like to be questioned.

"Nice!" she complimented. "Where'd you find an open toy store in the middle of the night?"

Andrew finally acknowledged her presence, but not in the way she was hoping for. With a silent look of disgust, he wondered how intelligent his wife truly was if she thought he bought the Woody doll from a toy store. More so, how could she possibly want their daughter to hear a detailed explanation of the violence he wreaked to get it? Yes, he would answer, I took it from the child of a drug dealer who was skimming money from my boss. He had taken the toy because she could no longer hold it after he broke her fingers in front of her father. If the man tries stealing from Piranha again, Andrew knew, he would cripple the same child and make sure she would never walk for the remainder of her life.

"I-I'm sorry," apologized Daphne.

"There's a snake in my boots!" the Woody doll said after Helen pulled its string.

"Heeheehee!" the girl laughed. "Thanks, daddy!"

"Anything for you, hon," her father smirked.

Daphne walked over to her husband and placed her arms around him.

"Welcome home," she kissed his neck.

Andrew brushed her aside and distanced her from him and Helen. "Why was the back door unlocked?"

"I just...I just figured it was easier to slip Buddy in and out when he needed to go," she said of one of their Rottweilers.

"Buddy knows to stay in the house. He wouldn't go in the middle night and besides, dogs can't open doors. What the hell kind of logic is that? Do you think before you speak sometimes, huh?"

Daphne felt a lump in her throat; she didn't like disappointing him.

"No, I meant it makes it easier for me to open it for him. There are so many locks and—"

"Are you fucking listening to me? Don't leave the door unlocked like that. Shit might happen to Buddy. Lord knows his life is worth than yours."

"Ooooh, daddy, you said a bad word," chastised Helen, "two bad words!"

Daphne stared at the floor, comforting herself from the pain her husband had inflicted with his disrespectful words. *He didn't mean that*, she rationalized. *He loves me when it matters. He's just not thinking properly at the moment. Stressful day.* With fear of provoking him further, she silently backed away with her head down, making her way upstairs. Andrew is a good father, she knew, someone who protected and provided. Daphne guessed this must be what a good husband was like—her only comparison was her father, a bad husband who never worked and threw objects at her mother. She slowly pushed herself into her bed with the baby within her sound asleep. *Daddy loves us*, Daphne whispered to Winnie, *he's just had a bad night.*

———————

"So tell us about your day, Mr. Quan," asked the fat lady.

Cody looked at her in confusion for a moment, wondering if it was rust that caused him to possibly mishear the question. After all, it was his first job interview in over ten years. He was nervous that he wasn't apprehensive; perhaps this was another symptom of a soulless existence, he thought.

"Um...my...day?"

"Yes, your day. How was it?"

"It's...it's fine. I'm sorry—people usually ask me to tell them about myself. About what I do, that is. Not exactly about my day—"

"Are you usually so disagreeable to simple questions, Mr. Quan?"

He wished he could take his attention away from the plumpish woman's enormous double chin. She wore a necklace too, a string of pearls that clung together like a pair of arms hugging a tree stump.

"Well?" she persisted.

"N-No. No, I'm not disobedient and free thinking at all, sir. I mean, ma'am. My...my day was fine. It was good. I ate a foot-long chili dog. Um, it didn't rain."

"Humph," the fat lady snorted, unimpressed with Cody's tactless answers. He should be lucky his skill set was of immense value, she thought, lest he would be kicked out of the interview right then and there for such babbling imprudence.

"Okay, just tell me about yourself, what it is that you do, how you could help us...all that."

"Well," Cody calmly resumed, putting down his cup of coffee, "I worked for seven years at the University of Houston as a hybrid senior graphic designer and web developer. The job had given me a lot of opportunity to polish up and develop a well-rounded set of skills. Uh, skills like Photoshop, Illustrator, Flash...basically all the Adobe products...and then extensive use of coding from HTML, CSS, PHP, RUBY, Javascript, JAVA, some C++ and I also do a lot of database entry with the SQL family. Particularly MySQL, but also Microsoft SQL. Other things I do include experience with video editing, particularly Final Cut Pro, and 3-D modeling. Just in case you guys need those sort of things."

She gave no reaction to his extensive reply; instead, she thumbed through his resume with the thick end of her pointer finger.

"It says here," the fat lady referenced his resume, "that you are a web developer, but I'd like to know if you are also in tune with social media and template sites like WordPress."

"Oh, certainly," replied Cody, "it goes without saying these days that understanding and frequently using social media is very important. If you look past the UH experience, you'll see that I also ran my own business in the past couple of years. The aspects of marketing with social media was something I got—"

"So you know how to use Twitter and Facebook, you're saying?"

"Of course. Yes," Cody answered. "Again, while I was growing my company I learned a lot about social media. One of the tricks I—"

"Back to your time at the University of Houston," the fat lady cleared her throat, "I see that you worked under supervised management. You are thus familiar with how we work here at our company. The team concept is exceptionally important. What you feel as an individual is less than the entirety of the group."

"Yes," Cody mindlessly nodded, "I agree. I will always do as I am told without question."

"Good," she smiled. "There are a few more candidates we have to interview. But we'll keep in touch with you to let you know our decision. Do you have any more questions for us?"

Cody tried to think of something he could ask, and then he laughed at himself, realizing it was silly to seek answers from a soul that was no longer there.

"No," he smiled, "no, I don't."

The humorless fat lady shook hands with him and escorted him out of her office. Cody liked the view from the building; they were on the top floor, dozens of stories high and in the focal point of Houston's Medical Center area.

"Have a good day," he nodded to her.

The fat lady responded with a slam of the office door.

As he waited for the elevator to come up, Cody realized how time had little meaning anymore in his new, lifeless existence. He couldn't tell if he had stood there for one minute or five. He didn't care about what time of day it was or what he might be doing next; apathy was such a lethal, numbing occurrence. All of this explained his delayed reaction when the elevator doors finally opened and a person with a familiar face exited, slapping him playfully on his left arm.

"Brother Cody!" smiled the short-bearded Asian man, "I am so blessed to see you!"

"..." Cody pointed at him, wanting his memory to react more quickly.

"Don't you remember me? It's your old pal, Henry. Henry Gao!"

"Yes...from Fellowship Communion Baptist Church."

"I've missed you, Cody. We all have."

"...'We'...?"

"Luke, Felix, Zoey, Marion, Deena, Ennis...er, even, Marco."

"Even Marco?" Cody questioned.

"Okay, I can't lie in front of the eyes of our Lord, but Marco is a good man. Deep within. Where Jesus resides."

They both stood awkwardly in silence, wondering what to say next.

"So are you here for an interview too?" Cody finally asked, glad that he was able to conjure up an inquiry.

"Oh no. No no no. Cody, the Lord has blessed me," smiled Henry. "I've come to patent a pill that brings back 20/20 vision. No more glasses, no more LASIK. I call it *John Nine Twenty-Five*."

"You're shitting...er, kidding...me, Henry."

"I would give one to you now, brother. But I have to make sure it's approved by the FDA."

"Alright, okay. Well. Good luck to that. So what else has been new?"

Henry indeed had been as blessed as he claimed. He had already struck it rich with a jewelry decorating app, one that allowed users to create and order jewelry that they customized. Cody also learned that his under-sized friend had married the most beautiful racing car model in Japan.

"She loves the Lord, and I love the Lord and, well, we married and procreated," his furry beard bobbed up and down as he nodded. "Christians have the most sex, you know."

"Congratulations on your kid. Or kids. Kidsss?"

"Seven kids."

"You know, you should probably wear a condom at this point, Henry. Or get her on the pill."

His Christian friend chuckled and patted him on the shoulder.

"The Lord will bless you too, Cody. Jesus always loves."

Cody looked shyly at the floor. "I...I don't think Jesus loves everyone equally, Henry. I'm happy for you though. It must be great to have God on your side. I'd like to know how that feels for once."

"You should come back and worship with us again, Cody."

"No, Henry...I...I can't. Not after Pastor Washington and Jay. I just...I mean, besides, hadn't Fellowship Communion Baptist Church shut down?"

Henry chuckled, "Yes, but the Lord never shuts down. Felix and Luke started their own church years ago."

It took a moment before Cody realized the uniqueness of what Henry was meaning.

"Wait," Cody stopped him, "you go to a gay church? Henry, you know they're gay, right? Felix and Luke. I'm okay with that, but it's...you know what I mean, it can't be too popular with the church community."

"A church is a church," Henry beamed.

They laughed and briefly shared the good times they had had in their youth. Cody learned that most of the original group had scattered. Ennis had permanently moved to the jungles of Guatemala—a "lifetime mission trip," he called it. Deena had married a white guy who looked like Jesus. Marion had gone on and become a college basketball star—"the female Jeremy Lin" Henry described.

"So what about Zoey?"

"Still single," Henry sighed.

"She was always the prettiest of all the church girls. Even prettier than...than...Daphne..."

Cody's voice trailed off as a part of his past haunted him again; not even his current state of indifference softened it. Henry excused himself and pointed at the office door.

"I've got to go, I'll be late, brother Cody." He handed a business card to him with Luke and Felix's new church address. "Come one of these Sundays. Jesus always has a place for you."

———

Dimitri admired his own reflection from his office window, believing himself a god among mortals. He had a visual representation in front of him—his translucent likeness from the glass presiding over the dancing mass beneath him. Such irony, he ridiculed, that people who believed themselves free were slaves to the hypnotic rhythms of the music. This was but a small example of the genius of the American elite—finding the ultimate tool to control its populace with bounteous streams of conditioned capitalism. What chance did average people have when they were habituated with instant gratification since childhood? Wasn't this the true catalyst of the country's drug problem? If people had more self-control, Dimitri boasted, the underworld could line up block after block of drug dealers and no one would purchase a gram.

Instead, the Russian was, in his opinion, merely an opportunist—someone who feasted on the spoils of a dilemma he did not cause. Drug lords were no different from banks that issued high-interest loans or plastic surgeons that offered a forty-eight-hour fix. Even religion took advantage of eager crowds, wanting feel-good, instantaneous resolutions to their complicated predicaments. Was it any coincidence then, he asked himself, that the music industry, organized orthodoxies and the underworld all relied on the same strategies of marketing that gave them such swift success?

He playfully squeezed the latest answer inside the right palm of his hand—a lethal conglomeration of addictive chemicals packaged in a pill no bigger than the size of an American dime. Of course, the Russian was keen to realize that calling it by its natural name of hypercathinone wouldn't catch on. The youth of today wouldn't give it a chance. But branding it in a commercialized package, white and smooth, with a concaved surface that made it appear sexy—why, the proselytized horde would lap it up, he smiled.

Dimitri proudly called this new drug White Vodka.

It was a pharmaceutical masterpiece with effects similar to Ecstasy, but with far greater hallucination potency. The drug instantaneously created short-term memory loss, fostering a false craving for its user. Anyone who took it would have no recollection of how often it was taken, masking its strong addictive properties and giving it a false perception of harmlessness.

Near the club's entranceway, the Russian observed his manipulable puppet, Wilbur Wang, being interviewed by a local female news reporter who was every bit as beauteous and fashionable as he was. Dimitri liked Wilbur—all criticism of his immaculate appearances aside, the young promoter was vigorously hard-working. The "You're the Celebrity" idea worked not so much because of its gimmick, but as a direct result of Wilbur's incessant tenacity. In many ways, he reminded Dimitri of himself, once hungry to make a name and eager to prove his worth.

The up-and-coming reporter also admired Wilbur, though for reasons distant from the Russian's. There, with the dazzling metrosexual a few feet in front of her, eyes locked and alluring, the girl found herself magnetized by his appearance. Despite his bumbling lack of speech proficiency, he was attractive like no man she had ever met. The captivation inspired her to question him with dexterous competence, smiling as she felt the honor of indulging in his presence.

"And what do you think is the main catalyst behind the instant success of 'You're the Celebrity,' Wilbur?" the reporter asked wide-eyed and exhilarated.

"I-I-I think t-t-that people are s-s-sick and t-t-tired of watching celebrities on T-T-TV," Wilbur stuttered. "W-w-when they p-p-party here t-t-they are p-p-picked up by our limo s-s-services, g-g-greeted b-b-by a red c-c-carpet. C-c-cameras taking s-s-snapshots, c-c-champagne on i-i-ice, VIP t-t-treatment, b-b-baby!"

"And how would you explain the overnight image change of The Platinum Star from a widely questionable establishment of underworld dealings to a venue of Houston's standard of class and entertainment?"

"I-I-I r-r-really think th-th-that we r-r-ran the c-c-criminals out! O-o-once they s-s-saw this is n-n-not what we-we-we're about th-th-they've moved o-o-on."

Wilbur's assumption was far from correct. Unbeknownst to him, White Vodka had already been implemented into the consciousness and regular usage of the frequent attendants of The Platinum Star. Its fun outer appearance camouflaged the drug among the sea of Hello Kitty phone covers, inextricable Coco Chanel sunglasses and Charlotte Russe party dresses. Whenever its perilous name did emanate from the lips of the clubbers, however, its reputation remained innocuous rather than cautionary.

Within a week, Dimitri's undercover dealers had already established who the excessive addicts were. One of them was among the most inner circle of Wilbur's group, a young man Dimitri was told was slightest in the intellectual spectrum. When the efficacious promoter finished with his interview, he soon found out just how prevalent the drug culture was in The

Platinum Star—and how the problem might have already reached new levels of destruction and enslavement within his circle of friends.

"Y-y-yo, have you seen my buddy DJ Zack?" Wilbur asked one of the janitors.

The custodian paused from his mopping and pointed in the direction of one of the restrooms. "Weird looking bald Asian kid with the headphones around his neck? Yeah, saw 'im in th' west corner men's room when I was cleaning up in there. He was huddled in one of the corners, lookin' like he was in a lotta pain."

Nearby, Jack saw the worried look on Wilbur's face and concluded something was wrong. When the effeminate promoter hastily made his way toward the designated restroom, Jack kept his distance and followed. They made their way past a horde of dancing partygoers, fighting from delaying their path to their destination.

Inside the west corner men's restroom, Wilbur found it unoccupied with the farthest stall door—the one for the handicapped—ajar.

"Z-Z-Zack?" called out Wilbur, discovering his friend lying face up beside the soiled toilet. "Zack!"

The cloddish deejay slowly opened his eyes and pushed Wilbur aside.

"Leave me alone, Wilbur," he grumbled. "I'm fine. Nothing's wrong."

"W-W-What do you m-m-mean nothing's w-w-wrong?"

DJ Zack let out an aberrant cough of blood and weakly waved his hand. "I'm alright, dude. Leave me...leave me...alone."

"W-W-What's wrong?!"

"I was...I was just taking a shit."

"You what?!"

DJ Zack slowly moved his head and directly faced Wilbur. "I was...I was taking a shit...and...I must've...fell...down."

"Y-y-you're l-l-lying! Y-y-your pants a-a-are still o-o-on!!!"

"The man said he was taking a shit, so he must've been taking a shit," countered a voice behind them.

Wilbur turned around and saw Jack.

"Yeah," Jack continued not believing his own words but remaining resolute. "Sometimes a man needs to go so bad he leaves his pants on. Simple as that."

Wilbur walked over and accursedly jabbed Jack with his finger. "Y-y-you c-c-can't be s-s-serious, m-m-man! A-a-and why a-a-are you f-f-following me?!"

DJ Zack stumbled as he stood up and brushed off the excrement that had stuck to his clothing.

"See?!" Jack scoffed. "The man's fine. Stop being like a woman worrying all the damn time."

"A-a-are you okay, DJ Z-Z-Zack?"

The deejay nodded unconvincingly.

"Hey Wilbur!" interrupted another familiar voice. "Heh, hah! There you are. I was, wah-eh, looking all over for you, heh."

Marty's entrance distracted the apprehensive promoter and reset his focus on the next task at hand.

"Mm-ah! You gotta see my new Wing Chun dummy, Wilbur. It just arrived and I've put it near your life-sized Jenga set. The partygoers are going wild with it. Psssh! WOO!"

The two left the restroom, leaving Jack alone with Wilbur's friend.

"Hey, man," Jack placed a hand on his shoulder, peering into the dazed deejay's eyes. "Look at me. Look. At. Me."

DJ Zack stared blankly back.

"You're high on something," Jack figured. "Your reactions are fucked up. Even more than usual, that is."

He snapped his fingers in front of DJ Zack and then around his ears. The action was met with delayed reactions, verifying what Jack had suspected.

"You're fucking kidding me," he remarked out loud. "This ain't your typical ex aftermath. What'd you take, you stupid motherfucker?"

Unknown to Jack, the deejay was trapped in a world of dazzling lights and two-headed dragons. There were sexy-figured women with box-shaped heads, riding on a wave of giant uprooting beanstalks. There was no up or down, left or right, or indication of gravity; the hallucinating addict was devoid of absoluteness. He watched the sun approach him and shrink into a tiny marble, where it shined a sharp beam of light directly through his forehead, leaving a perfectly round hole.

"HEY!" Jack made a deafening clap in front of DJ Zack's face. "Snap out of it! I'm talking to you, loser!"

"Huhhhhhhhhh?"

"You're fucking high. Really high. Where'd you get it?"

"From...from Grigor."

"Grigor? The weird foreign kid from Bulgaria or Vulgaria or whatever that European country is?"

"He's...he's not...really...Bulgarian..."

"You don't say, man," Jack raised an eyebrow.

"...His name's really...Charles. From...Detroit."

"Explains the horrible phony accent. Answer my original question. What'd you take? What'd this Grigor/Charles guy give you?"

The deejay's gaze averted Jack for a moment as he slowly began drifting into his imaginary world. Jack grabbed both of DJ Zack's shoulders and shook him.

"HEY! Come on! Answer me. What'd you take, dumbass?"

"White...Vodka..."

"White Vodka?" Jack thought out loud to himself.

"Someone mentioned that the other day. Thought it was some damn Tic Tac. Hmm."

A slow smile crept across Jack's face; he had suspected there was more going on other than The Platinum Star running legit. The owner had never changed; his cousin Marty and partner Wilbur were being used as pawns to get them mainstream clientele. He could see that the White Vodka effects were powerful, the evolution of a very financially lucrative narcotic. This knowledge gave Jack the upper hand; he planned to slowly find out who the dealers were, get a sample and synthesize the product and use it as leverage against the mysterious boss behind it all.

———————

Although he hadn't set foot in his native Hong Kong in over thirty-four years, Kelvin Min-Lo Quan felt like a fish returning to sea. He had decided to travel back for a few days on a whim, using up a portion of his enormous bank loan for recreation. It was a decision that filled him with exurberance; from the moment he stepped foot in his native city, he basked in its familiar character. Cody's father enjoyed being surrounded by signs and periodicals written in traditional Chinese. It was like he had regained a long-forgotten sense, recognizing things without having to think twice or resort to a portable translator. *That's more like it*, he smiled, admiring his environment, *a town where everyone looked like me, spoke like me and thought like me.* He took little time mingling with its people, conversing with strangers in his native tongue and never failing to take an opportunity to make jabs at America.

"<Back in the U.S.>," he told a woman at the Hong Kong International Airport baggage claim, "<they treated me like a second-class citizen. Worse, the food tasted bad. Everything is fried, everyone is fat and people like to get drunk. Mexicans and niggers run amok like wild animals, robbing us, getting free money from the government, but I outsmarted them all. I borrowed a lot of money from the bank, you see, and now I'm rich!>"

"<But don't you have to pay the bank back?>" inquired the woman.

"<Hah!>" laughed Mr. Quan. "<Yeah, slowly. Eventually. But better enjoy life now and seize the moment, you know what I mean?!>"

His jubilant return was further spirited when he was found by his celebrity brother-in-law and personal driver afterwards. Chef Mo had put on a few pounds, but more or less looked similar in appearance to the past, particularly with his decision to retain his recognizable caterpillar mustache and aviator sunglasses. Cody's father made himself comfortable in Chef Mo's palatial sedan and immediately initiated a conversation with the distinguished Hong Kong star.

"<It sure feels good to be back home!>" he exclaimed with a radiating smile. "<Can't wait to resume what I've been leaving behind since 1976! Food street dining, betting at the horse tracks, mahjong games with ol' Wong and ol' Big Toothed Ling, watching the latest episode of *Enjoy Yourself Tonight*.>"

Chef Mo paused for a few moments, calmly adjusting his sunglasses with the tip of his finger before answering him. "<Actually Hong Kong goes through a series of changes every couple of years. The city is always morphing, unrecognizable to anyone who has left even for a few months—certainly for those who've been gone for three decade.>"

The sedan approached a busy part of the Causeway Bay area where thousands of pedestrians overwhelmed them like waves on an ocean.

"<By the way, Ming Lo>" the celebrity chef added, "<ol' Wong is long dead and Big Toothed Ling found Christ and denounced gambling. *Enjoy Yourself Tonight* stopped production in 2007. Nobody watches that anymore. We've evolved.>"

The driver suddenly slammed on the brakes, missing a daring jaywalker by inches. More pedestrians braved the crossing and followed suit, angering the driver. After honking his horn continuously to no avail, the driver rolled down his window and chastised them with whimsical profanity.

"<Hey, dog shit turtles!>" he screamed. "<Put a finger in your assholes and move out of my way! You people are stopping the world from rotating!>"

"<Fuck your momma!>" replied one of the pedestrians with equally colorful cursing. "<Go back inside that big-tittied prostitute's cunt and never be born, you motherless castrated dick-faced bastard!>"

The driver remained poised, impervious to the kind of nonsense swearing he'd heard millions of times before. "<Don't believe I won't run you all over if you don't move!>"

When pedestrian after pedestrian ignored his warning, the driver pressed the accelerator and made his way forward, disregarding anyone their car might mow over. The walkers grew frightened and scattered out of the way of the sedan's path, reminding Mr. Quan of the parting of a sea.

"<Hunh!>" the driver grunted in satisfaction as he looked back, using the rearview mirror. "<Stick my dick in all your breasts, man!>"

The raunchy obscenities brought a comforting familiarity to Cody's father. How he had missed hearing such insulting banter, he smiled, putting him at ease in a blue-collar environment where cursing was the norm and classiness took a backseat. Hong Kong changed? he chuckled, it was probably just as condescending and crass as he had left it. The middle-aged returnee glanced at his sophisticated brother-in-law and figured he was probably still the same man from years past. Beneath the fame and dignified mellowness, there was still Skinny Mo, he believed, the vulgar plebeian who once enjoyed joking improperly just as much as he did.

By early evening, Cody's father had removed the stench of jet fuel with a long, alleviating shower inside of the celebrity chef's penthouse. It was one of Chef Mo's several luxury suites, overlooking the wall of opulent skyscrapers almost indistinguishable from various areas throughout south China's resplendent port town. When he was ready, his brother-in-law had his driver take them to a prestigious and exclusive restaurant, located near the Victoria Peak area of the city. From there, the view of Hong Kong was breathtakingly gorgeous, overlooking the mountainous terrain and more of its collection of skyscrapers that seemingly spread towards eternity.

Mr. Quan made sure to put on what to him was his best attire—a tacky faded purple blazer with a lime green tie. He paled in comparison with the rest of the guests who looked fitting of their high class and stature. Chef Mo had certainly done well for himself, he noted, these fellow diners with him were no ordinary people. Indeed, one by one they introduced themselves and their professions, ranging from established medical directors, real estate moguls, television producers and education administrators. None of it mattered, Mr. Quan thought, because they were from Hong Kong, he was from Hong Kong, and thus, he was among his people. All Hong Kong people are the same. That's how the world works, he reminded himself.

"<Can you believe this baby formula issue?>" laughed Cody's father, making himself comfortable with the dinner guests. "<Mainland China is putting chemicals into their milk. Glad that kind of stuff doesn't happen here! It's good to be Chinese free from Chinese issues!>"

"<Actually>," corrected one of the men next to him, "<it's caused plenty of Mainland Chinese to come into our city and buy off our imported baby milk supply. That stuff on the Chinese black market fetches for ten times the price. People would do anything to save their children. They're human, after all.>"

"<It's so unfortunate. Ironic actually>," added a woman. "<Many people here can't buy formula milk from either the regular stores or the black market. It's easier to buy illegal drugs in Hong Kong than baby milk.>"

"<Oh, is that so?>" Cody's father sheepishly backtracked. "<Well, you know how it is. The lower class will always take advantage of the well-to do, am I right?>"

"<They're Chinese and we're Chinese>," injected Chef Mo. "<I don't understand all this nonsense sometimes that some Hong Kong people regard themselves as 'real' Chinese. So the people who live in China aren't? It's ridiculous logic.>"

His brother-in-law surely must be speaking in jest, figured Mr. Quan. Of course, it was nonsense; everyone knew Hong Kong was the greatest city in the world and anyone not from it was clearly inferior. The celebrity chef had really taken his humor to another level, he admired, mastering punch lines with a straight face.

"<Haha! Only ridiculous because the mainlanders are so classless and Communist. Duh. It's because this city was educated and preserved from a white culture's perspective. We would never see that sort of criminal activity in Hong Kong, am I right?>" laughed Cody's father. "<Back in our day we could just walk freely on the streets. No one would mug us. People understood the necessity of civilization. Western civilization chose us and gave us an advanced way of living.>"

A man at the table—the television producer if Mr. Quan had remembered correctly—laughed at his questionable statement. "<Hah! What Hong Kong are you remembering, man? This place is dangerous! Always has been! There's plenty of criminal activity here from regular hoodlums to triad-related mobsters.>"

"<You'll have to forgive me for not telling you all sooner>," apologized Chef Mo. "<Quan Min-Lo here immigrated to America thirty-four years ago. Today was his first return.>"

"<Ah!>" they collectively acknowledged.

"<Welcome back!>" the same man earlier congratulated. "<How is it there in America? Where's your family? Did they travel back here with you too?>"

"<Agh!>" Cody's father dismissed in typical Chinese humbleness. "<Shouldn't have moved there. My son barely speaks Chinese, wasn't obedient for the longest time and waited until now to let me pick his wife. He even quit a job supplied by a white boss. A WHITE BOSS! Can you believe that?! He had the holy grail! It's just been an absolute nightmare. And the food...what they serve as gourmet there is stuff we'd just make soup with here.>"

"<I agree>," nodded another woman. "<My sister immigrated to a city named Orlando. She said the Chinese food over there is terrible. However, the people there are nice. Americans are nice people.>"

"<Hunh!>" Mr. Quan dismissed. "<Everyone says 'sorry' and 'excuse me' all the time. It's annoying. They're too nice to a fault. No one has discipline there. Look at all the gays and blacks we have running around there. They should keep them beneath society like the dust that they are...kind of like what we do to the Filipinos here in Hong Kong.>"

His comments caused an awkward silence in the table.

"<Mr. Quan>," replied one of the men, "<my wife is Filipina.>"

"<Hahaha, nice joke>," laughed Cody's father. "<Maybe you had to legally marry your housemaid to save her from some disaster? I think I follow you...>"

"<Why no, sir. We met at university during our time in Singapore. She's a doctor.>"

"<And my youngest son is gay!>" interrupted an offended woman.

"<My condolences>," Mr. Quan replied, "<but don't worry, I assure you this phase in young men will surely go away. Why, there was even a time I believed my own son was gay. He didn't have a girlfriend for ten years. I'm sure yours won't go through it that long. It depends. Sometimes it's a couple of months, other times it's, well, ten years.>"

With those controversial words, the table ignited into a cacophony of grumblings, turning the civilized dinner into a scattered, muddled discussion. The guests began pointing fingers at Cody's father, giving Chef Mo an aura of embarrassment and the need to rescue his brother-in-law.

"<Everyone, please excuse us>," announced the celebrity chef, standing up and taking Mr. Quan with him. "<I hadn't realized until now that we needed to visit a relative this evening. She lives all the way in Kowloon. I apologize for our haste departure and bid you all a good evening.>"

On the street, in an area where there were few passersby, Chef Mo took his visiting friend aside and thought deeply about how to deliver his message kindly. Kelvin Min-Lo Quan was a good man—at least, someone who was proud of his hometown and had no intentions of offending, but a part of him remained childlike, who still saw the world in simple black and white terms. It was a miracle he had gotten so far, let alone raised a family on his own with such antiquated viewpoints, though perhaps this was a sign that his brother-in-law had good principles embodied within his sectarian perspectives. It was enough to determine Mr. Quan worthy of being prescribed a more judicious outlook, one that might save him from embarrassing future encounters like the one they had just endured.

"<I messed up, didn't I?>" sighed Cody's father.

"<Hong Kong>," began Chef Mo, "<is a very multi-cultural city now. It has been for quite some time. When you see an Indian-looking person or a Western person or a Filipino person walking around, they might actually be born and raised in this city. The prevalent attitude is as such that people have welcomed all kinds of people. This even includes people like your son.>"

"<My son's not gay>," corrected Cody's father.

"<I didn't mean homosexual, although that's accepted here too. I meant your son as a foreign-born Asian. We see plenty of those.>"

"<Well, because English is symbolic of Western society>," laughed Mr. Quan. "<I doubt they'd accept him if he spoke Spanish or black people language.>"

Chef Mo calmly placed his palms on top of his brother-in-law's shoulders and sighed. He motioned for him to walk closer to an intersection where clumps of people were seen doing various activities.

"<Look around you, Min-Lo>," the celebrity chef gestured with his hands. "<Hong Kong is one of the most modern cities in the world. Look at all the state-of-the-art buildings around you. Look at the signs and the public transportations. This isn't the Hong Kong you remembered. Its people have changed. We're in an international spotlight all the time. How can you call yourself one of us when you've left and hadn't come back for three decades? You're not Chinese anymore. You're a man trapped in time, living in a bubble.>"

Cody's father was shaken up by the revelation; he had never considered the possibility that he had become an outsider. Mr. Quan was, indeed, preserved in a time capsule, finding himself without a place in the world that accepted him. His brother-in-law's words made a crude impact on his soul— perhaps it was time for him to change, he realized. He wanted to come back to America a better man, one who forgave the people who had hurt him and prevented fear from sprouting out of his emotions. Maybe then people would respect him the way they respected Chef Mo.

CHAPTER 30: TWIST AND TURNS

It was not difficult for Pete to say no, not anymore.

This personal triumph from compliance, however, only rewarded him with new enemies—at least, he figured, recently turned foes who were once his associates of The Platinum Star drug trade. Subordinates of Andrew Huynh, or perhaps the hit man himself, had responded to Pete's resignation with a bullet-riddled decoration of his family's front door. No additional messages were needed—Pete understood their intolerance of his leaving.

His family, though, misinterpreted their threats and saw it as a push for relinquishing the violent profession.

"Please quit!" cried his mother in broken English. "No more gangster!"

"I AM quittin'!" Pete clarified. "Them niggaz be shootin' at us BECAUSE I quit!"

His constrained mind prevented him from grasping why Piranha's enforcers were so resolute in keeping him on duty. After all, hadn't he fulfilled his promise from never snitching? he wondered. Pete thought himself replaceable; his former job could be easily performed by anyone with a pair of arms, legs and a brain. Pete grew more frustrated when even his own parole officer encouraged him to return to his former occupation.

"Yo, what up wit' this unemployment shit, ma-fuck?" Pete questioned. "Ain't your job to find me a job, huh, nigga?"

"Please, Mr. Mok, calm down," assured the parole officer. "These things take time. It's not easy to get someone a job with your.......record."

"Bitch, what Imma tell ya, man? I said it ain't matter what I do! I'll sweep floors and scrub toilets! You can't even find sumthin' like dat, nigga? What about McDonald's? Remix them beats and thump some hump for me!"

The parole officer gave a condescending laugh, one that revealed his underestimation of Pete's seriousness.

"McDonald's have children walking around, sir," he snorted, leaning back in his chair. "You think they'll just say yes to a convicted murderer?"

"I ain't kill no one!!!"

"That's not what your record says," he snapped. "You fed your best friend to a tiger."

"Nigga, I be framed, nigga!"

"Haha. Look, Mr. Mok, it's usually...advisable...that people of your...employment history find work with...people who may have helped you with that...profession in the past."

Pete remained seated, looking at him with a skeptical eye. The parole officer gave an encouraging smile in return.

"Now, Pete, consider the benefits of staying with your old ' job'—"

"I ain't goin' back to dat life! I ain't about dat life no mo'! Piranha can't pay you enough to make me!!!" Pete stood up and headed out.

The parole officer remained leaning back in his chair, watching the former convict storm out of his office.

"You think you can leave that life, Mr. Mok?!" he chastised. "Nobody ever leaves. They won't let you leave! You know too much!"

"Yeah? We'll see, nigga," Pete hollered on his way out.

His abrupt exit from the meeting left him with more time to roam around than he had intended. Fortunately, the parole officer's building was close to his day's main agenda: the location of a used food truck advertised for sale on Craigslist. Pete took out his new phone—a present from his sister a few days before—and checked out its various functions. He was told these types of devices were called smartphones, though it confused him whether or not it was because the gadgets themselves were intelligent or if the user had to be ingenious to use one. To his own embarrassment, he ended up seeking the aid of a passing stranger. The friendly woman was more than happy to show him how to use the global positioning application.

"Thanks, nigga," he responded, nodding with genuine appreciation. "Keep 'em rims shine, homie."

"Er, no problem," replied the woman, giving him a perplexed look.

At times he struggled with wondering if he coincided with the map's directions, walking forward while his blinking dot on the screen was moving west instead. When he turned left, the map twisted the other way, confusing him as to how he should follow the phone. Finally, he figured out a method by physically turning the phone so that his blinking dot went upwards no matter which direction he faced. The phone's estimated walking time was ten minutes—Pete ended up taking two hours.

Sweat, thirst and fatigue were plaguing him when he finally arrived at his destination, but the elation of reaching it was enough to renew his spirits. The area was a junkyard, surrounded by metal fencing and barbed wire that briefly reminded him of prison. He made his way toward a modest wooden shack nearby, happy to be soothed by the coolness from its sheet metal awning.

"May I help you?" inquired a voice from behind.

Pete turned around and observed a middle-aged black man walking toward him. The gentleman's bright pearly smile contrasted perfectly with his dark matte skin. His friendly demeanor and appearance allowed Pete to ease back and let his guard down.

"I'm Cid," the man introduced himself, offering a handshake, "Cid McCray. And as you might have guessed, I'm not Irish."

Cid let out a friendly laugh, tapping Pete on the arm.

"So you the nigga that put out the Craigslist ad?" asked Pete.

The man's joyous expression immediately turned into an appalled frown. "Did you just call me a nig—"

"Call you what, nigga?"

Cid shook his head and waved off the offending word. It was the way of the world now, he figured, every naive kid using it was oblivious to its past connotations.

"No, no," Cid sighed, "it's just...damn, you look Chinese. Why do you talk like that?"

"Product of my environment," nodded the former convict, "dun mind it."

"Product of what environment?" Cid scratched his head. "MTV?"

"Whateva, nigga, don't front, nigga. So you gonna tell me you the nigga puttin' out the ad or I gotta talk to some other nigga?"

"Yeah," the middle-aged man replied, operating on selective hearing, "I'm the one who put out the ad, but...look, can you talk normal? It's kind of offensive."

"Dis is normal, dude!" Pete answered with a hint of defensiveness. "Don't twist!"

"Okay. Alright. Well, anyway, follow me." He led Pete toward the abandoned food truck. "It's got some dust and cobwebs, but the ol' gal runs like brand new. She just needs a lot of renovation to make her more appealing. On a marketable level, that is."

"Mm. I figured," grunted Pete. "What you've use it fo' in the past?"

"Well, it belonged to my life partner, Enrique. It was more his dream than mine, going around selling burgers and fries. We called our little operation The Juke Joint. Basically, we played requested music and had a nice stereo system installed. That was our gimmick. All food trucks have one." They paused, standing a few feet from the vehicle. "Unfortunately, Enrique passed away a few years ago from cancer. I kept the truck around for sentimental reasons, but like I said, it was more his dream than mine."

Pete was given a tour. Cid opened the back of the truck, explaining where equipment could be installed. As the explanations went on, Pete's smile grew wider. When the Texas heat made the inside intolerable, they exited, still discussing the details of their potential transaction.

"Look, I'll sell it to you for cheap. I just want it gone," Cid confessed. He took out a napkin from his pocket and wiped his forehead.

"That right, my nigga? Why don't you just give it to me for free then, my nigga?" joked Pete.

"Can you please stop saying that word?"

"What word?"

"Never mind," replied Cid. "Okay, two thousand dollars and it's yours. How about that?"

The deal was too good to refuse. At the very least it gave Pete his own form of transportation—he was tired of asking people for rides.

"A'ight," nodded Pete. "You ain't bullshittin' when you said you just wanted it gone. That's a damn good price. I'll figure out a way to get you that money, no problem. Shit, I almost made that much working in prison."

The astounded usher dropped his stack of pamphlets when the voluptuous fashion designer made her way to the front doors of the modest church.

"H-Hello," he stammered, struggling to find his tongue. "W-welcome to New Union Trinity Church, Miss..."

"Lavender," she announced with a strong British accent, "Charlene Lavender. From London. Charmed."

It was difficult to fault his indiscreet reactions—her seductive appearance awakened the sensuous wanton appetites of most men, including ones infused with divine essence. Her beauty was further accentuated through her choice of church attire: a silk turquoise dress of her own design complemented by striking silver lipstick. Her long, velvety hair reached all the way to the back of her knees. To many in attendance of her first appearance, Charlene was Venus herself, emerging from the preservation of a mystical oyster shell. Her haughty behavior, however, was what solidified her celestial image because, although Charlene was indubitably enthralling, she was also a diva, designated to her place atop other mortals. At New Union Trinity Church, she took rare acknowledgement of her bountiful male admirers and relished great satisfaction in the jealousy of her female counterparts. Furthermore, the discussions she pretended not to hear gave approval to her continued narcissism.

"Wow, what a knockout..."

"*Humph!* Fake tits, gotta be..."

"Praise the Lord, my staff has risen to spread my flock..."

"Look at all the guys ogling her. What the hell does she have that I don't?"

The usher continued looking her way, craning his neck to the extremes.

"Hey there," interrupted a tap on his shoulder, "can I have one of those too?"

The usher remained fixated on Charlene's whereabouts, ignoring Cody Quan's request, but he did exhibit a slight degree of awareness as he handed Cody a pamphlet without looking. Completely understanding the reason for the usher's negligence, Cody forgivingly took the pamphlet and walked himself inside. He made thorough observations of his surroundings, pausing at times to take in the snazzy contemporariness of Luke and Felix's modern-stylized church. Cody had never seen one like this before—devoid of pews or stained glass windows. Instead, its decorative interior was garnished with solo table stands and dimmed lighting. Its stage was of minimalist design, with a few spotlights illuminating its dull wooden flooring, which, at the back end was concluded by a plain, brick wall. The appearance gave this church the atmosphere of a jazz lounge or comedy club, with the obvious exclusion of alcoholic beverages. Cody had a positive first impression, feeling a growing wave of excitement as he looked for a table and stool.

Meanwhile, the attention of the majority of New Union Trinity Church's male members was continually focused on the hypnotic Charlene.

"Oh please, please sit here," one of them begged as he offered her the stool next to him.

He was among several copycats who followed suit, contributing to the hankering for the British head turner that soon rose to the level of distraction. The winning suitor turned out to be the gentleman next to Cody, who was so determined in getting her a seat that he inattentively grabbed Cody's stool and nearly sent Cody falling to the floor.

"Here," he offered her. "This seat's not taken. Why don't you come near my table? It's close to the stage. I just want you to be closer to God."

As the alternative Christian rock band took the stage, signifying the beginning of the day's worship session, Cody ventured through his dim surroundings, looking for an empty table and stool to claim as his own. When Cody found all of them to be taken when the song ended, he resorted to leaning against a corner of the venue. Perhaps, he realized, there was a reason why churches had had pews for centuries; standing room—only services were not at all pleasing to the ones without accommodations.

Luke Lu made his way onstage as the clapping to the music faded, smiling and looking as handsome as ever. Now in his thirties, the son of Willy Lu had become fully mature-looking, his pronounced Roman nose even more distinguishable than before. The young pastor was resplendent, exuding a vibe of humbled charisma. He would make a great preacher, realized Cody, one who had the potential of comforting people in times of both euphoria and tribulation.

"Everyone, as always, thanks for coming," Luke gently said, his voice perfectly transferred and amplified without a hint of screeching from the microphone. "Let's start today's sermon off with a prayer."

He prayed for the love of each fellow Christian brother and sister, and the consideration of tending to the care of not just the very popular or the impoverished, but also for everyone in between. Luke's sermon followed up with that theme, exploring the necessity for indiscriminate concern. The ones who are neglected are sometimes the people who appear normal, he preached, in disguise from their need to be loved and understood. The message penetrated Cody's shell, a message that reached into his heart and appealed for him to believe again.

"And so," concluded Luke, "as commanded by Christ in Galatians 6:2, be one another's keeper, never stop caring, never turn a blind eye. I know most of you know the verse by heart, so let's recite it now. Say it with me."

The members collectively said the words, including Cody, who needed no Bible to speak the lines that once meant so much to him. "Bear one another's burdens, and so fulfill the law of Christ."

"We are all God's children," ended Luke. "Not one of us is more important than another."

After a follow-up prayer, the Christian rock group took the stage, turning the stylized church, once again, into a lively concert. With his misanthropy briefly lifted, Cody walked around and socialized with the various members of New Union Trinity Church. It was best, he thought, to approach any loners, perhaps making it easier for him to strike up a conversation. He summoned a bit of courage conversing with a random selection, though the chitchats inevitably reverted back to church gossip, celebrity heartthrobs or, most likely, the topic of Charlene Lavender. The lights were turned on, but Cody was invisible to them. When he made a more aggressive approach toward the nearest person—a man of about similar age who was standing on his tiptoes to get a better look at Charlene—Cody was shrugged off by a dismissive wave and back turn.

Luke shook a few hands, including Cody's, before making his way to the popular fashion couturier and enticing her to come back to their church. Cody faded back from the crowd, finding the same doorway usher who was still mesmerized by the beautiful visitor.

"Hey," Cody tapped his shoulder. "Today's my first time at New Union Trinity Church. You guys have a website or something where I can get more information about it?"

The usher remained focused on Charlene, oblivious to anything around him. Cody repeated the same question to others near the doorway, including girls who weren't locked in on Charlene's presence. The results were similar; only instead of neglecting his questions, they looked at him, shrugged and walked off. Cody exited the church like a ghost and felt his heart sink as he made his way to his car.

Like chewed gum, Super Duper Celebrity Night with Wilbur's "You're the Celebrity" program was rapidly losing its appeal to Phoebe Bowie. It was always the same, she realized, from its same party bus, its red carpet arrival, its fake paparazzi and the same phony reporter who "interviewed" the arriving partygoers. Even the sections of the club were indistinguishable; everything was labeled VIP—part of Wilbur's annoying belief that everyone was special and no one should be left behind.

It was all so corny, opined Phoebe, the directionless nights that felt more and more like wasted time.

She began isolating herself from the other girls, no longer captivated by the delight of being around other Asians. So what? she shrugged. She knew she was a class above these particular Asians, certainly on the scale of intelligence and ambition. Then again, she noted, she was also no different—if she was always around superficial bimbos and small-minded party girls, what did that say about her? Certainly it would be a hard case to make that she wasn't like them, as she wasn't doing anything but partying seven days a week while accelerating her aging through constant chain-smoking and hard liquor. At least she was fortunate enough to not partake of the new White Vodka drug so many of the other girls were trying. Something about it suggested it would be a bad idea for her to take it, and she was feeling more and more glad that she hadn't.

"Hey, Phoebeeee," greeted one of the more annoying girls. "Why are you still wearing that cheap bracelet, my dear? Here, look at mine. Louis Vuitton."

"That's nice," Phoebe deadpanned. "Meh."

The girl almost fumbled with the grip of her brandy, barely avoiding a ruinous spill on Phoebe's favorite red-orange shirt.

"Whoa," the annoying girl laughed, "almost made a mess."

Phoebe continued looking elsewhere, displaying a look of disinterest. Unfortunately, the girl ignored the hint and persisted with their conversation.

"So when are you going to go out with my cousin?"

Phoebe made a face. "The old guy? What is he, like, fifty-two?"

"Fifty-three. He's really rich. He works for Andrew Huynh now."

"Who's Andrew Huynh?"

"Oh, Phoebe! You don't know?"

"Is he a singer in Asia or something?"

The annoying girl broke out in laughter. "Hahaha! No! Andrew Huynh is a successful gangster! Not the thug kind. The powerful type. Only people in the know recognize him for what he does. He works for the biggest drug dealer in Houston. Don't tell anybody, okay? Just our inner circle secrets."

Phoebe shrugged, texting on her iPhone. She thought the girl had a big mouth.

"You really should date my cousin," the girl continued. "He says Korean girls are really hot!"

"I'm not really Korean," corrected Phoebe. "I'm adopted."

"Oh, adopted. So you must like white guys, huh? Hey! My coworker is white! He likes Asian girls a lot!"

"Meh. I'm not really looking."

"You should have a man! Someone to take care of you, Phoebe. Buy you things."

Phoebe grew irritated. "Well, maybe I don't need someone to take care of me. I'd rather be around someone who I can grow with as a person!"

She stood up and walked away from the idiot girl, hoping the conversation hadn't lowered her intelligence quotient. Phoebe admitted to herself that she missed Cody, regretting she had told him about her friendship with Marty and Wilbur. Now that she was around those two on a nightly basis, she understood Cody's disassociation from them. She, too, concluded that Marty was a nomadic parasite, a gutless con man whose sole talent was sponging off of his victims' hard work and money. Wilbur, while not malicious like Marty, was a spoiled man-child, too in love with himself to realize his charitable intentions were masking his primary motivation of boosting his prestige. She was tired of everything about them— from Marty's strange laughter to Wilbur's constant staring at his own appearance. Indeed, he was the only man she had ever seen carrying a compact mirror everywhere he ventured.

As if her thinking of him had somehow summoned the pansified promoter, she heard Wilbur calling out to her from the game table.

"P-P-Phoebe, c-c-come on!!!" he called out. "J-J-Jenga time!!!"

"JENGA! JENGA!" chanted the crowd.

Wilbur walked over and playfully dragged her towards the life-sized Jenga board. His action immediately irritated her, as she flung herself away from his grip, staring at him in disgust and repugnance. How could a grown man spend all of his time playing Jenga and other childish board games? she scoffed to herself. Other women may find his boyishness alluring, but to Phoebe it was a turnoff to think it was all that he could achieve.

"H-h-hey! W-w-what are you doing?!" he pleaded.

"I don't feel like playing your dumb games," she replied. "I'm going to the bathroom."

Phoebe avoided the chorus of playful boos. Once she was by herself in the ladies' room, she lit a cigarette and fixed her luxuriant hair, using one of the sinks' mirrors. She decided it was the last time she would attend a "You're the Celebrity" party—Wilbur's telephone number would be blocked. She might befriend a girl or two from the group before going her separate way. Suddenly, a spasmodic series of coughing from within herself interrupted her train of thought. Her lungs were on fire, her chest sweltering with pain. It became so intense that Phoebe immediately extinguished her cigarette and promised herself to quit smoking. It wouldn't be her first effort, but she was determined to seriously try this time.

Before she could contemplate further, an unforeseen extempore of screaming filled the hallway leading to the restrooms.

"HELP!" Wilbur's girlfriend Rosie could be heard. "Someone! Anyone!"

She frantically arrived inside the women's restroom, exhaling a sigh of relief as she saw Phoebe. "Oh, Phoebe. Thank God. Thank God."

"What's the matter, Rosie?"

"It's...it's..." Tears came out of the Filipina's eyes; she was shaking hysterically.

"Keep yourself together, what's wrong?"

"DJ Zack...he's...dead."

Phoebe blinked her eyes, wondering if she had heard correctly. "What do you mean he's dead?"

"In...ahh...ah..."

Rosie was too shocked to answer. Instead, she pointed towards the restroom's door, indicating the body was elsewhere, though not specifying anywhere in particular. Phoebe gave up on questioning her stunned friend and found courage within herself to investigate. The thought of potential danger paled in comparison to her growing curiosity, perhaps alongside the opportunity to prevent more danger from happening.

The hallway between the restrooms and dance floor was long and narrow. It also did not stop at the restrooms, extending farther beyond into a dark secluded area. Wherever DJ Zack was, alive or dead, Phoebe deduced, he was certainly not in the direction of the dance floor where the crowd was. She asked herself one more time if she dared to venture toward the isolated end of the hallway. Taking no more than a few seconds to decide, she resumed her valiant task. Feeling an adrenaline rush, she narrowed her focus to the point of absolute determination. As she made her way inward, the club music became less audible—the only distinct sound she heard was her own footsteps hitting the concrete floor. To her surprise, the lane widened a bit, consistently expanding until she was in a small area that led into a dull storeroom where drug activity had seemingly taken place. There, slumped across from her, was DJ Zack's body sitting on a stool. She had expected an overdose episode to conclude with the corpse lying on the floor, but in this rare instance, Wilbur's friend had retained his original position upon his narcotic-induced death. More importantly, Phoebe noticed White Vodka pills scattered around the body, indicating the exact drug that led to his demise.

"What you doing here?!" boomed a voice behind her.

The intrusion was so sudden that Phoebe couldn't help but to release a screeching scream. She turned around and faced the source, looking eye to one good eye with Li'l Bis.

"You ain't seen nuthin', got it?" ordered the eye patch–wearing bartender.

Frightened, she nodded her head in obedience.

The former Nam vet walked past her, tending to the body. He made plans to dispose of DJ Zack's carcass, removing it from the club before anyone began noticing. It was nothing out of the ordinary for The Platinum Star, he thought, just another loser who lost his life to an overdose. The girl, however, would have to be dealt with. His boss, Piranha, rarely advocated violence towards witnesses of overdose, believing they were not bystanders to murder. Besides, Li'l Bis knew, this girl wasn't that close to anyone—he had observed her distant disinterest on a nightly basis. He had, however, miscalculated on Rosie. Little did the club ownership know that she had also seen DJ Zack's body—and that she was Wilbur's girlfriend. Together, the couple spread word on the death of their friend.

Wilbur also demanded answers from Dimitri.

"Yes," acknowledged the Russian, "your friend had been found dead half an hour ago from a drug overdose. These things happen at our club and every other club. It's why your friends have to control themselves."

"B-b-b-b-b-b-but y-y-y-y-you..." Wilbur was too stressed to say anything more.

"I am sorry about what happened," Dimitri said.

"M-M-Marty! S-s-say s-s-something," Wilbur pleaded.

His business partner gulped and nervously laughed.

"Hmmm, heh, I...I don't know," replied Marty, wishing he wouldn't get involved. "DJ Zack...well, wah-eh, I told you he was a drug addict!"

Dimitri, devoid of sympathy, left them. He walked back toward his office, past the numerous dancing customers that didn't know or cared that a death had occurred within the club. While Wilbur and his friends were left convulsing with grief, Jack saw an opportunity and followed the Russian. He watched Dimitri go behind the bar and through a private door, then waited for a few moments before doing so himself. Li'l Bis was not around and the bartending girls were too busy to observe Jack's trespassing.

Inside of Piranha's office, where two of Piranha's unflappable bodyguards were stationed, Dimitri was offered a seat across from the drug lord.

"I thought you guys said your drugs were nonlethal," the kingpin frowned, calmly puffing his cigarette. "Who overdoses off ecstasy?"

"I assure you our product is a lot stronger than regular ecstasy," bragged the Russian. "That being said, you are right. Most people weren't supposed to be overdosing on it. This was an isolated case, however."

The large drug lord angrily pounded his enormous fists onto his desk. Objects were sent momentarily jumping, falling in scattered locations across the table.

"DAMN STRAIGHT THIS BETTER BE AN ISOLATED CASE!" threatened Piranha. "We don't want overly lethal drugs!"

"As opposed to the cocaine that you sell?" countered Dimitri.

"We don't give that to the regular clubbers."

The Russian laughed, showing he had little fear of Houston's premier narcotics seller.

"Are you criticizing your own orders?" he mocked. "I have given both of us a large increase in profits. This is what you wanted, yes? This is why you partnered with my group, yes? If this isn't something you agree with, we can always find ourselves another club."

Piranha assumed his former calm demeanor, eyes locked in on his Russian partner in a subtle acknowledgment he was right.

"Your men take care of the body?" he inquired, puffing his cigar.

"The bartender, Li'l Bis, helped. But yes, we took care of it the legal way by calling in an ambulance. However, my promoter's girlfriend had witnessed it and told a lot of people, including the promoter himself."

"And I'm sure you're smart enough you'll tell the police it was an isolated episode, am I correct? There better not be traces of White Vodka in the autopsy."

Dimitri cleared his throat. "The drug goes away from the body within a few hours after consumption. This is among one of the many unique advantages of White Vodka. It hides itself well in the body."

Their conversation was cut short by a third bodyguard entering the room. There was a reason for his abrupt interruption of the meeting: he was dragging in a reluctant, eavesdropping Jack.

"Sir," informed the guard, "I found him eavesdropping outside your office. Didn't buy his excuse that he was lost."

"I have seen this man before," the Russian pointed at Jack. "He is always following my promoter. What is your name again?"

"George," lied Jack.

"That is incorrect," replied Dimitri, knowing the real answer.

"Then why'd you ask, dickass?"

"Because I wanted to see how quickly you would resort to deception...Jack Tsing."

Jack was impressed. Did the Russian know everyone? He had access to undercover dealers and cameras, Jack figured, probably profiling each individual carefully with meticulous detail and research.

"You've something to tell us?" Piranha asked.

"Yeah I do, fucker. I know about the White Vodka. I know why you're getting promoters to attract new customers. I know who in the club are dealers. I know about the drug's effects."

"And you are foolishly thinking you're a hero?" laughed Dimitri.

Two of the bodyguard pulled out guns and pointed them at Jack, briefly making him nervous as he stared at their barrels in close proximity. With a slow wave of his hand, Piranha motioned for them to lay down their arms. The guards complied.

"No," answered Jack, "I want in. I can help."

"And what possible help can you provide?" Dimitri asked.

"Getting a majority of them hooked," replied Jack. "Look, I've built rapport with these idiots who come to your club. They've become fond of me. Your dealers are a pretty uncharismatic lot. Your fault. You should've chosen more charming people. Right now, sales are probably good, yeah, but you've yet to make users out of the majority of them. I can turn the tides, you know, speed things up."

Piranha gave him a steeled look.

"Of course," Jack boldly warned, "I could otherwise just tell everyone what's really going on around here. I could even update my Facebook status now. Tell all my thousands of friends about the truth."

"Not if we put a bullet into your brain first," Piranha objected.

The bodyguards raised their guns again.

"Whoa! Whoa whoa whoa," Jack chuckled. "Calm down, Captain Obvious. You guys misunderstand. I'm just a guy looking for employment. I wasn't really going to blackmail you. Calm the fuck down, everyone."

The drug lord smiled, admiring the young man's cunning and ruthlessness. He leaned forward to Jack and removed his cigar. "Okay. You take five percent of anything sold. Show me what you can do."

"Five? Five?!" Jack was appalled. "Could you at least make it seven percent?"

Piranha remained unmoved, daring Jack to resume his bluffing.

"Okay," relented Jack, "five it is."

———————

Cody sensed a change as he and his cousin Ace picked up his father from George Bush Intercontinental Airport. Mr. Quan had somehow arrived back to Houston an excessively altered man, similar in appearance, but whose essence was of a peculiar dissimilarity. His father's chattering mood gave clues about his inner transformation, giving explanations of "a new Hong Kong" and "your Uncle Mo giving me an international perspective." Cody would have shrugged off the metamorphosis if not for a request that was so out-of-character, he couldn't help but question his father's mysterious conversion—for the first time in Cody's life, his father desired a non-Chinese dinner.

"<Yes!>" his father repeated. "<How about Cajun? Why not? We should be around more black people! Broaden

our horizons! I can't wait to try gumbo! They said it's like congee! African congee!>"

"Not really dad," disagreed Cody, doing the driving, "it's nothing like congee at all."

"<I don't care! Fried chicken then!>"

"<Good idea!>" Ace chimed in. "<I like fried chicken, uncle!>"

Cody's eyebrows remained knotted in confusion as he glanced at his father from the rearview mirror.

"Fried chicken isn't necessarily Cajun," Cody clarified. "Fried alligator maybe—are you talking about soul food, dad?"

"Hey!" Cody's father barked back in English. "Don't be so correct, okay? I say Cajun and fried chicken, we go! No ask! Just want to be with black people."

"Fine," Cody sarcastically replied. "You want a regular black place or an extra black place?"

"Whatever. Just do whatever! Go wherever!" his father responded, hands flailing in the air.

With the help of the Yelp application from his cousin's iPhone, they sought out a nearby Cajun restaurant in north Houston. It wasn't predominated by African-American customers and staff as his father oddly wanted, but Cody welcomed it, judging the establishment solely from its ambrosial aroma.

"Hello," greeted their waiter, "what would y'all like to drink?"

Cody's father gave the server a stink eye, shaking his head in disapproval because he was Hispanic.

"Um, I want a black waiter," requested Mr. Quan. "Can you get out and give a black waiter?"

"Huh?"

"You not black! I want black! I love black people!"

Cody looked at his father in bewilderment, opening his own mouth in shocked but stunned silence.

"I don't..." the waiter paused and tried to put together his train of thought. "I'm sorry, I'm not following here."

"Go away!" waved off Mr. Quan. "Bring us a black man. Or woman. Whatever, okay? Just whatever."

"Look," apologized Cody, pointing at an adjacent African-American server, "can we just have that guy right there? I'm sorry. I don't know what's going on either. Just...please do it. I'm really sorry. Thanks."

Though the current waiter was confused, he complied regardless, leaving Cody to inquire about his father's atypical behavior.

"What's the matter with you?" asked Cody. "Why are you acting like this? Did you contract SARS while you were in Hong Kong?"

"I try to like black people," he explained. "Maybe they like me back. Too much white yin, must include the black yang."

"What?!"

The wheels inside of Cody's head began turning into high gear. It was now even more essential for him to solve the sudden mystery, no longer because he was merely curious, but for the reason of preventing their potential humiliation. Perhaps he could call his mother and ask for Chef Mo's number, and inquire of his uncle if there were a possible reason for his father's reconditioning. That would, however, be too frantic a decision and besides, he realized, it was six in the morning Hong Kong time. There had to be an easier way, he thought, as he grew more frustrated that his father gave him only cryptic, nonsensical answers. Before Cody could contemplate further, however, they were interrupted by a new waiter—one who was, by request, black.

"Hello," he awkwardly greeted, "can I get you guys something to drink?"

"Yes, my black friend," smiled Mr. Quan.

"Sprite," answered Ace.

"What you want Sprite for?!" scolded Cody's father. "Sprite is white! Coke is black! Get Coke!........or Dr. Pepper."

"<But, uncle, I like Sprite.>"

"Three cokes!" Cody's father ordered.

The waiter gave him a weird expression. "Are you...guys sure?"

"Yeah, we sure!" insisted Mr. Quan. "We love black people!!!!"

Much to Cody's dismay, his father's eccentric demeanor extended beyond their time at the airport and restaurant. He had even questioned his own annoyance about it a week later, considering its positive aspects that it reflected from his father. It opened Mr. Quan's eyes, for example, of the African-American demographic who exemplified virtue and morality—decent people who had always been around him, but were obscured by his own discerning perceptions. Still, Cody felt irritated about the extremes that were driving his father into his newfound admiration. They were, he realized, from the same ones that originally fueled his father's past loathing. Who knew if it would return to the hostile end of the spectrum someday?

It was during an early evening when Cody thought to bring this up to his father. They were jogging among their cordial neighbors, enjoying the beautiful trail that ran around their area's magnificent lake. As he had done for the past few weeks, Mr. Quan made expatiated efforts into greeting the random black strangers that caught his eye.

"Hi, black friend!" he smiled with a grin as wide as his exercise headband. "Run fast like an African!"

"Dad," Cody huffed, "I think it's better if you kept that to yourself."

"What you mean?" Mr. Quan inquired, waving at another passing black jogger. "Good job, black guy! Bless your Motown soul!"

Cody abruptly slowed his pace and switched to walking.

"Ffft," laughed his father, slowing down with him. "You tired already? I'm twenty-six years older than you!"

"We've got to talk."

"We are talking."

"No, I mean..." Cody sighed, his disposition for obedience fighting him over expressing his thoughts. "I like that you're starting to say good things about black people. But..."

"<Yeah?>" his dad switched to Cantonese. "<So what's the problem?>"

"<People different good some bad perhaps.>" Cody's poor grip of Chinese grammar discouraged him from continuing.

"Speak English!" ordered his father.

"Not every black person in this neighborhood is a good person, do you understand?"

"What? Good bad what what?"

Cody stressed himself, angry that his words weren't defining what he wanted to express.

"Of course they good!" Mr. Quan continued. "Maybe you the one with problem. Find help."

As Cody watched, his father resumed jogging and greeted more of their black neighbors as he passed them by. Cody remained standing, contemplating as to how he should present his point in a clearer explanation. As his father jogged farther away, Cody saw that he remained consistent with his welcoming, but noticed it wasn't given to everyone. He felt foolish in believing his father was a changed man, because in all his familiar attributes, the same subjectivity remained in the elder Quan.

CHAPTER 31: SAME OLD SHIT

There was an old Japanese saying, Cody recalled, about the pointlessness of climbing Mount Fuji twice after already conquering it once. He was sure he had butchered the exact wording, but as he stared out of his new cubicle's twenty-sixth floor window, he had no doubt about its meaning. Was it vanity to not settle and to be unthankful for having a job during a recession? He wished he had cared enough to answer that, though he wondered what was the point in doing so—he'd been down this philosophical road before.

Besides, he thought, "pointlessness" had its benefits.

There was a certain bliss he felt once he had accepted its uniformity, his body gaining weight as a result of its stress-free expectations. It remained a bit difficult to brush his teeth every morning without his reflection, though forgotten notions such as frustration and anger made the hindrance tolerable. His only defining characteristic these days was an ethereal patience—the kind that enabled him to endure lengthy boardroom meetings without a word or a yawn. Obedience wasn't so bad now that he had given in to it. At the very least, he was responsible for nothing.

"<You see?>" his father had told him earlier that morning. "<This is how it's supposed to be. Following orders, showing up on time, never questioning what you're told. Repeat.>"

He then placed more youtiao alongside Cody's milk bowl, insisting his son take another serving. Cody slowly did as he was told, putting the soggy bread pieces into his mouth and eating them without reaction.

"<Good boy. Good boy. Thirty-three more years of this and you'll be retiring without worry>," smiled his father. "<Just working, eating and making my grandchildren. Yep. Working, eating and making my grandchildren. Oh!—that reminds me, don't forget to invite your girlfriend Kiki here for dinner tonight.>"

Kiki didn't need reminding, of course. If anyone was happier than Cody's father with their newly forged relationship, it was the styleless nerdette herself. She was more than willing to assume her role as a doting girlfriend, visiting her newly dubbed sweetheart ten minutes before noon on workdays. Kiki brought him her home-cooked specialties—fermented tofu, steamed eggs and orange cuttlefish—and savored every spoonful she placed into his mouth.

"<Say ahhhhh>," she giggled, slipping a lump of tofu near him.

Cody followed her orders and opened his mouth, "<AHHHHHHHHHHH.>"

She watched him consume it, then handed the bowl and spoon to him.

"<Mmmm, now you feed me>," insisted Kiki, "<like a birdie mama feeding a birdie baby.>"

Cody didn't bother to question her illogical analogy. Instead, he watched her expand her mouth within a few feet away from him, exposing its imperfections in close proximity. He could see her crooked and discolored teeth—some with remnants stuck in them from her previous meals—and her wavering tongue, inviting him to insert pieces of cuttlefish on it. Even with Cody's neutered sense of individualism, the revolting scene gave him displeasure in the guise of a wince.

"<Come on>," she repeated, mouth left opened, "<this is romantic.>"

He quickly slid the spoon close to it and flicked the food inside, like a lacrosse player scoring a goal. Kiki coughed as most of the cuttlefish landed in her throat.

"<What...>" she coughed, "<...what was that?>"

"<Sorry am I used not this I do.>"

They heard footsteps approaching Cody's cubicle—his coworkers must have been returning from their lunch breaks, he figured.

"Hey, you gotta go," urged Cody.

"<Mmm, okay, mmmm>," Kiki laughed, her breath now smelling like cuttlefish and eggs. "<Kiss?>"

Cody froze, resisting his urge to obey. At least she said it in question format, he figured, maybe that could be interpreted as a loophole.

"<Kiss later shy am I wedding after only>," he stammered.

"<Okay!>" she acknowledged, bobbing her head side to side. "<Mmm, don't forgot to remind me to come to your house for dinner tonight! Kekekekeke! BYE!>"

Cody nodded, glad to be rid of her for a few hours.

Later that evening, inside the Quans' exorbitant new home, Kiki brought more of her fermented tofu, steamed eggs and orange cuttlefish. Her dishes were placed alongside the gourmet extravaganza Cody's father had prepared, resulting in a savory smell that permeated throughout the house. The overall amount of Chinese food was enough to feed them twice over, though Mr. Quan had cause to celebrate so excessively: the potential daughter-in-law he had chosen was joining them for their first family dinner.

Both of Cody's parents and Ace were taken in by Kiki. Mr. Quan, in particular, was unapologetically up front with the topic of grandparenting, at times annoying Cody's mother when he brought the subject up.

"<We absolutely must have a son>," Mr. Quan demanded, picking up an eggplant with his chopsticks. "<Cody is the last male with the family name. And this child must be tall because the two of you are short. Time your mating after marriage to the Year of the Tiger. That's next year, but there's still time. Also, be sure that once you two are in the process of child-bearing, be sure to have all doors opened so as to allow the chi to flow with the orgasms—>"

"<Quan Min-Lo!>" interrupted his wife beside him. "<For everyone's sake, don't talk about such intimate things!>"

"<What?>" he laughed. "<I'm just trying to help them!>"

"<You're not helping anyone here digest their food!>" she countered.

Kiki giggled and used her chopsticks to give Cody's father some pieces of tofu. She did the same for Cody, his mother and Ace.

"<Mmmmm, don't worry>," the girl snickered. "<I'm sure things will happen when they happen.>"

Ace laughed at her reply as he got up. "<Ehhh, I'm going to get another bowl of rice. Does anyone need me to fill up their bowl for seconds?>"

"<I do! Kekeke!>" Kiki obnoxiously giggled.

"<Wow, you sure eat a lot!>" Ace commented.

"<You know what they say!>" she laughed, handing Cody's scholarly cousin her finished bowl. "<The bigger the appetite, the bigger the brain!>"

"<Eeeh, that's sounds scientific. What school did you go to in Hong Kong?>"

"<Mmmm, HKUST!>" she answered proudly.

"<Ehhhhh!>"

"<Mmmm!>"

Their eyes locked for the briefest of moments, though it was enough to ignite a spark which manifestly tugged at their hearts. Ace's fingers reacted to the sudden sentiment by dropping her bowl. It landed face down, scattering rice on the Quans' sleek new carpeting.

"<Aiya!>" Mr. Quan shook his head. "<Don't be so clumsy, Ace! Girls won't like you!>"

"<Oh, I don't know about that>," giggled Kiki.

Afterwards, Cody's father knew something was wrong when he saw his son washing dishes with his mother. His son's display of passivity gave him great displeasure. Mr. Quan urged Cody to involve himself once again in the relationship he had chosen for Cody.

"<Hey!>" he grabbed his son's arm. "<What are you doing?>"

Cody stared blankly at him, not able to comprehend the deeper meaning of his question.

"I'm washing dishes," Cody soullessly replied.

The elder Quan squinted, looking at his son in disbelief. "<Why are you washing dishes?>"

"Because I was told to by mom."

Mr. Quan shook his head and dragged his son away; Cody's hands were still soapy from his current chore.

"<Must I do everything?>" seethed his father. "<I have to chase your women now too? Go spend some time with your girlfriend!>"

Their attention was immediately diverted by the gentle strumming of a guitar—the beautiful tune originating from Ace's guest room. They both walked upstairs and peeked into the young man's bedroom, finding a sight that broke the elder Quan's heart.

"<Kekeke!>" admired Kiki, sitting at the edge of Ace's bed. She was leaning on his shoulders as he sat next to her, his instrument's enrapturing melody charming its way into her senses. "<I love the way you play. It's so soft and gentle.>"

"<Ehhh>," blushed Ace, "<I'm not that good.>"

"<I loveee itttt!>"

Cody's father began making a motion to halt their newfound tenderness, but then abruptly stopped as their innocent love reminded him of something long forgotten. Instead, he turned around quickly and motioned for his son to follow, leaving Ace and Kiki alone in their moment of infatuation.

Outside the backyard, father and son strolled around undisturbed. The area was blessed with generous moonlight, giving the scenery a calm aura. The quietness enabled him to clearly attune with his thoughts. Mr. Quan felt saddened that his earlier joyous anticipation had dissipated so quickly. He could've put a premature end to the fondness that surprisingly sprung up between Kiki and his nephew, stamping it out like a small fire that hadn't yet spread. But it was so similar to his sweet memory of how he had met Cody's mother and the way they had succumbed to love's magical power. He wasn't supposed to marry her—his family advised against it because she was too short, too independent and too average a cook—but he did so anyway. For thirty-three years and counting, things remained happy; he considered returning his son to those same rebellious tendencies, but then, just as quickly, he returned to his original resoluteness in his duty of Confucian fatherhood.

"<Stop>," he commanded Cody.

His son did so without objection, following his orders like a robot.

"<Min-Guang>," he began, referring to his son by his Chinese name, "<you do know why I do things for you, right? I need to protect you. You're not smart and I don't believe you have much to offer. If you were like your cousin Duke or even me, perhaps you would stand a chance, but I've concluded

through your failures that you have poor judgment. As the last male Quan of our family, I can't afford to let you make mistakes. Some mistakes are irreversible, and who you are, the genetics you carry, they are far more important than the person inside. You're an investment, do you understand?>"

He patted Cody's head, fortunate that he was finally at his utmost obedience.

"<I was going to tell you something else tonight>," laughed his father, "<about how I married your mother against the wishes of our family. About how it turned out okay. But...well...I've also always envisioned choosing your bride. I enjoy the safety I feel knowing where you are, of seeing you within eyesight, even at this age. That type of thing, I was asked to abandon it once you grew up. But I can't do it, son. I just can't. Letting go of this power is too much for me to bear. Until you're married, you are still a child and you must listen to your elders. You are my property. But I promise you, I won't ever steer you wrong. A Chinese father is always right and it is his son's duty to obey and serve.>"

Cody looked downward, too defeated to offer anything in contradiction. He finally nodded with a smile.

"<Good boy, good obedient Chinese boy>," approved his father. "<Don't worry about losing Kiki. I will find you another one. You are exactly who I've always wanted you to be, submissive to your parents. One family, under one roof, united together for every meal!>"

———————

"Damn, what's takin' so long," complained Pete. "I'm hungry."

The body shop workers applying the vinyl to Pete's food truck quickly discovered that patience was not among his virtues. It was past midnight, but they had estimated at least one more hour before his mobile enterprise would be completed. The crew also repeatedly noted that an hour was wasted acquiring more royal purple material—a color he was adamant about and which he had refused to substitute.

"Gotta look like a king," Pete insisted. "Ain't no higher respectin' power than dark purple! Put some gold and watch all eyez on me."

He paced nervously, excited about his first venture into entrepreneurship—its intoxication far more addicting than any drug he ever put into his body. Their labor today was just for the exterior, of course; the interior was another issue, it had passed the regulations, but he still needed to feel comfortable working within it. His culinary experience was, after all, solely derived from his time in prison.

"I made sushi in jail," he bragged, trying to make conversation with a nearby worker. "Think how hard that is, nigga. Sushi. In prison. Sheyt. Gave me everyone's full respect for how well I made gourmet with prison food."

The body shop's graphic artist approached him and produced the latest draft of Pete's logo. He wanted a cartoon version of himself.

"Yo, how about this?" asked the artist, holding the printout in front of him.

Pete winced and shook his head in disapproval.

"Bitch! Dat dun look like me!" Pete criticized. "Dat look like Mr. Potato Head! You sayin' I look like Mr. Potato Head, huh?!"

"Actually, you kinda do," chuckled the worker he was talking to.

"Just try again," said Pete, handing the printout back to the artist. "I want this shit done right. Once-in-a-lifetime opportunity, my nigga."

The sound of screeching tires caught everyone's attention as a familiar silver Audi sports utility vehicle careened onto the body shop's premises. It approached Pete and stopped close to him, flashing its high beams for the purpose of intimidation. The former thug reacted with shielding arms, squinting towards the direction of the car. He watched as the recognizable hefty figure of Andrew Huynh got out of the passenger side, hands in both pockets, calmly approaching him.

"Man," quipped Pete, eyes concealed from the brightness, "you niggas still using the same car all these years?"

Andrew ignored the derisive comment and stopped a few feet from Pete. The enormity of his figure blocked the glaring lights, mercifully giving Pete a break from covering himself.

To Pete's surprise the veteran hit man began speaking in a serious tone he was not used to hearing from Andrew.

"You must the dumbest fool alive," Andrew opined, "and I don't know how much longer 'alive' would be a part of that description."

"Shit, fat nigga," challenged Pete, "you come to kill me, here I stand before you! Just do what you gotta do, nigga...otherwise, I'm a businessman now. Don't need you niggaz wastin' my time!"

"A businessman," Andrew scoffed. "I fail to see the comedy in this."

"Ain't no joke, nigga. I left prison a free man and dat's what I 'tend to remain—dead or alive."

The assassin walked closer to Pete, challenging him with an unblinking stare. Pete met the provocation and did the same, giving Andrew secret admiration for his bravery.

"You may think I'm here to offer you a chance to come back, to reason with you and put some sense into your dull, imbecilic brain," seethed Andrew. "But this visit is not about a warning. No. You're already a dead man, Pete. I'm not going to kill you tonight or tomorrow. When you least expect it, I'm going to destroy your food truck and burn it to the ground. I'm going to have my men torture and rape your mother and sister and put the footage on YouTube. Then, I will put a gun into your hands and force you to shoot them. Next, I will cut your arms, legs, eyes, ears, asshole and dick off and feed it to my dogs and only then, when you're blind, lame, deaf, unable to fuck and can't shit, when there's nothing more for you to dare and hope again, I'm going to bury you alive in the remote regions of some uncharted island and there, you will lose whatever remains of your life one by one through maggots tearing at your skin. No one will remember you, no will even know you existed. Count the days, Pete. Count the days."

With his message delivered, the cold-blooded enforcer straightened his collar in composed fashion and made his way back to the Audi. The car slowly pulled away from the body shop and noiselessly departed the scene.

"Wow," commented the graphic artist, "hell of a thing to say to a goon like that."

Pete continued with his determined expression of grit, his jaw locked in a stance of fortitude and fearlessness.

"Only way to escape the game, my nigga," nodded Pete. "Can't let 'em think they own ya. I meant every word of living or dying a free man."

"Like I said, one brave son of a gun," the artist shook his head.

Pete turned to him with an annoyed look. "Say, you gonna work on my cartoon logo or am I hirin' ya for your looks, ma'fucka?"

"Oh, right," the graphic artist replied, leaving Pete alone.

The former convict resumed his actions prior to the interruption, making his way toward the food truck. To his delight, the vinyl wallpaper was almost finished, causing him to smile and see the grandness of his ideas before him.

"My nigga," he playfully tapped the crew chief's shoulder. "This it right hea'! You on it

———

Hannah and Kiki took in the blaring crunk rap like a bitter pill. Granted, they surprisingly found the overly redundant hooks and earthquake-inducing thumps to be incontrovertibly catchy, but the majority of it was, in their opinion, haphazard noise. The days of the Happy Lotus have now become what Mr. Quan termed "blackified"— overwrought pandering to predicated African-American stereotypes. It was a mystery to the two women as to where Cody's father received his change of heart; it certainly hadn't originated from their customers' treatment of him. The majority of the low-income black patrons continued giving their boss the stink eye, now more irritated because of his disingenuous cordiality.

"What is up, my black friend?" he greeted one of his

regular customers walking through the door. "I know you! I know what you want! Shrimp fried rice and moo shu pork! I call it Martin Luther King combo!"

"Mannn, just take my order," hissed the customer, "and add a hot and sour soup in there."

"Okay!" nodded Mr. Quan. "Hot! Like a big black ass. Sour! Like—"

"Shut the fuck up, Bruce Lee. I liked you better when you were quiet and angry."

Cody's father laughed, interpreting the slander as a lighthearted zinger. He relayed the order to Hannah, who had taken on cashier duty. She glanced nervously at Mr. Quan as he walked from table to table, greeting the customers in a similarly reckless manner. At least back when he was intolerant of black people, she thought, he was protective of her and Kiki. This amiable version of him helped no one and, worse, placed them in harm's way. The three of them were outnumbered forty to three on a packed day—the situation was a powder keg, set to be ignited by any mistaken provocation.

More potential trouble arrived when her least favorite customer made his way into the restaurant. *Great,* Hannah sighed to herself, *Stuck Up couldn't have chosen elsewhere to have lunch today.* Stuck Up was the nickname she had given the quiet, frowning black man with the inordinately oily skin and disheveled dreadlocks. She had grown tired of making conversation with him, dismissing his silence as a prejudicial attitude toward Chinese women. If she could bet on any customer that was most likely to snap, it was surely him.

Kiki, meanwhile, had her mind far from her current whereabouts. The absentminded girl was too busy dreaming of her beloved Ace, taking orders without focus or concern. Her concentration was so far removed that she hardly noticed a discernible feature of her current table: the customers sitting there were all Asian. The Happy Lotus had hardly any Asian customers, but this particular threesome proved even more peculiar when they were just as distracted from realizing she had taken the wrong orders.

"What would you like?" recited the dazed waitress.

"Lemon chicken and Szechuan vegetables," one of the men said.

"Okay, chicken chow mein and ma po tofu," she wrote down, "anything else?"

The sole woman in the group waved her off in a dismissive gesture, impatient to be rid of Kiki's presence. When they were left to their own table again, the woman resumed discussing her plans. The goals were coarse and extremely perilous but necessary.

Her name was Ping and many years ago a malevolent executioner named Andrew Huynh had come into her house and shot her in the stomach, killing her unborn child. He came back a week later and clubbed her husband to death with a crowbar while his driver burned her three-year-old daughter in the process.

"<Many a day had I not forgotten what that awful man did to my family>," the now hardened woman said in her native Cambodian tongue. <"The planning is now towards fruition. We strike next month, on the first Wednesday."

The two men could do without her dramatic exposition. They were mercenaries in their own right, enlisted through proper underworld channels. For the right price, any target was qualified; both had long ago concealed their birth names, going by aliases that marked their reputation. Red Eye was an insomniac, a well-known pharmaceutical addict from Myanmar who specialized in weaponry and long-range assassinations. His skin was rough and dirty, souvenirs from the days as a freedom fighter for his country. Knife, on the other hand, was tall and clean-cut, a former Laotian soldier who was well-trained and experienced in hand-to-hand combat. Rumor had it that he had killed over a hundred men, often times with merely razors.

"<This is the bastard right here>," Ping said, showing a printed image of Andrew. "<Make him suffer.>"

"<I was under the impression we were after his boss>," noted Knife, whose Cambodian speech was a bit accented.

Ping took out another printed photo, this time of Piranha.

"<That's his boss>," she explained. "<Kill everyone involved with the 2006 attack. They must pay for what they did. I have spent years accumulating the money to hire your services. Don't disappoint me.>"

"<Miss>," replied Red Eye in his best attempt at Cambodian, "<our reputation is on the line. These two men are as good as dead.>"

Before they could continue their conversation, Kiki came back with three bowls of egg drop soup.

"<Did we order that?>" wondered Knife.

"HEY BITCH!" shouted a black customer at the table next to theirs. "That there soup is ours! Whatcha servin' it to them for?"

Kiki turned and faced the other table, blankly staring at what the man was talking about. She had suddenly become aware of her senses, yanked from her pleasant reverie about soaring the heavens with precious Ace.

"I'm sorry," she apologized to both tables.

She walked over and gave the soups to the right customers. As she turned around, one of the bowls were thrown in her direction, splattering remnants of egg drop soup along the backside of her waitressing shirt.

"That's what you get!" yelled the same customer who threw it. "Slant-eyed bitch, trying to serve your own kind over us! You better suck my dick as an apology!"

Kiki turned and bowed to him, terrified with fear. "I-I'm sorry, I didn't know, it was an accident, I was daydreaming, I—"

The customer stormed out of his chair, revealing the full stature of his gigantic presence. The black man's physique encompassed its shadow over the fragile waitress, freezing Kiki with intimidation. From the other end of the small restaurant, Mr. Quan paused from his vexatious conversing and turned around just in time to witness the large man pushing Kiki toward the floor. The delicate waitress lay on the floor, covering herself in mortified fear.

"Chink girl!" the man cursed at her. "Dog eating squat shitting tight pussy duck flossing egg roll bitch whore!"

An elderly customer came between them, hoping he could calm him. "Now now. She didn't mean it, man. Watch your temper, son. I—"

The bully pushed him too, smacking him aside with one swing of his forearm.

"Don't be helping these people! They hate us, don't you know?"

Kiki started crying, helpless on the floor. Cody's father ran over to the ruckus, pleading for the angry customer to stop. He looked at the other customers, hoping they would do something.

"Stop! Hey! I love black people!" pleaded Mr. Quan. "Please stop! Black people good!"

The giant put a hand on Cody's father's throat and watched as he gasped for air.

"I'm going to kill you, Chinaman. You hate me because I'm black. I'm gonna show you what a nigger can do to your chink throat. I'm going to make you wife a widow and she's gonna know what a nigger can do to your people. Niggers like me hate chinks like you. Fuck you, ching chong small dick

China Vietnam Japanese piece of shit. I'm going to murder you! How you like my nigger ass now?!!!!"

Cody's father began losing consciousness. He regretted that perhaps his last thoughts would not be of how much he loved his son, but the quickly returning racism he had long suppressed. Was it his fate to be at war with a group of people he hadn't even known existed for half his life? He began contemplating this question as his consciousness began dissipating.

From a nearby table, Red Eye slowly reached for his handgun inside his jacket. Ping stopped him, nodding toward another occurrence that was unfolding before them. The customer Hannah had nicknamed Stuck Up had approached the situation, standing in front of the bully and giving him a lengthy stare down.

"Negro, get out of my way," threatened the giant.

Stuck Up remained standing, veins protruding from his forehead as an indication of his displeasure and rage.

"What the hell are you doing?!" the giant shouted.

Stuck Up began clutching his fists.

"Fine!"

The giant released Cody's father and watched him fall towards the floor with a thud. Mr. Quan lay close to Kiki on the ground, gasping for air. The bully stormed out of the Happy Lotus, still shouting threats with his arms in the air.

"Fuck with me and be late on my egg drop soup, sheyttttt..."

The restaurant erupted with scattered conversation. Exaggeration of the situation had already begun via word of mouth. Cody's father slowly made his way up, helping a hysterical Kiki off the floor. She flicked off his hand, uncharacteristically screaming at him with animosity.

"<Don't touch me! Don't touch me!>" she sobbed. "<I can't work here anymore! I hate black people! They're monsters! All of them!">

Mr. Quan stood silently, watching the chaos around him. He stared at the customers, almost all of them black, picking out the bad qualities in them that allowed him to hate again. His soul welcomed back the immersion, reminding him of how easy it was to give in to it. Cody's father slowly closed his eyes and imagined a field of black people—the men, the women, the children, the elderly—chained together, lying on an open road. He imagined riding in a giant tank, slowly driving over their bodies one by one, hearing the crushing sounds of steel flattening flesh, the squashing of their blood joining the fracas. It was a sweet, violent fantasy, one that satisfied his predilection towards revenge.

———————

The Happy Lotus looked different after hours. It was tranquil; its unlit state blended in with the dark surroundings of Houston's Third Ward. Knife returned to his car nearby, thinking it was as good a place as any to make his phone call. With his car engine cut off and a few harmless bums around, he enjoyed the last few puffs of his Camel cigarette and let his mind wander off to nowhere in particular. He flicked the used cigarette out of the car window and took out his flip phone and dialed a recently acquired number.

The phone rang three times before the other end answered.

"Did you get any new info?" asked Andrew.

"Yes," Knife replied in decent English. "First Wednesday, next month."

"Good. I'll let Piranha know."

"Hey, you guys remembered the price, right?"

"Yes, of course we remember."

"Okay, because it's priceless to save your life. Don't forget, without me, you would be dead."

"Certainly. You did well, Knife. You did well."

Knife ended the call and lit another cigarette. Double-dealing was a part of the mercenary world, he smirked. Ping should have realized this. So should have Red Eye.

CHAPTER 32: ANGELS AND DEMONS

Underneath their silky, palatial bed covers, Xia placed her teeth on her husband's bewhiskered right nipple, playfully gnawing it. She had been doing this every morning now, a reward for the opulent lifestyle they would soon be enjoying.

"Muuaarrrhh," her husband moaned.

She nibbled faster, sending his body into slow, rhythmic spasms that indicated his pleasure. *He deserves it*, she thought. True, they were still living in the same moderate home off the same dreary income, but this time she believed they would succeed in escaping their subpar social stratum. She had seen the current success of The Platinum Star with her own eyes, authenticating a promise for riches.

The nipple gnawing session drew to a conclusion as Xia moved her way upwards towards Marty's lips in a route bathed with kisses. She then looked into her husband eyes with enamored admiration.

"<Mmm, I love you>," she murmured, pressing her tiny, petite body over him and twirling her pointer finger around his left nipple. "<Do you know how jealous my coworkers are of me? They tell me I've got the perfect husband.>"

"Hurrrrrrmmmmm." He closed his eyes, nodding and enjoying the moment of ecstasy.

She smiled wickedly, recalling the enviousness. "<You should've seen the look on Wanda's face. When she saw that necklace you got for me, I could see her jealousy. I love it when they're jealous of us.>"

"<Hah-arrrr, anything for my Shanghai queen.>"

"<I know>," she softly kissed his nose. "<And you need to continue treating me like I am. That's what husbands do.>"

"<Of course, of course>," he chuckled. "<Heh...hah!...It's such tough work. All of it. But, heh, what would my life mean without making you happy, you know? Eh?">

Marty, of course, attributed his current streak to good luck. More so, he believed the cosmos had been erroneously delaying it—someone of his scheming caliber ought to have received greater rewards in the first place. Everything in the past had always been thwarted by a meddling x-factor, as if he had done something wrong. There was nothing reprehensible, he thought, about taking things from others that they could replenish. No different from farmers taking corn from the soil.

"Honey," Xia interrupted in her delicate Shanghai accent, "let's go look at new homes again."

"<Gahhh>," Marty hesitated. "<Wah-heh, my legs are tired from all the homes we were looking at yesterday.>"

"<But I haven't found one I liked yet. None of them have the perfect baby room.>"

She smiled, hoping Marty would get the hint.

He reacted with an expression of wide-eyed shock, "You...you're..."

Marty quickly placed a hand on her stomach, searching for signs of pregnancy. Xia reacted to his overreaction with rolling eyes. She gently grabbed his inquiring arm and pushed for him to stop.

"<No, stupid. I'm not pregnant. You don't even aim right. But that's beside the point—Wanda's pregnant and I want a baby too.>"

"<Well, that explains a lot. Heh, ha! I thought she had let herself go.>"

"<Now that we'll be rich, we should start a family.>"

"<Whoa heh, Xia. Heh. Let's not get too hasty. The money's not coming until—>"

Xia frowned with suspicion. "<Until what?>"

"<Heh, er, well, until, ah...emmm...>"

"<You told me you had it handled. You told me that club was going to pay you after it was done and it was guaranteed. Is something not right about that?">

"<Ah, no no",> Marty lied, knowing that the windfall wasn't assured yet. "<Wah-gah, heh heh. HA! Heh. Of course, the money's guaranteed to come in a few weeks.>"

Xia eased off on her furious expression, returning to her alluring smile. With a surprising exhibit of strength, the dainty woman suddenly grabbed her husband by his wrists and pinned him on the bed.

"<Now about that baby>," she requisitioned. "<I think we shall start making love from now with purpose.>"

"<Heh, ah, er, ah, darling...you're...you're hurting me.>"

"<Create, husband. Create like you've never created before.>"

Without further words, Xia infringed her lustful prerogative upon him, commanding the action with an expeditious pacing. The process was coarse, testing his body's prowess to its limits and not particularly concerned of its coping. Marty's consciousness flickered off and on, leaving her to unleash an auxiliary of endurance she had reserved from her body. Fortunately, Xia's sensational stamina proved enough for the both of them, finding its conclusion forty minutes later. She collapsed on top of her lethargic husband, mixing her sweat with his. The wimp had immediately passed out, she observed between deep breaths. She flipped around and lay on her back, facing the contents of their muck-stained ceiling. A baby, she promised herself. They'd have one regardless of how many times it took. She hoped it would be a girl; if so, she would name her Angel.

———

Cody Quan.

In the instance Cody heard an indistinguishable voice whisper his name, he immediately took notice of his surroundings. There was, he observed, nothing to recognize; in all directions, including above and below him, he was enveloped by the blank entity of whiteness. It surprised him how naturally he stood without the aid of a floor or an indication of depth. The vacuum of his environment caused him to close his eyes and seek refuge within its darkness. There, without sight, he tried to recall how he ended up in this expressionless, blank reality. It wasn't a dream nor had he ventured into this otherworld through an application of prayer—someone had summoned him here, he realized. But by who or what?

He opened his eyes again, confronting the background-less reality. Within moments he began walking, hoping that it would help him think. Had he died? Was this another one of Jesus' sadomasochistic sessions? Perhaps I should try a different sense, he figured. Since nothing appeared by sight, he concentrated on noticing a breeze or a distinguishable temperature change.

No such luck, he realized.

Cody grew frustrated as he began running out of theories—it soon turned into an urgency to escape. He began running, hoping he would stumble upon a checkpoint. His trotting evolved into a full-speed sprint until he suddenly stopped when he began noticing a change in his surroundings. There was moisture in the air, he realized, replacing the dryness from before. Cody held out a hand and felt the vapor. But why? he wondered. Where was it coming from? The mystery gave him further annoyance, causing him to wish for its source.

To his gratifying surprise, he turned around and saw a nearby waterfall. The blankness was gradually replaced by a new reality, one with forests and streams, stone roads and wooden bridges. Mere moments later, Cody found himself within a jungle of some sort, though he knew it was a fraudulent one due to its absence of life. Where were the bugs, birds, wildlife or fish? Then again, he was thankful that this jungle was devoid of them as insects made him flinch and animals brought potential danger.

Codddyyyy.

That voice again, he mused, looking up and around. It seemed distant. Maybe it's from afar, Cody figured, wishing he could see a greater scope of the jungle. Suddenly, his head ached as he observed the ground shrinking away—no, not shrinking—he realized he was growing into an enormous size. As the giant Cody stood dumbfounded among the many trees, he felt disappointment in seeing a never-ending jungle. The voice had not come from a distance or the sky above, but from his head. He waited, hoping for the sound again.

Cody Quan.

"Who are you?" roared the giant Cody, his voice echoing miles across. "Show yourself!"

With this command, the scenery of trees and streams transformed into yet another incarnation for the environment. This time, he was inside a dark tunnel—he found his size was now in proportion to it, ending his brief tenure as a giant. At one end of the tunnel emerged a resplendent light, obvious in its hint as the source for answers. Cody began walking towards it as he heard the voice become clearer and louder.

Come, Cody.

The brightness grew with intensity, becoming so unbearable that Cody eventually stopped and succumbed to its prevailing luminosity. Instead of blinding Cody, however, the intense brightness slowly evolved into a new environment, one that confounded Cody but was recognizable to him: a small barbershop room.

The area of it was small, no bigger than the size of his own bedroom. The floors were checkered in a black and white pattern, nothing unusual except for the lack of a doorway among its four walls. Most noticeably, however, was a petite Asian woman standing beside a lone barber chair. Cody had never seen her before, though oddly he was recognizable to her.

"Hello, Cody Quan," the woman greeted, taking out a pair of scissors. "I'm Charlotte. Thanks for coming."

"Where am I?" he asked. "Is this a dream? Am I dead?"

"Neither," she replied, patting the seat of the chair. "Come, let's take a look at you and talk about why you're here."

Cody hesitated for a second before obliging. She walked in a circle around, observing the contents of his head. She then turned toward his reflection in the mirror. Cody was surprised to see his reflection and even more shocked to find that he had long hair. Still, he was pleased to see his long-absent likeness, greeting his depicted counterpart with a smile that grinned back at him.

"Tsk," Charlotte winced, sifting through his hair with her tiny fingers. "Look at all this negativity."

She began her work, placing a barber's cape over him and snipping at Cody's hair with her scissors. As each clump of hair dropped on the checkered floor, his spirit began feeling a sense of ease.

"Do you know," she began, "that every cause is a result of an effect?"

Cody silently repeated her words, swearing to himself that it must have been the other way around.

"You're mistaken," he corrected, "every effect is a result of a cause."

The celestial hairstylist offered no pause from her actions as she moved on to Cody's sideburns.

"That is not untrue," she agreed, "but what encouraged an action or a decision to take place? Things don't just move by themselves and decisions aren't made on a whim. Perhaps it can be said that causes don't exist, only effects creating effects."

"An endless loop," Cody nodded, almost causing the side of his head to collide with the scissors.

"Watch it," she warned. "Don't move your head."

He considered the meaning of what Charlotte had said, though he failed to understand how it related to who she was, why she was cutting his hair and whichever part of the cosmos they were in.

"What exactly are you?" Cody finally asked. "And what is this place?"

"I am merely what you need, Cody Quan. Your soul has been greatly endangered, and so, it seeks to repair itself by notifying you, the owner."

"I...don't exactly follow."

Charlotte turned the chair slightly towards the left and then towards the right, pleased that she was finished with his haircut. Cody sat patiently, waiting for her to continue their existential discussion. Instead, she tapped him on the shoulder and pointed towards the shampoo bowl with her chin.

"Come," she ordered, "let's rinse and shampoo the rest of your negativity."

He followed her and leaned against the shampoo bowl's chair. Warm water began flowing across his scalp as the cosmic hairstylist softly applied shampoo and conditioner while lightly scratching his scalp with her nails. Cody let out a gratifying moan, enjoying the pampered session.

Slowly, she leaned closer and began whispering softly into his ear, "Would you like to know the meaning of life?"

The question, he believed, was rhetorical. But under the exceptional pleasure he was experiencing, he replied anyway with a nod and a smile.

"Everything is a cycle," she began. "Beginnings end and endings begin. Round and round they go."

As she said this, Cody could feel her thumbs making soothing, massaging circles on his scalp.

Charlotte cleared her throat and continued, "We create beings that, in turn, create us. God made man, man made God. All truth is interpretational until it becomes concrete. Not long ago, I was but a figment of your imagination. Your soul was tortured, your subconscious desiring to be free from your negativity."

She washed away the remaining shampoo from his hair and, with a tap on his shoulder, signaled for him to get up. He was motioned to sit back in the barber's chair where she brought out a towel and began drying his hair.

"But what about Jesus?" he countered.

"Who do you think Jesus is?" she asked, drying his hair with the towel.

"An abusive and bipolar omnipotent being that takes joy out of torturing his creations?"

"Yes."

A look of surprise fell on Cody's face. "Really?"

"If that's what you see in your heart. That's what you get."

She finished drying his hair and began styling it with gel.

"So you're saying I...created Jesus? But I couldn't have. Other people saw Jesus too."

"An artist can create something alone, or a group of artists can create a piece of art together. The result is an accumulation of their ideas and interpretations. And as Picasso once said...'we're all artists deep inside.'"

With that, she finished styling his hair and made him look at his reflection. He saw himself, handsome and confident, fresh with newfound vigor.

"Never sell yourself short, Cody," she finished. "If you knew how much power your mind can wield, you could control your reality. Don't succumb to fears or allow the opinions of others to dictate that."

———————

"Hi there," greeted a middle-aged black man, handing a flyer to Cody's Aunt Mei. "Can I have a moment of your time please?"

Their encounter took place one evening at Mei's apartment mailbox. She instinctively clutched her pepper spray, preparing for an incursion.

"No, I no English," she waved off.

The black man insisted on handing her the flyer, which consisted of a sketch of another black man. She couldn't tell if the person in the sketch was the same as the man in front of her.

"Well, I just wanted you know that there's been a burglary committed in our neighborhood and this is who witnesses say to look out for."

She gave him a quick defensive glance, signaling for him to back away. Noting her skepticism, the man slowly placed the flyer on top of a nearby platform.

"Please, just make a note of the person on the flyer, okay?" he assured her by pointing at it. "I'm part of the home owners association. I just want you to be safe. Have a good day, ma'am."

Mei watched the black man leave and repeat his message to the other people around the building. A robber warning other people of robbers, she scoffed. She walked over to the flyer and studied the sketch—there was nothing discernible about the black face on it.

This could be anyone in my area, she thought.

She had grown discontented with Houston's financially diverse zoning patchwork. It made no sense that one city could intermingle new neighborhoods with slums. Because of this, she was becoming less pleased with the condo her son Duke had purchased for her. As more and more of her new neighbors were black, she figured they came from the nearby tenement housing. Additionally, she had found herself on the losing end of her status competition with her brother—he wouldn't stop bragging about how much better his new luxury house was.

"Oh yeah? Your neighborhood has black people too," she countered a week ago.

"Twenty-three," Cody's father stated, "that's only how many we have. Yours have sixty-eight. That's a forty-five black person difference. Plus we have more white people in my neighborhood, and you have more Mexicans and Asians. HAHA!"

Mei recalled how hot her face felt when he cited those statistics. She knew him well enough to believe he had actually ventured into her neighborhood and tallied those results himself. It was true, though, she thought, about the growing fear she felt whenever she took a stroll around her condo area. The blacks were starting to look the same—they had red eyes and deviled horns, mouths capable of spewing fire. Her brother believed them to be a simian species, an experiment by the human race to cohabit as pets or useful servants. Mei, however, believed herself to know better. Black people were actually Yaoguai, she surmised, demonic spawns from Diyu, the Taoist hell. They were straight out of Chinese legend—a modern day variant of Asia's archenemies.

She dreaded the long walk from the mailbox area back to her condo. The sun had recently set, making the demons more invisible than ever. As she quickly pocketed her mail and started her journey home, she viewed the people passing by her with increased suspicion. Two black teenagers tossing a football paused in their activity and turned their heads, revealing glowing red eyes and sharp pointy teeth. As a black woman with a stroller passed by her, the head of a baby demon popped out from the buggy and stuck out a long green tongue. Mei clutched her purse tightly, once again gripping the pepper spray within it.

BUZZZZZZZZZ!

"AH!"

The vibrations from her Samsung Galaxy phone startled her as she collected herself and glanced at who was calling her: Quan Min-Lo.

"<What do you want, little brother?>" she answered.

"<I just want you to know I just took father to Chinatown today and he's already got his groceries.>"

"<What? You can't do that. I'm supposed to that tomorrow.>"

"<Too bad. He says I'm great.>"

"<You forget your boundaries, little brother. Remember, my son still makes more money than yours and he's about to be married soon.>"

"<That's several months away and you know it. Besides, Cody's got plenty of time to marry before Duke... now that I have a major credit line to fund for his wedding. I can see it now. Seven course meals at Ocean Palace—abalone goose feet, shark fin soup, stir fried pawns, glutinous rice...>"

Mei clenched her teeth, suspending her walking in preparation for a counter. "<Oh yeah? How's your son going to do that when he doesn't have his perfect little Hong Kong girlfriend anymore?>"

"<W-What...how...?>"

"<Yeah, I know what's happening, little brother. The girl left your son for your nephew, Ace. Hahahahahaha!">

"<She and Ace are just friends!>"

"<I saw them holding hands just now at the Chinese supermarket>," she smirked.

"<Well, I guess this is as good a time as any to reveal that we've found an even better girlfriend for him. One that we've kept secret.>"

Mei let out a mocking laugh. She was so entertained with her brother's bluff that she tripped over an elevated curve on the sidewalk. As she collided with concrete, the impact caused her phone to slip out of her hands, landing somewhere on the grass.

"<Hello?>" she could hear Cody's father nearby. "<Hahaha. Speechless?>"

She cursed herself for becoming too engaged with the conversation; all the neighbors had gone back to their homes, leaving her all alone in a dark part of the condos.

"<Yeah, that's right>," he continued mocking. "<Her name is...uh...Chu...er...Chu Hua...>"

The soft glow illuminating from the Galaxy screen helped Mei determine its whereabouts quickly. She shook her head and approached the dropped phone, thinking of a witty comeback to such an obviously fake Chinese name: "Chrysanthemum" was the best her brother could do? Just as she was about to retrieve her Galaxy, however, the world suddenly flipped upside down. The immediate numbness on the right side of her face delayed a strong feeling of pain. Mei shook her head, trying to match the blurred objects she saw into one.

"Don't. Move," a voice ordered behind her ear.

As her vision returned to normal, she saw a large silhouette staring down at her.

"<Hello?>" repeated the phone. "<Big sister, are you there? What's going on?>"

The moonlight had revealed her assailant to be one of the demons. He had beast-like glowing yellow eyes, scaly skin, lengthy ears and a long, slippery tail.

"Hand over your purse. NOW!"

"<Hey! What's going on???!>" Mr. Quan's voice repeated with concern.

"Hold still—"

The thief was given a dose of Mei's vociferous screaming before turning back and running away. Her wailing hysterics continued until neighbors of all colors came to her aid. Their faces spun around her, giving her a headache with their coinciding questions.

"Oh my God."

"Is she breathing?"

"I got here as fast as I could."

"Is that a black eye?"

"Ma'am! MA'AM." It was the same demon she had seen earlier that night at her mailbox. "Ma'am, calm down. Are you okay? Did you see which direction your attacker went?"

Cody's hefty aunt shoved him aside, fearing he was in cahoots with the mugger. He suddenly morphed into an abhorrent creature, similar in fiendish detail as most of the other black neighbors.

"Ma'am!"

The demon now had no arms and legs, becoming an advancing serpent whose mouth was belching waves of scorching, searing fire. Suddenly, with remorseless effort, it took in a deep breath and unleashed upon Mei a blast that decimated her existence.

"MA'AM!"

The neighbors gathered around her collapsed body, petrified by the purgatory that had overcome her.

CHAPTER 33: TO TAKE AWAY LIFE

"Easily molding phenoxymethylpenicillin moderates the prevention of infection into what experts call Streptococcus pyogenes or, simply put, an orally ingested antibiotic. The multitude of defenses provided by the phenoxymethylpenicillin includes everything from exerting penicillin-sensitive microorganisms to living in the biosynthesis area of the peptidoglycan. The recommended dosage is set at two times a day, most notably for rheumatic fever and parenteral benzylpenicillin."

"What the hell is this?" the fat lady scolded, throwing the typed report back at Cody.

He stood there in front of her desk, oblivious to the tossed papers floating around him.

"Well?" she waited. "What is it?"

"It's the beginning paragraph of my report," replied Cody in a soft voice.

"IT'S WRONG."

He remained standing with his head facing the floor. The papers that were now near his feet lay in stark contrast to the smudgy yellowness of his boss' decades-old office tiling. Some of the tiles had wide cracks with what appeared to be carcasses of dead ladybugs between them.

"Blah bubble blah lorem ipsum blah blah womp womp wha boba ba la dee de da and blah bee ba boo blah blah blah?"

He looked up and blinked twice. "Excuse me?"

"I said: 'How could you NOT know that Streptococcus pyogenes are catalase-negative and why isn't there any mention that phenoxymethylpenicillin is done during the stage of active multiplication?'"

The long pause following her convoluted questioning only infuriated the fat lady further. Her probing eyes suggested to Cody that she was searching for a brain, one that would give her the exact answers she was looking for. He had worked there long enough to know she was like this, but struggled to adapt anyway with the compliant necessities of corporate America.

He intuitively answered what was in his head, "I...I did my best. I didn't know what phenoxeemorphinrangers—"

"Phenoxymethylpenicillin," she corrected. "Nine syllables. Come on."

"Yeah, that. Look, I'm a web developer and...and I didn't expect to be writing these scientific articles myself. I had initially assumed—"

"Don't ever assume, because you can't spell it without being an A-S-S," she cut him off. "Now write the report again and this time get your head out of the clouds. Stop making these simple, easy mistakes."

Cody left the office, closing her door in the method she had instructed him to do—with the handle turned before the door closed all the way, then releasing it so that it didn't make a *click-clacking* noise. It was one of her many pet peeves that the employees were taught to avoid. He had done well following her preferences, though he still had trouble avoiding the usage of "y'all" and he still occasionally stared at her enormous double chin.

As he sat in his cubicle again, he resumed the tedious task of researching the scientific mumbo jumbo. Phenoxymethylpenicillin. Hypovitaminosises. Dendrochronology. Mitochondrion. Chemosynthesis. Oligosaccharide. Cyanobacteria. Somatic-cell mutation.

Paraphimosis. Aspergillus nidulans. Heterothallic. Carbonic anhydrase. Methoxytryptamine. Streptomycetaceae. Catenulisporales.

Pneumonoultramicroscopicsilicovolcanoconiosis.

Cody suddenly bent over and clutched his chest. There was a rapid decline in energy; *a heart attack*, he figured. He placed two fingers on his wrist, trying to detect any irregularity with his pulse, only to discover normal beats. Reality, however, began bending around him, distorting itself like a fun house mirror. It was the only clue needed for him to suspect its origin was supernatural; no, he corrected himself, not supernatural— metaphysical. Picking up a nearby CD, he flipped it to its shiny back side and searched for his reflection, realizing it was fading.

His cubicle's phone rang.

Cody fumbled for a few moments before he mustered enough energy to answer.

"H...Hello?" he answered.

"And you screwed up on your pie chart!" boomed the fat lady's voice. "25.7% of the cyanobacteria lipopolysaccharide is obviously a deviation of 903.20189% of the first 20.934% sample of secondary metabolites notwithstanding the 0.005 probability error alongside the data shown in the ecotoxicology chart. Jesus, Cody, are you retarded?"

"O...Okay."

"ALSO! High susceptibility on pseudomonas aeruginosas based on lack of acquisitions of hypermutated resistances? Really? REALLY?! "

"I don't...I don't under...understand this...science..."

He could barely hold on to the phone. He was fading in and out of existence, his grip no longer as tangible as moments before.

" Obviously the true pathogen can be resisted based on an induced systemic resistance from the host plant which, like pseudomonas aurantiaca, actively influences diacetylfluoroglucylemethane for the positive organisms."

"I'm just...I'm just a web developer..."

Her harsh criticism of him only furthered his demise. *My soul*, he gasped, *it's permanently removing itself this time.*

"CODY QUAN...ARE YOU LISTENING?!"

"Can't...can't..."

"WHAT?"

"I can't do it. Not...not my job...description..."

"Doesn't matter," she hissed. "You're a team player. You do as you're told. A cog in the machine."

Cody collapsed to the floor, his spirit leaving him as he floated toward the ceiling. He watched his own body from above, stiffening and finalizing its last phase as a conforming tool. The person it would become, the identity it would end up as, would define him for the remainder of his life. With a long forgotten sense of urgency, Cody recalled the words of the cosmic hairstylist—*if you knew how much power your mind can wield, you could control your reality.*

His floating spirit concentrated, not sure of how he could combat this silent battle.

"Besides," the fat lady added, "if you want to be promoted you better not question me again. Your opinions don't matter here. Only your soul."

"NOOOOOOOOOO!" his shouts were only audible from the metaphysical plane, though the outburst helped him discover a long- contained desire he thought disappeared. With renewed vigor, Cody pushed his floating spirit closer and closer toward his body, fighting each setback with continual determination.

He was not going to take blind orders. He was not going to think this was all he could be. He was not going to trade safety and comfort for stagnation. He deserved to be cared for by a God that wanted him. He would speak his mind no matter how often his community disapproved of it. He was going to fall in love despite how much society made him feel unwanted.

Cody's soul and body began melding together, creating an explosion of bright light. He had entered the blank white canvas of the otherworld again. With merely a thought, he quickly created mountains and oceans, skies and stars. Cody laughed as he flew around the metaphysical realm, appearing like a comet in the conceived night sky.

Emerge, Cody Quan. Your life is yours to take.

Charlotte's prevalent voice beckoned him back into his cubicle, where he pushed himself up off the floor and confronted the phone with revived poise.

"Listen, you," he began with a steely, imposing voice.

"What?" the fat woman challenged back.

Cody was ready to unleash his frustration in a pent-up, eviscerating reply, something that would express his full displeasure throughout the short time he had worked for the woman. This vile, self-indulgent contemptuously overweight shrew, whose only means of management was to antagonize the livelihood of her laborers, was due to receive her comeuppance—a retribution that would come in the words from Cody Quan's mouth. It would be under an expression so grand, so vilifying that she would clearly understand how much pain she had inflicted upon him.

"FFFFFFFFFFFFFFFUUUUUUUUUUUUUUUCCCCK KKKKKKK YOUUUUUUUUUUUUUUUU!!!"

With that said, Cody slammed the phone down and emptied his cubicle.

———

Andrew Huynh sat calmly and smoked his last cigarette, patiently awaiting for Li'l Bis' return to the bar counter. He admired the new look of The Platinum Star, thinking it was classier, cleaner and devoid of the thugs that used to populate it. He also liked the new clientele—mostly college kids too sheltered and naive to distinguish danger from style—who whispered his name in hushed, admirable tones. Of course, they only knew the word "Andrew," oblivious to the unassuming face that came with the legend.

"Excuse me," asked a female voice beside him, "like, are these stools next to you taken?"

His eyes glanced sideways, mildly annoyed that his thoughts were disrupted. The college-aged girl and her friend seemed so much like the other overly materialistic and skittish Asian suburbanites with an excessive amount of self-importance. Still, he thought, their lascivious framework did serve some value to his eyes, perhaps even satisfying to the prehensile hormones that remained abundant in his mid-forties body.

"They're already taken," he said with cigarette in hand, "but I'm sure I'll fight off the abandoning assholes who left 'em. Have a seat."

"Are you sure?"

"Why wouldn't I be?" Andrew muttered, flicking off tobacco remnants in a nearby ashtray.

The two girls claimed the seats and began chirping away at their gossip, most of which was trivial to the hit man until he delightfully heard his name among the ensuing small talk.

"—and I was, like, trying to hook Phoebe up with my fifty-two year old cousin who knew Andrew Huynh and, like—"

"Excuse me, did you just say 'Andrew Huynh?'" he smirked.

The girls abruptly halted their conversation and curiously faced him.

"Yeah," one of them said, "you know him?"

"Just wondering who your cousin is that knew him. What's his name?"

"Why should it be any of your business?"

"It isn't," he shrugged, "but I doubt Andrew knows any fifty-two-year-olds that hang out in a place like The Platinum Star."

"Bullshit," one of the girls rolled her eyes at him, "what do you know about Andrew, you ugly fat old fart?"

He paused and looked at his cigarette. "Just curious, have either of you ever laid eyes on him?"

They shook their heads.

"My cousin says he's the ultimate badass," the first girl replied, "six feet tall, flat stomach, skinny leather jeans and salon groomed hair."

Andrew raised his eyebrows and nodded his head in amusement.

"I heard he wears Armani Exchange," added the second girl, "everything from head to toe, black and striped like Lee Min-Ho from the Korean dramas."

"Yeah, perfectly trimmed eyebrows too," agreed the first girl.

"Well," Andrew scoffed in a dismissive chuckle, "I doubt those metrosexual Korean 'Prince'-sses could really find the balls to squeeze the trigger in front of another man's eye, all the while laughing in front of the victim's beloved ones without conscience—a hit man so vicious that he finds sport in bashing the skulls of children and then returns home reading Dr. Seuss to his own flesh and blood the same night, all the while patting their heads with the same psychopathic hands that stain themselves in sin."

He smiled, looking at them with a suggestive gleam in his eyes.

"No," he concluded, "such a fearsome man will remind you that the grim reaper is an unassuming, frigid force of nature, dismissive of what anyone thinks, who takes pleasure only in immersing himself within an environment of torment."

The two girls looked at one another, trying to comprehend the full message of Andrew's elaborate soliloquy.

"Well, I still think he's probably cute," giggled the first girl.

"Flat stomach, tall, long hair, emo to the bone," nodded the other.

"Come on, let's go check out Wilbur and see if he's playing Jenga."

Andrew reacted to their dismissal in quiet laughter, flicking his finished cigarette down on the bar's dark concrete floor. He watched the last sizzle of its dull fire subsisting in the blackness before extinguishing it with a swift, brutal stomp.

"Hey, killer," he heard Li'l Bis call out to him, "Piranha's ready to see you now."

Both of them knew why Andrew was called; it was time for the hefty hit man to undertake his primary occupation. Better for it, he thought to himself while following the grizzled bartender through the familiar private hallway. Things had gotten boring for Andrew. Training new talent and crippling late-paying associates were all unsatisfactory replacements for his appetite of murder. It had been so long since his boss wanted someone dead.

"You called me, Piranha?" asked Andrew as he entered the drug baron's modest office.

He noticed the years had taken its toll on Piranha, whose advanced aging was derived from the stress and constant concentration required to maintain his criminal empire. He gestured for Andrew to close the door behind him, sealing themselves from outer interference. Once they were unbothered, Piranha carefully passed a folded letter-size paper to his trusted herald of death. Andrew smirked before unfolding it, knowing it was the anticipated kill list.

"Interesting choices for victims," he remarked, scanning through the names.

"Clean like always," Piranha commanded. "None of the theatrical flair like the time you fed that boy to a tiger."

"That was years ago," chuckled Andrew. "Everyone still remembers that one. No worries. Clean this time. Like always."

"I trust you, Andrew. I always have."

"By the end of the week, these people are as good as dead."

"See to it," the kingpin nodded.

The hefty hit man glanced at the list one more time and grinned at the final name on it:

- Jack Tsing
- Ping Narendrapong
- Red Eye
- Dimitri
- Pete Mok

He sighed as he folded the paper eight times, putting it into his pocket. He began formulating a strategy. The Cambodian woman and her hired gun would provide the heaviest chance of resistance, he noted, but he had the element of surprise on the Russian, who didn't know of Piranha's upcoming betrayal. Jack would not be a problem at all and Pete, he grinned—Pete's death would be savored.

"<You what?!>"

"<Today job quit I did>," nodded Cody.

His father had been hoping the night's dinner would be a remedy for their family's incursions over the past week. After inviting his sister Mei, Cody's Aunt Hannah and Kiki over, he was ready to unleash his passionate hatred for the black race in a rare, openly accepted opportunity for unfiltered grievance. It would be good that they released their tension, he thought, one where they didn't worry about political correctness and just speak on his perception of truth.

But Cody, who had been pleasantly deferential since his move back in with his parents, decided to shock them with his defiant news. Mr. Quan hoped he had perhaps heard wrong, that his son's poor grasp of Cantonese meant he quit the day's work because he was tired.

"<You didn't mean that>," Cody's father nervously laughed off. From across the table he saw Mei smiling. He thought his sister looked ridiculous with her black eye. He turned back to face Cody. "<Sometimes your Chinese is so bad it's almost like you are saying something else, I—>"

"I quit my job today, dad," Cody reiterated, this time in perfect English.

"<Hahaha!!!!!!!>" Mei burst with laughter. "<I knew it! Your son is a loser again, little brother. My son Duke wins!>"

"<We'll discuss this later>," Mr. Quan grunted while picking up pieces of cloud ear fungi and gingko nuts. "<Here,

eat some Buddha's Delight. Let it purify the rebellion within you.>"

Cody stared at the contents his father had inserted into his bowl. He loved Buddha's Delight, but something about eating it because he was told to irked him. Using his chopsticks, he quickly picked it up and returned it back into his father's bowl, looking at the elder Quan in defiance.

"<What are you doing?>" Mr. Quan asked.

"I don't want anything to go with my rice," Cody replied in a mutinous tone.

"<Don't be disagreeable. It's rude.>"

"It's my choice. I like my rice tonight to be plain and tasteless."

Father and son looked at one another in silent, challenging stares. The other dinner guests glanced at one another, wondering if they should intercede. With one final try, Mr. Quan picked up the Buddha's Delight with his chopsticks and transferred it back into his son's bowl.

Cody frowned and returned the food again.

"<Ehhh, cousin Cody>," Ace interrupted, "<why don't you give that to me? I love fungi.>"

Mr. Quan quickly dipped his chopsticks into the large bowl of Buddha's Delight and gave Ace a cluster of it. He then resumed staring back at his son.

"<Cody, be a good boy>," insisted his Aunt Hannah. "<Just eat what your father generously put into your bowl. Food is love. Think about it, there are starving kids in Africa.>"

The mere mention of the continent temporarily took Mr. Quan's attention away from Cody.

"<Don't feel pity for Africa. It's karma what's happening to those people—all the crime and suffering those blacks have done. I'm glad millions of them are dying. I hope they get more diseases and end horrifically disfigured. They can serve as examples of what people can reincarnate into when

they do bad things! That's why I always give more than my fair share to the temple. I hope in my next life I'll have the blondest hair and the bluest eyes and—>"

"STOP BEING SUCH AN IGNORANT UNCLE TOM, DAD!" screamed Cody.

Without a moment's hesitation, he got up and walked upstairs into his room, taking his bowl of rice with him.

"<Hey, come back!>" Cody's mother called after him. "<You'll attract bugs into your room with that food!>"

When she heard Cody slam his bedroom door, she glared at her husband and shook her head in disgust.

"<What? Was it something I said?>" inquired Cody's father. "<And who's Uncle Tom?>"

"<My sister's husband in Macau is named Tom>," suggested Hannah.

"<The loser with the gambling problem?>" Mr. Quan scratched his head. "<That makes no sense, how am I like him?>"

He shrugged, deciding to deal with his son later.

———

Sometime during the middle of the night, a loud noise woke up Cody. It was the distinct sound of smashed glass. *Plates or glass bowls*, concluded Cody, *it had to be. Perhaps the cat—?*

"Meow," Toby purred.

He shook his head in relief as he saw the feline's bulky silhouette walking in front of the window. Drifting back into sleep, he was shocked to suddenly hear another sound of smashed glass from below. This time he quickly rose, debating his next course of action. He supposed he could turn on the lights; though, if it really were an intruder, Cody thought, making himself known would be dangerous. Instead, he opted for a stealth approach, tiptoeing his way towards his bedroom door. Opening it slightly ajar, he peeked into the darkness of the second floor hallway. The hallway's visibility was limited— the only light seeping out of the Buddha room from the dull red lights of the Guan Yin statue. However, it was enough to indicate the coast was clear. He quietly made his way into the storage closet halfway across.

Crunch!

Cody's heart almost gave out when he heard yet another noise that came from downstairs. *It was definitely near the kitchen area*, he deduced. With adrenaline flowing in his veins, his temporarily sharp senses enabled him to feel his way towards what he was looking for in the closet: his Little League aluminum baseball bat.

Before making his bold descent downstairs, however, he questioned whether or not he should wake up his parents. They were close by, sleeping at the other side of the hallway. He quickly dismissed that thought, concluding they would panic and make the situation worse. Regardless, he admitted it was crucial to seek an ally.

"Ace?" he whispered, discreetly knocking on the guest room door.

No answer.

Cody tried the door handle, discovering that Ace had unlocked his room.

"Ace," he repeated in hushed tones as he walked in the darkness. "Wake up."

When he reached near the head of the guest bed, he saw that the covers had been pulled over the pillows. Cody reached for the protruding lump, figuring it was Ace's head. Instead, his hand caught a cluster full of blanket. He immediately removed the covers, revealing nothing but linen.

Gone, he realized. Had his cousin heard the noise too?

It was possible the original crash that had awakened Cody might not have been the first one. Perhaps Ace had gone before him and investigated it for himself. Could his cousin be in danger? With bat in hand, he quickly left the guest room, descending downstairs two steps at a time.

His mind calculated many of the possibilities that could occur should he see the burglar. Should he deliver a warning or attack by surprise? Maybe he should head back upstairs and call the police instead. Why didn't his father install a security system? Perhaps the house had come with one and no one had thought of activating it.

Think, Cody. Think.

However, before he could contemplate any more, he immediately saw a figure walking awkwardly around the kitchen. Cody leaned near the doorway, quietly observing its actions. Whoever this was, he concluded, displayed movements contrary to someone trying to steal—the person was pacing in circles, not particularly searching or even knowing which direction to go. In fact, Cody realized, they were patterns of a sleepwalker, one he had seen before.

"Hey, Ace!" Cody called out.

He turned on the kitchen lights and approached his cousin, still pacing in his slumbering trance. A sigh of relief came over him as he chuckled and shook Ace into consciousness.

"AH!" his cousin shouted.

"It's okay, it's okay, man," chuckled Cody.

"<Ehhh, cousin Cody. What am I doing in the kitchen?>"

"You sleepwalked again, you dick! Hahaha. Boy, did

you scare me when you crashed at something onto the...floor...I...thought..."

Cody immediately paused and looked around the kitchen.

"<Something wrong, cousin Cody?>"

"Ace, did you crash into anything?" Cody asked, suddenly feeling a bout of fear again. "I don't see any glass or objects on the floor."

He looked at his cousin only to find Ace's wide-eyed reaction toward something behind him. Cody turned around just in time to see a dark-skinned fist smack across his face. The impact immediately sent him to the floor, causing him to lose possession of his bat. Cody heard sounds of struggle as he shook his head to recover from the dizziness.

"<OOOF!>" Ace puffed, taking a blow to the stomach.

Though his young cousin wasn't putting up much of a fight, Cody found that it stalled the intruder enough. He quickly leapt toward the intruder, realizing in dismay he hadn't a clue what to do once he tackled him. The intruder immediately gave Cody an elbow, separating himself from their entanglement and making a break towards the front door. To the burglar's surprise, Ace suddenly popped out of the sofa and swung the bat at his legs, causing him to crash towards the living room wall.

"<Cousin Cody!!!>" screamed Ace. <"What do I do?!>"

They were now in the partially lit living room, too dark to make out what was going on. As Cody ran over to help, he heard more noises of struggle with Ace seemingly on the losing end of it.

"<OW! AH!>" his cousin yelped.

Cody grabbed the intruder in the darkness, both colliding on the floor again. With animal-like instinct, Cody bit into his arm, wounding the assailant before taking more elbows to the head. The blows did not succeed this time in making Cody release his hold. The robber was light, Cody realized, as much a novice in fighting as he was, probably not even a full-grown adult.

"Ace..." Cody mustered, "...help me...grab...him..."

"<Ehhh, I can't see, cousin, I—>"

The burglar gave Ace a swift kick, causing Ace to kneel down in pain. He then delivered clumsy elbow after clumsy elbow until he was free. Both the intruder and Cody ran and fought around the house until they reached the front door with the burglar struggling to unlock it. There, Cody charged at him full-speed, barely missing the intended target and accidentally slamming into the front door.

As he saw light coming from upstairs, Cody witnessed the burglar running back into the living room.

"<What's going on?>" he heard his father's voice.

"<UNCLE!>" Ace shouted. "<WE HAVE A ROBBER! HE'S HEADING THROUGH THE BACK DOOR!>"

Cody gathered himself quickly and ran another route. There were two ways to the backyard, he knew—the path the burglar had taken across the living room was much longer. With merely a couple of turns, Cody had already reached the other door to the backyard. In the moonlight he easily spotted the intruder making a break towards the lake. Both of them were high on adrenaline, running with disregard to fatigue. Cody found the chase easy, eventually catching up to the thief and tackling him once more.

"Uahh!" shouted the robber, landing a soft, uninspired punch to Cody's face.

He was tired, Cody realized.

"You...huff...puff...you hit...like a girl!" he mocked.

This time, the burglar submitted, with his body lying on the ground facing Cody. Cody placed a knee on top of his chest, fists in position to punch him. With the moonlight gleaming at them unhindered, the intruder's appearance became fully visible: a dark-skinned African-American teenager whose adolescent features were still very much in development. The youth looked frightened, knowing he had done a wrongful thing and feared the consequences.

The natural luminescence suddenly gave way to the brilliant radiance of artificial light; Cody's parents were heard coming out along with Ace's nervous chattering.

"<Where are they, do you see them?>" his father asked. "<Why is it so quiet?>"

"<Oh my God, my son...my son...>" stammered Cody's mother nervously.

From the sounds of their footsteps, Cody knew they were coming closer, though he dared not turn around and face them lest he give the teenage boy an opportunity to fight back.

"<There they are!>" Ace announced.

The three of them surrounded Cody and the intruder. With his Lorcin .22 pistol pointed at the boy, Mr. Quan signaled for Cody to get off. Cody nodded and slowly released his knee from the boy's chest, backing off until he was beside his father.

"<You were really stupid to chase him on your own>," opined Mr. Quan. "<He could've been armed.>"

Cody remained silent, staring at the burglar.

"<Sweetheart, are you hurt?>" his mother asked him.

"<He's fine>," snapped Mr. Quan. "<Why don't you go back in and find me some rope to tie this nigger son-of-a-bitch. And Ace—?"

"<Yes, uncle?>"

"<Call the police. Tell them that we've been broken into and we caught the burglar.>"

"<Of course, uncle.>"

Both Cody and his father were left alone with the intruder. They stood in silence for a few moments until Mr.

Quan awkwardly handed his son the gun. Cody had never touched it before, nor knew of its existence. How many firearms had his father purchased since they had moved into this new luxury home?

"<Take it>," his father ordered.

Hesitantly, Cody held the cold piece of metal in his hand. It was much heavier than he anticipated, but he also felt an overwhelming power, as if it made him judge and jury.

"<Don't point it at the ground, silly boy>," Mr. Quan criticized. "<Point it at him. Make sure he stays put.>"

Cody did as he was told, pointing the gun at the burglar. The profusely sweating youth looked him in the eye. It frightened Cody how much influence the gun wielded and how it had suddenly turned him into a god. He started counting with each quickening heartbeat how soon it would be before the authorities would come.

"Shoot him," his father suddenly commanded in English.

"W...what?"

"Kill him."

"Y-You're joking, right?" Cody glanced at his father and saw from his scowling face that it was not a jesting statement.

"<No>," Mr. Quan replied in an eerily calm tone. "<He trespassed into our property. We could tell the police he was attacking us and we had to shoot him in self-defense. These people...they'll never learn. Since I've been in America, all I've ever encountered from them is hatred and uselessness. They've had thirty years to prove me wrong and never a day passes that I hadn't thought about how much I hate them. If I could put a mask on and hurt as many of them as I can, I would. I just always wanted to get even. They're un-evolved monkeys, no capable of contributing to society than discarded fish bones and yesterday's newspaper. They do nothing but rob innocent

Chinese people and make music talking about being gangsters and raping women. This nigger piece of trash deserves to have a bullet through his heart and have his soul fed by Diyu hellhounds. May the gods have mercy on his nigger soul and deliver us good karma for doing this good deed. Now do it, son.>"

Cody froze, looking at the teenager who was too frightened to speak. He thought about Derrick James and the other black children from elementary school who had pinned him to the monkey bars and frequently beat him. To further add to the humiliation, the same group called Cody names, such as slant-eyed, China Boy and egg roll. He thought about Aunt Mei's black eye and how it was given to her by a black man who had no reservations about hitting women. He thought about every media report of black violence and every hate-spewed hip-hop lyric degrading women, glorifying bloodshed, and embracing racism.

"<Do it>," Mr. Quan whispered in his ear.

But Cody also remembered his client Maxine Walters. And the music of Marvin Gaye. And the speeches of Nelson Mandela. And the many black people who taught him life's little things like how to put in contacts, or how to write better, or the usage of kitty litter to melt snow—among the many other countless favors he could probably recall in a calmer moment. And besides, he rationalized, this burglar didn't break into their house because he was black; he did it because he wanted to steal.

"<Please>," gently begged his father. "<Be obedient. Do as your father says. Bring honor to your family. Like a good Chinese boy.>"

Cody loved his dad. The man had a good heart and treated friends and family alike. He was kindhearted to strangers, often naively breaking into their comfort zones to help them. And despite his wife's frequent jabbering, Quan Min-Lo was a fantastic husband who never cheated or was cruel to her. He gave every last penny to his family and without him, Cody would never have had the coddled life that he enjoyed.

He owed his father everything, including gratitude.

Cody squeezed the trigger and sent an audible shock wave across the quiet neighborhood. When they heard it, the two recently arrived policemen quickened their pace as Ace led them through the backyard.

"What happened?!" barked one of the officers. "We heard a gunshot!"

They found Cody holding his father's gun upward in the air; he was too stunned and emotionless for normal interaction. Cody was staring not at them, but at his father, who seemed equally dispassionate with head bowed down. The intruder remained lying on the ground as he was, breathing heavily, quietly thanking the stars.

"Sir, are you shot?" asked the officer, flipping the teenager over and handcuffing him.

He remained silent. The officer searched him, finding no weapons or anything else out of the ordinary.

"He's clean," observed the officer. "No gunshot wounds or weapons on him."

His partner walked up to Cody and persuaded him to put down the gun.

"I fired into the air," Cody finally spoke in a solemn voice. "I couldn't do it. I just couldn't."

"Put the gun down on the ground, please," requested the officer.

Cody slowly kneeled and gently placed it on the grass, happy to be emancipated of its cold, steel touch. As he got back up, he stared at his father once again in an emotional mixture of disappointment, pity and shame.

Yes, his dad was a good man. But malice infected him like a disease.

CHAPTER 34: VENGEANCE

Dimitri hated cigarettes, but the nicotine was all he had to calm himself from mounting pressure. He was red-eyed—deprived of sleep from the sudden drop in sales. Yet, despite the lukewarm revenue stream, White Vodka was more popular than ever among the patrons of The Platinum Star. It disturbed him that perhaps his own dealers were blatantly skimming their cut, not so much for their audacity but for their foolishness. Russian mobsters were well familiar with how gruesome their punishment could be. More so, he was worried about himself, sweating at what his bosses had in store for him should he fail. Their patience, after all, had already been worn thin—why else had they sent him half a world away, to a place far different from Moscow?

He paced nervously around his office, deciding whether or not to vanish. It was still early evening, hours before the club opened. There was also plenty of leftover money that was set up for his promoters, Marty and Wilbur, but his own survival was of greater importance.

Perhaps...

He chuckled to himself, admitting that his sleep deprivation was causing him to overreact. It was best he found the answers directly.

"<Illarion. Mikhail>," he called out to his two doorway bodyguards in Russian.

"<Yes, Dimitri?>" asked Illarion.

Their boss waved them over, putting his arms around each of their shoulders.

"<If you've heard something, you'd tell me, wouldn't you?>"

"<Of course>," nodded Mikhail.

"<What have you been hearing concerning our dealers? Do you think they're pocketing the profits?>"

"<I do not know, sir>," Mikhail shook his head.

Illarion was a different story; his obvious fidgeting was arousing suspicion.

"<You are shaking, Illarion. Why?>"

"<I have seen the customers buying White Vodka from other people.>" Illarion admitted, sheepishly relaying the bad news.

Dimitri slowly nodded; his worst fear had been realized—somehow Piranha had found a way to synthesize the drug. If that were the case, the Russian feared it would only be a matter of time before he was marked for death.

"<Get the car ready>," ordered Dimitri. "<This is dangerous news. We are sitting ducks now.>"

Illarion immediately headed out, placing a hand near his gun holster in case of trouble. However, no sooner had he opened the office door, two bullets came flying through, penetrating his heart. Dimitri watched in horror as his loyal bodyguard collapsed lifelessly to the floor with blood flowing from his mouth.

Andrew Huynh, with his calm demeanor, entered with gun in hand.

Mikhail immediately drew his pistol on the assassin, though he proved too slow as the hit man fired a quick bullet to his head. Fortunately, the action bought enough time for Dimitri to throw a lamp at Andrew, distracting the contract killer enough for a run at the door. From there, Dimitri darted down the stairwell, barely slipping a few times in the process.

The hit man coolly walked to the top of the stairwell, watching the Russian clumsily descend the spiraling steps. He aimed his gun at the panicked Dimitri and fired. The Russian felt a sharp wound in his shoulder and stumbled the rest of the way, collapsing on the ground floor. Slowly, Andrew whistled his way downstairs where Dimitri's body was.

"Piranha sends his regards," spat Andrew.

He kneeled down and fired twice into the Russian's chest.

One down, four to go.

———

Ever since the death of DJ Zack, Marty noticed a drastic difference in Wilbur's body language. The once frenetic exaltation the promoter displayed had now given way to a gloomy stoic behavior. This was bad news for Marty, who had spent his advance payment on his wife, particularly now that she was pregnant and they needed more money than ever. He depended on The Platinum Star quota being fulfilled, but the contract's deadline was looming.

"I-I-I j-j-just can't d-d-do it any m-m-more!" screamed a crying Wilbur.

Marty patted his partner's arm and helped wipe away his smeared mascara. Patrons had begun filling the club, necessitating a move into a more clandestine setting.

"Waahhh, er, huh-ah," Marty nervously replied. "Mm, maybe we should discuss this over in the corner."

He gave the metrosexual a little nudge, hinting for them to move away from prying eyes. Wilbur, however, quickly brushed Marty's hand aside.

"N-n-n-no!!!" he wept, "I-I-I-I don't c-c-care if a-a-anyone sees me c-c-cry!"

"Heh, come now, Wilbur. We gotta look for the cameras, remember? Meh-heh? Ah-ah?"

Wilbur reluctantly followed him into a secluded area of the club, where Marty took out some used tissue for Wilbur to blow his nose.

"DJ Z-Z-Z-Zack died and w-w-we just act like it's n-n-nothing!"

"Ffft, ppppfff, now now, that's not, heh, you know that's not true. I had tears in my eyes all night long. Wah-uh, you know, Xia had to coax me to stop. I love DJ Mack."

"Z-Z-Zack! H-h-his name was DJ Z-Z-Zack!"

"That's what I just said," Marty protested. "Now come on, wah-eh, we both know that, heh, what DJ, huh, Zack wanted the most was for us to turn this place into a badass party, wah-mah? 'Asian Pride' and all that, you know? In fact, heh, he once told me that he was inspired by what you do, Wilbur. You're a winner. Wah-heh. Think about it—you showed Cody! Why do you think I'm not his best friend anymore? Heh-ha? Mmm-hmmm. You know?"

Wilbur nodded in understanding. "B-b-because y-y-you know that I-I-I take g-g-good care of my f-f-friends!!!!"

"Wer-emm, I was about to say because you're a, heh, pimp, but yeah, heh, you're a good guy. The best guy!"

He patted his partner's back, relieved that the tears had stopped flowing. Wilbur was a mess; at least, a disaster in terms of the metrosexual's usually finicky standards. His hair reached out everywhere like a wild virus running amok and the sporadic smearing of his makeup made his face look like the scene of an oil spill.

"I t-t-think I-I-I need some t-t-time off. I'm b-b-burned out."

Marty's heart sank. This was exactly not what he needed. "No, er, that's, heh, that's not what I meant, ah-hah?"

It was no use.

Wilbur pushed Marty aside and sat alone in a corner where he wallowed in self-pity. Having exhausted all of his psychological tactics, Marty gave up with a disappointed sigh; he knew his emotive partner well enough to understand the recovery would take time. It was now necessary for him to discharge the emergency plan of using Jack as backup. His cousin was a wild card, but the current momentum seemed to have flowed Jack's way. Besides, Marty noticed, the unruly black sheep had displayed a peculiar upbeat attitude since DJ Zack's overdose. There was no doubt an established connection between Jack's sudden rise in popularity and the growing trend of drug use.

Making his way around the club, he easily spotted his swindling cousin by the large clump of people around him. Jack sat leaning on one of the lounge sofas, surrounding himself with loose women and intermediary cronies.

"So I fucking told this bitch I bet I could buy you to suck my dick," bragged Jack. "Shit, I don't care what your principles are, it doesn't matter what your parents taught you, everyone can be bought for money."

"So what happened?" hollered one of the cronies.

"She sucked my dick," shrugged Jack, "too bad she was terrible at it!"

The crowd erupted in laughter. He pulled out a few wrapped White Vodka pills and tossed them to the floor. Like wild animals, members of his entourage leapt forth, wrestling amongst themselves for the drugs that compulsively controlled them. Jack was pleased to witness this coarse exhibit of depravity, acknowledging that humanity was always at its worse beneath the surface of civility.

From a distance, Marty's cloddish waving successfully caught his cousin's eye.

"Excuse me, assholes and bitches," Jack declared, not particularly minding which of the addicts he stepped on. "Family is calling."

He put an arm around Marty's shoulder and walked him aside.

"Can you believe these people, Marty? Damn if they aren't the sorriest tools of humanity I've ever seen. "

"Mmm-huh," Marty agreed, "nice shirt, man! Hah! Glad to see that you like the presents I bought for you."

"What are you talking about?" inquired Jack. "You didn't buy me this."

"What? I bought you that shirt? Oh yeah! I did! Heh. Hah! So I see that you're surrounded by friends now, eh? Guess that made Wilbur jealous, you know? Huh? Eh?"

Jack shook his head and dropped his arm from Marty's shoulder. "I see what you're doing. What do you want, Marty?"

"Huh? What do I want what?"

With a long sigh, Jack stopped and rolled his eyes at his hoodwinking cousin.

"This is either about the drugs or it's about the pussy," Jack stated matter-of-factly. "Don't fucking beat around the bush. We're family. Spill."

Marty chuckled, tugging at his collar with a finger.

"I, er, wha..."

"It's the fucking drugs," correctly guessed his cousin. "I've heard Xia's been giving you plenty. She's already bloating after two months. It's gonna be one big baby, man."

"Jack, you, wah-meh, you gotta help me," Marty pleaded.

"Heh. As I suspected. Yeah, I heard the pretty boy's been overwrought with emotion since his bestie died. What's the problem? The Russian's going to pay you guys anyway, isn't he?"

"Sigh, not...not exactly, merr -aaahh," Marty stammered, "heh, you know...heh...they...fffftt. There's a quota I gotta fulfill before I get the money."

Jack smiled. "Fucking A, Marty. Why didn't you tell me earlier? I could've taken over Princess Wilbur's place. Look at these people—I'm practically their king now ever since I took control of their drugs."

"Heh, yeah," Marty grinned, "you're the best! Woo! Ha! You're the man! I knew I should've gone with you."

He had apparently pressed all of Jack's right buttons; the troublemaker loved having his ego stroked.

"Sure, man," agreed Jack, "I'll help you out with the rest of the quota. How many do you need?"

"Three thousand new faces, give or take."

Jack turned around and gestured for his cousin to follow. "Not a problem, Marty, my man. Say, mind following me? I gotta take a piss and smoke."

"Mm-huh, the bathroom's that way." Marty pointed in the other direction.

"I said I gotta take a piss AND smoke. That means outside, fucker."

Making their way across the club, Marty observed the growing disinterest in the expressions of the clubbers. The 'You're the Celebrity' gimmick had run its course on them, no longer concealing its lameness. It was a sign for Marty to move on once he was paid. He needed to scheme and find another victim he could scrounge off—perhaps a trading card game that he could muster up funding for from some naive angel investors. That was a good idea, he smiled to himself.

Once they were outside, they made their way to a nearby alleyway. Jack spoke with much criticism about The Platinum Star's drug trade, predicting their recklessness would reveal the dirty secrets of White Vodka sooner or later. Marty waited at a lighted area while Jack relieved himself in a darker part of the alley.

"—and like I said," Jack continued while urinating, "you've gotta take advantage of the now. Sure it was a bold move, but I went right to the drug kingpin here—a guy named Piranha—and I pushed him into giving me a cut. Know what that asshole did? He had his goons point guns at me forcing me to take a shitty five percent. So I agreed, but I just marked up everything without him knowing it. Motherfucker thought he could scare me. What do I gotta be scared about except—"

Blam! Blam!

The sound of two sudden gunshots sent Marty tripping over himself. As he nervously tried to get back up, a hefty figure with a gun emerged into the alleyway lights.

"I, heh, eh, heh...please don't kill me," Marty pleaded in a whimpering tone. " I got, ah-mah, I got a wife and a kid. Please please please don't kill me."

"Your cousin messed with the wrong people," explained Andrew.

He walked and pointed his gun at Marty, who fell on his knees and prayed for mercy.

"Now, now, heh," pleaded Marty, "hey, let me to tell you a joke, heh. Er, ah, ahhhh...er, how do you plan a space party? You planet. Huh heh huh? Get it? Plan it? Planet? Okay, okay, heh, ah, ahhh, sighhhh, heh, ahhhhh..."

Marty began sobbing near Andrew's feet. The hit man observed him in fascination, dismissing him as a coward and an idiot.

"You're pathetic," Andrew said, putting his gun away. "You're a disgrace to Asian men. Grow some balls."

Marty remained on bended knees, closing his eyes as he felt his bladder surrendering. A puddle grew underneath him, encompassing his feet and knees. He dared not move until he heard the hefty man's footsteps venture away at a safe distance, signifying his exit. The gutless con artist slowly opened an eye, looking left to right before opening the other one, and slowly picked himself up. Though his jeans felt cold and sticky with his own urine dripping down his legs, Marty made the uncomfortable walk to the dark part of the alleyway, calling for his cousin.

"Jack? Er, hehrm, Jack?"

He took a deep breath, knowing what he was expecting. With an uncharacteristic display of courage, the former salesman brought out his iPhone and activated its flashlight application.

"Meh-ah, ah no. Noooo," moaned Marty. His own suspicions were confirmed: Jack Tsing was dead.

———

Persistent knocking from the counter of the Mokco Polo food truck disturbed Pete from his slumber. The new entrepreneur awkwardly collapsed in his own folding chair, causing a high-pitched laughter outside of the truck. He slowly rubbed his pained body as he picked himself back up. It was still daylight, Pete observed, but summer evenings were often deceptive from the brightness of the sky.

Pete heard the knocking again.

He peered out of his food truck window, unable to find the instigator. Believing it to be a hoax or his own imagination, he began turning around until he noticed a child's hand jutting from the top of the counter. He immediately peered down at it, noticing a Hispanic child.

"Whatchoo want, lil' nigga?" Pete nodded.

"Can I have a Chinese taco?"

"Which one? The Kung Pao Mokco or the Sweet and Sour Mokco?"

"I like the one with duck."

"I ain't sellin' the Peking Mokco no mo'. Just them two."

"Man, this shit weak."

Pete gave out an expression of disgust. "Nigga, watch ya language, lil' ma'fa. Small niggaz like you shouldn't curse. Fuckin' shit, dawg."

The kid made a face.

"So pick," Pete demanded.

"Which one's better?"

"Kung Pao, my nigga. Trust."

"Okay," replied the little Mexican kid, plopping down a five-dollar bill, "I'll take one."

Pete took the money and rang up the cash register, secretly happy that he had a customer. Things had been slower than anticipated for his food truck business, a start which tested his patience. Still, he thought, prison had taught him the value of humility, that survival was dependent on keeping calm and picking battles. He had forgotten that lesson on his first day of work when he took on other food trucks from the "hot circle," an area of town where the most popular food trucks gathered. Pete couldn't compete with the big dogs yet, he learned, making a mental note of his mistakes.

"Dammmmn," the kid complimented after first bite, "this is GOOD."

"Appreciate the words, li'l man," Pete grinned.

"Why ain't you got customers?"

"I got you, ain't I?"

"I mean more people. Adults, man."

"Fuck if I know. Maybe it's the purple paint color. Doesn't exactly look like a food truck, know what I'm sayin'? Thinkin' maybe we make it orange instead."

"You should make a Twitter account and shit. Facebook it too."

"Nigga," Pete sighed, knowing he didn't know much about computers. "Nigggaaaaaa..."

"Man, you don't know how to do all that shit, eh?"

"'Course I do, li'l man," lied Pete.

"I'll do it for you," the kid insisted.

"What? For free, nigga?"

"Hell naw. Wanna cut."

Pete rolled his eyes and shooed him off, too embarrassed to admit the child's advice was right. He had so much to learn about this new world, one that was now immersed in social media and smartphones. All this dependence on technology was enough to make the thirty-one-year-old feel like an antique.

As it loomed closer to nine o'clock in the evening, Pete reluctantly accepted that he had served only one customer for the day. He folded back the counter and closed the window, double-checking the food storage while properly strapping the sauce drums. It would be helpful to get an assistant, he sighed, almost tripping over a large hot sauce container. He shook his head and carried it, looking around for storage space, but the folding chair had taken up the remaining area.

"Guess you'll just have ta sit in the passenger seat," Pete muttered to the container.

He brought it to the front seat of the truck, strapping it with the passenger seat belt. Still disappointed by the low sales,

Pete took his time walking towards the driver's side, hoping there would be a last-minute customer; he was willing to take out all the equipment again if that was the case. When passersby showed no interest, he gave up and sat behind the steering wheel.

It took three tries with the keys before the old engine obliged.

When it finally started, Pete set the gear to drive, fiddling with the radio stations while making his way out of the parking lot. There was little to no traffic when he got on the freeway; cars honked and passed him. They occasionally flashed their lights to complain of his truck's slow speed.

"Dang," he laughed out loud, "what y'all hurryin' fo'? Impatient ass motherfuckas."

The radio played an old rap song he used to like. Tupac Shakur's "I Ain't Mad at Cha" spoke to him, digging into his soul's trials and tribulations. Pete didn't want the song to end, mouthing out the lyrics he had memorized since he first heard it two decades ago. He felt sad at how quickly time flew, missing the days he thought himself invincible, when it was possible to know about death but never truly believing it could happen. He used to joke that maybe when people turned thirty, they'd learn that death was one big hoax.

Too bad it wasn't, he sighed.

An annoying light from the side mirror immediately terminated his reminiscing. He cursed at yet another tailgating car behind him.

"Just pass me, damn," hissed Pete.

The car continued to follow him, with no hint of changing lanes. Annoyed, Pete signaled and decided to move out of the way. To his surprise, the car did the same, remaining behind him.

"Yo, what the hell?"

He eased his acceleration, hoping it would encourage the follower to pass him. When the car remained behind him, Pete accelerated again, this time to eighty miles an hour. The car followed suit.

"Too slow, too fast, what do you want?"

Suddenly, the shadowing vehicle flashed its high beams twice, indicating it was personal. Pete began breathing hard, anxious to know who it could be. Perhaps his sister? A friend? Maybe someone who was so hungry he wanted Pete to stop his food truck in the middle of the freeway? Leaving little to mystery, the car suddenly accelerated to the left of the Mokco Polo, revealing itself as Andrew Huynh's silver Audi SUV.

"Oh, SHIT!" shouted Pete.

Slowly the tinted passenger side window of the Audi opened, disclosing the hefty hit man with a Smith & Wesson M&P15-22P semiautomatic.

"Farewell, Petey boy," Andrew muttered.

Pete slammed on the breaks as bullets sprayed out of the assassin's machine gun. Passing cars honked their horns while barely avoiding the slowing food truck. Frightened, yet filled with excitement, Pete accelerated full speed toward the right-most lane, knowing he would be a harder target on the smaller streets.

"Chase him! CHASE HIM!" Andrew ordered the driver as they saw the Mokco Polo speeding through.

The food truck exited at the next off-ramp, running through the feeder lane's red lights and turning onto the regular streets away from the freeway. Both cars weaved through traffic as pandemonium reigned around the nearby buildings and restaurants.

"Get close!" the hit man demanded. "Enough for me to shoot his tires out or get him through the window!"

"I'm trying!" pleaded the driver, "but other cars are in the way!"

Andrew lost his patience and began firing in the direction of the other cars. The vehicles began pulling over to the side as traffic unfolded for a clear shot of Pete's food truck. The SUV sped up, following the Mokco Polo, running red light after red light. Andrew quickly tossed out the used magazine as he reloaded his gun with another.

"Just a few yards closer..." he smiled.

Suddenly, a Metrorail train buzzed right behind Pete's vehicle, causing Andrew's driver to slam on the breaks, barely missing a collision.

"Fucking Main Street," cursed Andrew. "Go around. A big food truck like that can't be too hard to find."

Pete could feel his heart pounding, knocking on his chest as if it wanted to burst out. Now that the SUV was no longer in his rearview mirror, he pulled into a tight one-way back road, bringing the Mokco Polo to a stop. He placed his hand across his forehead and wiped a large pool of sweat from his face. Panicked, he remembered Andrew's warning a week ago when he promised to hurt his family. Pete shifted the transmission into park and took out his iPhone, nervously trying to figure out how to make a call.

"Shit, why 'dem things so complicated?" he shouted, frustrated that he had to poke through a few menu items to find a numeric keypad. When he typed in his sister's number, he scratched his head, wondering why the phone wasn't making the call. It was then that he realized he had accidentally opened the phone's calculator application, causing him to scream a few obscenities before finding the correct keypad.

"Hello?" finally answered his sister. Korean pop music could be heard playing in the background.

"This Pete. Anything happen?!"

"Huh? What're you talking about?"

"He said he was gonna rape you and mom and film that shit on YouTube!"

"Who?"

"Andrew, bitch!"

"Who's Andrew?"

"The motherfucka who be tryin' to kill me! Shit, lay off that weed, nigga! I mentioned who he was so many times!"

A sudden tap at the driver's window frightened Pete, causing him to drop his phone. He slowly turned his head around and saw a stranger.

"W-What you want, man?" asked Pete, who followed through on the stranger's request to lower the window.

"Hey, bro, your food truck opened, bro?" asked the man.

"N...nah, man. Nah."

"Then what are you just parking here for?"

"Man, some niggas be tryin' to kill—"

High beams from the silver Audi suddenly pulled over in front of Pete's food truck.

"Fuck!" Pete spat. "How'd they find me so fast?"

Andrew wasted no time and unleashed a barrage of bullets at the food truck. Its windows were garnished with holes as were its headlights, tires, hood and bumper. With calm certainty that the former thug was dead this time, Andrew smirked and calmly removed the used magazine from his Smith & Wesson.

"Sorry, Pete," he muttered to himself, "I was going to be more melodramatic than this as I had initially promised you, but time was of the essence. You'll just have to settle for a quick death."

The hit man nodded to the driver, indicating it was time for them to pull back and speed away. As they left, the stranger found the courage to peek out from his cover, witnessing Pete's slumped and stained body. Soon, other witnesses of the ruckus came out and investigated the riddled Mokco Polo.

"Oh my God."

"There's so much blood. So much blood!"

"I don't have my mobile phone with me! Somebody please call 911!"

"Sir? Sir? He's not responding, he's not responding!"

"I just bought a mokco from him days ago. He seemed nice."

"Hello? 911? There's been an emergency. A food truck just experienced a drive-by. The owner's been killed."

"Wait! He's still breathing! He's not dead!"

"What do you mean he's not dead? Look at all that blood!"

"This...wait, this isn't blood. It's some kind of hot sauce..."

"Hey, you're right! He's still breathing. This guy's still breathing! The fool just fainted!"

Ping, Red Eye, and Knife were now honorary members of the Happy Lotus; at least, that's what they were led to believe with the restaurant's free meals and warmer-than-usual reception. Mr. Quan saw them as protection, accurately guessing that they were mercenaries of some sort and believing they would defend the restaurant should another violent incident occur again. When Cody's Aunt Hannah asked why he felt this way, the elder Quan chastised them for seeking such an obvious answer: Asians, he claimed, always defended Asians.

Thus far, the lack of drama had seemingly proved him correct. The Happy Lotus owner was still convinced that violence was the way to prevent danger, particularly in the form of weaponry or enforcement. It was the only language the black race understood, he figured, and had it not been for his own son's cowardice, he would have easily practiced what he preached with the house intruder a few nights ago.

"Order's up!" shouted the cook.

Before Kiki could take the dishes, however, Cody's father took the young woman aside and instructed her to stall off the mercenaries. It was near closing time, he reminded, the moment when the restaurant was most prone to danger. With the money being taken out of the cash register and the lack of customers in the vicinity, everything was vulnerable.

"<That's why they have to stay>," explained Mr. Quan. "<The NAACP could be gathering right now, preparing for an attack.>"

Kiki nodded and resumed her waitressing duties.

"Here you go!" she smiled, serving them their dishes. "We made sure the chef give you extra portions! Take your time, okay? No rush."

Ping simply nodded without making eye contact, mildly annoyed that her meeting was frequently interrupted. She couldn't blame Kiki though—the waitress did not know the magnitude of their table's discussions. In just under twenty-four hours, Houston's most popular nightspot, The Platinum Star, would be attacked and burned and both its drug kingpin owner and key right-hand man executed.

She spent the next twenty minutes giving both Knife and Red Eye specific instructions to inflict maximum torture— slow deaths that satisfied the spirits of the husband and children taken away from Ping.

"<Remember to trip the alarms off and taking out the security cameras>," explained Ping in her native Cambodian language. "<The main way is through the small hallway at the back of the bar. Wait until the bartender is distracted and—>"

"Is everything okay?" interrupted Kiki. "Do you want some more napkins?"

The three of them observed their already large stack of napkins and shook their heads.

"We're almost done here," replied Ping. "Can we have the check, please?"

"Er, ah, don't you want to stay longer?" Kiki nervously suggested.

"We just want our check. Thank you."

Kiki quickly walked back to Cody's father and relayed him the situation. It wasn't preferable, explained Mr. Quan, there were still a couple of tables with black customers and one of them was the troubling Stuck Up. Perhaps they were waiting for the mercenaries to leave, ready to text their friends for a robbery.

"<That is not acceptable>," countered Cody's father. "<Let's treat them to some red bean soup. That'll buy us ten more minutes.>"

"<But I think they really want to leave>," Kiki replied.

"<Listen, I'm giving them red bean soup. Who could resist that? They'll understand. Asians helping Asians. That's the secret code.>"

Over on the other side of the restaurant, Hannah once again had difficulty getting Stuck Up to acknowledge her. She simply handed him a glass of water and took his usual order without asking him: sweet and sour pork and a cup of wonton soup. It was what he always stoically pointed at on the menu

.   "We're closing in twenty minutes," she announced to him. "You better eat fast."

Hannah returned to the register and shook her head in disgust.

"<Why don't these people just order to go?>" she tsk-

tsked.

"<Did you tell him we're closing soon?>" reminded Cody's father with his arms crossed.

"<Definitely>," Hannah replied. She noticed another car pulling up to the restaurant. "<Hey look, another customer. Want me to tell 'em we're closed?>"

"<Yeah...>" Mr. Quan initially answered, but then he saw the skin color of the two men getting out of the SUV. "<...Wait, they're Asian. It's okay. Tell them we're still opened.>"

Outside in the Happy Lotus parking lot, Andrew and his driver got out of their silver Audi. They took a moment to access the situation, spotting Ping and her mercenaries at the back of the restaurant, just like their mole Knife had informed them. From his long, dark gray trench coat, Andrew gripped his Para-Ordnance P-18 tightly, anticipating the final two deaths of the night. It was his preferred weapon of choice, much more intimate and accurate than the MP15-22P semiautomatic used on Pete an hour earlier.

"Text Knife," ordered Andrew to his driver. "Tell him to take a long bathroom break."

"Hey, man!" interrupted a homeless man, "got some spare change?"

Andrew flashed his gun and smirked.

"Oh fuck." The homeless man panicked, running in the opposite direction.

"Done," acknowledged the driver.

They watched as Knife checked his phone and closed it. From the window, they saw him excusing himself, leaving both targets ripe for a quick killing.

"Let's go," Andrew commanded.

The two men quickly walked up to the front door, eyes locked on Ping and Red Eye.

"Hello," greeted Hannah, "How many people—AHHHHH!!!"

With a fervor straight from the gates of hell, Andrew and his driver unleashed a barrage of bullets in the direction of their prey. In the same split second, using his catlike reflexes, Red Eye pushed his employer down and kicked their table on its side as a cover. Kiki clung to the corner of a booth, screaming at the top of her lungs. It provided an adequate diversion for Ping to unveil the semiautomatic concealed in her purse, and she began firing it at the perpetrators with a vengeance.

Hannah lost consciousness as she witnessed Andrew's driver being torn to shreds by Ping's wrath, his body now permeated with bullet holes and clumped on the ground like bloodied Swiss cheese.

As the shootout ensued, customers found cover under tables, the fish tank and potted plants. Cody's father slowly began crawling to the counter, hoping he could get behind it for safety.

"<God damn it, I'm hit!>" Ping screamed in Cambodian.

"<Where?!>" inquired Red Eye.

"<My leg...my leg...>"

More bullets tore through their table as Andrew grew bolder, firing away with each closer step. Red Eye momentarily popped out from behind the table and fired several rounds in Andrew's direction with his own gun.

"<How close is he?>" she asked in a short breath. "<Did you get him?>"

"<No. He's hiding behind cover as well.>"

"<Damn it, where's Knife? Is he a coward?>"

"<We need a table. This one's got too many holes.>"

Andrew unleashed another round of shots, as he moved from scattered table to scattered table. When he reached the halfway mark—the fish tank—he grabbed the customer there and shoved him into the line of fire. The man shouted in horror as Ping's and Red Eye's bullets barely missed him. With their focus momentarily distracted, Andrew took the offense and unloaded his third round of bullets, directly hitting Red Eye as he fell to the floor dead.

"Just you and me, bitch!" yelled Andrew.

Ping fired at the large fish tank, sending water and aquatic life on to the stooping Andrew. The cold and wet surprise caused the hefty hit man to drop his gun. He watched it slide across the floor near the counter and inches away from the crawling Mr. Quan.

Moving in for a closer shot, the injured Ping limped from behind the table. Every time he tried leaving from the cover of the fish tank platform, Ping fired at the floor, intimidating him to stay put. She gripped her semiautomatic tightly as she struggled closer to where he was hiding. Memories of what the monster had done to her family began flooding her emotions—Andrew Huynh deserved death in the worst way, for the countless lives he took and the pleasure he received doing in so. She was finally going to get her revenge, she viciously smiled, and as a bonus, rid Houston of its most nefarious killer.

"Watch out!" one of the customers suddenly warned her.

She turned just in time to dodge Knife's attack, his switchblade missing her by inches. As he attempted to stab her again, Ping instinctively fired her weapon at him, instantly killing the traitor.

Andrew took the opportunity to dart for his weapon, sprinting toward the counter where Cody's father had almost reached the gun. To the hit man's surprise, the Happy Lotus' owner was spry for his age and made it to the weapon in the same instance as Andrew.

"No! You cannot have!" Cody's father declared in bad English as the two wrestled for the gun.

Andrew easily overpowered him, shoving the elder Quan to the floor and critically wounding him with a bullet into his stomach.

"MISTER QUAN!" Kiki screamed.

The hit man's victory was short-lived as several of Ping's shots successfully tore through his left arm and leg.

"Ahhh..h...hhh," Andrew shouted, squeezing his eyes in pain.

Ping was right beside him now, her gun barrel directly in front of Andrew's forehead.

"<I know you don't understand me>," she breathed hard in Cambodian, "<but you killed my unborn daughter, my other daughter and my beloved husband. For that, you will spend an eternity in hell where your boss shall soon join you.>"

She squeezed the trigger, hearing only the empty sounds of a metal click. Nothing.

"<No!>" she cursed, realizing the gun had run out of bullets.

With his remaining good hand, Andrew punched her and threw her to the floor. He slowly stood up and regained possession of his own gun.

"I don't...I don't miss in this distance," he grinned. "Where is your God now? Why didn't he save you? Hahaha!"

He fired at her stomach, watching blood flow out of her mouth. Ping looked at him wide-eyed before permanently looking straight ahead, passing away to the hereafter.

"There's...nothing out...there...bitch," declared Andrew. "I...don't suffer....the....consequences."

With all the energy he could muster from his working leg, Andrew limped and hopped his way away from the crime scene and into the silver Audi. As she watched the car slowly drive away and with dead bodies all around her, the recovering

Hannah's first instinct was to dial 911. Her nervousness, however, kept screwing with her coordination. 912. 921. 912 again.

"<Cody's father is bleeding a lot!>" realized Kiki, now kneeling next to her boss. "<We need to stop it!!!>"

Stuck Up grabbed Hannah's phone and punched in 911 for her, then handed it back.

"No!" she hesitated. "Your English good! Mine no!"

He continued to shove the phone back into her possession, turning instead to help Cody's father.

"Hello," answered the operator, "this is 911. What is your emergency?"

"Someone come...shoot! Table firing fish tank explode! We are in restaurant!"

"Ma'am, calm down. Please explain your emergency."

Using her rudimentary English, Hannah described to the best of her ability the situation that had transpired. The operator finally decided it was best to transfer her to a Chinese-speaking translator.

Meanwhile, Stuck Up stormed into the kitchen, searching for a first-aid kit. At the sight of the intimidating black man, the chef ran out, leaving Stuck Up to find it on his own. With time running out and having no luck, the silent savior took whatever he could find, particularly alcohol wipes, to attend to Mr. Quan's bleeding.

"Please.......don't hurt me...black man bad....bad..." Mr. Quan moaned as he looked up and saw Stuck Up on top of him.

"<Shhhh, Uncle, mmmm. Please, he is trying to help you, I think>," replied Kiki.

There was no reply back; Cody's father had fainted.

"Daphne!" Andrew summoned. "DAPHNE!"

Sections of the Huynh's lavish household began lighting up one by one as the pregnant mob wife worriedly searched for her husband's whereabouts. When she finally found him in the first floor bathroom, he was unrecognizably bloodstained and irate, destroying the furnishings and wallpaper.

"What's wrong?...Oh, honey...you're bleeding all over..."

"YOU'RE GOD DAMN RIGHT I'M BLEEDING ALL OVER!!!" he screamed.

"What happened?"

"Are you SERIOUSLY going to ask me that?!"

Daphne froze in terror, not knowing what to do with him in such an enraged mood. She had never seen her husband so defeated, so vulnerable, always believing the bad boy was invincible from the war games that men play.

"I'm just trying to...look, please stop. You're scaring me," Daphne began crying hysterically. "I've never seen you like this, Andrew..."

"WHERE'S THE GODDAMN FIRST AID KIT? AND CAN YOU SHUT HELEN UP?"

The sudden stress did not mix well with her unstable hormones. She could feel Winnie kicking inside of her, not knowing what was happening but sensing discontent from her mother. Matters were made worse when Helen ran towards them, screaming in tears and demanding attention.

"Mommy!!!"

"No! Go back!" Daphne blocked her from going into the bathroom. "You can't see daddy like this."

"Mommy, what's happening?!" she cried. "What's going on?!"

"HELP ME GET THIS BULLET OUT, GODDAMNIT!"

He was going into shock, losing too much blood and control over his rage. Daphne went over to him, doing her best to apply pressure and control the bleeding. Ultimately, she gave up, not knowing how to treat Andrew's wounds.

"You're...so...useless," Andrew blurted, "...you...and that goddamn...kid..."

"I can't—I let this happen to you," said Daphne amid tears. "I love you so much. I'm going to save you, honey. You can't be killed. Nothing can kill you. You're strong and powerful and...and..."

"...should have...never...married...you..."

"I'm going to call the ambulance, honey. I know how much you told me not to, but...but I can't let you die...wait right here, okay? Everything's going to be okay. Everything's going to be okay."

Andrew sat still, leaning towards the wall and conserving whatever blood he had left. He watched as his wife left the room, scrambling to find her phone. Helen slowly walked into the shattered bathroom, viewing for the first time the consequences of her daddy's boisterous lifestyle. His gruesome appearance did not frighten her, but he seemed obscure, incapable of loving anyone except himself.

"...ugly...kid...I could...sell...you...by...the...time...you're...fourteen..."

"Daddy, why are you saying those horrible things?" she frowned.

"...killed...so...many...don't...care...you...all...deserve...to... die..."

"Daddy...."

"...I...deserve...to...die..."

"That won't be a problem," he suddenly heard a familiar Russian voice reply.

Andrew's eyes widened when Dimitri appeared near the bathroom entrance, forcing Daphne and now Helen at gunpoint.

"I'm sorry, honey," apologized Daphne, "He just appeared. I—"

"Surprised?" mocked Dimitri, unbuttoning his vest to reveal a bulletproof jacket. "Next time, make sure your target is bleeding."

"...kill you...KILL...you..."

"It was easy to find where you lived, Andrew. You've made far too many enemies who were eager to expose things about you. Did you really not think this day would happen?"

Using whatever energy that remained in him, the hefty assassin pulled out his gun and fired in the direction of Dimitri and his own family. The aim was entirely off, though that didn't stop both Daphne and Helen from screaming in fright.

"Daddy!!!" screamed Helen, "why're you shooting at us?!"

Dimitri chuckled, "You are left-handed, I see. Can't aim properly with your right."

As the enervated hit man squeezed the trigger again, the recoil caused the gun to fall from his loose grip and drop on the marble floor where it accidentally went off upon impact. Neither misfire resulted in a victim.

"Is that it?" the Russian ridiculed, pointing his gun at Andrew. "You know in Russia people like you are nothing."

Blam!

Andrew howled in pain after the Russian fired into his good leg.

"Let this be your final thought, comrade," he grinned. "You had this coming to you."

"No!" Daphne screamed. She threw herself at Dimitri, trying to wrestle the gun away from his grip. With a strong push, the Russian got her off, but not before the gun slipped into the determined woman's hands.

"Get away from my husband," she sternly threatened amidst dry tears.

The bathroom was cramped, far too little space for three adults.

"Are you really going shoot me?" Dimitri laughed, slowly backing up near Andrew's gun.

"Don't," threatened Daphne.

Unfazed, the Russian calmly kneeled down and picked up the weapon.

"See?" he shrugged, pointing her husband's gun at her. "You don't have it in you."

Without a moment's hesitation, Dimitri turned and fired a shot at Andrew's head, killing him instantly.

"NOOOOOOOOOOOOO!" Whatever hesitation Daphne had of killing another human being disappeared as she fired the gun over and over at the Russian until all the bullets were spent.

Helen stood frozen, unable to comprehend the carnage she had seen. She watched as her mother kneeled over her lifeless father and closed his eyelids with her fingers. Daphne looked at her own blood-soaked hands and began weeping, praying that it was all a bad dream.

Suddenly, she heard the Russian moaning in agony, still clinging on to life.

"H-how...?"

The weakened Dimitri opened up his vest and revealed his bulletproof vest again, the same one that had saved him earlier in the night from the assassination attempt.

"Make sure..." he gasped breathlessly, "...that your...target...is...bleeding..."

Summoning up enough strength to control her emotions, Daphne gave him a hateful look and pointed her gun at his head. The Russian lifted his gun and pointed it at her stomach. Helen screamed as she witnessed both weapons firing at the same time.

Twenty minutes later, the ambulance crew broke through, trying to find the woman who had called them. Instead, the medics found a war zone in the first-floor bathroom with two dead bodies, a hysterical child, and a pregnant woman who was unconscious but alive. They immediately placed Daphne into an ambulance, taking her to the hospital where she would later survive, but her unborn child was dead upon arrival.

CHAPTER 35: BAD ENDING

The steady rhythms of the electrocardiograph machine indicated Kelvin Min-Lo Quan would survive—he did, after all, live in Houston: the city with the greatest medical treatment in the world.

Now if only he'd shut up, joked his family.

Of course, only now were they capable of saying such a thing, knowing he would be okay. It was preferable to the uncertainty they had faced twenty-four hours ago when Cody's father, shot and left for dead, was rushed into the emergency room with tremendous blood loss and cardiac arrest.

"<So there I was>," proclaimed the triumphal restaurant owner, "<standing there near the counter like always, and just when those guys came in, I immediately pegged them as troublemakers.>"

"<Because they were black?>" interrupted Cody's Aunt Mei.

"<What? No. Why would you say such a thing? They were Asian. It was because they were holding guns.>"

"<But they didn't take out their guns until after they got in>," corrected Cody's Aunt Hannah.

"<No, they took their guns out before they came in. Trust me, I was there>," nodded Mr. Quan.

"<Well, so was I!>" protested Hannah.

"<You're old. What can you remember?>"

"<Old? I'm four years younger than you are!>"

Regardless of the ever-changing versions, "The Shot" had instantly become a part of the Quan family legend. Sometimes Cody's father was shot wrestling for the killer's gun; other times he single-handedly took on all five assailants in a heroic attempt to protect the Happy Lotus. The degree of exaggeration more or less depended on whether or not Kiki and Hannah were present at the time of storytelling.

Interestingly enough was the consistent detail of being saved by Stuck Up. In all accounts of what happened, Cody's father had used it as a platform to advocate judging someone through content of character. It was more than enough to surprise Cody, who had long given up on changing his father's prejudices.

So what was the lesson here? he wondered.

For once, Cody was happy that perhaps justice wasn't served in this situation, or, at least, what he would have deemed was coming to his father for his hate-filled antics. Deep inside, Cody feared the animosity would end up destroying his dad, skeptical of change ever coming into his father's heart during the later stages of his life. Instead, Mr. Quan was granted mercy, surrounded by beloved friends and family, all thanks to someone he now saw not as a "good" black person or a "bad" black person, but as a valiant, humanitarian person who saved him.

"<Anthony>," he told Cody one night at the hospital, long after everyone had left them, "<his name is Lieutenant Anthony B. Miller. He's mute, you know. We had always thought he was...well...stuck up.>"

"<This don't talk I want>," pleaded Cody.

"<Do you think I deserve this, son?>" Mr. Quan asked, ignoring his son's request. "<For every action there is a reaction. I don't know what good I've done to deserve such a fortunate fate. I'd like to take credit for it, but in all honesty, just between

you and me...I can't recall a single thing that led to me being alive today.>"

Cody looked at his father and struggled to come up with something profound. It would have been a good opportunity to chastise his father's lifelong dependency on silly superstitions. But then again, he realized, life also wasn't as simple as believing in something and having it come true. He was still searching for the answers himself, and somehow he doubted he would ever find truth in its entirety.

"I'm just happy you're alive, dad." Cody patted his father's hand, a tear rolling down his eye. "That's all that should matter."

Mr. Quan nodded, satisfied with the answer. However, it would be something he would partially disagree with. He refused to test his luck any further by risking his family's financial safety for his own indulgences.

"<Son, I've decided to sell our new house>," he proclaimed. "<Being near death has caused me to appreciate a new kind of wealth. Having you and your mom, your grandfather, my health, food on the table—I was greedy to believe I needed more.>"

"But if you do that, we'd be nearly broke," Cody expressed with some concern.

"<Were we ever rich?>" his father laughed. "<We were just blindly in debt.>"

They both chuckled, not so much for its humor but because of its irony.

"<It will hurt>," admitted his father. "<We'll be scraping by again. Living in a modest home, eating home-cooked meals, being thrifty with the bills. But at least we'll have each other. Most people would be gratified just to have a roof over their heads. I wouldn't call this a great ending. Just a thankful one.>"

"Some ask if God is so loving, then why is there death?" began the preacher as Andrew Huynh's coffin was slowly set to go six feet into the ground.

The funeral was quiet and nearly empty; aside from the newly widowed Daphne and her daughter Helen, scattered attendants included various members of the Vietnamese community and some long-forgotten friends from Daphne's past.

"God has seen all evil," the preacher continued. "He has seen all the suffering, all the pain that has endured during our time on earth. At some point, this madness has to stop. It stops for those who receive it and it stops for those who deliver it. Andrew Huynh was once a child. He laughed, he cried, he sinned. May God have mercy on his soul."

He briefly paused as Daphne's clamorous weeping penetrated the silent, solemn atmosphere.

"Let us commend Andrew to the mercy of God, so that he may be forgiven and receive the everlasting love of Christ. We therefore commit his body to the ground; earth to earth, ashes to ashes, dust to dust; in the sure and certain hope of the Resurrection to eternal life. Amen."

With a flip of a switch, the mechanical devices lowered the coffin. The funeral workers soon took their shovels and began tossing dirt on it. What few attendees there were began scattering, leaving the widow to weep alone. Her daughter remained motionless, absent of the emotional outburst her mother was displaying. In her blemished mind, Helen could still see her father's shattered skull, a bullet hole right through the middle of his head; she could also see the same type of fatal wound on the man who did it to him—a man that was slain by her mother, who, in her darkest moments, displayed a thirst for killing no different than the two monsters who were dead in their bathroom. Helen knew she was the spawn of atrocious, sinister people—but at least her father was strong enough to embrace that pernicious side.

"I often wondered what you saw in him," chimed in a voice from behind. "Even after all these years."

Daphne's expression turned into anger as she instantly knew whom the voice belonged to.

"Zoey?! But how—"

Daphne paused for a moment to take in Zoey's current look. She, too, had aged, but it was a graceful aging, one without the wear and tear from the stress that Daphne endured.

"His death was all over the news," Zoey calmly explained. "It wasn't difficult to locate the funeral service."

"So you're here to give me your sympathy?!" barked Daphne. "I'm sorry to say you've wasted your time."

"No. That's not it at all. You know, you don't have to go alone from here."

"I've made my decision and I don't regret it."

"Your husband was a murderer, Daphne. He took lives and ruined families. How many funerals like this did he create?"

"PEOPLE DIE EVERY DAY," the widow scowled. "It wasn't in God's plan for me to be the Sunday school teacher, sitting in some obscure job where life passed me by. It was never me, can't you see? I was meant to witness this man—his greatness as a person, as a husband, as the father to my child. God put me with him for a reason, and I never questioned it because what I felt for him was always normal and effortless— despite its eccentricities."

"Excuse me?!" blurted Zoey. "'Eccentricities'? Is that what you call it, Daphne? You know...I admit I used to despise you. Always the judgmental sort, always someone who entitled herself above others, but I would trade that Daphne back from the person you are now—a lost soul too in love with a bad life decision."

Daphne felt her eyes watering again, too prideful to look in Zoey's direction.

"Look," Zoey softened, "Luke and Felix started a church a few years back. I came here to be your sister in Christ. I want you to join us."

Helen watched her mother's expression. Daphne had a concentrated look to her, staring off into the far distance, looking within herself.

Zoey slowly reached out and, in a gesture of friendship, touched her arm. "You don't need to go through this alone."

"No," Daphne swatted her hand away, "you'll...you'll never understand. None of you'll ever understand. I've seen things, Zoey. That man that just got buried? He was the closest thing to a god. And darn it if I'll let his legacy end like that."

The widow took her daughter's hand and together they headed out of the cemetery, leaving Zoey alone to scratch her head. Soon, a sharp breeze fell over the area; it was stubborn and powerful, forcing Zoey to plant her feet on the ground lest she might topple over. She watched from a distance as Daphne pulled Helen closer to her, buttoning up the child's coat in preparation for stormier weather.

Despite a few raindrops, Zoey continued observing until her former friend and daughter were merely indistinguishable dots among the rest of the cemetery. A sweeping wave of sadness overcame her as she wondered if the moment was their last together—and if it wasn't, what enigmatical plans would God have in store for a future reunion?

"Let it go, Zoey."

She didn't know how long Felix had been standing beside her, but she was glad her best friend displayed the same impeccable timing that always rescued her from doubt and apprehension.

"I tried to reach out to her, Felix," she replied. "I really did."

"I know," he replied, putting a hand behind her shoulder. "We'll leave it to God, okay? Come on, it's starting to rain. I parked the car close by."

He opened an umbrella and escorted her out of the cemetery. Birds flew past them, seeking shelter among the scattered trees. As some of them perched on the branch directly on top of Andrew's grave, they began tweeting, communicating with one another the gossip of their natural world. One by one they excreted, decorating the callous hit man's tombstone until a visible coating of pasty droppings furbished it—a white frosting on a gray memorial.

———

Homer Flacco rubbed his bald spot, wondering if he could pull off one more miracle for Marty Ho. It wasn't like it was his long-term client's first jam; Marty had always schemed, evading lawsuits and payments, fines and jail time. But this situation was different—they were taking the offense and trying to sue someone, new territory that they had always avoided.

"I...I can't help you. They're criminals, Marty. And they're dead." Homer handed The Platinum Star contract back to him.

"Wah-eh, pout, ffft," Marty puffed his face for maximum sympathy. "Come on, heh, you...you're the best, heh, there's got to be a way!"

"You and your new partner should've asked me about this contract before you signed it. Why didn't you? I would've at least added a few loopholes. Look, you didn't even fulfill the quota."

"But couldn't we get something? You got to help me. My mom, wah-mah, has cancer!"

"My condolences, Marty, but that wouldn't be a reason I could bring to court. Your contract is void. This Piranha character was found dead by the same man who signed your contract who, in turn, is also dead. What happened at the club and the murders that took place there were also well-known to everyone watching the news in the past few weeks. Frankly, your promotions had helped the drug activity that was going on. No judge or jury would be sympathetic to your contract. Bottom line, you're lucky you got out without loss of reputation. Again."

Upon hearing this news, Marty's heartbeat quickened. The expensive Brooks Brothers three-piece he was wearing was soon saturated in perspiration as he did a mental calculation of all the purchases he and his wife made with credit. The total was in the hundreds of thousands.

"And we threw away the receipts too," stammered Marty.

"Hey," consoled Homer, giving him a sympathetic pat in the back, "maybe it's time you got a regular job."

Marty nodded slowly and left his lawyer's office. The thought of getting a legitimate career disgusted him; among his arsenal of lying, scheming, manipulating and psychological deception, he really had no valuable skill to offer a company. At least, not to one that would believe he wouldn't be using those same specialties against them. He had a few hours to brainstorm something before Xia asked him about the money. Perhaps, he thought, he could use his forged degrees in English and psychology, trick a trust fund baby, start a pyramid scheme, or...

As he made his way into the main hallway of the building, he noticed something unusual among the bustling crowd. Marty dropped his jaw and did a double take, making eye contact with a man who showed no discretion about following him. Doing his best to recall who the person may be, his memory was nevertheless unable to evoke someone who was Asian, in his early thirties, tall, clean-cut and extremely serious. The pursuit continued through various twists and turns until Marty decided it was safest to remain in an open area full of people.

"Mah...uh...ahhhh," he puffed and moaned in nervousness.

To his utter disbelief, he looked behind him and saw that his pursuer remained in stride, approaching him without regard to the abundance of witnesses surrounding them. Marty held his breath, summoning whatever courage he had to plaster a grin. He hoped the man was well-intended, perhaps another bone sent by the mercy of the universe.

"You," the stranger pointed.

"Me? Heh...me?" Marty nervously chuckled. "Wrong person. Hah! Huh-eh, ah! I'm Marty. Marty Ho. Nice to meet you, I—"

Wasting no time, the man immediately placed a hand on Marty's crotch and tightly squeezed it.

The crowd gasped.

"OOFFFFFF!!!" puffed Marty.

The combination of shock and pressure sent Marty into a state of intimidation.

"Do you know what I'm doing?" the man asked.

Amid proliferating sweat and involuntary urination, Marty swiftly shook his head.

"I'm squeeeeezing your dick," he explained. "How do you like it? Do you like how it feels when somebody else has you by the balls? I know who you are, Marty Ho. You're the son-of-a-bitch that tricked my cousin and blew up much of our family's savings."

Marty's eyes widened when he realized who this man was and the terrifying descriptions Cody had often portrayed of him.

"D-D...Dukkkeee," he blurted.

"Oh my God! Someone call security!" shouted a random woman.

"Are you kidding me?" laughed another spectator, recording the incident with his iPhone. "This is awesome! I'm putting this on YouTube!"

Marty was about to pass out from the intense pain. "But... how... did...you... find...me..."

"Luck," Duke explained. "Plain, dumb coincidence. I was just exiting the Wells Fargo in this building when I spotted you. Cody used to put your photo up on Facebook so I knew. You have a distinguishable betaness about you. My alphaness picked it up right away."

"Let...me...tell...you...a...funny...story...heh...ah...ha..."

"No. No stories. This is the story right here, right now."

Duke handled Marty's crotch like a water faucet and twisted it into a 90-degree angle. The action resulted in a snapping sound as Cody's avenging cousin finally let go and remorselessly watched him collapse on to the ground. The spineless con artist assumed a fetal position where he remained long after Duke had left him. With no sympathy from the bystanders, the crowd soon dissipated, leaving Marty to wallow alone in self-pity. Despite the incident, however, Marty was more worried that the incident would not be the worst thing to happen to him that day. Indeed, in just a few hours he would have to explain to Xia how they would have to pay off a lifetime of credit card debt.

———————

Phoebe sat in the classroom, irritated that her professor's cascading style sheets weren't properly connecting with his id tags. Clearly, she scoffed, he was still stuck on the old HTML4 system with his abundant use of tables and embedded framework.

"And for some reason, the form isn't sending when I hit Submit...I..." The rookie professor was nervously scratching his neck.

She rolled her eyes. "You forgot to put in an action sequence, and when you did, you didn't refer back to the same file where your JavaScript was stored. Really, you should make it into an external file."

The rest of the class turned around and glanced at her with irritation; no one liked a prodigy, they thought, especially when her brains meant they would be saying good-bye to a bell curve.

"Show off," detested one of her classmates.

"Ah!" the professor smiled, finding out the code now worked. "How...silly of me. Of course. There it goes. Thanks, Phoebe."

711

Once the class ended, she endured the same cold treatment from her peers. Her smiles were returned with their disapproving glares, isolating her as the role of the teacher's pet. The webmistress extraordinaire didn't let it bother her, however—she knew that their grudge was merely derived from their callowness.

"You're really good," the professor complimented. "Like, really, really good. That last assignment you did, I was like...wow! Geez! You could teach this class!"

"Meh. Thanks," laughed Phoebe. "Figured it'd be an easy A."

"Where did you learn all those tricks? Some of those aren't even in the textbook!"

"I...well...a really good friend taught me."

"He must really know his stuff!"

"He sure did."

"Ah, well," the professor shrugged. "Thanks for correcting me again. I've got another class to teach. See you later.......genius!"

Phoebe appreciated the compliment, but it was an empty remedy to an unfulfilled existence. It was true that things were better now since her return to school; it was what she deemed progress in comparison to those quickly forgotten party nights at The Platinum Star. She was, however, yearning again for the empowering nectar of aspiration, a gift Cody had given to her, which she had never forgotten. It was all she could think of these days whenever she took breaks on the rooftop of the Cullen College of Engineering. There, she found at just the right time of day, it was cool enough that she could sit around and enjoy a nice smoke.

Just as she was about to relish her daily nicotine rendezvous, however, the sudden interruption of her vibrating iPhone momentarily delayed the action. Better for it, Phoebe laughed to herself; she had been trying to quit for awhile and it would be convenient to be disturbed whenever she was lighting up a cigarette. The cell phone ID suggested an unrecognizable number, perhaps someone who had called in error or maybe one of Wilbur's promoting cronies. She allowed the phone to vibrate for an extra few seconds when another thought entered her mind: maybe it was Cody calling from a new number to apologize and reconcile. The theory was ridiculous, she knew, but nevertheless the hope was enough for her to answer the call and leave it to chance.

"Hello?" she answered.

"Hello? Is this Phoebe?" replied a female voice.

"...yes?"

"Hi! I was hoping it was you. Glad your cell phone number from your business card still works!"

"Who...is this?"

"Oh, haha. Sorry, forgot to say. It's me, Doreen!"

"Doreen?"

"Yeah, we met at the networking event all those months ago! You met my husband too, Mitch."

"Oh, oh yeah!" laughed Phoebe, remembering Cody's little nickname for Mitch. "I had a little too much that night, sorry!"

"It's okay!" Doreen assured. "Listen, I apologize we haven't followed back with you. We really did mean to. Do you and your boyfriend Cody want to come to our house for dinner some time?"

Phoebe blushed. "Cody's not...um...well, that is, I'll have to call him and see."

"Great! You could see our baby Papyrus too!"

"Papyrus, haha. What a cool name. Um, okay! If he can make it, what day would you like us to be there?"

"Ah, anytime next week. Just let us know! I'll make us some crawfish etouffee! Hope you guys can make it!"

Phoebe ended the call with a prodigious smile, knowing it would be a justifiable reason to contact Cody. Of course, a part of her was still livid from their fight, but the stubborn pride that resulted was never worth the exceptional camaraderie they had built. She realized this now as she quickly looked his number up from her cell phone's contact list.

"Hello—" came after a few rings.

"Cody, it's me Phoebe. I—"

"—I'm currently not available right now. Please leave your name, number and message and I'll reply back as soon as possible. Thanks."

The automated greeting momentarily nullified Phoebe's forgiving mood, giving her mere seconds to hang up and resume their silent treatment game.

No, she decided, silent treatments are what children do.

"Hi, uh, Cody," she stammered, "it's me, Phoebe. Remember me? Heh. Um, anyway, the couple from that networking night when we were drunk, Doreen and...and Mitch, you know Mitch Bitch?....anyway...they've invited us to have dinner with them at their house next week. Yeah, I know, pretty out there, huh? Well, I don't know if you're up for it, but I certainly am. I miss you and I hope you can call me back. Just to say hi again. Like we used to. I mean, I dunno, I just want to talk to you again. Please call back. I miss you."

As she remained on the engineering building's rooftop past sunset, she found herself repeating her voice mail, pondering if she could've sounded more conciliatory. She looked above toward the stars and savored their interminable allurement, wondering if certain things were meant to be. *We take so much for granted,* she thought, *never appreciating them as gifts but, instead, thinking them as privileges.*

It was close to ten o'clock in the evening when her phone rang again. At first, it excited her that it might have been

Cody; instead, it was from a loose end of The Platinum Star days.

"Phoebe, thank God," Rosie answered, "we need to talk, girl! I don't think Wilbur loves me anymore. I need you to help me come up with a trap to win his heart over."

Phoebe rolled her eyes, wondering if she should simply hang up and block her number. "Rosie, how many times do I have to tell you? I don't want to get involved in the drama between you and your emo boyfriend."

"Come on, girl! I need your help!"

With a quick apology to herself, Phoebe did what she originally wanted to do and disconnected. Rosie, Wilbur, Marty. Now all blocked, she smirked. She remained on the roof with her spirit still flickering with hope for Cody's reply.

Her message remained unanswered.

CHAPTER 36: HAPPILY EVER AFTER

Splash!

It had been ten years to the day since Cody had been baptized—now it was his turn among the crowd, observing a new flock that was being plunged into the purifying sanctity of holy water. Like he had once done, they were experiencing a transformative journey, transcending through time and space while watching their young lives flash into a compendium of memories and emotions.

One by one, the newly denominated came out convinced of Jesus' existence; Cody, however, knew what he perceived to be the truth. No doubt their strong faith had conjured up a literal image of the Messiah in the implemented version set by media and literature: that of a blue-eyed, blonde-haired, Roman toga-sporting Anglo-Saxon god whose arms were outstretched in a gesture of liberation and salvation. How each of their subconscious creation would end up treating them would vary among individual experience. Cody only hoped the Christian experience would be more pleasant for them than it had been from his personal time with the "Savior."

Nonetheless, he enjoyed the comforting, casual atmosphere of New Union Trinity Church, and his recusant views of organized religion did not impede his happiness for the occasion. It was Megan's baptism and he was invited to share her enthusiasm in a temperament without hesitation or judgment. More so, at least his cousin chose to hold it in an equitable and open-minded church, one that had the rare reverence of being sermonized by homosexual pastors Luke Lu and Felix Lin.

"Oh, this is dreadfully dull," commented Charlene Lavender, the sensational British fashion designer in attendance. "They ought to think of a more systematic way of going through the baptism. And I'm thirsty. I wish someone'd get me a glass of water."

At the moment of her declaration, eight of the male church members quickly shot off their stools and raced towards the water cooler. Cody snickered at the sight of this as he recognized the irony of thirsty men fetching water for a thirsty woman.

"Upon your profession of faith and in accordance with the Lord's command," Luke pronounced, "I baptize you, Megan, in the name of the Father, Son and Holy Spirit. Buried in the likeness of His death and raised in the likeness of His resurrection."

After the baptism was over and the photo opportunities with Megan were done, Cody's family expected to leave in anonymity until a long-forgotten squeal made Cody turn around and momentarily bask in the spotlight.

"Cody!!!!!!!"

"Zoey!" laughed Cody, embracing his old friend. "Wow, it's been...years..."

"Don't give me that!" she scolded. "You were here several months ago. You ignored everyone! You saw me and you didn't come to say hi."

"I...well..." Cody bowed his head in embarrassment. "Well, I didn't think anyone wanted to say hi to me."

"Don't be foolish, Cody," interrupted another familiar voice—Luke.

Cody squirmed a little at the touch of the gay pastor,

giving in to his subconscious homophobia. It was something that he needed to work on, he realized, knowing how well-received Luke's embraces once were before he knew of his sexuality.

"We missed you," smiled the young pastor.

"How's your dad?" Cody asked.

"He's doing fine. Still running the old church."

"Even after the incident with Pastor Washington and Jay?"

"Well, one can't just let tough times get in the way. I only hope that when this church gets its big test, I'd be able to stand just as firm. Lord willing. For now, I just hope Dad and I can talk again someday."

"I'm not surprised he rejected your lifestyle, though hopefully he'll turn around to it."

"That's what I pray for, Cody. And I have faith it will happen."

Their reunion was joined by Marion, Henry and Felix, all sharing recollections of happy memories and hopeful circumstances. Megan, the ever impatient teenager, tugged at her cousin's sleeve and insisted on leaving. It eventually got Cody to comply, bidding his former church friends farewell before heading to the door with the rest of his family.

"Listen, Cody, before you go," Luke insisted, "we've...all heard of your...exiting as a Christian. Everyone goes through those times. But perhaps you should reconsider your decision. It is, after all, faith that gives us peace."

Although the young pastor's sincerity flattered him, Cody had already made a final decision.

"I eventually did find faith," Cody replied. "Real faith. It's believing in something with enough certainty that it inevitably happens. Sometimes it's a good thing, other times not so much. Faith is something we have as a responsibility, to make sure that what we believe in guides us in a positive way.

Through difficult times I've learned what that is—and I'm at peace with it."

Bearing a cryptic smile, Cody bid them farewell, winking to the beautiful cosmic hairdresser that only he could see. He had no remorse about leaving Christianity. Not anymore.

———————

Rain Yoon couldn't believe it.

She had finally finished her graphic novel, thanks to the breathtaking scenery from the top of the Tokyo Sky Tree. There, sitting at one of the tables inside of the tower's 634 Musashi Restaurant, she irrevocably found the inspiration that activated a much needed epiphany. Maybe it was the beatific collection of mankind's potential or the celestial feeling of being among the heavens in the world's tallest building. Whatever it was, her iPad's Sketchbook Pro file was finally saved, completing the young artist's masterpiece.

"Yuki!" she called out to her traveling companion. "Hey, Yuki!"

Yuki let out an elongated sigh. She loved Rain and enjoyed taking trips with her, but sometimes she wished the impatient girl would just leave her alone—at least for a short while. This was one of those "whiles" as she was practicing her Japanese with their waitress while deciding on what to order next. Between choosing the Poisson or the Riz d'ail, it was hard enough to communicate in a foreign language, let alone doing so while her own name was being recited to her.

"Hold on, hold on," Yuki dismissively waved, continuing her order with the waitress.

"Yuki!" Rain repeated.

"*Sakana ryōri o onegaishimasu,*" Yuki pointed at the menu, not sure if her Japanese was quite correct. "*Orenji jūsu wa arimasu ka?*"

"*Hai,*" the patient waitress bowed. "*Go-chuumon wa okimari desu ka?*"

"You know," Rain continued to interrupt, "I can understand you guys. Hey Yuki, I've finally finished it! My graphic novel is done! I finished it on my iPad! Helloooo..."

The talented artist flipped her iPad around to show both her friend and the waitress. Despite the annoyance that came with her persistency, the gifted art on display negated any ill will from the other two women as they stared with their jaws dropped. One by one, Rain slid her finger across the touch screen, flipping virtual comic page after virtual comic page.

"*Anata wa sugoku sainou ga aru to omoimasu!!!*" admired the waitress with a solid thumbs-up.

"*Douka kanojowo sonnani odatenide kudasai,*" warned Yuki. "*Sorewa kanojowo unubore saseru deshow.*"

"*Watashiwa gengides. Korega itsumo no watashides!*" Rain scowled.

Sensing they wanted to be left alone, the waitress quickly took their orders and departed. Yuki smirked and gently took hold of the impetuous artist's iPad. The digital comic book was quite beautiful, she thought, maybe it was best to give her young friend the just due she deserved.

"It's beautiful, Rain," Yuki admitted. "You know that and so do I."

"Thanks!" she giggled, "the nighttime Tokyo landscape brought out the best in me."

"Maybe we should live here forever."

"Really?!"

"No," laughed Yuki, "even with all my abundant amount of early retirement funds we couldn't afford it here for the rest of our lives. Certainly not the rest of yours. Besides, don't you want to travel to other places? I hear Australia's nice this time of year."

"Wait, I thought we were going to Barcelona next."

"I'm sure we can squeeze in Sydney somewhere."

"Ah, who cares! Maybe I'll sell enough of these books that I'll be able to treat you for once!"

Long after their meal had been served and finished, the two world travelers remained at their table and watched the infinite sea of lights beneath them. Rain did most of the talking while Yuki half listened and occasionally nodded. The rest of her mind was focused on the more philosophical aspects with a life already half lived and finding peace from what she has yet to experience. It wasn't the happy ending a younger Yuki Yee once had in mind, but she discovered that one didn't need to keep love to find love—company and companionship were always around. Certainly there was more to life than the textbook example of how it should be lived. Happiness was a choice, and she chose to be happy. Happily ever after, in Maui. Barcelona. Sydney. Rio de Janeiro. Seoul. Zurich. Singapore. Crete. The Bahamas. Never alone, always at peace.

"Yuki?"

"Yeah?"

"I wonder what happened to Cody?"

Rain whipped out a box of Pocky from her duffle bag and offered a piece to Yuki. Yuki munched on it for awhile before letting out her deep, thought-out answer:

"Cody who?"

———————

Wilbur peered at his Hollywood trailer's dressing room mirror and freaked.

"I-I-I s-s-said no n-n-nose hairs!!!" the pretty boy demanded.

"Sir," the makeup assistant pleaded, "we've trimmed and plucked all the major ones out. The rest won't show up on camera. Besides, I have issues with your mascara. There's just too much—"

"Get ready!" interrupted the producer. "We're about to film!"

It had been a crazy few months for the son of the Wang's Restaurant empire. The notoriety brought by his "You're the Celebrity" concept garnered national headlines, especially after the incident with the drug trafficking bust. After peculiar negotiations that included biweekly Brazilian waxing sessions, a constant supply of Clinique BB Cream and a Velocity HP1000 tanning bed, "Wilbur's Future Celebrities" proved to be a big hit despite his stuttering monologues, odd guest choices and a lengthy segment involving giant Jenga blocks.

The makeup assistant struggled. "Sir, if you'd stop moving so much maybe I can fix your—"

"H-h-hey don't t-t-touch my h-h-hair!!!"

"Come on, come on!" the producer pushed.

Wilbur checked his reflection one more time—he was ready. Amid the glittering lights and all-encompassing cameras, he knew this was where his soul wanted to be.

Finally, he had found his home.

"S-s-s-s-s-show t-t-time!!!" he declared.

As the producer hurried him out, the makeup assistant couldn't help but notice Wilbur's phone intensely vibrating across the makeup desk. She wondered for a moment who it might be, and then thought the better of it, knowing it was none of her business. After she closed the door, the vibrating stopped and a message was recorded:

"Ah-huh...heh...hah! Wilbur! Ffft, wah-heh, I knew you could do it! Didn't I, heh, didn't I tell you that you were the chosen one? Heh. Ha! How do you say 'You're the Man' in dinosaur? Heh! It's 'Rawr'! Mah-hah. Heh. Ah heh heh. You sure showed your dad!...Mahhh...Come on, man, heh. I...I need you to answer my calls. Waaaaerrr...ah, ah-heh-heh, please...I got...I got testicular cancer, man! You know? Emotional support, remember? Double dragon, me and you, heh...hah! Wah-ha...ehhh...please call me back. Please. My wife's gonna kill me. I need you, man. HA! Heh hah. Ma-heh."

———

One look at the so-called Texas preacher and it was obvious that he wasn't from the state at all; at least, that's what Duke was convinced of as he observed the ten-gallon hat, bolo tie, pointy-toed boots, and oversized belt buckle. Yet, despite his own displeasure of selecting the Rent-a-Texan, the phony minister appealed to his bride, whose decision ultimately triumphed in a surprisingly assertive *coup d'état*. She felt he was perfect for their wedding's out-of-town attendees who desired a stereotypical Texas experience. It was one of many victories in a string of decisions in which Annebelle had gotten her way—Duke's subjugation had exposed him as a weak, defeated beta.

Of course, what made it worse for his ego was that she was right.

The preacher's over-the-top antics proved to be a hit with the guests, most of whom were not religious or offended by the extremities of his manufactured persona. They often used him as a mascot, giving him plenty of photo opportunities and reveling in his companionship. And now, in their moment of vow exchanges, the caricaturized preacher looked no less ridiculous as he recited from the note cards between the pages of his open Bible.

"Duke Feng," he began in an accent straight from a spaghetti western, "do y'all reach out in love to receive this here pretty gal and choose to share y'all's life together? Will y'all promise always to give together y'all's expression of the ever growing love, comfort, and sensitivity to express feelings, listen to one another, put y'alls trust, and forsaking all others, be the intimate friend and honor y'allselves as equal partners?"

The question's proposition tested Duke's principles, foreshadowing a life of sacrifices, occasional submissiveness and accommodation—something he did not expect in his original forecast of a patriarchal marriage. Still, he realized, something deep within his heart disallowed him from defecting, perhaps as a gesture to remain in good standing with his promise, but more so, he feared, from a feeling he dared not admit he was capable of bearing: love.

In a rare display of vulnerability, the indomitable egotist found himself lost in his betrothed's eyes and rumbled his answer in a voice filled with candidness and devotion, "I do."

The genuine reply sent several of the bridesmaids into a stream of tears, which, in turn, pushed the bride into a trembling state, letting loose her heart's contentment in the form of a weeping grin.

Pleased at their response so far, the overplayed cowboy minister faced her and offered the same inquiry.

"And what about you, Annebelle Wu? Same question, too long to repeat."

His humor was well-received by the crowd as Annebelle took little time in giving out her portion of the couple's reply.

"I reckon I sure do," she smiled.

The preacher nodded in affirmation as he located the next line from the note card taped between the pages of his Bible.

He cleared his throat and resumed, "Please repeat after me."

Both bride and groom echoed the pastor's words as they vowed to give each other unconditional love through good times and bad; a marriage devoid of secrets where two become one, filled with an openness which nourishes their growth as a couple. In between it all, members of Cody's family seized the sentimental moment and contributed with their own tear-filled displays of emotion.

"<My son!>" cried Duke's mother. "<Since the day you were sucking on my breasts, I knew I bore a winner!>"

"<Oh my Buddha, that didn't need to be said>," moaned Cody's father.

Kiki nudged her boyfriend, Ace, and gave him a wink through her coke-bottled glasses. "<Mmmm, all this romantic

atmosphere makes me want to study biochemistry and listen to your soft guitar.>"

"<Ehhhh, I love it when you, ehhh, feed me chicken feet congee while I play my guitar>," fantasized the musical young man.

"<Ugh!>" cried out Winston. "<When is this shit over? I want to race my car.>"

"I'm pregnant!!!" blurted his wife Wanda in English.

"<Wait, what?!!>" he exasperated.

When the exchange of vows had finally neared its conclusion, the attendants collectively turned silent and happily listened to their favorite part of the ceremony.

The preacher's tone gradually became stronger as he spoke more and more with confidence. "Now that y'all have given y'allselves to each other by solemn vows, with the joining of y'all's hands and the giving and receiving of this here ring, I now pronounce y'all wife and husband, in the name of the Father, and of the Son, and the good ol' Holy Spirit. Those whom God has joined together, let no one put asunder."

Duke held Annebelle's hands in a firm and assuring manner. In one pertinacious act of figurative telepathy, his silent fervor assured her of a stable lifestyle that included a consistent stream of revenue, a beautiful house in a good neighborhood, and a dominant baby—one that would take the best of their genes and offer the world a human being even more perfect than Duke himself.

"Ladies and gentlemen," the spurious cowboy concluded, "it is my pleasure to introduce to you, Mr. and Mrs. Duke Feng: husband and wife!"

Jubilation erupted as all in attendance shared in the two newlyweds' happiness, basking in the common bond that temporarily eliminated all rivalries, jealousies and bitterness. With confetti raining down upon them and Annebelle overjoyed by the assemblage of congratulations, Duke needed a moment to absorb his new reality. He was frightened at how much he was enjoying the euphoria and the feeling of attachment.

Delicacy. Accommodating. Gratefulness. These were, in Duke's terms, the signs of a happy beta male.

———————

Just like any other weekday at noon time, the people of downtown Houston began scurrying out of their offices like ants from an anthill. They then split into groups and cluttered around the various food trucks that were eager to satisfy their appetites. Included among them was the newest addition of the "hot circle," Mokco Polo, where Pete's dream venture was now brimming with business—so much so that he had to employ two full-time staff members to complete a day's work. Indeed, everyone loved the Asian-themed Mexican food they had come to know as mokcos, mokrittos and mokjitas. Nearby, an old friend found ample shading from the blistering Texas summer heat.

Cody, of course, was with his own motley group of friends, a scattered assortment of individuals who were just getting to know one another as well as the sensational discovery of Pete's nomadic gourmet enterprise.

"Man, this is so good, man!" Mindy complimented.

"And you're saying...he came up with this in prison?" admired Diana.

Her question did not receive an answer; instead, Cody merely continued observing Pete's success, happy that the former convict had broken out of the cycle of drug dealing and violence. More so, it inspired Cody to realize he also wasn't tied to fate, encouraged to repeatedly rise with courage and determination until he found—.

"HEY!" Mindy interrupted his thoughts with a slap across the back of Cody's head.

"Damn it, Mindy!" scolded Cody, rubbing the sore spot. "I told you to stop doing that!"

"Your friend asked you a question, Bobbie! Answer her!"

"No, it's okay," laughed Diana. "Cody drifts in and out all the time. It's like he's talking to himself. He just stares into space and moves his mouth."

"Humph!" Mindy shook her head. "It's still rude to ignore a friend!"

More of Cody's friends joined them under the shade, each with a second helping of mokcos in hand.

"Man," laughed Mitch, "I love Houston's food trucks! Your friend kicks ass!"

"Yeah," agreed Doreen, holding their toddler, "Papyrus just loves the mokcos. Of course, I have to chop them into little pieces for her to crunch on them."

Mitch and Doreen were good examples of the company he now kept: honest, well-intentioned people who did not judge or care about looks, money and social status. Despite Cody's pennilessness, he was a frequent invitee to their home, being allowed to be himself around them. It let him know that the world, indeed, had good people, perhaps filled with them if he obligated his viewpoint with an open mind and a positive heart. From his dearly departed grandmother, his grandfather, his parents, his uncle Chef Mo, Mindy, Diana, Kiki, Ace, Felix,

Luke, Zoey, Yuki, Rain—the list was much longer that he initially realized.

"<Mmm, there's only one more left on our plate>," observed Kiki to her new boyfriend, Ace. "<You take it, kekeke!>"

"<Eeeh, no, you take it.>"

"<Mmm, no, you take it!>"

"MINE!" Herman suddenly approached and whisked their mokco away. "See how fast I was? Tiger Balm Speed!!!"

No one lifted a finger to challenge the dubious self-proclaimed martial arts master—there was already a new tray of mokcos arriving, thanks to Cody's better half.

"Your friend Pete snuck out a tray for us," Phoebe winked, bringing more exquisite goodness to the famished group. "He says sorry he couldn't say hi, Cody."

"I'm sure he said it more thuggishly than that," Cody laughed.

"Meh," she shrugged, "paraphrasing."

"Gimme it! Gimme it!" grabbed Herman. "Nom nom nom!"

Mindy's twin four-year-old girls stepped on his foot.

"No no!" Mindy scolded her daughters. "There's enough for all of us."

There were indeed enough mokcos for everyone, though Cody and Phoebe stepped aside, allowing enough distance for themselves to observe the contentious chomp fest from afar.

"They're good people," quipped Cody, "but, man, do they eat like carnivores."

Phoebe let out a chuckle. "I've seen worse from Hula Hoops Shakes."

They held hands, glad to know that Phoebe had made the effort in resuscitating their reunion. Well, she admitted, Mitch and Doreen also deserved some of the credit—Cody had never responded to their original dinner invitation, but Phoebe had showed up that night and the couple took it as an opportunity to learn of the fight she had with Cody. Through persistency, Mitch and Doreen helped mend what seemed like a previously unrecoverable acquaintanceship and miraculously bonded the two back together into a substantially deeper one.

"You're smiling," Phoebe rested her head on his shoulder. "You've been doing that a lot these days."

"I've been thinking."

"You don't say?" she laughed. "That's quite a burden for someone who's currently unemployed, nearly broke and hitting his mid-thirties."

"And yet none of it matters now that I know what I want and what I can have."

"Oh?" Phoebe inquired, clutching the left hand of the man who believed he had everything. "And what can you have?"

Cody had waited a lifetime to answer that question—finally, he had the answer.

"The sky," he replied. "The sky is the limit."

ACKNOWLEDGEMENTS

I've always told my father that I'm supposed to achieve more than him and my mother. Without their help and hard work, I wouldn't have had the opportunities to exceed them. That's the sign of progression and the ultimate way of rewarding a previous generation's lifetime of dedication and sacrifice. I will never forget that they were the ones who brought me here and they were the ones who stuck with me during a struggling time in my life. The existence of this book shall long outlive us and future generations of the Leung family. By showing my parents proper recognition here, their loving and unselfishness will hopefully be immortalized. I know it's not enough to repay them as wonderful parents, but it's a start. I would also like to thank a very good friend in Nori Choy who encouraged and pushed me to start and finish this book. Her constant feedback and early grammar fixing made writing this book very enjoyable. To my editor, Ron Lewis, I thank him for his professionalism and hard work; like all great editors, he's made me look smarter than I really am. Finally, I'd like to give a special appreciation to everyone who gave this book a chance; whether you love it or hate it, you gave me your time and for that, I will always be thankful and never take it for granted.

Please write your honest thoughts on Amazon.com.

Simply log on to Amazon.com, search "Cody Quan" and click on the <u>Write a Customer Review</u> button. Thanks!

PLEASE LIKE US ON FACEBOOK:

www.facebook.com/louisleungauthor

PLEASE FOLLOW US ON TWITTER:

@ricedaddy7

WEBSITE:
www.louisleungauthor.com

www.ingramcontent.com/pod-product-compliance
Lightning Source LLC
Chambersburg PA
CBHW022142130726
47905CB00004BA/940